Books by James Grippando

*Got the Look**
*Hear No Evil**
*Last to Die**
*Beyond Suspicion**
A King's Ransom
Under Cover of Darkness
Found Money
The Abduction
The Informant
*The Pardon**

*Jack Swyteck series

The Pardon

James Grippando

Beyond Suspicion

AVON BOOKS

An Imprint of HarperCollins*Publishers*

The Pardon was originally published in hardcover by HarperCollins in September 1994 and in paperback by HarperPaperbacks in November 1995.

Beyond Suspicion was originally published in hardcover by HarperCollins in September 2002 and in paperback by HarperTorch in July 2003.

HarperCollins books may be purchased for educational, business, or sales promotional use. For information please write: Special Markets Department, HarperCollins Publishers Inc., 10 East 53rd Street, New York, NY 10022.

FIRST EDITION

ISBN-13: 978-0-06-089472-6
ISBN-10: 0-06-089472-5

06 07 08 09 JTC/RRD 10 9 8 7 6 5 4 3 2 1

THE SWYTECK SERIES: AN INTRODUCTION

What's it like to be Miami criminal defense lawyer Jack Swyteck? Simply imagine that your father is Florida's governor, your best friend was once on death row, and your love life could fill an entire chapter in *Cupid's Rules of Love and War* (Idiot's Edition). Throw in an indictment for murder and a litany of lesser charges, and you'll begin to get the picture.

When readers first met Jack in my debut novel, *The Pardon*, he was a young lawyer defending death row inmates and struggling to understand women, learning such important personal lessons as "there is no line more palpable than the one that runs down the middle of the bed." He learned his lessons so well, in fact, that I wrote five novels over the next six years with no mention of Jack. I had no intention of creating a series.

It wasn't until 2001, after I wrote *A King's Ransom*, that I considered a sequel to *The Pardon*. The inspiration was due in part to the fact that the lead character in *A King's Ransom* is a young Miami lawyer, and in my mission to make him different from Jack I found myself thinking more and more about Jack and the other characters—my old friends—from *The Pardon*. But Jack's resurgence is really a testimony to the power of e-mail. *"What ever happened to Jack?"*

became a common refrain from readers around the world. When these e-mails started to outnumber even the unwanted efforts to sell me Viagra and diet pills, the verdict was in: Jack would be back.

From the earliest drafts of *Beyond Suspicion*, I developed a new level of respect for my favorite authors who have managed to keep a series fresh over the years. The challenges are formidable. How much of the old story can you tell for the benefit of new readers without boring everyone else? How do you grow your hero without disappointing those fans who have been rooting for him from book one? Jack would probably brood over these questions forever. I needed answers—quick. Enter Theo Knight, Jack's best friend. "Theo the Not-So-White Knight" is Jack's investigator, bartender, best friend, confidante. Jack (like me) is cautious by nature, and often it is Theo's crude but plainspoken manner that stirs him (and me) into action. As Theo likes to say, *"There are two kinds of people in this world, risk takers and s--t takers. You gotta decide which you wanna be when you grow up, Jack."*

As you'll see from this special two-in-one edition, Jack still has plenty of growing up to do. Thankfully, he has Theo along to make sure that he lives through it, and to make doublesure that both you and I have fun watching.

James Grippando
Miami, Florida
April 2006

The Pardon

To my parents

ACKNOWLEDGMENTS

I am indebted to a great many people who helped make this dream come true.

A very warm thank-you to my first readers—Carlos Sires, James C. Cunningham, Jr., Terri Pepper, Denise Gordon, and Jerry Houlihan—who were good enough friends to suffer through the truly rough drafts. Jerry was a special help. His advice and courtroom instincts proved as invaluable to me as a writer as they were to me as a young lawyer. Thanks also to James W. Hall, Deputy Sheriff and Search and Rescue Coordinator in Yakima County, Washington, for his law-enforcement expertise.

From the very start, I had the extremely good fortune of dealing with the best in the book business. Special thanks to my literary agents, Artie and Richard Pine, for patiently waiting until I got it right, and for running—and howling—like the wolves when they knew we had something. I am equally grateful to Joan Sanger, whom I met through Artie, and whose editorial guidance helped turn an outline into a novel. And Rick Horgan, my editor, was an amazing teacher. He has left his mark not just on the book, but on the writer as well. Rick is one of the many reasons I am eternally thankful for the backing of a publisher of the quality and repute of HarperCollins.

Thanks also to the lawyers, paralegals, secretaries, and staff at Steel Hector & Davis for their support and enthusiasm. I'm happy to say I've spent the last ten years working with friends and colleagues who are rightfully proud of what they do for a living.

Finally, my deepest gratitude goes to my wife, Tiffany, and to my family. Without your love, prayers, and encouragement, I would still be just talking about writing a book.

PART ONE

•

October 1992

Prologue

•

The vigil had begun at dusk, and it would last all night. Clouds had moved in after midnight, blocking out the full moon. It was as if heaven had closed its omniscient eye in sorrow or just plain indifference. Another six hours of darkness and waiting, and the red morning sun would rise over the pine trees and palms of northeast Florida. Then, at precisely 7:00 A.M., Raul Fernandez would be put to death.

Crowds gathered along the chain-link fence surrounding the state's largest maximum-security penitentiary. Silence and a few glowing lights emanated from the boxy three-story building across the compound, a human warehouse of useless parts and broken spirits. Armed guards paced in their lookout towers, silhouettes in the occasional sweep of a searchlight. Not as many onlookers gathered tonight as in the old days, back when Florida's executions had been front-page news rather than a blip next to the weather forecast. Even so, the usual shouting had erupted when the black hearse that would carry out the corpse arrived. The loudest spectators were hooting and hollering from the backs of their pickup trucks, chugging their long-neck Budweisers and brandishing banners that proclaimed GO SPARKY, the nickname death-penalty supporters had affectionately given "the chair."

The victim's parents peered through the chain-link fence with quiet determination, searching only for retribution, there being no justice or meaning in the slashing of their daughter's throat. Across the road, candles burned and guitars strummed as the names of John Lennon and Joan Baez were invoked by former flower children of a caring generation, their worried faces wrinkled with age and the weight of the world's problems. Beside a cluster of nuns kneeling in prayer, supporters from Miami's "Little Havana" neighborhood shouted in their native Spanish, *"Raul es inocente, inocente!"*

Behind the penitentiary's brick walls and barred windows, Raul Fernandez had just finished his last meal—a bucket of honey-glazed chicken wings with extra mashed potatoes—and he was about to pay his last visit to the prison barber. Escorted by armed correction officers in starched beige-and-brown uniforms, he took a seat in a worn leather barber's chair that was nearly as uncomfortable as the boxy wooden throne on which he was scheduled to die. The guards strapped him in and assumed their posts—one by the door, the other at the prisoner's side.

"Barber'll be here in a minute," said one of the guards. "Just sit tight."

Fernandez sat rigidly and waited, as if he expected the electricity to flow at any moment. His bloodshot eyes squinted beneath the harsh glare as the bright white lights overhead reflected off the white walls of painted cinder block and the white tile floors. He allowed himself a moment of bitter irony as he noticed that even the guards were white.

All was white, in fact, except the man scheduled to die. Fernandez was one of the thousands of Cuban refugees who'd landed in Miami during the Mariel boat lift of 1980. Within a year he was arrested for first-degree murder. The jury convicted him in less time than it had taken the young victim to choke on her own blood. The judge sentenced him to die in the electric chair, and after a decade of appeals, his time had come.

"Mornin', Bud," said the big guard who'd posted himself at the door.

The prisoner watched tentatively as a potbellied barber with cauliflower ears and a self-inflicted marine-style haircut entered the room. His movements were slow and methodical. He seemed to enjoy the fact that for Fernandez every moment was like an eternity. He stood before his captive customer and smirked, his trusty electric shaver in one hand and, in the other, a big plastic cup of the thickest-looking tea Fernandez had ever seen.

"Right on time," said the barber through his tobacco-stained teeth. He spat his brown slime into his cup, placed it on the counter, and took a good look at Fernandez. "Oh, yeah," he wheezed, "you look just like you does on the TV," he said, pronouncing *TV* as if it rhymed with *Stevie*.

Fernandez sat stone-faced in the chair, ignoring the remark.

"Got a special on the Louis Armstrong look today," the barber said as he switched on his shaver.

Curly black hair fell to the floor as the whining razor transformed the prisoner's thick mop to a stubble that glistened with nervous beads of sweat. At the proper moment, the guards lifted Fernandez's pant legs, and the barber shaved around the ankles. That done, the prisoner was ready to be plugged in at both ends, his bald head and bare ankles serving as human sockets for the surge of kilovolts that would sear his skin, boil his blood, and snuff out his life.

The barber took a step back to admire his handiwork. "Now, ain't that a sharp-lookin' haircut," he said. "Comes with a lifetime guarantee too."

The guards snickered as Fernandez clenched his fists.

A quick knock on the door broke the tension. The big guard's keys tinkled as he opened the door. Raul strained to hear the mumbling, but he couldn't make out what was being said. Finally, the guard turned to him, looking annoyed.

"Fernandez, you got a phone call. It's your lawyer."

Raul's head snapped up at the news.

"Let's go," ordered the guard as he took the prisoner by the arm.

Fernandez popped from the chair.

"Slow down!" said the guard.

Fernandez knew the drill. He extended his arms, and the guard cuffed his wrists. Then he fell to his knees so the other guard could shackle his ankles from behind. He rose slowly but impatiently, and as quickly as his chains and armed escorts would let him travel, he passed through the door and headed down the hallway. In a minute, he was in the small recessed booth where prisoners took calls from their lawyers. It had a diamond-shaped window on the door that allowed the guards to watch but not hear the privileged conversation.

"What'd they say, man?"

There was a pause on the other end of the line, which didn't bode well.

"I'm sorry, Raul," said his attorney.

"No!" He banged his fist on the counter. "This can't be! I'm innocent! I'm *innocent!*" He took several short, angry breaths as his wild eyes scanned the little booth, searching for a way out.

The lawyer continued in a low, calm voice. "I promised you I wouldn't sugarcoat it, Raul. The fact is, we've done absolutely everything we can in the courts. It couldn't be worse. Not only did the Supreme Court deny your request for a stay of execution, but they've issued an order that prevents any other court in the country from giving you a stay."

"Why? I want to know *why*, damn it!"

"The court didn't say why—it doesn't have to," his lawyer answered.

"Then *you* tell me! *Somebody* tell me why this is happening to me!"

The line was silent.

Fernandez brought his hand to his head in disbelief,

but the strange feeling of his baldness only reinforced what he'd just heard. "There has . . . some way . . . look, we've gotta stop this," he said, his voice quivering. "We've been here before, you and me. Do like the last time. File another appeal, or a writ or a motion or whatever the hell you lawyers call those things. Just buy me some *time*. And do it like quick, man. They already shaved my fucking hair off!"

His lawyer sighed so loudly that the line crackled.

"Come on," said Fernandez in desperation. "There has to be *something* you can do."

"There may be one thing," his lawyer said without enthusiasm.

"Yeah, baby!" He came to life, fists clenched for one more round.

"It's a billion-to-one shot," the lawyer said, reeling in his client's overreaction. "I *may* have found a new angle on this. I'm going to ask the governor to commute your sentence. But I won't mislead you. You need to prepare for the worst. Remember, the governor is the man who signed your death warrant. He's not likely to scale it back to life imprisonment. You understand what I'm saying?"

Fernandez closed his eyes tightly and swallowed his fear, but he didn't give up hope. "I understand, man, I really do. But go for it. Just go for it. And thank you, man. Thank you and God bless you," he added as he hung up the phone.

He took a deep breath and checked the clock on the wall. Eight minutes after two. Just five hours left to live.

Chapter 1

•

It was 5:00 A.M. and Governor Harold Swyteck had finally fallen asleep on the daybed. Rest was always elusive on execution nights, which would have been news to anyone who'd heard the governor on numerous occasions emphasizing the need to evict "those holdover tenants" on Florida's overcrowded death row. A former cop and state legislator, Harry Swyteck had campaigned for governor on a law-and-order platform that prescribed more prisons, longer sentences, and more executions as a swift and certain cure for a runaway crime rate. After sweeping into office by a comfortable margin, he'd delivered immediately on his campaign promise, signing his first death warrant on inauguration day in January 1991. In the ensuing twenty-one months, more death warrants had received the governor's John Hancock than in the previous two administrations combined.

At twenty minutes past five, a shrill ring interrupted the governor's slumber. Instinctively, Harry reached out to swat the alarm clock, but it wasn't there. The ringing continued.

"The phone," his wife grumbled from across the room, snug in their bed.

The governor shook himself to full consciousness, realized he was in the daybed, and then started at the blinking red light on the security phone beside his empty half of the four-poster bed.

He stubbed his toe against the bed as he made his way toward the receiver. "Dammit! What is it?"

"Governor," came the reply, "this is security."

"I *know* who you are, Mel. What's the emergency?"

The guard shifted uncomfortably at his post, the way anyone would who'd just woken his boss before sunrise. "Sir, there's someone here who wants to see you. It's about the execution."

The governor gritted his teeth, trying hard not to misdirect the anger of a stubbed toe and a sleepless night toward the man who guarded his safety. "Mel— please. You can't be waking me up every time a last-minute plea lands on my doorstep. We have channels for these things. That's why I have counsel. Call *them*. Now, good—"

"Sir," he gently interrupted, "I—I understand your reaction, sir. But this one, I think, is different. Says he has information that will convince you Fernandez is innocent."

"Who is it this time?" Harry asked with a roll of his eyes. "His mother? Some friend of the family?"

"No, sir, he . . . well, he says he's your son."

The governor was suddenly wide awake. "Send him in," he said, then hung up the phone. He checked the clock. Almost five-thirty. Just ninety minutes left. *One hell of a time for your first visit to the mansion, son.*

Jack Swyteck stood stiffly on the covered front porch, not sure how to read the sullen expression on his father's face.

"Well, well," the governor said, standing in the open doorway in his monogrammed burgundy bathrobe. Jack was the governor's twenty-six-year-old son, his only offspring. Jack's mother had died a few hours after his birth. Try as he might, Harold had never quite forgiven his son for that.

"I'm here on business," Jack said quickly. "All I need is ten minutes."

The governor stared coolly across the threshold at Jack, who with the same dark, penetrating eyes was plainly his father's son. Tonight he wore faded blue jeans, a brown leather aviator's jacket, and matching boots. His rugged, broad-shouldered appearance could have made him an instant heartthrob as a country singer, though with his perfect diction and Yale law degree he was anything but country. His father had looked much the same in his twenties, and at fifty-three he was still lean and barrel-chested. He'd graduated from the University of Florida, class of '65—a savvy sabrefencer who'd turned street cop, then politician. The governor was a man who could take your best shot, bounce right back, and hand you your head if you let your guard down. His son was always on guard.

"Come in," Harry said.

Jack entered the foyer, shut the door behind him, and followed his father down the main hall. The rooms were smaller than Jack had expected—elegant but simple, with high coffered ceilings and floors of oak and inlaid mahogany. Period antiques, silk Persian rugs, and crystal chandeliers were the principal furnishings. The art was original and reflected Florida's history.

"Sit down," said the governor as they stepped into the library at the end of the hall.

The dark-paneled library reminded Jack of the house in which he'd grown up. He sat in a leather armchair before the stone fireplace, his crossed legs fully extended and his boots propped up irreverently on the head of a big Alaskan brown bear that his father had years ago stopped in its tracks and turned into a rug. The governor looked away, containing his impulse to tell his son to sit up straight. He stepped behind the big oak bar and filled his old-fashioned glass with ice cubes.

Jack did a double take. He thought his father had given up hard liquor—then again, this was the first time he'd seen him as *Governor* Swyteck. "Do you have to drink? Like I said, this is business."

The governor shot him a glance, then reached for the Chivas and filled his glass to the brim. "And *this*"—he raised his glass—"is *none* of your business. Cheers." He took a long sip.

Jack just watched, telling himself to focus on the reason he was there.

"So," the governor said, smacking his lips. "I can't really remember the last time we even spoke, let alone saw each other. How long has it been this time?"

Jack shrugged. "Two, two and a half years."

"Since your law-school graduation, wasn't it?"

"No"—Jack's expression betrayed the faintest of smiles—"since I told you I was taking a job with the Freedom Institute."

"Ah, yes, the Freedom Institute." Harry Swyteck rolled his eyes. "The place where lawyers measure success by turning murderers, rapists, and robbers back onto the street. The place where bleeding-heart liberals can defend the guilty and be insufferably sanctimonious about it, because they don't take a fee from the vermin they defend." His look soured. "The *one* place you knew it would absolutely kill me to see you work."

Jack held on tightly to the arm of the chair. "I didn't come here to replow old ground."

"I'm sure you didn't. It's much the same old story, anyway. Granted, this last time the rift grew a little wider between us. But in the final analysis, this one will shake out no differently than the other times you've cut me out of your life. You'll never recognize that all I ever wanted is what's best for you."

Jack was about to comment on his father's presumed infallibility, but was distracted by something on the bookshelf. It was an old photograph of the two of them, together on a deep-sea fishing trip, in one of their too-few happy moments. *Lay in to me first chance you get, Father, but you have that picture up there for all to see, don't you?*

"Look," Jack said, "I know we have things to talk about. But now's not the time. I didn't come here for that."

"I know. You came because Raul Fernandez is

scheduled to die in the electric chair in"—the governor looked at his watch—"about eighty minutes."

"I came because he is innocent."

"Twelve jurors didn't think so, Jack."

"They didn't hear the whole story."

"They heard enough to convict him after deliberating for less than twenty minutes. I've known juries to take longer deciding who's going to be foreman."

"Will you just *listen* to me," Jack snapped. "Please, Father"—he tried a more civil tone—"listen to me."

The governor refilled his glass. "All right," he said. "I'm listening."

Jack leaned forward. "About five hours ago, a man called me and said he had to see me—in confidence, as a client. He wouldn't give me his name, but he said it was life and death, so I agreed to meet him. He showed up at my office ten minutes later wearing a ski mask. At first I thought he was going to rob me, but it turned out he just wanted to talk about the Fernandez case. So that's what we did—talked." He paused, focusing his eyes directly on his father's. "And in less than five minutes he had me convinced that Raul Fernandez is innocent."

The governor looked skeptical. "And just what did this mysterious man of the night tell you?"

"I can't say."

"Why not?"

"I told you: He agreed to speak to me only in confidence, as a client. I've never seen his face, and I doubt that I'll ever see him again, but technically I'm his lawyer—or at least I was for that conversation. Anyway, everything he told me is protected by attorney-client privilege. I can't divulge any of it without his approval. And he won't let me repeat a word."

"Then what are you doing here?"

Jack gave him a sobering look. "Because an innocent man is going to die in the electric chair unless you stop the Fernandez execution right now."

The governor slowly crossed the room, a glass in one hand and an open bottle of scotch in the other. He sat in the matching arm chair, facing Jack. "And I'll ask you one more time: How do you *know* Fernandez is innocent?"

"How do I *know?*" Jack's reddening face conveyed total exasperation. "Why is it that you *always* want more than I can give? My flying up here in the middle of the night isn't enough for you? My telling you everything I legally and ethically can tell you just isn't enough?"

"All I'm saying is that I need *proof.* I can't just stay an execution based on . . . on *nothing*, really."

"My word is worth nothing, then," Jack translated.

"In this setting, yes—that's the way it has to be. In this context, you're a lawyer, and I'm the governor."

"No—in this context, I'm a witness, and you're a murderer. Because you're going to put Fernandez to death. And I *know* he's innocent."

"*How* do you know?"

"Because I met the *real* killer tonight. He confessed to me. He did more than confess: He *showed* me something that proves he's the killer."

"And what was that?" the governor asked, genuinely interested.

"I *can't* tell you," Jack said. He felt his frustration rising. "I've already said more than I can under the attorney-client privilege."

The governor nestled into his chair, flashing a thin, paternalistic smile. "You're being a little naive, don't you think? You have to put these last-minute pleas in context. Fernandez is a convicted killer. He and everyone who knows him is desperate. You can't take anything they say at face value. This so-called client who showed up at your door is undoubtedly a cousin or brother or street friend of Raul Fernandez's, and he'll do anything to stop the execution."

"You don't *know* that!"

The governor sighed heavily, his eyes cast downward. "You're right." He brought his hands to his temples and began rubbing them. "We never know for certain. I suppose that's why I've taken to *this*," he said as he reached over and lifted the bottle of scotch. "But the cold reality is that I campaigned as the law-and-order governor. I made the death penalty the central issue in the election. I promised to carry it out with vigor, and at the time I meant what I said. Now that I'm here, it's not quite so easy to sign my name to a death warrant. You've seen them before—ominous-looking documents, with their black border and embossed state seal. But have you ever really *read* what they say? Believe me, I have." His voice trailed off. "That kind of power can get to a man, if you let it. Hell," he scoffed and sipped his drink, "and doctors think *they're* God."

Jack was silent, surprised by this rare look into his father's conscience and not quite sure what to say.

"That's all the more reason to listen to me," he said. "To make sure it's not a mistake."

"This is no mistake, Jack. Don't you see? What you're *not* saying is as significant as what you're saying. You won't breach the attorney-client privilege, not even to persuade me to change my mind about the execution. I respect that, Jack. But you have to respect me, too. I have rules. I have obligations, just like you do. Mine are to the people who elected me—and who expect me to honor my campaign promises."

"It's not the same thing."

"That's true," he agreed. "It's not the same. That's why, when you leave here tonight, I don't want you to blame yourself for anything. You did the best you could. Now it's up to me to make a decision. And *I'm* making it. I don't believe Raul Fernandez is innocent. But if *you* believe it, I don't want you feeling responsible for his death."

Jack looked into his father's eyes. He knew the man was reaching out—that he was looking for something from his son, some reciprocal acknowledgment that Jack didn't blame *him*, either, for doing *his* job. Harold Swyteck wanted absolution, forgiveness—a pardon.

Jack glanced away. He would not—could not—allow the moment to weaken his resolve. "Don't worry, Father, I won't blame myself. It's like you always used to tell me: We're all responsible for our own actions. If an innocent man dies in the electric chair, you're the governor. You're responsible. You're the one to blame."

Jack's words struck a nerve. The governor's face flushed red with fury as every conciliatory sentiment drained away. "There is *no one* to blame," he declared. "No one but Fernandez himself. You're being played for a sucker. Fernandez and his buddy are *using* you. Why do you think this character didn't tell you his name or even show you his face?"

"Because he doesn't want to get caught," Jack answered, "but he doesn't want an innocent man to die."

"A *killer*—especially one guilty of this sort of savagery—doesn't want an innocent man to die?" Harry Swyteck shook his head condescendingly. "It's ironic, Jack"—he spoke out of anger now—"but sometimes you almost make me glad your mother never lived to see what a thick-headed son she brought into the world."

Jack quickly rose from his chair. "I don't have to take this crap from you."

"I'm your *father!*" Harry blustered. "You'll take whatever I—"

"No! I'll take *nothing* from you. I've never asked for anything. And I don't *want* anything. *Ever.*" He stormed toward the door.

"Wait!" the governor shouted, freezing him in his tracks. Jack turned around slowly and glared at his father. "Listen to me, young man. Fernandez is going to be executed this morning, because I don't believe any of this nonsense about his being innocent. No more than I believed the eleventh-hour story from the last 'innocent man' we executed—the one who claimed it was only an accident that he stabbed his girlfriend"—he paused, so furious he was out of breath—"twenty-one times."

"You've become an incredibly narrow-minded old man," Jack said.

The governor stood stoically at the bar. "Get out, Jack. Get out of my house."

Jack turned and marched down the hall, his boots punishing the mansion's hard wooden floor. He threw the front door open, then stopped at the tinkling sound of his father filling his empty scotch glass with ice cubes. "Drink up, Governor!" his voice echoed in the hallway. "Do us all a favor, and drink yourself to death."

He slammed the door and left.

Chapter 2

•

Death was just minutes away for Raul Fernandez. He sat on the edge of the bunk in his cell, shoulders slumped, bald head bowed, and hands folded between his knees. Father José Ramirez, a Roman Catholic priest, was at the prisoner's side, dressed all in black save for his white hair and Roman collar. Rosary beads were draped over one knee, an open Bible rested on the other. He was looking at Fernandez with concern, almost desperation, as he tried once more to cleanse the man's soul.

"Murder is a mortal sin, Raul," he said. "Heaven holds no place for those who die without confessing their mortal sins. In John, chapter twenty, Jesus tells his disciples: 'Whose sins you forgive are forgiven them, and whose sins you hold bound are held bound.' Let me hear your sins, Raul. So that you may be forgiven them."

Fernandez looked him directly in the eye. "Father," he said with all the sincerity he could muster, "right now, I have nothing to lose by telling you the truth. And I'm telling you this: I have nothing to confess."

Father Ramirez showed no expression, though a chill went down his spine. He flinched only at the sound of the key jiggling in the iron door.

"It's time," announced the guard. A team of two stepped inside the cell to escort Fernandez. Father Ramirez rose from his chair, blessed the prisoner with the sign of the cross, and then stepped aside. Fernandez did not budge from his bunk.

"Let's go," ordered the guard.

"Give him a minute," said the priest.

The guard stepped briskly toward the prisoner. "We don't have a minute."

Fernandez suddenly sprung from his chair, burrowing his shoulder into the lead guard's belly. They tumbled to the floor. "I'm innocent!" he cried, his arms flailing. A barrage of blows from the other guard's blackjack battered his back and shoulders, stunning the prisoner into near paralysis.

"You crazy son of a bitch!" cried the fallen guard, forcing Fernandez onto his belly. "Cuff him!" he shouted to his partner. Together they pinned his arms behind his back, then cuffed the wrists and ankles.

"I'm innocent," Fernandez whimpered, his face pressing on the cement floor. "I'm *innocent!*"

"The hell with this," said the guard who'd just wrestled with the condemned man. He snatched a leather strap from his pocket and gagged the prisoner, fastening it tightly around the back of his head.

Father Ramirez looked on in horror as the guards lifted Fernandez to his feet. He was still groggy from the blows, so they shook him to revive him. The law required that a condemned man be fully conscious and alert to his impending death. Each guard grabbed an arm, and together they led him out of the cell.

The priest was pensive and disturbed as he followed the procession down the brightly lit hallway. He'd seen many death-row inmates, but none was the fighter this one was. Certainly, none had so strongly proclaimed his innocence.

They stopped at the end of the hall and waited as the execution chamber's iron door slid open automatically. The guards then handed the prisoner over to two attendants inside who specialized in executions. They moved quickly and efficiently as precious seconds ticked away on the wall clock. Fernandez was strapped into the heavy oak chair. Electrodes were fastened to his shaved head and ankles. The gag was removed from his mouth and replaced with a steel bit.

All was quiet, save for the hum of the bright fluorescent lights overhead. Fernandez sat stiffly in his chair. The guards brought the black hood down over his face, then took their places along the gray-green walls. The venetian blinds opened, exposing the prisoner to three dozen witnesses on the dark side of the glass wall. A few reporters stirred. An assistant state attorney looked on impassively. The victim's uncle—the only relative of the young girl in attendance—took a deep breath. All eyes except the prisoner's turned toward the clock. His were hidden behind the hood and a tight leather band that would keep his eyeballs from bursting when the current flowed.

Father Ramirez stepped into the dark seating area and joined the audience. The guard at the door raised his eyebrows. "You really gonna watch this one, padre?" he asked quietly.

"You know I never watch," said the priest.

"There's a first time for everything."

"Yes," said Ramirez. "There is, indeed. And if my instincts are correct, let's hope this is the *last* time you kill an innocent man." Then he closed his eyes and retreated into prayer.

The guard looked away. The priest's words had been pointed, but the guard shook them off, taking the proverbial common man's comfort in the fact that *he* wasn't killing anyone. It was Governor Harold Swyteck who'd signed the man's death warrant. It was someone else who would flip the switch.

At that moment, the second hand swept by its highest point, the warden gave the signal, and lights dimmed throughout the prison as twenty-five hundred volts surged into the prisoner's body. Fernandez lunged forward with the force of a head-on collision, his back arching and his skin smoking and sizzling. His jaws clenched the steel bit so tightly his teeth shattered. His fingers pried into the oak armrests with such effort that his bones snapped.

A second quick jolt went right to his heart.

A third made sure the job was done.

It had taken a little more than a minute—the last and longest sixty-seven seconds of this thirty-five-year-old's life. An exhaust fan came on, sucking out the stench. A physician stepped forward, placed a stethoscope on the prisoner's chest, and listened.

"He's dead," pronounced the doctor.

Father Ramirez sighed with sorrow as he opened his eyes, then lowered his head and blessed himself with the sign of the cross. "May God forgive us," he said under his breath, "as He receives the innocent."

PART TWO

•

July 1994

Chapter 3

•

Eddy Goss was on trial for an act of violence so unusual that it amazed even him. He'd first noticed the girl
when she was walking home from school one night in
her drill-team uniform. At the time, he thought she
must be sixteen. She had the kind of looks he liked—
long blond hair that cascaded over her shoulders, a
nice, curvy shape, and most important of all, no
makeup. He liked that fresh look. It told him he would
be the first.

By the time he'd caught up to her, she'd known
something was wrong. He was sure of that. She'd
started looking over her shoulder and walking faster.
He guessed she must have been really scared—too
scared to react—because it took him only a few seconds to force her into his Ford Pinto. About five miles
out of town, in a thick stand of pines far from the main

highway, he held a knife to her throat and warned her to do everything he asked. Naturally, she agreed. What choice did she have? She hiked up her skirt, pulled off her panty hose—all the drill-team members at Senior High had to wear nude hose, he knew—and sat perfectly still as Eddy probed her vagina with his fingers. But then she started crying—great wracking sobs that made him furious. He hated it when they cried. So he wrapped the nylon around her neck—and pulled. And pulled. He pulled so hard that he finally did it: He actually severed her vertebrae and decapitated her. *Son of a bitch!*

Eddy Goss was on trial for his proudest accomplishment. And his lawyer was Jack Swyteck.

"All rise!" the bailiff shouted as the jury returned from its deliberations. Quietly, they shuffled in. A nursing student. A bus driver. A janitor. Five blacks, two Jews. Four men, eight women. Seven blue collars, two professionals, three who didn't fit a mold. It didn't matter how Jack categorized them anymore. Individual votes were no longer important; their collective mind had been made up. They divided themselves into two rows of six, stood before their Naugahyde chairs, and cast their eyes into "the wishing well," as Jack called it, that empty, stagelike area before the judge and jury where lawyers who defended the guilty pitched their penny-ante arguments and then hoped for the best.

Jack swallowed hard as he strained to read their faces. Experience made him appear calm, though the adrenaline was flowing on this final day of a trial that had been front-page news for more than a month. He looked much the same now as he had two years ago, save for the healthy cynicism in his eye and a touch of gray in his hair that made him look as though he were more than just four years out of law school. Jack buttoned his pinstripe suit, then glanced quickly at his client, standing stiffly beside him. *What a piece of work.*

"Be seated," said the silver-haired judge to an overcrowded courtroom.

Defendant Eddy Goss watched with dark, deep-set eyes as the jurors took their seats. His expression had the intensity of a soldier dismantling a land mine. He had huge hands—the hands of a strangler, the prosecutor had been quick to point out—and nails that were bitten halfway down to the cuticle. His prominent jaw and big shiny forehead gave him a menacing look that made it easy to imagine him committing the crime of which he was accused. Today he seemed aloof, Jack thought, as if he were enjoying this.

Indeed, that had been Jack's impression of Goss four months ago, when Jack had watched a videotape of his client bragging about the grisly murder to police investigators. It was supposed to be an open-and-shut case: The prosecutor had a videotaped confession. But the jury never saw it. Jack had kept it out of evidence.

"Has the jury reached a verdict?" asked the judge.

"We have," announced the forewoman.

Spectators slid to the edge of their seats. Whirling paddle fans stirred the silence overhead. The written verdict passed from jury to judge.

It doesn't matter what the verdict is, Jack tried to convince himself. He had served the system, served justice. As he stood there, watching the judge hand the paper back to the clerk, he thought of all those homilies he'd been handed in law school—how every citizen had a right to the best defense, how the rights of the innocent would be trampled if not for lawyers who vindicated those rights in defense of the guilty. Back then it had all sounded so noble, but reality had a way of raining on your parade. Here he was, defending someone who wasn't even *sorry* for what he had done. And the jury had found him . . .

"Not guilty."

"Noooooo!" screamed the victim's sister, setting off a wave of anger that rocked the courtroom.

Jack closed his eyes tightly; it was a painful victory.

"Order!" shouted the judge, banging his gavel to calm a packed crowd that had erupted in hysteria. Insults, glares, and wadded paper continued to fly across the room, all directed at Jack Swyteck and the scum he'd defended.

"Order!"

"You'll get yours, Goss!" shouted a friend of the dead girl's family. "You too, Swyteck."

Jack looked at the ceiling, tried to block it all out.

"Hope *you* can sleep tonight," an angry prosecutor muttered to him on her way out.

Jack reached deep inside for a response, but he found nothing. He just turned away and did what he supposed was the socially acceptable thing. He didn't congratulate Eddy Goss or shake his hand. Instead, he packed up his trial bag and glanced to his right.

Goss was staring at him, a satisfied smirk on his face.

"Can I have your business card, Mr. Swyteck?" asked Goss, his head cocked and his hands planted smugly on his hips. "Just so I know who to call—next time."

Suddenly, it was as if Jack were looking not just at Goss, but at all the remorseless criminals he had defended over the years. He stepped up to Goss and spoke right into his face. "Listen, you son of a bitch," he whispered, "there'd better not *be* a next time. Because if there is, not only will I *not* represent you, but I will personally make sure that you get a class-A fuck-up for an attorney. And don't think the son of the governor can't pull it off. You understand me?"

Goss's smirk faded, and his eyes narrowed with contempt. "Nobody threatens me, Swyteck."

"I just did."

Goss curled his lip with disdain. "Now you've done it. Now you've hurt my feelings. I don't know if I can forgive you for that, Swyteck. But I do know this," he said, leaning forward. "Someday—someday soon, Jack Swyteck is gonna *beg* me to forgive him." Goss pulled back, his dark eyes boring into Jack's. "*Beg* me."

Jack tried not to flinch, but those eyes were getting to him. "You know nothing about forgiveness, Goss," he said finally, then turned and walked away. He headed down the aisle, scuffed leather briefcase in hand, feeling very alone as he pushed his way through the angry and disgusted crowd, toward the carved mahogany doors marked EXIT.

"There he goes, ladies and gentlemen," Goss shouted over the crowd, waving his arms like a circus master. "My *ex*-best friend, Jack Swyteck."

Jack ignored him, as did everyone else. The crowd was looking at the lawyer.

"Asshole!" a stranger jeered at Jack.

"Creep!" said another.

Jack's eyes swept around, catching a volley of glares from the spectators. He suddenly knew what it meant, literally, to *represent* someone. He represented Eddy Goss the way a flag represented a country, the way suffering represented Satan. "There he is!" reporters shouted as Jack emerged from the bustling courtroom, elbow-to-elbow with a rush of spectators. In the lobby, another crowd waited for him in front of the elevators, armed with cameras and microphones.

"Mr. Swyteck!" cried the reporters over the general crowd noise. In an instant microphones were in his face, making forward progress impossible. "Your reaction? . . . your client do now? . . . say to the victim's family?" The questions ran together.

Jack was sandwiched between the crowd pressing from behind and the reporters pressing forward. He'd never get out of here with just a curt "No comment." He stopped, paused for a moment, and said: "I believe that the only way to characterize today's verdict is to call it a victory for the system. *Our* system, which requires the prosecutor to *prove* that the accused is guilty beyond a reasonable—"

Shrill screams suddenly filled the lobby, as a geyser of red erupted from the crowd, drenching Jack. The panic continued as more of the thick liquid splattered Jack and everyone around him.

He was stunned for a moment, uncomprehending. He wiped the red substance from around his eyes—was it blood or some kind of paint?—and said nothing as it traced ruby-red rivulets down his pants onto the floor.

"It's on you, Swyteck," his symbolic assailant hollered from somewhere in the crowd. "Her blood is on you!"

Chapter 4

•

Jack drove home topless in every sense of the word. His blood-soaked shirt and suit coat were stuffed in the back of his '73 Mustang convertible, and the top was rolled back to air the stench. It was a bizarre ending, but the press *had* been predicting an acquittal, and the prospect of a not-guilty verdict had apparently angered someone enough to arm himself with bags of some thick red liquid—the same way animal-rights extremists sometimes ambushed fur-coated women on the streets of New York. He wondered again what kind of ammunition had been used. Animal blood? Human blood infected with AIDS? He cringed at the thought of the photo and headline that would appear in the next day's tabloids: "Jack Swyteck—Bleeding Liberal." *Shit, does it get any worse than this?*

It was after dark by the time he got home. He noticed

immediately that there was no red Pontiac in the driveway, which meant his girlfriend, Cindy Paige, wouldn't be there to listen to the day's events. *His girlfriend*. He wondered if he was kidding himself about that. Things hadn't been the best between them lately. The story she'd handed him about staying with her friend Gina for a few days "to help her with some problems she's been having" was starting to sound like just an excuse to get out from under all the baggage he'd been carrying these past few months. Hell, he couldn't blame her. When he wasn't up to his eyeballs in work, he was having these dialogues with himself, questioning where his life was going. And most of the time he left Cindy on the outside looking in.

"Hey, boy," said Jack as his hairy best friend attacked him on the porch, planting his bearlike paws on his master's chest and greeting him nose to cold nose. His name was Thursday, for the day Jack, Cindy, and her five-year-old niece picked him up from the pound and saved him from being put to sleep—the most deserving prisoner he'd ever kept from dying. He was definitely part Lab, but mostly a product of the canine melting pot. His expressive, chocolate-brown eyes made him an excellent communicator—and at the moment, the eyes were screaming, "I'm hungry."

"Looks like you have a case of the munchies," Jack said, gently pushing him away as he entered the house. He went to the kitchen and filled the dog's bowl with Puppy Chow, then dug the pizza-bones appetizer out of the refrigerator. Cindy never ate the crust or the pepperoni. She saved them for Thursday.

He set the bowl on the floor and watched the dog dig in.

Fortunately, the blood—or whatever it was— washed off easily in the shower. As he toweled himself dry, Jack could hear Thursday pushing his empty bowl across the kitchen floor with his nose. Jack smiled and pulled on his boxer shorts. Then he went to the bedroom and sat on the edge of the king-size bed. His eyes scanned the room, finally coming to rest on a framed photograph of Cindy that stood on the nightstand. In it she was standing on a rock along some mountain trail they'd hiked together in Utah. She had a big, happy smile on her face, and the summer wind was tossing her honey-blond hair. It was his favorite picture of her, because it captured so many of the qualities that made her special. At first glance, anyone would be struck by her beautiful face and great body. But for Jack, it was Cindy's eyes and her smile that told the whole story.

On impulse, he reached for the phone. He frowned when Gina Terisi's machine picked up: "I'm sorry I can't come to the phone right now . . ." said the recorded message.

"Cindy, call me," he said. "Miss you," he added, and put the receiver down. He fell back on the bed, closed his eyes, and began to relax for the first time in more than a day. But he was disturbed as he realized that Gina would get the message first and convince Cindy he was pining away for her. Well, he was, wasn't he?

Idly, he flipped on the TV and began channel-surfing, searching for any station that didn't have something to say about the acquittal of Eddy Goss. He fixed on MTV. Two mangy-looking rockers were banging on their guitars while getting their faces licked by a Cindy Crawford look-alike.

He switched off the set, nestled his head in the pillow, and lay in the darkness. But he couldn't sleep. He looked straight ahead, over the tops of his toes, staring at the television on the dresser. There was nothing he wanted to watch. But as the day's ugly events played out in his mind, there was one thing he suddenly *had* to watch.

He rolled out of bed, grabbed his briefcase, and popped it open, quickly finding what he was looking for, even in the darkness. He switched on the television and VCR, shoved in the cassette, and sat on the edge of the bed, waiting. There was a screen full of snow, a few rolling blips, and then . . .

"My name is Eddy Goss," said the man on the screen, speaking stiffly into a police video camera. Goss's normally flat and stringy hair was a tangled, greasy mess. He looked and undoubtedly smelled as if he'd been sleeping under a bridge all week, dressed in dirty Levi's, unlaced tennis shoes, and a yellow-white undershirt, torn at the V and stained with underarm sweat. He sat smugly in the metal folding chair, exuding a punk's confidence, his arms folded tightly. Four long and fresh red scratches ran along his neck. The date and time, 11:04 P.M., March 12—four and a half months ago—flashed in the corner of the screen.

"I live at four-oh-nine East Adams Street," Goss continued, "apartment two-seventeen."

The camera drew back to show the suspect, seated at the end of the long conference table, and an older man seated on the side, to Goss's right. The man appeared to be in his late sixties, gray-haired, with a hawk nose that supported his black-rimmed glasses.

"Mr. Goss," said the man, "I'm Detective Lonzo Stafford. With me, behind the camera, is Detective Jamahl Bradley. You understand, son, that you have the right to remain silent. You have the right—"

Jack hit the remote, fast-forwarding to the part he'd seen at least a hundred times before. Visible in the frame now was a different Goss, more animated, boasting like a proud father.

". . . I killed the little prick tease," Goss said with a carefree shrug.

Jack stopped the tape, rewound, and listened again, as if flogging himself.

". . . I killed the little prick tease," he heard one more time. Just the way thousands of other people had heard it—with expletive deleted—and were probably hearing it again tonight, on the television news. The tape rolled on, and Jack closed his eyes and listened as Goss described the deed in grisly detail. The car ride to the woods. The knife at the young girl's throat. The tears that had stemmed his vulgar attempts at gentle caresses. The struggle that had ensued. And finally, pulling the nylon tight around the girl's neck . . .

Jack sighed, keeping his eyes closed. The tape continued, but there was only silence. Even the police interrogators, it seemed, had needed to catch their breath. Had they been allowed to hear it, a jury probably would have reacted the same way. But he'd prevented that. He'd kept the entire videotape out of evidence by arguing that Goss's constitutional rights had been violated—that his confession had been involuntary. The police hadn't beaten it out of him with a rubber hose. They hadn't even threatened him. "They tricked him," Jack had argued, relying on one questionable remark by a seasoned detective who so desperately wanted to nail Goss that he pushed it a little too far—though the detective had still played good odds, knowing from experience that only the most liberal judge would condemn his tactics.

"We don't want to know if you did it," Detective Stafford had assured Goss. "We just want you to show us where Kerry's body is, so we can give her a decent Christian burial." That was all the ammunition Jack had needed. "They induced a confession by playing on my client's conscience!" he'd argued to the judge. "They appealed to his religious convictions. A Christian burial speech is patently illegal, Your Honor."

No one was more surprised than Jack when the judge bought the argument. The confession was ruled inadmissible. The jury never saw the videotape. They acquitted a guilty man. And the miscarriage of justice was clear. *Nice going, Swyteck.*

He hit the eject button on his VCR and tossed the confession aside, disgusted at himself and what he did for a living. He grabbed another cassette from the case beside the television, pushed *To Kill a Mockingbird* into his VCR, and for the fifteenth time since joining the Freedom Institute, watched Gregory Peck defend the innocent.

Peck's Atticus Finch had just launched into his peroration when a shrill ringing startled Jack from a state of half sleep.

He snatched up the telephone, hoping to hear

Cindy's voice. For a few moments, though, all he heard was silence. Finally, a surly voice came over the line. "Swyteck?" it asked.

Jack didn't move. The voice seemed vaguely familiar, but it also seemed raspy and disguised. He waited. And finally came the brief, sobering message.

"A killer is on the loose tonight, Swyteck. A killer is on the loose."

Jack gripped the receiver tighter. "Who's there?"

Again, there was only silence.

"Who's there? Who are you?" Jack waited, but heard only the sound of his own erratic breathing. Then, finally . . .

"Sleep tight," was the cool reply. The phone clicked, and then came the dial tone.

Chapter 5

●

Governor Harold Swyteck jogged down a wood-chip jogging path. He muttered a soft curse as he reflected on the political repercussions of Jack's victory the previous day. The governor and his advisers had been speculating for weeks on how the trial might affect his bid for re-election. They figured a few tough anticrime speeches would probably counter Jack's involvement. Never, however, had they figured he'd actually win an acquittal. Had they considered it, they might have had a comeback when the media issued its hourly reports that it was indeed the governor's son who'd gotten a confessed killer off on a technicality.

"Damn it all!" Harry blurted with another husky breath, his arms pumping to a quicker cadence. As his legs surged forward he felt his anger building. It was a father's anger, tinged more with disappointment than with vitriol.

The governor struggled to maintain his pace. Since the Fernandez execution, he'd taken up jogging and sworn off the booze. In some twelve hundred days in office, he'd jogged about as many miles and thought about that one disturbing night at least as many times, wishing he'd just listened to his son and stopped the execution—if only for a few days, long enough to investigate Jack's story. Jogging gave him a chance to reflect on events and feelings without yielding to the urge to confide. His advisers pleaded with him about security, but he avoided escorts, except late at night or in big cities. "If some crazy is gunning for me," he'd always say, "he won't come looking on a back road for some guy in frumpy jogging sweats and a baseball cap." So far, he'd been right.

Harry slowed as he neared a cluster of sprawling oak trees and royal poincianas that marked the halfway point of his route. He reminded himself of the rules: The first half of his run was for venting anger; the second was reserved for positive thoughts.

"My fellow Floridians," he silently intoned as he reached his halfway marker, jogging beneath the fire-orange canopy of a royal poinciana. He could feel his attitude changing. His troubles were falling behind him; this morning's speech and throngs of loyal supporters were looming ahead. In just a few hours he would officially launch his re-election campaign.

". . . in this election, you have a choice," the speech continued in his mind. But his feet went out from under him, and he found himself sprawled on the ground, his right elbow and knee skinned and bleeding. At first he thought he'd tripped over something, but as he looked behind him a dark blur raced out from the shadow of a huge old oak and pounced on top of him, knocking him flat again. Their bodies locked together as they tumbled down a steep ravine along the deserted jogging path. They landed hard amid the tangled weeds and cattails beside a scummy green canal. The governor quickly reached in his pocket for his electronic pager to alert security, but before his finger could hit the red button, his attacker knocked the wind out of him with a fist to the solar plexus. In a split second, Harry was flat on his belly, his face pushed into the dirt.

"Heh!" the governor gasped, his head moving just enough to the side to allow his mouth to work. But a cold steel blade was at his throat before he could utter another word.

"Don't move," the man ordered.

Harry froze, his body trembling as he forced himself to remain facedown and perfectly still. His right cheek was pressed to the ground, but out of the corner of his left eye he could see a bruiser of a body sitting on his kidneys. Its sheer weight nearly prevented him from breathing, let alone moving. It was a man, he presumed. The voice was deep; the hands covered by black leather gloves were very large. The features, however, were indiscernible. He wore camouflaged marine fatigues, and his face was covered by a ski mask.

"Well, what do we have here," the man taunted in a thick, raspy voice. "Mr. Big-Time Politician out for his morning jog."

The governor clenched his fists, not to defend himself but to bring his fear under control. All was silent, except for a sucking sound the man made when he breathed. He must have been drooling from the wads of cotton or whatever he had in his mouth to disguise his voice.

"Hey, Governor," the attacker said, mocking him now with a friendly tone. "I hear you politicians like to deal. Well, here's one for you, my man. How about I give you proof that Raul Fernandez was innocent?"

Raul Fernandez? Harry started at the name. His mind ran in a dozen different directions, trying to make sense of why that name was being dredged up now.

"And in exchange for me being such a stand-up guy," the attacker continued, "for saving this big-time job of yours by not letting it slip that you and Junior killed an innocent man, you give me some money. A shitload of it."

The governor remained silent.

The man squeezed the back of Harry's neck, as if the knife were not already commanding enough attention. "Or maybe you prefer I just have a conversation with the newspapers."

The governor forced himself to put his fear aside long enough to ask a question. "What do you want from me?"

"There's a drugstore at the corner of Tenth and Mon- roe—Albert's. Be at the pay phone out front. Noon, Thursday. Alone. And don't even think about calling the cops. If you do, I go right to the newspapers. You hear what I'm saying?"

The governor swallowed hard. "Yes," he replied.

The man pushed the governor's face into the ground and sprung to his feet. "Before you even twitch a finger, count to a hundred, out loud, nice and slow. *Now*."

"One, two," Harry counted off, listening carefully as the man's footsteps faded into the distance. He lay still until he reached thirty, when he figured it was safe to move. Then he quickly rolled over and snatched the transmitter from his pocket. If he pushed the red button, security would be there in less than a minute. But he hesitated. What would he tell them? That some thug had threatened to reveal he'd executed an innocent man?

He tucked the transmitter into his pocket, still thinking. His attacker had warned him: Alert security and the Fernandez story goes straight to the media. Would that really be so disastrous? No question, it would be bad, but inside he felt an even deeper fear. That the attacker *wouldn't* go to the newspapers. That if he didn't show up at Albert's, he'd never hear from the man again. And he'd never know the truth about Fernandez.

He cast a forlorn look over the weeds, toward the thick woods where his attacker had disappeared. Tenth and Monroe was a crowded intersection—a very public and safe place. It wasn't like a face-to-face meeting in a dark alley. Hell, if the guy'd wanted to kill him, he'd be dead already. The decision was clear.

"Noon," he said aloud, confirming their telephone conference. "Tomorrow."

Chapter 6

●

Grateful for smart lawyers and legal loopholes, Eddy Goss was back on the streets of Miami, following the familiar cracked sidewalk to his favorite hangout. It was in a desolate part of town, where women stood alone on street corners to pay for their hundred-dollar-a-day crack habit and married men drove slowly by to satisfy their twenty-dollar urges. Goss, however, always avoided the women, ignoring their blunt offers of a quick "up and down." He would pass right by them on his way to the bright yellow building with no windows and huge black triple X's covering the length of the door. Inside, the windowless walls were lined with cellophane-wrapped magazines sitting in floor-to-ceiling racks. Goss liked the magazines because the girls were always so much prettier than the women on the street.

He moved around the adult bookstore like he owned

the place, familiar with every rack. He liked the way the materials were organized. Oral sex on the east wall. Group sex on the west. If he wanted messy sex, the south wall was the place. His favorite was the back wall, the place for those who liked really young girls.

"You buying anything?" asked the very fat man seated by the cash register behind the counter.

"Huh?" Goss responded, realizing that the man was talking to him.

The man rolled his eyes as his dirty, stubby fingers shoved an overstuffed sandwich into his mouth. "I said," he repeated with his mouth full, bits of lettuce and mayonnaise stuck in his straggly salt-and-pepper beard, "are you gonna buy anything, asshole?"

Goss shoved a magazine entitled *Pixie Vixens* back into the rack. "I'm just lookin' around."

"Well, an hour and a fucking half is long enough to look. Out, pal."

Goss stood rigidly, his furor-filled eyes locked in an intense stare-down. At first the clerk's expression was tough, but after a few seconds he seemed to lose heart. Just three weeks on the job and already he'd seen hundreds of weirdos in the shop. No one, however, had *ever* looked at him with such bone-chilling contempt.

"Do you know who you're talking to?" Goss seethed.

The clerk swallowed hard. "I don't care who—"

"I'm Eddy Goss."

The clerk froze. He'd seen the news coverage on television, and suddenly the face was familiar.

Goss took a couple of steps forward, toward the bin in the center of the room that was full of plastic dildos and other adult paraphernalia. He stopped short and stared at the clerk. "*I'm* Eddy Goss," he said, as if there were no need to say more. Then, with a quick jerk of his hand he sent an armful of merchandise sailing across the store.

The barrage of paraphernalia galvanized the clerk. Instinctively, he reached under the counter and came up with a pistol aimed at Goss. "Get outta here," his voice trembled. "Or I'm gonna blow your fucking head off!"

Goss scoffed and shook his head.

"You got ten seconds!" the clerk warned.

Goss just glared at him.

The clerk shifted his weight nervously. His arms strained to hold the pistol out in front of him. Beads of sweat began building on his brow, and the gun started shaking. "I'm not foolin', asshole!"

Goss was unshaken, convinced that this clerk didn't have the nerve to shoot him. But he'd had enough of this place for one day. "I'm outta here," he said as he headed for the door and stepped outside.

The sun had been shining brightly when he'd arrived at the bookstore, but it was overcast now, and dusk was near. He was hungry and thirsty, so he cut through the parking lot to the 7-Eleven next door. The store was empty, except for the Haitian clerk behind the counter. Goss opened a pack of Twinkies on his way down the aisle and stuffed them into his mouth as he reached the coolers in the back. He opened the glass doors, tossed the Twinkie wrapper behind the cold six-packs, and grabbed himself a tall can of malt liquor. He paid the clerk for the drink and left. He checked over his shoulder to see if the man was looking. He wasn't, so he grabbed a newspaper from the stand. He tucked it under his arm and headed down the dimly lit alley that led to the back of the store. He chugged down his malt liquor and threw the empty can onto the pavement. He found a secluded spot behind the store, by the Dumpster, and sat on some plastic bread crates beside a tall wooden fence that offered plenty of privacy. It was time.

Goss tore into the paper and pitched the sports, classifieds, and other useless sections onto the ground until he found something suitable—a Victoria's Secret special advertising pullout. He flipped the pages until he found the right girl, one with a particularly demure expression, then he spread the pullout on the ground at his feet. He hurriedly unzipped his pants, spit into the palm of his hand, and reached down between his legs. His eyes narrowed to slits as he imagined himself on top of the girl. His breathing became deeper and more rushed as his hand moved rhythmically back and forth.

"Fucking bitches," he gasped as his body jerked violently. He closed his eyes completely, then a second later opened them and inspected his handiwork. *Son of a bitch*.

Slowly he stood up and zipped his fly, towering over the smeared pictures on the ground. He reached inside his pocket and tossed down something tiny that landed with a tick on the wet surface. It was a seed. A chrysanthemum seed.

"My card," said Goss with a quick, sinister laugh.

Chapter 7

•

Governor Swyteck woke at six o'clock Thursday morning. As he showered and shaved, his wife, Agnes, lay awake in bed, exhausted after a night spent tossing and turning. Harold Swyteck was not a man who kept secrets from his wife. Yesterday he'd fabricated a story about a bad fall to explain his disheveled appearance to his security guards. But he told his wife the truth—as much out of concern for her safety as out of a need to be honest.

Agnes listlessly flipped on the television with her remote, tuning in to the local "News at Sunrise." Harry was in it again, this time appearing with a group of ministers, priests, and rabbis who were endorsing his candidacy. As her husband gratefully acknowledged the clergy's words of praise, she felt a surge of pride, but then her thoughts returned to what he'd told her the previous evening.

Agnes had always feared that a lifetime of public service could put her Harry in danger—that eventually one of his enemies might do something more than just threaten. But her fear gave way to more complicated feelings when Harry told her that this particular attacker had special knowledge about the Fernandez case. Agnes knew all too well how her husband had anguished over the decision not to grant a stay of execution—how he'd second-guessed the clarity of his own judgment. She understood her husband's pain. She shared it. Not just because there was no way to know whether the right decision had been made, but because of Jack.

She'd pretty much botched it as a stepmother. She knew that. She'd tried to reach out to her stepson countless times, but there was nothing left but to accept the reality of his bitterness. She might have had a fighting chance of winning his love but for a low moment twenty-three years before. It had happened the day that her doctor broke the news that she and Harry would never have children, and the awful truth had caused her to reach for the bottle.

She'd been too drunk to pick Jack up after kindergarten, so a neighbor had dropped him off. Jack came in quietly through the back door, making a conscious effort to avoid his new "mother," whom he still didn't trust.

"Jack," Agnes had muttered as her eyes popped open. Her tongue was thick as frozen molasses. "Come here, sweetie."

Jack tried to scoot past her, but Agnes reached out and managed to grab him by the back of his britches as he passed. She wrapped her arms around him in an awkward embrace and mashed her lips against his cheek. "Give Mommy a big hug," she said, stinking of her gin martini. He struggled to get out of her grip, but Agnes squeezed him tighter. "Don't you want to give Mommy a hug?" she asked.

"No," he grimaced. "And you're not my mommy!"

Resentment flared within her. She pushed little Jack off her lap but held him tightly by the wrist, so he couldn't go anywhere. "Don't you *dare* talk to me that way," she scolded. Then she slapped him across the face. The boy burst into tears as he struggled to get loose, but Agnes wouldn't release him.

"Let me go, you're hurting me."

"Hurt is the only thing you understand, young man. You don't appreciate anything else. I'm the one who changed your dirty diapers. I'm the one who . . . who"—she struggled to find the words—"lost sleep with all your crying in the night. Not your mother. *I* did it. *I'm* your mother. I'm all you've *got!*"

"You're *not* my mommy. My mommy's in heaven!"

Agnes didn't know where the ugly words were coming from, but she couldn't stop them. "Your mother isn't dead, you little brat. She just didn't *want* you!"

Jack's hands trembled as he stared at his stepmother. "That's a lie!" he cried. "A lie, lie, lie! That's all it is! That's—"

". . . the news at sunrise," The anchorman's voice drew Agnes out of her past. "From all of us at channel seven, have a great day."

Agnes hit the off button as she returned from her memories. The governor stepped from the bathroom, dressed and ready to take his phone call at the corner of Tenth and Monroe, ready to find out the truth about Raul Fernandez. However, last night he'd promised his wife that he wouldn't go without her blessing. She'd promised to sleep on it. As he stood at the foot of the bed, adjusting his necktie, she knew it was time for her to give him an answer.

"Well?" he asked.

Agnes sighed. It wasn't an easy decision. Even taking a phone call could be dangerous. The man *did* have a knife. But if this was a way to ease Harry's pain, a way to fix the rupture between her husband and her stepson, she couldn't stand in his way.

"Don't you dare take any chances, Harry Swyteck."

The governor smiled appreciatively, then came to her and kissed her on the lips. "I'll call you when it's over. And don't worry—I'm the original Chicken Little, remember?"

Agnes nodded but without conviction. In the beginning of their marriage, when Harry had been on the police force, such assurances were offered on a daily basis. It was her knowledge of her husband's innate bravery that worried her so much.

He pulled away, then stopped as he reached the door. "But if I don't call by one—"

"Don't say it, Harry," she said, eyes glassy now with tears. "Don't even think it."

He nodded slowly. "I'll call you," he promised. Then he was out the door.

More out of an ingrained sense of obligation than passion for his work, Jack put on jeans and a polo shirt—

typical summer attire at the Freedom Institute—gave Thursday a friendly pat on the rump, and headed out the door. In the car he brooded on whether he would tender his resignation. When he arrived at nine o'clock, he still hadn't come to a decision. It was his first day back in the office in almost three weeks, since the Goss trial had begun. He stood in the foyer, taking a hard look at the place where he'd worked for the past four years. The reception area was little more than a hallway. Bright fluorescent lighting showed every stain on the indoor-outdoor carpet. A few unmatched chairs lined the bare white walls. An oversized metal desk was at the end of the hall. It belonged to the pregnant woman who served as both the Institute's receptionist and only secretary. Behind her were four windowless offices, one for each of the lawyers. Beyond that was a vintage sixties kitchen, where the lawyers did everything from interviewing witnesses to eating their bagged lunches.

"Victory!" chorused Jack's colleagues as he stepped into the kitchen. All three of the Institute's other lawyers were smiling widely and assuming a celebratory stance around the Formica-topped table. There was Brian, a suntanned and sandy-haired outdoor type who moved as smoothly in court as he did on water skis. And Eve, the resident jokester who helped everyone keep sanity, the only woman Jack had ever known to smoke a pipe. And Neil Goderich, who'd lost his ponytail since establishing the Institute twenty-eight years ago, but who still wore his shirt collar unbuttoned beneath his tie—not just to be casual, but because his neck had swollen more than an inch since he last bought a new dress shirt.

The home team cheered as they broke out a six-dollar bottle of cold duck and popped the cork.

"Congratulations!" said Neil as he filled four coffee-stained mugs.

They raised their cups in unison, and Jack smiled at their celebration; although he didn't share the festive mood, he appreciated the gesture. He considered them all friends. At his first interview four years ago he'd learned they were down-to-earth people who believed in themselves and their principles. They were honest enough to tell even the son of a prominent politician that anything "politically correct" was a walking oxymoron. It was the strength of their collective character that made it hard for Jack to leave. But suddenly, he knew the time had come.

"Excellent job!" said Neil, a sentiment echoed by the others.

"Thank you," said Jack, hoping to stem any further backslapping. "I really appreciate this. But . . . as long as everyone's here, I might as well take this chance to tell you." He looked at them and sighed. "Guys, Eddy Goss was my last case. I'm leaving the Institute."

That took the fizz right out of their cold duck.

Jack placed his cup on the table, turned, and quietly headed toward his office, leaving them staring at one another. The announcement had been awkward, but he didn't feel like explaining. With no other job offer in hand, he was having a hard time explaining it to himself.

He spent a couple of hours packing up his things, going through old files. At eleven o'clock Neil Goderich appeared in his doorway.

"When you first came here," Neil began, "we honestly wondered if you'd ever fit in."

Jack picked up some books, placed them in a box. "I wondered the same thing."

Neil smiled sadly, like a parent sending a kid off to college. He took a seat on the edge of Jack's desk, beside a stack of packed boxes. "We never would have hired your type," he said as he stroked his salt-and-pepper beard. "You had 'big greedy law firm' written all over your résumé. Someone who clearly valued principal and interest over interest in one's principles."

"Then why'd you hire me?"

Neil smiled wryly. "Because you were the son of Harold Swyteck. And I could think of no better way to piss off the future law-and-order governor than to have his son come work for a long-haired leftover from a lost generation."

It was Jack's turn to smile. "So you put up with me for the same reason I put up with you."

"I suspected that was why you were here," he said, then turned serious. "You were tired of doing everything your old man said you *should* do. The Institute was as far off the beaten path as you could get."

Jack fell silent. He and Neil had never spoken about his father, and Neil's unflattering perception of the relationship was more than a little disturbing.

Neil leaned forward and folded his hands, the way he always did when he was speaking on the level. "Look, Jack. I read the papers. I watch TV. I know you're catching hell about Goss, and I know the bad press can't be doing the governor's campaign any good. Maybe you feel guilty about that . . . maybe your old man is even pressuring you to leave us. I don't know, and that's none of my business. But this much is my business: You've got what it takes, Jack. You're an incredibly talented lawyer. And deep down, I know you're not like all those people out there who are perfectly content to put up with poverty and drugs and homelessness and all the other problems that turn children into criminals, so long as the criminal justice system allows them revenge. The Freedom Institute deprives them of that revenge—of *their* sense of 'justice.' But we are doing the right thing here. *You've* done the right thing."

Jack looked away, then sighed. He had never been as sure about right and wrong as Neil was, though there had indeed been times when he saw the higher purpose, when he actually believed that each acquittal reaffirmed the rights of all people. But it took more than vision to defend the likes of Eddy Goss day after day. It took passion—the kind of passion that started revolutions. Jack had felt that passion only once in his life: the night his father had executed Raul Fernandez. But that was different. Fernandez had been innocent.

"I'm sorry, Neil. But the lofty goals just don't drive me anymore. Maybe I wouldn't be leaving if I'd defended just *one* murderer who was sorry for what he'd done. Not innocent, mind you. Just sorry. Someone who saw a not-guilty verdict as a second chance at life, rather than another chance to kill. Instead, I got clients like Eddy Goss. I hate to disappoint you, but I just can't stay here anymore. If I did, I'd be nothing but a hypocrite."

Neil nodded, not in agreement but in understanding. "I *am* disappointed," he said, "but not in you." He rose from the edge of the desk and shook Jack's hand. "The door's open, Jack. If ever you change your mind."

"Thanks."

"Got time for lunch today?"

Jack checked his watch. Almost eleven-thirty. He had no official plans, but right now he figured he needed a stronger dose of good cheer than Neil could provide. "I'd like a rain check on that, okay?"

"Sure thing," Neil said, giving him a mock salute as he turned and left.

Ten minutes later, Jack's thoughts were on Cindy as he walked toward his car, weighed down with three of the ten boxes he'd packed. He'd still had no return call from her. Which meant either she hadn't gotten his messages or she was sending him a message of her own.

He thought back to the last night they'd been together, how she'd told him she was going over to her best friend Gina's to console her. The story might have been believable if it had been anyone but Gina—a woman to whom the adjective *needy* didn't apply. Certainly Jack had never thought of her that way, and he knew her quite well. It was through her that he'd met Cindy. Fourteen months ago, a mutual friend had fixed him up on a blind date with Gina. It was their first and only. She'd kept Jack waiting in her living room nearly an hour while she got ready. Cindy was Gina's roommate back then, and she kept Jack entertained while he waited. He and Cindy clicked. Boy, did they click. He spent the rest of the evening with Gina just trying to find out about Cindy, and Cindy was the only woman he'd dated ever since. At first, Gina had seemed upset by the turn of events. But as he and Cindy became more serious, Gina came to accept it.

He checked the traffic at the curb, waited for the light to change, then started across the boulevard toward the Institute's parking lot. He was still wrapped up in his thoughts and struggling under the weight of the boxes when he noticed a car rolling through the red light. He picked up his pace to get out of the way, but the car increased its speed. Suddenly, it swerved sharply in his direction. He dove from the street to the sidewalk to keep from getting run over. As he tumbled to the concrete, he caught a glimpse of the retreating car. The first letter on the license plate was a Z. In Florida, that meant it was a rental.

His heart was in his throat. He couldn't stop shaking. He looked to see if there were any witnesses, but he saw no one. The Freedom Institute wasn't in a neighborhood where many people strolled the sidewalks. He remained on the ground for a moment, trying to sort out whether it was an accident, some street gang's initiation rite, just another crazy driver—or something else. He didn't want to be paranoid, but it was hard to dismiss the event as an accident. He picked himself up, then froze as he thought he heard a phone ringing. He listened carefully. It was *his* phone, a cheap but reliable car phone he'd installed at Neil Goderich's insistence, just in case his twenty-year-old Mustang happened to leave him stranded in one of those questionable areas that were breeding grounds for Freedom Institute clientele.

He looked around. He was still alone. The phone kept ringing. He walked to his car, disengaged the alarm with the button on his key chain, and opened the door. The phone must have rung twenty times. Finally, he picked up.

"Hello," he answered.

"Swyteck?"

Jack exhaled. It was that voice—that raspy, disguised voice on his home telephone two nights ago.

"Who is this?"

There was no answer.

"Who is this?"

"You let the killer loose. *You're* the one who let him go."

"What do you *want* from me?"

There was a long pause, an audible sigh, and then the response: "Stop the killer, Swyteck. I *dare* you."

"What—" Jack started to say. But he was too late.

The line clicked, and they were disconnected.

Chapter 8

●

At 11:40 A.M. Harry Swyteck put on his seersucker jacket, exited the capitol building through the rear entrance, and headed to Albert's Pharmacy at the busy intersection of Tenth Street and Monroe. The bright morning sun promised another insufferable afternoon, but the air wasn't yet completely saturated with the summer humidity that would bring the inevitable three o'clock shower. It was the perfect time of day to hit the streets, press the flesh, and do some grass-roots campaigning.

He reached the drugstore a few minutes before noon, masking his anxiety with campaign smiles and occasional handshakes along the way. Albert's was a corner pharmacy that hadn't changed in forty years, selling everything from hemorrhoidal ointment to three-alarm chili. Most important for the governor's purposes,

though, it was one of the few places in town that still offered the privacy of a good old-fashioned phone booth
out front. Harry wondered if his attacker had that in
mind when he selected it.

"Mornin', Governor," came a friendly greeting. It
was seventy-nine-year-old Mr. Albert, sweeping up in
front of his store.

"Morning," Harry said, smiling. "Great day to be
out, isn't it?"

Mr. Albert wiped the sweat from his brow. "I suppose," he said as he retreated back inside. Harry felt
that he, too, should be on his way. But he couldn't go
anywhere until his phone call came—and, above all, he
couldn't arouse suspicion by hanging around in front of
a drugstore. So he stepped inside the booth and tucked
the receiver under his chin, giving the appearance that
he was deeply engaged in private conversation. He casually rested his hand on the cradle, concealing from
passersby that he was pressing the disconnect button. He
checked the time on a bank marquee down the block.
Exactly twelve o'clock. He was suddenly very nervous—not about taking the call, but about the possibility
that it wouldn't come at all. To his quick relief, the phone
rang, and he immediately released the disconnect button.

"I'm here," he said into the phone.

"So you are, my man." There was still that thick
sucking sound to the man's speech. "Let's make this
quick."

"Don't worry, I'm not tracing the call."

The man seemed to scoff. "I'm not worried at all.
You're not about to call in the cops."

Harry bristled, annoyed that the caller had him figured for an easy mark. "How can you be so sure?"

"Because I can read you like a book. I saw the way your eyes lit up when I told you I had information about Fernandez. You've been thinking about that one for a while, haven't you?"

The governor listened carefully as pedestrians and cars buzzed by outside the booth. It disturbed him that this stranger understood him so well—this stranger who spoke like a punk but had the insight of a shrink. *Part of his disguise*, he figured. "What's your proposal?" he asked.

"Simple. I'll give you the evidence. The same evidence I showed your son two years ago, so you can see with your own eyes it was *me* who slit the bitch's throat. All you gotta do is come up with the cash."

Harry's mind was reeling. *This* was the man who had visited Jack the night of the Fernandez execution? Could he be on the level—could he really be the killer?

"Wait a minute, you're saying *you* killed that young girl?"

"You need a hearing aid, old man? That's exactly what I'm saying."

The governor felt as if a deep chasm were opening up in front of him and he was plummeting downward with no end in sight. It took a few seconds to collect himself. "You said something about money?"

"Ten thousand. Unmarked fifties."

"How do I get it to you?" he asked, though he could hardly believe he was actually negotiating. "And how do I get this evidence you claim you have?"

"Just bring the money to Bayfront Park in Miami. Go to where the carriage rides start, by the big statue of Christopher Columbus. Get in the white carriage with the red velvet seats. The driver's an old nigger named Calvin. Get the nine P.M. ride. When you get to the amphitheater, he'll stop for a break and get himself an iced tea from the roach-coach señorita with the big tits. When he does, check under your seat on the right-hand side. The seat cushion flips up, and there's storage space underneath. You'll find a shoe box and a note. Leave the money, take the box, read the note—and do *exactly* as it says. Got it?"

"What if the carriage driver doesn't stop?"

"He'll stop, if you get the nine o'clock ride. You can set a fucking clock by him. He always stops."

"I can't just go for a carriage ride with a sack full of money."

"You can—and you *will*."

The governor quickly sensed the nonnegotiability of the terms. "I'll need a little time. When do you want it?"

"Saturday night. And like I said: Take the nine o'clock ride. Gotta go, my man. I don't think you're tracing the call, but just in case you are, my seventy seconds is about up."

The governor heard a click on the other end of the line. Slowly he placed the receiver back in the cradle, then took a deep breath. He worried about getting in deeper, but he had to be certain that what this man was telling him was the truth. He didn't know what he'd do once he confirmed it, how he'd be able to live with himself or explain it to Jack, but he had to be certain.

Besides, it could be worse. Paying a single dime to

this low-life would be too much, but the truth was that ten thousand dollars would not devastate his and Agnes's finances. The man could easily have asked for much more.

He wondered why the man *hadn't* asked for more. He was taking quite a risk exposing himself like this. Why not go for the big payday? Unless he was playing a different game altogether, one Harry couldn't even begin to fathom.

Somehow the possibility of that filled him with an even deeper dread.

Chapter 9

•

"To my good buddy, Jack," said Crazy Mike Mannon, proprietor of Mike's Bikes and Jack Swyteck's best friend. He raised a bottle of Michelob. "May you come to your senses and never find another job as a lawyer."

Jack smiled, then tipped back his Amstel and took a long pull. After a day of phone calls to friends about potential job openings, he'd let Mike talk him into dinner on South Beach. A couple of beers and cheeseburgers at a sidewalk cafe sounded good.

They enjoyed the ocean breezes and watched bronzed bodies on roller blades weave in and out of bright-red convertibles, classic Corvettes, and fat-tired jeeps blaring reggae and Cuban salsa. By eight o'clock the sun had gone down and everything trendy, sexy, and borderline illegal was parading down Ocean Drive beneath colorful neon hues.

"Whoa," said Mike as a deeply tanned blonde with a seriously plunging neckline sent a ripple of whiplash through the cafe.

Jack smiled with amusement. Mike was one of those guys who was forever on the make—a frat boy stuck in a man's body. Even so, he had an irrepressible spirit that most people found charming. He had a way of not taking life too seriously, of following his own desires and not worrying about what others thought or said. Jack envied him for that.

"You know, Mike, there's an orthopedic surgeon over at Jackson Memorial who would love to see your X rays. She's doing a paper on swivel heads."

"Easy for you to be so pious, Mr. Monogamous. But some of us don't go to bed every night with Cindy Paige."

"Yeah, well," Jack said, looking away, "I'm beginning to wonder how much longer that's going to last."

"Uh-oh. Trouble in Camelot. That's okay, I'll find a honey for you, too. How about that one?" Mike said, nodding at a leather-clad bodybuilder with spiked burgundy hair.

"Perfect. She looks like the type who'd go for a guy without a job. And if she seems undecided, I'll just mention that some maniac wants to turn me into roadkill."

Mike gave him an assessing look. "Any new theories about that car thing yesterday?"

"Your guess is still as good as mine," Jack said, shrugging. "I suppose it could be Goss having fun with me. This 'killer on the loose' stuff is his style. But I'm not sure he has the attention span. First the phone call three days ago. Now this. It's a real campaign. Someone is obviously furious about the verdict."

Mike's head swiveled to follow two halter-topped women who'd emerged from the ladies' room. "Maybe you should call the cops."

Jack smiled. "The Miami Police Department would like nothing better than to hear Jack Swyteck is being hassled. They'd probably offer the guy the key to the city. I don't think the cops are an option right now."

"Well, you watch your back," Mike said with emphasis. He grinned. "You might even want to consider a new line of work—you know, greeting-card salesman or something."

Jack nodded. Maybe Mike had a point. Maybe he did need a clean break—even a move to another state. Away from Goss, and out of the shadow of his father, for whom the best was never enough, and Cindy who was always pushing him to open up. Hell, why *couldn't* he open up? Everyone else in America was unloading their thoughts. You couldn't turn on a talk show these days without watching someone turn his guts inside out in front of the camera.

"Hey, Mike," Jack asked, his mind drifting. "Do you get along with your family—you know, do you chew the fat regularly with your mom and dad?"

Mannon had made eye contact with some woman in tight purple capri pants. "Huh," he said, refocusing on Jack. "Oh, family . . . well, yeah, you know. My mom and I talk. It's mostly her that does the ear-bending. Always wants to know when I'm going to get married and give her grandchildren."

"And your dad?"

"We get along." He smiled, but with a hint of sadness. "When I was a kid, we were real tight. Horsed around, went to the Hurricanes games. We took the boat down toward Elliot Key nearly every weekend. Came back with our limit every time, it seemed." He paused. "After I got out of school, though, it was more formal—you know, brisk handshake and 'how's the business going, son?' That sort of thing. But we're always there for each other."

Jack thought of that picture he'd seen on his father's bookshelf the night of the Fernandez execution. Deep-sea fishing. Just the two of them.

"Waiter," he called out. "Two more over here, please."

Driving back from South Beach at 1:45 that Saturday morning, Cindy leaned over, turned off the A.C. in Gina's car, and opened her window to let in some warmer air.

"Why'd you do that?" Gina said petulantly.

"Because it's getting cold in here."

"I like the cold air. It keeps me awake—especially after I've had a few drinks. Besides, these pants I'm wearing are hot."

Cindy looked over at her girlfriend. Oh, they were hot all right, but not in a thermal sense. The clingy black spandex molded Gina's body perfectly—a body that could get her anything from dinner at world-class restaurants to full service at self-service gas stations. She was gorgeous, and she worked at it, still striving at age twenty-four for "the fresh look" that had earned her a thousand dollars a week as a sixteen-year-old model.

They'd first met six years ago in college, two eighteen-year-old opposites who were thrown together by the administrative fiat of dorm-room assignments. Cindy was the more serious student; Gina, the more serious partyer. For the better part of a semester they simply put up with each other. Then late one Saturday night Gina came back to their room in tears. It took until dawn, but Cindy finally convinced her that no college professor, no matter how good a lover, was worth a fifth of bourbon and a bottle of sleeping pills. Cindy was the only person who ever learned that a man had pushed Gina Terisi to the edge. A friendship grew out of that night's conversation, and over the years Cindy had witnessed the slaughter of countless innocent men who came along later and paid for the sins of Gina's first and only "true love." Cindy knew that the predatory Gina wasn't the real Gina; but it was hard convincing others who hadn't seen her at her most vulnerable.

"Have you ever driven a car with your eyes closed?" Gina asked.

"Can't say I have," said Cindy as she fiddled with the buttons on the car radio trying to find something she liked.

"I have. Sometimes when I see there's a car coming at me, I get this feeling that I want to hold the wheel steady, close my eyes, and wait for that *whooooooosh* sound as the car whizzes by."

Cindy rolled her eyes. "Just drive, Gina."

Gina made a face. "You're in one hell of a mood."

"Sorry. I guess I don't feel like I should be out partying tonight. I'm having second thoughts about telling Jack I want to break up."

"We've been over this a hundred times, Cindy— you're getting out of that relationship."

Cindy blinked. "It's just that we were so close. We were even talking about making it permanent."

"Which means that I rescued you without a moment to spare. Believe me, it's no accident that the word *married* rhymes with *buried*," she said, mashing the pronunciation. "Life's no dress rehearsal, okay? Find some excitement without standing on the sidelines and living your life through me. You've got a great opportunity right in front of you. It's not every twenty-five-year-old photographer who gets hired by the Italian Consulate to go traveling around Italy taking pictures for a trade brochure. Jump on it. If you don't—if you stay behind because you think you're gonna lose Jack—you'll end up hating him for it someday."

"Maybe," Cindy said. "But that doesn't mean I have to dump him. I could just tell him that the time apart will give us both a chance to decide whether our relationship should be permanent or not."

"Just *stop it*, will you? You've been living with Jack for months. After that much time, you either know it's right or it's wrong. And if you're still saying you're trying to make up your mind—believe me, it ain't right."

"It felt right at times."

"That was a long time ago. I know you, Cindy. And I know you've been unhappy with Jack for months. Here's a guy who claims to be talking about 'making things permanent,' yet half the time he won't even give you a hint of what's *really* on his mind. And whatever the hell this big secret is that keeps him from talking to his big-shot father is too weird. I think he has a screw loose."

"There's nothing wrong with Jack," Cindy said defensively. "I just think the way his mother died and how his family handled all these problems has him confused about a lot of things."

"Fine. So while he sorts it all out, you go have yourself a ball in Italy."

"I don't know—"

"Well," Gina huffed, "do what you want then. But it's a moot point, anyway. Once Jack hears who your traveling companion will be, it'll be over between you two anyway."

Cindy didn't answer. Gina had a point, but she didn't want to think about that right now. She just listened to the radio for a few minutes, until the early-morning jazz gave way to the local news at 2:00 A.M. The lead story was still Eddy Goss.

". . . the confessed killer," said the newscaster, "who was acquitted by a jury Tuesday afternoon on first-degree murder charges." This report was about Detective Lonzo Stafford's diligent efforts to link Goss to at least two other murders, to get him off the streets so that, according to Stafford, "Goss will never kill again."

Cindy and Gina both pretended not to listen, though neither had the other one fooled. Jack's involvement in the Goss case had brought this killer a little too close to home. Cindy thought of Jack, probably by himself, back at the house. Gina thought of Eddy Goss. Out there. Somewhere.

Gina steered her champagne-colored BMW, a gift from her latest disappointed suitor, into her private townhouse community, a collection of twenty lushly landscaped units facing the bay. Gina could never have afforded waterfront property on her salary as an interior designer, so she "leased" this place from an extremely wealthy and married Venezuelan businessman who, as Gina once kidded, "comes about three times a year, all in one night, to collect the rent."

Cindy's car was parked in Gina's garage, so Gina parked in a guest space across the lot. They stepped tentatively from the car with the disquieting newscast about Eddy Goss still fresh in their minds.

"Nothing like a killer on the loose to make a marathon out of a two-minute walk to the front door," Cindy half-joked as they briskly crossed the empty parking lot.

"Yeah," Gina replied, her nervous laughter ringing flat and hollow in the stillness of the dark night. She ran up the front steps two at a time. Cindy trailed behind, moving not quite as fast in heels as her long-legged friend. The porch light was on and the front door was locked, just the way they'd left it. Gina fumbled through her cosmetic-packed purse for her key and poked awkwardly at the lock. Finally, she found the slot and pushed the key home. With two quick turns she unlocked the dead bolt, then turned the knob and leaned into the door, opening it—but just a foot, as her body jerked to an unexpected halt. The door caught on the inside chain.

They froze as they realized they couldn't possibly have gotten out of the townhouse had *they* put the chain on the door.

Gina glanced at the clay pot on the porch that hid her extra key—a spare only a few people knew about. The pot had been moved.

Before Gina could back away, the door slammed shut, pushing her back and spilling the contents of her purse onto the porch.

Panic gripped the two women as they grabbed for each other. When they heard the chain coming off the door, they screamed in unison as they raced down the stairs. Gina led the way, kicking off her shoes and negotiating the steps like a steeplechase racer. Cindy's left heel caught on the bottom step, and she tumbled to the sidewalk.

"Gina, help!" she cried, sprawled out on her hands and knees. But her friend never looked back.

"Gina!"

Chapter 10

•

"**H**ey!" Jack shouted as the door flew open at the top of the steps. "Hey! It's me!"

Gina kept running, but Cindy stopped and looked up from the foot of the stairs. "Jack?" she called out as she picked herself up from the sidewalk.

Jack waved from the top of the stairs. "It's okay. It's just me."

"You son of a bitch!" Gina shouted on her way back from the parking lot. "What the hell are you doing here?"

Good question, thought Jack. Back at the bar, he'd yielded to Mike's urging and switched from beers to Bahama Mamas. And in no time flat he was feeling the effects of the grain alcohol. He rarely drank hard liquor, so when he did, it went straight to his head. Rather than kill someone trying to drive all the way home, he'd stopped at Gina's, hoping to find Cindy.

"I don't know *what* I'm doing here," he said with a shrug, speaking to himself more than anyone else. Then he looked at Cindy. "Sorry, guess I had a little too much to drink. I just wanted to talk to you, find out what was going on with us."

"Jack," Cindy sighed, "this is not the place—"

"I just want to *talk*, Cindy. You owe me at least that." As he spoke he wobbled slightly and used the railing to regain his balance.

Cindy struggled. Seeing Jack made her regret the way she'd handled their problem. "I'm not sure I *can* talk—at least tonight. I honestly haven't made up my—"

"Her mind *is* made up," Gina contradicted. "Forget it, Jack. She's leaving you. Like it or not, she's a better person without you. Just let her go."

Cindy shot an exasperated look at her friend.

Jack was suddenly embarrassed by the spectacle he was making of himself.

"Just forget it," he said as he shook his head and then started down the stairs.

Cindy hesitated a moment, then moved to stop him. "No, you're right, we do need to talk. Let me get my car keys. We can talk at home."

He looked back at Gina, then turned to Cindy. "You're sure?"

She gave a quick nod, avoiding his eyes. "Go ahead, get in your car. I'll follow."

There is no line more palpable than the one that runs down the middle of the bed. The room may be dark. The eyes may be shut. But it is there, silent testament to the deep division that can separate a couple.

The line between Jack and Cindy began to emerge as they drove from Gina's in separate cars, parked in their driveway, and headed into the house single file. It became more pronounced as they undressed in silence, and by the time they tucked themselves into their respective corners of the king-size mattress, it was the Berlin Wall born again. Jack knew they had to talk, but after a night of drinking, he was afraid of what he might say. He played it safe. He flipped off the light, mumbled a clipped "night," and pretended to be asleep, though it was actually hours before his troubled mind finally let his body rest.

Cindy didn't try to keep him up, but she couldn't fall asleep either. She was thinking of how he'd asked her to move in with him, almost ten months ago. He'd covered her eyes with his hands and led her to his bedroom, and when he took his hands away she saw little yellow ribbons tied to the handles on half the dresser drawers, marking the empty ones. "Those are yours," he'd told her. Now, lying in their bed, she closed her eyes and thought of yellow ribbons—ribbons and lace and streamers. As her thoughts melted into sleep, the last waking image was of a room decorated for a party. A lavish party with hundreds of guests. Instinctively, she knew that it was important Jack be there, but when she looked for him, when she called out his name, no one answered.

"Jack," she whispered barely three hours later as the heat from the morning sun warmed her forehead. The sound of her own voice speaking in a dream woke her, and she rolled over onto her side. "Jack," she said, nudging his shoulder. "We need to talk."

"Huh?" Jack rubbed his eyes and turned to face her. He stole a look at the alarm clock and saw that it was just 7:00 A.M.

"Be back in a second," he said as he slid to the side of the bed, stood up, then sat right back down. "Whoa," he groaned, feeling the first throb of a hangover so massive that had someone suggested amputation as the only cure, he might have considered it. He sighed, resigning himself to remaining seated. "Listen," he said as he glanced over his shoulder at Cindy, "I'm sorry about last night, okay?"

Cindy sat up, then hesitated, deciding whether to cross the line between them. It was strange, but after ten months of living with him, she suddenly felt uncomfortable about Jack, sitting there in his striped underwear, and about herself, wearing only an oversized T-shirt.

"I'm sorry too," she said as she slid tentatively across the bed. She sat on the edge, beside him, though she kept her distance. "But it's not enough just to exchange apologies. We need to talk. I've been giving this a lot of thought."

"Giving *what* a lot of thought?"

She grimaced. "I've been offered a photo shoot for the Italian Trade Consulate. In Italy."

He smiled, relieved it was good news. "That's fantastic, absolutely terrific," he said as he reached out and squeezed her hand. "That's the kind of thing you've always dreamed about. Why didn't you tell me before?"

"Because I'd have to leave right away—and it'll take me away for three or four months."

He shrugged it off. "We can survive that."

"That's just it," she said, averting her eyes. "I'm not so sure we can."

"What do you mean?" he asked, his smile fading.

She sighed. "What I mean is, we have problems, Jack. And the problem isn't really *us*. It's something inside you that for some reason you just won't share."

He looked away. She was right. The problem *was* inside him.

"We've been over this before," he said. "I mope—get in these lousy moods. A lot of it's work—the job I do." He thought for a second of telling her he'd quit the Freedom Institute, but decided that being jobless wouldn't help his case. "But I'm dealing with it."

"There's just something that makes you unable or unwilling to communicate and expose yourself emotionally. I can't just dismiss it. As long as we've been together, you've been completely incapable of reaching out to your own father and solving whatever it is that keeps you two apart. It worries me that you handle relationship problems that way. It worries me so much that I took the Goss trial as an opportunity to get away from you for a few days. To think about us . . . whether we have a future. I honestly wasn't sure how I was going to leave it. Whether I'd say, 'Let's just go our separate ways' or 'I still love you, I'll phone and write and see you when I get back from Europe.' "

"And you were going to make that decision by yourself?" he asked, now somewhat annoyed. "I was just supposed to go along with whatever you announced?"

"No, I knew we had to talk, but it just wasn't that easy. It gets a little more complicated."

"In what way?"

She looked at her toes. "I'm not going alone," she said sheepishly. "It's me and Chet."

His mouth opened, but the words wouldn't come. "Chet," he finally uttered. Chet was Cindy's old boss at Image Maker Studios, her first employer out of college—and the man in her life before Jack had come along. Jack felt sick.

"It's not what you think," Cindy said. "It's purely professional—"

"Why are you doing it this way?" he asked, ignoring her explanation. "Do you think I'm gonna go over the edge if you just tell me the truth and dump me? I won't, don't worry. I'm stronger than that. For the past month, every time I turn on the nightly news or read a newspaper, it's one story after another about confessed killer Eddy Goss and his lawyer, Jack Swyteck—always mentioned in the same sentence, always in the same disgusted tone. I walk down the street, and people I know avoid me. I walk down the other side of the street, and people I've never even *seen* spit at me. Lately, it's been worse." He thought of his near rundown just two days ago. "But you know what? I'm gonna come out of this okay. I'm gonna beat it. If I have to do it without you, that's your choice. But doing it without your pity—that's *my* choice."

"I'm not pitying you. And I'm not leaving you. Can't you just accept what I'm telling you as my honest feelings and be honest with me about your own feelings?"

"I've never lied to you about my feelings."

"But you never *tell* me anything, either. That bothers me. Sometimes I think it's me. Maybe it's my fault. I don't know. Gina thinks it's just the way you are, because of the way you and your father—"

"What the hell does Gina know about my father?"

She swallowed hard. She knew she'd slipped. He was shaking his head, and his fists were clenched. "Did you tell her the things I told you?"

"Gina's my best friend. We talk. We tell each other the important things in our lives."

"Damn it, Cindy!" he shouted as he sprung from the bed. "You don't tell her *anything* I tell you about me and my father. How could you be so fucking insensitive!"

Cindy's hands trembled as her nails dug into the mattress. "Don't talk to me that way," she said firmly, "or I'm leaving right this second."

"You're leaving anyway," he said. "Don't you think I can see that? You're going to Italy with the boss you used to sleep with. You're out with Gina till two in the morning, checking out guys and prowling the nightclubs—"

"That's not what we were—"

"Oh, bullshit!" His emotions had run away so completely that he'd forgotten his own whereabouts the night before. "You're not hanging with Mother Teresa, you know. Hell, I've had more meaningful conversations with tollbooth attendants than Gina's had with half the men she's slept with."

"I'm not Gina. And besides, Gina's not that way. Just stop it, Jack."

"Stop what?" he said, raising his voice another level. "Stop looking behind what this is really all about? Stop taking the fun out of Cindy and Gina's excellent adventure?"

She sat rigidly on the side of the bed, too hurt to speak.

He charged toward the bedroom door. "You want to go?" he asked sharply, flinging the door open. "Go."

She looked up, tears welling in her eyes.

"Go *on*," he ordered. "Get outta here!"

She still didn't move.

He moved his head from side to side, looking frantically about the room for some way to release months or maybe even years of pent-up anger that Cindy hadn't caused but was now the unfortunate recipient of. He darted toward the bureau and snatched the snapshots of them she'd tucked into the wood frame around the mirror—their memories.

"Jack!"

"There," he said as he ripped one to pieces.

"Don't do that!"

"You're leaving," he said as he took the picture of them taken in Freeport from his stack.

She jumped up and dashed for the walk-in closet. He jumped in front of her.

"I need to get some clothes!"

"Nope," he said, holding another photo before her eyes. "You're leaving right now. Go back to Gina— your confidante."

"Stop it!"

He ripped the entire stack in half.

"Jack!" She grabbed her car keys and headed for the door, wearing only her T-shirt. She stopped in the doorway and said tearfully, "I didn't want it to turn out this way."

He scoffed. "Now you sound like the scum I defend."

Her face reddened, ready to burst with tears or erupt with anger. "You *are* the scum you defend!" she screamed, then raced out of the house.

Chapter 11

•

At eight-thirty that Saturday evening, Harry Swyteck parked his rented Buick beneath one of the countless fifty-foot palm trees that line Biscayne Boulevard, Miami's main north-south artery. The governor was alone, as he'd promised his blackmailer. It was a few minutes past sunset, and the streetlights had just blinked on. Harry sighed at the impending darkness. As if he didn't already have enough to worry about, now he had to carry around ten thousand dollars in cash in Miami after dark. He checked the locks on his briefcase and stepped quickly from the car, then scurried across six lanes of traffic to the east side of the boulevard, following the sidewalk into the park.

Bayfront Park was Miami's green space between bustling city streets and the sailboats on Biscayne Bay. Granite, glass, and marble towers lit up the Miami skyline to the south and west of the park. Across the bay toward South Miami Beach the lights of Caribbean-bound cruise ships glittered like a string of floating pearls. Cool summer breezes blew off the bay from the east, carrying with them the soothing sound of rolling waves breaking against the shoreline. At the north end of the park was Bayside Marketplace, an indoor-outdoor collection of shops, restaurants, and bars, and the starting place for the horse-and-buggy rides through the park that were favored by tourists.

Tonight it was Governor Swyteck's turn to take a carriage ride. He hoped to blend in as a tourist, which was the reason for his white sailing pants, plaid madras shirt and Marlins baseball cap. But the leather briefcase made him feel conspicuous. He bought a stuffed animal from one of the cart vendors, just to get hold of the paper shopping bag, and stuck the briefcase in the bag. Now his outfit was complete: He didn't *look* at all like a governor, and that was the whole idea—though he did have a plan in case anyone recognized him. "Another stop on my grass-roots campaign trail," he'd say, and they'd probably buy it. Four years ago he'd manned a McDonald's drive-through, taught phonics to first-graders, and worked other one-day jobs—all just to look like a regular Joe.

"Carriage ride?" one of the drivers called out as he reached the staging area.

"Uh—I'm thinking about it," Harry replied.

"Forty bucks for the half hour," the driver said, but the governor wasn't listening. He was trying to figure out which of the half dozen carriages belonged to Calvin, the man he'd been told to hire for the nine o'clock ride. By process of elimination he zoomed in on a sparkling white carriage with red velvet seats, pulled by an Appaloosa with donkeylike ears poking through an old straw hat. The governor felt nervous as he approached the wiry old black driver, but he told himself once again that he had to see this mission through. Sensing he was being watched, he looked one way, then the other, but could see nothing out of the ordinary.

"Are you Calvin?" he asked, looking up at the driver.

"Yessuh," he replied. Calvin was in his eighties, a relic of old Miami, when the city was "My-amma" and truly part of the South. He had frosty white hair and the callous hands of a man who had worked hard all his life. He seemed exaggeratedly deferential, making Harry feel momentarily guilty for his race and the way this old codger must have been treated as a young man.

"I'd like to take a little ride," said the governor as he handed up two twenty-dollar bills.

"Yessuh," said Calvin as he checked his watch. "Fair warnin' for you, though: You're my nine o'clock ride. I always stop at the concession stand on my nine o'clock ride. Get myself an iced tea."

"That's fine," said the governor as he climbed aboard. *I wouldn't have it any other way.*

Calvin made a clicking sound with his mouth and gave the reins a little tug. His horse pulled away from the rail and started toward the waterfront, as if on automatic pilot, while the governor looked on with amusement as the animal navigated the route. "How long you been doing this, Calvin?"

"Lot longer than you been guvnuh, suh."

So much for anonymity.

The journey began at the towering bronze statue of Christopher Columbus and headed south along the shoreline. Palm trees and musicians playing saxophones and guitars lined the wide pedestrian walkway of white coral rock, the south Florida version of a quaint cobblestone street. Calvin played tour guide as they rolled down the walkway. He was a veritable history book on wheels when it came to the park and its past, talking about how they had filled in the bay to build it in 1924 and how the sea had tried to reclaim it in the hurricane of 1926. He spoke from memory and years of practice, but he was clearly putting a little more emotion into it for his distinguished guest. The governor listened politely, but he was fading in and out, trying to remain focused on the purpose of his trip. His anxiety heightened as the carriage curled around the spewing fountain and headed west, away from the brightly lit walkway along the water to the interior of the park, where palm trees and live oaks cast shadows beneath street lamps that were becoming fewer and farther between. As they reached the amphitheater, the carriage slowed up, just as Calvin had warned and the blackmailer had said it would.

"Whoa," Calvin said gently to his horse, bringing the carriage to a halt. He turned and faced the governor. "Now, this is what I call the dark side of my tour, sir. For it was right here, where the old bandstand used to be, in the year of our Lord nineteen hundred and thirty-three, that President-Elect Franklin Delano Roosevelt addressed a crowd of fifteen thousand people. Amidst that huge crowd there stood one very angry young man—a man who doctors would later describe as a highly intelligent psychopath with pet schemes and morbid emotions that ran in conflict with the established order of society. That disturbed young man stood patiently atop a park bench until the president finished his speech, then took out his revolver and fired over the crowd at the dignitaries onstage, intending to kill Mr. Roosevelt. The president escaped unhurt, but five innocent people were shot. The most seriously injured was Anton Cermak, the distinguished mayor of Chicago, who, before he died, told the president, 'I'm glad it was me, instead of you.' "

Calvin saw the expression on the governor's face, then looked down apologetically. "Didn't mean to frighten you, Guvnuh. I always tell that story to all my passengers, not just to politicians. Just a part of our history, that's all."

"That's quite all right," he said, trying to ignore the chill running down his spine. But he wondered if his blackmailer knew that Calvin did indeed tell this story to all his passengers. Maybe that was the reason he had selected this particular carriage ride for the exchange. It was certainly possible—the man had apparently been planning this for two years, since the Fernandez execution. The governor suddenly wanted to hear more. "So, Calvin," he said casually, "I imagine this assassination must have been pretty big news back in '33."

"Oh, sure. Was front-page news for about a month or so, as I recall."

"What happened to the assassin?"

Calvin widened his eyes and raised his bushy white eyebrows. "I don't mean no disrespect, sir. But this man pulled out a pistol in front of fifteen thousand people, fired six shots at the president of the United States, wounded five people and done killed the mayor of Chicago. They dragged him into court, where he proceeded to tell the world that his only regret was that he didn't get Mr. Roosevelt. And to top it all off, the man begged the judge to give him the chair. Now whatchoo think they done to that fool?"

"Executed him," he said quietly.

"*Course* they executed him. Four days after they laid Mayor Cermak's dead body in the ground they done did execute him. Swift justice was what we had back then. Not like we got these days. All these lawyers we got now, hemmin' and hawin' and flappin' their jaws. Appealin' this and delayin' that. Anyhow," Calvin said with a sigh, "that's enough bellyachin'. I'm gonna let Daisy rest a spell and get myself a nice iced tea. Somethin' for you, Guvnuh?"

"No, thank you, Calvin. I'll wait here." Harry watched the old man hobble over to the concession stand, and he began to wonder about this whole curious arrangement. Was the blackmailer revealing his deeper, darker side—the "morbid emotions that ran at conflict with the established order of society?" Could he be *that* clever, that he had purposefully sent the governor to this old tour guide who in his own melodramatic way could make so painfully obvious the difference between the relatively easy capital cases and the unbearably difficult ones, between a man who boasts of his crime all the way to the electric chair and a man who proclaims his innocence to the end—between a crazed political assassin and someone like Raul Fernandez? Or maybe the message was less subtle, less philosophical. Maybe he was simply telling the governor that the very site of Florida's most famous political assassination was about to be the site of its next political assassination—tonight.

Harry glanced nervously toward Calvin, who was smiling and chatting with the concessionaire, an attractive young Hispanic woman whose shapely appearance alone explained the regularity of Calvin's nine o'clock stops. He pulled the carriage blanket over his lap, even though it was seventy-five degrees outside, so as to hide his movements. Then he touched the edge of the red velvet seat cushion beside him and got ready to lift it off. His heart began to race as he suddenly wondered whether a pistol-wielding madman would leap from the darkness or a bomb would explode when he lifted the carriage seat, writing the final chapter to Calvin's history lesson. He took a deep breath and pulled up. The seat popped out, just as his blackmailer had said it would. No explosion. No rattlesnakes inside. He checked over his shoulder to make sure no one was looking. Again he sensed he was being watched. But he saw nothing. He looked down to see what was beneath the seat.

Inside the little cubbyhole was a brown shoe box, with a note on the side: "Leave the money. Take the box." There was no signature. Only this warning: "I'm watching you."

The governor didn't dare turn his head to look around. He opened the briefcase in his shopping bag, emptied two stacks of crisp fifty-dollar bills under the seat, stuffed the shoe box into his bag, and put the seat cover back in place.

Calvin returned a few minutes later, and the ride back to Bayside Marketplace took only a few minutes more, though it seemed like an eternity. Harry thanked Calvin for the ride and quickly retraced his steps across the busy street to his car. As soon as he was behind the wheel, he set the shopping bag on the front seat beside him and took a deep breath, relieved that no one had stopped him. He turned on the ignition, but before he could pull into traffic he was startled by a short, high-pitched ring. It stopped, and then started up again. It seemed to emanate from the box inside the shopping bag. He took the shoe box from the bag and unfastened the tape on the lid. The shrill ringing continued. He flipped off the top and found a portable phone inside, resting on top of a sealed white envelope. He switched on the "talk" button and pressed the phone to his ear.

"It's in the envelope," came the familiar, thickly disguised voice.

The governor shuddered. Of course it would be him, but he was disturbed by the voice nonetheless. "What's in the envelope?"

"You have to ask, Governor?" came the reply. "I have your money, and you've got the proof it was me, not Raul, who killed the girl. That was our deal, wasn't it?"

The governor was silent.

"*Was* that our deal, Governor?"

"Yes, I suppose so."

"Good," said the caller in a calmer voice. "Now open the envelope. Just open it. Don't take anything out."

Harry tucked the phone under his chin and unsealed the envelope. "It's open."

"There's two photographs inside, both of the girl Raul got the chair for. Take out the one on the left."

The governor removed the snapshot from the envelope and froze. It was a photo of a teenage girl from her bare breasts up. She was lying on her back with her shoulders pinned behind her, as if her hands were bound tightly behind her back. A red bandanna gagged her mouth. The long blade of a knife pressed against her throat. Her blood-shot eyes stared up helplessly at her killer. The rest of her face was puffy and bruised from unmerciful beatings.

"You see it, my man?"

"Yes," his voice trembled.

"That's real fear in those eyes. You can't fake that. Sometimes I wish I'd videotaped it. But no need, really. I play it over and over again in my mind. It's like a movie. I call it 'The Taming of Vanessa.' Vanessa was her name, you know. It's nice to know their name. Makes it all more real."

The photograph shook in the governor's hand as his whole body was overcome by fear and disgust.

"Take out the next picture," said the caller.

Harry closed his eyes and sighed. It would have been difficult to look under any circumstances, but it was doubly painful now, realizing that Raul Fernandez was not responsible for this girl's death. The enormity of the governor's mistake was beginning to sink in, and all at once he was filled with self-loathing. "I've seen enough," he said quietly.

"Look at the next one. Look what I did with the knife."

"I said I've seen enough," Harry said firmly as he shoved the photo back into the envelope. "You've got your money, you monster. Just take it. That was our deal. Take it, keep your mouth shut, and don't ever call me again."

The caller chuckled with amusement. "Harry, Harry—that's not how the game is played. We're just getting started, you and me. Next installment's in a few days."

"I'm not paying you another cent."

"Such conviction. I guess you still can't feel that noose around your neck. Here, give *this* a listen."

The governor pressed the phone closer to his ear, straining to hear every sound. There was a click, then static, then a clicking sound again—and then a voice he clearly recognized as his own: *"You've got your money, you monster. Just take it. That was our deal. Take it, keep your mouth shut, and don't ever call me again."*

Another click, and the caller was back on the line. "It's all on tape, my man. You, the esteemed Governor Harold Swyteck, bribing an admitted killer to keep his mouth shut to save your own political skin. Every word of it's on tape—and ready to go to the newspapers."

"You wouldn't—"

"I *would*. So consider your piddling ten grand as nothing more than a down payment. Because you're gonna take another ten thousand dollars to four-oh-nine East Adams Street, Miami, apartment two-seventeen. Be there at four A.M., August second. Not a minute before, not a minute after. The door will be open. Leave it right on the kitchen table. Be good, my man."

"You son of a—" the governor started to say, but the caller was gone. A wave of panic overcame him. He pitched the phone and the envelope into the box beside him, holding his head in his hands as a deep pit of nausea swelled in his stomach. "You idiot," he groaned aloud, sinking in his car seat. But it wasn't just his own stupidity that had him shaking. It was the whole night that sent a current of fear coursing through him. The "history lesson" in the park, the photographs of the young girl, the tape recording in the car—and, most of all, the dawning realization that in this confrontation with a cold-blooded killer, he was clearly overmatched.

Chapter 12

•

Jack Swyteck bent low to avoid the doorway arch as he carried the last stack of boxes into the house. Behind him, carelessly flicking ashes from a fat cigar and obviously enjoying his friend's huffing and puffing, was Mike Mannon.

"I do believe you're out of shape," Mike needled.

"Excuse me, Mr. Schwarzenegger, but I didn't notice you setting any weight-lifting records today. And get that stink-rod out of my house."

Mike shrugged and blew a thick cloud of smoke at Jack. "Not my job to lift. You said you needed wheels because your 'stang was in the shop. You *didn't* say I had to play donkey."

"Well, I guess that's about it," Jack said, surveying his office haul. "God knows why I went back to get all this stuff, but I suppose it'll come in handy one of these days when I find a new job."

Mike looked down at the stack of legal volumes poking out of the biggest carton. "Yeah," he said, "McDonald's crew chiefs find frequent reason to cite legal precedent."

"I'll remember that, Mannon, next time some collection agency's breathing down your deadbeat neck." Jack smiled bitterly. "Hell, what am I saying. I'll probably *be* the guy breathing down your neck. That's about the extent of my options in this town until this Goss thing blows over."

"Ah, don't sell yourself short, old boy. One of those big law firms can always use an unscrupulous man like you."

Jack gave a short laugh, then turned serious. "Sure you can't hang out for a while?"

"Nah, got to get back to the shop. It takes Lenny about two and a half hours to create a major crisis." He looked at his watch. "One should be brewing about now."

"Okay, then," Jack said, following him out the door. He looked down to see Thursday wriggling through his legs with a bookend in his mouth. "Hey, give me that," Jack said, reaching down and patting his head. He called out after Mike, who was walking down the wood-chip path. "Thanks for the help."

"No problem," Mike said, turning around. He gave a short wave as Thursday bounded after him and nipped at his heels. In a few seconds the car had pulled away from the curb, and Jack was left alone with his thoughts.

He closed the door and headed to the living room. The sofa felt good as he fell back onto it and propped his feet on the hassock. He looked around. Emptiness—a lot of emptiness. Sitting there, it seemed as if he were the only occupant of a grand hotel. Why had he ever bought such a huge house? Cindy once told him that as a girl she'd dreamed of living in a mansion. Sharing a small apartment with her parents and three brothers probably had something to do with it.

There he went again. Thinking of her. Ever since yesterday morning, when he'd made such an ass of himself and insisted she leave, he couldn't get her out of his mind. For perhaps the thousandth time since watching her go, he marveled at his stupidity. Deep down, he'd been worried that her relationship with Chet might be starting up again, and what did he do but drive her into his arms.

Brilliant move, Swyteck. Jack was tempted to call her, plead for forgiveness, but some inner voice told him he needed to get his life together—that he was too much at loose ends these days. For now, he stalled.

He had been reduced to counting the motes of dust that swirled in a shaft of sunlight when the phone rang. Cindy, maybe? His face darkened as he considered that it could be the guy who was hassling him. He decided to let the machine pick up.

"Jack," came a woman's voice. But it wasn't Cindy. "This is your—" she began, then stopped. "This is Agnes."

He felt a rush of emotion, of which most was confusion. He hadn't heard Agnes's voice since law school. She sounded worried, but he resisted the urge to pick up.

"I can't be specific, Jack, but there's something going on in your father's life right now that I think you

should know about. He's not sick—I mean, your father
is definitely healthy. I don't mean to worry you about
that. But please call him. And don't tell him I asked you
to do it. It's important."

He sat upright, not sure of what to make of the message. He couldn't remember the last time his stepmother had phoned him, but her voice had temporarily
taken his mind off Cindy. He *had* caught the slip at the
beginning of the message—Agnes's almost saying the
words "your mother." Brooding on that phrase, he felt
himself drifting back, to when he was five years old . . .

"Your mother isn't dead, she just didn't want you!"

"You're a liar!" Jack screamed as he ran from the
family room, leaving his stepmother alone with her gin
martini. Tears streamed down his face as he reached his
room, slammed the door, and dove into the bed. He
knew his real mother was dead. Agnes had to be lying
when he said his real mother didn't want him. He
buried his face in the pillow and cried. After a minute
or two he rolled over and stared up at the ceiling. He
was thinking about how he could prove to Agnes that
she was wrong. At the age of five, he was planning his
first case.

He rolled off the bed and went to the door. He peered
out and heard the television in the family room. It was
less than fifteen feet to his parents' room. As he approached the closed white door, he looked over his
shoulder. There'd be big trouble if he were caught. But
he went in anyway.

At the far corner of the room, he pulled out the bottom drawer of the Queen Anne highboy. It was his father's drawer. Jack had first rummaged through it two

months earlier, searching for some after-shave he could slap on his face after having "borrowed" his father's electric razor. He hadn't found the after-shave. But tucked beneath the T-shirts and underwear, he *had* found a box. It was a jewelry box, burl maple with fancy, engraved silver initials that Jack couldn't read. The initials were his mother's. His *real* mother's.

As he had that day two months earlier, he lifted the box and opened it. Quickly, he lifted out the top tray of jewelry to reveal the compartment below. There it was. A heavy brass crucifix, concave on the back, the way cookie dough curved when it stuck to the rolling pin, he thought, only not as much. The first time he'd seen the crucifix, the concave back had completely perplexed him. He'd never seen one like that. So, after swearing his grandmother to secrecy, he'd told her about his discovery, and she'd explained the strange shape. It was the crucifix that had lain flat atop the rounded lid of his mother's coffin. His mother was dead, and this was the proof.

He removed the crucifix and put the jewelry box back in the drawer. Squeezing his physical evidence tightly, he left the bedroom and walked determinedly down the hall.

He saw his stepmother on the couch. "You're a liar!" he called out.

Agnes slowly raised her aching head to see Jack standing in the doorway.

He brandished the crucifix from across the room. "See," he said smartly, "my mother's in heaven. You're a liar!"

"Come here, Jack."

He froze.

"Come here!" she shouted.

He swallowed hard, took one timid step back, then turned and ran. "Jack!" she shouted as he scampered down the hall.

He darted into his parents' room, pulled open the drawer to the highboy, and tried to stuff the crucifix back into the box. But Agnes grabbed his arm before he could close the box. "What is *that?*" she demanded.

He stared up at her with fright in his eyes. She saw the initials on the box, and her face was flush with anger. He cringed, waiting for the blow to fall, but when he looked at her again, she seemed lost in thought. "Go to your room," she said distractedly. Once he'd stepped into the hallway, she pulled the door shut . . .

The sound of screeching tires jarred Jack back into the present. He went to the window and parted the curtain. The heavy foliage in the front yard obscured his view of the street, but he thought he saw some movement in the lengthening shadows by the side of the garage.

He got up from the sofa and went to the front door. Outside, the wind was picking up, whipping the palm fronds against the house. He looked around but saw nothing. Slowly, he began walking toward the garage. He felt apprehensive, unsettled. That incident the other day as he was leaving work . . . Agnes's call . . . and now the sound of a car peeling out . . .

He walked along the side of the garage, then in back, squinting in the half-light. Nothing. He doubled around to the front, and that's when he saw Thursday. The dog was struggling to get on all fours, but his legs buckled and he fell on his side.

"Thursday!" Jack rushed to him and cradled his head, then quickly ran his hand along the dog's body to check for wounds. The dog whimpered softly at his master's touch. Red foam was coming from his mouth.

Jack looked around, panicky. No car. *Shit*. Then he remembered. Jeff Zebert, four doors down, was a vet. "Hold on, boy," Jack said. He gathered him up and started running.

Less than thirty seconds later, he was striding up the Zeberts' walkway. Jeff was in the front yard, watering his shrubs. "I've got an emergency here!" Jack called out breathlessly. "It's Thursday," he said. "I think he got into something, poisoned himself."

Jeff dropped the hose. "Do you know what it might have been?"

"Could be anything—here, take a look," Jack said, holding his pet out for the doctor's examination.

The vet glanced quickly at the dog, then instructed Jack to put him on the picnic table. He ran into the house. When he returned, he washed some solution down Thursday's throat with the hose.

"C'mon, boy," Jack said desperately. Thursday lifted his head a few inches, reacting to Jack's voice. He finally managed to bring something up, but it looked mostly like blood. Jeff tried the hose again, but got no reaction. The animal's paws had stopped shaking. Suddenly, his whimpering stopped and his chest stilled. There was only the sound of running water. Jack looked at the vet.

"I'm sorry, Jack."

Jack couldn't speak, just looked away. Jeff gave him a moment, then touched him on the shoulder. "There's nothing we could have done."

"I shouldn't have left him running around alone. I should have—"

"Jack, really. Don't blame yourself. I don't think it was some poison he just happened to come in contact with. Looks like somebody fed him about a pound of raw hamburger—with two pounds of glass mixed in. Poor guy about swallowed it whole."

"What—" Jack said, disbelieving. Then it began to click into place. "That sick bastard."

"Who?"

"Huh? Oh, nothing. I . . . I just can't believe it that someone would do this."

"Listen," Jeff said, "Why don't you leave him with me. I'll bring him in tomorrow morning and take care of it."

Jack nodded reluctantly. "Thanks." He stared down at Thursday, gave him a last pat on the head, and headed for home. As he walked the gravel path between the two houses, trying to maintain his self-control, it seemed like his whole life was spiraling downward—that he'd entered a dark tunnel and completely lost his bearings. He wondered when—or if—it would end.

He'd been in the house only a few minutes when the phone rang. He was seized with cold fury as he recalled how he'd nearly been run over outside the Freedom In-stitute, and then gotten a call a few seconds later. He snatched up the phone.

"Listen, you son of a bitch—"

"Jack, it's Jeff," said the vet.

Jack swallowed back his anger. "Sorry. I thought—"

"No problem. I just wanted you to know. After you left, I took a closer look at that stuff Thursday expelled from his stomach. There's not just glass in the meat. There's seeds too. Some kind of flower seeds, it looks like. I don't know if they're poisonous or not, but it was still the glass that killed your dog. I just thought I should mention it."

Jack nodded with comprehension. But he didn't share his thoughts with the vet. "Thanks, Jeff. Maybe it'll help me get a lead on the guy. I'll let you know if I turn up anything."

He hung up the phone. The seeds gave him a lead all right. In fact, they pointed right at Eddy Goss. Jack's most notorious client had explained the meaning of the seeds in Jack's very first in-depth consultation with him. The two of them had been locked alone in a dimly lit, high-security conference room at the county jail, about twelve hours after Goss had confessed on video-tape to Detective Lonzo Stafford. Jack had sat passively on one side of the table listening, as his client doted on the details of his crime. Now some of those details—the ones that had earned Goss the nickname "Chrysan-themum Killer"—were coming back.

"Did they find the seed?" Goss asked his lawyer.

Jack lifted his eyes from his yellow notepad, pen in hand, and looked across the table at his client. "The medical examiner found it. It was shoved somewhere beyond her vagina."

Goss sat back in his chair and folded his arms

smugly, obviously pleased. "It's a chrysanthemum seed, you know." He arched his eyebrows, as if his lawyer was supposed to see the hidden significance.

Jack just shrugged.

Goss seemed annoyed, almost angry that Jack didn't appreciate his point. "Don't you get it?" Goss asked impatiently.

"No," Jack said with a sigh. "I don't *get* it." *Sigmund Freud wouldn't get you, buddy*.

Goss leaned forward, eager to explain. "Chrysanthemums are the coolest flower in the world, man."

"They remind me of funerals," Jack said.

"Right," Goss answered, pleased that Jack was following along. "Nature *designed* them for funerals. Because funerals are dark, like death. And chrysanthemums love that."

Jack flashed a curious but cautious expression. "What are you talking about?"

Goss warmed to the topic. "The chrysanthemum seed is just really unique. Most flowers bloom when it's warm outside. They love summer and sunshine. But chrysanthemums are different. You plant the seed in the summer, when the ground is nice and warm, but it doesn't do anything. It just sits there. The seed doesn't even start to grow until summer's almost over, when the days get shorter and the nights get cooler. And the cooler and darker it gets, the more the seeds like it. Then, in November—when everything around it's dying, when the ground is getting cold, when the nights are long and the days are cloudy—that's when the big flower pops out."

"So," Jack said warily, "you planted your seed."

"In a warm, dark place," Goss explained. "And that place is going to grow darker and colder every day from now on—until it's the perfect place for my seed to grow."

Jack stared at Goss in stone-faced silence, then scribbled the words "possible insanity defense" on his pad. "How did you learn so much about flowers, Eddy?"

Goss averted his eyes. "When I was a kid in Jersey, there was this man in the neighborhood who had a greenhouse. He grew everything in there," he said with a sly smile. "Me and him used to smoke some of it, too."

"How did you learn about planting the seed? How did you get this idea about planting seeds in a warm, dark place?"

Goss's mouth drew tight. "I don't remember."

"How old were you?"

"Ten or eleven," he said with a shrug.

"And how old was the man?"

"Old . . . not real old."

Jack leaned forward and spoke firmly, but with understanding. "What did you used to do in there, Eddy? With that man?"

Goss's eyes flared, and his hands started to shake. "I said I don't *remember*. Something wrong with your ears, man?"

"No, I just want you to try to remember—"

"Just get the fuck outta here!" Goss shouted. "Meeting's over. I got nothing more to say."

"Just take it easy—"

"I said, get your ass outta here!"

Jack nodded, then packed up his bag and rose from

his chair. "We'll talk again." He turned and stepped toward the locked metal security door.

"Hey," Goss called out.

Jack stopped and looked back at him.

"You're gonna get me out of here, aren't you?"

"I'm going to represent you," Jack said.

Goss narrowed his eyes. "You have to get me outta here." He leaned forward in his chair to press his point. "You *have* to. I have a *lot* more seeds to sow."

As Jack stood in his living room recalling that conversation, the memory still gave him a chill. He sighed, shook his head. If the situation wasn't so serious, he'd laugh at the irony. He'd secured a psychopath's acquittal, only to find himself the man's next target.

But was he really Goss's target? Of his rancor, maybe. But Jack found it hard to believe that Goss would actually do him physical harm. He seemed more comfortable confronting overmatched women and small animals.

He had more than enough to get a restraining order against Goss, if he wanted one. But he wasn't sure that was the answer. The legal system had failed once before to stop Eddy Goss—thanks to him.

So it was up to Jack to find something that would work, once and for all.

It was just after 11:00 P.M.—bedtime at the governor's mansion. Harry Swyteck was in his pajamas, sitting up in bed against the brass headboard, reading a recent *Florida Trend* magazine article about acquitted killer Eddy Goss. Toward the end of the story, his irritation ripened into anger as the writer delivered a fusillade of criticism against Goss's "argue-anything" lawyer, Jack Swyteck. "They call this *balanced* journalism?" the governor muttered as he threw down the magazine.

A few seconds later, Agnes emerged from the bathroom in her robe and slippers. She stopped at the table by the window and tended to a bouquet of flowers, her back to her husband.

"Thank you for the flowers, Harry," she said, her body blocking his view of the bouquet.

"Huh," said the governor, looking over. He hadn't sent any flowers. Today wasn't a birthday, anniversary, or any other occasion he could think of that called for flowers. But it wasn't inconceivable that in all the campaign commotion he'd forgotten a special day and one of his staff had covered for him. So he just played along. "Oh," he replied, "you're welcome, dear. I hope you like them."

"It's nice to get things for no reason," she said with a sparkle in her eye. "It was so spontaneous of you." Her mouth curled suggestively. Then she stepped away from the table, revealing the bouquet, and the governor went white.

"Keep the bed warm," she said as she disappeared into her walk-in closet, but the governor wasn't listening. His eyes were fixed on the bouquet of big white, pink, and yellow chrysanthemums perched on the table. He rose from the bed and stepped toward the bouquet. The card was still in the holder. Harry's hand trembled as he opened the envelope. It suddenly seemed so obvious: the disguised voice, the threats, the photographs of a gruesome murder, and now the flowers. His mind raced, making a logical link between the

"Chrysanthemum Killer," whose weird pathology had been mentioned in the article he'd just been reading, and the blackmailer.

He read the message. Instantly, he knew it was intended for him, not his wife. "You and me forever," it read, "till death do us part."

"Eddy Goss," the governor muttered softly to himself, his voice cracking with fear. *I'm being blackmailed by a psychopath.*

Chapter 13

•

The following morning, Monday, Jack picked up his Mustang from the garage and went to A&G Alarm Company, where he arranged to have a security system immediately installed in his house. By noon he had new locks on the doors and was thinking about escape plans. He still couldn't bring himself to believe that Goss would try to kill him, but it would be foolish not to take precautions. He imagined the worst-case scenarios—an attack in the middle of the night or an ambush in the parking lot—and planned in advance how he would respond. And he called the telephone company. In two days he'd have a new, unlisted phone number.

But there was one basic precaution he decided not to take. He didn't call the police because he still felt the cops would do little to protect Eddy Goss's lawyer. Besides, he had another idea. That afternoon he bought ammunition for his gun.

It wasn't actually *his* gun. He'd inherited a .38-caliber pistol from Donna Boyd, an old flame at Yale. Most people didn't know it, but crime was a problem in certain areas of New Haven where many students lived off campus. After Jack's neighbor had been robbed, Donna had refused to sleep over anymore unless Jack kept her gun in the nightstand. Even for an independent-minded Yale coed, she was a bit unconventional. He agreed but took the precaution of signing up for a few shooting lessons at the local range. He didn't want to make a mistake they'd both regret.

As it turned out, the gun stayed in his drawer until after graduation, when he was packing for Miami. By that point, he and Donna had broken up and she'd been bitter enough to leave town without stopping by to pick up her things. A mutual friend said she'd gone to Europe. So Jack had just packed the gun away with her racquet-ball racket and Elvis Costello CD and forgotten about it until now.

Suddenly, he had a use for the gun that had lain in his footlocker for the last six years, last registered in Connecticut, in the name of Donna Boyd.

Jack had never considered violence an answer to anything. But this was something altogether different. This was truly self-defense. Or was it? Deep down, he wondered if he actually hoped Goss would break into his house. As he sat back in the sofa in his living room with the ammunition he'd just purchased, he thought hard about his real motivation for not calling the cops. But the possibility that he was subconsciously looking for a showdown with Goss was ridiculous. Goss was the killer. Not him.

The phone rang. Jack muted the nine o'clock Movie of the Week on TV and snatched it up.

"Have you checked your mail, Jack?" came the familiar voice.

He hesitated. He knew that stalkers thrived on contact, and that any "expert" would have told him just to hang up. But he was nearly certain he knew who it was, and if he could just get him to speak in his normal voice, he'd have confirmation. "This is not *clever*, Goss," Jack goaded. "Knock off the funny voice. I know it's you."

A condescending snicker came over the phone, then a pause—followed by a decided change in tone. "You don't know shit, Swyteck. So just shut up, and check your mail. *Now.*"

Jack blinked hard, frightened by how easily he'd set off the man's temper. "Why?"

"Just check it," the caller ordered. "And take the phone with you. I'll tell you what to look for."

Jack wondered whether it was wise to play along, but he was determined to get to the bottom of this. "All right," he answered, then headed down the hall with his portable phone pressed to his ear. He looked through the window before stepping outside but saw nothing. He opened the front door and stepped onto the porch. "Okay," he said into the phone. "I'm at the box."

"Look inside," the caller ordered.

Cautiously, Jack reached for the lid on the mailbox beside the door. He extended one finger, pried under the lid, and quickly popped it open, jerking his hand back as if he'd just touched molten lava.

"Do you see it, Swyteck?"

Jack stood on his toes and peered inside from a distance, fearful that he was about to see bloody gym shorts or torn panties or some other evidence of Goss's latest handiwork. "There's an envelope," he said, seeing nothing else inside.

"Open it," said the caller.

Jack carefully took the envelope from the box. It was plain white. No return address. No addressee. It had been hand-delivered, which meant the stalker had been on his porch—an unsettling thought. He unfolded the flap and tentatively removed the contents. "What is this?"

"What's it look like?"

He studied the page. "A map." A route had been high-lighted by yellow felt-tip pen.

"Follow it—if you want to know who the killer on the loose is. You *do* want to know, don't you, Swyteck?"

"I already know it's you, Goss. This is a map to your apartment."

"It's a map to the killer on the loose. Be there. Meet him at four-thirty A.M. tonight. And no cops. Or you'll be *very* sorry."

Jack bristled at the sound of the dial tone, then switched off the portable phone. At first it didn't even occur to him to actually go to Goss's apartment. But if Goss were going to kill him, would he do it in his own apartment? Would he *invite* Jack over and give him directions to the scene of the crime? No, he must be up to something else, and Jack's curiosity was piqued.

But it was more than just curiosity. He was thinking

of the night two years ago when he'd refused to give his father enough "privileged" information to stop Raul Fernandez's execution. His rigidity had resulted in Raul's death, and he was determined not to make the same mistake again. In dealing with a confessed killer who was continuing his evil ways, he *had* to be more flexible with privileged information.

It was time to issue an ultimatum. Months ago, when he and Goss had been considering an insanity defense, Jack had pumped him for information about his past crimes—some of which included murder. His client had told him plenty. Now it was time to confront Goss and let him know that if he wanted to stay out of the electric chair—if he didn't want a prosecutor to get an anonymous tip about his most perverted secrets—then he'd better change his ways.

He stepped to the window and looked outside. It was getting dark and starting to drizzle. A storm was brewing. If he was going to meet Goss, there was no reason to wait until four-thirty in the morning. In fact, it seemed safer *not* to wait. He started toward the door, then stopped. He went up to the attic, opened his footlocker, and found the .38. Downstairs, he spent several minutes cleaning the gun, then loaded it with bullets.

Just in case.

Chapter 14

•

Rain started to fall as Jack pulled his Mustang out of the driveway. The downpour was a continuation of a violent Florida thunderstorm that had flooded city streets that afternoon. The nasty weather didn't bring him down, though. He was determined to get to Goss's as quickly as possible, before he could change his mind. He raced his old eight-cylinder down the expressway at a speed only a fleeing fugitive would have considered safe, exited into a section of town that *no one* considered safe, and screeched to a halt outside Goss's apartment.

The old two-story building stretched nearly a third of the city block. It was bordered on one side by a gas station and on the other by a burned-out shell of an apartment building that some pyromaniac landlord had probably figured could generate more income in fire-insurance proceeds than in rent. Rusty iron security bars covered most of the ground-floor windows, plywood sealed off others, and noisy air conditioners stuck out of a few. Weeds popping up through cracks in the sidewalk were the closest thing to landscaping.

The rain beat loudly on the convertible's canvas top and seeped in where the twenty-year-old rubber window seals had rotted away. Jack jumped out and dashed through water that ran in wide rivulets down the street. He was at the apartment entrance in only fifteen seconds, but that was long enough for the rain to soak his clothes and paste them to his body. Dripping wet, he stepped inside the dimly lit foyer and checked the rows of metal mailboxes recessed into the wall. He had the right place. GOSS, APT 217, read one of them.

He ran up a flight of stairs to a long hallway lined with apartments on either side. It was even darker here than in the foyer, the tenants having stolen most of the bulbs to light their apartments. Spray-painted graffiti covered the walls and doors, forming one continuous mural. Most of the ceiling tiles had been punched out by kids proving how high they could jump. Rainwater leaked in from above and streaked down the water-stained walls, forming little puddles on the musty indoor-outdoor carpet. All was quiet, except for heavy raindrops pounding on the flimsy flat roof.

He started down the hall, checking the numbers on the doors that still had them. His pace quickened as he approached 217, the fifth door on the left. He was convinced that the only way to stop Goss was to threaten him—and to do so in a way that only his own lawyer could. If Goss was to report him to the Florida bar for threatening to reveal a client's secrets, it could end his career. But it didn't matter at this point. The stark contrast between his one tragic failure in the Fernandez case and his string of "successes" in sending men like Goss back onto the streets to prey on an unwary public had weighed on him too long. He'd reached the lowest point of his life.

Jack knocked on the hollow wood door to Goss's apartment, then waited. No one answered, but he refused to believe that Goss wasn't there. He knocked harder, almost banging. Still no answer. "Goss," he said loudly. "I know it's you. Answer the door!"

"Hey!" an angry man shouted from an open apartment doorway down the hall. "It's ten o'clock, man. I got a two-year-old here. Cut the racket."

Jack took a deep breath. He'd been so focused in his pursuit of Goss that he'd acted as if no one else lived in the building. That was a stupid approach, he realized. So he stepped back from the door and slowly headed down the hall, as if to leave. As soon as Goss's neighbor retreated into his apartment, Jack quietly but quickly returned to apartment 217 and turned the knob. It was unlocked. He hesitated and listened for footsteps on the inside. Nothing. He pushed the door open slowly, about a foot, and peered inside. All was dark and quiet. He pushed it open further, about halfway, and stood in the open doorway.

"Goss," he said in a firm voice. Then he waited.

There was no reply, only the sound of heavy tropical rain tapping on the roof and against the window on the other side of the room. Jack swallowed hard. As he saw it, he had two choices. He could turn and walk away, his tail between his legs. If he did, it would only be a matter of time before he got another threat, before the violence escalated further. His other choice—the only *real* choice—was to do something right then.

He discreetly checked the hallway, but saw no one. Then he stared nervously into the dark apartment. He could hear his heart pounding and feel his palms begin to sweat. He took a deep breath and reached deep inside himself for the strength he needed. Slowly and very cautiously, he entered the dark, deathly quiet apartment of Eddy Goss.

"Goss," Jack said again, standing just inside the open door. "It's Swyteck. You and I need to talk, so come on out."

When after a few seconds there was no response, Jack reached out and flipped the light switch by the door. But no lights came on.

A huge bolt of lightning cracked just outside, sending his heart to his throat. The storm was worsening, the heavy rain pelting against the room's only window. Another large bolt struck even closer, bathing the small room in a burst of eerie white light. Jack got a mental snapshot, hastening his eyes' adjustment to the layout of the apartment. The kitchen, dining, and living areas were one continuous room. A ghostly white bed sheet covered the window. Furniture was sparse—he noticed only a beaten-up old couch, a floor lamp, a kitchen table, and one folding chair. The walls were bare, but there were a few plants. Not your ordinary houseplants. These were big and colorful crucifixes, Stars of David, and other tributes to the dead, all made of chrysanthemums and other fresh flowers, apparently stolen by Goss from graves at the local cemetery. Jack felt anger rising in him as he read one pink ribbon inscribed OUR BELOVED DAUGHTER. He looked away in disgust, then noticed a door across the room that led to the bedroom. It was open.

Whit-whooooo, came a sudden shrill-pitched whistle from the bedroom, like a catcall at the girls on the beach. Jack coiled, ready for an attack.

Whit-whoooo came the sound again, a little louder this time.

His heart raced. The urge to turn and run was almost irresistible, but his feet refused to retreat. Slowly, he forced one foot in front of the other, surprising even himself as he moved closer to the bedroom. He took deliberate, stalking steps, trying to minimize the squeak in his rain-soaked tennis shoes. He stared at the open doorway as he steadily crossed the room, his eyes wide with intense concentration, his every sense alert to what might be inside the bedroom. He flinched slightly as heavy thunder rumbled in the distance. He halted just two steps away from the open door.

Whit-whooooo came the whistle again.

The whistling spooked Jack, but it was also beginning to anger him. The bastard was taunting him. This was all just a game to Goss. And Jack knew the rules by which Goss played his games. He took the loaded gun from his pocket.

"Eddy," he called out. "Cut the game-playing, all right? I just want to talk to you."

Thunder clapped as a flash of lightning filled the room with strobelike light. Jack took a half step forward, and then another. He glanced at the kitchen table beside him. There was a dirty plate with dried ketchup and remnants of Goss's fish-stick dinner. An empty Coke bottle. A fork. And a steak knife. The sight of the knife made Jack glad he had his gun. He raised his weapon to chest level, clutching it with both hands. His hands were shaking, but he wasn't about to stop now. He took the last step and peered inside the bedroom.

A sudden shriek sent Jack flying backward. He saw something—a figure, a shadow, an attacker! But as he took a step back and tried to squeeze off a shot, he lost his balance. He collided with the floor lamp, sending it careening across the carpet. For a second he was on his hands and knees, then he struggled to his feet, panting from the burst of excitement. The fight was over as quickly as it had started. "A stupid cockatoo," he said aloud, but with a sigh of relief.

Whit-whooooo, the bird whistled at him, perched on his pedestal.

Jack flinched, suddenly panicked by what sounded like footsteps in the hall. He didn't want to have to explain himself to someone checking on the noise. He shoved the gun into his pants, ran from the bedroom, and pushed up the window to open it. But it raised only six inches. A nail inside the frame put there by a previous tenant as a crude form of security kept it from opening all the way. Jack's heart raced as he thought he heard the footsteps in the hall getting closer. He quickly scanned the room, grabbed the steak knife from Goss's dinner table, and used it like a claw hammer to work the nail free. At first the nail wouldn't budge, but then it suddenly popped out. As it did, the knife slipped and sliced Jack across the back of his left hand. He was bleeding, but was too scared to feel the pain. He tossed the knife back toward the table and climbed out the open window. He climbed down the rickety fire escape like a middle-schooler on monkey bars, letting himself drop the last ten feet and landing with a splash in an ankle-deep puddle. He ran around the building and back to his car as fast as he could, then pulled away slowly, realizing that the faster he went, the more suspicious he'd look.

As he drove he took several deep breaths, trying to collect himself. He checked the back of his left hand. The cut was fairly deep and still bleeding, but it didn't look like he'd need stitches. He steered with his wounded hand and applied pressure with the other to stop the bleeding.

"Damn," Jack cursed at himself—and at that stupid cockatoo. That bird had scared the hell out of him. It seemed strange that Goss would own a bird—that he'd care about any living creature. But then it made sense as he thought of the bird pecking at his food around the pedestal. Seeds. There had been all kinds of seeds—the seeds of the Chrysanthemum Killer. Jack thought again of Goss's comment: "I still have a lot of seeds to sow."

As he put more distance between himself and Goss's apartment, he re-evaluated the events that had drawn him there—the phone call, the map, the invitation to meet the "killer on the loose." It made him think through Goss's gradual escalation of violence and what might be the logical next step after killing his dog. He was suddenly afraid his instincts had been right. Goss was not luring him to his apartment to kill *him* but, rather, someone else.

"Cindy," Jack said aloud, frantically weighing the

possibility. Maybe he was giving Goss too much credit, but on the other hand, this madman could have lured him to his apartment at exactly 4:30 A.M. to make sure Cindy would be alone—so that Goss could sow another seed.

Jack punched the accelerator to the floor and raced toward Gina's apartment, steering with one hand and dialing his car phone with the other. It wasn't even midnight yet, let alone 4:30 A.M., but he was not taking any chances.

"Come on," Jack groaned at the busy signal from Gina's apartment. He tried the number again. It was still busy, so he asked the operator to interrupt. "Yes, it is definitely an emergency," he said firmly.

But Gina refused to let him cut in.

"What do you mean, she won't *let* me?" he asked with disbelief. But the operator gave no explanation.

He switched off the phone and drove even faster, fearing the worst.

Chapter 15

•

Seven minutes later the Mustang careened over a speed bump and squealed to a stop outside Gina's condominium. Jack jumped out, devoured two steps at a time on the stairway to Gina's front door, and then knocked firmly. He paced frantically until Gina finally opened up.

"Is everything okay?" he asked. "Are you all right?"

Gina stood in the doorway, wearing a tight-fitting white denim mini and a loose red tank top that revealed as much of her breasts as any wandering eye cared to see.

"Where's Cindy?" he demanded.

"Cindy's out."

"Out where?"

Gina made a face. "Out being twisted like a pretzel by a squadron of Chippendale dancers. It's none of your business *where* she is. She's out."

"I have to find her. I think someone may be after her."

"Yeah," Gina scoffed, hands resting on her hips. "*You* are."

Jack stiff-armed the door to keep Gina from shutting it in his face. "I'm not making this up. Ever since the Goss trial ended, someone's been following me—making threats. Some guy with a raspy voice called me and said there was a killer on the loose. He tried to run me over with his car. He killed my dog. And now he might be after Cindy."

Gina's face finally registered concern. "Cindy's safe," she said coolly. "After you two had your little Saturday morning brawl, she decided to catch an earlier flight to Rome. We went by the house this afternoon, while you were out, and cleaned out her closet. Then I dropped her off at the airport. She's on her way to Italy."

"Oh," he said, "that's great." But he didn't feel great. He was relieved that she was safe, but he was having a hard time adjusting to the fact that she was actually gone. Some part of him was wishing he had had one last chance to explain himself to her.

Gina watched as he turned to leave. It amazed her the way Jack looked after Cindy, even after they'd split up. Gina had definitely felt rejected last year, when Jack had dropped her for Cindy after their one blind date. And although Jack and Cindy were both denying it to themselves, she was convinced that the trip to Italy would be the end of their relationship—which only made her wonder, as she'd often wondered before, just what it would take to get Jack to notice *her*.

"And what about me?" she said, arching her eyebrow as he looked back at her quizzically. "What if this lunatic comes looking for Cindy, and I'm here all alone?"

"What do you want me to do?"

"Stay," she said. "Just in case something happens."

His mouth opened, but his speech was on a several-second delay. "I don't think—"

"You think too much, Jack. That's your whole problem. Come on, I'll buy you a drink. Maybe I'll even give you the lowdown on how truly 'professional' Cindy's so-called business trip to Italy is," she said coyly as she stepped back, inviting Jack inside.

He flinched. He wanted to think that she was yanking his chain about Cindy, but her insinuation had the ring of truth—especially since she'd packed up her clothes and left this afternoon without giving him a chance to apologize. In any event, after everything he'd been through over the last week, he saw no harm in not being alone—especially if his company could fill him in on what Cindy was really thinking. "Make it a Scotch," he said. "On the rocks."

Jack followed Gina inside the townhouse, through the foyer and living room. The downstairs was one big room, done in white tile, black lacquer, chrome and glass, with some large abstract acrylic paintings, Persian rugs, and dried flowers for color.

"Here," she said as she tossed him a terrycloth robe. "Let me put those wet clothes in the dryer for you."

He hesitated, even though he *was* soaked.

"Believe me, Jack," she half-kidded, "if I wanted you out of your clothes, I'd be far less subtle. Now get in there and change before you catch pneumonia."

He retreated into the bathroom and peeled off his

wet clothes—which left him with the problem of what to do with the gun in his pants pocket. He didn't want to do any more explaining to Gina. He removed the bullets, wrapped them with the gun in a washcloth, and slid the wad into one of the robe's deep pockets. The knife wound on his left hand had stopped bleeding, so he carefully rinsed away some of the dried blood. He emerged with his hand in his pocket. Gina took his clothes and tossed them into the dryer, then led him to the kitchen.

"You did say Scotch," said Gina.

"Right," he replied. He watched from the bar stool across the kitchen counter as she filled his glass. The kitchen's bright fluorescent lights afforded him a really good look at his ex-girlfriend's best friend. *Gorgeous*, he thought, *absolutely gorgeous*. She had dark, glistening eyes, set off against a smooth olive complexion; he imagined there were no tan lines beneath her tight white miniskirt. Her only flaw was an ever-so-slightly crooked smile, noticeable only because it was accentuated by her bright red lip gloss. The imperfection was enough to have kept her from becoming a teenage supermodel, but Jack didn't see it as an imperfection.

"Here you are," she said as she handed him his glass.

He nodded appreciatively, then downed most of the drink.

"Tough night?" she teased, pouring him a refill.

"Tough month," he quipped.

A gleam came to Gina's eye. "I've got just the thing for you. Let's do Jagermeisters."

"Excuse me?"

"Shots," she said as she lined up a couple of glasses on the counter. "It's just a cordial."

"I don't think—"

"I told you," she interrupted, "you think too much." She poured two shots, more in Jack's glass than hers, then handed him one. "Prost," she said, toasting in German.

Their heads jerked back in unison as they downed the shots.

Gina smiled. "Good start. Have another," she said as she filled his glass.

The second was gone as quickly as the first.

"Whoa," Jack wheezed.

Gina filled his glass again.

"What's in this stuff?" he asked, his throat burning.

"Drink that one. Then I'll tell you."

He hesitated, reminding himself he was there to keep a lid on things. It wouldn't do to be half-in-the-bag if Goss showed up. "Gina, I think I've had enough."

"C'mon," she pouted. "Just one more. Relax"—she looked over her shoulder—"the lock on that door is strong enough to keep the bogeyman out."

It was no use. She raised the shot glass to his lips, and he reluctantly swallowed.

She smirked at the glazed look on his face. "It's from Germany. It's actually illegal in most of this country. Something about the opium in it."

"Opium?" his jaw dropped.

Gina smiled wryly. "You'll be totally shit-faced in about ninety seconds."

He took a deep breath. He was already feeling some-thing considerably more than an ordinary buzz. He grabbed the edge of the counter to keep his bearings. "I've got to go," he said.

She leaned across the counter and looked into his eyes. He blinked and looked away only to get an eyeful of cleavage, which made him shift awkwardly, as if his personal space had been invaded.

"I really should go," he said. But he didn't pull back.

"I know a couple of ways to make you stay," she said slyly.

"Such as?"

"Bribery, for one," she said quietly.

He swallowed hard. "And the other?"

Her eyes slowly narrowed. "Torture!" she said as she grabbed his ribs and pinched hard, laughing as she turned and stepped away.

"Oww!" Jack groaned. It had really hurt, but he knew she was just playing and tried to smile. "Could we maybe stick to bribery?"

"Whatever you want," she whispered as she handed him another Scotch, then directed him toward the living room with a casual wave of her hand. She twisted the dimmer switch, lowering the overhead lighting, then sauntered toward her stereo, walking the way she always did when she knew a man was watching her.

At first he couldn't help but admire the gentle sway of her curves as she crossed the room. He was certain Gina was coming on to him. And after a month of personal, professional, and public rejection, he was definitely starting to feel too weak, too lonely, and too drunk to put a stop to it, particularly after she'd rekindled his doubts about the "purely professional" nature of Cindy's trip.

"Take a load off," Gina said from behind, knocking him onto the couch. She fell in next to him, and they were instantly swallowed by the fabric of her over-stuffed couch. She kicked off her shoes and drew her knees up onto the cushion. She scooted closer to Jack, stirred the ice in his drink with her finger, and then licked it off.

She leaned into him, her firm breasts pressing against his arm and her hand falling onto his hip. He suddenly thought of Cindy, which made him tense up.

"What are you, a linebacker?" she grumbled as she gave him a little shove. She reached across his lap, grabbed the remote control from the end table, and flipped on the stereo, preset for Gato Barbieri's "Europa."

"Oh, sorry," he said with a nervous smile, now realizing what all the pushing was about.

"I *love* Gato," she interrupted him. "You like the sax?"

Jack coughed into his drink, thinking she'd said "sex."

"I think it's the sexiest instrument ever invented," she said as she leaned back, clearly enjoying the mood of the music. "Have you ever watched a man play the sax, Jack? I mean *really* watched him, in a jazz bar, late at night? The lighting is always dimmed, just so. The smoke rises in the room in a certain fuzzy way, as if it's all a fantasy. And then the musician makes love to his instrument, his lips pressed to the mouthpiece, his eyes closed tightly while his face displays his every emotion. It's like a man with the confidence, the courage, the balls, or whatever it takes to cry, or to make love or to reveal himself, all at the same time, with the whole world watching. How can they be so free? I don't know how they do it . . . but it affects me deep inside when they do." She leaned toward him and stared deeply into his eyes.

Once again he hesitated. That was the most articulate he had ever known Gina to be. *Bet you've given that little speech a few times before*, he wanted to say.

She moved closer. "Could you do that?" she whispered.

"Could I what?" he played dumb.

"Let yourself go," she answered. "Turn yourself inside out. And enjoy it."

He sighed. There was indeed a woman who made him feel that way, who could strip him down to a desire so intense that he could have stood naked to the world and yet felt like the most powerful man on the planet. Then something happened. It wasn't his fault or hers. It just happened. And nothing had been the same since. "I suppose it depends on who I'm with."

She smiled, only to have her next move interrupted by the shrill ring of the telephone.

Cindy? asked his guilty conscience.

Gina sprang from the couch, snatched up the phone, and carried it to the other side of the room, as far away from Jack as the cord would allow her to travel. She hissed something into the receiver, slammed it down, and walked back toward him, an intense look of desire having replaced the anger in her eyes.

"My old boyfriend," she volunteered as she took her place next to Jack, "Antoine. Guy buys me a BMW and he thinks he owns me for life. He calls whenever he figures I have a date. Kind of pathetic," she shrugged, "but he just doesn't want anyone else to have me."

"Does this Antoine own a gun?" Jack only half-kidded.

The phone rang again. Gina jumped up, angrier than before. She grabbed the phone and threw it at the floor. "Asshole!" she shouted, as if Antoine could hear her. She sighed deeply to collect herself, then returned to Jack and knelt beside him on the couch. "Now," she said softly, "where were we?"

He edged away from her. "I think we were talking about . . . Antoine," he said nervously.

"Antoine," she scoffed. "What I wouldn't give for someone who could make me forget I ever knew a silly *boy* named Antoine."

Their eyes met and held. Jack started to say something, but the clothes dryer buzzed, and he looked away, distracted. "I think I'm ready. I mean, my clothes are ready," he said as he pushed himself up from the couch. His knees shook, the room spun, and he was back on the couch in a split second.

"I don't think you're going anywhere tonight."

"I really should go."

"No way," she said as she jiggled the car keys she'd taken from his pants before tossing them into the dryer. "Friends don't let out-of-town girlfriends' ex-boyfriends drive drunk. You're staying here tonight."

"I—"

"Don't argue," she interrupted him. "It's already after midnight, and your clothes probably aren't even dry yet. I'll sleep in Cindy's bed—too many bad vibes in there for you. You can sleep in mine. Come on," she said as she rose from the couch, pulling him by the elbow.

He wobbled to his feet, drunker than he'd been since college. He knew he couldn't drive, and part of him was glad he couldn't. "All right. I'll stay."

Gina held on to his arm and guided him across the room, toward the stairway. They were both startled as they heard the sudden pulsating noise of the phone off the hook. Together they glanced at the screaming receiver on the floor and then at each other, as if to see whether either would make the move to put it back on the hook. The noise stopped on its own, and they let the phone lie on the floor. No more Antoine. No more interruptions. It was just Jack and Gina. Gina the man-eater. Jack shook his arm loose from her grasp and followed her up the stairs.

"Time for bed," she sang as she led him to her bedroom. The hallway lighting gave the room a warm glow. He sat on the edge of the bed and watched as she turned down the sheets. He wondered how many men had been in Gina's bed. He figured he'd be the first to sleep in it without sleeping *with* her.

"If you need anything, I'm right across the hall."

"Good night," he said.

Gina disappeared into the hallway, leaving the door open. She turned off the hallway light, and Jack was in total darkness. He started to remove his robe, but felt uncomfortable about being naked in Gina's bed, so he left it on. He removed the washcloth containing the gun and the bullets from his pocket and laid it on the nightstand, then crawled between the sheets. His head was buzzing. The shots Gina had poured him would surely give him a splitting headache in the morning, but at least they would speed him toward a deep and much needed sleep. He was nearly gone when a light suddenly flashed in his eyes, stirring him from his rest. It was the hallway light, but it seemed to shine like a flashlight right into his eyes. He raised his head groggily from the pillow and strained to make out the figure in the darkness. Someone was standing in the doorway, the backlighting from the hallway making the image a silhouette.

"I couldn't sleep," Gina's voice cut through the darkness.

He propped himself up on his elbow, his eyes adjusting. She was posing like a pinup, one hand on her hip and the other on the door frame. Her long brown hair was pulled to one side in a bushy ponytail that seemed to flow from her ear like water from a hydrant. A gold hoop earring dangled from the other side. She was naked, except for a silk sash around her waist.

"I need my own bed," she said.

Jack pulled back the covers and stood up, but she was already on him, pushing him gently toward the bed.

"Let me find my own way," she said in low voice.

He searched for his conscience as his head hit the pillow, but Gina's earlier remarks had him feeling foolish about waiting for Cindy while she traveled around Italy with her old boyfriend, and in his drunken, semi-dream state he was well beyond resistance. Gina started at the foot of the king-size bed and worked her way up, touching and tasting beneath his robe, demonstrating skills that he had only known as fantasies—until the caresses turned to pain.

"Oww!" Jack withdrew. "That hurt!"

"Oh, come on," Gina smiled playfully, looking up from between his legs. "It's a fine line, isn't it—pleasure and pain?"

"Not *that* fine. I'm gonna have fucking bruises."

"Just relax," she said as she removed his robe. Then she swung her leg over him and sent him into a state of arousal that bordered on the uncontrollable. She was on top of him, but not touching him. She was teasing, tempting, torturing him. She kissed him on the chest, gently pulling his hair with her teeth. He winced at the pain, then felt the pleasure of her gentle kiss around his mouth. In a sudden lucid moment, it flashed through his mind that he hadn't made love to anyone but Cindy in a long time. But this wasn't about making love.

"Tell me," Gina breathed heavily down his neck, her lips touching his as she spoke. "Tell me what you want."

"I want you," he said, caught up in her passion.

She probed and pressed with her fingers, touching him at his center of gravity. "Tell me exactly what you want," she whispered.

"I want to be inside you," he said.

She stared down at him, amused by his euphemism. "I want you to *fuck* me," she said with fire in her eyes, then pressed her body against his and rolled, pulling him on top of her. He entered with a rush, pushing out a horrible month's worth of anger, frustration, and rejection, taking delight in her moans and groans as her long, red nails attacked his back.

Suddenly, Jack froze. "Did you hear that?" he asked quickly, his body completely rigid.

"Hear what?" Gina said with a satisfied smile.

"That thumping noise."

Gina answered with a flick of her tongue. "That's the headboard pounding against the wall, you stud."

"No. It's downstairs."

"Stop it," she said sharply. "Don't do this to me, Jack."

"I'm not fooling around, Gina. Did you lock the front door like you said?"

"Of course."

"And the sliding doors in back?"

"Always locked," she replied, "when the A.C. is on."

"That wouldn't stop Goss—if it is Goss." He slid out from between her thighs. "I know I heard something." He rolled off the bed without a sound, walked cautiously toward the bedroom door, and leaned forward, listening intently. He put the robe back on and took the gun from the nightstand.

"You brought a *gun* into my house," she said angrily.

"Yeah—and aren't you glad I did?"

"No. Please, Jack. No shoot-outs. Just call the police."

"I can't. The phone's off the hook."

Gina grimaced, as if for the first time in her life she regretted her craziness.

He checked the chambers to make sure the gun was fully loaded. It was. "I'll take a look downstairs," he said. "You stay here."

"Don't worry," she assured him.

He opened the door carefully, holding the pistol out in front of him. The hall was dark. The apartment was still. He quietly stepped out and closed the bedroom door. He heard Gina lock it behind him; there was no turning back. He peered down the stairway but saw nothing. He stepped forward and slowly descended the first four steps. From his vantage point he could see most of the downstairs, but none of the kitchen. He noticed the phone on the floor by the couch, still off the hook. He took a few more steps and waited at the bottom of the stairs. He saw nothing, heard nothing, felt only the pounding of his heart. Slowly, he crossed the living room and placed the phone back on the hook. He turned and gasped as he noticed the front door—it was wide open.

He jumped back at a sudden burst of noise from outside. Then he realized it was his car alarm, blasting from the parking lot. Instinctively, he bolted out of the apartment and raced down the steps, leaving the door open behind him. He reached his car and froze as he saw firsthand one of the more obvious reasons that even a twenty-year-old convertible needed an alarm: The black canvas top was in shreds, sliced open from windshield to rear window.

"I can't believe this," Jack said to himself. An instant later his head was snapped around by the sound of a shrill scream from inside Gina's townhouse. He rushed back up the stairs and dashed inside.

"Jack!" Gina cried from upstairs—in Cindy's bedroom.

He led with his gun as he raced up the stairs and burst into the room. Gina stood in her green satin robe, frozen beside Cindy's brass bed. She was alone. He caught his breath and stared. The pink bedspread had been neatly turned down, revealing clean white sheets that were smeared with something bright red and wet that looked like blood. He reached down and touched it.

"Ketchup," Gina said, nodding toward the empty

bottle on the floor, which had been taken from her re-frigerator.

He cautiously approached Cindy's bed, his gut wrenching as he imagined what might have happened here tonight. He knew better than to touch anything, but he could tell there was something beneath Cindy's pil-low—something, he figured, that whoever had been here tonight had wanted him to find. He gently took the corner of the pillowcase between his fingertips. Slowly, with arms fully extended so that he could stand as far away as possible, he raised the pillow.

"Jack," her voice trembled, "what the hell are you doing?"

He ignored her. He kept lifting, slowly, until he saw it. A flower—a chrysanthemum.

"Goss," he said as he lowered the pillow back into place.

Suddenly, the phone rang. Jack's eyes locked with Gina's. Her panicked expression said there was no way she was going to pick up. "Hello," he answered, trying to sound calm.

Four blocks away at a pay phone on the street, a man in torn blue jeans and a yellowed undershirt stood in the murky shadows of a flickering streetlight, pressing the receiver to his ear and covering the mouthpiece with a rag. "You came early to my party," he said accusingly.

Jack took a deep breath. It was the same voice, but the tone was different. The man was breathing heavily, as if he'd been running, and his voice trembled as he spoke.

"You came early, Swyteck. And now I'm *very* angry."

Jack stayed on the line but was unable to speak, paralyzed by the crazed panting of a madman so furious he was gasping for breath. "Please," Jack said, "let's talk."

"I said four-thirty A.M.," he seethed. "And I meant four-thirty A.M. This is your last chance. Be there—at *four-thirty*."

Jack started to say something, but the phone went dead. His hand shook as he hung up.

"What was that?" Gina asked with fear.

He looked at her. "My final invitation," he said.

Chapter 16

•

Two hours later, Miami was in its deepest phase of sleep, that eerie, silent period just after the last drunk makes it home for the evening and just before the first early bird leaves for work. There was a knocking, then a pounding at the door. Eddy Goss rose from his bed and listened, wondering if he'd really heard something. Another round of pounding told him he wasn't dreaming. He rolled out of bed and paused, letting his eyes adjust to the darkness. He couldn't switch on a light; they'd shut the power off when he failed to pay his last bill. He took small, precarious steps out of his bedroom and toward the door, somewhat leery of answering the knock. He reached under the couch cushion and retrieved his revolver, then pressed his face to the door and looked through the peephole. The bulb hanging outside his apartment was out, and all he could distinguish was a distorted silhouette. He recognized the dark blue police uniform, however, so he tucked the gun away. Convicted felons weren't allowed to have guns. He opened the door and presented himself in the same cocky way he always addressed cops.

His face showed confusion as he stared into the eyes of the man in uniform. "What the hell—" he started to say, but before he could get the next word out, the intruder burst inside the apartment, slammed the door behind him, and shoved Goss against the wall. He had no time to think, no time to fully understand what was happening. In half a second, the look of horror that he'd seen in so many of his own young victims overtook his face as he stared down the marksman's tunnel of death and swallowed two silenced bullets that pierced his cheeks and blew his brains out the back of his skull. He slid to the floor, smearing a bright red streak against the wall and landing with a thud, a twisted heap in a pool of blood. His lifeless body lay in the dark shadow of his executioner. Then the door opened quietly, and in an instant the shadow was gone—down the dimly lit hall, down the stairs, and back onto the street, carried away from the scene and into the night by the lonely echo of worn leather heels pounding on the pavement . . . like just any other beat cop making his rounds.

PART THREE

•

Tuesday, August 2

Chapter 17

•

At 5:25 A.M. a frantic 911 call came in to the department. A crimson pool of blood had seeped beneath the
closed door to Goss's apartment, staining the hallway's
dirty green carpet. A neighbor had spotted it coming
home from her night shift at the county hospital. The
address she gave to the dispatcher would have been familiar to any homicide detective in the city, with all the
publicity the Goss trial had received. Any one of them
would have been tickled to see Goss get his due. But the
chief of the homicide division knew exactly who
should answer the call.

"Jump in your car, Lon," he said as he rushed into the
office of Detective Lonzo Stafford. The venetian blinds
rattled against the glass door as it swung open. "Sun
ain't even up, and I'm about to make your day."

Stafford looked up from the *Miami Herald* sports

section spread out on his desk. As usual, he was in his cubicle of an office a full ninety minutes before his 7:00 A.M. shift officially began, sipping coffee and dunking doughnuts. Stafford had been in law enforcement for almost forty-five years, a detective for nearly twenty. He was an ex-marine and a workaholic who filled nearly all his free time with overtime. Some said he worked longer hours because he'd lost a step with age—that he had to push a little harder to get less satisfactory results, like a magic lamp that had to be rubbed three times to yield one wish. In his prime, however, Lonzo Stafford had been the best homicide detective on the force. He didn't make mistakes. Except one time in forty-five years, and it had been so big that it cost a prosecutor a sure conviction. He'd played on a murder suspect's conscience during a videotaped interview and induced a 'confession by giving a "Christian burial speech." He'd botched the case against Eddy Goss. And Lonzo Stafford despised Jack Swyteck for nailing him to the wall with that one.

"Whatchya got for me?" Stafford asked.

"Cold one," the homicide chief replied with a smirk. "Four-oh-nine East Adams Street. Apartment two-seventeen."

A satisfied grin came to Stafford's face as he instantly recognized the address. "Praise Jesus," he said, rising from his old Naugahyde chair. "I'm on my way."

"Lon," said the chief as he stepped inside and closed the office door. Stafford was stopped in his tracks by the chief's pointed look. "I know how you felt when that bastard Goss walked. I felt the same way. And I want you to understand that I won't be upset if, just this once, your investigation turns up goose eggs."

Stafford looked back plaintively, without disagreement. The chief turned to leave, then stopped before opening the door. "Actually," he said, sighing, "there's more to it than that. Right after Goss's neighbor called nine-one-one, we got another call. Some guy who didn't want to get involved. Wouldn't leave his name, and he called from a pay phone outside the building so we couldn't trace it back. Claims he saw someone in a police uniform leave apartment two-seventeen—right about the time Goss got blown away."

Stafford raised an eyebrow but said nothing.

"We don't know anything for sure," the chief continued, "but I suppose it's possible that when the jury didn't give Goss what he deserved, one of our men decided to take matters into his own hands. Can't say I'd be terribly shocked if that's what happened. Can't say I'd be terribly disappointed, either. You've been around long enough to know what I'm saying. Your job isn't to catch a killer. It's to kill a rumor."

Stafford smiled wryly. "Second call sounds like a dead end already."

"Good. Now, on your way, Detective. And give my regards to Eddy Goss."

The two men chuckled as they headed out the door together, smiling the way men smile when they're in complete agreement.

"Morning, Lon," Detective Jamahl Bradley said to his partner as he ducked his six-foot-six frame beneath the yellow police tape that spanned the width of the hall outside Goss's apartment. The building had been completely secured, with uniformed police officers standing guard at the staircase and at either end of the hall. The door to apartment 217 was wide open, a yellow tarp draped over the bloody corpse that blocked the entrance. Dawn's eerie glow seeped in through the apartment's only window. All was quiet, save for the occasional squawk and static of a police walkie-talkie.

Stafford glanced at Bradley as he folded his arms across his signature attire: red tie, white shirt and twenty-year-old blue blazer—"the colors," the flag-waving ex-marine liked to say. "About damn time you got here," Stafford grumbled.

Bradley gave him a look that typified the mutual disrespect this young African-American and old Florida cracker outwardly demonstrated toward each other. But their banter belied their true feelings. Deep down, they knew they worked well together, basically liked each other, and, most of all, loved giving each other unmitigated hell. "You're lucky my black ass is here," Bradley snapped back. "Your daughter wouldn't let me out of bed."

A joke like that would normally have drawn a nuclear reaction out of Stafford. But he wasn't listening. The old master was absorbed in details, standing squarely in the open apartment doorway as he peered inside with narrowed, discerning eyes. He'd been on the scene for over an hour already. He needed just one more hard look before turning things over to the department's "lab rats," who would collect blood, fingerprints, fibers, and whatever else they could find.

"Let's go," said Stafford.

"Go?" asked Bradley.

"Yeah," he nodded. "You and me gotta be at Jack Swyteck's house before he turns on the morning news."

Bradley winced with confusion. "What for?"

"Justice," he quipped, the corner of his mouth curling in a wry smile. "I can't wait to see that cocky bastard's expression when I tell him that half his client's ugly face is splattered on the living room wall."

Detective Bradley returned the smile. Like everyone else in the police department, he was familiar with the way Eddy Goss's lawyer had skewered Stafford on the witness stand. "I'll drive," he said.

They left Goss's apartment building at 7:00 A.M., just as rush hour began, but they were headed against traffic. They reached Jack's house in fifteen minutes, pulled into the driveway, and marched up to the front door, Stafford leading the way. The detective gave three loud knocks and waited. There was no answer. Jack's car was in the driveway, though, so he knocked again, louder this time. He listened carefully, then smiled with success as he and his partner heard someone stirring inside.

Jack lumbered out of his bedroom and shuffled through the living room to the door. His eyes were puffy slits, and his hair stuck out in all directions. He wore no shoes and no shirt, only the baggy gray gym shorts he'd slept in. He yawned as he pulled aside the curtain and looked out the window next to the front door. He recognized the beige sedan in the driveway as an unmarked police car, and his brow furrowed with curiosity. Then his curiosity turned to concern as Lonzo Stafford's familiar face appeared in the window. Right behind the crusty old detective was his young black partner, whom Jack recognized from Goss's video-taped confession. Bradley seemed even taller and more formidable in person. He had the thick neck of a weight lifter, and his hair was cropped short on the sides and flat on the top, like a pencil eraser. Jack's heart fluttered as the black detective glanced at the Mustang in the driveway. Fortunately, the top was still down so the slash wasn't visible. Relieved, Jack took the chain off the door and opened it.

"Good morning," Stafford said matter-of-factly.

"It certainly is morning," Jack answered.

"We need to talk."

"What about?" asked Jack.

"You mind if we come in?"

"What's it about?" Jack repeated, this time more firmly.

Stafford showed no expression. "It's about Eddy Goss."

Jack shook his head. "Then we have nothing to talk about. I don't work at the Freedom Institute anymore. I don't represent Goss anymore."

"He's dead," said Stafford.

Jack froze. "What?"

"Goss is dead," he repeated, as if he liked the sound of it. "We found him in his apartment a few hours ago. Somebody killed him."

"Are you sure?"

"I seen a few dead bodies in my day," Stafford said. "I know a homicide when I see one. Now," he arched an eyebrow, "you mind if we come inside for a minute?"

"Sure," said Jack.

"You do mind?" Stafford asked, pretending to have misunderstood.

"No," Jack said, flustered. "I mean, I don't mind."

"Because you don't have to talk—"

"I don't mind," Jack asserted, a little too forcefully. "Come on in," he said as he stepped aside, allowing Stafford and Bradley to pass.

As he entered, Stafford reflected on the irony of the situation. Had a homicide detective shown up at the door of any of Swyteck's clients the night after a murder, Swyteck would have been the first to tell him to get lost. It amazed Stafford how lawyers never seemed to heed their own advice.

"Have a seat," said Jack as he cleared the newspapers off the couch.

Stafford watched him carefully. Jack's movements were jerky, a little nervous. Stafford noted the fresh red scratches on his bare back. *Could have been a woman,* he thought. There was a purple bruise on his ribs, too. *Would have taken a pretty aggressive woman.* And the back of Jack's left hand had a nasty cut—like from a knife. *Not something a woman delivers in ordinary course.*

"That's quite a gash you got there," said Stafford as he and his partner took their seats on the couch.

Jack glanced down, picking up on the detective's nod at his hand. It suddenly hurt more now than when he'd stabbed himself with the steak knife. It looked worse, too. *Everything* looked worse than it had last night. There was a dead body and two nosy detectives looking for an explanation.

"It's nothing, really," said Jack. "Just a scratch."

"Pretty deep for a scratch," observed Bradley. "More like a puncture."

Jack shifted uneasily, feeling somewhat double-teamed now that Stafford's partner was talking too. He glanced at Stafford, then at Bradley. They seemed to want an explanation. So he gave them one. "Yesterday, I was doing some work on my Mustang," he lied. "I was loosening a really tight nut, you know—one of those ones that gets rusted on real tight. I just pushed and pushed," he said, demonstrating with his left hand. "The wrench slipped, and I cut my hand."

Stafford arched an eyebrow suspiciously. "Didn't know you were a lefty, Jack."

Jack hesitated, measuring his response. "I'm not. But I use both hands."

"You're ambidextrous?" Bradley followed up.

"No, not exactly, but whenever I work on my car I use both hands. One gets tired, I use the other. You know how it is," he smiled nervously, "especially on the really tough nuts."

Stafford gave a slow, exaggerated nod, as if to say, *"You're a fool and a liar, but let's move on."*

"So," said Jack, "you didn't come here to talk about cars."

"No," Stafford agreed. "We're here about Goss. Some routine stuff. Just a few minutes of your time. You mind answering a few questions?"

"Sure," Jack shrugged.

"You do mind?" said Stafford, taunting again.

"No, I don't mind," Jack snapped. The detective took mental note of his agitated tone.

Stafford continued the game. "It's okay, really, if you don't want to talk, Jack. I mean, you don't have to talk to us."

"I know that," Jack said dryly.

Stafford's eyes narrowed. "You have the right, you know, to remain silent."

Jack rolled his eyes.

"You have the right to an attorney," Stafford continued. "If you can't afford an attorney—"

"Are you reading me my rights?" Jack asked. "I mean, for real?"

Stafford's expression was deadly serious.

"Look," said Jack, "I know you guys are just doing your job. But the truth is, nobody is going to be terribly upset if you don't catch the guy who blew away Eddy Goss."

"How'd you know he was shot?"

All expression drained from Jack's face. "I just figured he'd been shot," Jack backpedaled. "I just meant killed, that's all."

Stafford gave him that slow, exaggerated nod again, his old detective's eyes brightening as he pulled a little pad and pen from his inside coat pocket. "You mind if I take a few notes?"

Jack thought for a moment. "I think this has gone far enough."

"That's certainly your right," Stafford said with a shrug. "You don't have to cooperate."

"It's not that I don't want to cooperate."

"Hey," Bradley intervened, as if to calm Jack down. "It's no problem."

Jack swallowed hard, completely unaware of how obvious it was that they'd rattled the hell out of him.

The detectives rose from the couch, and Jack showed them to the door.

"See you again, Jack," Stafford promised.

Jack showed no reaction. He just closed the door as soon as they stepped outside and went to the window, watching as the two detectives walked side-by-side to their car. He looked for some feedback, but they didn't even look at each other until Bradley got behind the wheel and Stafford was in the passenger seat.

"There was a steak knife on the floor at Goss's apartment," said Stafford as his partner backed the car out of the driveway.

Bradley glanced at his passenger, then looked back at the road as he backed into the street. "So?"

Stafford sat in silence, thinking. "Check with forensics for prints. First thing."

"Sure," Bradley shrugged, "no problem."

"Then call the Florida bar. They keep a set of fingerprints on all attorneys. Tell them you need a set for Swyteck."

"Come on, Lon," Bradley groaned. "We had a little fun with the guy in there, playing with the Miranda rights and the whole bit. But you don't *really* think he killed Goss?"

"You heard me," Stafford snapped. "Check it out."

Bradley sighed and shook his head. "Swyteck, huh?"

Stafford stared at the dashboard. He cracked his window, lit a cigarette, and took a long, satisfying drag. "Swyteck," he confirmed, smoke and disdain pouring from his lips. "Defender of scum."

Chapter 18

•

The steak knife found in Goss's apartment yielded a nice set of prints, and by the following Monday afternoon Detective Stafford thought they looked even nicer, when Jack Swyteck's prints came from the Florida bar.

"We got a match!" Stafford blurted as he barged into the state attorney's office.

Wilson McCue peered out over the top of his rimless spectacles, his working files spread across the top of his desk. Stafford closed the door behind him and bounded into the room with boyish enthusiasm. "Swyteck's prints are all over the steak knife," he said with a grin.

The prosecutor leaned back in his chair. Had anyone but Lonzo Stafford charged unannounced into his office like this, he would have tossed him out on his tail. But Lonzo Stafford enjoyed a special status—acquired more than half a century ago, when an eleven-year-old Lonnie entered into a pact with an eight-year-old Willie to remain "friends forever, no matter what." As boys they'd hunted in the same fields, fished in the same ponds, and gone to the same school, Lonzo always a couple of steps ahead of Wilson on the time line, but Wilson always a notch higher on the grading curve. Now, at sixty-five, Wilson looked at least seventy-five, even on a good day.

"I want you to convene a grand jury," said Stafford.

The prosecutor coughed his smoker's hack, then lit up a Camel. "What for?"

Stafford snatched the lit cigarette from his friend and smoked it himself, pacing as he spoke. "Because I got a suspect," he replied, "in the murder of Eddy Goss."

"Yeah," McCue scoffed, "so do I. About twelve million of them. Anybody who has seen that animal's videotaped confession is a suspect. Eddy Goss *deserved* to die, and everybody wanted him dead. There ain't a jury in the world that would convict the guy who did the world a favor by blowing Goss's brains out."

Stafford arched an eyebrow. "Unless the guy who did it was the same slick defense lawyer who got him— and others like him—off the hook and back on the street."

McCue was apprehensive. "And I can see the headlines already: 'Republican State Attorney Attacks Democrat Governor's Son.' It'll be ugly, Lon. With the gubernatorial election just three months away, you'd *better* have plenty of ammunition if we're gonna start that war."

Stafford took a drag on his cigarette. "We got

plenty," he said, smoke pouring through his nostrils. "We got Swyteck's prints on the handle of a knife we found on the floor. I also had the blade checked. There was blood on the tip. AB negative. Very rare. Same as Swyteck's. Lab found some fish-stick remnants on there, too, which is what the autopsy showed Goss had for dinner. And best of all, the blood came later, after the fish sticks."

"Which means?"

"Which means that on the night Goss was murdered I can place Jack Swyteck in the victim's apartment, after dinner, wielding a steak knife."

"And you got a victim who was shot to death," the prosecutor fired back. "I'd say we need more."

"There is more. Just a few hours after the murder, about seven in the morning, we interviewed Swyteck. This was before he was a suspect. Swyteck came to the door in a pair of gym shorts, right outta bed. Nervous as a cat, he was. Big bruise on his ribs. Looked like a bite mark on his belly. Fresh red scratches on his back. Had an open cut on the back of his left hand, too. It looked like a stab wound, to me and Bradley both. Just to look at him, I'd say he'd been in a pretty recent scuffle."

"And he would say he fell down the stairs."

"Maybe," said Stafford, his voice gathering intensity. "But he's gonna have a hard time explaining how he knew Goss had been shot before we ever told him so."

"What do you mean?"

"I checked with the media. No news reports were out about Goss's murder until almost eight o'clock. We showed up at Swyteck's house at seven, and we told him Goss had been killed—but we didn't tell him how.

Swyteck knew he had been shot. He said so. It was a slip of the tongue, I think, but he was talking about a shooting before we were."

McCue listened with interest. "We're getting there," he said. He paused to rub at his temples and think for a second. "Why don't you just arrest him, Lonnie. You know, maybe B and E or something, if all you want to do is rattle his cage?"

Stafford's eyes narrowed with contempt. "I want to do more than rattle him. I want to *convict* his ass."

"Because of what he did to you in the Goss trial?" McCue asked directly.

"Because he's guilty. The fact that I would thoroughly enjoy nailing his ass doesn't change that. I wouldn't tag him or any one of those crusaders at the Freedom Institute just to get even. Swyteck *did* it. I'm convinced of it. He wigged out and blew away his scumbag client. He screwed up—big time. And I want to be the guy who makes him pay."

The prosecutor sighed heavily. "We can't be wrong about this one."

"I'm *not* wrong. And if you'd seen Swyteck's face that morning after the murder like I did, you'd *know* I'm not wrong. I've got a feeling about this one, Wilson. Not some flaky feeling you get when you wake up one morning and read your horoscope. This one's based on a lifetime of police work. And in all the years you've known me, have my instincts ever steered you wrong?"

McCue averted his eyes. He had complete trust in his friend, but the pointed question reminded him that there may very well have been one instance when

Lonzo Stafford had steered him wrong—dead wrong. It was a first-degree murder charge that Stafford had built on circumstantial evidence. McCue had gone ahead and prosecuted the case, but by the time it was over, even he was beginning to wonder whether Stafford had tagged the right man. It was academic now, of course. The jury had convicted him. Governor Swyteck had signed his death warrant. The state had put him to death. He was gone. McCue would never forget him, though. His name was Raul Fernandez.

"Let me sleep on it," McCue told his friend.

"What more do you want?"

He shrugged uneasily. "It's just that there are so many people who wanted to see Eddy Goss dead. We need to talk to other suspects. We need to talk to neighbors. You need to make sure there isn't some witness out there, somewhere, who'll gut the whole case by saying they saw somebody running from Goss's apartment with smoke pouring from the barrel of a .38-caliber pistol. Somebody who couldn't possibly be Swyteck. Like a woman, a seven-foot black guy, a friend of one of Goss's victims, or—"

"A cop," Stafford interjected, his tone disdainful. "That call to nine-one-one about the cop being around Goss's apartment has you spooked, doesn't it?"

McCue removed his eyeglasses. "I'm concerned about it, yeah. And so's your boss. That's why he told you about it when he put you on the case."

Stafford shook his head. "You know as well as I do, Wilson, that if it'd really been a cop who'd blown Goss's brains out, he wouldn't have showed up at his apartment wearing a uniform. He would've stopped Goss on the street, shot him in 'self-defense,' and laid a Saturday-night special in his cold, dead hand."

"Maybe," said McCue. "But the fact of the matter is that we're talking about the governor's son here. And we're talking about a first-degree murder charge. I'm not taking *that* case to the grand jury until you've got some good, hard evidence."

Stafford's eyes flared. He looked angry, but he wasn't. He took it as a challenge. "I'm gonna get it," he vowed. "I'm gonna get whatever you need to bring Swyteck down."

McCue nodded. "If it's out there, I'm sure you will."

"It's out there," Stafford replied, his tone very serious. "I know it's out there. Because in here," he thumped his chest, "I *know* Swyteck's guilty." He rose quickly from his chair and started for the door, then shoved his hand in his coat pocket and stopped short, as if he'd suddenly found something. "What the hell's this?" he asked, clearly overacting as he pulled a plastic bag from his pocket.

McCue smiled. He knew his old friend was up to something.

"Well, I'll be damned," said Stafford as he smacked his hand playfully against his forehead. The Cheshire-cat smile he'd been holding inside was now plastered from ear to ear. "I almost forgot to tell you the best part, Wilson. You see, nobody heard any gunshots at the time of Goss's murder. Doesn't seem possible, really, that nobody hears nothin' in a building like that—unless, of course, the man who plugged Goss had a silencer on his thirty-eight-caliber pistol. Which is why *this* is so important," he said as he raised the plastic evidence bag before the prosecutor's eyes.

"And just what is *this?*"

"A silencer," Stafford said smugly, "for a thirty-eight-caliber pistol."

"Where'd you get it?"

"Underneath the front seat of Jack Swyteck's car."

McCue's eyes widened with interest, then concern. "Hope you had a search warrant?"

"Didn't need one. This came to us via Kaiser Auto Repair—Swyteck's mechanics. Seems our favorite lawyer brings in his Mustang every other day for something—it's a real Rent-A-Wreck. Thursday morning, he leaves his car to get the convertible top fixed. A few hours later, the owner of the shop catches one of his mechanics stealing things from the customers' cars and calls us. One of the cars the grease monkey robbed happened to be Swyteck's. And what do you suppose shows up in the guy's loot?" Stafford gave a huge grin. "One silencer."

"That's a pretty strange coincidence, Lonnie, that some punk was rifling through Swyteck's car. You sure it happened that way?"

"Shop owner will back me up a hundred percent," he said, giving McCue an insider's wink.

McCue sat back in his chair, folding his hands contentedly on his belly. "Lonnie," he said with a power grin, "*now* we're on to something."

Chapter 19

●

"You had forty-three press calls, Governor," Harry Swyteck's secretary reported, trailing at the heel of the candidate-by-day/governor-by-night as he rushed into his spacious office. "And that's just in the last hour."

"Oh, for Pete's sake," the governor groaned as he tossed his charcoal suit coat onto the couch, loosened his tie, and plopped into the high-back leather chair behind his carved mahogany desk, exhausted. Before the campaign, he found it relaxing to nestle into his position of power between the state and American flags, amidst the brass chandeliers, white coffered ceilings, and big arching windows with red velvet drapes that reminded him he was indeed governor. But now that the campaign was in full swing, the opulent surroundings were stark reminders that he had to be re-elected to keep these trappings of power for another four years. "Who did I insult this time?" he asked, only half kidding.

"No one," his secretary assured him as she placed his hot cup of tea with lemon on his desk. She served without a smile, her expression all business. With her gray hair pulled back and a white silk scarf wrapped tightly around her neck, she had all the warmth of a nun on a vow of silence. When it came to political staffers, however, personality was a small sacrifice for eighteen years of efficiency and undivided loyalty. "I'm sure they're all trying to get the scoop before the six o'clock news," she said, "that's all."

The governor froze as he brought his teacup to his lips. Even after all these years it still bothered him that Paula always seemed to know everything about late-breaking news before he knew *anything* about it. "The scoop on what?" he asked with some trepidation.

Her look was more somber than usual. "Your son, of course."

His trepidation turned to concern. "What about my son?"

"Campbell's on his way up," she said, avoiding the question. "He'll explain."

Moments later the door flew open, and the governor's chief aide, Campbell McSwain, rushed into the office, nearly mowing down Paula on her way out. Campbell was a handsome, thirty-eight-year-old Princeton graduate who looked as if he wouldn't know a blue collar unless it was pinpoint Oxford cloth, but his uncanny ability to portray Harold Swyteck as a regular Joe to the average voter had gone a long way toward winning the election four years ago. Campbell wore his usual Bass loafers, khaki slacks, and a Brooks Brothers blazer over a white polo shirt, but his wide-eyed expression was far less understated.

"Sorry, sir," Campbell said as he gasped for breath. He'd run all the way to the governor's office. "I just got off the phone with the Dade County State Attorney's Office."

"The state attorney?"

"It's your son, sir. Our sources tell us he's the target of a grand jury investigation. He's the prime suspect in the murder of Eddy Goss."

The governor's mouth fell open, as if he'd just been punched in the chest. "Goss is dead? And they think Jack did it? That's preposterous. It's *impossible*. Jack is no murderer. It has to be a mistake."

"Well, whether it's true or not, Governor, this is a terrible setback for us. Until a month ago, no one thought a former state insurance commissioner would be a serious challenge to a popular incumbent like yourself. But he's making a damn good showing. He made quite a name for himself rooting out fraud, and he had the good sense not to push so hard that big business wouldn't open its wallets when the campaigning got under way. The polls have you up by just four points at last tally. *This*, however, could change everything. The press is already pouncing all over it. Forty-three calls, Paula said."

The governor leaned forward in his chair and glared at his aide. "This is my son we're talking about," he said angrily. "We're not talking about bad press, or about points on an opinion poll."

Campbell stood in check. "I'm sorry, Governor," he said quietly. "I mean—it's just that, I know you and your son haven't been close. At least not as long as I've known you. I guess I should have been more sensitive."

The governor rose from his chair, turned, and walked slowly to the floor-to-ceiling window that overlooked the garden in the courtyard. "It's true," he said, speaking as much to himself as to his aide, his voice trailing off as if he were retreating deep into his innermost thoughts. "Jack and I have not been as close as I'd like."

Campbell watched with concern, searching for something to say. "Your son is only a grand jury *target*—a suspect," he said. "The lawyers tell me there's at least a theoretical possibility he might not actually be indicted."

Harry nodded appreciatively at Campbell's attempted consolation. But in his mind he could already see the chilling accusation: "John Lawrence Swyteck did with malice aforethought knowingly commit murder in the first degree." Sometimes he couldn't help wondering if fate meant him to be separated from Jack, if the alignment of the stars foreordained a rift between them. But he knew that was a cop-out, an attempt to deny his own complicity in the shaping of Jack's . . . what were they? Neuroses? Problems? Confusion, certainly. With a deep sense of guilt, Harry thought back to the *first* time his son was accused of murder—when he was five years old . . .

Harry had pulled into the driveway around supper time and walked briskly up the sidewalk to the front door. He could see his young son peering sadly out the bedroom window as if he were being punished for something. Before Harry had even closed the front door and stepped inside, Agnes was screaming at him about Jack and the crucifix he'd found. Harry tried to calm her, but she was determined to have it out. He rushed to the kitchen and closed the door, so Jack couldn't hear, but the bitter argument continued.

"I told you I didn't want these things in the house anymore," Agnes said. "*I'm* your wife now. Give up the past, Harry. I won't tolerate you having your own little shrine."

"It's not for me. I'm saving them for Jack, when he's old enough to understand."

"I don't believe that for a second," she shouted. "You're not thinking of Jack. You're thinking of yourself. You're living in the past—ever since you took that boy home and left her behind. You won't let go. Admit it, Harry, you hate me for not being her. And you hate your own son for killing her."

"Shut up!" he shouted as he rushed toward her.

"Don't you dare raise a hand to me! It's sick, Harry! And I'm *sick* of it!"

Just outside the kitchen, five-year-old Jack trembled in shock and fear of what he had done to his mother. He'd snuck out of his room and tiptoed down the hallway, finding a spot behind a large spider plant, just outside the kitchen, where his father and stepmother had dug in to do battle. He had wanted to hear the truth— but the truth was more than any five-year-old could handle. He stepped back in a daze, then tripped over the pedestal holding the plant, sending himself and the plant crashing to the floor.

The noise from the hall immediately silenced the argument in the kitchen. Harry rushed out and saw Jack lying on the floor, beside the overturned plant. Their eyes met, but neither one spoke. Harold Swyteck didn't have to ask how much his son had heard. The look on his face told him he'd heard it all. And from that day forward, they'd never looked at each other the same way . . .

"Are you listening to me, sir?" Campbell asked. The governor looked at him blankly. His mind was elsewhere.

"I'm sorry," he said, trying to shake himself loose of his memories. But he was still thinking of Jack. After so many disappointments and regrets, he wanted to help his son. But with their turbulent history, it wouldn't be that simple. Jack would surely rebuff any overtures he made.

"Governor," Campbell interrupted, "obviously this isn't something you want to focus on now. I'm not trying to be insensitive. I do understand that, for all your differences, Jack is still your son. That's really none of my business. It is my business, however, to get you re-elected. And, like it or not, we have to evaluate your son's predicament in political terms. Personal tragedy aside, sir, the simple fact is that if Jack Swyteck loses his trial, Harold Swyteck loses his election. Politically speaking," he said coolly, "*that* is the bottom line."

Harry was angered by Campbell's mercenary view, but he also appreciated the simple logic of his words. Campbell was right: Helping Jack *would* help his campaign. And that was the answer to the problem—a kind of reverse psychology. Jack wouldn't accept help if his father were doing it only for his son. But if the governor were doing it for himself, for his own political reasons,

Jack would owe him nothing—not even gratitude. That would be the way he could help Jack—and, more important, be assured that Jack would *let* him.

"You're absolutely right," said the governor, smiling inwardly. "I guess I have no choice but to help my son—any way I can."

Chapter 20

•

After just a week in Rome, Cindy Paige returned to Miami that afternoon. The photo shoot in Italy was officially off. It turned out that Chet had a much more recreational view of their "business" trip than she did—which became clear the moment she found out he'd reserved one hotel room with one king-size bed in each of the cities on their tour. It had hurt to find out that it wasn't her talent with a camera that had landed her the job.

Gina met her at the baggage claim, but she wasn't a very chatty chauffeur on the ride home from the airport. She told Cindy she wasn't feeling very well, and she wasn't. Of all the things Gina had done in her life, she realized now that bedding Jack was the lowest. Somehow it had seemed easy to view Jack as "fair game" the other night, when she'd thought Cindy was jetting off to the Eternal City with her old lover. But her friend's quick return simply confirmed what Gina had suspected all along: Despite the ugly words Jack and Cindy had exchanged the last time they were together, they were far from through.

When they got back to the townhouse, Gina retreated right to her bedroom. She flopped onto the bed and escaped into a rerun of "Lifestyles of the Rich and Famous."

Cindy left her suitcase by the door and went straight to the kitchen. The so-called snack on the airplane had been about as appetizing as boiled lettuce. She quickly microwaved herself some french fries, then opened the refrigerator in search of ketchup.

"Gina," she called out, "where's the Heinz?"

Gina didn't answer.

"Oh, well," Cindy said, shrugging. Balancing the plate of fries in one hand and a Diet Coke in the other, she headed for the living room. She grabbed the remote control as she sat on the couch and flipped on the television.

The lead story on every local evening-news broadcast was the same. She was just in time to catch the south Florida version, the hometown approach to the breaking story of how, "in a shocking development, the grand jury investigation into the murder of Eddy Goss had now targeted murder suspect Jack Swyteck."

She stared dumbfounded at Jack's face on the television screen, framed by an imposing graphic of the scales of justice. "Oh, my God," she muttered. She punched the buttons on the remote control and flipped frantically from one channel to the next, as if trying to watch them all at once. She couldn't believe it, even after hearing it straight from the mouth of every news anchor in the city. After ten minutes she'd had enough, since coverage on every station had degenerated to "live and exclusive" interviews with virtually every publicity hound in town who claimed to "know" Jack Swyteck. She switched off the set in disgust. Not one of these people knew Jack the way she did. He was no killer.

Her hands were shaking as she sank into the couch. She wasn't sure what to do. Should she just let him know she was back in town—if he needed a friend? She wondered why, indeed, she *was* back in town. Had it really been necessary to call off the photo shoot in Italy? She probably could have laid down a few ground rules with Chet and gotten the job done—unless, of course, her relationship with Jack had subconsciously drawn her back to Miami.

She glanced at the phone. Talking to him wouldn't be good enough. Not after the blowup they'd had when they were last together. She needed to *see* him. She grabbed her purse from the coffee table. "I'll be back later," she shouted up the stairway, then hurried out the door.

The sun had set and the streetlights had popped on by the time Cindy reached Jack's house. Even when she'd lived there, she'd never liked driving up alone after dark. Jack professed to like landscaping, but what he really meant was that he liked foliage of any kind, and lots of it. His "lawn" was a thick blanket of bromeliads, bushy ferns, and practically anything else that didn't look like a weed. Large, bushy palms and leafy ficus trees were scattered everywhere, creating an array of menacing shadows. It was enough to make any twenty-five-year-old blonde in blue denim shorts and sleeveless white shell a bit on edge. At night the scene always made her feel a bit like Dorothy in the land of Oz contending with the talking apple trees.

Anxiety propelled her to the front door in a matter of seconds. The porch light flipped on before she could knock, and the door swung open.

Jack stood in the doorway, looking perplexed. "Cindy, what are you doing here?"

"I saw the story on the news. I thought you might need to talk."

"You're too much," he said, opening his arms. She stepped forward to accept his embrace. "After you left I wanted to call you and tell you how sorry I was, but I felt like such a jerk." He held her tighter and looked into her eyes. "Can you forgive me?"

"Let's try to forget that ever happened," Cindy said. "I felt terrible about what I said, too."

"No, no, you were right," he protested, "I totally lost it. But—" he shook his head in confusion. "What happened with Italy?"

She slipped from his embrace and gave him a look of concern. "That's not nearly as important as what's happening to you."

His spirits soared. Just an hour ago, after having watched the six o'clock news, he'd thought it would be a very long time before he'd ever feel happy again.

"I guess you know all about the grand jury investigation," he said, still not quite believing the turn of circumstances.

She nodded.

"Do I need to tell you I didn't do it?"

She looked into his eyes. "I know you didn't."

He went to embrace her again, but his attention was diverted by a car pulling into his driveway. It was a police car—not one but two in fact. And inside the lead car was Detective Lonzo Stafford.

"I've got to talk to these guys," Jack said to Cindy as he gestured for her to go inside. At first she hesitated, but then she entered the house.

Stafford trudged up the path and took Cindy's place on the porch. His blue blazer was even more wrinkled than usual, his necktie was loosened, and a few extra lines seemed to have appeared in his tired old face. He'd clearly been working some long hours, but the gleam in his gray eyes made it equally clear that he thought his hard work was about to pay off.

"Got a warrant here, my friend. Time for a little search party."

Jack sighed, relieved that it wasn't an arrest warrant. "You won't find a murder weapon here," he assured the detective. For a moment, Jack felt like leading him right to his footlocker and the old .38. A simple ballistics test would prove it wasn't involved in the Goss shooting. But the gun was never registered in Florida, a problem in itself, and possessing it would only prove his familiarity with the same type of weapon the newspapers said had killed Goss. Jack figured the less grist the detective had for wild conjecture, the better.

Stafford glanced over his shoulder to make sure the other officers couldn't hear him. "Do you think I'm stupid enough to get a warrant to look for a murder weapon?" he asked contemptuously. "Then I'd have to tell the jury we looked for it and didn't find it, wouldn't I, Swyteck? Besides," he said smugly, "I don't need to find the gun. Not since Ballistics determined a silencer was used to kill Goss. Not since that mechanic down at Kaiser pulled a silencer out of your convertible."

"A mechanic did *what?*"

Stafford smiled wryly. "You'll hear all about it soon enough, counselor. Right now," he said with a wink as he flashed the warrant in Jack's face, "baby needs a new pair a' shoes. Reeboks to be exact. You may recall that it was a rainy night when you visited your favorite client. Your footprints are all over the apartment."

Jack fell silent. Things were getting worse by the minute, but he had nothing to gain by sparring with the old detective. "Just get what you came for," he said flatly. "And be on your way."

Stafford signaled back to his team with a jerk of his head. Jamahl Bradley and two other officers filed into the house, heading straight for the master bedroom. Jack followed closely behind, his stomach in knots.

"What's happening?" Cindy asked Jack, her voice trembling as the officers whisked by her in the living room.

Stafford stopped to field the question. "We're gonna prove your boyfriend here was traipsing around Eddy Goss's apartment the night of the murder. That's what's happening, miss." Stafford took another step, then stopped and arched a suggestive eyebrow at Cindy. "You sure you want to sleep here tonight, sweetheart?"

"Shut the hell up, Stafford," Jack snapped.

Stafford just shrugged and continued on toward the

bedroom. Jack started to follow but stopped when he saw the look on Cindy's face. He wanted to watch the police conduct their search, just to make sure they stuck to the warrant, but he couldn't let Stafford's remark linger. He had to keep Cindy's trust, so he took her by the hand and led her quickly through the kitchen, into the backyard by the gazebo where they'd be out of earshot.

"Were you really at Goss's apartment the night he was murdered?"

He looked into the middle distance, obviously struggling with what he was about to say. "Listen, Cindy, there are going to be things I won't be able to tell you from here on out. Not because I'm guilty, but because it's possible you may end up being a witness at trial—and the less you know, the better. But I may as well tell you this, because the footprints are going to prove it anyway. Yes, I was there that night. I went to Goss's apartment. But I didn't kill him. I went because of some threats I was getting. Someone was calling me, telling me there was a 'killer on the loose.' And then I was nearly run down, and Thursday—he killed Thursday."

Cindy brought her hand to her mouth. "Oh, my God . . . oh, my God, Jack."

Jack touched her cheek gently to console her. "I figured it was Goss, and sure enough, that day you left for Italy I got a call inviting me to his apartment. He didn't identify himself, but that was just part of the game-playing. I had to confront him, Cindy. But I didn't kill him."

"Are you going to tell the police all that?"

"No way." He laid his hands on her shoulders for emphasis as he spoke. "It's very important that you understand this. We can *never* tell the police about the harassment. Not unless they force us to tell them."

"Why not?"

He sighed. "Right now, they're trying to build a case against me for killing Eddy Goss. I don't know how good it's going to be, but off the top of my head, I can see one glaring weakness: motive. Why would I kill Goss? Without any evidence that Goss was stalking me, all the prosecution can say is that I killed him because I felt guilty about having gotten him acquitted. Their whole case boils down to whether or not a lawyer—a *criminal defense lawyer*—had a guilty conscience. Now, how many jurors would even believe a lawyer actually *has* a conscience, let alone one strong enough to make him into a killer?"

She listened carefully, considering his explanation.

"It's simple," he continued. "If I were to tell the police about the threats I started getting after Goss's trial, I'd be handing them a motive on a silver platter. The moment they find out Goss was after me, that's it. Bingo! They've got a motive. Understand?"

Cindy sighed. She felt like she was going to cry, not so much because of what was happening at the moment, but because she realized that this was all just the beginning of a new and terrible set of events. "Yes," she said quietly, "I understand. Don't worry, Jack. I'm with you."

Jack and Cindy ordered out for Chinese after Stafford left the house. At first they tried to keep the conversation light, but as Jack finished his last spring roll, he turned the discussion in a more serious direction. "I'm sorry we didn't get to talk before you left for Italy—at least to say good-bye."

"More than that needed to be said," Cindy answered. "There's a side of you that always seems cut off from me. And it's not just me—you seem to deal with your father the same way. The whole time I've known you, you've never made an effort to contact him, and he's never called you either."

"I don't blame you for being confused about that."

"It's not about blame, Jack. It's just something you've got to deal with."

He averted his eyes as he fiddled with an empty soy sauce packet. "I've wanted to. Oddly enough, just before this thing got really crazy, my stepmother phoned. Said I should give my father a call. I don't know how to explain it . . . it's absurd, really, but as long as I don't call him, there's hope we'll work things out. If I do take a chance, and there's a blowup, I'm not sure we can ever put the pieces back together. It's like they say, if you take your shot and miss, the dream is over. But if you don't, there's always *someday*."

"C'mon, Jack, you know better than that. You can't trudge along, status quo, hoping things will change. There comes a point when you have to do something. That's what I did with us. I'm not saying I handled it perfectly, but I had to do something." Her eyes sought his. "You need to know that it was strictly business between me and Chet." She shook her head, rolled her eyes. "It turned out that *he* wanted it to be more, and that's why I came right back home. I didn't feel it was over between us—which is why I told Gina to give you the number at my hotel."

"Gina never gave me a number," said Jack.

"Oh . . ." Cindy looked confused. "She promised me she would. I guess she forgot."

"Yeah," he said skeptically. He'd really allowed Gina to sucker him in. His feelings of guilt were overwhelming.

After they'd cleared the dinner plates, Jack glanced at his watch. They'd been talking longer than he thought. It was nearly eleven-thirty. He asked Cindy if she'd be all right getting back to Gina's.

"I want to stay here tonight," she said, avoiding direct eye contact. "But 'tonight' means just that. No commitments yet, okay?"

"That's fine," he said, his expression showing both gratitude and relief.

Twenty minutes later, Cindy emerged from the bathroom wearing a big football jersey Jack had loaned her to sleep in. She shuffled toward the bed, then paused as she noticed the dresser mirror. "You replaced all the torn snapshots."

"Yeah, I dug out the negatives and made some new prints," he said sheepishly. "I didn't have much of a choice. Every time I looked at the mirror, it reminded me of how awful I was the last time we were together."

She flashed a wide smile. "Come to bed," she said as she led him by the hand.

As he drew back the sheets, thoughts of his impending arrest took the edge off his desire. He looked at

Cindy and felt an enormous burden of guilt. She was *so* willing to give him a second chance, *so* willing to support him as he weathered this latest crisis. He wondered how she'd react if she heard that his best shot at an alibi was her own best friend.

Chapter 21

•

Stafford and his assistants left Jack's house at about eight o'clock. Jack's tennis shoes were in the lab by eight-thirty. Stafford and his partner hung around the police station for the preliminary results, patiently waiting in the senior detective's office. Stafford was at his desk, still in that faded blue blazer he never seemed to take off, his white shirt collar unbuttoned and wide polyester tie dropped over his chair. He was busying himself smoking cigarettes and straightening out paper clips. Bradley was in the chair beside the window, wadding up yesterday's newspaper into little balls and shooting free throws into the wastebasket in the corner.

The phone rang at ten. "Stafford," the detective answered eagerly, cigarette smoke pouring from his lips as he spoke.

Bradley watched expectantly as his partner nodded and grunted.

"Got him!" Stafford proclaimed as he hung up. He leaned back in his chair and folded his arms smugly across his chest. "Perfect match on the Reeboks. Twenty-seven glorious prints all over the apartment, and even one on the windowsill. Can't say I'm surprised. I knew in my gut Swyteck did it. But I'm pleased as hell we can *prove* it."

Bradley nodded slowly. "Congratulations," he said, though he spoke without heart.

Stafford looked questioningly at his partner. "I would have expected a little more excitement than that, Jamahl."

Bradley hesitated, but there was something he needed to say. "Frankly, Lon, you just seem a little too eager to nail this guy. That's all."

Stafford's eyes flared with anger, but he kept control. "Listen to me," he lectured. "I've been a cop more than forty years, son. I know enough to listen to my instincts. And my instincts say that Jack Swyteck lost his cool after that trial, and he blew Goss away. I know what I'm talking about," he growled, then took a drag from his cigarette. "The system is just a game to these criminal defense lawyers. They don't care about the truth. They'll say or do whatever it takes to win: 'My client ate too many Twinkies,' or 'My client watched too much television.' I've heard it all and I've seen 'em all, and Swyteck ranks up there with the worst. I listened to Eddy Goss confess murder right to my face. Right to my damn *face*. And then I watched Fancy Jack Swyteck convince a jury his client wasn't guilty. That boy made a *fool* out of me. I've watched that son of a bitch do it time and time again. And every time he wins, another killer goes back on the street. Usually it's on a technicality or some flaky defense. And Swyteck's just getting warmed up. He's a tenderfoot. Can you imagine him doing this for the next twenty-five, thirty years?"

Bradley swallowed apprehensively. He knew the dangers of a cop who let the ends justify the means—especially one who seemed out for revenge. "So what are you saying, Lon? Somebody's got to stop him?"

Stafford's expression turned very cold. "No," he snapped. "All I'm saying is that this slick defense lawyer has got himself into deep trouble, and I'm gonna make damn sure he pays for it. So excuse *me* if I seem a little too happy about catchin' myself a killer, okay?"

Bradley nodded slowly. "Okay, chief," he shrugged, seeming to back off. "After all, you *do* have twenty-seven footprints."

"You're damn right I do."

"But don't forget," said Bradley, shooting him a look. "There's still an unidentified footprint right outside the apartment door. We know it's not from Goss. It's not the right shoe size. And we know it's not from Swyteck, either, since he was wearing the Reeboks."

"So what," said Stafford, waving it off. "It's from the janitor or somebody else in the building."

Bradley shook his head. "No, it's not, Lon. That's a very clean print. You can see the insignia on the heel very plainly: two crossed oars. Those are Wiggins wing tips—three-hundred-dollar jobs. There ain't no janitor and nobody in that slum of an apartment building who wears three-hundred-dollar wing tips."

"Look, Jamahl," Stafford grimaced. "We got twenty-seven footprints from Jack Swyteck *inside* the apartment. We got one stray footprint *outside* the apartment. Quit bein' a pain in the ass, will ya?"

Bradley sighed. His doubts weren't alleviated, but he didn't want to provoke his partner. "Maybe you're right," he said as he rose from his chair and stepped toward the door. Then he stopped. "But let me put it to you this way, Lon. Twenty-seven footprints from the same pair of shoes adds up to how many people?"

Stafford shrugged, as if the question were stupid. "One, of course," he said.

"That's right. And no matter how you look at it, one single footprint from a different pair of shoes adds up to what?"

"One person," Stafford answered reluctantly.

"Right," said Bradley, "as in one *other* person. Think about it," he said.

Chapter 22

•

Sometime after 2:00 A.M. Jack finally fell asleep with Cindy in his arms. He awoke at about ten o'clock, and he smiled at the sight of her sleeping at his side. She looked great even in the morning, he thought. Cindy was the woman he loved, the only woman he really wanted. Her coming back to him was like a dream come true.

He heard a pounding on the front door. He immediately sat upright; he knew who it was. Grand juries normally convened at nine. As much as he'd expected the visit, he still shuddered at the thought that he was no longer just someone the prosecutor had labeled a grand jury "target." If his guess was correct, in the last hour he'd been formally indicted for murder in the first degree.

He jumped out of bed and pulled on khaki slacks and loafers. The pounding continued.

Cindy sat up. "What is it?"

He slipped on a blue oxford shirt, decided against a tie, then spoke in a voice that strained to be upbeat. "I think it's time . . . they probably handed down an indictment." He went to the bureau, checked himself in the mirror, and quickly brushed his hair. He fumbled through his wallet and took out all the pictures and credit cards, leaving only his driver's license, voter's registration, and fifty dollars cash. He shoved the wallet into his back pocket, tucked in his shirt, and took a deep breath. In the mirror he saw Cindy looking at him, and he turned to meet her stare.

"I love you, Jack," she said quietly.

He felt a rush of emotion, which he managed to control, then, smiling a sad smile, said, "I love you, too."

The knocking continued, louder this time.

"It won't be bad," he assured her. "It's not like they're about to lock me up and throw away the key. They'll book me at the station, and then I'll go before the judge, who'll probably release me on bail. I'll be home this afternoon. No sweat." He leaned down and kissed her on the forehead.

She nodded slowly. A tear rolled down her cheek as she watched him turn and disappear into the hallway. Another loud knock, and it was definitely time to go.

"Coming," Jack said as he walked briskly toward the front door. He grabbed the knob, then stopped to collect himself. He was as ready as he'd ever be. Ironically, he'd coolly and calmly counseled scores of clients on how to prepare for arrest, but now he realized that this was one of those events that no amount of preparation could completely smooth over.

Jack swallowed his apprehension and opened the door.

"Manny?" he said with surprise.

"How you doing, Jack?" replied Manuel Cardenal, Florida's preeminent criminal defense lawyer. Jack knew him from the courthouse. *Everyone* knew Manuel Cardenal from the courthouse. He'd started his career twenty years ago as a murder-rape-robbery public defender, making his name defending the guilty. He'd spent the last ten years at the helm of his own law firm, making a fortune defending the wealthy.

"What are *you* doing here?" asked Jack.

"I'm your attorney. Can I come in?"

"Of course."

Manny stepped inside. He wore a blue double-breasted suit, black Italian shoes, and a colorful silk necktie with matching handkerchief showing from the left breast pocket. He stopped to check his reflection in the mirror beside the door and obviously liked what he saw. At forty-three, Manny's life with women was at its peak; younger women still found him handsome, while older women were drawn to his youthfulness. He had a smile that bespoke confidence and experience, yet his eyes sparkled with the vibrancy of a teenage heartthrob. He wore his jet-black hair straight back, no part, as if he were looking into a windstorm. He turned and faced the man in the eye of a real storm.

"I didn't hire you," said Jack. "Not that I wouldn't want to. I just can't *afford* you."

Manny took a seat on the couch. "Sorry for the short notice, but just this morning your father retained me on your behalf."

"Excuse me?"

"Your father regrets that you have to suffer at his expense."

"At *his* expense?"

Manny nodded. "You're going to have one hell of a day, Jack. If you weren't Harry Swyteck's son, you wouldn't be dragged out of your house in cuffs and carted away in a squad car with the lights flashing. You wouldn't be locked up like a crack dealer pulled off the street and forced to wait in the pen for arraignment. You'd be allowed to surrender yourself and immediately be released on your own recognizance, or at worst for some token signature bond. It's politics," Manny explained, "and your father regrets that."

"Are you saying that the indictment was politically motivated?"

"No. But everything after the indictment will be."

"Great . . . so I'm going to be dragged through the system by my father's political enemies."

"I'm afraid so, Jack. I called the state attorney to see if they'd just let you come in and surrender quietly. No go. They want a spectacle. They want publicity. Your case is already a political football. Your father recognizes that. And he knows that however your case goes, so goes his election."

"Is *that* the reason you're here, Manny? To save my father's election?"

"All I know is what your father told me, Jack."

Jack narrowed his eyes and took a good look at Manny, as if he were searching his face for the truth. "I'm not stupid, Manny. And I know my father. At least I know him well enough to know that this can't be entirely about politics. And I know you, too. I don't believe a man like *you* would get involved in this case if my father didn't genuinely want to help me. So what gives? Why did the two of you have to come up with this little charade to make it look like the governor is doing it not for me, but for his own political gain? Is he too proud or too afraid to tell the truth? Why the hell doesn't he just be my father and *tell* me he wants to help?"

Manny's warm eyes seemed to convey more than he was saying. "Maybe that *is* what he's telling you, Jack."

Jack fell silent. Manny's answer had him thinking.

A loud knock on the door interrupted his thoughts. "Open up!" came the order.

Jack and Manny exchanged glances.

"So, what do you say, Jack? Shall we dance?"

Jack took a deep breath, and a thin smile crept onto his face. "Just don't step on my toes, Cardenal." Then he opened the door.

"Police," said Detective Lonzo Stafford, flashing his badge. Stafford wore his usual blue blazer and an unmistakable smirk. Detective Bradley was at his side. "You're under arrest," Stafford announced with relish, "for the murder of Eddy Goss."

Jack was stiff but composed as he surveyed the situation. Manny appeared to be right about being put through the wringer. It wasn't the low-profile, cooperative approach he'd hoped for. They'd driven up in a patrol car rather than Stafford's unmarked vehicle, and they'd left the lights flashing, a blue swirl of authority in his yard.

A crowd of nosy neighbors and probing reporters

gathered at the end of Jack's driveway, just off his property. Jack could hear their collective "there he is" when he appeared in the doorway, followed by a barrage of clicking cameras with telephoto lenses.

"You have the right to remain silent," Jack heard Stafford say, but he wasn't really listening to the Miranda litany until Stafford said to his partner, "Cuff him, Jamahl."

"What?" Jack asked in disbelief.

"Cuff him," Stafford repeated with pleasure.

"Look, Detective. I'm willing to cooperate—"

"Good," Stafford cut him off. "Then cuff his hands in front, instead of behind his back."

Jack knew better than to resist. He obediently stuck his hands out in front of him, and Bradley quickly clamped the steel cuffs around his wrists.

"Let's go for a ride," said Stafford.

Jack stepped onto the porch and turned to close the door. He reached with his right hand, the left one following as the chain pulled it along. He froze as he saw Cindy standing in his bathrobe at the end of the hallway, staring at him and his handcuffs with shock and utter fear.

"Stay by the phone," he called to her, no longer so sure that he'd be coming home that afternoon. She nodded quickly, and he closed the door.

Stafford took Jack's left arm and Bradley took his right as they led him down the winding wood-chip path to the squad car. Jack said nothing and looked straight ahead. He tried not to look worried or ashamed or, worst of all, guilty. He knew his neighbors were watching and the reporters had their video cameras running.

He hoped to God that Cindy wasn't looking out the window.

Manny joined Jack in the backseat and the detectives sat in front. As Detective Bradley steered slowly onto the street, faces and cameras pressed against the car windows, all eager for a peek at the lawyer who'd allegedly killed his client, as if Jack were in the midst of those famous fifteen minutes Andy Warhol had talked about.

Jack was whisked downtown in a matter of minutes, and the crowds came into view a block from the station. Mobs of reporters filled all three tiers of granite steps in front of the Metro-Justice Building, like so many expectant fans in the grandstands.

Jack's gut wrenched. He looked at the crowds, then down at his cuffed hands. "Can't we lose these?" he asked, holding up the cuffs. "This really is *not* necessary."

"Sorry, counselor," Stafford said smugly. "No professional courtesy between defense lawyers and cops."

Jack tried to show no reaction, since he knew it would only please Stafford to elicit one. But he was angry and more than a little scared.

"As soon as we're at the curb," said Stafford, "we're outta here. We won't run, but it won't be a stroll either. Just stay close behind us. Got that, Swyteck?"

Jack remained silent.

"Just shut up and drive," Manny responded.

Bradley punched the accelerator, and in a moment they could see the station with its flock of reporters, photographers, and the just plain curious. The car squealed around the final corner, and Bradley slammed on the brakes. "Here we go!" he shouted.

The detectives popped open the front doors and jumped out of the car, then they threw open Jack's door and pulled him out. Reporters were all over them before Jack could get both feet on the sidewalk. Manny and Stafford each grabbed an elbow and pushed him into the crowd, but the mob pushed back, turning Jack into a pigskin in a lopsided rugby match.

"Outta the way!" Stafford shouted, pushing reporters aside and forging ahead toward the crowded steps, taking the accused killer into custody as the flock assaulted them with flailing hands, wires, and microphones.

"Mr. Swyteck!" someone yelled, "will you represent yourself?"

More arms, more wires, more microphones. *Keep moving*, Jack thought, *just keep moving*.

"Mr. Swyteck!" they shouted, their voices indistinguishable.

Jack had never been so aware of putting one foot in front of the other, but forward progress had never been more important.

"Will the Freedom Institute defend you, Mr. Swyteck?" The reporters' questions kept coming, but Jack and his escorts inched steadily up the granite steps, past the video cameras that taped their every movement.

"Gonna craft another insanity defense, Jack, baby?" a photographer taunted, trying to get Jack to look his way.

Stafford kept them moving forward through the mass of wires, cameras, and bodies. They finally reached the station's bottlenecked entrance, pried themselves away from the heaving crowd, and disappeared from view through the revolving door.

Inside, the steady clatter of a busy station house replaced the mob's raucous din. The station had a thirty-foot ceiling, like a huge bank lobby, but the glass dividers with venetian blinds that sectioned the space into individual offices were only nine feet high, so if seen from the ceiling, the station would have appeared to be a sprawling rat maze. Men and women in dark blue police uniforms whisked by, glancing at Detective Stafford's latest and biggest catch.

Jack and Manny knew the routine. This was where the lawyer left his client behind for fingerprinting and snapshots along the booking assembly line. *In* the front door as a private citizen, *out* the back door as an accused criminal. They'd meet again in the courtroom for arraignment, when Jack would enter his plea.

"See you at the other end of the chute," Manny told his client.

"Let's go," Detective Stafford grumbled.

Manny's look soured. "And Stafford," he said, catching him just as he started inside. The detective glared back at him.

"If you think Jack Swyteck ripped into you on the stand," Manny warned, "just wait 'til Jack's lawyer rips into your hide."

Stafford was stoic. He turned and hauled Jack away, satisfied that, for now at least, Jack Swyteck was his.

Chapter 23

•

That same morning, Governor Harold Swyteck stood tall on a raised dais in the courtyard outside the old legislative chambers, a gray two-story building with arches, columns, and striped-canvas window canopies that provided a nostalgic backdrop. The courtyard was his favorite place for press conferences because of its size—large enough to hold everyone who cared to attend, yet small enough to create a crowded, newsworthy feeling. Clusters of red, white, and blue helium balloons decorated surrounding trees and fences. Above it all, a slickly painted banner read FOUR MORE YEARS—a more inspiring message than either LAWYER TURNS KILLER, SON OF THE GUV WAS GOSS'S LOVER, or the other recent headlines that threatened to send the governor plunging in public-opinion polls.

"Thank you all for coming," Harry Swyteck said after he finished his answer to the final question. Cameras clicked and reporters jostled for position as he stepped away from the lectern, smiling and waving to one side and then the other, flashing his politician's smile and pretending to know everyone.

"One more question, Governor?" came a friendly voice from the crowd.

He returned the smile, expecting a lob at this stage of the game. "All right."

"What about mine?" shouted the one reporter no politician could stomach. It was David Malone, a smooth, good-looking, and notoriously unethical tabloid-television reporter who thrived on scandal. He was the kind of sleazy journalist who, on a slow news night, could take a video camera and microphone into a local tavern and make six drunken loudmouths falling off their bar stools look like the raging nucleus of a community-wide riot on anything from race relations to the Eddy Goss trial. Today, however, Malone didn't have to reach for controversy. All he needed was a few minutes, one-on-one, with Jack Swyteck's father. "You afraid of my questions, Governor?"

Harry cringed inside. Malone had been pushing toward the front of the crowd since the beginning of the press conference, and the governor had simply ignored him. But he couldn't just walk away from someone who had publicly called him chicken. "A quick one," he acquiesced. "What's your question, Mr. Malone?"

Malone's eyes lit up, eager for the opportunity. "Four years ago," he read from his tattered spiral notepad, "you campaigned on a 'two-fisted approach' to law and order. Specifically, you promised to ensure that the death penalty was carried out 'with vigor,' I think were your exact words."

"Do you have a question?"

"My question, sir, is this: Do you intend to keep that promise in the next term?"

"I've kept all my campaign promises. And will continue to honor them after I'm re-elected. Thank you." As he closed he started to move away from the lectern.

"More specifically," Malone pressed, raising his voice. "If the jury convicts Jack Swyteck of murder in the first degree, are you going to sign his death warrant?"

The governor halted in his tracks. His plastic smile faded, and his eyes flared with anger. But Malone waited for an answer. "The answer," said the governor, "is definitely no."

"Why not?"

The governor glared at his interrogator. "Because Jack is innocent. And I would never execute an innocent man."

"How would you know?"

"I know my son's not a murderer."

"No," said Malone. "I meant, how do you know that you haven't already executed an innocent man?"

The governor glared menacingly at the reporter, but his eye twitched nervously. A sign of weakness, Malone detected.

"First of all," said the governor, "most of them admitted they were guilty before—"

"Not all of them."

"No, but—"

"What about the ones who didn't confess? What

about the ones who went down swinging? What about the guys who swore their innocence to the end?"

"What about Raul Fernandez?" someone shouted from the rear.

The governor went cold. That was a name he hadn't heard since his blackmailer had threatened him— since the death of Eddy Goss. He looked out to see who had asked the question, but the faces in the crowd were indistinguishable.

"What *about* Fernandez?" Malone picked up the question. Heads bowed, as legions of reporters scribbled down the name.

The governor shifted nervously. He was clueless as to who had shouted out Fernandez's name, but he was suspicious of the way Malone's line of questioning had prompted the outburst. "I'm sorry. I'm not going to get into individual cases today, no more than I'm going to discuss my son's individual case. It's just not appropriate. That's all for today," he said as he started toward the exit.

"Governor!" others called out in unison, wishing for a follow-up. But he'd lost his concentration. There would be no more questions. "Thank you," he said with a wave as he exited the stage through a side door, into a private room.

The governor's aide was there to greet him and to close the door on pursuing press. Harry wiped little beads of sweat from his brow, relieved to have the conference behind him.

"Went well, I thought," said Campbell as he handed his boss a cold drink. The governor chugged down the

Coca-Cola but didn't respond. "Except for that little exchange about your son," Campbell added. "I'm telling you, that son of yours is killing you, Governor. We checked the polls again this morning. You've lost another point and—"

Campbell droned on, but Harry had stopped listening. He glanced out the window, strangely amused by the irony. It seemed that Jack was always being accused of killing someone. His father. His client. And a long time ago, on a day Harold Swyteck would never forget—his own mother. It had been nearly a quarter century since Agnes, in a drunken state, had made the accusation, and then added to the boy's confusion by suggesting that Harry reckoned his son accountable. Harry's own role in that ugly interchange had been the worst, however, because he had yet to look Jack in the eye and deny it.

"Jack isn't killing anyone," Harry suddenly objected in a loud voice. Campbell was a bit taken aback. He watched, curious, as the governor seemed to retreat into his thoughts.

"I killed *him*," Harry finally said in a low voice. "By my silence—a long time ago."

Campbell was about to follow up, but the governor quickly changed the subject—to someone he may have *really* killed. "Who was that reporter who yelled out the name of Raul Fernandez?" he asked, trying not to sound too interested.

"I don't know. I sent a security man after him, but he was long gone before anyone really knew what was going on. You want me to follow up on it?"

"No," he said, a little too forcefully. The last thing he

wanted was someone else poking into this. "It's not worth the trouble," he said in a more reasonable tone. Then he stepped toward the window and sighed. "Could you give me a few minutes, please?"

Campbell nodded. His boss looked like he could use some time alone. "I'll be in the car," he said, then left the room.

Harry lowered himself into a chair. He was still weak in the knees from the pointed Fernandez questions. *Could he be back?* The chrysanthemums had led him to believe that Goss was the blackmailer. And since he hadn't heard from the man since Goss's murder, he had been convinced he was right. But this was too strange for coincidence. It couldn't have been a heckler or someone making a lucky guess who'd shouted out Fernandez's name. And Malone's line of questioning had been deliberate. He trembled at the thought: Not only had his blackmailer returned, but one of Florida's sleaziest television reporters knew something about it.

Don't jump to conclusions, he told himself. Raul Fernandez had been the most controversial execution of his administration. A reporter or a protester didn't have to *know* anything to draw a comparison between the execution of the governor's son and the execution of a man who had proclaimed his innocence to the very end. It wasn't completely outside the realm of possibility that today had been coincidence—that Goss *had* been the extortionist, and that his extortionist was dead. Then it occurred to him that there was a way to find out for sure if it had been Goss. The first time Harry had been attacked, his assailant had identified himself as the man who confessed to Jack the night of Fernandez's execution. Surely, Jack would know if that very same man was Goss.

Now all he had to do was figure out a way to get Jack to tell him.

Chapter 24

●

"**S**tate versus *Swyteck*," the bailiff finally announced, ending Jack's ninety-minute wait in the holding cell. The cavernous courtroom came to life as Manuel Cardenal met his client at the prisoners' side entrance and escorted him across the marble floor to a mahogany podium, where they stood and faced the judge. Clusters of newscasters and curious spectators looked on from the public seating area as Jack passed before them, his head down and eyes forward, the accused murderer of the infamous Eddy Goss. Goss was indeed on Jack's mind. The entire scene was hauntingly reminiscent of the Goss arraignment, when Jack had accompanied the confessed killer to the very same podium to enter his not-guilty plea. Now, as Jack was about to enter his own plea, it was more plain than ever that a simple "not guilty" was no assertion of innocence. Innocence was a moral judgment—a matter of conscience between mortals and their maker. "Not guilty" was a legalistic play on words, the defendant's public affirmation that he would stand on his constitutional right to force the prosecutor to *prove* guilt beyond a reasonable doubt. Manuel Cardenal seemed sensitive to that fine distinction when he entered Jack's plea.

"My client is more than not guilty," Manny announced to the judge. "Jack Swyteck is *innocent*."

The pale old judge peered down from the bench over the top of his bifocals, his wrinkled brow furrowed and bushy white eyebrows raised. He didn't approve of defense lawyers who vouched for the innocence of their clients, but he didn't make an issue of it. "Register a plea of not guilty," he directed the clerk. "And Mr. Cardenal," he said sharply, pointing menacingly with his gavel, "save the speeches for your press conference."

Manny just smiled to himself.

"There's also the issue of bail, Judge," came the deep, gravelly voice from across the room. It was Wilson McCue, the state attorney, wearing his traditional three-piece suit. His pudgy face was nearly as round as his rimless spectacles, and a heavy gold chain from his pocket watch stretched across a bulging belly. Jack knew that the aging state attorney rarely even went to trial anymore, so seeing him at a routine matter like an arraignment was a bit like noticing a semiretired general on the front lines. "The govuhment," McCue continued in his deep drawl, "requests that the court set bail at—"

"I'm quite familiar with the case," the judge interrupted, "and I know the defendant. Mr. Swyteck is no stranger to the criminal courtrooms. Bail is set at one hundred thousand dollars. Next case," he announced with a bang of his gavel.

McCue's mouth hung open momentarily, unaccustomed as he was to such abrupt treatment from anyone, including judges.

"Thank you, Your Honor," said Manny.

Jack moved quickly across the courtroom to the clerk, continuing along the assembly line. Thankfully, the politicians hadn't gotten the judge to deny bail. Now all Jack had to do to get back on the street was pledge his every worldly possession to José Restrepo-Merono, the five-foot-tall, two-hundred-pound Puerto Rican president of "F. Lee Bail-Me, Inc."—the only bail bondsman ever known to have a sense of humor.

Jack returned to the holding cell for another hour or so while Manny's assistant handled the mechanical aspects of posting bail. Late that afternoon he was released, thankful he could spend the night in his own bed. He didn't have a car, since Stafford had driven him to the station. Manny's assistant was supposed to swing by and take Jack home, so he wouldn't have to wait for a taxi while fighting off reporters eager for their shot at eliciting a little quote that might make theirs the breaking story. As it turned out, though, Manny himself showed up at the curb behind the wheel of his Jaguar. The look on his face told Jack he wasn't just playing chauffeur.

"Get in," Manny said solemnly when Jack opened the door.

Jack slid into the passenger seat, and Manny pulled into the late-afternoon traffic.

"I wasn't expecting to see *you*," said Jack.

"Your father called me," Manny replied, as if that were enough to explain his appearance. He looked away from the road, just long enough to read Jack's face. "He told me about Raul Fernandez. I heard all about your request for a stay that night, and his response."

Jack smoldered, but said nothing. Instead, he made a conscious effort to look out the window.

"Okay," he said finally, "so now you know the Swyteck family secret. We not only defend the guilty. We execute the innocent."

Manny steered around the corner, then pulled into a parking space beneath a shady tree. He wanted to look right at his client as he spoke. "I don't know everything, Jack. I only know what your father knows about that night. And he's missing a key piece of information. So we both want to know if there's more to this case than whether Jack Swyteck killed Eddy Goss. He and I *both* want a straight answer from you: Did Raul Fernandez die for Eddy Goss?"

"What?" Jack asked, thoroughly confused.

"The night before Fernandez was executed, was Eddy Goss the guy who came to you and confessed to the murder? Was Raul Fernandez innocent, and Eddy Goss guilty?"

"Where did you dream up—" Jack paused, calmed himself down. "Look, Manny, if my father wants to talk, *I'll* talk to him. Fernandez is between him and me. This has nothing to do with your defending me for the murder of Eddy Goss."

"Wrong, Jack. This could have *everything* to do with

the murder of Eddy Goss. Because it bears directly on your motive to kill—or to 'execute'—Eddy Goss. You can't risk letting Wilson McCue flesh out this theory before I do. So answer me, Jack. And I want the truth."

Jack looked Manny right in the eye. "The truth, Manny, is that I didn't kill Eddy Goss. And as far as who it was who came to me the night Fernandez was executed, the honest answer is that I don't know. The guy never gave me his name. He never even showed me his face. But I do know this much: It was *not* Eddy Goss. The eyes are different, the build is different, the voice is different. It's just a *different person*."

Manny took a deep breath and looked away, then gave a quick nod of appreciation. "Thanks, I know this isn't an easy subject for you. And I'm glad you leveled with me."

"Maybe it's time I leveled with my father, too. I think he and I need to talk."

"I'm advising you not to do that, Jack."

"It's kind of a personal decision, don't you think?"

"From a legal standpoint, I am *strongly* advising you not to speak to your father. I don't want you talking to anyone who might jeopardize your ability to take the witness stand in your own defense. And talking to your father is very risky."

"What are you implying?"

Manny measured his words carefully. "Right after I spoke to your father," he began, "I had an uneasy feeling. It was just a feeling, but when you've been doing this as long as I have, you follow your gut. So I went and took another look at the police file."

"And?"

"I wasn't looking for anything in particular. But I noticed that the police report showed an extraneous footprint, right outside Goss's apartment. It wasn't from you, and it wasn't from Eddy Goss. It was from someone else. Now, that's a definite plus for us, because it can help us prove that someone else was at the scene of the crime. But what has me concerned is that the footprint is very clear." He sighed. "It's from a Wiggins wing tip."

Jack's expression went white. He said nothing, but Manny read the message on his face.

"How long has your father worn Wiggins wing tips, Jack?"

"As long as I can remember," he said with disbelief. "But, you can't possibly think my father—"

"I don't know what to think. There was just something about the urgency in your father's voice—his curious tone—that concerns me. I don't know if there's something he's not telling me or what. But I do know this: I don't want my client talking to him. I can't take the risk that he'll confess something to you, and then you won't be able to take the witness stand, for fear you might incriminate your own father. Or, even worse, I don't want you being evasive on the stand because you're trying to protect your father. So until I get to the bottom of this, I want you to stay as far away from him as possible. Can I have your word on that?"

Jack felt sick inside. But he knew Manny was right. A tough judgment call like this one was precisely the reason that lawyers should never represent themselves.

He needed someone like Manny to put the personal issues aside and counsel him wisely. "All right," he said with resignation. "I haven't spoken to my father in two years. I can wait a little longer. You have my word."

Chapter 25

•

Jack woke the next morning with the memory of his conversation with Manny still vivid. He ran all sorts of hypotheses through his head but was unable to explain why his father would be involved with Goss. It just didn't make sense. He needed to find some answers, and he knew they wouldn't come to him if he sat around the house.

So, after showering and downing a quick cup of coffee, he threw on a jacket and tie and headed for the police station. He arrived at the document section around ten o'clock and asked the clerk to pull the investigative file on *State* v. *Swyteck*. He wanted to see for himself what this business of an "extraneous footprint" was all about.

Only the police, the prosecutor, the defendant, or the defendant's attorney can pull the file in a pending murder case, but Jack had done it so many times as a lawyer with the Freedom Institute that he didn't even have to show his Florida bar card to the clerk behind the counter. He just signed his name in the registry and filled in his bar number. Out of curiosity, he checked to see who else had been reviewing his file. Detective Stafford and his assistant, of course . . . Manny had been there twice, as recently as yesterday . . . and someone else had been there: Richard Dressler, an attorney.

He had never heard of any attorney named Richard Dressler, so he checked with the file clerk to see who he was.

"You putting me on, Mr. Swyteck?" said the young black woman behind the counter. She had large, almond eyes and straightened black hair with an orangey-red streak on one side. Other than Jack, she was the only person in the busy station who wasn't a cop, and she was the only person he'd ever seen with ten different glittering works of art on two-inch fingernails of curling acrylic. "Richard Dressler's a lawyer," she told Jack, looking at him as if he were senile. "Said he was *your* lawyer."

Jack was stunned, but he put on his best poker face. "You know," he shook his head with a smile, "my lead counsel has so many other young lawyers helping him on this case, sometimes I can't keep track of them. Dressler . . ." Jack baited her, as if he were trying to place the man. "Tall guy—right?"

She just rolled her eyes. "I don't know what he looked like," she said, fussing with a little ornamental rhinestone that had loosened from her thumbnail. "I got five hundred people a day coming through here."

Jack nodded slowly. He definitely wanted to know

more about this Richard Dressler, but the last thing he wanted to do was make an issue out of it in the middle of the police station—deep in the heart of enemy territory. He had an idea. "I changed my mind," he said as he slid the file back over the counter to her. "Thanks anyway. I'll check it out later."

"Suit yourself," she said with a shrug.

He left the police station quickly and headed for a pay phone at the corner. He dialed the Florida bar's Attorney Information Service and asked for some basic information on Richard Dressler.

"Mr. Dressler's office is at five-oh-one Kennedy Boulevard, Tampa, Florida," the woman in the records department cheerfully reported.

A hell of a long way from Miami. "And what kind of law does he practice? Does he do criminal defense?"

The woman checked the computer screen before her. "Mr. Dressler is a board-certified real estate attorney. Would you like a listing of criminal defense lawyers in that area, sir?"

"No, thank you. That's all I need." He slowly replaced the receiver and leaned against the phone, totally confused. Why would a real estate attorney from Tampa come three hundred miles to look at a police file in Miami? And why would he pose as Jack's criminal defense lawyer? Jack could think of no reason—at least no *good* reason. He shook his head, then walked back to his car. He started thinking about the extraneous footprint that had drawn him to the police file in the first place. He wondered if Dressler had also been curious about Wiggins wing tips.

Chapter 26

•

Harry Swyteck may not have liked the way his campaign manager had phrased it, but if Jack wasn't actually "killing" him, the publicity certainly wasn't doing his campaign any good. It was only August, and the November election was still arguably far enough away to dismiss the plunging public-opinion polls as not the pulse of the people but merely the palpitations of the times. The governor, however, was not one to sit around and wait for things to change. A road trip was in order—one of those whirlwind, statewide tours that would allow him to press the flesh and pick a few wallets in face-to-face meetings with Rotarians, Shriners, and virtually any other group that wanted a breakfast or luncheon speaker.

He finished the first of what would be many fifteen hour days on the speaking circuit at 9:30 P.M. and retired to his motel room. The Thunderhead Motel was one of those roadside lodges familiar to any traveler who'd been forced to spend the night in some small town where the nicest restaurant was the Denny's across from a bowling alley. It was typical of those long and narrow two-story motels where the rooms on one side faced the parking lot and the rooms on the other faced the algae-stained swimming pool. The rooms facing the parking lot, however, didn't directly abut the rooms facing the pool. An interior service corridor ran through the middle of the building, for use by house-keepers and other hotel employees. That didn't seem very important, unless you also knew that the walls in the corridor were a paper-thin sheet of plaster-board, and that employees sometimes poked holes in them to satisfy their perverse curiosity.

Harry, in his second-floor room, was completely un-aware of this as he peeled off his clothes and stepped into the tub for a nice hot shower. The incredibly tacky brown, orange, and yellow floral-print wallpaper made it impossible to detect any holes in the wall that sepa-rated the bathroom from the service corridor. In fact, there *was* a small hole right next to the towel rack, which offered a full view of the governor's left profile. Eight inches below that was a larger hole that accom-modated the barrel of a .38-caliber revolver pointed di-rectly at the governor's ear.

"Don't move," came a muffled voice from the other side of the bathroom wall.

The governor was both startled and confused by the sound of a strange voice over running water. He froze when he saw the barrel of the gun.

"I'll kill you if you move," came another warning,

followed by the cocking of the hammer. "You know I will. You *do* recognize the voice, don't you, my man?"

Goose bumps popped up beneath the soap and lather on the governor's body. He knew the voice all right. "You're still alive?" he said with a mix of fear and wonder. It hadn't been Eddy Goss who was blackmailing him; and it couldn't have been Eddy Goss who confessed to Jack. "Why are you here?"

"Just wanted to make sure you knew it was me who fucked up your press conference, Governor."

Harry swallowed apprehensively. "And what about the reporter—Malone? What does he know?"

"Squat. I just told him Fernandez was innocent. That's all. Just enough to let *you* know I'm serious about going to the press. Didn't show him any proof—*yet.*"

The governor trembled. He could barely find the nerve to ask another question, but he had to know: "Did you tell him I received a report that Fernandez was innocent before"—he paused—"before he was executed?"

"No. But I will, my man. Unless you pay up."

"You already have ten thousand."

The scoff was audible even over the sound of the still cascading shower. "You stiffed me on the last installment. You went all the way to Goss's apartment, just like I told you to. I watched you walk right up to the fucking door. And you chickened out. You turned and walked away. You didn't leave my money. And now, with interest and all, I'd say you owe me an even fifty grand."

"Fifty thousand! I don't have—"

"Don't lie to me!" he snapped. "You and that rich society bitch you married have it. And you *will* give it to me. Don't forget, Governor. I still have our last conversation on tape. No money, and the tape goes right to Malone—along with the proof that Fernandez was innocent. You hear me?"

Silenced by fear and utter disbelief that this could be happening to him, the governor stood quietly as the water from the shower pelted his body.

"Do you hear me!"

The governor shifted his eyes slowly toward the gun. "This is the end of it, right? This is the last installment."

"That's why it's fifty grand, my man. I want the whole enchilada in one big bite. So shut the fuck up and listen. Since this is the last one, I want you to buy a big bouquet of flowers—chrysanthemums, to be exact. Get one with a nice big pot. Put the money in the pot. And just for fun, put your shoes in there, too—those Wiggins wing tips you like to wear. This Friday night, seven o'clock, take the whole thing to Memorial Cemetery in Miami. Row twelve, plot two thirty-two in the west quadrant. Leave it right there. It's a flat marker."

"How do I find plot two thirty-two? Who's buried there?"

"It's a new grave. You'll recognize the name on it."

"Eddy Goss?" the governor swallowed his words.

"Raul Fernandez, asshole. Go pay your *respects*."

The barrel of the gun suddenly disappeared through the hole, and the quick footsteps and the slam of a door in the service corridor told the governor that his blackmailer was gone—for now.

Chapter 27

•

Two hours after Jack had requested his file at the police station and turned up the information about Richard Dressler, he met Manny in his offices for a brainstorming session. Manny knew nothing about Dressler. He'd reviewed the police file before that name had been entered into the registry. He knew about as much as could be expected of someone who'd been retained just forty-eight hours earlier, having picked up bits and pieces from the file and a brief talk with Jack after the arraignment. Jack had a lot to tell him, and he was eager to hear Manny's assessment of the case. But after a brief overview of the salient facts, and at the risk of sounding like so many of his guilty clients at the Institute who were so quick to assert their innocence, Jack couldn't help but get to the bottom line.

"I've been framed," he said.

"Whoa," Manny half kidded. "Turning paranoid on me already, are you?"

"It's not paranoia. It's a fact, Manny. Somebody wanted me to think Goss was stalking me. Why else would they have given me a map to Goss's apartment? Why else would they have left the chrysanthemum under Cindy's pillow the night I stayed at Gina Terisi's townhouse? That was when I, of all people, should have known it wasn't really Goss who was harassing me. Goss never left flowers anywhere. His signature was *seeds*. He had this perverse connection between chrysanthemum seeds and his own semen. He was a nut case, but he was consistent about his signature."

"So, somebody wanted you to think Goss was after you," said Manny, moving the theory along. "Why?"

"I don't know exactly why. I guess because they planned to kill him. And they planned to make it look like I did it. That's why the silencer showed up in my car at the repair shop. Somebody planted it there."

Manny stroked his chin, thinking. "And why would someone want to pin you with the murder of Eddy Goss?"

"Again," Jack said with a shrug, "I don't know. Maybe to retaliate against me for getting Goss acquitted. Friend of the victim, or somebody like that. Maybe even a cop. All the lawyers from the Freedom Institute have lots of enemies on the force. And we already have that nine-one-one call about a cop being on the scene right after Goss was killed."

That much was true. They did know about the cop. The prosecutor had disclosed that information under rules established by the Supreme Court, which required the government to disclose helpful information to the defense. "We have a recorded phone message," said Manny, putting the evidence on the cop in perspective, "but we don't have a witness, because we don't have a name and we don't know who the caller is." Then he sighed, swiveled in his leather chair, and looked out the window.

Jack studied his lawyer's face, trying to discern his thoughts. It was important to Jack that Manny believe him, not just because Manny was his attorney, but because he was the only person other than Cindy to whom Jack had proclaimed his innocence—and he was a man whose judgment people valued. That was obvious, Jack thought as he admired the way income from praiseworthy clients had helped Manny furnish his oversized office. Primitive but priceless pre-Colombian art adorned his walls and bookshelves. Sculptured Mayan warriors lined the wall of windows overlooking the glistening bay, as if worshiping the bright morning sun. A touch of sentimentality rested atop his sleek marble-top desk: a glass vase with a white ribbon around it, containing the black soil of a homeland the Cardenal family had left more than three decades ago, fleeing a Cuban revolutionary turned despot.

"Let me say this, Jack," Manny said as he turned to face his client. "I *do* believe you're innocent. Not that guilt or innocence is relevant to whether I would defend you. I want you to know it, though, because it's important you continue to tell me *everything*.

"That said," he continued, "I hope you'll understand if I don't appear overly enthusiastic about your frame-up theory. I've been doing this for twenty years. Every client I've ever represented claimed he was framed. Juries are skeptical of these kind of claims, as I'm sure you're aware. That makes it a tough defense to prove."

"Tough—but not impossible."

"No," Manny agreed. "Not impossible. And I think we already have a couple of very important leads to follow, which may prove key to your theory. One is this Richard Dressler. Who is he, and why is he snooping in your file? And second, we need to find out who made that nine-one-one call and reported they saw a police officer leaving the scene of the crime. Obviously, we need to get on both these leads immediately. It could take some time, especially tracking down the nine-one-one caller."

"We don't have time," said Jack.

"Well, we have a little time. Trial is two months away."

"The trial isn't our deadline."

"I know, but—"

"I think you're overlooking something," said Jack in a polite but serious tone. "We don't have two months. We may not even have two minutes. Whoever framed me, Manny, is a cold-blooded killer. Which means one thing: We have to find the nine-one-one caller—before *he* does."

If the newspapers Jack read over lunch were any indication, the public couldn't hear enough about the brilliant young son of the governor who'd wigged out and blown away his client. Jack was a veteran when it came to bad press, but still, it helped when he called home and picked up messages on his machine from Mike Mannon and Neil Goderich, both offering any help they could.

One newspaper story in particular had Jack concerned. After summarizing the evidence against him, it made prominent mention of the anonymous 911 call. "A little something," the article observed, "that a lawyer of Jack Swyteck's ability could seize upon to blow the case wide open."

The article made Jack feel uneasy. It was bad enough that anyone who'd looked at the police file could have learned about the 911 caller. Now, anyone who read the newspaper would know about it, too.

Jack drove the five minutes to the police station and requested the recorded 911 message. He played it over and over, until the caller's voice was one he'd recognize. The man had spoken partly in English, partly in Spanish, a hybrid that made it easier to remember.

From the station he drove to Goss's apartment building and checked the mailboxes. There were seventeen Hispanic surnames, which he wrote down. He walked to the corner phone booth, confirmed there was a telephone book, then matched the names and addresses to numbers. He then went back to his car to make the calls. He posed as a pollster from a local radio station seeking views on U.S. immigration policy, as a salesman, as someone just getting a wrong number—anything to get the person on the other end of the line to speak long enough so that he could compare his voice to the one on the 911 recording.

A few of the people weren't home. One line had

been disconnected. Those people Jack did reach had clearly not made the call. After thirty minutes of calling, he still didn't have a match. *Damn.*

Sitting there outside Goss's apartment building, watching the last rays of the setting sun glint off the Mustang's windshield, he wondered if it might already be too late.

Chapter 28

●

The next morning, a Thursday, Jack and Manny were scheduled to meet in Manny's offices with their first potential witness: Jack's alibi, Gina Terisi.

From the moment he'd called Gina to arrange the meeting, Jack had been ambivalent. He considered the frame-up theory his best defense, and as the minute hand on his watch drew closer to their eleven o'clock appointment, he found himself wanting to drop the whole idea of an alibi, rather than deal with her. Manny, however, had a different point of view.

"Humor me, Jack," said Manny, seated behind his desk. "Just for the moment, let's put this frame-up and grand-conspiracy theory of yours aside. It may sound like a good defense. But even if my investigator makes headway on this Dressler lead, a frame-up is very hard to prove. Your best defense is always going to be an alibi. Because no human being—framed, or unframed—can be in two places at one time."

"I understand that."

"And I understand your reluctance about Gina. It certainly won't sound good when the tabloids print that kinky hot sex with girlfriend's roomie is your alibi. But it will sound a lot worse if a jury comes back and says you're guilty of murder in the first degree. So," he said as he reached for his desktop telephone, "let's not keep Ms. Terisi waiting. All right, Jack?"

Jack took a deep breath. There were so many reasons he would have liked to leave Gina out of this and just forget using her as an alibi. But it was too late for that. "All right. Let's see how cooperative she is."

Manny hit the intercom button and spoke to his secretary. "Shelley, send in Ms. Terisi, please."

"Yes, Mr. Cardenal."

The office door opened, Manny's secretary stepped aside, and Gina Terisi entered the spacious corner office. Manny politely rose from his chair to greet her, and Jack followed suit, though with considerably less enthusiasm.

"Good morning," said Manny, his face alight with the expression most men wore when they first laid eyes on Gina Terisi. She was wearing a cobalt blue dress, not tight, but flattering in all the right places. Her long brown hair was up in a twist, tucked beneath a black, broad-brimmed hat, revealing sparkling diamond-stud earrings, two on the left ear, one on the right. At least a karat each, Jack observed, and undoubtedly "gifts" from one of her admirers.

"Nice to see you, Jack," she said through a forced smile.

He nodded courteously as Manny flashed a chivalrous smile and stepped forward to greet her. "Please," he said, offering her the winged arm chair in which Jack had been seated.

"Thanks," said Gina, making a production out of taking her seat. Jack moved to the couch beneath the window, and Manny returned to the black leather chair behind his desk. Both men faced their guest. Gina crossed her long legs comfortably, as if constructing a barrier between her and her interrogators.

"Can I get you some coffee?" Manny offered.

Gina didn't acknowledge the question. She was busy checking her makeup in the reflection of the glass-top table beside her.

Manny was completely unaware that he was staring as Gina applied her lipstick slowly and seductively to the bottom of her pouty lip. "Nothing for me," she said finally. "This will be a short meeting. I assure you of that."

"What do you mean?" asked Manny.

"It means that although I tentatively told Jack on the phone that I'd support his alibi, I need to have some questions answered before I commit to anything."

"That's fair enough," answered Manny. "I'll do my best to answer them."

Gina narrowed her eyes, stressing the import of her question. "What I need to know is this: Exactly what time of the morning was Eddy Goss shot?"

"Why do you need to know that?" asked Jack.

Gina ignored him and looked only at Manny. "Never mind why. Just answer my question."

Manny leaned back in his chair. He, too, was curious about the reason for the question. "We don't know exactly. But some time after four A.M. is the medical examiner's preliminary estimate, based on the fact that the blood had not yet dried by the time the police arrived on the scene."

"Four o'clock, then, was the earliest possible time he could have been shot," Gina pressed.

Manny shrugged. "If you accept the medical examiner's report, yes. There's not much doubt that death was instantaneous."

Gina seemed satisfied. "That's all I need to know," she said to Jack. "I can't testify for you. And I *won't*. The time of Goss's death changes everything."

Jack's gut wrenched. Manny shot him a glance, but he just looked away uncomfortably. "How does it change things?" Manny asked her.

"If Goss was shot after four A.M., then that makes me a very flimsy alibi. Granted, if I were to say that Jack and I went to bed, it might help Jack explain how he got his"—she smiled with false modesty—"scratches and bruises. But that's as far as it goes. It's not like I can place him somewhere else at the time of the murder."

"But you slept together," said Manny.

"No. We fucked each other. Nobody got any sleep. And, most important, he *didn't* spend the night. Jack left my townhouse before three. I'm certain of that."

Manny again glanced at his client, but Jack wouldn't look him in the eye.

Gina rose from her chair and headed for the door. "Sorry, fellas," she said as she reached the door. "I'm not going to tell the world I betrayed my best friend and went to bed with her boyfriend, when the truth really isn't much help."

Manny leaned across his desk to make his point in a firm but not quite threatening manner. "You realize we can subpoena you. We can make you testify."

"You can make me show up at the courthouse. But you can't *make* me say Jack was with me. Not unless I want to say it."

Manny knew she was right. He tried another angle. "You *should* want to," said Manny. "You should want to help Jack."

"That's just the point: I *don't* want to. Good day, gentlemen," she said coolly, then left the room, closing the door behind her.

The two men sat in uncomfortable silence, until Jack looked into Manny's piercing black eyes and said, "I warned you about her."

Manny seemed concerned, but not with Gina. "I don't think she's lying," he said sharply. "And now I understand why you were having second thoughts about the alibi. I think *you* lied to me, Jack. You told me you spent the night with her. *All* night. That was a lie, wasn't it?"

Jack sighed and averted his eyes, then responded in a quiet tone. "It happened almost exactly the way I told you before, Manny. While we were making love or having sex or whatever you want to call it, somebody *did* sneak into the townhouse and smear ketchup on the sheets and put a chrysanthemum under Cindy's pillow.

And whoever it was called me and tried to get me to go back to Goss's place—which I *definitely* wasn't going to do at that point. But I didn't stay either. I honestly didn't want to leave Gina by herself—especially after seeing that some lunatic had taken a knife to my convertible. But I didn't want to wake up the next morning with Gina by my side, either. Cindy and I were technically split up at the time, but that didn't seem to matter. I just had to get the hell out of there. So I left."

"Before three o'clock."

"Right."

"At least an hour before Goss was killed."

Jack sighed. "I'm afraid so."

"Unbelievable," Manny groaned, shaking his head. "Or maybe it's not unbelievable. I suppose it's understandable that someone charged with murder might try to reach for something that's not there. But honestly, Jack: What the hell were you thinking? Did you think she was going to have amnesia about what time it was when you left her apartment?"

"I don't know," Jack grimaced. "I guess I just hoped she wasn't going to be so damn certain about the time. After all, we'd had a lot to drink. I thought she might be a little fuzzy on the time. Or maybe even she'd be wrong about the time and say I left at four-thirty."

"You were hoping she was going to lie for you."

"Not lie, no. I mean—I don't know. I don't know what I was thinking, Manny."

Manny's face showed deep disappointment. Then his eyes narrowed with suspicion. "Are there any more lies, Jack, and more important, is your alibi the *biggest* lie you've told me?"

Jack became indignant. "Are you questioning my innocence?"

"Not based on what I've heard so far. But I can't live with deception from a client who, at the very least, was willing to put himself in a position where he might *have* to kill Eddy Goss."

"I resent that. I'd never kill *anyone*."

"Really? Then why did you go inside Goss's apartment that night—before you went to Gina's? And just what were you planning to do with that pistol you were packing?"

Jack paused. It was a difficult question. "Maybe I don't know *what* I was going to do with it."

Manny looked his client straight in the eye. "You can do better than that," he said, speaking in a tone that forced Jack to search his own soul. Manny's look was not accusatory. It was not judgmental. But it still made Jack uncomfortable.

"Look, Manny. The bottom line is this: I didn't kill Eddy Goss."

"Then don't kill your chances for an acquittal," he said, "and don't manipulate your lawyer."

Jack looked him in the eye. He said nothing, but they'd reached an understanding. Then he rose from his chair and stepped toward the window. "We're really better off without Gina anyway. Better this blew up now than at trial."

Manny leaned back in his chair. "One thing still bothers me, though. When I told Gina she should help you, she said she didn't want to. That disturbs me."

"That's just Gina."

"Maybe. But when she says she doesn't want to help

you, is that all she's saying? Or is she saying she wants to *hurt* you?"

Jack froze. His throat felt suddenly dry. "I don't think so. But with her, you really never know."

"We *need* to know."

"I suppose I could talk with her. I think she'd say more if it were just the two of us."

"All right," Manny nodded. "Try the personal approach. The sooner the better. Let's talk again as soon as you've had a conversation with her."

"I'll call you first thing." He shook Manny's hand, then started across the room.

"Oh, Jack," Manny called out as his client reached the door. Jack stopped short and looked back at his lawyer.

"This Gina is a key player," said Manny. "Don't get into it with her. Be polite. And if it's not going well, just ask her if she'll meet with me. Then let me handle her. And don't worry. I'm good with witnesses. Especially women."

"Thanks," Jack replied, his expression deadpan. "But you've never known a woman like this one."

Chapter 29

•

Seventy-three-year-old Wilfredo Garcia stood in his kitchen before his old gas stove cooking dinner, *bistec palamillo* and *platanos fritos*—flank steak and fried plantains. A Cuban who'd come to the United States with grown children in 1962, he had never become completely conversant in his adopted tongue, often shifting to Spanish to get his point across. He was a likable sort, though, and even his English listeners easily forgave his linguistic limitations.

Wilfredo was pudgy, with warm, deep brown eyes and chubby cheeks. He loved to eat, and most nights he dined at home, since the area of Adams Street wasn't really safe after dark.

Tonight, just as he was smothering his steak with chopped onions and parsley, the phone rang. He glanced up, but he didn't answer. He'd been ignoring his phone calls for the past couple days, ever since he'd read that article in the newspaper about how important the 911 call could be in the case against Jack Swyteck. He knew it was only a matter of time before they'd come looking for the man who'd been so ambivalent about getting involved that he'd called from a pay phone to keep the police from tracing it. He still didn't want to get involved. So until things blew over, he'd decided to live like a hermit.

But the phone kept on ringing—ten times, and then more than a dozen. It had to be important, he figured. Maybe it was his daughter in Brooklyn. Or his bookie. He turned off the stove and picked up the phone.

"*Oigo*," he answered in his native Spanish.

"Wilfredo Garcia?"

"*Sí.*"

"This is Officer Michael Cookson of Metro-Dade Police. How you doin' this evening, sir?"

Wilfredo's heart sank. He instantly wished he hadn't answered. "Am fine." He answered in English, though his heavy accent was detectable even in his two-word response.

"Mr. Garcia, I'm just doing some routine inquiries about the murder of Eddy Goss. I understand you live on the same floor as Mr. Goss used to live on."

"Same floor, *sí*. But—*por favor*. I know nothing. I no want me involved."

"I can understand that, sir. But this is important. We're looking for the man who dialed nine-one-one from a pay phone outside your building the night Mr. Goss was killed."

Wilfredo grimaced. "I no want—"

"Hey, listen, my man," the officer said, speaking in a friendly tone, "I understand where you're coming from. Between you and me, I don't care if they ever catch the guy who killed this Goss character. But it's my job to follow up on all these things. So if you know who made the call, you might just want to pass it along to him that it's really much better to talk to the police before all the lawyers come looking for him. Will you do that for me?"

Wilfredo had a lump in his throat. "All right."

"In fact, let me make it real easy for you, Mr. Garcia, because I know how people hate to get involved in these things. I don't want you or anyone else to have to come down to the station, or even make a phone call to the station. Let me give you my personal beeper number. If you hear anything, or if one of your friends knows anything, just beep me. All I want is information. I promise I won't use your name unless I absolutely have to. Sound fair, my man?"

"*Sí.*"

"Write this down—five, five, five, two, nine hundred. Got it?"

"Uh-huh."

"Excellent. Thanks for your time, sir."

"Good-bye." Wilfredo was short of breath as he hung up. It surprised him that he'd actually written down the beeper number. He really did hate to get involved, but the same instincts that had prompted him to dial 911 in the first place were gnawing at him again. It was a long time ago that he'd been naturalized as a citizen, that he'd sworn an oath to support his country and be a good American, but his memory of it was still vivid.

He glanced at the number he'd just scribbled down. The policeman had seemed nice enough. Maybe it wouldn't be as bad as he feared. Maybe it was time to come forward and get the monkey off his back.

Wilfredo drew a deep breath. Then he picked up the phone. His hand was shaking, but he managed to dial the number.

Chapter 30

•

Jack put the top down and took a long drive along the beach after leaving Manny's office. Cindy had called him a couple of nights before—just to chat, but they'd talked about being apart, and suddenly he heard her saying she'd move back in. Unfortunately, the euphoria he'd felt then had been severely dampened by the past two days' events. They'd settled on tonight for her to bring her stuff over, and he knew she'd be at the house, unpacking, when he arrived. He needed time to think before facing her.

The meeting today with Gina had been a real reality check. Any prior illusions about keeping his "evening" with her a secret were beginning to dissipate. He kept looking for a way to steer a course with her that would help his case and not affect his relationship with Cindy, but nothing was coming to him.

It was shortly after six o'clock when he finally pulled into the driveway and turned off the engine, and by then he'd received a call from Manny in his car that made him even more ill at ease. He thought about the call as he got out of the Mustang and walked up the wood-chip path.

The front door opened before he'd even mounted the stairs. "Hi there," Cindy said. She stood smiling in the doorway, and although he felt miserable it was impossible for him not to throw his arms around her.

"How's the unpacking going?" he asked, closing the door behind them.

"Getting there," she said, taking his hand as they walked into the living room. "It's mostly just clothes, but I spent most of my time sifting through Gina's closet, looking for things she borrowed from me."

As they sat down on the couch, she noticed that he was brooding about something. "You're not having second thoughts, are you?"

He sighed. "Cindy, as much as I want us to be together, after today I wonder if it's such a great idea for you to move in."

"What do you mean?"

"It's not a question of loving you. I'm crazy about you. It's just that I'm not sure it's safe for you here."

"Why not?"

He exhaled, then launched into a selective summary of the events of the past two days, focusing on the Tampa real estate attorney by the name of Richard Dressler.

"So why is Dressler so interested in this?" she asked.

"He's not. I got a call from Manny driving back here. His investigator met with Dressler in Tampa. Turns out his wallet was stolen two months ago. Somebody got all his identification. Including his Florida bar card."

"So somebody's been using his bar card to pose as an attorney?"

"Exactly. This somebody used his name to check out the police file in my case *after* Goss was dead. I think the guy, whoever he is, is trying to frame me. If I'm right, it was *him* who was hassling me all along, not Goss."

Her eyes widened. "Are you saying—"

"I don't know exactly what I'm saying. I haven't thought it all the way through yet. But I'm pretty sure there's still a killer on the loose. Whoever was after me is still out there."

She took a step back. "Who is it, then? If it wasn't Eddy Goss, who could it be?"

"I don't know. But I'm going to find out. And until I do, I think it's best if you take a vacation or just get out of town for a few—"

"No. I'm staying with you, Jack. I'm not going to leave you at a time like this. We'll deal with this together."

He took a deep breath, then put his arms around her again. "We still can't call the police. I can't tell them that whoever was after me is still out there. Because the minute they find out I thought Goss was threatening me, the prosecution goes from no evidence of motive to iron-clad proof."

Cindy bit her lip. It was bad enough that a stalker was still out there, but not being able to tell anyone was against common sense. Yet everything Jack had said seemed logical. "All right," she said with a sigh. "No police. We'll look out for ourselves, and we'll look out for each other."

That same Thursday evening, Governor Harold Swyteck checked into a room on the thirty-second floor of Miami's Hotel Intercontinental. He was scheduled to speak at a fund-raiser later that evening, but first he had to give away some money of his own. The bouquet of chrysanthemums he'd ordered was waiting for him in his room. He took the money from his briefcase—fifty thousand dollars—and placed the bills in the oversized pot. Then he took his shoes from his suitcase, all the while fighting to keep his anger under control. It was demeaning, really—like stealing a man's clothes and leaving him stranded on a street corner. But if that was the kind of cheap power trip this lunatic needed, so be it. At this point, Harry would have given much more than fifty grand to be rid of his blackmailer, once and for all.

He checked his watch. Six-thirty. With traffic, it would be about a twenty-minute drive to Memorial Cemetery. For perhaps the hundredth time that day, the governor mentally ran through his options, trying to find some way out of this ludicrousness. But both of his alternatives—calling the police or letting his tormentor do what he'd threatened—seemed unacceptable. At least, by following his blackmailer's instructions, he had a *chance* of holding on to the life he'd struggled so hard to create.

He grabbed the pot and the keys to his rental car and he was off, wondering with a growing dread if the grave he was about to visit was his own.

Chapter 31

•

Jack and Cindy were in bed by 9:00 P.M., and they didn't stop making love to the sounds of "Love Jazz" on the radio until well after the deejay said, "Thank God it's Friday." Afterward, Jack decided he *had* to find some way to tell Cindy the truth about Gina. She was risking too much for him to be dishonest with her. Before breaking the news, however, he wanted to confirm Gina's position. He wanted to be able to tell Cindy that Gina wouldn't be telling their sordid story to the world—as a witness for the prosecution.

The following afternoon Jack was deep in thought as he headed to Gina's townhouse, driving so slowly that even carloads of tourists zoomed by him on the expressway.

Gina had just returned from jogging when Jack knocked on her door. She wore orange nylon shorts,

Nike running shoes, and a skimpy tank top that had been pasted to her body by a good hard sweat. Her long brown hair was pulled back and tied behind her head.

"Can I come in?" he asked, standing in the open doorway.

Gina sipped her Gatorade Lite, her expression as cool as the ice in her glass. "Sure," she said with a shrug.

He stepped inside and closed the door, then followed her to the kitchen. "I realize this isn't your favorite subject, Gina. But the way you left Manny's office yesterday, I felt like we should talk."

Gina went to the refrigerator for a refill on her drink. "I've pretty much said it all, haven't I?"

"That's what I'm here to find out. That crack you made yesterday about not wanting to help me. That worried me."

"Well," she said with a wry smile, "maybe I did lay it on a little thick. But you got the point of my performance: I don't want to get involved. That shouldn't surprise you, Jack. I honestly don't think it even upsets you. I could see it on your face. The *last* thing you wanted was for me to be your alibi."

"You don't know what I want, Gina."

"Oh, no?" she said coyly, switching to a low, sexy voice. She suddenly felt challenged. She moved closer to him, so close that he could feel her breath on his cheek and smell the sweat that reminded him of things he should never have done. She reached behind her head and tugged on the sweatband, letting her hair down. "Let me put it another way, Jack. Did you actually *want* me to say I touched this body," she said, gliding her open hand lightly over his chest, a half inch away from touching him, but never making physical contact. "That I felt the weight of it on top of me. That we tangled and sweated and screamed in the night, that with each thrust I dug my nails into your back and sunk my teeth into your chest, crying out for more, even though you were more than enough for any woman. Is that *really* what you wanted? And if you did," she whispered, now looking deeply into his eyes, "did you want Cindy in or out of the courtroom when I said it?"

Jack pulled himself away from her. "What happened between you and me was a mistake. I think we both regret it. And you certainly could have been my alibi without making it sound so lurid."

Gina emptied her Gatorade into the sink and opened the liquor cabinet. She filled her glass with Campari and ice. "Are you negotiating with me?"

"Negotiating for what?"

She arched an eyebrow, then sipped her drink. "Do you want me to say you didn't leave my townhouse until after four o'clock?"

Jack knew her serious look, and she was definitely being serious. "Just hold it right there, Gina. You've totally got the wrong idea. I didn't come here for that."

"I didn't say you did. But, then again, think about the last time you came here. You didn't come here to make love to me. But you did."

"And I wish it had never happened."

"Do you? Or do you just wish Cindy would never find out about it?"

He looked away, trying not to lose his temper. He brought his emotions under control, then gave her a very lawyerly look. "Listen, Gina, I didn't come here to talk you into being my alibi. I just wanted to make sure you weren't going to testify *against* me."

Her eyes widened. "Don't be absurd, Jack. I would never do that."

"And as far as what happened between you and me— no, I haven't told Cindy yet. But she'll know everything. Just as soon as I find the right time to tell her."

"There is no *right* time, Jack. I know Cindy. I know her better than you do. If she finds out about us, you can bet that neither one of us will ever see her again. The only reason there'd ever be to tell her anything is if I were going to be your alibi. And I'm not. So it's final. I won't have you shooting your mouth off to Cindy in some juvenile attempt to soothe your conscience. I won't allow it."

"It's not up to you."

"Oh, yes, it is. Because I'm taking back what I said earlier. I can't say I would *never* testify against you. Because there *is* one way I would. If you tell Cindy about us, I swear I'll tell the police everything—including how you came to my apartment thinking Eddy Goss was after you and Cindy.

"And that's only the half of it. I'll tell the world what really happened between us—how you *really* got your scratches and bruises. I'll tell them how I invited you inside my townhouse because you had scared me to death about Eddy Goss. How I trusted you when you said you'd sleep on the couch. And how I scratched and bruised you only after you snuck into my room, tore off my nightgown, and forced yourself on me." She took a long sip and finished the rest of her drink. "It's your choice. Just grow up and keep what happened between us to yourself. Or face the consequences."

Jack stared with disbelief. "Why are you doing this? Why not just live with the truth?"

"Because the truth helps no one. If I tell the truth to the police, it hurts you. If you tell the truth to Cindy, it hurts us both. So those are my terms. Neither of us talks. Or we both talk. Take your pick."

He would have loved to tell her to butt out of his relationship with Cindy, but he couldn't. Maybe she was bluffing—he certainly couldn't believe she would fabricate a rape claim. But he was in no position to take that kind of risk. "All right," he said with resignation. "I'll take your terms, Gina. And just be glad I don't have a choice."

"Smart boy," she said, smiling. She raised her glass. "Can I offer you some Campari?"

He didn't bother to answer as he let himself out.

At 5:30 A.M., Wilfredo Garcia was awakened by a loud knock on the door. He'd been up most of the night, his mind racing. It had been almost thirty-six hours since he'd beeped Officer Cookson, but he still hadn't heard back. He was beginning to worry.

The knocking continued. Wilfredo rolled from his mattress, which lay on the floor.

"Un momento." He put on his robe and stepped into his slippers, then shuffled toward the door.

There was a place for a peephole in the door, but the little window had been removed and replaced with a wad of putty. Wilfredo removed the putty and peered into the hallway. It was dark, as usual, but he could see well enough to recognize the midnight blue uniform.

"It's Officer Cookson," came the voice in the darkness.

The old Cuban gentleman opened the door just a crack and peered through the opening. He was a foot shorter than the policeman and nearly twice as old.

"Can I come in, sir?"

Wilfredo felt a mixture of relief and anxiety. He didn't know what to expect, but he certainly didn't expect a cop to show up at this hour. Nonetheless, he nodded his head obediently and opened the door the rest of the way. The officer stepped inside and closed the door behind him. Wilfredo switched on a lamp with no shade, then turned and faced his visitor.

The old man froze at the sight. He hadn't been able to make out the features in the dark hallway, but in the better lighting it was clear. The build, the complexion, the sweeping dark eyebrows. A thousand different things were hitting him at once, and each screamed out the similarities between this man and the man he'd seen on the night Goss was murdered. His hands trembled and his heart hammered in his chest as he suddenly realized he was staring into the eyes of a killer. He turned to run, but the man in the uniform grabbed him by the shirt and pulled him back. Wilfredo opened his mouth to cry out for help, but before he could utter a word, the deadly hand of a trained killer came up from below and delivered a powerful jolt to the base of his chin. His head snapped back with the force of a rear-end collision, cracking the frail old vertebrae in his neck until the crown of his head met the middle of his back. In an instant Wilfredo went limp.

The killer released his grasp of the old man's nightshirt, and let the body fall to the floor. He bent down and felt for a pulse. There was none. His job was done.

He straightened his stolen uniform, put on his dark glasses, and then quietly left the apartment, closing the door behind him. Once again, he left behind his handiwork at 409 East Adams Street. Once again, his footsteps echoed through the empty hallway—like just another beat cop making the rounds.

PART FOUR

•

Tuesday, October 11

Chapter 32

•

"**A**ll rise!" were the words that set everything in motion, like the blast from a starter's pistol. After nine weeks of preparation, the stage was finally set. On one side of the courtroom sat a publicity-craving prosecutor, cloaked in the presumption of validity that came with his office. On the other sat a beleaguered defendant, clinging to the presumption of innocence that came with his predicament. Wilson McCue would go it alone for the government. Jack and his lawyer would see this through together, a joint defense, unified in their resistance.

Judge Virginia Tate emerged from her chambers through a side entrance to the courtroom. She was black and white in motion, with pasty white skin, salt-and-pepper hair, steely dark eyes, and a long, double strand of pearls swaying against her black robe. The thunderous clatter of reporters and spectators rising to their feet only added to the effect of her entrance. As she sat in a black leather chair, she looked first at the lawyers and then at the reporters, momentarily shedding her dour expression for a pleasant but tough smile.

"Let's get moving," she said and with those distinctly unceremonial words began the first of what would be nine days of jury selection, the phase lawyers referred to as voir dire. It was during this phase that opposing counsel would summon their best psychoanalytic powers, divining who should serve and who should be rejected. Jack could only feel helpless in these circumstances. Manny called the shots, displaying his finely honed skills for all to admire; Jack sat in silence, passing an occasional breath mint or a scribbled message, at once useless yet indispensable to the performance, like a page turner for a concert pianist. And it would remain that way for weeks. He would speak only through Manny. Wear clothes approved by Manny. Take his place at the polished walnut table beside Manny. He was on display as much as he was on trial.

Judge Tate had been apprehensive throughout jury selection. She was well aware of Wilson McCue's reputation for abusing voir dire—for using it to present his case to the jury or to prejudice his opponent, his questions doing less to elicit information than to advocate his position. McCue had behaved himself, for the most part—until Friday of the second week of selection, when they were finally on the verge of empaneling a jury.

"Do any of the jurors know Mr. Swyteck personally?" McCue began innocently enough. The prospective jurors simply shook their heads. "Surely you have *heard* of Mr. Swyteck," was his follow-up, eliciting a few nods. "Of course you have," he said with a smirk. "Mr. Swyteck was the lawyer who defended the infamous Eddy Goss, the man he is now charged with having murdered." Then that gleam appeared in his eye as he put his first drop of poison into the well. "Let me ask you this, ladies and gentlemen: Would anyone here be less inclined to believe Mr. Swyteck because he's a slick lawyer who was able to persuade twelve jurors to find a confessed killer not guilty?"

"Objection," said Manny.

"Sustained."

"Your Honor," McCue feigned incredulity. "I'm a little surprised by the objection. I'm just trying to ensure a fair panel. I mean, there are people who might even want to hold Mr. Swyteck responsible for all those grotesque murders his guilty clients committed—"

"That's enough!" the judge rebuked. "You are much more transparent than you realize, Mr. McCue. Move on. *Now.*"

"Surely," he agreed, having already made his point.

"I mean it," the judge said sternly. "I'll have no more of that."

Like a man testing fate, McCue seemed to get more outrageous with Manny's repeated objections, each of which was sustained and followed by increasingly stern reprimands from the judge. His antics pushed jury selection well into that Friday afternoon. But by the middle of that ninth interminable day the judge finally had some good news.

"We have a jury," she announced with relief.

A burly black construction worker who carried his lunch every day in the same crinkled paper sack; a retired alligator poacher with cowboy boots, tobacco-stained teeth, and a crew cut; and a blue-haired widow whose juror identification number, fifty-five, might have been half her age were just three of the twelve "peers" who would decide whether Jack Swyteck would live or die.

It was nearly four o'clock in the afternoon, and normally Judge Tate would have called it a day at that point, recognizing that there wasn't enough time for both the state and the defense to present opening statements. But in light of McCue's conduct during jury selection, she had a plan that would allow her to finish opening statements and still have plenty of time to watch herself on the six o'clock news.

"Mr. Cardenal," the judge said with a nod, "please proceed for the defense."

Manny rose slowly, giving the judge a confused look.

McCue also rose. "With all due respect," he interjected in his most folksy manner, "the govuhment usually gives the first opening statement."

The judge glared, then spoke explicitly, so that the jury would understand exactly what she was doing.

"We know the government *usually* goes first," she said. "But we warned you repeatedly—you were making your opening statement while selecting a jury. So now the defense gets its turn; you've had yours."

McCue was dumbstruck. "Your Honor, that seems pretty draconian, don't you think? I mean, if I could just have a couple of minutes. That's all—"

"Very well. You have two minutes."

"Well," he backpedaled, "I mean two min—"

"You've just wasted ten seconds of your two minutes."

At that, McCue scurried across the room, putting on his jury face. His big, dark eyes were full of life as they peered over the spectacles that he wore low on the bridge of his prominent nose, Teddy Roosevelt-style. Even in a serious moment like this, a trace of a smile lit up his happy, round face, making it clear why people said Wilson McCue was simply an overgrown good ol' boy at heart.

"Ladies and gentlemen of the jury," he said, pacing as he spoke, "this case is about murder, about power . . . the power over life and death. By the will of the people, we *do* have capital punishment in this state: We recognize the power of the government to put convicted killers to death. What we don't recognize, however, are the misguided efforts of private citizens to exercise that power at will. We do not allow vigilantes to take the awesome power of the state into their own hands. We do not permit men to carry out their own private executions, whatever their motive.

"As the evidence in this case unfolds, ladies and gentlemen, you will come to know a man who did indeed take that power into his own hands. This man was a lawyer. A lawyer who had devoted his professional life to defending men and women who were accused of some of the most violent murders this community has ever seen. Most, if not all, of his clients were guilty. A few were convicted. Now, there's nothing wrong with that. Some lawyers would say it's even admirable to defend the rights of the guilty. It's in the public interest, they might argue."

McCue moved closer to the jury, addressing each of the twelve as individuals, as if it were just the two of them sitting on his front porch, sipping lemonade and watching the sun set. "But it's not the public interest or even this lawyer's public service that is at issue here," he said in a low but firm voice. "You are here as jurors today because this lawyer," his voice grew louder, "the defendant in this case, has a private side—a very dark private side. The evidence will show that on August second, at roughly four o'clock in the morning, he burst into an apartment—another man's *home*—and made himself judge, jury, and executioner. He took out his thirty-eight-caliber pistol, fired off two quick shots, and slew his own client. And ladies and gentlemen, the defendant—the man who did this deed—is sitting right here in this courtroom," McCue said solemnly, scowling as he pointed an accusing finger. "His name is Jack Swyteck."

Jack suddenly felt the weight of the government's case, as if McCue's pointed finger had brought it to rest on his shoulders at that very moment. *How true it all sounds!* he thought morosely as the hallowed courtroom seemed to transform even this blowhard state attorney into something dignified, the way dirt becomes soil just because it's in a nursery, or spit becomes saliva when in a dentist's office.

"You have fifteen seconds left," the judge intoned.

"My time is short," McCue grumbled, "and I don't have nearly enough to lay out all the evidence against Mr. Swyteck. But you will see and hear all of it over the next several days. And at the end of the case, I will come back before you—and then I will ask you to find Jack Swyteck *guilty* of murder in the first degree."

McCue paused, the silence in the room seeming to reinforce his words. Then he headed back to his seat.

Manny rose and stepped toward the jury, exchanging glances with McCue as he passed. Manny stood comfortably before the jury, made eye contact with each of the jurors, and then held up the indictment in one hand and read loudly: "*The State* versus *Jack Swyteck.*" He let his hand fall to his side, still clutching the indictment. "*The State,*" he repeated, this time with emphasis, "versus *Jack Swyteck.* Now, *that,*" he said, his resonant voice making his audience shiver, "is power. And Mr. McCue is right in one respect: This case *is* about power. And what you have seen so far is simply the power to accuse," he said as he flipped the indictment irreverently on the prosecutor's table, then faced the jury squarely. "Because that's all an indictment is, ladies and gentlemen: an accusation. In a criminal case, the government has no *power*. It has only a burden. It has the burden of proving its case beyond a reasonable doubt. Over the next few weeks, the testimony, the evidence, the *facts,*" he hung on the last word, "will show you that the government is powerless to meet that heavy burden . . . because Jack Swyteck is an innocent man."

Jack's gut twitched. Just how innocent did he have to be, he wondered. Just how much would this jury make McCue prove? Jack knew that his lawyer would address all those things in his opening statement, and he wanted to hear every word of it. But he was having trouble focusing. McCue hadn't said anything that he hadn't expected him to say, but finally hearing the accusations directly from the prosecutor's mouth had deeply affected him. It was as if Jack had convinced himself that the prosecutor didn't really have any evidence, and now he had to deal with the fact that McCue just might have all the evidence he needed.

"And when you evaluate the testimony of the government witnesses," Manny told the jurors, "remember that not a single one of these witnesses *saw* my client commit a crime. The government's case is based entirely on circumstantial evidence: Not a single government witness will say they saw Mr. Swyteck do *anything* illegal with their own two eyes."

Jack scanned the courtroom. All eyes were on Manny except . . . What was it? He looked around again, more slowly this time, focusing. There it was. A man seated in the last row of public seating was staring at him—not the way a curious observer would stare, but in a penetrating, communicative way. He looked familiar. Tall and broad-shouldered. A very round, clean-shaven head. The sparkle of a diamond stud on his left earlobe. And then the image of the man merged with another. Jack could see himself standing outside Goss's apartment on the night Goss was killed. He was pounding on the door. A man had stepped into the hall, a few doors down from Goss's apartment, and shouted, "Cut the racket." Without question, this was that same man.

Jack quickly looked away from the man. He tried to listen to Manny's opening statement but couldn't keep his concentration. *What the hell's that guy doing here?* he asked himself. It seemed odd that Goss's neighbor would be in the courtroom. He could have been a compelling witness for the prosecution. He could identify Jack and place him at the scene of the crime. But he obviously wasn't going to be a witness. As a lawyer, Jack knew that the rules of court prevented potential witnesses from being in the courtroom at any time before they testified. He glanced again at the man. The cold, unnerving look in his eye was definitely one of recognition, which only increased Jack's confusion.

The next thing he knew he was hearing Manny say "Thank you very much," to the jury. He couldn't believe it! He pried his tight, starched collar from his throat and sighed. After weeks of anticipation, he'd missed his own lawyer's opening statement. But it didn't seem to matter. Curiosity now consumed him. Who *was* that guy?

"Ladies and gentlemen," said the judge, "we will break for the weekend now. But due to the inordinate amount of publicity attending this trial, I am exercising my prerogative to sequester the jury. The jurors should check with the clerk about accommodations. Thank you. Court's in recess until nine o'clock Monday morning," she announced, banging her gavel.

Jack rose quickly as the shuffle and murmur of spectators and reporters filled the courtroom. He didn't wait for Manny to offer him a ride home. "I gotta get out of here," he said, his eye still on the man in the last row. "Can you keep the press busy while I duck out and find a cab?"

"Sure," said Manny as he closed his briefcase. "But what's the rush?"

"There's something I have to check out," he said, giving Manny no time to ask what. He quickly stepped away and passed through the swinging gate that separated the lawyers from the audience, pushing his way through the crowded aisle and ignoring calls from reporters. Manny was a few steps behind. With his height Jack could see over the crowd just well enough to keep a bead on the back of the man's shaved head.

"I'll take all your questions right over here," Jack heard Manny announce as the crowd poured from the courtroom into the lobby. Most of the reporters moved in one direction, and Jack immediately went the other way, toward the elevator, where the clean-shaven head was just then passing through the open doors of a packed car, going down. Jack dashed through the maze of lawyers, reporters, and spectators, trying to keep his target in sight. A couple of reporters tagged along, persisting with their probing questions. He was just ten feet from the closing elevator doors when he broadsided a blur of pin-striped polyester, a five-foot-tall personal-injury lawyer with files tucked under both arms. The collision sent papers flying and bodies sprawling, like the violent end of a bowling lane.

"You jerk!" the man cried from the floor.

"Sorry," said Jack, though he was sorry only that the elevator had just left without him. He left the man on the floor and his manners behind as he sprinted toward the stairwell and barged through the emergency door. He leaped down two and three steps at a time, covering five flights in little longer than it would have taken his hundred-and-ninety-pound body to fall down the shaft. He burst through the metal door at the bottom, catching his breath as he scanned the main lobby. The place was bustling, as it always was, but the crowd was scattered enough for him to see that he'd been too slow. The elevator had already emptied, and the man with the clean-shaven head was nowhere to be found. Jack charged out of the courthouse and stood atop the granite steps, searching desperately. The sidewalks were full of rush-hour traffic, but the man had disappeared. Dejected, Jack lumbered down the steps, hailed a cab, and jumped into the backseat.

"Where to?" asked the driver.

Jack started to give his home address, hesitated, then replied, "Four-oh-nine East Adams Street."

Adams Street was twenty long blocks from the court-house, each block representing a geographic uptick in the crime rate. The sun was setting as the taxi entered Eddy Goss's old neighborhood, steering past mountains of trash and vandalized buildings. The driver left Jack off at the curb right in front of Goss's apartment building. Jack passed a twenty through the open car window for a ten dollar fare, and before he could ask for change the driver was gone.

Once inside, Jack retraced his journey of eleven weeks earlier up to the second floor, to a very long, graffiti-splattered hallway with apartments on either side. It was just as dark as the last time; not even the murder of tenant Wilfredo Garcia had prompted the landlord to replace a single burned-out or missing bulb.

Jack walked briskly down the dimly lit hall and came to a halt before number 217, Eddy Goss's old apartment. Yellow police tape barricaded the doorway, but Jack had no intention of going inside. He stood in front of the door just long enough to look down the hall and determine the apartment from which the neighbor had emerged that night. It was only a second before he was certain: four doors down—apartment 213, the one with a swastika spray-painted on it. He walked the thirty feet, knocked firmly on the door, and waited. There was no reply. He knocked a little harder, and the force of his knock pushed the door halfway open.

"Hello?" he called out. But no one answered. With a gentle push, the door swung all the way open, revealing a dark efficiency that had been completely ravaged. Huge holes dotted the plasterboard walls like mortar fire. Newspapers, bags, empty boxes, and other trash covered a floor of cracked tile and exposed plywood. Broken furniture was piled up in the corner. The room's only window had been boarded up from the outside. He checked the number on the door to verify he was in the right place. He was, so he stepped inside, sending a squealing rat scurrying to the kitchen. He looked around in confusion and disbelief.

"What the hell you doing here?" demanded a man in the doorway. Jack wheeled around, expecting to see Goss's neighbor. But it was an old man with yellow-gray hair and a scowl on his pasty white face. He was wearing a T-shirt stained with underarm perspiration, and a toothpick dangled from his mouth.

"The door was open, so I came in. I'm looking for someone. Tall guy. Shaved head. He was living here on the second of August."

"The hell he was," the old man said, the toothpick wagging as he spoke. "I'm the manager of this dump, and there wasn't *nobody* livin' here on no second of August. Ain't nobody lived in this rat hole goin' back more than a year."

"But—he said he had a two-year-old kid."

"Kids?" the manager scoffed. "Here?" Then his look soured. "I'm puttin' the padlock back on the door one more time. And if it's broken off again, I'm gonna remember you, mister. We've had two murders in three months in this building—both of them on this floor. So get your butt outta here, or I'm callin' the cops."

Jack didn't argue. He lowered his head and left the way he had come, down the hall, down the stairs, and out the front door.

It was nearly dark outside when he stepped out of the building, but the streetlights hadn't yet come on. From the top of the steps he saw someone on the sidewalk across the street, standing in the shadows of what little daylight remained. Jack looked at him carefully, and the man glared back. He felt a chill of recognition: *It's him.*

Suddenly the man bolted, running at an easy pace back toward the courthouse. Jack instinctively gave chase, sprinting across the street and down the sidewalk as fast as he could in his business suit and black-soled shoes. The man didn't seem to be trying to pull away. He was taunting Jack, as if he wanted him to catch up. Jack came within fifteen feet, and then the man pulled away, effortlessly disappearing into the Greyhound parking lot two blocks down the street. Jack tried to follow, stopping and starting again and again, catching a glimpse of him every second or two as he weaved between coaches bound for New York, Chicago, and Atlanta. Revving engines filled the air with window-rattling noise and thick exhaust. Thoroughly winded, Jack stopped between two coaches and looked frantically for his target. He scanned in one direction, then the other. Nothing. The door to the empty bus beside him was open. Cautiously, he stepped inside and peered down the aisle.

"I know you're in here," Jack called out, though he was far from certain. There was only silence. He took one step down the dark aisle, then thought better of it. If his man were crouched down between the seats, he had to come out sometime. Jack decided he'd wait for him outside.

He turned to leave, but suddenly the door slammed shut. He wheeled around to see that someone was standing behind him, but a quick blow to his head and then another to the gut doubled him over in pain. Another blow to the back of the head and he was facedown on the floor. His attacker threw himself on top of him from behind and pressed a knife to his throat.

"Don't even *think* of moving."

Jack froze as the blade pinched at his neck.

"I'd really *hate* to have to slit your throat, Swyteck—after all the trouble I've gone to."

Jack clenched his fist tightly. "Who are you?"

"Think back. Two years ago. The night before Raul Fernandez was executed."

Jack felt a chill as the voice came back to him. "What do you want from me?"

"I want justice. I want you to die like Raul died—in the chair for a murder you didn't commit."

"That's not justice," he struggled to say. "This is sick. And it won't work."

"It'll work," the man said, laughing as he drew a little blood with a slight twist of the knife. "Remember:

You're alive only because I let you live. You might think you're safe. The locks on your doors. The alarm on your car. All that's just bullshit. It's like that warm, safe feeling people get by closing the drapes in their house at night, when for all they know there's a guy with an axe outside their window with his face up against the glass. There's no protection from that, Swyteck. All you can do is play by the rules. *My* rules."

"Such as?"

"There's only one. This trial is me against you, one-on-one. You try to turn it into anything else, and I promise you, innocent people are gonna get hurt."

"What does that mean?"

"You're smart. Figure it out, asshole."

"Why—"

"Why must you die?" The man leaned forward until Jack felt his breath on the back of his neck. "Because there's a killer on the loose," he said in a cold whisper. "And the killer is *you*."

Jack gasped as he felt the knife press harder against his throat. Then his attacker sprung to his feet and vanished into the night. Jack just lay there, his face resting on the gritty floor, feeling like he did when he was five years old. Like he was all alone.

Chapter 33

•

Ten weeks had passed since Harry Swyteck followed his blackmailer's instructions and left the final payoff at Memorial Cemetery. Thankfully, the dark forebodings that had plagued him that night turned out to be false apprehensions. The journey to the cemetery passed without incident—though the governor did experience profound discomfort as he looked down at Raul Fernandez's final resting place.

Harry had not been in the courtroom today for opening statements. But he'd received a full report from one of the young lawyers who served as governor's counsel. The purpose of opening statements was for each side to give the jury a road map identifying the evidence that they intended to present during trial. After analyzing the direction the defense seemed to be taking, it struck Harry as odd that Manny hadn't made a reference to the 911 caller's report of a man in a police uniform leaving the scene of the crime.

The governor had promised Manny that, although he was paying the bills, the legal strategy would be up to Manny and Jack. Therefore, he was reluctant to second-guess Manny's opening statement. But he feared the lawyer might have gotten the wrong idea. Perhaps Manny hadn't brought up the 911 call because Harry had once been a police officer. If that was the case, Harry needed to set Manny straight. He caught the next flight from Tallahassee, and by eight o'clock that evening he was sitting across from his son's attorney.

"Thanks for meeting me on such short notice," Harry said as he studied the exotic decor of Manny's office.

"My pleasure," Manny replied. "You mentioned on the phone that you had some concerns about my strategy."

"Yes," Harry said, "Well, not concerns really, just areas that I needed clarified."

"Such as?"

"Well, the nine-one-one call, for one. I'm told that you didn't mention it in your opening statement today." The governor looked at him appraisingly. "I don't mean to insult you, Manny, or question your integrity. But I want to make it clear that I hired you to represent Jack for one reason only: because you're the best in the business, and because I think that if anyone can get my son acquitted, you can. *How* you go about it is up to you and Jack. If that means making the police look bad—well, so be it. I'm a former cop. But I'm a father first."

Manny nodded slowly, seeming to measure his response. "I understand what you're saying. And I'm not insulted. You're not the first concerned parent who's walked into my office. You are, however, the first concerned parent to leave a footprint outside the door of the murder victim's apartment."

The governor went rigid. All expression ran from his face. "What are you talking about?"

Manny was a master at reading reactions. He was testing Harry, and Harry had flunked. "Please, don't say anything. Let's just say I know you didn't come here because I decided not to mention the nine-one-one call. You're here because I didn't mention the footprint."

"What *footprint?*" Harry was genuinely confused—and concerned.

Manny frowned, sat up straighter in his chair. "I honestly don't think we should discuss this any further, Governor. Rest assured, I'll use the footprint at trial, if it's necessary to win Jack's case. That I didn't mention it as a matter of argument doesn't mean that I won't offer it later as a matter of *evidence.*"

"But Manny, I honestly have no idea what footprint you're talking about."

"And that's precisely the response I would expect from you. Like I said. I don't think you and I should discuss this any further. I'm Jack's lawyer, not yours. And you should have a lawyer."

"Me?" he chuckled nervously. "Why do *I* need a lawyer?"

Manny leaned forward, not to threaten him, but to convey the import of what he was about to say. "Let me spell it out for you. You've told me some things about the night Raul Fernandez was executed—about what happened between you and Jack. But I don't think that's the end of the story."

"What do you mean?"

"Well, I'm sure you heard about that old man in Goss's apartment building who got his neck snapped a few weeks ago. Tragic thing—a real mystery. The police don't even have a motive, yet. Can you think of one, Governor?"

Harry's face showed irritation. "No, except that there are lunatics out there who like to kill innocent people."

"There's more to it than that, I think. I reviewed the investigative file in that old man's case. There were extraneous footprints in his apartment. Turns out that the lunatic who snapped the old man's neck in apartment two-oh-one was wearing wing tips. Wiggins wing tips. The *same* Wiggins wing tips that left a very clear footprint outside Eddy Goss's door on the night *he* was killed."

The governor went cold. He'd been wearing the same brand the night he'd gone to Goss's apartment. And now he realized the purpose of the seemingly silly "souvenir" he'd left on the grave of Raul Fernandez, along with the money and flowers—right before the old man had been murdered.

"Now," said Manny, "you're the former cop, Governor. Maybe it's time for you to remind yourself of your right to remain silent. And of your right to an attorney. Your *own* attorney."

The governor shook his head slowly, but said nothing more than "thank you" and "good night."

Chapter 34

•

A taxi took Jack from the bus station and dropped him at the end of his driveway just before nine. He was still shaken from the attack, but fortunately he had time to recuperate. It was Friday night, and there was a weekend between opening statements and what would surely be the worst Monday of his life—the day the first witness for the prosecution would take the stand against him.

He stepped slowly up the stairs of his front porch and reached out wearily with his key, but the front door flew open and Cindy greeted him with a smile.

"I hope you have a reservation," she said.

"What?"

"All right," she said, pretending to give in. "I'll let you in this time, but no complaints about the evening's menu."

She looked great in her short black skirt and paisley blouse.

As he walked into the house, he was met by the mixed scent of her perfume and a tangy, buttery smell coming from the kitchen. A quick glance at the dining room table revealed flickering candles.

Okay, I get it, Jack thought to himself. To take some of the edge off my first day in court, she's knocked herself out and prepared a candlelit dinner.

As he passed into the bright light of the front hall, she noticed the scratches on his face and his soiled clothes. "What happened to you?" she asked.

He swallowed hard. "I met him tonight. The guy who's been stalking me."

She froze. "You *what?*" Eyes wide with fright, she took him by the arm and led him into the living room. She switched on the lamp and took a closer look at his scratches. "It doesn't look serious," she said. "But what happened?"

He lowered himself onto the couch. She sat beside him and listened as he told her everything, beginning with the night Goss was killed: Jack's banging on Goss's door, the man stepping out of the apartment down the hall to complain about the noise, the same man staring at Jack in the courtroom, the return to East Adams Street, and finally the attack on the bus.

With some difficulty he also told her about the night Raul Fernandez was executed, and his inability to persuade his father to grant a stay.

After listening to his monologue, she felt like she'd finally met Jack for the first time. "I'm glad you told me—about you and your father. But this attack. What does it mean?"

He took a deep breath. "It confirms that Eddy Goss was never after me. And it confirms that I'm being framed. This guy killed Goss, and then made it look like I did it. It's poetic justice in his eyes. Raul Fernandez died an innocent man. I'm his killer. So I have to die, too—for a crime I didn't commit."

"But that doesn't make sense. Why you? After all, you pleaded with your father to stop the execution. If this guy is trying to avenge Fernandez's death, why are you the target, instead of your father?"

Jack shook his head. "I don't know. I don't know how his crazed mind works."

"And what's his motive? I understand that he's punishing you for the execution. But why's he so attached to Raul Fernandez? What's the connection?"

Jack sighed. "I don't know that either."

"Oh, Jack," she said, holding him close. "Why would anyone hate you this much? It scares me that he *enjoys* hating you so much. He's taunting you, Jack. He's playing with you like this is a game."

Jack nodded in agreement. He looked into her eyes, then repeated the suggestion he'd made to her weeks ago. "I really think you should get out of Miami. The man put a knife to my throat, Cindy. I still can't tell the police about it. I need to call Manny, but I'm sure he'll agree with me. It's no different now than it was before: I still can't give the prosecutor proof of my motive to kill Eddy Goss."

A knock at the door interrupted them.

"Did you invite someone else for dinner?" he asked.

"Of course not."

The knocking continued. "I'll get it," he said.

"What if it's *him?*"

"I know what he looks like now. I'll know if it's him before I open the door." Jack walked briskly through the living room and stopped in front of the door. A third round of harsh knocking began, then it stopped as he flipped on the porch light. He peered out through the peephole and saw a man staring back at him with a dour expression. He wore a beige short-sleeve shirt, chocolate-brown pants, and black patent-leather shoes that glistened in the porch light. And he had a gun with a pearl-white handle tucked in to a heavy black shoulder holster. His official license to bear a sidearm—a shiny gold badge—was pinned to his chest. Jack opened the door.

"Evenin'," the officer said in a polite but businesslike tone. "I'm with the county sheriff's department. I'm looking for Miss Cindy Paige."

A lump came to Jack's throat, followed by second thoughts about opening the door.

"I'm Cindy Paige," she said, standing behind Jack.

"This is for you," the sheriff announced as he handed her an official-looking document.

Jack intercepted the delivery.

"What is it?" Cindy asked.

"It's a subpoena."

"A trial subpoena," the sheriff clarified.

"What it's for?" she asked.

"Be at the courthouse, Monday, nine A.M.," the sheriff commanded. "You're the government's first witness in *State* versus *Swyteck.*"

"The *government's* first witness?"

"Don't say another word," Jack advised her. He quickly closed the door on the sheriff.

"I can't believe this," she said as her eyes welled with tears. "Why me? Why do they want *me* to go first?"

"Maybe because you're honest," he said. "The prosecutor probably thinks he can get you to say something to hurt me."

She pulled back and looked into his eyes. "Never."

"I know you wouldn't," he said as he pulled her close. As he pulled her close, he noticed that smoke and the smell of their burning dinner had begun to seep in from the kitchen. *At least not intentionally*, he thought.

Chapter 35

•

The air seemed electric with possibility that Monday morning as the players in the drama of *State* v. *Swyteck* assembled for the opening act. The script called for the prosecution to present its version of events first. After Jack's character was thoroughly impugned and his actions given the most sinister interpretation, the defense would come on and try to reverse the brainwashing. It seemed almost amazing, really, that juries so often reached the right result. But the lofty notion that this was the best system in the world was little consolation for an innocent man who might well be put to death.

"Call your first witness, Mr. McCue," the judge ordered.

"The State calls Cindy Paige," McCue announced.

Jack's heart sank. It was no bluff.

A sea of heads turned in unison toward the rear of the courtroom as Cindy emerged through the twelve-foot swinging doors. She looked nervous, but only Jack could detect just how nervous she truly was. He knew the little signs—the tightness in her lower lip, the stiffness in her walk, the way she pressed her thumb against her forefinger.

She wore a beige skirt and matching jacket, with a powder-blue blouse. "Look soft and sympathetic," Manny had told her last night. And she did.

"Do you swear to tell the truth, the whole truth . . ." the bailiff said, administering the familiar oath. Jack looked on from across the courtroom, watching Cindy's raised right hand tremble just slightly. It was ironic, he thought, that she appeared so anxious. If ever there was a person who could be counted on to tell the truth, it was her.

Wilson McCue allowed the witness to settle into the old Naugahyde chair, then began innocuously enough. "Please state your name," he requested.

Cindy shifted in her chair, as if even this easy question caused discomfort. "Cindy Paige," she replied in a soft voice.

"Miss Paige, how long have you known the defendant?"

"A year and a half," she said.

"How well do you know him?"

She shrugged. "Better than anyone, I suppose."

"Is it fair to say you two are romantically involved?"

"Yes. We live together."

"You're not married, though," said McCue, sounding more than a little judgmental.

Cindy glanced at the jurors. She saw grandmotherly disapproval from a blue-haired retired schoolteacher in the second row. "No, we're not married."

"And how long have you two lived together?"

"About a year. Except for a couple of weeks a while back."

"Let's talk about that little hiatus," said the state attorney. "When was that?"

She sighed, not because her memory failed her, but because it was a time in her life she'd rather have just forgotten. "Almost three months ago."

"It was right after the trial of Eddy Goss, wasn't it?" he asked, sounding a little less friendly now, more like an interrogator. "Right after Mr. Swyteck defended him and got him off."

"Objection as to characterization," said Manny as he rose from his chair.

"Sustained," groaned the judge. "I won't tolerate cheap shots, Mr. McCue. The jury is reminded that Mr. Swyteck is on trial for the alleged murder of Eddy Goss," she instructed the jurors, "and not because he represented Mr. Goss in another trial."

A few jurors exchanged glances, as if they were torn as to which of the two was the real crime.

"The witness may answer the question," said the judge.

"Jack and I split a couple of days after the Goss trial," Cindy responded. "But that trial had nothing to do with our breakup."

"It was your decision to move out, wasn't it."

"Yes, it was my decision."

"And Mr. Swyteck was pretty upset about that."

She hesitated, surprised at how personal the questions were, and suspicious of where this was leading. She glanced at Jack, then looked the prosecutor in the eye. "It was hard on both of us."

"Well, let me be a little more specific. The two of you had a nasty fight before you left him, didn't you?"

"Objection," said Manny. "Judge—"

"Overruled."

Cindy shifted nervously in her chair. "We had a disagreement, yes."

McCue smirked. "And I suppose the battle of Gettysburg was also a disagreement."

"Objection!" said Manny.

The judge frowned at McCue. "Sustained. I'm warning you for the last time about the cheap shots, Mr. McCue."

McCue was unfazed. "Isn't it true, Miss Paige, that the defendant literally threw you out of his house?"

"He never laid a hand on me. We had an argument. Every couple I know has arguments."

"But this wasn't just like any other argument," McCue said, moving closer to the witness. "On the morning you left him, Mr. Swyteck really lost control," he said in a low, serious voice. "He was a different person. Wouldn't you say?"

"Objection," said Manny. "Your Honor, this line of questioning is getting ridiculous."

The judge glared at the prosecutor. "I'd tend too agree."

"If we could have a sidebar," said McCue, "I think I can explain the relevance."

"Make it brief," the judge said as she waved them for ward.

The lawyers stepped quickly toward the bench and huddled beside the judge, out of earshot of the jury.

"I've been patient," Manny argued quietly, "waiting to see where Mr. McCue is going with this. But lovers' spats between my client and Miss Paige are completely irrelevant to the issues in this case. This is simply humiliating and improper."

"It goes right to the heart of the government's case," McCue countered, his expression deadly serious. "We have an all-American defendant who looks like the last person on earth who'd kill another human being. But on the inside, Your Honor, Mr. Swyteck is wound a little too tightly. He snapped after the Goss trial. And when he did, he killed his own client. I need the testimony of this witness to prove that he snapped. To prove that *stress* made him into a different person—someone capable of murder."

"Miss Paige is not a psychiatrist," Manny said with sarcasm.

"I don't want a medical opinion," McCue fought back. "I want to know what this woman perceived—the woman who has lived with the defendant for the last year, and who has already testified that she knows him better than anyone."

The judge wasn't completely persuaded, but she deferred to the state attorney. "I'll allow it," she muttered. "But not for much longer."

"Judge," Manny groaned, "I—"

"I've ruled," she said sharply.

"Thank you," said McCue. Manny shook his head, then returned to his seat beside Jack. The prosecutor resumed his position in front of the witness, a little closer than before, almost close enough to touch her.

Cindy tried to be ready for anything as she stared back at McCue. She wondered what the judge had said to him. She hoped he'd move on to another topic, but knew from the gleam in his eye that he wasn't finished yet.

"How about it, miss?" McCue continued. "On that morning you left your boyfriend—right after Eddy Goss was acquitted, and right before he was murdered—would you say you saw a side of Jack Swyteck that you'd never seen before?"

She looked at Jack, then back at McCue. "I wouldn't say that . . . exactly."

"He scared you though, didn't he?"

Cindy reddened. "I don't know. He could have."

"*Could* have, huh? Well, let me clarify a few things. The morning you left him, you didn't bother to kiss him good-bye, did you?"

"No."

"You didn't even shake his hand, did you?"

"No."

"In fact, you didn't *walk* out on him. You *ran* out."

"Yes, I ran."

"You ran out so fast you didn't even have time to dress."

"No."

"You ran out half-naked, wearing nothing but a T-shirt."

She gulped, her eyes welling. "It's what I sleep in."

"You ran out because you were scared for your own safety, weren't you?"

She was flustered. She licked her lips, but her mouth was desert-dry.

"Isn't it true," he said, "that you *told* Mr. Swyteck that the Goss trial had changed him?"

Cindy shook her head with confusion. "I don't remember anything like—"

"Miss Paige!" McCue bellowed, his voice filling the courtroom like a pipe organ. "You thought Jack Swyteck had changed so much, that you told him he was no different from the scum he defended. Isn't that right!"

"I—" Cindy gasped.

"Isn't that right, Miss Paige!"

"No, not exactly. I said, 'You are the scum you defend,' but—"

"He *is* the scum he defended!" McCue exclaimed, pouncing on her words for having dared to equivocate. "Thank you, Ms. Paige. Thank you very much for clearing that up for us. I have no further questions," he announced as he turned away from the witness and headed back to the prosecutor's table.

She sat limply in the witness chair, her head down and shoulders rounded. Manny approached slowly, to give her time to compose herself before his cross-examination. "Good morning, Miss Paige," he said in a conversational tone, trying to put her at ease.

Jack listened as Manny tried to rehabilitate her. She explained that she'd spoken purely out of anger on that ugly morning, that she'd never meant a word of it, and that they were now back together. But Jack couldn't lis-

ten. He knew Cindy had told McCue the truth, and
nothing could change the truth. The best strategy was to
minimize the importance of her testimony, and the
longer Manny kept her on the stand, the more important
her testimony would seem. Thankfully, Manny didn't
keep her long.

"That's all the questions I have," said Manny, dis-
missing the witness. "Thank you."

Cindy stepped down and headed for the swinging
gate that separated the players from the spectators. As
she laid her hand atop the polished mahogany banister,
she paused and gave Jack a look that asked for forgiveness.

"We got a problem," he whispered to Manny.

"It's only round one," Manny said, shrugging it off.

"No, you're missing the point," Jack said. "It was
just me and Cindy in my bedroom that morning she left
me. We were *alone*."

"So? Why is that a problem?"

"If Cindy and I are the only two people who know
what went on in that room, how did McCue know how
to ask her all the right questions?"

For a moment they just stared at each other. Then
Jack's eyes shifted from Manny to Wilson McCue, who
was seated at the prosecutor's table across the room.
The state attorney looked up from his notepad and returned the glance, as if sensing the weight of Jack's
stare. He was smiling, Jack noticed, albeit just around
his eyes. Jack fought a rising tide of anger. He was
ready to leap from his chair and drag it out of him if he
had to: *How did you know, you bastard? How did you
know what to ask her?*

"Is the State ready to call its next witness?" asked the judge.

Jack was so engrossed he didn't hear the words. Then it came to him. Of course McCue had an informant. *Who else could it be?*

"Your Honor," the prosecutor announced to the hushed courtroom, "the State calls Miss Gina Terisi."

Chapter 36

•

The big mahogany doors in the back of the courtroom swung open, and Gina Terisi strode down the center aisle like a model on the runway. Though her dazzling beauty attracted stares, she didn't have her usual seductive air. Her makeup was understated. Her navy-blue suit and peach silk blouse were stylish but conservative.

"Do you swear to tell the truth, the whole truth, and nothing but . . ."

Please, God, Jack prayed as the oath was administered. The truth was bad enough, but "the *whole* truth"? He wasn't sure he—or his relationship with Cindy— could survive it. "Please state your name," the prosecutor began.

Jack watched carefully as she testified, searching for some sign that she resented McCue's questions. A downturned lip, clenched teeth, lowered eyes. But, to his consternation, she seemed articulate, cooperative, willing.

"Do you know the defendant?" McCue asked.

"Yes, I do." Jack listened impassively to the interrogation, trying not to panic as Gina told the jury how she'd met Jack and how long she'd known him.

"Now, Miss Terisi," the prosecutor shifted gears, "I'd like to turn to the night Eddy Goss was murdered. Did you see Mr. Swyteck on the night of August first?"

"Yes, I did," she answered. And from that point forward her testimony moved from a wide-angle view to a punishing close-up. Wilson McCue was no longer eliciting bits of background generalities; he had Gina poring over every detail about the night Jack showed up at her door. He wanted specifics, from how Jack looked and what he was wearing, to what he said and how he said it. Jack's fear that he was being stalked by Goss, and his outrage when he discovered that an intruder had broken into Gina's townhouse received particular attention. Reporters in the gallery scribbled down every word as Gina's damning story unfolded and Jack's motive to kill Eddy Goss became clear. Strangely—*very* strangely, Jack thought—Gina didn't mention that Jack had had a gun in his possession.

By late afternoon, though, the damage to his defense was clear. The State had plugged the gaping hole in its case: The defendant's motive to kill Eddy Goss had been the weakest part of the prosecution's case, and Gina's testimony had transformed it into the strongest. Jack tried to show no reaction, but he wondered whether things would get worse. Though Gina had been on the witness stand nearly four hours, she had yet to breathe a word of their "indiscretion." With Cindy sitting right behind him, he could only hope she never would.

"Now, Ms. Terisi," McCue continued, "did you call the police after all this happened?"

"No," she replied, "I didn't."

"I see," said the prosecutor as he stroked his chin. "That may seem a little odd to some of our jurors, Miss Terisi. After someone broke into your house, you say you didn't call the police. Can you tell us *why* you didn't call the police?"

Gina glanced at Cindy, then looked back at the prosecutor. "I really don't have an explanation."

McCue did a double take. He hadn't expected that answer. Indeed, it was far different from the answer Gina had given him several times before, when they'd rehearsed her testimony. "Are you saying you don't remember?" he asked politely. "Because I can refresh your recollection if—"

"I'm saying I don't have an explanation," she said firmly.

McCue narrowed his eyes and stepped out from behind the podium. If he was going to have to impeach his own witness, he needed to let her feel his presence. "Miss Terisi," he said, his tone decidedly less friendly, "when I interviewed you in my office, you told me that Mr. Swyteck had insisted that you not call the police. Isn't that correct?"

Gina shifted nervously in her chair, but she remained firm. "Yes. I said that. But I wasn't telling you the truth when I said it was Jack's idea. *I* was the one who insisted on *not* calling the police. Not him."

Wilson McCue stood in silence. He'd hoped to convince the jury that Jack had prevented Gina from calling the police because he wanted to take care of the problem himself—that Jack had intended to murder Goss. Gina's sudden switch had thrown him a curve. McCue didn't know the reason for the change. But he had to make at least one attempt to put his witness back on course.

"It's okay, Miss Terisi," he said in a sympathetic tone. "I understand that Mr. Swyteck is the boyfriend of your best friend. And I can understand how you might be reluctant to hurt her and her boyfriend. But come on, now, level with us. You have to admit that it's a little hard to believe that *you* were the one who didn't want to call the police after some stranger had just broken into *your* apartment."

Manny rose from his chair. "Is that a question?" he asked sarcastically.

"Objection sustained."

"My question is this," the prosecutor said to his witness. "Did you want to call the police, or didn't you?"

Gina swallowed hard. "Of course I wanted to."

McCue felt a rush of satisfaction. It had taken a little maneuvering, but he'd placed his witness right back on track. Or so he thought. "Then tell us, please: Why didn't you call the police?"

"I wouldn't let myself."

"Excuse me?" Again he'd received an unexpected answer.

"I refused to call the police because—" Gina

stopped herself. She looked away and wrung her hands in her lap. "I didn't call," she said, lowering her head in shame, "because I didn't want to have to tell the police that Jack and I had slept together."

The prosecutor's mouth fell open, and a murmur of disbelief filled the courtroom. Reporters feverishly flagged their notes with stars and arrows. Jack felt like a man impaled, but he couldn't allow himself the slightest reaction. He didn't dare look behind him, knowing that if he did, he'd lose all self-control.

"Order," said the judge with the bang of her gavel.

Jack couldn't fight the impulse any longer. He looked over his shoulder at Cindy. Their eyes met for just a split second—long enough for him to see something he'd never seen before. It wasn't anger or embarrassment or heartbreak or disbelief. It was *all* of those things.

"All right, miss," McCue said to his witness. He took a deep breath. Gina had diverted widely from the script, and at the moment his chief fear was that her admission about having lied was something the defense would seize on in cross-examination. He had to prevent that from happening. If ever there was a time to turn lemons into lemonade, this was it. "That was a very painful admission you just made, and I'm glad you made it. It shows that you're an honest person—you tell the truth, even when it hurts."

"Objection," said Manny.

"Sustained," the judge said. "Let's not vouch for our witnesses, Mr. McCue."

"Sorry, Your Honor. But I'm just trying to elicit a very simple point." He turned and faced the witness.

"Ms. Terisi, when you and I talked in my office and you told me that little falsehood about it being Mr. Swyteck's idea not to call the police, you were not under oath, were you?"

"No, I wasn't."

"Today, however, you are under oath. You *are* aware that you're under oath?"

"Yes."

"Very well. So, tell us, Miss Terisi. What about all the other things you've testified to today, under oath: Are those true, or are they false?"

"They're true," she said resignedly. "All of them are true."

The prosecutor nodded slowly. "And tell us one more thing, please, if you would: Did Mr. Swyteck voice any objection when you told him that you did *not* want to call the police?"

"He didn't fight it," she said.

"What *did* he do?"

Gina shrugged. "He left."

"What time did he leave?"

"I don't know exactly," she said shaking her head. "Sometime before three o'clock."

"Before three," he repeated, as if to remind the jury that Goss was not murdered until four. The point seemed to register with most of them. "Was he drunk or sober?"

Gina's mouth was getting dry. She sipped some water, then answered, "He still appeared to be a little drunk."

"Did he take anything with him?"

"His car keys."

"Anything else?"

She nodded. "He took the flower with him—the chrysanthemum he found under Cindy's pillow. The one he said was from Eddy Goss."

"And did he say anything at all before he left?"

Gina took a deep breath. "Yes, he"—she looked into her lap—"he said, 'This has got to stop.' "

McCue turned and faced the jury, looking as if he were about to take a bow. "Thank you, Miss Terisi. I have no further questions."

McCue buttoned his jacket over his round belly and returned to his chair. The courtroom filled with the quiet rumble of spectators conferring among themselves, each seeming to confirm to the other that the accused was most definitely guilty as charged.

"Order," said the judge with a bang of her gavel. The courtroom came to a hush. The judge checked the clock on the wall. It was almost five o'clock. "I see no reason to keep the jury any longer today," she said. "We'll resume tomorrow morning with defense counsel's cross-examination of this witness."

"Your Honor," Manny politely interrupted. He had to do something to keep the day from ending on this devastating note. "If I might just begin my cross-examination. Perhaps just twenty minutes—"

"The defense will have all the time it needs—tomorrow. This court is in recess," she announced as she ended the day with another sharp bang of the gavel.

"All rise!" shouted the bailiff, but his instruction was totally unnecessary. Everyone in the courtroom immediately stood and sprung into action. Television reporters rushed to meet five o'clock deadlines. Print journalists ran for the rail, hoping to get an interview with the prosecutor, the defense—or maybe even the government's star witness.

Jack jumped up, too, immediately looking behind him. He needed to say something to Cindy, but she was already gone. She'd darted from her seat the instant Judge Tate's gavel had landed on the block.

He stood beside his chair as he scanned the buzzing courtroom. *Where is she?* He flinched as he felt Manny's hand on his arm. "You and I have to talk," his lawyer said.

Jack sighed. He could barely speak. "Cindy and I have to talk," he said quietly.

Chapter 37

•

Jack raced home as quickly as he could, weaving in and out of rush-hour traffic. He was relieved to see Cindy's car in the driveway. She hadn't left him—at least not yet. He rushed into the house, then froze as he heard the sound of dresser drawers slamming shut in the bedroom.

"What are you doing?" asked Jack as he appeared in the bedroom doorway.

Her half-filled suitcase was lying open across the bed. "What's it look like I'm doing?" she said as she dumped a drawer of panty hose into her suitcase.

He sighed. "It looks like you're doing exactly what I would do. Looks like you're giving me exactly what I deserve. But I'm asking you not to."

She wouldn't even look at him. She just kept packing. "Why shouldn't I leave?"

"Because I'm sorry. You just don't know how sorry I am. You don't know how much I love you."

"Stop it," she glared. "Just *stop* it."

"Cindy," he pleaded, "it's not what you think. You've got to remember: This all happened right after the Goss trial, when everything was so crazy. I was being stalked by some guy who had tried to run me over and who'd just killed Thursday. I'd just come from Goss's apartment after stabbing myself in the hand. And then Gina managed to convince me that I was being naive to think you'd ever come back to me. She told me you and Chet were definitely not going to be 'just friends' over there."

"Hold it," she said, looking at him with utter disbelief. "Are you listening to what you're saying? Less than twelve hours after I left for Italy, you were in bed with my best friend because *you* were afraid that you couldn't trust *me*. That makes a lot of sense, Jack," she said with sarcasm, then resumed packing.

"You don't understand, I was drunk—"

"I don't care. Have you been drunk for the past two months, too? Is that why you didn't tell me about it? Or maybe you just thought it was best for me to hear about it for the first time in a crowded courtroom, so I could be humiliated in front of the entire world."

"I was going to tell you," he said weakly.

"Oh, *were* you? Or did you just think you could sweep this problem under the rug, like you do with all the problems between you and your father? Well, that obviously hasn't worked very well with *that* relationship, has it? And it won't work with me anymore, either. What you and Gina did is bad enough. But keeping it from me is unforgivable," she said, then closed up her suitcase and bolted out the bedroom door.

He stepped out of the way, then followed her down the hall. "Cindy, you can't leave."

"Just watch me," she said as she opened the front door.

"I mean, you can't leave town. You're still under the trial subpoena. It's possible you could be recalled as a witness. And if you don't appear, you'll be in contempt of court."

She shook her head in anger. "Then I'll just move into a hotel."

"Cindy—"

"Good-bye, Jack."

He searched desperately for something to say. "I'm sorry," he called as she headed down the front steps.

She stopped and turned around, her eyes welling as she looked back. "I'm sorry, too," she said bitterly. "Because you *ruined* it, Jack. You just ruined *everything*."

He felt completely empty inside, like a lifeless husk, as he watched her toss her suitcase into the car and pull out of the driveway. He tried to feel *something*, even anger at Gina. But another voice quickly took over. He could hear his father repeating that lesson Jack had never seemed to learn as a boy, probably because Harold Swyteck had tried so hard to teach it to him. It was the same lesson Jack had fired back at his father the night Fernandez was executed. "We're all responsible for our own actions," Jack could hear his father telling him. The memory didn't help Jack with his sense of loss. But somewhere deep inside, he felt a little stronger because of it.

"I'll always love you," he whispered over the lump in his throat as Cindy drove away. "Always."

Chapter 38

•

Harry Swyteck received a full report on the day's events in his Tallahassee office. Gina's testimony was the first he'd heard of Jack's stalker. While the rest of the world took the story as Jack's motive to kill Eddy Goss, he saw it differently, because he also had been harassed before the murder—and he, too, had believed it was Goss.

His first instinct was to make a public statement, but it was quite possible that going public with what had happened to him could *strengthen* the case against Jack. From the jury's standpoint, evidence that both Swytecks were being threatened would only double Jack's motive to kill Goss. And even telling Jack wouldn't be wise, because he'd have to divulge everything he knew when he testified in his own defense.

A knock on the door interrupted his thoughts. "This

just came," his secretary said as she entered his office, handing him a large, sealed envelope. "I didn't want to interrupt, but the courier said it relates to your son's trial."

"Thank you, Paula." It was a brown envelope, with no return address. He was immediately suspicious. He waited for her to disappear behind the closed office door, and then he cautiously slit the seal with his letter opener and peered inside. He paused. Photographs—again. He feared it was more of the same horrible photographs his blackmailer had shown him after his carriage ride in the park. But there was only one photo this time. Slowly, he removed the large black-and-white glossy, then froze. He'd never seen the shot before, but the subject was certainly familiar. It was taken on the night of the murder. It was a photo of the governor walking away from Goss's apartment, after he'd chickened out and decided not to go inside, toting the shoe box full of cash his blackmailer had told him to deliver to apartment 217 at four o'clock in the morning.

His hands shook as he laid the photograph facedown on his desk. Only then did he notice the message on the back. It was a poem—brief, but to the point:

> *One word to your son,*
> *one word to the cops,*
> *we double the fun,*
> *the other shoe drops.*

The governor went rigid in his chair, disgusted by the way he was being manipulated. But he knew exactly what "shoe" would drop. This was one last threat—a solemn promise that if he came forward in defense of his son, the police would shortly come into possession of the wing tips that could connect the governor and his extraneous footprints not only to the murder of Eddy Goss, but to that of Wilfredo Garcia as well. And there was more still: The tape recording of the bribe, the payoff for the victim's photographs—all of it would bring into public focus that this entire tragedy was rooted in the execution of an innocent man.

The governor held his head in his hands, agonizing. He felt compelled to act, yet at the same time paralyzed. He had to make sure he didn't play into the hands of the enemy. He had to figure out a way to help his son—without self-destructing.

Chapter 39

●

Jack didn't want to stay in the empty house after Cindy had left, and he'd lost all appetite for dinner. So he drove to Manny's office to prepare for the next day of the trial.

The first thing he mentioned to his lawyer was Gina's glossing over that he'd had a gun that night he came to her apartment. The question was never asked, and so Gina never answered it. Perhaps she'd sensed that saying anything about the gun would be driving the last nail into Jack's coffin? Maybe that was too much even for Gina.

Manny was as perplexed as Jack. What she *had* said, though, had been devastating. He wanted a powerful cross-examination of Gina, and by ten o'clock that night, the two lawyers had mapped out an impressive assault. Jack feared, however, that it was the kind of legal warfare that could impress only a lawyer. Manny couldn't disagree. They both knew the bottom line. Gina had told the truth. And there was only so far a criminal defense lawyer could push a truthful witness on cross-examination before the jury would start to resent the lawyer *and* his client.

To say the least, Jack wasn't feeling very optimistic when he got home—until he checked his answering machine.

"Jack," came the familiar voice. "It's Gina."

There was a long pause. He turned up the volume, then stood frozen as he listened.

"I think we should talk," she said finally. "Face-to-face. Come by tonight, please. I'm sure I'll be up."

He took a deep breath. He detected no gloating in her tone. No animosity. No seductiveness. Just honesty.

He picked up the phone, then put it down. If he called her, he was afraid she might change her mind. But if he showed up at her door, he was certain she'd talk to him. He grabbed his car keys and rushed out.

Twenty minutes later, Gina opened her front door. She was dressed in soft slippers and a white bathrobe. Her chestnut hair was wet and a little tangled, as if she'd washed it an hour ago, started combing it out, then lost the energy to finish the job. She wore no makeup, and in the same strange way that her toned-down appearance in the courtroom had made her more attractive, she was even prettier now, Jack thought—except for one thing. She looked sad. Very sad.

"Come on in," she said in a subdued voice.

"Thanks." He stepped inside, and she closed the door behind him.

"Something to drink?"

"No, thanks."

"A Jagermeister, maybe?" A smile briefly bloomed on her face, then withered. She crossed the room to a hammock-style chair, sat down, and brought her knees up to her chin. She kept her back to Jack as she enjoyed the balmy breezes that rolled in through the open sliding-glass doors.

Jack took a seat on the couch, on the other side of the cocktail table. They said nothing until Gina turned her head and looked at him plaintively.

"You don't have to tell me if you don't want to," she said. "But what happened with Cindy?"

He hesitated. For a second he felt as if she were intruding. But this wasn't just idle curiosity. She really seemed to care.

"She packed up and left."

"I'm sorry," she said. Then she rolled back her head, closed her eyes, and sniffled. "I don't know why I do the idiotic things I do," her voice cracked. "I really don't."

Jack moved to the edge of his seat. The last thing he'd expected tonight was to be consoling Gina. But he found himself doing it. "Everyone makes mistakes."

She shook her head and suddenly snapped out of her malaise. "Mistakes? Do you have any idea how *many* mistakes I've made? You don't know me, Jack. Nobody knows me. Not even Cindy. Everyone thinks that a great body has gotten me anything I've ever wanted in life. And it did, for a while. When I was sixteen years old, I made over a hundred grand modeling for the Ford Agency. But then the next year I gained twenty pounds and was all washed up—out of work. A real wake-up call, that was. 'Use it while you got it' is what I learned.

But then I learned something else: The more you use it, the more you *get* used. And believe me, there's no shortage of users out there."

He nodded slowly.

"Anyway," her voice quivered. "That's why I called you. I'm through being used. I'm through feeling like shit even when I *try* to do the right thing. Like today. All I did was tell the truth on the witness stand. Yet I feel like *I've* done something wrong."

"You *didn't* mention the gun. I wondered about that."

"Yeah, well, maybe it's because they were licking their chops too much over everything else I told them. I didn't feel like volunteering it, you know?"

"But why volunteer anything? I'm confused."

"Welcome to the club," she said, running her hands through her hair. "They want you to play the game, but they don't tell you the rules."

Jack was confused. "What game?"

She started to speak, then stopped. Finally she said, "The whole charade that landed me in that court-room—*that's* the game. I've been playing it ever since you asked me to be your alibi. Everything I did and said was designed to make you think that I didn't want to get involved—or that if I did get involved, it would be to help you, and not to hurt you. The whole idea was to make sure you'd be totally shocked when I took the stand and testified against you. That was part of my deal."

Jack's eyes narrowed with suspicion. "Your deal with who?"

"With that cop, Stafford," she said, then looked away

in shame. "The truth," she said with a lump in her throat, "is that right after you were indicted, he came over to question me. I let the creep use my bathroom, and he comes out saying he just saw enough amphetamines sitting out in plain view to put me away for years. I use them to lose weight. It's not smart, but I do it. Anyway, he said he wouldn't bring any charges if I'd help him out. And all I did was tell him the truth. It's just the sneaky way he made me do it that has me so disgusted. I mean, how do you think the prosecutor knew every little detail about the morning Cindy left you? She told me all about it. And I told Stafford. And then Cindy got creamed on the witness stand."

Jack felt a rush of anger, but he kept cool—because a tremendous opportunity was within his grasp. "Gina," he said in a calm, understanding tone, "this is important. What Stafford made you do isn't just sleazy. It's illegal. The prosecution has violated the law by failing to tell Manny and me that Stafford cut a deal with a government witness. This could get the whole case against me dismissed. The trial could be over tomorrow. I could go *free*."

"What do you want me to do?" she asked cautiously.

"All I want you to do is to get on the witness stand tomorrow morning and say exactly what you told me. That's it. Just tell the truth."

"And then what happens to *me?* I'll go to jail on drug charges?"

He thought fast. "The state will have to honor its deal with you. Stafford made the promise. You've already lived up to your end. You told the truth. It's Stafford's fault if it blows up in his face, not yours."

"I don't know—"

"Gina," he pressed. "You've told the truth so far. I respect you for that. But if you told the truth for Stafford, the least you can do is tell the truth for me."

She sighed. "This is so crazy. But in the last twenty-four hours, it's like I've suddenly got this feeling that it's time to start making up for all the lies I've told my entire life. I just feel like it's time to tell the truth."

"The truth is best," he said. "Even when it hurts."

She swallowed hard. "All right. I'll do it."

Jack's heart was in his throat. "In fact, why don't I call Manny now, and we can go over some things—"

"No. I don't want to do this according to a script."

"I understand," he said, sensing that he shouldn't push too hard.

Gina rose. "I'll see you at the courthouse at eight-thirty," she said, leading him out. "Right now, I need some sleep."

He nodded in agreement. "I'll see you then," he said as they reached the door.

She laid her hand on his shoulder and stopped him. "I'm sorry about you and Cindy," she said. "I really am."

"Thanks," he said.

As he drove home, he was barely conscious of the tires gripping the road. He felt like he was floating on air. His conversation with Gina had made him feel alive again. Suddenly he felt hope.

Chapter 40

•

At 3:30 A.M., just as Jack and Manny had finished planning a case-saving cross-examination of Gina Ter-isi, bare-breasted women were dancing one last set at Jiggles, a rundown, smoke-filled strip joint where stiff drinks came as cheap as the thrills. A buxom black woman wearing only spike heels and a holster was lit by an orangey-red spotlight as she strutted up and down the long bar top, thrusting her hips to the delight of the drunk and howling crowd each time the rap vocalist on the jukebox screamed "I like big butts!" Around the room women danced on little round tables, each wearing only boots or bow ties or maybe a Stetson, and all of them wearing a garter on one thigh so the men they teased could stuff them with cash and extend their fantasies.

Just before closing, a tall, broad-shouldered man

with a clean-shaved head and a diamond-stud earring presented himself at the entrance. A bearded bouncer who looked like he was moonlighting from the pro wrestling tour stepped in front of him. "We close in fifteen minutes," he said.

"That's all the time I need," the man replied as he started inside. The bouncer grabbed him by the shoulder.

"Ten-dollar cover, chief."

"Shee-it." But he was in a hurry, so he paid it and stepped inside. He looked around the room, first checking the bar top and then each individual table for the woman he knew as Rebecca. She knew him as Buzz, a name she'd given him not simply because of his shaved head, but because of his whole look. She said his hook nose, folds of leathery skin, and skinny neck made him look like a buzzard. Especially at night, when his eyes were bloodshot. Rebecca usually worked until closing, but Buzz didn't see her anywhere. Then his eyes lit up as he saw her standing by the cigarette machine, having a smoke.

She had short, wavy hair—black, this week—and the best body of all the dancers. She was dressed tonight, or as dressed as women ever got here. A sleeveless V-neck undershirt with the neck-line ripped down to her navel revealed ample cleavage and a long chain necklace as thick as a dog leash. Tight black leather shorts with silver studs on the pockets were cut up to the middle of her round rear end, and shiny patent-leather boots rose up to the butterfly tattoo on her inner thigh. He caught her eye from across the room and walked over to her.

"I'm done for the night," she said, blowing smoke in his face.

He shook his head, as if he knew better. "How much?"

"Three hundred."

"Fuck you."

"That would be extra."

He emptied his pants pockets. "I got a hundred sixty dollars. Take it or leave it."

"Deal." She snatched the money and stuffed it into the top of her boot. "But I ain't goin' back to the car with you for no hundred sixty. We do it in here."

"Here?" he winced.

"Over there," she said, pointing to a dark and isolated corner. "Meet you there."

He nodded in agreement, then headed for the corner. Rebecca stepped up to the bar. "The crazy-man's usual," she told the bartender. "Margarita, just salt." The bartender smirked and handed her a glass filled only with margarita salt, moistened with a squirt of lemon juice. "Thanks," she said, then strutted toward the darkest corner of the bar.

"I missed you," he said when she returned.

Rebecca put the glass on the table, threw her shoulders back, and placed her hands on her hips. "Don't talk shit," she barked like a drill sergeant.

"You're right," he said in a husky whisper. "I've been bad."

"Just as I thought," she spat, her voice growing menacing. "You know what happens when you're bad."

He nodded hungrily.

She raised her index finger, stuck it in her mouth, and sucked it sensually, from base to tip. She immersed it in the glass of lemony margarita salt and stirred, then removed it and held it before his eyes. The crystals stuck to her moistened finger. "How bad were you?" she demanded.

He got down on his knees and looked up sheepishly. "Very bad," he assured her.

Slowly, she lowered her coated finger and rubbed the salt deep into his eye. He cringed and moaned, his head rolling back with perverse pleasure. His intermittent cries of pain were drowned out by the loud music. She knew he liked her to remain tough, but she had to fight to keep a look of fear from crossing her face. She'd seen men approach ecstasy in the bar before, usually the creeps who got tossed out for masturbating. But he was beyond ecstasy. This was utter rapture.

He regained his composure, still on his knees. He looked up at her through his one good eye. The other was puffy and closed. Lemon and salty tears streamed down his cheek. For a hundred sixty bucks, he knew he'd have her for at least another song. "Put the salt away," he said. "I've been very, very bad."

Rebecca sighed; she knew what that meant. She lit up another cigarette. "What did you do?"

He took a deep breath, then with his left hand he reached deep inside his pocket and discreetly squeezed a handkerchief that contained two bloody nipples. "Nothing I haven't done before," he whispered, a thin smile coming to his face. Then his body jerked and his head rolled back in another fit of ecstasy, as Rebecca crushed out the glowing end of her cigarette in the burn-scarred palm of his right hand.

Chapter 41

•

Jack and Manny arrived in the crowded courtroom just before nine that morning. Jack was a bit worried that he hadn't been able to spot Gina in the courthouse lobby earlier, but he told himself that she must have been delayed. She'd show up, he was sure. Something in her eyes the night before convinced him that she was determined to set the record straight.

Quite quickly, though, he sensed something was wrong. McCue, who normally arrived early, was conspicuously absent from the courtroom, and the bailiff seemed to have disappeared as well.

Ten minutes passed. The murmur of the spectators built as there was still no sign of the prosecutor. Finally the bailiff appeared, showing no expression as he stepped up to the defense table. "Mr. Cardenal," he said politely, "Judge Tate would like to see you and Mr. Swyteck in her chambers."

Jack's heart sank as he and Manny exchanged glances. This was not standard procedure. Something had to be wrong. "All right," said Manny, and they followed the bailiff to a side exit.

The judge's chambers had the air of a funeral parlor. Judge Tate sat in the leather chair behind her imposing desk, framed by the state and American flags. Wilson McCue sat in an armchair to her left, before a wall of law books. Their expressions were somber.

"Good morning," said Manny as he entered the room.

"Please sit down," the judge said formally, her tone suggesting that this was *very* serious.

Jack and Manny sat in the Naugahyde chairs facing McCue. Jack swallowed hard, fearing the worst—perhaps some wild accusation that he had threatened Gina. The judge folded her hands on her desk and leaned forward to speak.

"Mr. McCue has just informed me that Gina Terisi is dead," she said.

"What?" Manny uttered with disbelief.

"She was murdered," said the prosecutor.

"That can't be," Jack said, stunned.

"Mr. Swyteck," said the judge, "you would be advised to remain silent."

He sat back in his chair. The judge was right.

Judge Tate glanced at Manny, then at McCue. "I am not trying to be cold or unsympathetic, gentlemen, but I didn't assemble this group to discuss the how and why of Ms. Terisi's murder. The purpose of this meeting is to decide what impact the murder will have on Mr.

Swyteck's trial. Fortunately, we have a sequestered jury, so they won't hear anything about it."

"But, Your Honor," said Manny, "the jury has already heard the witness's testimony, and now I won't have an opportunity to cross-examine her. My client can't get a fair trial under these circumstances. The court has no choice but to declare a mistrial. We have to start all over again—without Gina Terisi."

McCue slid to the edge of his chair, unable to contain himself. "Judge," he implored. "I knew they'd try to pull this. You *can't* grant a mistrial. You'd be playing right into their hands. Look at the sequence here, Judge. And look at the motive. This is no coincidence. The government was building an ironclad case. Gina Terisi devastated Mr. Swyteck on the witness stand. And then a few hours later she turns up dead. Now, you don't have to be a genius to see—"

"That's an outrageous suggestion!" said Manny.

"The hell it is!" McCue fired back. "Swyteck's car was spotted at Gina Terisi's last night."

Jack's jaw dropped. "Now wait just a minute—"

"Gentlemen!" the judge barked. "That's enough."

There was silence. The prosecution and defense exchanged glares. Jack glanced at the judge, then looked away. Judge Tate was no easy read, but her suspicious eyes had revealed a glimpse of her feelings. And Jack didn't like what he saw.

"I will not declare a mistrial," she announced, shaking her head. "Mr. Swtyeck's trial will proceed. However, Miss Terisi's testimony will be stricken. I will instruct the jury that it must disregard her testimony, and I will further instruct them that they are to draw no inferences whatever from the fact that she has not returned to the courtroom."

"Judge," Manny argued, "a curative instruction isn't going to help anything. The jury has already heard her testimony. You can't tell them to ignore it. That's like telling a shark to ignore the blood."

"Mr. Cardenal," she said sternly, "I've made my decision."

McCue's face was aglow. "It may go without saying, Judge," he said in his folksy manner, "but I presume that Ms. Terisi's disappearance would be fair game on cross-examination, assumin' Mr. Swyteck were to take the witness stand in his own defense. The court's instruction will not curtail my ability to question him about that, will it?"

The judge leaned back in her chair, thinking. "I hadn't thought about that. But I would have to agree with you, Mr. McCue. If Mr. Swyteck takes the witness stand, the door is open. You're free to question him."

Manny shook his head incredulously. Even the judge, it seemed, had concluded that Jack was guilty. "Your Honor, you have just made it impossible for Mr. Swyteck to testify on his own behalf. I can't put him on the stand if you're going to allow the prosecutor to suggest that my client murdered the government's star witness. Your ruling is a death sentence. I strenuously object and urge you to reconsider—"

"That's all," said the judge, heading off any further argument. "You understand my position. Now, I'm giving both the prosecution and defense twenty-four hours to regroup. We shall reconvene at nine o'clock tomorrow morning. Mr. McCue, be prepared to call your next witness. Thank you, gentlemen," she said with finality.

"Thank *you*," McCue told the judge.

The lawyers rose and turned away. Jack stood more slowly, in a state of disbelief. He followed his lawyer down the hall, past the water cooler. Neither said a word until they reached the exit and McCue caught up with them.

"Better circle your wagons, Swyteck," the old prosecutor said sarcastically, all trace of his good-old-boy accent having vanished. "Because if you don't get the electric chair for killing Eddy Goss, you can bet I'll be coming after you for the murder of Gina Terisi." He nodded smugly, like a gentleman tipping his hat, then headed out the door.

Jack stood in the open doorway, looking at his lawyer with dismay. "This can't be happening," he said quietly. But it was. Innocent people kept getting killed. Fernandez, Garcia, now Gina—and Jack, it seemed, was next in line. The only thing more unfathomable was the *reason* it was happening—why his life, like Gina's, might end before his thirtieth birthday. Never to be a husband or a father . . . never to achieve his dreams—for the first time since the trial began, the weight, the enormity of what was at stake pressed down on him, nearly crushing him with its load.

Being convicted. A death sentence. The electric chair. All those things had seemed so abstract before, but suddenly they were palpable, real. A memory came to him—of lying in bed as a young boy and trying to scare himself, trying to imagine what death felt like. He'd picture himself crouched over a hole in the earth, a dark hole. And then he'd see himself falling into it. It

was a descent that never ended. Nothing could stop
it . . .

He shook off the memory and tried to focus. What
had the stalker said when he attacked Jack on the bus?
Something about "innocent people" getting hurt if he
turned to others for help. He looked at Manny with apprehension, then sprinted down the hall to a bank of pay
phones near the rest rooms. He quickly dialed Cindy's
work number.

He nearly fainted with relief as the sound of her
voice came on the line. "Thank God you're all right."

"I just heard about Gina," she said. "Her brother
called me."

"They're saying I did it."

"They're liars," she said. "The things that animal did
to her . . ." She shuddered. "No sane human being
would *do* that."

He didn't know the details, but he didn't have to ask.
"*Please*, be careful," he said, "I'm worried about you. If
there's anything you need or want, just call me."

"I'll be all right," she said. "Really, I will."

He wanted to say something else, anything, to keep
her on the line, but words eluded him.

"Good luck," she said, meaning it.

"Thanks," he said softly. "Cindy, I—"

"I know," she said, "you don't have to say it."

"I love you," he blurted out.

He heard what he thought was a sob on the other end
of the line, and then she said, "Good-bye, Jack."

Chapter 42

•

"**C**all your next witness, Mr. McCue," Judge Tate announced from the bench.

Trial had reconvened at nine o'clock, Wednesday. As promised, the judge had instructed the jurors that they were to disregard Gina Terisi's testimony and that they were to infer nothing from her failure to return to the courtroom to complete her testimony. The instruction, of course, had evoked nothing but suspicious glares from the jury—all of them directed at the defense. With that, the government spent the morning with some technical witnesses, then moved directly after lunch to its final big witness—an experienced fighter who could hardly wait to take his best punch at Eddy Goss's staggering lawyer.

"The State calls Lonzo Stafford," said McCue.

The packed courtroom was silent as Detective

Stafford marched down the center aisle, the click of his heels on the marble floor echoing throughout. After taking the oath and stating his name and occupation, Stafford allowed himself to be guided by McCue in a summary of the physical evidence against Jack Swyteck.

Stafford's testimony unfolded like a script: The defendant's fingerprints matched those on the steak knife in Goss's kitchen; twenty-seven footprints matched the tread on his Reeboks; his blood type matched the blood on the blade; Mr. Swyteck appeared nervous and edgy the next day, when Detective Stafford interviewed him; he had scratches on his back and a bruise on his ribs, as if he'd been in a scuffle; and Swyteck knew that Goss had been killed by gunshot before the detectives had mentioned anything about a shooting. And, just as McCue had planned, the witness saved the best for last.

"When you say Goss was killed by gunshot," asked McCue, "what kind of gun do mean, exactly?"

"It was a handgun. A thirty-eight-caliber, for sure. And there was definitely a silencer on it."

"Was the murder weapon ever found?"

"Not the gun, no. However, we did locate the silencer."

"And where did you find the silencer that was used to kill Eddy Goss?"

Stafford's eyes brightened as he looked right at Jack. "We retrieved it from Mr. Swyteck's vehicle."

A murmur filled the courtroom. The jurors glanced at each other, as if the case were all but over.

"No further questions," said the prosecutor. He turned and glanced at counsel for the defense. "Your witness," he said, dripping with confidence.

Manuel Cardenal was at his best in the spotlight, and this one was white-hot. His client, the jurors, the packed gallery, and especially the witness were filled with anticipation, everyone wondering if the skilled defense counsel could rescue his client. Manny stepped to within ten feet of the government's final witness and stared coldly at his target. "Detective Stafford," he began, "let's start by talking about the alleged victim in this case, shall we?"

"Whatever you want, counselor."

"Anyone who is alive and breathing in this town has heard of Eddy Goss," said Manny. "We all know the awful things Mr. Goss was alleged to have done. And we all know that Mr. Swyteck was his lawyer. But there's one thing I want to make clear for the jury: You were personally involved in the investigation that led to Mr. Goss's arrest, were you not?"

"Yes," he replied, knowing he was being toyed with. "I was the lead detective in the Goss case."

"You personally interrogated Mr. Goss, didn't you?"

"I did."

"In fact, you elicited a full confession from Mr. Goss. A confession on videotape."

"That's right."

"But that confession wasn't used at Mr. Goss's trial."

"No," he answered quietly. "It was ruled inadmissible."

"It was ruled inadmissible because you broke the rules," said Manny, his tone judgmental.

Stafford drew a sigh, controlling his anger. "The judge found that I had violated Mr. Goss's *constitutional rights*," he said, spitting out the words sarcastically.

"And it was Mr. Swyteck who pointed out your violation to the court, wasn't it?"

Stafford leaned forward, his eyes narrowing. "He *exploited* it."

Manny stepped to one side, closer to the jury, as if he were on their side. "That must have been very embarrassing for you, Detective."

"It was a travesty of justice," replied Stafford, using the words the prosecutor had coached him with the night before.

Manny smirked, sensing that he was getting under Stafford's skin. Then he approached the witness and handed him an exhibit. "This is a copy of a newspaper article from June of this year, marked as Defendant's Exhibit 1. It reports certain pretrial developments in the case against Eddy Goss. Could you read the bold headline to us, please? Nice and loud," he added, gesturing toward the jurors, "so we all can hear."

Stafford scowled at his interrogator, then cleared his throat and reluctantly read aloud: "Judge throws out Goss confession."

"And the trailer, too," said Manny. "Read the little trailer underneath the headline."

Stafford's face reddened with anger. "Seasoned cop botched interrogation," he read. Then he laid the newspaper on the rail in front of him and glared at Manny.

"And that's your photograph there beneath the headline, isn't it, sir?"

"That's my picture," he confirmed.

"In forty years of police work, Mr. Stafford, had you *ever* gotten your picture on the front page of the newspaper?"

"Just this once," Stafford grunted.

"In forty years," Manny continued, "had you ever screwed up a case this bad?"

"Objection," said McCue.

"I didn't screw it up," Stafford said sharply, too eager to defend himself to wait for the judge to rule.

"Overruled," said the judge.

"I'm sorry," Manny said, feigning an apology. "In forty years, had you ever been *blamed* for a screw-up this bad?"

"Never," he croaked.

"Yet, there you are, page one, section A, in probably the least flattering mug shot the newsroom could dig up: the 'seasoned cop' who 'botched the interrogation.' " Manny moved closer, crouching somewhat, as if digging for the truth. "Who do you blame for that?" he pressed. "Do you blame yourself, Detective?"

Stafford glared at his interrogator. "At first I did."

"But you don't blame yourself anymore, do you," said Manny.

Stafford fell silent—he knew exactly where Manny was headed. "Come on, Detective. We *know* who you *really* blame. *This* is the man you blame," said Manny, pointing toward his client, his voice much louder now. "Isn't it!"

Stafford glanced at Jack, then looked back at Manny. "So what," he scoffed.

Manny locked eyes with the witness. "Yes or no, Detective. Do you blame Mr. Swyteck for your own public disgrace?"

Stafford stared right back, hating this lawyer almost

as much as he hated Jack. "Yeah," he said bitterly. "I do blame him. Him and Goss. Both of them. They're no different in my eyes."

Manny paused, allowing the answer to linger. A quiet murmur passed through the courtroom as Manny's point struck home.

"But that doesn't make it okay for Swyteck to kill him," Stafford blurted, seeming to sense that he was in trouble.

"Let's talk about that," replied Manny. "Let's talk about just who *did* kill Eddy Goss. The time of Mr. Goss's death was about four A.M., right?"

"Yes," replied Stafford.

"What time did you get to the police station that morning?"

"Five-fifteen," he answered, "same as always."

"Can anyone corroborate where you were before then?"

"No. I live alone."

Manny nodded, as if to emphasize Stafford's response, then forged ahead. "Now, after you arrived at work that morning, an anonymous phone call came in to the station, right?"

"I don't know what you mean," Stafford played dumb. "We get lots of calls—"

"I'm not talking about *lots* of calls," Manny bore in. "I'm talking about the caller who reported that someone in a police uniform was seen leaving Goss's apartment about the time of the murder."

"Yes," he answered. "Someone did call and report that."

"You used to be a patrolman, didn't you?"

"Yes. Twenty-eight years, before I became a detective."

"And I'll bet you still have your old police uniform," said Manny.

Stafford fell silent. "Yes," he answered quietly.

"I thought so," said Manny. "Now, Eddy Goss was shot twice in the head, at close range, was he not?"

"That's right."

"Thirty-eight-caliber bullets."

"Correct," said Stafford.

"You carry a thirty-eight-caliber, don't you, Detective?"

"Eighty percent of the police force does," Stafford snapped.

"Including *you*."

"Yes," he grudgingly conceded.

Manny paused again, allowing time for suspicion to fill the jury box, and then he continued his roll. "Now, after Mr. Goss was killed by not just one, but two gunshots, you interviewed all the neighbors in the apartment building, didn't you?"

"I did."

"And not *one* of those neighbors heard any gunshots."

Stafford was silent again. "No," he finally answered, "no one heard a gunshot."

"And that was one of the reasons you suspected that a silencer had been used to kill Goss."

"That's correct," he said. Then he took a free shot. "And we found a silencer in your client's car," he added smugly.

Manny nodded slowly. "How convenient," he said sarcastically, his eyebrow arching. "But let's take a closer look at that incredible stroke of luck, Detective. Let's talk about how, incredibly, you seemed to have found the one man in the world who was smart enough to be graduated summa cum laude from Yale University, yet stupid enough to leave a silencer under the front seat of his car."

"Objection," McCue groaned.

"Sustained."

Manny pressed on, unfazed. "You, personally, did not find that silencer in Mr. Swyteck's car. Did you, Detective?"

"No."

"You got it from a patrolwoman, isn't that right?"

"Yes."

"And she got it from the owner of Kaiser Auto Repair—the shop where Mr. Swyteck's convertible top was being fixed."

"That's right."

"And the owner of the shop got it from one of his mechanics."

Stafford's eyes narrowed. "Yeah."

"Am I leaving anybody out, Detective?"

Stafford just glared. "No," he said angrily.

"What do you mean, *no*," Manny rebuked him. "You didn't stand guard over Mr. Swyteck's car while it was in the repair shop, did you?"

"No."

"So," said Manny, pacing before the jury, "as far as you know, scores of people could have come and gone from Mr. Swyteck's car over the two-day period it was in the shop."

"I don't know," he evaded.

"Precisely," said Manny, as if it were the answer he wanted. "You *don't know*. Or, to put it another way, maybe you have a reasonable doubt."

"Objection," McCue shouted.

"Overruled."

"I don't know who went into his car," Stafford snarled. "That's all."

"Isn't it possible, Detective, that any one of the people walking by or fixing Mr. Swyteck's car could have put the silencer there?"

"Objection," McCue groaned. "Calls for speculation."

"Let me ask it another way," said Manny. He stepped closer, moving in for the kill. "Detective Stafford: Do you happen to own a silencer for your own thirty-eight-caliber pistol?"

"I object!" shouted McCue. "Your Honor, this is insulting! The suggestion that Detective Stafford would—"

"Overruled," said the judge. It wasn't the first time she had seen a defense lawyer turn a cop inside out. "Answer the question, Detective Stafford."

The courtroom fell deadly silent, awaiting the detective's answer. "Yes," he conceded. "I do."

Manny nodded, checking the jurors to make sure the response had registered. It had. He started back to his chair, then stopped, pointing a professorial finger in the air. "Just one more question, Detective," he said as he turned back toward the witness. "When I asked you who you blamed for your own public disgrace, you did say *both* Jack Swyteck *and* Eddy Goss—didn't you?"

"Objection," shouted McCue. "The question was asked and answered."

"Withdrawn," said Manny, smiling with his eyes at the jurors. "I think we all heard it the first time. No further questions. Thank you, sir."

"The witness is excused," the judge announced.

Stafford remained in his chair, his face frozen with disbelief. He'd been coveting this moment—his opportunity for revenge against Jack Swyteck, the lawyer who'd humiliated him. The last laugh was supposed to have been his. But a lawyer had humiliated him again. He'd been more than humiliated. This time he wasn't just the stupid cop who'd botched the investigation. He'd been painted as the *bad* cop who'd done the deed. He'd been pushed too far—and he wasn't going to just sit there and take it.

"It's irrelevant, you know," he groused at Manny, as if no one else were in the courtroom.

"You are excused," the judge instructed the witness in a firm voice.

"It wasn't my silencer that was used to kill Goss," he said angrily.

"*Detective,*" the judge rebuked him. But Stafford was determined to have his say.

"It was the silencer we found in Swyteck's convertible!"

"Detective!" the judge banged her gavel.

"Swyteck's silencer was used on Goss," he shouted, "and he used a silencer to kill Gina Terisi, too!"

"Your Honor!" Manny bellowed, rising to his feet. "Your Honor, may I approach the bench? I have a motion to make."

The judge held up her hand, stopping Manny in his tracks. She knew what he wanted—that she declare a mistrial. And if all the other evidence against Jack Swyteck hadn't been so strong, she would have done it. But she was not going to throw out the state's entire case just because one witness had lost his temper and spouted something he shouldn't have.

"Save your motion, Mr. Cardenal," she said. Then she turned toward the jurors. "Ladies and gentlemen of the jury," she said in a very serious tone, "I am instructing you to disregard that last outburst. Those remarks are not evidence in this case. As I instructed you earlier, you are not to draw any inference whatsoever from the fact that Ms. Terisi did not return to the courtroom to complete her testimony against the defendant."

Jack's heart sank as, yet again, he listened to the judge deliver the dreaded "curative instruction." It was any criminal defendant's nightmare. In theory, the instruction was supposed to "cure" any mistake at trial by telling the jury to disregard it. In reality it was, as lawyers often said, like trying to "unring" a bell. Jack knew the bottom line. Manny's beautiful cross-examination had been ruined. The *only* thing the jury would remember was what the judge insisted they forget.

"As for you, Mr. McCue," the judge's reprimand continued, "Detective Stafford is your witness, and I'm holding you responsible, at least in part. Five-hundred-dollar fine!" she barked. "And Detective Stafford, you're an experienced officer of the law. You know better. Why don't you spend a night in the county jail to think about what you've done. And next time," she warned, pointing menacingly with her gavel, "I won't be so lenient. Bailiff," she said with finality, "take the witness away."

The bailiff stepped forward and led Stafford from

the witness stand. He should have been ashamed, but he was looking at Jack and smiling. Jack looked away, but Stafford wasn't going to let him off easy. He stopped, rested his hand on the table at which Jack was seated and looked him right in the eye. "I'll save a seat for ya, Swyteck," he whispered, loud enough only for Jack and the bailiff to hear.

"Detective," the judge said sternly. "On your way!"

Jack looked up at Stafford but said nothing. The detective flashed a thin smile, then the bailiff tugged his arm and they headed for the exit.

"Mr. McCue," the judge intoned, "do you have any more witnesses?"

McCue rose slowly, resting his fists on his chest with contentment, his thumbs tucked inside the lapels. "Your Honnuh," he said, speaking like a Southern gentlemen, "on that note, the State most respectfully rests."

"Very well," she announced. "We'll reconvene tomorrow, nine o'clock sharp. Mr. Cardenal: If you plan to put on a defense, be prepared to proceed. If not, we'll conclude with closing arguments. Court's in recess," she said, then banged her gavel.

The crowd rose at the bailiff's instruction and stood in silence as the jury filed out of the courtroom. Jack and Manny exchanged glances as the judge stepped down from the bench. The irony of her comments wasn't lost on either of them. The fact was, as they both so painfully knew, that it wasn't at all clear the defense *had* a defense.

Chapter 43

•

At six o'clock the next morning, Governor Harold Swyteck was in his robe and slippers, shaving before a steamy bathroom mirror, when he heard a ring on the portable phone in his briefcase. It was the same phone he'd been given in Miami's Bayfront Park. Realizing who was calling, the governor gave a start and nicked himself with the blade.

Annoyed, he dabbed his shaving wound with a washcloth, then dashed from the bathroom, grabbed the phone from his briefcase, and disappeared into the walk-in closet, so as not to wake his sleeping wife. "Hello," he said, sounding slightly out of breath.

"Me again, Governor," came the thick but now familiar voice.

Harry bristled with anger, but he wasn't totally surprised by the call. Clever as this maniac was, he seemed to thrive on letting his victims know how much he enjoyed their suffering, like a gardener who planted a rare seed and then had to dig it up to make sure it was growing.

"What do you want now?" he answered. "A pair of argyle socks to go with your wing tips?"

"My, my," came a condescending reply. "Aren't we testy this morning. And all just because you're gonna have to sign your own son's death warrant."

"My son is *not* going to be convicted."

"Oh, no? Seems to me that his last chance at getting off is lying on a slab in the morgue. I'm sure you've heard that the fox who testified against him had him over for a little chat—and then ended up a bloody mess on her bedroom floor. Too bad, because if you happened to be the eavesdropping type"—he snickered, remembering how he'd perched outside her sliding-glass doors—"you'd know that she was going to get back on the stand and bail him out of trouble."

"I knew it was you," Harry said in a voice that mixed frustration with outrage. "You butchered that poor girl."

"Jack Swyteck butchered her. I told him the rules. It's just me against him. I warned him that whoever tried to help him was dead meat. He went and asked for the bitch's help anyway. That son of yours did it again, Governor. He killed another innocent person."

Harry shook with anger. "Listen to me, you sick son of a bitch. If you want your revenge for Raul Fernandez, go ahead and take it. But don't take it out on my son. *I'm* the one responsible."

"Now, isn't that noble—the loving father who's willing to sacrifice himself for his son. But I'm not stupid"—his voice turned bitter—"I know Jacky Boy didn't even make an effort. If he had, his own father would have listened to him in a heartbeat."

Harry sighed. *You'd think so, unless that father were a pigheaded fool.*

"You're not going to get away with this," Harry said firmly.

"And just who's gonna stop me, Governor?"

"I am."

"You *can't*. Not unless you want to turn the case of *State* versus *Swyteck* into *State* versus *Harold Swyteck*. And not unless you want the whole world to know you've been paying off a blackmailer to cover up the execution of an innocent man. Didn't you get the point of my poetry, my man? You're as powerless to save your son as I was to save Raul."

The governor's hands began trembling. "You bastard. You despicable *bastard*."

"Sticks and stones—well, I think now you get the point. Gotta go, my man. Big day ahead of me. Should be a guilty verdict coming down in the Swyteck case."

"You listen to me! I won't allow my son—" he said before stopping midsentence. The caller had hung up.

"Damn you!" He pitched the phone aside. He was boiling mad, but he was feeling much more than that. He was scared. Not for himself, but for Jack.

He turned and saw his wife standing in the doorway.

"It was him again, wasn't it?" she asked.

Sensing her fear, he took her in his arms and held her close. "Agnes," he asked with a sigh, still holding her, "would you still love me if I weren't the governor of Florida?"

"Of course I would, Harry," she replied without hesitation. "Why would you ask such a silly question?"

He broke their embrace and stepped back, pondering his next move. "Because I think I've made a decision."

Chapter 44

•

At twenty minutes past nine, Judge Tate's cavernous courtroom was packed with thirty rows of spectators, yet quiet enough to hear the scratch of a reporter's pencil on his pad. Trial had been scheduled to begin at nine, but the jury had yet to be seated. Judge Tate presided on the bench with hands folded, her dour expression making it clear she was infuriated by the delay. The prosecutor sat erect and confident at the table closest to the empty jury box, pleased that the judge's wrath would soon befall his opponent. Jack was seated at the other side of the courtroom—nervous, confused, and alone.

"Mr. Swyteck," Judge Tate demanded from the bench, her tone more threatening than inquisitive, "just *where* is your lawyer?"

Jack rose slowly. Manny had phoned him a few minutes before nine and told him to stall until he got there.

That made Jack the sacrificial lamb, for he knew the one thing that absolutely incensed Judge Tate was a lawyer who kept her waiting. "Your Honor," he said apprehensively, "I'm sure there's an excellent explanation for Mr. Cardenal's tardiness."

Judge Tate scowled, but before she could tell Jack just how excellent his lawyer's explanation had better be, the double mahogany doors in the back of the courtroom flew open and Manny walked down the center aisle. The steady tap of his heels echoed over the quiet murmur of the crowd.

"You're late, counselor," the judge said severely.

"I apologize, Your Honor," Manny said as he passed through the swinging gate on the rail, "but there was a last-minute development—"

"Two-hundred-dollar fine, Mr. Cardenal! Bailiff, call in the jury!"

"Your Honor," he pleaded, "could I please have a word with my client? Just a couple minutes is all I need."

"All rise!" came the bailiff's announcement, and with it Manny's plea was drowned out by the shuffle of six hundred spectators rising to their feet. The jurors filed in and took their seats. The bailiff called the court to session, proclaiming "God save this honorable court." The judge bid a pleasant "good morning" to everyone, then turned to the defense.

"Mr. Cardenal," she said with an unfriendly smile, "will you be putting on a defense?"

Manny swallowed hard. He'd been meeting with his witness all morning, but Jack still knew nothing about it. It was Manny's duty to inform his client what was going on. "Your Honor, if I could have just a brief recess."

"Obviously you didn't hear me," she interrupted. "I asked you a question, Mr. Cardenal: Will there be a defense?"

He nodded. "I may have one witness, Your Honor, but—"

"Call your witness, or rest your case. And I mean it. You've kept us waiting long enough."

Manny took a deep breath. He wanted Jack's approval, but there was no time for discussion.

"Mr. Cardenal," the judge pressed, "we're waiting."

Manny paused, his eyes locking with Jack's for a moment. Jack gave a quick nod, as if he instinctively sensed that whatever Manny had planned was the right thing to do. Manny smiled briefly, then looked up at the judge. "If it please the court," he announced in a resounding voice, "the defense calls Governor Harold Swyteck."

A wave of surprise hit the courtroom like a huge breaker on the beach. The heavy wood doors in the rear of the courtroom swung open, and in walked a tall, handsome man whose gold cuff links and graying around the temples added color and distinction to a dark suit and crisp white shirt. Harold Swyteck never just appeared. He was the kind of man who made an appearance. Being governor amplified that trait. Being both governor *and* the surprise witness in his own son's murder trial made *this* the appearance of a lifetime.

The courtroom was electric yet silent as the governor came down the aisle. As he passed, heads turned in row after row like a wheat field bending in the breeze. Everyone knew who he was, but no one knew what he would say—not even Jack. A strange sensation filled the courtroom as he stepped to the witness stand and swore the oath. It was as if the bailiff had stood up and officially announced that the young man on trial was indeed the governor's son. The prosecutor's gut wrenched. The jurors stared in anticipation. Jack's heart filled with hope and with something else, too—something pleasant, if unfamiliar: genuine pride.

"Good morning," Manny greeted the distinguished witness from behind the lectern. "If you would, sir, please introduce yourself to the jury."

The governor swiveled in his chair and faced the jurors. "I'm Harold Swyteck," he said cordially. "Most people call me Harry."

A few jurors showed faint smiles of familiarity. If it were possible for one man to look at twelve people simultaneously and make each one of them feel like the only person on the planet who mattered, Harold Swyteck was doing it. He responded directly to them after each of Manny's introductory questions, as if the jurors, not the lawyer, were eliciting the testimony.

"Now, Governor," said Manny, marking the transition from introductory questions to more substantive testimony, "I want to focus on the events that took place immediately after the trial of Eddy Goss. Did anything out of the ordinary happen to you?"

The governor took a deep breath, glanced at Jack, and then looked back at the jury. "Yes," he replied solemnly. "I was attacked."

"You were *what*?" the judge asked. The stunned reaction was the same throughout the courtroom.

Jack watched with concern as his father explained

not just the attack, but also the reason for it. Harry admitted that his attacker had blackmailed him and that he had paid the man thousands of dollars.

And then he explained why.

"The man threatened to reveal that I'd executed an innocent man," he said. His voice was low and subdued. His eyes filled with remorse. "A man named Raul Fernandez."

A buzz of whispers filled the courtroom. Reporters scribbled down the new name, some of them recalling it from the outburst at the governor's press conference. Every word was another nail in the governor's political coffin.

"Order," said the judge, banging her gavel.

Jack went cold. Long ago, he'd come to the conclusion that he and his father would never discuss Fernandez again, not even privately. His public confession was overwhelming—and a bit confusing, really, until Manny's next line of questioning brought it all into focus.

"Did you come to any conclusion, Governor, about the identity of the man who was threatening you?"

"Yes," he said with conviction. "I firmly believed it was Eddy Goss."

The whispering throughout the courtroom became a quiet rumble. Jurors exchanged glances. No one seemed quite sure whether to feel sympathy or suspicion.

"Order!" the judge intoned, more loudly this time, and with a few more cracks of the gavel.

Manny waited for the courtroom to settle, then proceeded, still standing behind the lectern. "Governor," he asked gently, though pointedly, "why did you think it was Eddy Goss who was blackmailing you?"

Harry took a deep breath. "I first thought it was Goss when one of the messages I received was accompanied by a bouquet of chrysanthemums. I'm sure you recall that Goss was known as the Chrysanthemum Killer. But what really convinced me was when I learned that the address the blackmailer had told me to deliver the ten thousand dollars to—four-oh-nine East Adams Street—was where Goss lived."

"And did you in fact go to Goss's address?"

"Yes, I did—at four o'clock in the morning, on the second of August."

The courtroom exploded once again in a torrent of whispers—followed immediately by the rapping of Judge Tate's gavel. "Order!"

"Judge," the prosecutor croaked. "I move to strike all of this testimony. It's—it's," he stammered, searching desperately for some way to stop this assault on his ironclad case. "It's prejudicial!"

The judge frowned. "I don't doubt it's *prejudicial*, Mr. McCue. I hardly think Mr. Cardenal would call a witness to *help* your case. Overruled."

McCue grimaced as he lowered himself into his chair.

Manny smiled briefly, then continued. "Just a few more questions," he told his witness. "Governor, is there any way you can prove you were at Eddy Goss's apartment on the night he was murdered?"

"Yes," he nodded, "because on the night I went there I was wearing the same kind of shoes I'm wearing now. The same kind of shoes I've worn for twenty-five years. I was wearing—"

"Hold it!" McCue shouted, seemingly out of breath

as he shot to his feet. "Just one second, Your Honor."

"Is that an objection?" the judge groused.

"Uh, yes," McCue fumbled. "I just don't see the relevance of any of this. Governor Swyteck is not on trial. His son is."

"Your Honor," Manny countered, "this testimony is highly relevant, and for a very simple reason. We now have not just one, not just two—but *three* people with the means and motive to kill Eddy Goss. We have Detective Stafford. We have Governor Swyteck. And we have the defendant. Ironically, it's the man with the weakest motive of all who's been charged with the crime. We submit, Your Honor, that under the evidence presented in this case, it is impossible for any reasonable juror to decide which, if any, of these three men might have acted on his motive and killed Eddy Goss. If it could have been any one of them, then it might not have been my client. And if it might not have been my client, then there is reasonable doubt. And if there is reasonable doubt," Manny said as he canvassed the jurors, "then my client must be found not guilty."

The judge leaned back in her chair and pursed her lips. "Very nice closing argument, Mr. Cardenal," she said sarcastically, though in truth she was more impressed than annoyed by Manny's speech. "The objection is overruled."

The prosecutor's round face flushed red with anger. He felt manipulated, and he feared that clever lawyering was stealing his case from under him. "But, Judge!"

"*Overruled*," she rebuked him. "Mr. Cardenal, repeat your question, please."

Manny nodded, then turned toward the governor. "My question, Governor, was whether you can prove you were at Eddy Goss's apartment on the night he was murdered."

"Yes, because I was wearing my Wiggins wing tips."

Manny stepped toward the bench, waving an exhibit as he walked. "At this time, Your Honor, we offer into evidence as defendant's exhibit two a copy of the footprint that was left outside Mr. Goss's apartment on the night of the murder. This document was prepared by the police. It is an imprint from a Wiggins wing tip."

The judge inspected the exhibit, then looked up and asked, "Any objection, Mr. McCue?"

"Well, no. I mean—yes. I object to this whole presentation. I—"

"Enough," she groaned. "Overruled. Do you have any further questions, Mr. Cardenal?"

Manny considered. He was sure the governor's testimony had planted the seed of doubt, but with Jack's life hanging in the balance, he owed it to his client to pursue *every* avenue of inquiry—even if it cast further suspicion on the governor. "Just one more question, Judge." He turned back to Harry.

"Tell me, Governor, how did your life of public service get its start—have you always been a politician?"

McCue rolled his eyes. Where was Cardenal heading now?

Harry smiled. "Well, my mother would say I've been a politician since birth." A few of the spectators tittered. "But no, my first years of public service were as a police officer. I spent ten years on the force," he said proudly.

"And do you still have your patrolman's uniform?"

"I do," the governor conceded.

Over a loud murmur, Manny called out to the judge, "I have no further questions, Your Honor."

Jack felt a lump in his throat. He was nearly overcome by his father's selfless act. The governor was a destroyer on the witness stand. He was destroying the prosecution's case against Jack—as well as his own chances for reelection.

"Mr. McCue," the judge queried, "any cross-examination?"

McCue sprung from his chair. "Oh, most definitely," he said. He marched to within a few feet of the witness, his stance and expression confrontational, if not hostile. "Governor Swyteck," he jabbed, "Jack Swyteck is your only son. Your *only* child, is he not?"

"That's true," the governor replied.

"And you love your son."

There was a pause—not because the governor didn't know the answer, but because it had been so long since he'd said it. "Yes," he answered, looking at Jack. "I do."

"You love him," McCue persisted, "and if you had to tell a lie to keep him from going to the electric chair, you would do it, wouldn't you!"

A heavy silence lingered in the courtroom. The governor leaned forward, his eyes narrowing as he spoke from the heart. "Mr. McCue," he said in a low, steady voice that nearly toppled the prosecutor, "if there's one thing I always taught my son, it's that we're all responsible for our own actions. Jack even reminded me of that once," he added, glancing over at the defense table. "My son didn't kill Eddy Goss," he said, looking each of the jurors right in the eye. "Jack Swyteck is innocent. That's the truth. And that's why I'm here."

"All right, then," McCue said angrily. "If you're here to tell the truth, then let's hear it: Are you telling us that *you* killed Eddy Goss?"

The governor looked squarely at the jurors. "I'm not here to talk about me. I'm here to tell you that Jack did *not* kill Goss. And I'm telling you that *I know* he did not."

"Maybe you didn't hear my question," McCue's voice boomed. "I am asking you, sir—yes or no: Did *you* kill Eddy Goss?"

"It's like you said earlier, Mr. McCue. I'm not the one on trial here. My son is."

McCue waved his arms furiously. "Your Honor! I demand that the witness be instructed to answer the question!"

The judge leaned over from the bench. "With all due respect, Governor," she said gravely, "the question calls for a yes or no answer. I feel compelled to remind you, however, of your fifth amendment right against self-incrimination. You need not answer the question if you invoke the fifth amendment. But those are your only options, sir. Either invoke the privilege, or answer the question. Did you or did you not kill Eddy Goss?"

Time seemed to stand still for a moment. It was as if everyone in the courtroom suddenly realized that *everything* boiled down to this one simple question.

Harold Swyteck sat erect in the witness stand, calm and composed for a man facing a life-and-death decision. If he answered yes, he'd be lying, and he'd be hauled off in shackles. If he answered no, he'd be telling the truth—

but he'd remove himself as a suspect. Invoking the privilege, however, raised all kinds of possibilities. His political career would probably be over and he might well be indicted for Goss's murder. And, of course, there was the one possibility that truly mattered: Jack might go free. For the governor, the choice was obvious.

"I refuse to answer the question," he announced, "on the grounds that I might incriminate myself."

The words rocked the courtroom. "Order!" the judge shouted, gaveling down the outburst.

The prosecutor stared at the witness, but the fire was gone. He knew it was over. He knew there was reasonable doubt. This witness had created it. "Under the circumstances," he said with disdain, "I have no further questions."

"The witness may step down," announced the judge.

Governor Swyteck rose from his chair, looking first at the jurors and then at his son. He wasn't sure what he saw in the eyes of the jurors. But he knew what he saw in Jack's eyes. It was something he'd wanted to see all his life. And only because he'd finally seen it did he have the strength to hold his head high as he walked the longest two hundred feet of his life, back down the aisle from the witness stand to the courtroom exit.

"Anything further from the defense?" the judge asked.

Manny rose slowly, feeling the familiar twinge that all defense lawyers feel when it's time to either put their client on the stand or rest their case. But the specter of Gina Terisi gave Jack and Manny no choice, really—and, more important, the governor had given Jack all the defense he needed. "Your Honor," Manny announced, "the defense rests."

The judge looked to the prosecutor. "Any rebuttal, Mr. McCue?"

McCue sighed as he checked the clock. "Judge, it's almost one o'clock, and the governor has shocked everyone—including me. I'm simply not prepared to rebut something as unforeseeable as this. I would like a recess until tomorrow morning."

The judge grimaced, but this *was* a rather extraordinary development. "All right," she reluctantly agreed. "Both sides, however, should be ready to deliver closing arguments tomorrow. There will be no further delays. We're in recess until nine A.M.," she announced, then banged the gavel.

"All rise!" cried the bailiff. His words had the same effect as "There's a fire in the house!" Spectators flooded the aisles and exits, jabbering about what they'd just seen and heard. Journalists rushed in every direction, some to report what had happened, others to pump the lawyers for what it all meant, still others to catch up with the governor. A few friends—Mike Mannon and Neal Goderich among them—shook Jack's hand, as if the case were over.

But Jack knew it wasn't over. Manny knew it, too. And one other man in the courtroom knew it better than anyone. He lingered in the back, concealing his shiny bald head and diamond-stud earring beneath a dark wig and broad-brimmed hat.

He glared at Jack through an irritated eye.

"Should have been Raul," he muttered to himself, "not you, Swyteck." He took one last look, imagining Jack telling his pretty girlfriend the good news. Then he stormed from the courtroom, determined to give the Swyteck family something else to think about.

Chapter 45

•

The parking lot at Jiggles strip joint was full from the Thursday evening crowd, so Rebecca had to find an empty spot on the street. She was wearing baggy jeans and a sweatshirt, her usual attire on her way to and from the bar. There was just one cramped dressing room inside for all the dancers, which was a hassle—but it was safer changing in there than walking the parking lot in some skimpy outfit that was sure to invite harassment or worse. Rebecca checked her watch. Ten after ten. "Damn," she muttered, realizing she was late for her evening shift. She locked her car and started across the parking lot. In one hand she carried a gym bag, which held her dancing clothes and makeup. In the other was her mace, just in case.

"Hey, Rebecca," came a low, husky voice from somewhere to her left.

Her body went rigid. Her name wasn't really Rebecca, which meant that it had to be a customer calling. She quickened her walk and clutched her can of mace, making sure it was ready. She jerked to a halt as a man jumped out from between cars.

"Get back!" she shouted, pointing the mace.

"It's Buzz," he said.

She took a good look, then recognized him beneath his hat and behind the dark, wraparound sunglasses that he wore, even after dark, to conceal his irritated eye. "Let me by," she said sternly.

"Wait," he replied, his tone conversational. "I have a proposition for you."

"Not *now*," she grimaced, her jaws nervously working a wad of chewing gum. "I'm supposed to punch in by ten, or I can lose my job. Come inside."

"Not that kind of proposition," said Buzz. "This is something different. I want your help."

"Why should I do anything for you?"

"No reason. But I'm not asking you to do it for me. I want you to do it for Raul."

Rebecca averted her eyes. The name clearly meant something to her. "What are you talking about?"

"I'm talking about revenge. I'm gonna nail the fuckers who put Raul in the chair."

Her shoulders heaved with a heavy sigh, then she just shook her head. "That's history, man. Raul was a punk. He treated me like dirt, even when I was giving it to him for free. Shit happens to punks."

Buzz stifled his fury. He would have liked to put her in her place with the hard truth that to Raul she was just a free blow job, but that wouldn't advance his purpose.

"Fine," he said with a shrug. "Just go on pretending you weren't nuts over him. Don't do it for him. Just do it for the money."

Her interest was suddenly piqued. "How much?"

"Ten percent of my take."

Rebecca rolled her eyes. "I've heard that one before. Ten percent of nothin' is still nothin'."

"Yeah. But ten percent of a quarter million is more money than you'll ever make sucking cocks."

She flashed a steely look, but she was more interested in the proposition than in refuting the insult. "Don't bullshit me. Where you gonna get that kind of money?"

"I'm not bullshittin' you. I'm serious. We're talking high stakes. And all you gotta do is make one phone call. That's it. A cush job."

She paused. "I don't believe it."

"*Believe* it. I've already conned sixty grand out of him. I'll show it to you. Count it, if you want. It's all right in my van. And that's just the tip of the iceberg. So what do you say? You in?"

Rebecca pressed her tongue to her cheek, mulling it over. "Sure," she said with a crack of her gum. "But I want ten percent of the sixty grand you already got, up front. Then I'll know you're for real."

Buzz flashed a thin smile. "I'm for real. You can have your six thousand. But you gotta come with me now."

She twitched, practically kicking herself for not having asked for the whole sixty thousand. "I can't come now. I gotta go to work."

"Six thousand dollars," he tempted her. "You can come now. Fuck work."

She cracked her gum, then sighed. "All right. I'll go. But I *want* my money."

He smiled and nodded toward his van. "Just get in."

"And I want to know more about what I'm getting into," she said as she heaved her gym bag over her shoulder and started walking. "I want to know *everything*."

He focused on the wiggle in her rear end as she reached the other side of the van, his eyes narrowing and a smirk coming to his face. No way you *really* want to know everything, he thought.

Chapter 46

•

Cindy received a bouquet of flowers when she arrived at the studio that Friday morning. They were from Jack.

"Please be there for me today," the card read. "I need you."

She wanted to pretend that the message didn't affect her, but it did. Leaving Jack hadn't made her stop loving him. In fact, leaving him was the easy part. It was staying away that was the test. Tuesday morning, after attempting to be cool and distant with him, she'd felt her resolve eroding. Gina's death had reminded her of how little time there is to do anything in life—of the purposelessness of grudges and resentment. Gina had probably died believing that Cindy hated her. Cindy didn't want the same thing—God forbid!—to happen to Jack.

By the time she received the phone call, at ten

o'clock in the morning, she'd already made up her mind to go over to the courthouse.

"Miss Paige," a woman said over the phone. "This is Manuel Cardenal's paralegal. Sorry to bother you, but he asked me to call you right away."

"Yes," she said with trepidation, afraid the trial had already accelerated to a verdict.

"Both Mr. Cardenal and Mr. Swyteck are in court right now, so they couldn't call you themselves. But they need you to come down to the courthouse. Mr. Swyteck needs you to testify for him. It's extremely important."

Cindy was confused. How could anything she had to say help Jack's case?

"I was about to go over there." She looked at her watch. "I can be there by ten-twenty—will that be in time?"

"Yes, I believe so," the woman said, "but *please* hurry."

Once Cindy heard the click on the other end, she sprung into action. She picked up her bag and rushed out of the office to the parking lot. The tires of her Pontiac Sunbird squealed as she accelerated out of the lot. She weaved in and out of traffic as she raced toward Frontage Road—the quickest route to the courthouse.

Ordinarily, Cindy was no speedster, but now was the time to see just how fast her Pontiac could go. She jammed down the accelerator and squeezed the steering wheel tightly, glancing intermittently at the speedometer as it pushed its way toward uncharted territory, past eighty-five miles per hour. The road was nearly deserted, and she was covering the distance in record time until she rounded a wide turn and suddenly the engine started to sputter. She was quickly losing speed.

"Come *on*," she urged as she pumped the accelerator. The car lunged forward a little, but the engine just gasped, then died. She coasted to a stop and steered off the road to the gravel shoulder. She pressed the pedal to the floor and turned the key. The ignition whined, but the engine wouldn't fire. She tried again. Same response.

"Not now," she groaned, as if she could reason with the vehicle. She didn't see a single car on the road, and she suddenly wished she had a car phone. She glanced in her side-view mirror and gave a start as she was suddenly staring into the face of a stranger.

"Can I help you, miss?" he said—loud enough to be heard through her window.

Cindy hesitated. The man's voice sounded pleasant enough, but the way he'd suddenly appeared out of nowhere seemed strange. She looked in the rearview mirror and saw an old gray van parked a short distance down the road. She looked at the man but couldn't read his expression, since most of his face was covered by the brim of his baseball cap and big dark sunglasses. Then she remembered: *Jack needs me.* She cracked the window half an inch. "My car—"

"Has sugar in the carburetor," he finished for her.

Cindy gulped. "I need—"

"To get to the courthouse," he interrupted again.

Her eyes widened with fear, but before she could react, the window suddenly exploded, and she was covered in a shower of glass pellets. She screamed and pounded the horn, but her cries for help quickly turned to desperate gasps for air as the hand of a very strong man came through the open window and wrapped tightly around her throat.

"Ja—ack!" her strangled voice cried.

"It ain't Jack, baby," came the snide reply. Then he reached for his sheath and showed her the sharp steel blade that had grown very cold since it had been used on Gina Terisi.

Chapter 47

●

Jack had wanted to see his father before returning to the courtroom on Friday morning, but Manny insisted that father and son have absolutely no communication until the trial was over. Since McCue had reserved the right to call rebuttal witnesses, the possibility remained that he'd recall the governor, and anything Jack and his father discussed would be fair game for cross-examination.

As it turned out, McCue called no further witnesses, and closing arguments were finished by one o'clock. Manny was brilliant, expanding on the speech he'd delivered during the governor's testimony. He reminded the jurors that the law did not require Jack to prove he was innocent—that it was the government's heavy burden to prove him guilty "beyond a reasonable doubt."

McCue did the best he could, then retreated to his office. Jack and Manny waited in the attorneys' lounge, down the hall from Judge Tate's courtroom. At five-fifteen, the courtroom deputy stuck her head into the lounge and gave them the news.

"The jury has reached a verdict," she told them.

In a split second they were out the door, walking side-by-side as quickly as they could without breaking into a dead run down the hall and into the courtroom. The news of a verdict had traveled fast, and the expectant crowd filed in behind them. Wilson McCue was already in position. Manny and Jack took their places at the defense table. Jack glanced behind him, toward the public seating. Ten rows back, Neil Goderich gave him a reassuring wink. On the opposite side of the aisle, Mike Mannon looked worried but gave him a thumbs up. Cindy, Jack realized with a pang, wasn't in the courtroom. Not even the flowers had worked.

"All rise!" cried the bailiff.

Judge Tate proceeded to the bench, but Jack gave her only a passing glance. He was focused on the twelve jurors who were taking their seats for the final time. He was trying to remember those indicators jury psychologists relied on to predict verdicts. Who had they selected as foreman? Did they look at the defendant, or at the prosecutor? At that moment, however, he couldn't think clearly enough to apply any of those tests. He was consumed by the feeling of being on trial—of having twelve strangers hold his life in their hands.

"Has the jury reached a verdict?" Judge Tate asked.

"We have," responded the foreman.

"Please give it to the clerk."

The written verdict was passed from the foreman to

the clerk, then from the clerk to the judge. The judge inspected it, then returned it to the clerk for public disclosure. The ritual seemed to pull everyone to the edge of his seat. Yet the courtroom was so deathly quiet that Jack could hear the fluorescent lights humming thirty feet overhead.

This is it, he thought. *Life or death*. He struggled to bring his emotions under control. Everything seemed so encouraging moments ago, when he and Manny had assessed his chances. But odds were deceiving. Like a year ago, when Cindy's mother had been diagnosed with breast cancer. They'd all taken comfort in the doctor's assurance that her chances of survival were 80 percent. Those odds sounded pretty good until Jack had started thinking of the last hundred people he'd laid eyes on—and then imagined twenty of them dead.

"The defendant shall rise," announced the judge.

Jack glanced at Manny as they rose in unison. He clenched his fists tightly in anticipation.

"In the matter of *State* versus *Swyteck*, on the charge of murder in the first degree," the clerk read from the verdict form, "we, the jury, find the defendant: *not* guilty."

A roar filled the courtroom. On impulse, Jack turned and embraced Manny. Never had he hugged a man so tightly—not even his father. But had the governor been there, Jack would have cracked his ribs.

"Order!" said the judge, postponing the celebration. The rumble in the courtroom quieted. Manny and Jack returned to their seats, smiling apologetically.

"Ladies and gentlemen of the jury," the judge intoned, "thank you for your service. You are discharged.

A judgment of acquittal shall be entered. Mr. Swyteck," she said, peering over the bench, "you are free to go. This court is adjourned," she declared, ending it all with one last crack of the gavel.

Happy cries of congratulation flew across the courtroom. Neil and Mike and the other friends who'd never stopped believing hurried forward and leaned across the rail that separated players from spectators, slapping Jack's back and shaking the hand of an innocent man. Jack was elated but dazed. He canvassed the buzzing crowd, still hoping for a glimpse of Cindy. Then he thought of the other person who was missing.

"Where's my father?" Jack asked Manny. His voice was barely audible in the thundering commotion of the crowded courtroom.

Manny smiled. "We've got a special celebration planned," he said with a wink. "Back at my office."

Jack was overcome with a sense of euphoria. He felt like a death-row prisoner released into the bright light of day. He'd never been so eager to see his father. As he and Manny started toward the gate, they were stopped abruptly by Wilson McCue.

"I'd lose the smiles if I were you," the prosecutor said bitterly. He spoke in a low, threatening voice that couldn't be overheard by the noisy crowd on the other side of the rail. "This is only round one, boys, and round two is about to begin. It's just a matter of how fast I can assemble the grand jury and draft the indictment, that's all. I warned you, Swyteck. I said I'd come after you for the murder of Gina Terisi, and I meant it. Right now the only question is whether I'll do it before or *after* I indict your old man for the murder of Eddy Goss."

Jack's eyes flared with contempt. "You just won't take those blinders off, will you, McCue?"

"Jack," Manny stopped him. "Say nothing."

"That's right," McCue countered. "Say nothing. Take the fifth. It runs in the family." He shook his head with disgust, then turned and stepped through the swinging gate, into the rabble of reporters clamoring at the rail.

Jack desperately wanted to rush after McCue and set him straight, but Manny held him back. "Just take it easy, Jack," he said, pulling him toward the bench, away from the media frenzy. "McCue can afford to talk out of anger, but you can't. So for now, just let me handle the press. The best thing you can do is to say nothing and go back to my office. We need to regroup and talk with your father."

"My father . . ." Jack said slowly, as if tapping into a source of strength. Then he nodded. "All right, I'll meet you there." Then he opened the gate and pushed his way into the swarming press. He kept his head lowered, ignoring all questions until he reached the elevators. Less than three minutes later, he was behind the steering wheel of his Mustang, ready to pull out of the courthouse parking lot.

He'd just put the car into gear when he heard the ringing of his car phone. *Cindy*, he hoped. But why would she use this number? Could she have already heard the verdict? It didn't seem possible.

He moved the shift back into park and picked up the phone.

"Jack," he heard her voice. "It's me, Cindy."

He started to say something, but words wouldn't

come. "Cindy," he said finally, just wanting to say her name. "Where are you?"

"Balcony scene's over, Romeo," came the ugly reply. It wasn't Cindy's voice anymore. It was the same voice he'd heard while on his belly in the bus. "She's with me."

Jack's hand shook as he pressed the phone to his ear. Some part of his brain that wasn't absolutely terrified directed his other hand to turn off the ignition. He moved slightly forward in his seat. "What have you done with her!"

"Nothing," the caller said coolly. *"Yet."*

"It's me you want, you bastard! Just leave her out of it."

"Shut up, Swyteck! I'm through fooling around. Your legal system has fucked everything up again. This time we'll play on my turf. And this time I want real money. I want a quarter million. Cash. Unmarked fifties."

Jack's head was spinning. He tried to focus. "Look, I'll do whatever you want. But that's a lot of money. It'll take time to—"

"Your girlfriend doesn't have *time*. Talk to your father, asshole. He's so eager to help you."

"Okay. Please, just don't hurt her? Just tell me how to get you the money."

"Take it to Key West. Just the two of you."

"The *two* of us?"

"You and your father."

"I can do it myself—"

"You'll do it the way I *tell* you to do it!" the caller snapped. "I need to know where everybody is who knows anything about this. I'm not gonna be ambushed. No police, no FBI, no National Guard—not even a meter maid. Any sign of law enforcement and your pretty girlfriend's dead. If I see any roadblocks on U.S. 1, any choppers in the air, any news reports on television, anything that even *looks* like you called in the cavalry—she's dead, *immediately*. It's me against the Swytecks. End of story. You got it?"

"I got it," Jack said, though he could barely speak. "When do you want us there?"

"Saturday night, October twenty-ninth."

"That's tomorrow," Jack protested.

"That's right. It's the Key West Fantasy Fest weekend. Nice, big Halloween street party. Like the Mardi Gras in New Orleans. Everyone's going to be in costume. And so will I. No one could possibly find me in that mess, Swyteck. So don't even try."

"How will we contact you?"

"I'll contact you. Just check into any one of the big resort hotels. Use your name. I'll find you. Any questions?"

Jack took a deep breath. "No," he replied.

"Good. Very good. Oh—one other thing, Swyteck."

"What?"

"Trick or treat," he taunted, then hung up the phone.

It should have been a night of celebration, beginning with him and his father sipping Dom Perignon, then blossoming into a fairy-tale reunion with Cindy. Instead, the nightmare was continuing.

Jack went to Manny's office as planned, where he

met up with his father. They sat alone in Manny's conference room, considering their options.

"Agnes and I can certainly come up with the money," the governor assured his son. "That's not a problem. And, naturally, I'm in a position to bring in the best law enforcement available. All I have to do is make a phone call. I can do it right now."

Jack shook his head. "We can't," he said emphatically. "He'll kill Cindy, I know it. He'll spot anything we try to do."

The governor sighed. "You're probably right. He may be crazy, but he's brilliant-crazy. I'm sure he's monitoring a police radio even as we speak. And if there's anything I learned in my ten years on the force, it's that police departments are sieves."

Father and son sat staring at each other. "All right," the governor finally said, "we don't bring in the police. But I have lots of friends in the private sector—retired FBI agents, retired Secret Service. They can help. They can at least give advice."

Jack wrestled with it. "That makes sense, I guess. But any advisers have to be just that—advisers. Ultimately, it comes down to me."

"No," the governor corrected him. "You *and* me."

Jack looked at his father across the table. The governor gave him a reassuring smile that was meant to remove any doubt that he could count on his old man.

"Let's do it, then," said Jack. "We'll nail this bastard. Together."

PART FIVE

•

Saturday, October 29

Chapter 48

•

Jack and Harry Swyteck reached the end of U.S. 1 and the city limits of Key West at about noon the next day. They followed the palm trees along the coastline and parked Harry's rented Ford Taurus near Duval Street, the main thoroughfare that bisected the tourists' shopping district. Both sides of Duval and the streets leading off of it were lined with art galleries and antique shops housed in renovated white-frame buildings, booths advertising snorkel tours, T-shirt emporiums, bicycle rental shops, and open-air bars blaring a mélange of folk, rock, and calypso.

At the north end of Duval was Mallory Square, a popular gathering spot on the wharf where magicians, jugglers, and portrait artists entertained crowds and turned sunsets into a festival every day of the year. During Fantasy Fest, the square was simply an extension of a ten-day party that stretched from one end of Duval to the other.

Fantasy Fest was already in its ninth day when the Swytecks arrived, and the party in the streets was still nonstop. Some tourists were buying their feathers, beads, and noisemakers for the annual but hardly traditional Halloween parade on Saturday night, others were just people-watching. Many were already in costume. Men dressed as women. Women dressed as Martians. A brazen few were undressed, covering their bare breasts or buttocks with only grease paint.

"Check that out," Jack said from his passenger seat, pointing to a man outfitted in a lavender loincloth and a pink bonnet.

"Probably the mayor," the governor deadpanned.

Harry parked the car in the covered garage near their hotel. They grabbed their overnight bags and a briefcase from the trunk and headed up the old brick sidewalk, grateful for the shade of hundred-year-old oaks and a cool ocean breeze. Hotel rooms were hard to come by during Fantasy Fest—especially if requested at the last minute—but the governor had a few connections. They checked in at the front desk and carried their own luggage to a suite on the sixth floor.

The sliding-glass doors offered a stunning, eight-hundred-dollar-a-night view of the Gulf of Mexico. Jack walked out onto the balcony and looked at the Pier Point, one of those outdoor waterfront restaurants where the food was never as good as the atmosphere. It all seemed so surreal, he thought. He wanted to think that at any moment Cindy would join them, and then they'd get caught up in the party, walk on the beach or head over to the original Sloppy Joe's and find the table Ernest Hemingway used to like. But they had business to tend to—someone to meet. And at 1:00 P.M., the man they wanted to meet was at their door.

"Peter Kimmell," said the governor, "meet my son, Jack."

Jack closed the balcony's sliding-glass doors and pulled the curtains shut. "Glad to meet you," he said, reaching out to shake the man's hand.

Kimmell was tall, about six feet four inches, with a lean body that moved with catlike grace. His face registered little emotion, but his eyes seemed to be constantly assessing, processing information. They gave Jack the uncomfortable feeling that he was being evaluated, measured against some personal set of standards.

Old habits die hard. Kimmell was a twenty-year veteran of the Secret Service who'd burned out two years before and retired to his bass boat in the Florida Keys. But he'd quickly grown bored with fishing, so he took up cycling, then swimming, then running—and before he knew it, the same energy that had made him a top agent made him one of the top competitors in the age-fifty-and-above Ironman triathlon. He still did some work as a private investigator when he wasn't training, and Harry Swyteck used him as a consultant on special events that raised thorny security problems. The governor considered Kimmell the best in the business. And, most important, he was the only man Harry trusted to give Jack and him the expertise they needed without any danger of a leak to the press or police.

"So *you're* Jack," Kimmell said, smiling. "Your dad's told me a lot about you—all good." He shifted his gaze from son to father. "You ready to get right to it, men?"

"Ready," they both answered.

"Good. Now let me show you some toys I've brought along for you," he said with a wink. He hoisted onto the bed a gray metal suitcase that was nearly as big as a trunk. "Voila," he said as he popped it open.

The Swytecks stood in silence as they peered at the cache inside. "What did you do," asked the governor, "mix up your bag with James Bond's?"

"You won't need half this stuff," said Kimmell. "But whatever you will need is here. I got everything from voice-activated wires to infrared binoculars."

"I think we should keep it simple," said Jack.

"I agree," he replied. "First, let's talk weapons. You ever fired a gun, Jack?"

Jack smiled at the irony. How would Wilson McCue have answered that question for him? "Uh-huh"—he nodded—"back when I was in college. I had a girl-friend who didn't feel safe at night without a gun in the apartment, so I learned to use it."

"Good. Now, for you, son," he said as he removed a sleek black pistol from the holster, "I recommend this baby—the Glock Seventeen Safe Action nine-millimeter pistol, Austrian design. It's completely computer-manufactured of synthetic polymer. Stronger than steel, but weighs less than two pounds even with a full maga-zine, so you can hold it nice and steady. Deadly accurate, too, so you don't have to be right in this lunatic's face to blow him away. And it's got a pretty soft recoil, consid-ering the punch it packs: You got seventeen rounds of police-issue hollow-point para-ammunition that'll drop a charging moose with an attitude dead in its tracks." He handed it to Jack. "How's that feel, partner?"

Jack laid it in his hand and shrugged. "Feels like a gun."

"Like a part of your hand, Jack. *That's* what it feels like." He took the pistol back, then dug into his suitcase. "Now, let's talk real protection: body armor. It's gonna be hot as hell, but you gotta wear a vest. This is the top of the line in my book. Made of Kevlar one twenty-nine and Spectra fibers. Full coverage. Protects your front, back, and sides, and the shirttails keep it from riding up on you. Stops a forty-four-magnum slug at fourteen hundred feet per second—that's point-blank range. Excellent multihit stopping power, too"—he winked—"but I think I'd still hit the deck if he pulls out an Uzi. Best of all, it weighs less than four pounds and gives you full range of motion. Beneath your baggy black sweatshirt, your kidnapper won't even know you got it on. Governor, got a Glock and body armor for you, too. I know you never used to like to wear the vest, but—"

"I'll wear one," he said without hesitation.

"Good," replied Kimmell. "Now—the plan. If I'm gonna help you men get ready to meet this character face-to-face, I need to get a fix on who he is. I need to know everything *you* know about him. So let's start at the beginning. Tell me about the murder he confessed to. Who was the woman he says he killed?"

"A teenager, actually," Jack answered. "She got herself into a nightclub with a phony ID, then she was abducted in the parking lot on the way to her car. The next morning, they found her on the beach. Her throat had been slit."

"What else—" Kimmell asked, but he was interrupted by the shrill ring of the telephone. "You guys expecting a call?"

"No," answered the governor.

The phone was on its third ring. "Answer it, Jack," Kimmell directed.

"Hello," he answered, then listened carefully. "No, thank you," he finished the conversation, and then hung up. His father and Kimmell were staring expectantly. "There's a package at the front desk for us."

"From who?" asked Kimmell.

"No name on it. But it must be him. When he called me yesterday, he said we should just check into one of the big hotels and that we'd hear from him. There's only a handful of possibilities on the Key. Looks like he found us."

Kimmell nodded. "Tell them to send it up."

Jack phoned the manager and asked him to deliver the package to their room personally. The manager was glad to accommodate. In two minutes he was at their door with the delivery. Kimmell answered, then brought the shoe-box-sized package inside and lay it on the bed. He took a metal detector from his suitcase and ran it across the package.

"There's metal inside," said Kimmell.

"You think he sent us a bomb?" asked the governor.

"Can't be," Kimmell answered. "If he was going to blow you up, he would have done it two years ago. Open it."

Jack carefully removed the string and cut the tape with the care of a surgeon. He lifted the lid. Inside the bubble wrap was a cellular phone. Across the top lay a business-sized envelope with a handwritten message on the outside. "Switch on the phone at midnight," it read.

"At least we know your kidnapper hasn't lost his nerve," said Kimmell. "He's still in the game. Which means there's still hope."

"What's in the envelope?" asked the governor.

Kimmell opened it and unfolded its contents. "It's a certificate of death," he said.

"Not Cindy?" the governor asked with sudden fear.

" 'Raul Francisco Fernandez,' " he read from the first line. "It's from the County Health Department. An exact duplicate, except for Box thirty—the cause of death. You can still make out the original, typewritten entry. 'Cardiac arrest,' " he read aloud, " 'as a consequence of electrocution.' But someone has crossed out the coroner's entry and penciled in a different cause of death." He handed it to the governor.

" 'Jack Swyteck,' " Harry read aloud, his voice cracking.

A heavy silence permeated the room. Then Kimmell took a closer look at the certificate. "Why'd he do this?" he asked.

"That's been his message all along," Jack said. "He's blamed me from the beginning."

"I'm talking about something different," said Kimmell. "There's another message here—one that's a little less obvious. Maybe even unintended. Box seven," he said as he pointed to it, "is the space for the 'informant.' That's the person who provides personal data for completion of the certificate. The named informant here is Alfonso Perez."

"Who's that?" asked Jack.

"There are lots of men named Alfonso Perez. But from my days in law enforcement I know that at one time it was also one of the aliases used by a guy known as Esteban. Every federal agent based in Miami in the eighties knew about this character. Brilliant guy. Speaks English as well as he does Spanish. Every so often he changes his name and identity. The feds can't keep up. I heard they almost nabbed him two years ago, but he took off to somewhere in the Caribbean. Anyway, he's a suspect in at least five murder-kidnappings in this country alone."

"He's wanted in other countries, too?" asked Jack.

"Came here from Cuba. He was a thug in Castro's army, years ago. Trained with the Russians during the war in Angola, then distinguished himself by torturing political prisoners—a merciless bastard. Earned himself a nice promotion to the Batallon Especial de Seguridad, Castro's elite military force. But when they cut off his daily routine of driving nails into molars and bashing heads with bayonets, they say he snapped. He craved the violence. Went on a killing spree. Raped and murdered about a dozen women in Havana—all prostitutes. The Cubans threw him in a booby hatch for a couple years. Then Castro sent him over to Miami in 1980, when he opened the jails and asylums and turned the Mariel boat lift into a Trojan horse. Esteban just snuck in with the hundred and fifty thousand other Marielito refugees. FBI and Immigration have been looking for him ever since."

"Raul Fernandez came to Miami in the Mariel boat lift too," said Jack.

"Probably not a coincidence," Kimmell speculated. "That doesn't mean Fernandez was a criminal, though.

Only a small number of the Marielitos were."

Jack and his father sat in silence. "You think it could be him?" Jack asked.

Kimmell sighed heavily. "I really can't say for sure. But for your sake," he added, "I sure as hell hope not."

Jack rose and stepped toward the window, pulling back the drapes just enough to peer out at the vast ocean. "It's not *me* who I'm worried about," he said with more than a touch of fear.

Chapter 49

●

On the other side of Key West, near the tourist land-mark designated "The Southernmost Point in the Continental United States," beneath the rotting pine floorboards of an abandoned white frame house, Cindy Paige blinked her eyes open. She wasn't sure if she was awake. Although her eyes were open, her world was total blackness. She tried to touch her eyes to make sure she wasn't blind, but her hands wouldn't move. They were bound. She struggled to get loose, but her feet were bound too. She screamed, but it didn't sound like her. She screamed again. It was muffled, as if a hand were covering her mouth. Was someone there? Was someone *with* her? Suddenly it came back to her—the last two things she could remember: a sack being thrown over her head and then a jab in her arm.

She heard a pounding above her. Her heart raced.

More pounding, and then a blinding light was in her eyes. A wave of fresh air hit her face, making her painfully aware of how stifling hot her hell really was. Her blurry vision focused, and then her eyes widened with fear. The image had returned—the man in the cap and wraparound sunglasses who'd attacked her in the car.

"Quiet, angel," Esteban said softly. He was seated on the floor and speaking down into the hole. "No one is going to hurt you."

She'd never been so frightened in her life. Her teeth clenched the gag in her mouth. Her chest heaved with quick, panicky breaths. *Please*, she cried out with her eyes, *don't hurt me!*

"If you'll promise not to scream," he said, "I'll take off your gag. If you'll promise not to run, I'll take you out of your hole. Do you promise?"

She nodded eagerly.

Esteban's mouth curled into a sinister smirk. "I don't believe you."

Cindy whimpered pathetically.

"Don't blame *me*," he said. "Your boyfriend is to blame. Swyteck *forced* me to do this. I didn't want it to be this way. So many times I could have hurt you, had I wanted to. But I never did. And I won't hurt you . . . so long as Jack Swyteck does what I tell him to do. You do believe me, don't you?"

Cindy's eyes were still wide with horror. But she nodded.

"Good," he replied. "Now, I can't let you out of your little hiding place. But I'll make a deal with you." He displayed a syringe. "This is secobarbital sodium. It's what made you sleep so deeply. I must have gotten the dosage right. But now I've got a problem. You see, I don't know how much of it is still in your system. Which means that I don't know how much to give you. If I give you too much, you're not gonna wake up. So promise me you'll lie real quiet, and we can skip the injection. Deal?"

Cindy nodded once.

"Smart girl." He stood up and put one of the loose floorboards back in place. At the sound of Cindy's muffled cry, he stopped and wagged his finger at her. "Not another peep," he reminded her, like a loving parent telling a four-year-old she can't sleep with Mommy and Daddy tonight.

Cindy swallowed hard. Somehow she managed to stop crying.

"Good girl. Now, don't you worry, I've already found better accommodations for us. You'll be out of there before long."

She quivered as she lay in the hole, hoping for a miracle as he reached for the other floorboard. Her world went dark as he laid it in place.

"Night, angel," she heard him say through the wooden barrier.

Esteban got up off his knees and pulled off his cap and sunglasses. The humidity in the boarded-up house was nearly as sweltering above the floor as it was below. He was in a living room of bare wooden floors and water-stained walls. A few trespassing transients had left behind their aluminum cans, cardboard blankets, and cigarette butts. Esteban had brought only what he absolutely needed: a couple of lounge chairs, a fully stocked ice chest, his ham radio, and three battery-operated fans that pushed stale air around the room. He didn't dare open the boarded-up windows, for fear of being detected. But the chances of that were slim. The old house was so overgrown with tropical foliage that he'd practically needed a machete to reach the front door. And so far as he could tell from the police band on his radio, no one was searching for him.

"What's this *angel* crap?" Rebecca groused from across the room, startling him. She'd been standing in the doorway, listening.

He gave her a quick once-over. She was wearing very short blue-jean cutoffs, a loose tank top, no shoes, no bra, and no makeup. She had the deep suntan of a woman who worked nights, yet her skin didn't look all that healthy.

"Something a whore like you wouldn't know anything about," he snarled.

"Right," she said indignantly, then walked across the room to the ice chest and grabbed a Coke. "If she's such an angel, then why you got her under the floorboards? Huh?"

His expression went cold. "She's *alive*, isn't she? And you know why she's alive?"

"Because she's no good to you dead."

"No," he spat, "because I've been watching her for months. Because I *know* she's not a slut like her girlfriend—or like *you* and all the other cocksuckers who dance on tables."

Rebecca leaned against the wall, shifting her weight nervously. She was afraid but tried not to show it. "Listen, I don't know what your problem is. If anyone should be complaining, it's me. I said I'd make the phone call, and I did. I called the bitch. You paid me the

six thousand dollars, and that's fine. But you didn't tell
me I was going to have to come all the way to Key West
with you to collect the rest of my stinking twenty-five
grand. You didn't tell me we were going to have Sleeping Beauty in the back of the van. And you sure as hell
didn't tell me we'd have to hole up in this dump, or in
this other place you're bringing us to. So maybe I deserve a little more. Or maybe I walk out right now."

He glared at her. "You'd do *anything* for money.
Wouldn't you, Rebecca."

"Oh," she said, "and you're not doing this for the
money."

"I'm doing this for Raul! Because Raul was fucking
innocent!"

Beneath the floorboards, Cindy shuddered with fear.
She could overhear everything, and the tone in the
man's voice made her wish she was still unconscious.

Inwardly, Rebecca also trembled at his tone. "Just
cool your jets," she said, feeling a lump rising in her
throat. "I just want my fair share, all right?"

Esteban stepped toward her slowly, looking as
though he were deliberating. He reached into his
pocket. "You'll get your share," he assured. "But you
gotta earn it. Here," he said as he crumpled up a twenty
and threw it at her. He stopped a foot away from her and
stared into her eyes. "Here's twenty bucks, bitch. Do it."

Rebecca stepped back in fear, her back to the wall.
"Do *yourself*."

He slapped her across the face. "Do *me*."

She tried to slide away, but he grabbed her by the
wrist and squeezed hard. "Do *it*."

She was about to scream, but was silenced by the

look in his eyes. She had been in bad situations before. Men who pulled knives on her. Men who urinated on her. She was streetwise enough to sense whether a scream would make him stop or make him snap. This time, she didn't *dare* scream.

Rebecca lowered herself onto her knees, her hands shaking as she unzipped his pants. His head rolled back and he moaned with pleasure. She worked fast and furiously to finish the job as quickly as she could. "Quickies" were her trade, with hundreds or maybe even thousands of them under her belt. But she didn't swallow for any of her customers, for fear of the deadly virus. She heard Esteban groan, signaling that he was near. She prepared to pull away, but this time the routine was different. She felt his hand clasp the back of her neck, pressing her head down further, forcing her to take in much more than she could. His groaning grew louder. She gagged. He was in so deep she was unable to breathe. She tried to back off, but he forced even harder. She needed out. So she bit him.

Esteban smacked her across the head, knocking her to the floor. "Watch the fucking teeth!"

Rebecca gasped for air, looking up in fear. "I couldn't breathe!"

He grabbed her by the hair, jerking her head back. "That's the *least* of your problems," he said, his eyes two vacuous pools.

Beneath the floor, Cindy began to shake uncontrollably. She closed her eyes tightly to shut off the tears, but no matter how hard she tried, she couldn't shut her ears.

"I got plans for you, Rebecca," Cindy heard him say—and the laugh that followed chilled her to the bone.

Chapter 50

•

Kimmell, Jack, and Harry spent the rest of that Saturday going over everything—main plans, backup plans, contingency backup plans. Each plan revolved around the same basic triangle. Jack and his father would be out in the field, following the kidnapper's instructions. Kimmell would remain in the hotel suite, a kind of central command station operator who could be reached by phone or beeper in case of emergency.

By 10:00 P.M. they'd about reached the point of information overload. They ordered room service and ate dinner in total silence, save for an occasional happy scream or blast of fireworks from the burgeoning Halloween crowd on nearby Duval Street. The increasing level of noise was a steady reminder that the midnight phone call was just two hours away.

When he finished eating, Kimmell tossed his napkin

to his plate and rose from the table. On average, he smoked two, maybe three cigarettes an entire year. Already tonight he'd exceeded his annual quota. He grabbed the ashtray and retreated to the adjoining room to take another look at the photographs and notes sent by the kidnapper, as if by absorbing all available information he could get into his mind.

Jack and Harry sat across from each other at the dining table. The governor watched as Jack picked at his food.

"I'm sorry, Jack," he said sincerely.

Jack wasn't sure what he meant. "We both are. I just pray we get Cindy back. Then there'll be nothing for anyone to be sorry about."

"I pray we get her back, too. No question—that's the most important thing. But there's something else I'm sorry about," he said with a pained expression. "It has to do with pushing a kid too hard when he was already doing his best—and then pushing him away when his best wasn't good enough. I mean, hell, Jack, sometimes I look back on it and think that if you'd been Michelangelo, I probably would have walked into the Sistine Chapel and said something like, 'Okay, son, now what about the walls?'" He smiled briefly, then turned serious again. "I guess when your mother died I just wanted you to be perfect. That's no excuse, though. I'm truly sorry for the pain I've caused you. I've been sorry for a long time. And it's time I told you."

Jack struggled for the right words. "You know"—his voice quivered with emotion—"in the last two days, the only thing I've been able to think about besides the kidnapping is how to thank you for what you did at the trial."

"You can thank me by accepting my apology," Harry said with a warm smile.

Jack's heart swelled. Of course he'd accept it; he felt like *he* should be the one to apologize. So he expressed it another way. "You're gonna love Cindy when you get to know her."

The governor's eyes were suddenly moist. "I know I will."

"Hey," said Kimmell as he entered the room, "time to get dressed."

Jack and his father looked at each other with confidence. There was strength in unity. "Let's do it," said Jack. The governor gave a quick nod of agreement, and they marched off to the adjoining room, where Kimmell helped them get ready. Both wore dark clothing, in case they had to hide. Sneakers, in case they had to run. And both wore the Kevlar vests Kimmell had brought them, in case they couldn't hide or run fast enough.

"What's that?" Jack asked as Kimmell wired a battery to his vest.

"It's a tracking device," he answered. "The transmitter sends out a one-watt signal. It's on intermittent-duty cycle, so it'll be easy for me to recognize your signal— and the battery will last longer, too, just in case this takes longer than we think. Any time I need a location on you, I can do it in an instant from my audio-visual indicator here in the room."

Kimmell went ahead and rigged the antenna and was tucking the pistol into Jack's holster when the portable phone rang.

It was exactly midnight.

Jack took a deep breath, then reached for the phone. Kimmell stopped him.

"Be cooperative," Kimmell reminded him, "but insist on hearing Cindy's voice."

He nodded, then switched on the receiver. "Hello," he answered.

"Ready to trick or treat, Swyteck?"

Be cooperative, Jack reminded himself. "We've got the money. Tell us how you want to do the exchange."

"Ah, the *exchange*," Esteban said wistfully. "You know, no kidnapper in the history of the world has ever really figured out the problem of the exchange. It's that one moment where so many things can go wrong. And if just *one* little thing goes wrong, then *everything* goes wrong. Do you understand me, Swyteck?"

"Yes."

"Good. Here's the plan. I'm splitting you up. Your father will deliver the money to me in a public place. You'll pick up the girl in a private place. Brilliant, isn't it?"

"What do you want us to do?"

"Tell your father to take the money to Warehouse E off Mallory Square and wait outside by the pay phone. When I'm ready for the money, I'll come by in costume. Believe me, he'll recognize me."

"What about Cindy? How do I get her?"

"When we hang up, take the portable phone with you and start walking south on Simonton Street away from your hotel. Just keep walking until I call you. I'll direct you right to her. And so long as your father hands over the money, I'll direct you to her in time."

"What do you mean *in time*?" Jack asked.

"What do you *think* I mean?"

"I need to speak to Cindy," he said firmly. "I need to know that she's all right."

The line went silent. Ten long seconds passed. Then twenty. Jack thought maybe he had hung up. But he hadn't.

"Ja—ack," Cindy's voice cracked.

"Cindy!"

"Please, Jack. Just do what he says."

"That's all," said Esteban. "If you want to hear more, you gotta play by my rules. No games, no cops, nobody gets hurt. Start walking, Swyteck." The line went dead.

Jack breathed a heavy sigh. "No fear," he added, speaking only to himself.

Chapter 51

•

After some last-minute advice from Kimmell, Jack and his father told each other to be careful. Then they left the hotel and headed in separate directions. The governor went west toward Mallory Square, an assortment of big, wide piers that had once been a waterfront auction block for wine, silks, and other ship salvage hauled in by nineteenth-century wreckers. During Fantasy Fest, the square was more or less a breaker between the insanity on Duval Street and the peaceful Gulf of Mexico. Jack walked south on Simonton, a residential street that ran parallel to Duval. The neighborhood was a slice of wealthy old Key West, with white picket fences and one multistory Victorian house after another, many of them built for nineteenth-century sailors, sponge merchants, and treasure hunters, many of them now bed-and-breakfasts.

He walked two blocks very quickly, then slowed down, realizing that he had no official destination. The Flintstones danced by on their way to the festival, singing their theme song. Others in costume streamed by on foot or on motor scooter, since cars were useless during Fantasy Fest.

Jack's portable phone rang, startling him. "Yes," he answered.

"Turn left at Caroline Street," said Esteban, "and stay on the phone. Tell me when you hit each intersection."

Jack crossed Simonton and headed east on Caroline Street. The noise from Duval was beginning to fade, and he saw fewer pedestrians on their way to the party. It was darker, too, since there were fewer street lamps, and the thick, leafy canopy blocked out the moonlight. The sidewalk was cracked and buckled from over-grown tree roots. Palm trees and sprawling oaks rustled in the cool, steady breeze. Majestic old wooden houses with two-story porches and gingerbread detail seemed to creak as the wind blew. Jack just kept walking.

"This is not about your girlfriend," said the voice over the phone.

Jack exhaled. The phone obviously was not just for directions. "I'm at Elizabeth Street."

"Keep going," said Esteban, and then he immediately picked up his thought. "This is *all* about Raul Fernandez. You know that, don't you?"

Jack kept walking. He didn't want to agitate, but after two years of wondering, he had to keep him talking. "Tell me about Raul."

"You know the most important thing already." His

tone was forceful but not argumentative. "It wasn't Raul's idea to kill that girl."

"Tell me about *him*, though."

There was silence on the line—one of those long, pivotal silences Jack had heard so many times when interviewing clients, after which the flow of information would either completely shut down or never shut off. He heard the man clear his throat. "Raul had been in prison in Cuba for nine years before we came over on the boat. And after nine years in jail, what do you think he wanted most when he got to Miami?"

Jack hesitated. The story about the boat fit Kimmell's theory that the kidnapper was Esteban. But he wasn't sure whether this was meant to be a monologue or a dialogue. "You tell me."

"A *whore*, you dumb shit. And he was willing to pay for it. But there are so many whores out there who just won't admit what they are. Just pick one, I told him. He did, but he still needed encouragement. So I went with him, to show him how easy it was."

"You and Fernandez did it *together*?"

"Raul didn't *kill* anyone. The knife was just to scare her. But the stupid bitch panicked and pulled off his mask. Even then, Raul *still* didn't want to kill her. I was saving his ass by doing it. So how do you think it felt when *he* was the one arrested for murder? I did everything I could to keep him from getting the chair. I even confessed! But you didn't do *your* part, Swyteck. The governor, the man who could stop it all, was your father, and you did *nothing*."

Jack resisted the temptation to educate the kidnapper, but he felt a certain vindication—not for himself, but for his father. Since the murder had begun as a rape or attempted rape by Raul Fernandez, Fernandez was as guilty as the man who had slit her throat. By law, anyone who committed a felony that brought about an unintended death was guilty of murder, even if the murder was committed by an accomplice. It was called "felony murder." It was a capital crime. And most important, it meant that his father had *not* executed an innocent man after all.

"So you and Raul were prison buddies. Is that it?"

"Prison buddies," he said with disdain. "What do you think—we were a couple of fags, or something? Raul was my brother, you son of bitch. You fucking killed my little brother."

Jack took a deep breath. It didn't seem possible, but the stakes had suddenly risen. "I'm approaching William Street."

"Stop now. Face south. Do you see it?"

"See what?"

"The house on the corner."

Jack peered through the wrought-iron fence toward a stately old Queen Anne-style Victorian mansion that was nearly hidden from view by thick tropical foliage and royal poinciana trees. It was a three-story white frame house with a widow's walk and a spacious sitting porch out front, due for a paint job but otherwise in good repair. Blue shutters framed the windows, purely for decoration. But the windows themselves and even the doors were covered with corrugated aluminum storm shutters—the kind that winter residents installed to protect their property during the June-to-November hurricane season.

"I see it," said Jack. "It's storm-proofed."

"Yes," replied the voice on the other end of the line. "But your girlfriend's inside. And she's not coming out. You have to go in and get her. And don't even think about calling the police to go in and get her for you. It's a big old house, and she's very well hidden. Maybe she's in the attic. Maybe she's under the floorboards. The only way you'll find her alive is if you stay on the phone and listen to me. I'll direct you right to her. But you have to move fast, Swyteck. I fed her arsenic exactly five minutes ago."

"You bastard! You said you wouldn't hurt her!"

"*I* didn't hurt her," he said sharply. "The only one who can hurt her is *you*. You'll kill her, unless you do as I say. She can last twenty minutes without an antidote. The sooner you find her, the sooner you can call the paramedics. The back door is open. I took the storm shutters off. So go get her, Jacky Boy. And stay on that phone."

Jack felt anger, fear, and a flood of other emotions, but he realized he had no time to consider his options. He yanked open the squeaky iron gate, sprinted up the brick driveway, and leaped over a three-foot hedge on his way to the back door—the only way into the desolate Key West mansion.

Chapter 52

•

Harold Swyteck was pacing nervously outside the waterfront warehouse where he'd been instructed to deliver the ransom. He was alone, but the noise from the nearby festival made it sound like he was in the Orange Bowl on New Year's night. He was as close as he could be to the madness on Duval Street and still be in relative seclusion. Occasionally someone in costume passed by, coming or going to the dimly lit parking lot behind the old warehouse to have sex, take a leak, or smoke a joint.

The governor checked his watch. It was almost 1:00 A.M., and he still hadn't heard from Jack or the kidnapper. Strange, he thought. He was alone in the dark with a suitcase full of money, and he wasn't the least bit concerned about himself or the cash. He was worried about Jack. He stopped pacing and lifted the receiver on the pay phone to make sure it was still working. He got a dial tone, then hung up.

He sighed heavily. He was trying to stay alert, but the noise from the festival was impossible to block out. Laughter, screaming, and every kind of music, from kazoos to strolling violins, had him constantly on edge. A rock band was blasting from the nearby Pier House Hotel. He could hear the bone-rattling bass and the beat of the drum. It was annoying at first, like a dripping faucet in the night. Then it became a thunder in his brain. He wished it would stop, but the pounding continued. He shook his head—and then he froze as he realized that the bass and drum were coming from one direction, but the *real* pounding was coming from the opposite direction. He wheeled and checked behind him. The pounding was right there, coming from somewhere near the pay phone.

"Who's there?" he called out. No one replied. The pounding grew louder and more frantic by the second, like the palpitations of his heart. He took two steps forward, then stopped. There was an old, rusted van parked just beyond the telephone. The rear doors bulged with each thudding beat. The pounding was coming from inside. It was like a kicking noise. Someone was trying to get out! The metal doors flew open. The governor drew his gun.

"Freeze!" he shouted. "Who's there?"

The violent motion stopped, but there was no reply. The governor stepped closer to the van. He knew it would do no good to ask again. If he wanted an answer, he'd have to go in and get it.

Chapter 53

•

Jack threw open the back door of the old mansion and rushed into a pitch-dark kitchen. He ran his hand along the wall and found a light switch. He flipped it on, but the room remained dark—*totally* dark, since every window in the house was covered by hurricane shutters.

"There's no power!" Jack shouted into the phone.

"It's off," said Esteban. "Take the flashlight from the kitchen table."

Jack bumped into a chair and found the table, then snatched up the flashlight and switched it on. His adrenaline was flowing, but he suddenly realized that he was terrified. His white beam of light cut like a laser across the room, and he felt like an intruder—not just in this house, but in another world. The old wooden house seemed to come alive, creaking and cracking with each breath it drew. The Victorian relic had a musty, shut-in smell, and everything in it was ancient—the furniture, the wallpaper, even the old hand pump by the sink. It was as if no one had lived here in a hundred years. No. It was as if the same people who'd lived here a hundred years ago were still living here now.

"Where's Cindy?" he screamed into the phone.

"Go through the door on your right. Into the dining room."

Jack shined the light ahead of him and walked hurriedly toward the door. The floorboards creaked with each step. He turned the crystal doorknob and entered the dining room. His flashlight's bright beam skipped across the long mahogany dining table, chair by chair. Cindy wasn't there. He searched higher, but the crystal chandelier only scattered the light. He scanned the walls, fixing on a hundred-year-old portrait of some crusty old sea captain who'd probably lived and died here. He almost seemed to scowl at Jack.

"Where *is* she!" he demanded.

"Easy," said Esteban. "You've got time. You've got as much time as *you* gave *me* to convince you that Raul should live. And now," he said, "it's *your* turn to convince *me*."

Jack felt a sinking dread. It was dawning on him that he was way out of his depth, that he was a pawn being manipulated at will. Sweat poured from his brow as he pressed the portable phone to his ear. "Listen, please—"

"I said *convince me!* Convince me she shouldn't die!"

"I'll give you anything you want. Just name it—whatever you want."

"I want *you* to feel what I felt. I want *you* to feel as helpless as I did. Let's start with groveling. Beg me, Swyteck. Beg me not to execute her."

Jack stood speechless for a second, fearful that precious time was wasting. He shined the flashlight into the living room and down the long hall. He wanted to sprint away and search for Cindy. But the house was huge. He could never find her in time. "Please," his voice shook, "just let her go."

"I said *beg!*"

"*Please.* Cindy doesn't deserve this. She's never hurt anyone."

"Try the cabinet. Beneath the breakfront."

Jack darted across the dining room, tripping over the Persian area rug. He pulled open the cabinet and shined the light inside. "She's not—"

"Of course she isn't. Begging and pleading gets us nowhere—remember? Try something else."

Jack rose to his feet, taking short, panicky breaths as he squeezed the portable phone in his hand. "You miserable son of a bitch. Just tell me where she is."

"*Anger,*" he taunted. "Let's see where *that* takes us. Try the living room—the closet at the base of the stairway."

Jack pointed the light across the room, revealing a grand stairway worthy of Scarlett O'Hara. It curved majestically up to the second floor, then curled in tight, smaller steps all the way to the third.

"The closet!" ordered Esteban, as if he somehow sensed that Jack hadn't moved.

Jack felt the seconds ticking away. He was a puppet, but following orders was his only hope. He darted toward the stairway, leading with the flashlight as he zigzagged through a maze of antiques in the living room. He found the closet and yanked open the door. Nothing. "You bastard!" his voice echoed in the dark, cavernous stairwell.

"Time is short," came the voice over the phone. "What are you going to do now?"

"Just stop the game! I'm the one you want. Take me. Just take *me*."

"Yessss," said Esteban, hissing with satisfaction. "A confession. It's your last chance. That's exactly the conclusion I reached, Swyteck. See if it works *this* time. Confess to me."

"I'll confess anything. I'm the one you want."

"Why?" he played his game. "What did *you do*?"

"Whatever you say I did. Whatever you say. I did it—"

"No!" he said bitterly. "You have to mean it. Confess to me and *mean* it!"

"I did it!"

"You killed Raul! Tell it to me!"

"Where is she?"

"Confess!"

"Yes! Yes!" he shouted into the phone. "I killed Raul Fernandez, all right? I did it! Now *where is Cindy*?"

"She's right behind you."

Jack wheeled, looked up into the stairwell and saw a body plunging like a missile through the stale air. "Cindy!" he cried out. But the next awful sound was the cracking of a neck at the end of a rope. Her feet never hit the ground. Jack screamed in agony. He recognized the clothes. A black hood covered her head—execution-style. "Oh, God, no . . ." he cried, all of his senses recoiling in horror. He dropped the portable phone and rushed halfway up the stairs to try to pull her down. But he couldn't reach her. He climbed a couple more steps and stretched out as far as he could. He still couldn't reach. He ran to the living room to grab a chair on which to stand, then rushed back toward the stairs.

"It's no use," came a deep, booming voice from somewhere in the pitch dark stairwell. "She's dead."

Jack's body went rigid. He was not alone.

He dropped the chair and drew his gun. He shined the flashlight behind him, then swept it forward and above. He didn't see anyone. "I'll kill you!" he shouted into the darkness.

"Revenge!" came a thundering reply that rattled the stairwell. "Now we *both* want it! Come get me, Swyteck!"

Jack thought only of Cindy hanging from her neck, and for one crazy moment he was willing to trade his own life for her killer's. He ran up the stairway with no conscious thought of his own safety, his gun in one hand, the flashlight in the other. He was at full speed when he reached the top of the steps. But as he turned the corner and started down the hall, a deafening blast sent him flying backward. *Pain . . . feet leaving ground . . . falling back . . . out of control.*

His gun and flashlight flew out of his hands as he crashed through the wooden banister. He was falling in what felt like slow motion. He heard himself cry out as he crashed onto a table and tumbled to the living-room floor. Then he sensed himself lying on his back. *Can't breathe . . . God, the pain.*

Seconds passed. The room was total blackness. Then a bright beam of light hit him in the eyes.

Esteban stared down from the top of the stairs. A smile crept onto his face at the sight of the body squirming and writhing on the floor. It pleased him that Jack was still alive. He pointed his flashlight up into the towering stairwell, as if admiring his work. The limp, lifeless body dangled overhead, twirling slowly on the rope. He tucked his gun into his belt, then pulled out his switch-blade. "Let the games begin," he said dryly. Then he shined the flashlight back down the stairway toward Jack—and his satisfied smile disappeared. In the few seconds he'd taken to savor the moment, his prey had quietly vanished.

Esteban scanned the living room floor with the flash-light. A look of confusion crossed his face. He saw no blood. No blood at all—anywhere. He grit his teeth in anger, realizing that his quarry must have been wearing a vest. Quickly, he jerked the flashlight from downstairs to upstairs. Jack's gun and flashlight were lying on the floor.

Esteban's smile returned. Jack was unarmed, and he couldn't have gone far. The house was completely dark, yet he'd snuck away without a sound. To do that, he had to have stayed within the glow from Esteban's flash-light. Esteban laid the flashlight down on the floor right where he stood at the top of the stairs, so as to mark the outer limits of Jack's escape. The dim, eerie glow ex-tended all the way across the living room, into the par-lor on one side, down the hall that led to the library on the other. It was large enough to make this *fun*. Esteban put his knife away, then pulled out his pistol. This time, Jack Swyteck would *not* get away.

Chapter 54

•

Outside the warehouse four blocks away, Governor Harold Swyteck stepped cautiously toward the wide-open doors of the old Chevy van. His gun was drawn and his heart was racing. He froze ten feet from the van when he saw that a sack the size of a body bag was lying across the van's floor, jerking back and forth.

"Don't move!" he shouted.

The motion stopped, but a steady whimpering followed. It was a muffled, desperate sound. The governor stepped closer and focused on the license plate. It was a Dade County tag—from Miami.

"This is Harold Swyteck," he announced as he reached the back of the van.

The whimpering grew louder, more urgent.

"Lie perfectly still," he ordered. "I have a gun." He stepped up into the dark van and knelt down beside the body. He pointed the gun with one hand and quickly untied the strings on the sack with the other.

"Cindy!" he said, recognizing her from Jack's description.

She stared up at him with wide, horrified eyes.

"It's okay," he tried to calm her. "I'm Jack's father." He began to open the sack, then stopped, realizing she was naked. The monster had taken her clothes. He untied the gag.

She drew a deep breath and tried to move her stiffened jaw. "Thank God," she cried in a trembling voice.

"Are you all right?"

"Yes, yes!" she answered. "But you have to call the police. He's going to kill Jack! He told me he would, right before he knocked me out with some injection. He was moving to another house, said you'd find me in this van. I'm his messenger to you." She raced on without catching her breath. "He said he's going to kill Jack, and he wants *you* to find the body. We may already be too late to save him. He said Jack would be dead by the time I woke up."

"Where are they?"

"He didn't tell me. He's not looking for a showdown with you. He wants you to search for your son, hoping you can save him. He wants you to be too late. He just wants you to find Jack's body."

The governor snatched a portable phone from his vest and punched the speed dial. "Code red, Kimmell! I've got Cindy. She's okay. Jack's in trouble. Need a location."

"Roger," replied Kimmell. He punched a button on his terminal. In seconds, it would pick up the signal from Jack's pulsating transmitter. At least it should have picked it up. He punched it again. Still nothing. Again. Nothing.

"Dammit, I'm not getting a reading," he said.

"What?"

"It's not coming through."

"How can that be?"

Kimmell shook his head, trying to think. "I don't know—maybe, maybe he lost the transmitter? I'm sorry, Governor. I can't find him."

The words cut to Harold Swyteck's core. "God help him," he uttered. "Dear God in heaven, please *help* him."

Chapter 55

●

A determined Esteban stepped quietly down the staircase, beneath Rebecca's dangling corpse. He'd left the flashlight on the top step, pointing into the stairwell. He needed light, but he didn't want to reveal his whereabouts by being its source. In the eerie yellow glow, his tall, lean body cast a lengthy shadow into the living room. His movements were quiet as a snake's. The gun felt warm in his hand. His heart actually beat at a normal pace—just another day at work for an experienced killer. He could either wait for Jack to come out of hiding, or he could go and get him. The choice was easy. Esteban *loved* flushing his quarry out of the bush.

Behind the staircase, at the end of the long, dark hallway, the heat in the tiny bathroom was nearly suffocating Jack. Sweat poured from his body. The bulletproof vest cloaked him like a winter parka, but he didn't dare take it off. It had saved his life once already—though a constant sharp pain told him the blow from the bullet had probably cracked a rib. He drew shallow breaths to minimize the pain. But pain was the least of his problems. He had no gun, no flashlight, and no contact to the outside world. He'd lost everything in the tumble down the stairs, and the gunshot had destroyed Kimmell's transmitter. Surprise was his only weapon. He stood perfectly still, hiding behind the open bathroom door with his back against the wall. He listened carefully for his stalker and accepted the brutal fact that only one of them would walk out of the house.

Leading with his gun, Esteban crept down the hall behind the stairway, one slow and silent step at a time. The fuzzy light from the stairwell grew dimmer with each step, but this was familiar territory. He had walked the entire house several times before Jack's arrival. He knew that just a few feet ahead, just beyond the faint glow from the flashlight, there was a bedroom on the right and a bathroom straight ahead. He moved closer to the wall and stopped just five feet away from the open bathroom door.

Jack was in total darkness, but his eyes were adjusting. From behind the open door he peered with one eye through the vertical crack at the hinges. There was light in the living room at the other end of the hall, but the hallway itself was barely illuminated. Jack's night vision improved with each passing second. Finally, he could see Esteban—a black silhouette with a gun in its hand.

Jack could feel his hands shaking and his heart pumping even more furiously. He could taste his own blood from a cut on his lip. The shadow slowly inched closer. He couldn't see his eyes or the features of his face. But there was enough light in the background to know he was right there. He was staring into the face of the enemy—but the enemy was a shadow. He wondered whether Esteban—or whoever he was—could see *him*, whether he was toying with him, knowing that his prey was unarmed and defenseless. Jack would find out in a moment. Esteban had two doors from which to choose—the bedroom or the bathroom. Jack held his breath and waited.

Go into the bedroom, he prayed.

Time stood still. Then Esteban moved—just a few inches. He was coming closer. He'd chosen the bathroom.

Jack could hear Esteban breathing. Jack's own lungs were about to explode, but he didn't dare take a breath. He was frozen against the wall. The open door was in his face. Esteban was at the threshold. His hand had crossed the imaginary plane. Another step and he'd be inside.

Suddenly, Jack pushed against the door with all his might, slamming it shut. Esteban cried out. His wrist was caught in the door, and his hand with the gun was in the bathroom. A shot roared in the pitch-dark bathroom, shattering the mirror. Another shot exploded the basin. Esteban was firing wildly. Jack put all his weight behind one last shove, and then he heard the sound of metal crashing on ceramic tile. The gun was on the floor. And Esteban was pinned.

Still braced against the door, Jack groped with one foot in the darkness, searching for the gun. He found it. His foot was right on it. He heard a piercing sound above his head, like a nail puncturing wood. Another piercing sound, and Jack cried out with pain as the point of Esteban's switchblade passed through the door and punctured his forearm. Jack dove to the floor and grabbed the gun, expecting Esteban to come crashing through. He pointed and shot twice in the darkness. But no one fell. Through his terror, he registered the sound of footsteps in the hall. Esteban was running. Jack opened the door and fired another quick shot, but his target had already turned the corner.

Jack dashed from the bathroom and followed in Esteban's footsteps. He heard a crash in the kitchen. The killer was escaping. Jack sprinted to the kitchen just as the back door slammed shut, then ran out to the porch. He looked left, then right. He saw a man dressed in black running down the sidewalk toward Duval Street. Jack knew Esteban would disappear forever if he made it back to the madness at Fantasy Fest. Jack's ribs were sore from the gunshot, his forearm had a puncture wound, and he was bleeding badly from the forehead, but his fall hadn't broken any bones in his legs. So he tucked the gun into his belt and began sprinting.

He was running faster than he had ever run, despite the vest, and he was gaining ground. As they drew closer to Duval, they started passing peacocks, tin men, and drunks who'd spilled over from the crowded street festival. Rock music rumbled in the night. A sudden burst of firecrackers drew piercing screams and a round of laughter.

"Hey, watch it!" a woman dressed as Cleopatra shouted, but Esteban plowed through her like she didn't exist, then plunged into the safety of a shoulder-to-shoulder parade of costumes on Duval. Jack followed right behind, trying desperately to keep his target in sight as he weaved his way through the heaving mass. He could hardly breathe. All at once the sea of beads and feathers and painted faces swallowed him up, and when he broke free Esteban was gone.

"You stupid jerk!" he heard someone shout. He looked ahead in time to see Esteban dashing through the middle of a long and twisted Chinese dragon, ripping it right in half. Esteban wasn't just trying to vanish in the crowd, Jack realized. He was *going* somewhere specific. He was headed north, toward the marina off Mallory Square. Jack had a sudden flash. A *boat!* Esteban was going to escape by boat. Jack hesitated only a second— just long enough to think of Cindy. Then he darted in the same direction, bumping into the Beatles and Napoleon, pushing aside Gumby and Marilyn Monroe.

Esteban was untying a sleek racing boat from its mooring just as Jack reached the long wooden pier at the end of Duval. The triple outboard engines cranked with a deafening blast. Jack stopped short, pulled out his gun, and took aim. A clown screamed and the crowd scattered, since Jack's gun looked too real, even for Fantasy Fest. A caveman suddenly turned hero and whacked the pistol from Jack's hand with a quick sweep of his club.

"No!" Jack shouted as his weapon skidded across the dock and plunked into the marina.

Esteban's boat drifted away from the dock, slowly at first, until it was clear of the other boats. Instinctively, Jack sprinted ahead and leaped from the dock to the covered bow of the boat just as Esteban hit the throttle.

The powerful engines roared, and the bow rose from the water, knocking Jack off balance as he landed. He scrambled to his feet on the wet fiberglass as the boat cut through the darkness.

Realizing that Jack was aboard, Esteban kept one hand on the steering wheel and with the other slashed at his unwanted passenger with a long fishing gaff. The engine noise grew deafening as the needlelike boat shot from forty, to sixty, then seventy miles per hour, bouncing violently on the waves. Jack fell to his knees as the hull slammed through a big whitecap. With a quick jerk of the wheel, Esteban shifted the boat to the right and Jack tumbled across the bow. In a split second he was overboard, head over heels, bouncing like a skipping stone across the waves at seventy miles per hour.

He emerged dizzy and coughing up salt water. He was trying to swim when his foot hit bottom. In less than ninety seconds the speeding cigarette boat had taken them nearly a mile offshore, where they'd reached a coral reef. He could stand flat-footed with his head above water. He cursed as he stood in the middle of a zipper of white foam that was Esteban's wake, forced to watch as the boat grew smaller in the distance. Then he froze as he saw that Esteban was turning around. He was coming back—at full throttle, headed right at him.

The bastard is going to flatten me.

Jack dove beneath the surface and pressed himself against the reef. He cut his hands and knees on sharp coral that projected like huge fingers and fans from the floor, but it saved his life. He held fast as the boat zipped overhead. The churning propeller missed him by less than a foot. He emerged for air, saw the boat coming back for another pass, and went under again. This time, though, the boat approached more slowly. Esteban wanted to check his work. After two years of waiting, he *had* to see the blood.

"Are you fish food, Swyteck?" he called into the darkness. He was nearly certain he'd cut the miserable lawyer in half. He'd felt the thud. But the water was so shallow it was possible the boat had hit bottom rather than pay dirt. He looked left, then right, searching intently as the boat slowly arrived at the spot where he'd last seen his prey.

Jack clung to the reef, struggling to stay underwater. But he desperately needed air. The boat was right overhead, puttering at no-wake speed. A few seconds passed, and he couldn't stand it any longer. He broke the surface and grabbed onto the diving platform on the back of the boat. He looked up. Esteban hadn't seen or heard him. The triple engines still rumbled loudly, even at a slow speed. Carefully, Jack pulled himself onto the platform and peered up over the stern. Esteban was studying the waves, longing to see little pieces of floating flesh.

Jack moved silently across the diving platform, toward the outboard engines. He was after the fuel lines. Without them, Esteban might get another mile from shore, but then he'd be stranded at sea. Jack reached for them and tried to muffle his cry as he scorched his hand on the hot engine block—but Esteban heard the stifled groan.

"Die!" he screamed, bringing the gaff down like an axe across Jack's back.

Jack cried out in pain, but he grabbed the gaff and pulled as he tumbled into the water, taking Esteban with him. They plunged into just three feet of sea water, both hitting the jagged coral bottom simultaneously. Esteban emerged first, thrashing like a marlin on the end of a line as he struggled to hold Jack underwater. Jack tumbled over the coral, trying to find his footing so he could get his head above water. But Esteban's powerful fingers found Jack's throat before he could plant his feet. Jack kicked and swung with his fists, but the resistance of the water made his blows ineffective. His nostrils burned as he sucked in more salt water. He gasped for air but drew only the sea into his lungs.

He reached frantically on the shallow bottom for a rock to use as a weapon. There were none. But there was the coral that projected from the bottom like a fossilized forest. It was hard and sharp, and it cut like a knife. He groped and found a formation that felt like the stubby antler of a young buck. He grabbed it, snapped it off, and swung it up toward Esteban's head. It hit something. Jack was blinded by the churning foam, but he sensed the penetration upon impact. He jabbed again, and finally the death grip around his throat loosened somewhat. He broke free and shot to the surface, coughing as he emerged.

Jack spit out the last of the salt water just in time to see Esteban, less than fifteen feet away, once again raising the gaff, which had floated back into his grasp. As he lifted it overhead, Jack could see the blood pouring from his throat.

"You bastard!" Esteban cried out. "You fucking bastard!" His arm shot forward in an attempt to impale, but Jack jinked to his left and grabbed the gaff's wooden shaft. By now, Esteban's eyes were glassy and his grip insecure. The loss of blood was taking its toll, but Esteban was still coming at him.

"No more!" Jack called out fiercely.

He drove forward, shattering the Cuban's teeth with the blunt end of the gaff and pushing it into his throat. The force of the movement jerked Esteban's body backward, then headfirst under the waves as Jack leaned forward and maintained steady pressure on the pole. Only after a full minute, when the bubbles had stopped floating to the surface, did he unclench his hands and swim toward the boat.

Once aboard, he watched intently, still unwilling to believe that the fight was over. He sat for ten minutes, staring at the spot where Esteban had gone under, half expecting him to rise again like the mechanical shark in *Jaws*. But this was real life, where people paid for their actions. The full moon hung like a big bright hole in the darkness. A shooting star appeared briefly on the horizon, and the gentle lapping of the waves against the hull reminded Jack that even this drama had done nothing to disturb nature's rhythms.

He heard a flutter behind him and looked up. A Coast Guard helicopter was approaching from shore. Jack sat perfectly still as the warm, gentle current washed across the reef and dispersed the dark, crimson cloud of Esteban's blood. It was ironic, he thought. Hundreds, maybe thousands of oppressed refugees had fled Cuba in little rafts and inner tubes, only to be caught in the Gulf Stream and lost somewhere in the Atlantic. Finally, one of the oppressors was on his way to the bottom. And with God's grace, the sea would never give him up.

Jack looked up as the pontoon helicopter hovered directly overhead, then came to rest on the surface. The glass bubble around the cockpit glistened in the moonlight, but he could see his father inside. Jack waved to let him know he was all right, and the governor opened the glass door and waved back.

"She's okay," his father shouted over the noise of whirling blades. "Cindy's okay!"

Jack heard the words, but couldn't assimilate them. *She can't be alive.* He'd seen her with his own eyes. Seen her hanging there. The part of his soul where she'd resided had been ripped out of him. Still, he wanted to believe. Oh, how he wanted to believe . . . He looked at his father intently, allowing himself some small measure of hope.

"She is *definitely* okay," Harry said, seeing the confusion on his son's face. "I just saw her. I just held her in my arms."

The governor threw him a line, but Jack was too stunned to move. Slowly, the realization sank in. Cindy was *alive*. His father was with him. And the danger was behind them. He reached for the lifeline and swam toward the helicopter. The swirling wind from the chopper blades blew water in his face, but he didn't mind. All the cuts and scrapes, the bruises—even his cracked rib—were glorious reminders that he was alive—alive with something to live for.

That much was obvious from the face that greeted him. As he looked up, Jack saw tears of joy in his proud father's eyes.

Epilogue

•

Before Esteban's body was borne by currents out to sea, his story had washed ashore with the force of a tidal wave. The media blitz began that Sunday morning and lasted for weeks, but the essential elements of the story were out within twenty-four hours. It was front-page news in every major Florida newspaper. It was the lead story on local and national network newscasts, and CNN even ran several hours of continuous coverage.

By Monday afternoon the Swytecks had revealed all to the media, and the truth was widely known about Esteban's two-year campaign to avenge his brother's execution. The public knew that neither Jack nor his father had killed Eddy Goss. Esteban had, as part of his plan to frame Jack and have him executed for a murder he'd never committed. The public knew that Esteban, not Jack, had murdered Gina Terisi, in a last-ditch effort to ensure

Jack's conviction. And the public knew that Governor Swyteck had not executed an innocent man. As Esteban had admitted to Jack, Raul Fernandez was in the act of raping the young girl when Esteban had killed her; both Esteban and Fernandez had gotten what they deserved.

By Monday evening the Swytecks were heralded as heroes. They'd eliminated not just a psychopathic killer, but one of Castro's former henchmen. The governor received congratulatory telegrams from several national leaders. A petition started in Little Havana to create "Swyteck Boulevard." Amidst all the hoopla, a cowardly written statement was issued quietly from the state attorney's office, announcing that Wilson McCue would promptly disband the grand jury he'd empaneled to indict the Swytecks.

And on the following Tuesday—the second Tuesday in November—the voters went to the polls. Florida had never seen a larger turnout. And no one had ever witnessed a more dramatic one-week turnaround in public opinion.

"The second time is sweeter!" Harry Swyteck proclaimed from the raised dais at his second inaugural ball.

Loud cheers filled the grand ballroom as three hundred friends and guests raised their champagne glasses with the re-elected governor. The band started up. The governor took Agnes by the hand and led her to the dance floor. It was like a silver wedding anniversary, the two of them swaying gracefully to their favorite song, the governor in his tuxedo and his bride in a flowing white taffeta gown.

Couples flooded onto the dance floor as Jack and Cindy watched from their seats at the head table. It had been a long time since they were this happy. They had their wounds, of course. Cindy had nightmares and fears of being alone. Both she and Jack constantly remembered Gina and what she'd gone through. Slowly, though, they regained some semblance of normalcy, and their love for each other became the source of their strength. Cindy returned to work at her photography studio. Jack started his own criminal-defense firm and enjoyed the luxury of picking his own clients. By Christmas, their lives had vastly improved—psychologically, emotionally, and most of all, romantically.

Jack couldn't hide his look of wonder and admiration as he stared at Cindy across the table. She was spectacular in a deep purple gown that featured an elegant hem and sexy décolletage. Her hair was up in a swirling blonde twist; her face was a radiant portrait framed by dangling diamond earrings that Agnes had loaned her.

"Come on," he said as he took her by the hand. "There's something I want you to see." They walked arm-in-arm away from the crowded ballroom to one of the quiet courtyards that had made this classic Mediterranean-style hotel so special since its opening in the 1920s.

Soft music flowed through the open French doors, making it even more romantic beneath the moon and stars on this cool, crisp January evening. They strolled arm-in-arm amidst trellised vines, a trickling fountain, and potted palms on a sweeping veranda the size of a tennis court. Jack rested their champagne glasses on the stone railing where the veranda overlooked a swimming pool forty feet below. He took Cindy in his arms.

"What's that for?" she asked coyly, enjoying the hug.

"Forever," he answered. Then, covertly, so she

wouldn't notice, he took a diamond ring from his pocket and dropped it into Cindy's glass.

"Well, *here* you are," said the governor with a smile as he came around the corner. "I've been trying to have a word alone with you two all evening."

Jack wasn't sure how to the handle the untimely interruption.

Cindy returned the smile. "And we've been waiting for a minute with you, too, Governor. To drink our own private toast to another four years."

"A wonderful idea," he replied, "except I'm out of champagne."

"Well, here," she offered, "have some of mine."

"Wait—" Jack said.

Cindy reached for her glass but knocked it off the railing.

"Oh, my God," Jack gasped, looking on with horror as it sailed over the edge and plunged forty feet down, exploding on the cement deck by the pool.

"Oh, I'm so clumsy," she said, looking embarrassed.

Jack continued to stare disbelievingly at the impact area below. Without a word, he turned and sprinted down the stone stairway that led to the pool, then began furiously searching the deck. Hunched over and squinting beneath the lanterns by the pool, he scoured the area with the diligence of an octogenarian on the beach with his metal detector. But he found only splinters of glass. He got down on his knees for a closer look, but the ring was gone.

"Looking for this?" Cindy asked matter-of-factly. She was standing over him, extending her hand and displaying the sparkling ring on her finger.

Jack just rolled his eyes like a guy caught on "Candid Camera." "You saw me drop it into the glass?" he asked, though it was more a statement than a question.

She nodded.

"You had the ring all along . . . it didn't go over the edge?"

"I fished it out when you were looking at your father," she said, smiling.

He laughed at himself as he shook his head. Then he looked up and shrugged with open arms. "Well?"

"Well," she replied. "So long as you're on your knees . . ."

Jack swallowed hard. "Will you?"

"Will I *what*?"

"Will you *marry* me?"

"Mmmmmm," Cindy stalled, then smiled. "You *know* I will." She pulled him up by the hand and threw her arms around him.

For one very long, happy moment, they were lost in each other, oblivious to their surroundings. But a sudden round of applause reminded them that they were in public. Perched on the veranda and smiling down on them were the governor and Agnes, and perhaps ten other couples the governor had rustled together after Cindy had shown him the ring.

Jack waved to them all, then took a quick bow.

"Your father's proud of you," Cindy said, looking into Jack's eyes. "And when we have a little Jack or Jackie running around our house, you can be proud, too."

" 'Jackie' sounds good," he said with a shrug, "if it's

a girl. But if it's a boy I'd like to call him 'Harry,' " Jack said thoughtfully. "For his grandfather."

She drew him close. "I'm happy he'll have a grandfather," she said.

"I am, too," Jack said.

He'd finally earned the governor's pardon. And the governor had earned his.

Beyond Suspicion

To Tiffany, always.
And forever.

Acknowledgments

•

Beyond Suspicion is a sequel to my first published novel, *The Pardon*. That first Jack Swyteck story was a true labor of love that came into being only after I'd spent four years, nights and weekends, writing a big, fat, multigenerational murder mystery that now collects dust on a closet shelf. Six novels later, I have to say that the best part about returning to my debut was the time spent reflecting on a point in my life when I didn't have time to start writing until eleven o'clock at night, and when I wouldn't stop pecking away until long after Tiffany had fallen asleep on the couch with the latest draft pages spilled at her side. Thanks, Tiff, for being there when it all began, and thanks for putting up with me all these years later.

A big thank-you goes to my editor, Carolyn Marino, and my agent, Richard Pine. Both were early fans of *The Pardon*, and both have left their mark on *Beyond Suspicion*. I'm also grateful to my team of first readers who endured some very rough drafts, Dr. Gloria M.

Grippando, Cece Sanford, Eleanor Rayner, and Carlos Sires. Probate attorney Clay Craig lent his usual expertise, Patrick Battle and Joseph N. Belth provided insights on viatical settlements, and the World Federation of Neurology offered a wealth of information on amyotrophic lateral sclerosis.

The people who helped most with my research wish to remain anonymous, which is perfectly understandable in the case of cops who work undercover. Their insights into the growth of Russian organized crime in South Florida were invaluable.

Finally, character names are often a pain to come up with, so I want to thank Mike Campbell and Jerry Chafetz for making my job easier. Through their generous contributions at fund-raising auctions for the benefit of St. Thomas Episcopal Parish School in Coral Gables and for The Gold-Diggers Inc. of Miami, they have lent their names to two of Jack Swyteck's buddies in *Beyond Suspicion*.

1

.

Outside her bedroom window, the blanket of fallen leaves moved—one footstep at a time.

Cindy Swyteck lay quietly in her bed, her sleeping husband at her side. It was a dark winter night, cold by Miami standards. In a city where forty degrees was considered frigid, no more than once or twice a year could she light the fireplace and snuggle up to Jack beneath a fluffy down comforter. She slid closer to his body, drawn by his warmth. A gusty north wind rattled the window, the shrill sound alone conveying a chill. The whistle became a howl, but the steady crunching of leaves was still discernible, the unmistakable sound of an approaching stranger.

Flashing images in her head offered a clear view of the lawn, the patio, and the huge almond leaves scattered all about. She could see the path he'd cut through the leaves. It led straight to her window.

Five years had passed since she'd last laid eyes on her attacker. Everyone from her husband to the police had assured her he was dead, though she knew he'd never really be gone. On nights like these, she could have sworn he was back, in the flesh. His name was Esteban.

Five years, and the horrifying details were still burned into her memory. His calloused hands and jagged nails so rough against her skin. The stale puffs of rum that came with each nauseating breath in her face. The cold, steel blade pressing at her jugular. Even then, she'd refused to kiss him back. Most unforgettable of all were those empty, sharklike eyes—eyes so cold and angry that when he'd opened his disgusting mouth and bit her on the lips she saw her own reflection, witnessed her own terror, in the shiny black irises.

Five years, and those haunting eyes still followed her everywhere, watching her every move. Not even her counselors seemed to understand what she was going through. It was as if the eyes of Esteban had become her second line of sight. When night fell and the wind howled, she could easily slip into the mind of her attacker and see things he'd seen before his own violent death. Stranger still, she seemed to have a window to the things he might be seeing now. Through his eyes, she could even watch herself. Night after night, she had the perfect view of Cindy Swyteck lying in bed, struggling in vain with her incurable fear of the dark.

Outside, the scuffling noise stopped. The wind and leaves were momentarily silent. The digital alarm clock on the nightstand blinked on and off, the way it always did when storms interrupted power. It was stuck on midnight, bathing her pillow with faint pulses of green light.

She heard a knock at the back door. On impulse, she rose and sat at the edge of the bed.

Don't go, she told herself, but it was as if she were being summoned.

Another knock followed, exactly like the first one. On the other side of the king-sized bed, Jack was sleeping soundly. She didn't even consider waking him.

I'll get it.

Cindy saw herself rise from the mattress and plant her bare feet on the tile floor. Each step felt colder as she continued down the hall and through the kitchen. The house was completely dark, and she relied more on instinct than sight to maneuver her way to the back door. She was sure she'd turned off the outside lights at bedtime, but the yellow porch light was burning. Something had obviously triggered the electronic eye of the motion detector. She inched closer to the door, peered out the little diamond-shaped window, and let her eyes roam from one edge of the backyard to the other. A gust of wind ripped through the big almond tree, tearing the brownest leaves from the branches. They fell to the ground like giant snowflakes, but a few were caught in an upward draft and rose into the night, just beyond the faint glow of the porch light. Cindy lost sight of them, except for one that seemed to hover above the patio. Another blast of wind sent it soaring upward. Then it suddenly changed direction, came straight toward her, and slammed against the door.

The noise startled her, but she didn't back away. She kept looking out the window, as if searching for whatever it was that had sent that lone leaf streaking toward her with so much force. She saw nothing, but in her heart she knew that she was mistaken. Something was definitely out there. She just couldn't see it. Or maybe it was Esteban who couldn't see it.

Stop using his *eyes!*

The door swung open. A burst of cold air hit her like an Arctic front. Goose bumps covered her arms and legs. Her silk nightgown shifted in the breeze, rising to midthigh. She somehow knew that she was colder than ever before in her life, though she didn't really feel it. She didn't feel anything. A numbness had washed over her, and though her mind told her to run, her feet wouldn't move. It was suddenly impossible to gauge the passage of time, but in no more than a few moments was she strangely at ease with the silhouette in the doorway.

"Daddy?"

"Hi, sweetheart."

"What are you doing here?"

"It's Tuesday."

"So?"

"Is Jack here?"

"He's sleeping."

"Wake him."

"For what?"

"It's our night to play poker."

"Jack can't play cards with you tonight."

"We play every Tuesday."

"I'm sorry, Daddy. Jack can't play with you anymore."

"Why not?"

"Because you're dead."

With a shrill scream she sat bolt upright in bed. Confused and frightened, she was shivering uncontrollably. A hand caressed her cheek, and she screamed again.

"It's okay," said Jack. He moved closer and tried putting his arms around her.

She pushed him away. "No!"

"It's okay, it's me."

Her heart was pounding, and she was barely able to catch her breath. A lone tear ran down her face. She wiped it away with the back of her hand. It felt as cold as ice water.

"Take a deep breath," said Jack. "Slowly, in and out."

She inhaled, then exhaled, repeating the exercise several times. In a minute or so, the panic subsided and her breathing became less erratic. Jack's touch felt soothing now, and she nestled into his embrace.

He sat up beside her and wrapped his arms around her. "Was it that dream again?"

She nodded.

"The one about your father?"

"Yes."

She was staring into the darkness, not even aware that Jack was gently brushing her hair out of her face. "He's been gone so long. Why am I having these dreams now?"

"Don't let it scare you. There's nothing to be afraid of."

"I know."

She laid her head against his shoulder. Jack surely meant well, but he couldn't possibly understand what truly frightened her. She'd never told him the most disturbing part. What good was there in knowing that her father was coming back—*for him*?

"It's okay," said Jack. "Try to get some sleep."

She met his kiss and then let him go, stroking his forehead as he drifted off to sleep. He was breathing audibly in the darkness, but she still felt utterly alone. She lay with eyes wide open, listening.

She heard that sound again outside her bedroom window, the familiar scuffle of boots cutting through a carpet of dead leaves. Cindy didn't dare close her eyes, didn't even flirt with the idea of sliding back to that place where she'd found the cursed gift of sight. She brought the blanket all the way up to her chin and clutched it for warmth, praying that this time there'd be no knocking at the back door.

In time the noise faded, as if someone were drifting away.

2

.

Jack Swyteck was in Courtroom 9 of the Miami-Dade courthouse, having a ball. With a decade of experience in criminal courts, both as a prosecutor and a criminal defense lawyer, he didn't take many civil cases. But this one was different. It was a slam-bang winner, the judge had been spitting venom at opposing counsel the entire trial, and Jack's client was an old flame who'd once ripped his heart right out of his chest and stomped that sucker flat.

Well, two out of three ain't bad.

"All rise!"

The lunch break was over, and the lawyers and litigants rose as Judge Antonio Garcia approached the bench. The judge glanced their way, as if he couldn't help gathering an eyeful of Jack's client. No surprise there. Jessie Merrill wasn't stunningly beautiful, but she was damn close. She carried herself with a confidence that bespoke intelligence, tempered by intermittent moments of apparent vulnerability that made her simply irresistible to the knuckle-dragging, testosterone-toting half of the population. Judge Garcia was as susceptible as the next guy. Beneath that flowing black robe was, after all, a mere mortal—a man. That aside, Jessie truly was a victim in this case, and it was impossible not to feel sorry for her.

"Good afternoon," said the judge.

"Good afternoon," the lawyers replied, though the judge's nose was buried in paperwork. Rather than immediately call in the jury, it was Judge Garcia's custom to mount the bench and then take a few minutes to read his mail or finish the crossword puzzle—his way of announcing to all who entered his courtroom that he alone had that rare and special power to silence attorneys and make them sit and wait. Judicial power plays of all sorts seemed to be on the rise in Miami courtrooms, ever since hometown hero Marilyn Milian gave up her day job to star on *The People's Court*. Not every south Florida judge wanted to trace her steps to television stardom, but at least one wannabe in criminal court could no longer mete out sentences to convicted murderers without adding, "You *are* the weakest link, good-bye."

Jack glanced to his left and noticed his client's hand shaking. It stopped the moment she'd caught him looking. Typical Jessie, never wanting anyone to know she was nervous.

"We're almost home," Jack whispered.

She gave him a tight smile.

Before this case, it had been a good six years since Jack had seen her. Five months after dumping him, Jessie had called for lunch with the hope of giving it another try. By then Jack was well on his way toward falling hopelessly in love with Cindy Paige, now Mrs. Jack

Swyteck, something he never called her unless he wanted to be introduced at their next cocktail party as Mr. Cindy Paige. Cindy was more beautiful today than she was then, and Jack had to admit the same was true of Jessie. That, of course, was no reason to take her case. But he decided it wasn't a reason to turn it down, either. This had nothing to do with the fact that her long, auburn hair had once splayed across both their pillows. She'd come to him as an old friend in a genuine crisis. Even six months later, her words still echoed in the back of his mind.

•

"The doctor told me I have two years to live. Three, tops."

Jack's mouth fell open, but words came slowly. "Damn, Jessie. I'm so sorry."

She seemed on the verge of tears. He scrambled to find her a tissue. She dug one of her own from her purse. "It's so hard for me to talk about this."

"I understand."

"I was so damn unprepared for that kind of news."

"Who wouldn't be?"

"I take care of myself. I always have."

"It shows." It wasn't intended as a come-on, just a statement of fact that underscored what a waste this was.

"My first thought was, you're crazy, doc. This can't be."

"Of course."

"I mean, I've never faced anything that I couldn't beat. Then suddenly I'm in the office of some doctor who's basically telling me, that's it, game over. No one bothered to tell me the game had even started."

He could hear the anger in her voice. "I'd be mad, too."

"I was furious. And scared. Especially when he told me what I had."

Jack didn't ask. He figured she'd tell him if she wanted him to know.

"He said I had ALS—amyotrophic lateral sclerosis."

"I'm not familiar with that one."

"You probably know it as Lou Gehrig's disease."

"Oh." It was a more ominous-sounding "oh" than intended. She immediately picked up on it.

"So, you know what a horrible illness it is."

"Just from what I heard happened to Lou Gehrig."

"Imagine how it feels to hear that it's going to happen to you. Your mind stays healthy, but your nervous system slowly dies, causing you to lose control of your own body. Eventually you can't swallow anymore, your throat muscles fail, and you either suffocate or choke to death on your own tongue."

She was looking straight at him, but he was the one to blink.

"It's always fatal," she added. "Usually in two to five years."

He wasn't sure what to say. The silence was getting uncomfortable. "I don't know how I can help, but if there's anything I can do, just name it."

"There is."

"Please, don't be afraid to ask."

"I'm being sued."

"For what?"

"A million and a half dollars."

He did a double take. "That's a lot of money."

"It's all the money I have in the world."

"Funny. There was a time when you and I would have thought that *was* all the money in the world."

Her smile was more sad than wistful. "Things change."

"They sure do."

A silence fell between them, a moment to reminisce.

"Anyway, here's my problem. My *legal* problem. I tried to be responsible about my illness. The first thing I did was get my finances in order. Treatment's expensive, and I wanted to do something extravagant for myself in the time I had left. Maybe a trip to Europe, whatever. I didn't have a lot of money, but I did have a three-million-dollar life insurance policy."

"Why so much?"

"When the stock market tanked a couple years ago, a financial planner talked me into believing that whole-life insurance was a good retirement vehicle. Maybe it would have been worth something by the time I reached sixty-five. But at my age, the cash surrender value is practically zilch. Obviously, the death benefit wouldn't kick in until I was dead, which wouldn't do *me* any good. I wanted a pot of money while I was alive and well enough to enjoy myself."

Jack nodded, seeing where this was headed. "You did a viatical settlement?"

"You've heard of them?"

"I had a friend with AIDS who did one before he died."

"That's how they got popular, back in the eighties. But the concept works with any terminal disease."

"Is it a done deal?"

"Yes. It sounded like a win-win situation. I sell my three-million-dollar policy to a group of investors for a million and a half dollars. I get a big check right now, when I can use it. They get the three-million-dollar death benefit when I die. They'd basically double their money in two or three years."

"It's a little ghoulish, but I can see the good in it."

"Absolutely. Everybody was satisfied." The sorrow seemed to drain from her expression as she looked at him and said, "Until my symptoms started to disappear."

"Disappear?"

"Yeah. I started getting better."

"But there's no cure for ALS."

"The doctor ran more tests."

Jack saw a glimmer in her eye. His heart beat faster. "And?"

"They finally figured out I had lead poisoning. It can mimic the symptoms of ALS, but it wasn't nearly enough to kill me."

"You don't have Lou Gehrig's disease?"

"No."

"You're not going to die?"

"I'm completely recovered."

A sense of joy washed over him, though he did feel a little manipulated. "Thank God. But why didn't you tell me from the get-go?"

She smiled wryly, then turned serious. "I thought you should know how I felt, even if it was just for a few minutes. This sense of being on the fast track to such an awful death."

"It worked."

"Good. Because I have quite a battle on my hands, legally speaking."

"You want to sue the quack who got the diagnosis wrong?"

"Like I said, at the moment, I'm the one being sued over this."

"The viatical investors?"

"You got it. They thought they were coming into

three million in at most three years. Turns out they may
have to wait another forty or fifty years for their investment to 'mature,' so to speak. They want their million
and a half bucks back."

"Them's the breaks."

She smiled. "So you'll take the case?"

"You bet I will."

•

The crack of the gavel stirred Jack from his thoughts.
The jury had returned. Judge Garcia had finished perus-
ing his mail, the sports section, or whatever else had
caught his attention. Court was back in session.

"Mr. Swyteck, any questions for Dr. Herna?"

Jack glanced toward the witness stand. Dr. Herna
was the physician who'd reviewed Jessie's medical history on behalf of the viatical investors and essentially
confirmed the misdiagnosis, giving them the green light
to invest. He and the investors' lawyer had spent the
entire morning trying to convince the jury that, because
Jessie didn't actually have ALS, the viatical settlement
should be invalidated on the basis of a "mutual mistake." It was Jack's job to prove it was *their* mistake,
nothing mutual about it, too bad, so sad.

Jack could hardly wait.

"Yes, Your Honor," he said as he approached the
witness with a thin, confident smile. "I promise, this
won't take long."

3
•

The courtroom was silent. It was the pivotal moment in the trial, Jack's cross-examination of the plaintiff's star witness. The jury looked on attentively—whites, blacks, Hispanics, a cross section of Miami. Jack often thought that anyone who wondered if an ethnically diverse community could possibly work together should serve on a jury. The case of *Viatical Solutions, Inc. v. Jessie Merrill* was like dozens of other trials underway in Miami at that very moment—no media, no protestors, no circus ringmaster. Not once in the course of the trial had he been forced to drop a book to the floor or cough his lungs out to wake the jurors. It was quietly reassuring to know that the administration of justice in Florida wasn't always the joke people saw on television.

Reassuring for Jack, anyway. Staring out from the witness stand, Dr. Felix Herna looked anything but calm. Jack's opposing counsel seemed to sense the doctor's anxiety. Parker Aimes was a savvy enough plaintiffs' attorney to sprint to his feet and do something about it.

"Judge, could we have a five-minute break, please?"

"We just got back from lunch," he said, snarling.

"I know, but—"

"But nothing," the judge said, peering out over the top of his wire-rimmed reading glasses. "Counselor, I just checked my horoscope, and it says there's loads of leisure time in my near future. So, Mr. Swyteck, if you please."

With the judge talking astrology, Jack was beginning to rethink his reavowed faith in the justice system. "Thank you, Your Honor."

All eyes of the jurors followed him as he approached the witness. He planted himself firmly, using his height and body language to convey a trial lawyer's greatest tool: control.

"Dr. Herna, you'll agree with me that ALS is a serious disease, won't you?"

The witness shifted in his seat, as if distrustful of even the most innocuous question. "Of course."

"It attacks the nervous system, breaks down the tissues, kills the motor neurons?"

"That's correct."

"Victims eventually lose the ability to control their legs?"

"Yes."

"Their hands and arms as well?"

"Yes."

"Their abdominal muscles?"

"That's correct, yes. It destroys the neurons that control the body's voluntary muscles. Muscles controlled by conscious thought."

"Speech becomes unclear? Eating and swallowing becomes difficult?"

"Yes."

"Breathing may become impossible?"

"It does affect the tongue and pharyngeal muscles. Eventually, all victims must choose between prolonging their life on a ventilator or asphyxiation."

"Suffocation," said Jack. "Not a very pleasant way to die."

"Death is rarely pleasant, Mr. Swyteck."

"Unless you're a viatical investor."

"Objection."

"Sustained."

A juror nodded with agreement. Jack moved on, knowing he'd tweaked the opposition. "Is it fair to say that once ALS starts, there's no way to stop it?"

"Miracles may happen, but the basic assumption in the medical community is that the disease is fatal, its progression relentless. Fifty percent of people die within two years. Eighty percent within five."

"Sounds like an ideal scenario for a viatical settlement."

"Objection."

"I'll rephrase it. True or false, Doctor: The basic assumption of viatical investors is that the patient will die soon."

He looked at Jack as if the question were ridiculous. "Of course that's true. That's how they make their money."

"You'd agree, then, that a proper diagnosis is a key component of the investment decision?"

"True again."

"That's why the investors hired you, isn't it? They relied on *you* to confirm that Ms. Merrill had ALS."

"They hired me to review her doctor's diagnosis."

"How many times did you physically examine her?"

"None."

"How many times did you meet with her?"

"None."

"How many times did you speak with her?"

"None," he said, his tone defensive. "You're making this sound worse than it really was. The reviewing physician in a viatical settlement rarely if ever reexamines the patient. It was my job to review Ms. Merrill's medical history as presented to me by her treating physician. I then made a determination as to whether the diagnosis was based on sound medical judgment."

"So, you were fully aware that Dr. Marsh's diagnosis was 'clinically possible ALS.' "

"Yes."

"*Possible* ALS," Jack repeated, making sure the judge and jury caught it. "Which means that it could possibly have been something else."

"Her symptoms, though minor, were entirely consistent with the early stages of the disease."

"But the very diagnosis—possible ALS—made it clear that it could've been something other than ALS. And you knew that."

"You have to understand that there's no magic bullet, no single test to determine whether a patient has ALS. The diagnosis is in many ways a process of elimination. A series of tests are run over a period of months to rule out other possible illnesses. In the early stages, a seemingly healthy woman like Jessie Merrill could have ALS and have no idea that anything's seriously wrong with her body, apart from the fact that maybe her foot falls asleep, or she fumbles with her car keys, or is having difficulty swallowing."

"You're not suggesting that your investors plunked down a million and a half dollars based solely on the fact that Ms. Merrill was dropping her car keys."

"No."

"In fact, your investors rejected the investment proposal at first, didn't they?"

"An investment based on a diagnosis of clinically possible ALS was deemed too risky."

"They decided to invest only *after* you spoke with Dr. Marsh, correct?"

"I did speak with him."

"Would you share with the court Dr. Marsh's exact words, please?"

The judge looked up, his interest sufficiently piqued. Dr. Herna shifted his weight again, obviously reluctant.

"Let me say at the outset that Dr. Marsh is one of the most respected neurologists in Florida. I knew that his diagnosis of clinically possible ALS was based upon strict adherence to the diagnostic criteria established by the World Federation of Neurology. But I also knew that he was an experienced physician who had seen more cases of ALS than just about any other doctor in Miami. So I asked him to put the strict criteria aside. I asked him to talk to me straight but off the record: Did he think Jessie Merrill had ALS?"

"I'll ask the question again: What did Dr. Marsh tell you?"

Herna looked at his lawyer, then at Jack. He lowered his eyes and said, "He told me that if he were a betting man, he'd bet on ALS."

"As it turns out, Ms. Merrill didn't have ALS, did she?"

"Obviously not. Dr. Marsh was dead wrong."

"Excuse me, doctor. He wasn't wrong. Dr. Marsh's diagnosis was clinically *possible* ALS. You knew that he was still monitoring the patient, still conducting tests."

"I also know what he told me. He told me to bet on ALS."

"Only after you pushed him to speculate prematurely."

"As a colleague with the utmost respect for the man, I asked for his honest opinion."

"You urged him to *guess*. You pushed for an answer because Ms. Merrill was a tempting investment opportunity."

"That's not true."

"You were afraid that if you waited for a conclusive diagnosis, she'd be snatched up by another group of viatical investors."

"All I know is that Dr. Marsh said he'd bet on ALS. That was good enough for me."

Jack moved closer, tightening his figurative grip. "It wasn't Ms. Merrill who made the wrong diagnosis, was it?"

"No."

"As far as she knew, a horrible death was just two or three years away."

"I don't know what she was thinking."

"Yes, you do," Jack said sharply. "When you reviewed her medical file and coughed up a million and a half dollars to buy her life insurance policy, you became her second opinion. You convinced her that she was going to die."

Dr. Herna fell stone silent, as if suddenly he realized the grief he'd caused her—as if finally he understood Jack's animosity.

Jack continued, "Ms. Merrill never told you she had a confirmed case of ALS, did she?"

"No."

"She never guaranteed you that she'd die in two years."

"No."

"All she did was give you her medical records."

"That's all I saw."

"And you made a professional judgment as to whether she was going to live or die."

"I did."

"And you bet on death."

"In a manner of speaking."

"You bet on ALS."

"Yes."

"And you lost."

The witness didn't answer.

"Doctor, you and your investors rolled the dice and lost. Isn't that what really happened here?"

He hesitated, then answered. "It didn't turn out the way we thought it would."

"Great reason to file a lawsuit."

"Objection."

"Sustained."

Jack didn't push it, but his sarcasm had telegraphed to the jury the question he most wanted answered: *Don't you think this woman's been through enough without you suing her, asshole?*

"Are you finished, Mr. Swyteck?" asked Judge Garcia.

"Yes, Your Honor. I think that wraps things up." He turned away from the witness and headed back to his chair. He could see the gratitude in Jessie's eyes, but far more palpable was the dagger in his back that was Dr. Herna's angry glare.

Jessie leaned toward her lawyer and whispered, "Nice work."

"Yeah," Jack said, fixing on the word she'd chosen. "I was entirely too *nice.*"

4
.

Jack and Jessie were seated side by side on the court-house steps, casting cookie crumbs to pigeons as they awaited notification that the jury had reached a verdict.

"What do you think they'll do?" she asked.

Jack paused. The tiers of granite outside the Miami-Dade courthouse were the judicial equivalent of the Oracle of Delphi, where lawyers were called upon daily to hazard a wild-ass guess about a process that was ultimately unpredictable. Jack would have liked to tell her there was nothing to worry about, that in twenty minutes they'd be cruising toward Miami Beach, the top down on his beloved Mustang convertible, the CD player totally cranked with an obnoxiously loud version of the old hit song from the rock band Queen, "We Are the Champions."

But his career had brought too many surprises to be that unequivocal.

"I have a good feeling," he said. "But with a jury you never know."

He savored the last bit of cream from the better half of an Oreo, then tossed the rest of the cookie to the steps below. A chorus of gray wings fluttered as hungry pigeons scurried after the treat. In seconds it was in a hundred pieces. The victors flew off into the warm, crystal-blue skies that marked February in Miami.

Jessie said, "Either way, I guess this is it."

"We might have an appeal, if we lose."

"I was speaking more on a personal level." She laid her hand on his forearm and said, "You did a really great thing for me, taking my case. But in a few minutes it will all be over. And then, I guess, I'll never see you again."

"That's actually a good thing. In my experience, reuniting with an old client usually means they've been sued or indicted all over again."

"I've had my fill of that, thank you."

"I know you have."

Jack glanced toward the hot-dog vendor on the crowded sidewalk along Flagler Street, then back at Jessie. She hadn't taken her eyes off him, and her hand was still resting on his forearm. *A little too touchy-feely today.* He rose and buried his hands in his pockets.

"Jack, there's something I want to tell you."

The conversation seemed to be drifting beyond the attorney-client relationship, and he didn't want to go there. He was her lawyer, nothing more, never mind the past. "Before you say anything, there's something I should tell you."

"Really?"

He sat on the step beside her. "I noticed that Dr. Marsh was back in the courtroom today. He's obviously concerned."

His abrupt return to law-talk seemed to confuse her. "Concerned about me, you mean?"

"I'd say his exact concern is whether you plan to sue him. We haven't talked much about this, but you probably do have a case against him."

"Sue him? For what?"

"Malpractice, of course. He eventually got your diagnosis right, but he should have targeted lead poisoning as the cause of your neurological problems much earlier than he did. Especially after you told him about the renovations to your condo. The dust that comes with sanding off old, lead-based paint in houses built before 1978 is a pretty common source of lead poisoning."

"But he's the top expert in Miami."

"He's still capable of making mistakes. He is human, after all."

She looked off to the middle distance. "That's the perfect word for him. He was *so* human. He took such special care of me."

"How do you mean?"

"Some doctors are ice-cold, no bedside manner at all. Dr. Marsh was very sympathetic, very compassionate. It's not that common for someone under the age of forty to get ALS, and he took a genuine interest in me."

"In what way?"

"Not in the way you're thinking," she said, giving him a playful kick in the shin.

"I'm not thinking anything."

"I'll give you a perfect example. One of the most important tests I had was the EMG. That's the one where they hook you up to the electrodes to see if there's any nerve damage."

"I know. I saw the report."

"Yeah, but *all* you saw was the report. The actual test can be pretty scary, especially when you're worried that you might have something as awful as Lou

Gehrig's disease. Most neurologists have a technician do the test. But Dr. Marsh knew how freaked out I was about this. I didn't want some technician to conduct the test, and then I'd have to wait another week for the doctor to interpret the results, and then wait another two weeks for a follow-up appointment where the results would finally be explained to me. So he ran the test himself, immediately. There aren't a lot of doctors who would do that for their patients in this world of mismanaged care."

"You're right about that."

"I could give you a dozen other examples. He's a great doctor and a real gentleman. I don't need to sue Dr. Marsh. A million and a half dollars is plenty for me."

Jack couldn't disagree. It was one more pleasant reminder that she was no longer the self-centered twentysomething-year-old of another decade. And neither was he.

"You're making the right decision."

"I've made a few good ones in my lifetime," she said, her smile fading. "And a few bad ones, too."

He was at a loss for the right response, preferred to let it go. But she followed up. "Have you ever wondered what would have happened if we hadn't broken up?"

"No."

"Liar."

"Let's not talk about that."

"Why not? Isn't that just a teensy-weensy part of the reason you took my case?"

"No."

"Liar."

"Stop calling me a liar."

"Stop lying."

"What do you want me to say?"

"Just answer one question for me. I want you to be completely honest. And if you are, I'll totally drop this, okay?"

"All right. One."

"Six months we've been working this case together. Are you surprised nothing happened between us?"

"No."

"Why not?"

"That's two questions."

"Why do you think nothing happened?"

"Because I'm married."

She flashed a thin smile, nodding knowingly. "Interesting answer."

"What's so interesting about it? That's the answer."

"Yes, but you could have said something a little different, like 'Because I love my wife.' Instead, you said, 'Because I'm married.'"

"It comes down to the same thing."

"No. One comes from the heart. The other is just a matter of playing by the rules."

Jack didn't answer. Jessie had always been a smart girl, but that was perhaps the most perceptive thing he'd ever heard her say.

The digital pager vibrated on his belt. He checked it eagerly, then looked at Jessie and said, "Jury's back."

She didn't move, still waiting for him to say something. Jack just gathered himself up and said, "Can't keep the judge waiting."

Without another word, she rose and followed him up the courthouse steps.

5

.

In minutes they were back in Courtroom 9, and Jack could feel the butterflies swirling in his belly. This wasn't the most complicated case he'd ever handled, but he wanted to win it for Jessie. It had nothing to do with the fact that his client was a woman who'd once rejected him and that this was his chance to prove what a great lawyer he was. Jessie deserved to win. Period. It was that simple.

Right. Is anything *ever that simple?*

Jack and his client stood impassively at their place behind the mahogany table for the defense. Plaintiff's counsel stood alone on the other side of the courtroom, at the table closest to the jury box. His client, a corporation, hadn't bothered to send a representative for the rendering of the verdict. Perhaps they'd expected the worst, a prospect that seemed to have stimulated some public interest. A reporter from the local paper was seated in the front row, and behind her in the public gallery were other folks Jack didn't recognize. One face, however, was entirely familiar: Joseph Marsh, Jessie's neurologist, was standing in the rear of the courtroom.

A paddle fan wobbled directly over Jack's head as the decision makers returned to the jury box in single file. Each of them looked straight ahead, sharing not a glance with either the plaintiff or the defendant. Professional jury consultants could have argued for days as to the significance of their body language—whether it was good or bad if they made eye contact with the plaintiff, the defendant, the lawyers, the judge, or no one at all. To Jack, it was all pop psychology, unreliable even when the foreman winked at your client and mouthed the words, "It's in the bag, baby."

"Has the jury reached a verdict?" asked the judge.

"We have, Your Honor," announced the forewoman. The all-important slip of paper went from the jury box to the bailiff and finally to the judge. He inspected it for less than a second, showing no reaction. "Please announce the verdict."

Jack felt his client's long fingernails digging into his bicep.

"In the case of Viatical Solutions Incorporated versus Jessie Merrill, we the jury find in favor of the defendant."

Jack suddenly found himself locked in what felt like a full body embrace, his client trembling in his arms. Had he not been there to hold her, she would have fallen to the floor. A tear trickled down her cheek as she looked him in the eye and whispered, "Thank you."

"You're welcome." He released her, but she held him a moment longer—a little too long and too publicly, perhaps, to suit a married man. Then again, plenty of overjoyed clients had hugged him in the past, even big burly men who were homophobic to the core. Like them, Jessie had simply gotten carried away with the moment.

I think.

"Your Honor, we have a motion." The lawyer for Viatical Solutions, Inc. was standing at the podium. He seemed on the verge of an explosion, which was understandable. One and a half million dollars had just slipped through his fingers. Six months earlier he'd written an arrogant letter to Jessie telling her that her viatical settlement wasn't worth the paper it was written on. Now Jessie was cool, and he was the fool.

God, I love winning.

"What's your motion?" the judge asked.

"We ask that the court enter judgment for the plaintiff notwithstanding the verdict. The evidence does not support—"

"Save it," said the judge.

"Excuse me?"

"You heard me." With that, Judge Garcia unleashed a veritable tongue-lashing. From the first day of trial he'd seemed taken with Jessie, and this final harangue only confirmed that Jack should have tried the case to the judge alone and never even asked for a jury. At least a half-dozen times in the span of two minutes he derided the suit against Jessie as "frivolous and mean-spirited." He not only denied the plaintiff's post-trial motion, but he so completely clobbered them that Jack was beginning to wish he'd invited Cindy downtown to watch.

On second thought, it was just as well that she'd missed that big hug Jessie had given him in her excitement over the verdict.

"Ladies and gentlemen of the jury, thank you for

your service. We are adjourned." With a bang of the judge's gavel, it was all over.

Jessie was a millionaire.

"Time to celebrate," she said.

"You go right ahead. You've earned it."

"You're coming too, buster. Drinks are on me."

He checked his watch. "All right. It's early for me, but maybe a beer."

"One beer? Wimp."

"Lush."

"*Lawyer.*"

"Now you're hitting way below the belt."

They shared a smile, then headed for the exit. The courtroom had already cleared, but a small crowd was gathering at the elevator. Most had emerged from another courtroom, but Jack recognized a few spectators from Jessie's trial. Among them was Dr. Marsh.

The elevator doors opened, and Jack said, "Let's wait for the next one."

"There's room," said Jessie.

A dozen people packed into the crowded car. In all the jostling for position, a janitor and his bucket came between Jack and Jessie. The doors closed and, as if it were an immutable precept of universal elevator etiquette, all conversation ceased. The lighted numbers overhead marked their silent descent. The doors opened two floors down. Three passengers got off, four more got in. Jack kept his eyes forward but noticed that, in the shuffle, Dr. Marsh had wended his way from the back of the car to a spot directly beside Jessie.

The elevator stopped again. Another exchange of passengers, two exiting, two more getting on. Jack kept his place in front near the control panel. As the doors closed, Jessie moved all the way to the far corner. Dr. Marsh managed to find an opening right beside her.

Is he pursuing her?

It was too crowded for Jack to turn his body around completely, but he could see Jessie and her former physician in the convex mirror in the opposite corner of the elevator. Discreetly, he kept an eye on both of them. Marsh had blown the diagnosis of ALS, but he was a smart guy. Surely he'd anticipated that Jessie would speak to her lawyer about suing him for malpractice. If it was his intention to corner Jessie in the elevator and breathe a few threatening words into her ear, Jack would be all over him.

No more stops. The elevator was on the express route to the lobby. Jack glanced at the lighted numbers above the door, then back at the mirror. His heart nearly stopped; he couldn't believe his eyes. It had lasted only a split second, but what he'd seen was unmistakable. Obviously, Jessie and the doctor hadn't noticed the mirror, hadn't realized that Jack was watching them even though they were standing behind him.

They'd locked fingers, as if holding hands, then released.

For one chilling moment, Jack couldn't breathe.

The elevator doors opened. Jack held the DOOR OPEN button to allow the others to exit. Dr. Marsh passed without a word, without so much as looking at Jack. Jessie emerged last. Jack took her by the arm and pulled her into an alcove near the bank of pay telephones.

"What the hell did you just do in there?"

She shook free of his grip. "Nothing."

"I was watching in the mirror. I saw you and Marsh hold hands."

"Are you crazy?"

"Apparently. Crazy to have trusted you."

She shook her head, scoffing. "You're a real piece of work, you know that, Swyteck? That's what I couldn't stand when we were dating, you and your stupid jealousy."

"This has nothing to do with jealousy. You just held hands with the doctor who supposedly started this whole problem by misdiagnosing you with ALS. You owe me a damn good explanation, lady."

"We don't owe you anything."

It struck him cold, the way she'd said "we." Jack was suddenly thinking of their conversation on the courthouse steps just minutes earlier, where Jessie had heaped such praise on the kind and considerate doctor. "Now I see why Dr. Marsh performed the diagnostic tests himself. It had nothing to do with his compassion. You never had any symptoms of ALS. You never even had lead poisoning. The tests were fakes, weren't they?"

She just glared and said, "It's like I told you: We don't owe you anything."

"What do you expect me to do? Ignore what I just saw?"

"Yes. If you're smart."

"Is that some kind of threat?"

"Do yourself a favor, okay? Forget you ever knew me. Move on with your life."

Those were the exact words she'd used to dump him some seven years earlier.

She started away, then stopped, as if unable to resist one more shot at him. "I feel sorry for you, Swyteck. I feel sorry for anyone who goes through life just playing by the rules."

As she turned and disappeared into the crowded

lobby, Jack felt a gaping pit in the bottom of his stomach. Ten years a trial lawyer. He'd represented thieves, swindlers, even cold-blooded murderers. He'd never claimed to be the world's smartest man, but never before had he even come close to letting this happen. The realization was sickening.

He'd just been scammed.

6

.

Sparky's Tavern was having a two-for-one special. The chalkboard behind the bar said WELL DRINKS ONLY, which in most joints simply meant the liquor wasn't a premium brand, but at Sparky's it meant liquor so rank that the bartender could only look at you and say, "*WELL,* what the hell did you expect?"

Jack ordered a beer.

Sparky's was on U.S. 1 south of Homestead, one of the last watering holes before a landscape that still bore the scars of a direct hit from Hurricane Andrew in 1992 gave way to the splendor of the Florida Keys. It was a converted old gas station with floors so stained from tipped drinks that not even the Environmental Protection Agency could have determined if more flammable liquids had spilled before or after the conversion. The grease-pit was gone but the garage doors were still in place. There was a long wooden bar, a TV permanently tuned to ESPN, and a never-ending stack of quarters on the pool table. Beer was served in cans, and the empties were crushed in true Sparky's style at the old tire vise that still sat on the workbench. It was the kind of dive that Jack would have visited if it were in his own neighborhood, but he made the forty-minute trip for one reason only: The bartender was Theo Knight.

" 'Nother one, Jacko?"

"Nah, I'm fine."

"How do you expect me to run this joint into the ground if you only let me give away one stinking beer?" He cleared away the empty and set up another cold one. "Cheers."

As half-owner of the bar, Theo didn't give away drinks to many customers, but Jack was a special case. Jack was his buddy. Jack had once been his lawyer. It was Jack who'd kept him alive on death row.

Jack's first job out of law school had been a four-year stint with the Freedom Institute, a ragtag group of lawyers who worked only capital cases. It was an exercise in defending the guilty, with one exception: Theo Knight. Not that Theo was a saint. He'd done his share of car thefts, credit card scams, small-time stuff. Early one morning he walked into a little all-night convenience store to find no one tending the cash register. On a dare from a buddy, he helped himself. It turned out that the missing nineteen-year-old clerk had been stabbed and beaten, stuffed in the walk-in freezer, and left to bleed to death. Theo was convicted purely on circumstantial evidence. For four years Jack filed petitions for stays of execution each time the governor—Jack's own father—signed a death warrant. At times the fight seemed futile, but it ended up keeping Theo alive long enough for DNA tests to come into vogue. Science finally eliminated Theo as the possible murderer.

Theo thought of Jack as the guy who'd saved his life.

Jack thought of Theo as the one thing he'd done right in his four years of defending the guilty at the Freedom Institute. It made for an interesting friendship. Best of all, Theo had kept his nose clean since his release from prison, but he could still think like a criminal. He had the kind of insights and street smarts that every good defense lawyer could use. It was exactly the point of view Jack needed to figure out what had gone wrong with Jessie Merrill.

"What are you laughing at?" said Jack.

Theo was a large man, six-foot-five and two-hundred-fifty pounds, and he had a hearty laugh to match. He'd listened without interruption as Jack laid out the whole story, but he couldn't contain himself any longer. "Let me ask you one question."

"What?"

"Was it the big tits or amazing thighs?"

"Come on, I'm married."

"Just what I thought. Both." He laughed even harder.

"Okay. Pile it on. This is what I get for feeling sorry for an ex-girlfriend."

"No, dude. Abuse is what you get for sitting too far away for me to slap you upside the head. Then again, maybe you ain't sitting so far . . ." He reached across the bar and took a swing, but Jack ducked. Theo caught only air and laughed again, which drew a smile from Jack.

"Guess I was pretty stupid, huh?" said Jack.

"Stupid, maybe. But it ain't like you did anything wrong. A lawyer can't get into trouble if he don't know his client is scamming the court."

"How do you know that?"

"Are you forgetting who you're talking to?"

Jack smiled. Theo had been the Clarence Darrow of jailhouse lawyers, a veritable expert on everything from writs of habeas corpus to a prisoner's fundamental right to chew gum. He was of mixed ancestry, primarily Greek and African-American, but somewhere in his lineage was just enough Miccosukee Indian blood to earn him the prison nickname "Chief Brief," a testament to the fact that some of the motions he filed with the court were better than Jack's.

Theo lit a cigarette, took a long drag. "You know, it's not even a hundred percent you were scammed."

"How can you say that?"

"All you know is that your client held hands in the elevator with this Dr. Swamp."

"Not Swamp, you idiot. Dr. Marsh."

"Whatever. That don't make it a scam."

"It was more than just the hand-holding. I flat-out accused her and Dr. Marsh of faking her tests. She didn't deny it."

"I didn't deny it either when the cops asked me if I killed that store clerk. Sometimes, even if you ain't done nothing, you just think you're better off keeping your mouth shut."

"This is totally different. Jessie wasn't just silent. She looked pretty damn smug about it."

"Okay. And from that you say Jessie and this big, rich doc got together and pulled a fast one on a group of Vatican investors."

"Viatical, dumbshit, not Vatican. What do you think, the pope is in on this too?"

"No, and I ain't even so sure this doctor was in on it."

"Why would you even doubt it?"

"Because this cat could lose his license. You gotta

show me more than a good piece of ass to make a doctor do something like this."

As bad as things had looked in the elevator, Theo had hit upon a crucial link in the chain of events. The criminal mind was at work. Jack asked, "What would you want to see?"

"Somethin' pretty strong. Maybe he needs money real bad, like right now."

Jack sipped his beer. "Makes sense. Problem is, I can't even get Jessie and her doctor friend to return my calls."

"I'd offer to give Jessie a good slap, but you know I don't rough up the ladies."

"I don't want you to slap her."

"How about I slap you then?" he said as he took another swing. This one landed. It was a playful slap, but Theo had the huge hands of a prize fighter.

"Ow, damn it. That really hurt."

" 'Course it did. You want me to slap Dr. Swamp, too?"

"No. And for the last time, moron, his name is Marsh."

"I'll get ol' swampy good—pa-pow, one-two, both sides of the head."

"I said no."

"Come on, man. I'll even do him for free. I hate them fucking doctors."

"You hate everyone."

"Except you, Jack, baby." He grabbed Jack's head with both hands and planted a loud kiss on the forehead.

"Lucky me."

"You is lucky. Just leave it to Theo. We'll get the skinny on this doc. You want to know if you got scammed, you just say the word."

Jack lowered his eyes, tugging at the label on his bottle.

Theo said, "I can't hear you, brother."

Jack shook his head and said, "It's not as if I can do anything about it. There's no getting around the fact that everything Jessie told me is protected by the attorney-client privilege. She could have pulled off the biggest fraud in the history of the Miami court system. That doesn't mean her own lawyer can just walk over to the state attorney's office and lay it all out."

"That's a whole 'nother thing."

"What the hell am I thinking, anyway? I'm a criminal defense lawyer. I don't do my reputation any good by ratting on my own clients."

"Listen up. What you do with the information once you get it ain't my department."

"You think I want to get even with her, don't you? That I want to nail my ex-girlfriend for playing me for a fool?"

"All I'm asking is this: Do you want to know for a hundred percent certain if the bitch stuck it to you or not?"

Their eyes locked. Jack knew better than anyone that Theo had ways of getting information that would have impressed the CIA.

"Come on, Swyteck. You didn't drive all the ways over here just to talk to Theo and drink a beer. Do you want to know?"

"It's not about revenge."

"Then why bother?"

He met Theo's stare, and a moment of serious honesty washed over them, the way it used to be when staring through prison glass. "I just need to know."

"That's good enough for me." Theo reached over the

bar and shook Jack's hand about seven different ways, the prison-yard ritual. "Let's get to it, then. We'll have some fun."

"Yeah," said Jack, raising his beer. "A blast."

7

.

Theo slammed the V-8 into fifth gear. The car almost seemed to levitate. Jack smiled from the passenger seat. No one could get his thirty-year-old Mustang to hum the way Theo could. Not even Jack.

"When you gonna give me this car?" asked Theo.

"When you gonna buy me a Ferrari?"

"I can get you a sweet deal on a slightly used one. You won't even need a key to start it."

Jack gave him a look, not sure he was kidding. "Some things I don't need to know about you, all right?"

Theo just smiled and downshifted as they turned off the highway and into Coconut Grove. Jack held on, trying not to land in Theo's lap as he dug his ringing cell phone from his pocket. He checked the display and recognized the incoming number. He wasn't in the mood to talk, but this was one call he never refused.

"Hello, *Abuela*."

It was his grandmother, an eighty-two-year-old Cuban

immigrant who, once or twice a week, would drop by his office unannounced to deliver excellent guava-and-cream-cheese pastries or little *tazas* of espresso straight from Little Havana. Her specialty was a moist dessert cake called *tres leches*. Not many people expected a guy named Jack Swyteck to have an *abuela*. It was especially interesting when Anglos would confide in him and say they were moving out of Miami to get away from all the Cubans. Funny, Jack would tell them, but my *abuela* never complained about too many Cubans when she was growing up in Havana.

He listened for nearly a solid minute, then finally cut in. "*Abuela,* for the last time, you did not invent *tres leches*. It's Nicaraguan. We're Cuban. *Cubano: C-U-B-A-N-O. Comprende?* . . . We'll talk about this later, okay? . . . I love you. Bye, *mi vida*."

The car stopped at a traffic light. Jack switched off the phone only to find Theo staring at him. "You and Julia Child going at it again?"

"My grandmother is the laughingstock of Spanish talk radio. She's been phoning in every afternoon to tell the world how she invented *tres leches*."

"*Tres leches?*"

"It's a cake made with three kinds of milk. White frosting on top. Very moist, very sweet."

"I know what it is. It's fucking great. Your grandmother invented that?"

"Hardly."

"Except I hate when they put those maraschino cherries on top. I bet that's not part of the original recipe. Call your *abuela,* let's ask her."

"She did *not* invent it, okay? It's Nicaraguan."

The light turned green. Theo punched the Mustang through the intersection. "You know, I think I read somewhere that maybe *tres leches* isn't from Nicaragua. Some people say it was invented by a Cuban lady in Miami."

"Don't start with me."

"I'm serious. It might even have been in the *Herald*. Long time ago."

"Since when do you read the food section?"

"Try spending four years on death row. You'll read the *TV Guide* in Chinese if they'll give it to you."

Jack massaged his temples, then tucked the phone back into his pocket. "Why do I even try to argue with you?"

After two minutes on Bayshore Drive they made a quick turn toward the bay and crossed the short bridge to Grove Isle condominiums. Grove Isle wasn't quite as chic as it was in its heyday, back when beautiful young women used to crash at poolside to meet rich young men or even richer old men. But it was still an exclusive address in an unbeatable setting. A short walk or bike ride to shops and restaurants in Coconut Grove, balconies with killer views of Biscayne Bay and downtown Miami in the distance.

Sandra Marsh lived alone in the penthouse apartment in Building 3. It was one of the many things she stood to acquire in the impending divorce from her husband of twenty-four years, Dr. Joseph Marsh. It had taken Theo just twenty-four hours to get through to her. It had taken all of thirty seconds on the phone to talk her into a meeting.

All he had to do was mention money and her soon-to-be-ex-husband.

They valeted the car and checked in with the security guard, who found their names on the guest list and directed them to the pool area. It was two-thirty in the afternoon. Palm fronds rustled in the warm breezes off the bay. As promised, Mrs. Marsh was dressed in a red terry-cloth robe and a big Kaminski sun hat, reclining on deck in a chaise lounge that faced the water, recovering from her two-o'clock deep-tissue massage.

"Mrs. Marsh?" said Jack.

She opened her eyes, tilted back her hat, and looked up from beneath the broad brim. She checked her Rolex and said, "My, you boys are prompt. Please, have a seat."

Jack sat on the chaise lounge facing Mrs. Marsh. Theo remained standing, his eye having caught an attractive sunbather in a thong bikini with a rose tattoo on her left buttock. Jack started without him.

"Mrs. Marsh, I'm Jack Swyteck. I was the lawyer for a woman named Jessie Merrill."

"I know you and your case. I have plenty of friends who keep me abreast of my husband's going-ons."

"Then you also know he was a witness."

"I know he was the doctor for that woman."

"Do you know *that woman?*" he asked, pronouncing the words the same way she had.

"What does that have to do with anything? Your friend told me this was about some financial dealings of my husband."

"It could be. But it depends, in part, on the nature of his relationship with Ms. Merrill."

"She was his little slut, if you call that a relationship."

"I do," said Theo.

Jack shot him a look that said, *Get serious.* "How long was that relationship going on?"

"I don't know."

"Did it start before or after she started seeing him as a patient?"

"I didn't find out about it until sometime after. But I can't say it wasn't going on longer."

"Did Jessie have anything to do with the two of you splitting up?"

She stiffened. "These questions are getting way too personal."

"I'm sorry."

"Well, I'm not," said Theo. "Look, lady, here's the bottom line. Mr. Swyteck here has to dance around the issue like a fly on horseshit because he thinks he still owes some loyalty to Jessie Merrill. Well, you and I don't have the same worries, so can we talk straight?"

"That depends on what you want to know."

"Let's say your husband suddenly came into a pile of money—say a million and a half bucks, or some share of it. Isn't that something you'd like to know about?"

"Surely. Our divorce isn't final yet. I'd have my lawyer adjust the property settlement immediately."

"You'd want a cut, naturally."

"I'd want more than a cut. After four kids and twenty-four years of marriage, I'm leaving that bastard broke. He'll be working till he's ninety-five just to pay my bar tab."

Jack and Theo exchanged glances, and she suddenly seemed to realize that perhaps she was giving two perfect strangers too much of what they wanted to hear.

"I think it's time I referred you gentlemen to my lawyer," she said.

"Just a few more questions."

"No, I'm not comfortable with this. I'll tell her to expect your call. She's in the book. Phoebe Martin."

Jack started to say something, but she extended her hand, ending it. Jack shook her hand, and Theo gave her a mock salute.

"Thank you for your time, ma'am."

"You're welcome."

She reclined into her chaise lounge, retreating into silence. Jack and Theo turned and walked across the pool deck toward the valet stand. As soon as they were out of Mrs. Marsh's earshot Jack asked, "What do you think?"

"Hell with tending bar, I'm opening a tattoo parlor," he said as he gathered one more eyeful of the woman with the pink rose on her tanned and firm buttock.

"Be serious," said Jack.

They stopped at the valet stand. Jack handed over his claim ticket, and the kid with the pressed white uniform and monster thighs took off running.

Theo lit a cigarette. "I think you got a middle-aged doctor, a hot new girlfriend with her hand on his balls, and a pissed off wife with two hands on his wallet."

"She's definitely not going to go easy on him."

"The ex gets at least half of everything he has. Probably more."

"Much more," said Jack. "If her lawyer is Phoebe Martin, our doctor friend really might be broke. I'll bet she gets eighty percent of every dime."

"You mean every dime she can find."

"Nothing like a million and a half bucks to keep a new girlfriend happy. Especially when the Wicked Witch of the West doesn't even know about it."

"True, true," said Theo. "Scam those investors and send that money right off to a Swedish bank account."

"You mean Swiss bank account."

"That's what I said. Swiss."

"No, you said Swedish."

"You think I don't know the difference between a bank and a fucking meatball?"

"Okay, forget it. You said Swiss."

Theo let out a cloud of smoke. "Hate them fucking Swiss anyway."

"What's to hate about the Swiss?"

"Cheese with holes in it. What's with that shit, anyway? Stinking thieves selling us all a bunch of fucking air."

"God, you really do hate everyone."

"Except you, Jack, baby." He grinned and pinched Jack's cheek so hard it turned red. The Mustang rumbled up to the valet stand, and Theo jumped ahead of Jack on his way to the driver's side. "Except you!"

Jack rubbed the welt on his face and retreated to the passenger side, smiling as he shook his head. "God help me."

8
·

It was their second-favorite indoor activity. Jack was a horrendous cook, but his wife was phenomenal, and as with all their favorite things, he fancied himself a pretty swift and eager learner. Tonight, he was taking total responsibility for dessert.

"What the heck are you making over there?" Cindy asked as she glanced across the kitchen counter. Jack was surrounded by a clutter of mixing bowls, milk cartons, and opened bags of flour and sugar.

"*Tres leches*," he said.

"You can't make *tres leches*."

"Watch me."

It had been an awful week, and goofing off with his wife in the kitchen was a good way to give his brain a rest. They hadn't spoken about Jessie since the verdict—that was his decision, not hers. In fact, six months earlier, Cindy had seen Jessie as a victim and even encouraged Jack to take her case. That was pretty big of her, given the history between him and Jessie. Maybe she didn't want to be the one to keep Jack from helping an old friend. Or perhaps she'd simply wanted Jack to realize for himself that representing Jessie wasn't exactly the thing to do with their own marriage on shaky ground.

"Is it a good recipe?" she asked.

"The best."

"Where'd you get it?"

"From the woman who invented it."

"Seriously?"

He smiled, thinking of *Abuela*. "Maybe."

Cindy wiped her hands clean and crossed the room to adjust the stereo. Maybe it was the Jessie experience lingering in his mind, but he couldn't take his eyes off Cindy.

Playing by the rules. Was that what their marriage was about? Lord knows they'd tried to make things work. A string of marriage counselors and more sessions than Jack could count. In the end it came down to how hard they were willing to work at the relationship. When it came to work, Jack was a regular beast of burden.

Cindy was no slacker, either. Even since their last counselor had basically given up on them, Cindy had made it her mission to keep their relationship fresh. It seemed she was always changing something about herself, and Jack couldn't help but wonder what all the changes were about. Was she really just trying to keep married life interesting, or was she still fighting off demons and struggling to find happiness? Tonight she had her blond hair pulled straight back with a wide headband, her Valley of the Dolls look, as she called it. Even music was an adventure with Cindy. Her tastes were eclectic and ever-evolving, and lately she'd been exposing him to the likes of Peggy Lee and Perry Como. Without a doubt, some of the most romantic tunes ever had come straight out of the 1940s, but the lyrics to this particular song she'd chosen were pretty aggravating. Even if your heart *was* "filled with pain," to Jack's ear it still didn't rhyme with "again."

"Jack, what are you doing?"

He glanced into the bowl. His hands were buried in a thick, sweet mixture of flour, sugar, and condensed milk. "Shoot, I forgot the eggs."

"You forgot your brain. You've got *tres leches* up to your elbows."

"I'm just following the recipe. It says beat fifty strokes by hand."

"As opposed to using an electric mixer, Einstein."

He flashed an impish grin. "Oh."

She handed him a wooden spoon and rolled her eyes. "Lawyers. You're so literal."

"Yeah," he said, thinking once more of Jessie's parting words. "Always playing by the rules."

"What's that supposed to mean?"

"Nothing."

"It wasn't nothing."

"I was just kidding around."

"But you weren't smiling. You meant something by that."

"I didn't mean anything by it."

She looked away, shook her head subtly and said quietly, "You think I don't know you?"

"Cindy, let it go, okay? We were having fun here."

She returned to her end of the kitchen counter. Jack could see the regret in her eyes, the way they'd slipped into their usual pattern. Without thinking, he ran a messy hand through his hair, giving himself an earful of sweet goo. Cindy snickered to herself. He chuckled, too, and sharing the moment helped to shake off some of the unwanted tension. As he snagged a paper towel to wipe it off, she came to him, grabbed his *tres leches*–coated forearm, and said, "Don't."

"What?"

"I think I'm ovulating."

"Huh?"

She arched an eyebrow, pointing with her eyes toward the bedroom.

He smiled and said, "Now that's the kind of non sequitur I can live with."

He started to wipe his face clean. "Don't," she said. She gently kissed a gob of the sweet mixture off the corner of his mouth, and the tip of her tongue was suddenly exploring his earful of *tres leches*.

It tickled, and he recoiled—but only slightly. There'd been times when it seemed their marriage was hanging by a thread. But every now and then, out came the old Cindy and, oh, what a thread. "My, you're a veritable box of surprises tonight."

"And you are one lucky boy," she whispered.

He smiled and touched her face. "Don't I know it."

•

Jack watched her as she slept, soothed by the rhythm of her gentle breathing. Even after a hot shower, the faint smell of *tres leches* lingered in the bedroom. Nothing like skipping dinner altogether and heading straight for dessert to send you off to dreamland.

Sex wasn't exactly a strong point of their relationship. In fact, it had been nonexistent when they were first married. What should have been the happiest time of their lives was marred by Cindy's recurring nightmares. The medical doctors had ruled out sexual assault, but probably no one would ever know the details of what her attacker had done or threatened to do. Five years was a long time; five years was yesterday. At times Jack felt as though he could only guess how long ago it was in Cindy's mind. The good news was that she'd finally pushed it far enough away to want to try to start a family. It had taken her all that time to convince herself that the world was not such an awful place that a child should never be brought into it.

Jack laid a hand lightly on her belly, wondering if this one would be the one.

The phone rang. It was down the hall in his home office, a separate phone line from the main number. Jack let it ring five times, and the machine got it. The caller hung up. A minute later the phone rang again. On the fifth ring it went to the machine. Another hang up.

Seconds later it was ringing yet again. It was as if someone had his number on redial and was determined to keep calling until a live person answered. If this kept up, Cindy would certainly wake. He knew she hadn't been sleeping well the last few nights, so he sprang from the bed, wearing only his underwear, and hurried down the dark hall. He caught it on the fourth ring, just before the machine would take it.

"Hello."

"It's me. Jessie."

He suddenly felt more naked than he was. "I've been trying to reach you. You didn't return my calls."

"That's because I didn't want to talk to you."

"Then why are you calling now?"

"Because you pissed me off."

"I pissed *you* off?"

"It's odd, don't you think? I was in a lawsuit for

months, and the viatical investors never once accused me of fraud. They thought the diagnosis was all just a mistake. Suddenly, the case is over, and they've become highly suspicious. They think they were scammed."

"How do you know that?"

"Because they're poking around, asking questions. And I think you have something to do with it."

"I haven't said a word to anyone."

"Liar. You and your investigator were on Grove Isle questioning Dr. Marsh's wife, weren't you?"

Jack couldn't deny it, so he steered clear. "Jessie, we should talk."

"I warned you, don't ask so many questions. You have ticked me off bad this time."

He bit back his anger, but he couldn't swallow all of it. "I'm tired of you acting as if *I'm* the one who did *you* wrong."

"If you blow the lid off this, you are really going to regret it."

"So you admit it was a scam. You did it."

"We did it."

He'd known since the elevator, but her admission still shocked him. "You've pushed it too far this time, Jessie."

"Not just me. All of us. So watch yourself, or I'll not only have you disbarred, I'll have you sitting in the prison cell right next to Dr. Marsh."

"What?"

"The simple truth is, I couldn't have done this without you. You were a key player."

"I didn't have anything to do with this."

"No one's going to buy that. Especially when I tell them the truth—that you were in on the deal all the way."

"I can't believe what you're saying."

"Believe it. Now watch your step—partner."

The line clicked in his ear. She was gone before he could say another word.

9
.

Jack met Theo for a late dinner. Jack had a burger smothered in cheese and mushrooms. Theo opted for the five-alarm chili. Both were staples on the simple menu at Tobacco Road.

In Jack's eyes, Tobacco Road was *the* place in Miami for late-night jazz and blues, and that wasn't just because his friend Theo was a regular sax player. By South Florida standards, it was steeped in tradition. It was Miami's oldest bar, having obtained the city's very first liquor license in 1912 and surviving Prohibition as a speakeasy. The upstairs, where liquor and roulette wheels were once stashed, was now a showcase for some of the most talented musicians in the area—including Theo. Tonight Theo and his buddies were slated to play at least one obligatory cut from Donald Byrd's *Thank You for . . . F.U.M.L. (Fucking Up My Life)*. It wasn't generally regarded as the talented Mr. Byrd's best work, and Jack was certain that the catchy title alone had put it near the top of Theo's all-time favorite list.

Theo splashed more hot sauce on his chili, wiped the beads of sweat from his brow, and asked, "What we gonna do about Jessie?"

Jack had been ignoring Theo's messages all week. It was clear that he'd viewed the interrogation of the soon-to-be-ex-wife of "Dr. Swamp" as just the beginning of the fun.

Jack said, "To be honest, I haven't had much time to think about it."

"What a crock."

"Unlike you, I work for a living. I've been in trial the last four days. We still got one more day of witnesses, then closing arguments on Friday."

"You gonna win?"

"Only if I can explain a miracle."

Jack took a minute to fill him in. His client was an accused serial stalker, not the kind of case Jack would ordinarily take, but the guy seemed to be getting a raw deal. The government's star witness was a woman who'd claimed to have seen him running from her building, even though he'd spent the last ten years in a wheelchair. The prosecutor claimed he wasn't paralyzed at all, just a fat and lazy pig who liked to buzz around town in a motorized wheelchair. "The Lazy Stalker," the media had dubbed him, and a dozen organizations were speaking out to protect the rights of stalking victims, the physically challenged, and the obese alike. Then came the first day of trial—the day of "the miracle." His wheelchair set off the metal detector at the courthouse entrance, so the idiot stood up and walked around the machine. Jack was left scrambling to salvage the case.

Theo yawned into his fist. "Can we just talk about Jessie Merrill? The rest of your life is way too fucking ridiculous."

"You have such a way about you."

"Least I don't talk shit. You trying to tell me that for the past week you haven't even thought about these Viagra-kill investors?"

Jack chuckled. "You just can't get that word, can you?"

"What?"

" 'Viagra-kill?' We're not talking about a terminal case of erectile dysfunction. It's 'viatical.' "

"What the hell kind of word is that, anyway?"

"Latin. The *viaticum* was the Roman soldier's supplies for battle, which might be the final journey of his life. Two thousand years later, some insurance guru thought it was a catchy way of describing the concept of giving someone with a life-threatening disease the money they need to fight their final battle."

"And I guess some of the soldiers live to fight another day. Like Jessie Merrill."

Jack poured some ketchup on his french fries. "She called me."

"When?"

"The day after we went to see Mrs. Marsh. She admitted it was a scam."

"Hot damn. Now we got her."

"No. We don't *got* anybody. You're not going to like this, but I've decided to let it go."

"What?"

"What's done is done. It's not my place to fix it."

"Aw, come on. Think in these terms: How much did she pay you in legal fees?"

"I gave her the friend's rate. Flat fee, twenty grand."

"There you go, my man. I can get you twenty times that much now."

"I'm sure you could. But that would be extortion, now wouldn't it?"

"I don't care what you call it. You can't just let her get away with this."

"I don't have a choice. I was her lawyer. All I can do at this point is be content with the knowledge that, yes, I was played for a sucker. If I start looking for something more than that, it's going to be trouble."

"Don't tell me you're scared."

"I need to move on with my life." As soon as he'd said it, he realized he'd used Jessie's own words. *Weird.*

Theo leaned closer, elbows on the table. "Did she and that doc threaten you?"

"It's not important."

"It is to me. Let me talk to her. She thinks she can threaten us, I'll straighten her out."

"Don't. The best thing I can do for myself right now is to forget about Jessie Merrill and the whole damn thing."

The deep thump of a bass guitar warbled over the speakers. Theo's band was tuning up for the first set. He pushed his empty bowl of chili aside and said, "You really think she's going to let you?"

"Let me what?"

"Forget her."

"Well, yeah. She's got her money. Got no more use for me."

Theo chuckled.

"What are you laughing at now?" said Jack.

Theo rose, tossed his napkin aside. The bass had broken into a rhythm, the drums and trumpet were joining in. "Hear that?" asked Theo.

"Yeah, so?"

"They're playing your song. Yours and Jessie's." He snapped his fingers to the beat. The song had no lyrics, but he sang out part of the album title anyway: "*Thank You for . . . Fucking Up My Life.*"

Theo was only half-smiling. Jack just looked at him and asked, "What are you talking about?"

"You got this old-girlfriend thing going on. Cuttin' her legal fees, cuttin' her a break. I'm talking about some kind of a strange love-hate thing going on here. *Thank you for . . .*"

"That's bull."

"Sure it is. But something tells me you ain't heard the last of Jessie Merrill. Not by a long shot, Jacko. Call me after your trial. Or after this squirrel comes back again for your nuts. Whichever comes first."

Jack watched from his table, alone, as Theo and the rest of the crowd moved closer to the music.

10

·

"**G**ood night, Luther."

The security guard started. Having worked two jobs for eleven years to support a wife and eight children, Luther was a master at sleeping with his eyes wide open. " 'Night, Mr. Swyteck."

The final day of evidence at trial hadn't done "The Lazy Stalker" any good. Perhaps it was the lingering effects of the Jessie disaster, but an embarrassing loss was the last thing he needed. He'd stayed at the office till almost midnight trying to rustle up a gem of a closing argument that would at least keep the jury out a few hours. The case was still a definite loser, but you do the best you can with the facts you're dealt. That was every good lawyer's mantra. It was what sustained you from one day to the next. That, and a good Chinese restaurant with late-night delivery.

"Good luck tomorrow," said Luther.

"Thanks."

Jack stepped through the revolving door and into the

night. It was warm and muggy for February, even by Coral Gables standards. The rain had stopped an hour or so earlier, but Ponce de Leon Boulevard was still glistening wet beneath the fuzzy glow of street lamps. A cat scurried across the wide, grassy island that separated eastbound traffic from westbound, except that at this hour there was no traffic. Storefronts were dark on both sides of the street. At the corner, the last of the guests at Christy's steakhouse were piling into a taxi. The humidity flattened their wine-induced laughter, making them seem much farther away than they were. Jack started up the sidewalk to the parking lot.

The car was still wet from the rain. As much as he loved his Mustang, rainstorms and thirty-year-old convertibles were no match made in heaven. He opened the door and wiped down the seat. He could have cursed the dampness that was seeping up through the seat of his pants, but the beautiful sound of that V-8 made all well again. He threw it into reverse, then slammed on the brake. Another car had raced up behind him and stopped, blocking his passage.

What the hell?

The door flew open, and the driver ran out. It was dark, and before Jack could even guess what was going on, someone was banging on his passenger-side window.

"Let me in!"

The voice was familiar, but it was still startling to see Jessie's face practically pressed against the glass. "What the hell are you doing?"

"Open the damn door!"

He reached across the console, unlocked it. Jessie jumped in and locked the door. She was completely out of breath. "I'm so scared. You have to help me."

"Help you?"

"*Look* at me, Jack. Can't you see I'm a wreck?"

She looked even more sleep-deprived than Jack was. Bloodshot eyes, pasty pallor. "That's no reason to ambush me like this. How long have you been waiting for me to come out?"

"I had to do it this way. I can't go anyplace where they might be waiting for me. I haven't been home in three days. If I had just popped by your office, they would have found me for sure."

"They, who? The police?"

"Farthest thing from it. These guys are thugs."

"What guys?"

"The viatical investors."

Jack shut off the engine, as if the noise were keeping him from hearing her straight. "Jessie, those investors aren't thugs. They're businesspeople."

"Hardly. That company that sued me—Viatical Solutions, Inc.—is just a front. The real money . . . I don't know where it comes from. But it's not legit."

"How do you know this?"

"Because they're going to kill me!"

"What?"

"They are going to put a gun to my head and blow my brains out."

"Just slow down."

Her hands were shaking. He could see her eyes widen even in the dim light of the street lamps. "Start at the beginning."

"You know the beginning. We scammed these guys."

"You mean you and Dr. Marsh."

"I mean all of us."

"Hold it right there. I didn't have any part in this."

"Don't act like you didn't know what was going on. You let me scam them."

"Wrong. I was completely shocked when—"

"Just cut the crap, all right? This is so like you, Swyteck. You come along for the ride to add a little excitement to your pathetic little life with Cindy Paige, and then when it all hits the fan, you throw up your hands and leave me twisting in the wind."

"What are you talking about?"

"I'm talking about—"

She stopped in midsentence. Her eyes bulged, and her shoulders began to heave. She jerked violently to the right, flung open the car door, and hung her head over the pavement. The retching noise was insufferable—two solid minutes of painful dry heaves. At last, she expelled something. Her breath came in quick, panicky spurts, and then finally she got her body under control. She closed the door and nearly fell against the passenger seat, exhausted.

Jack looked on, both concerned and amazed. "What are you doing to yourself?"

"I'm so scared. I've been throwing up all day."

"When's the last time you slept?"

"I don't remember. Three days ago, maybe."

"Let me see your eyes."

"No."

Jack held her head still and stared straight into her pupils. "What are you on?"

"Nothing."

"The paranoia alone is a dead giveaway."

"I'm not paranoid. These guys are serious. They stand to gain three million dollars under my life insurance policy just as soon as I'm dead. You've got to help me."

"We can start with the name of a good rehab center."

"I'm not a druggie, damn you."

He still suspected drugs, but that didn't rule out the possibility that someone was really out to get her—particularly since she had indeed scammed them. "If somebody's trying to kill you, then we need to call the police."

"Right. And tell them I scammed these guys out of a million and a half dollars?"

"I can try to swing a deal. If these viatical investors are really the bad operators you say they are, you could get immunity from prosecution if you tell the state attorney just who it is that's trying to kill you."

"I'll be dead by the time you cut a deal. Don't you understand? I have no one else to turn to. You have to do something, Jack!"

"I'm helping you the only way I know how."

"Which is no help at all."

"What do you want from me?"

"Call them. Negotiate."

"You're telling me they're killers. You want me to negotiate with them?"

"You've defended worse scum."

"That doesn't mean I do business with them."

"Can't you see I'm desperate? If we don't come to some kind of terms, they're going to make me *wish* I'd died of Lou Gehrig's disease."

"Then give them their money back."

"No way. It's mine."

"It's yours only because you scammed them."

"I'm not giving it back. And I'm not calling the police, either."

"Then I don't know how to help you."

"Yes, you do. You just want to stick it to me, you bastard."

"I'll do for you what I'd do for any other client. No more, no less."

"Fool me once, shame on you; fool me twice, shame on me. That's what you're thinking."

"I don't know what to think."

"Damn you, Swyteck! You never know what to think. That's why we blew up seven years ago."

He looked away, resisting the impulse to blow her off. A car passed on the street just outside the lot, its tires hissing on the wet pavement. Jessie pushed open the car door and stepped down.

"Where are you going?"

"As if you care."

"Leave your car here. Don't drive in this condition. Let me take you home."

"I told you, I can't go home. Don't you listen, ass-hole?" She slammed the door and started away from the car.

Jack jumped out. "Where can I reach you?'

"None of your business."

"I'm worried about you."

"The hell you are. I'm not going to let you talk me into calling the police just so you can ease your con-science." She fished her keys from her purse, and Jack started after her.

"Don't follow me!"

"Jessie, please."

She whirled and shot an icy glare that stopped him in his tracks. "You had your chance to help me. Now don't pretend to be my friend."

"This isn't just talk. I'm truly worried about you."

"Fuck you, Jack. Be worried for yourself."

She opened her car door and got inside. The door slammed, the engine fired, and she squealed out of the parking lot like a drag racer.

As the orange taillights disappeared into the night,

Jack returned to his car and locked the doors, his mind awhirl. He'd just finished the most bizarre conversation of his life, and four little words had given him the uneasy sensation that it wasn't over yet.

Exactly what had Jessie meant by *"Be worried for yourself"*?

He started his car and pulled out of the lot. He hated to admit it, but Theo's favorite song was playing in his head. *Thank you for . . .*

11

Cindy was staring into the eyes of a killer. Or at least it exuded a killer's attitude. It was a two-pound Yorkshire terrier that seemed to think it could take on a pack of hungry Rottweilers simply because its ancestors were bred to chase sewer rats. Scores of color photographs were spread across the table before her. A dozen more images lit up the screen on her computer monitor in an assortment of boxes, like the credits for *The Brady Bunch*, all of "Sergeant Yorkie" and his adorable playmate, a four-year-old girl named Natalie.

Cindy's South Miami studio had been going strong for several years, but she did portraits only three days a week. That left her time to do on-site shoots for catalogs and other work. The studio was an old house with lots of charm. A small yard and a white lattice gazebo offered a picturesque setting for outdoor shots. For reasons that were not entirely aesthetic, Cindy preferred outdoor shots when dealing with animals.

A light rap on the door frame broke her concentration. Cindy was alone in her little work area, but not alone in the studio. It had been five years since that psychopath had attacked her, and even though she was in a safe part of town, she didn't stay after dark without company. Tonight, her mother had come by to bring her dinner.

"Are you okay in there, dear?"

"Just working."

A plateful of chicken and roasted vegetables sat untouched on the table, pushed to one side. A white spotlight illuminated the work space before her. It was like a pillar of light in the middle of the room, darkness on the edges. A row of photographs stretched across the table, some of them outside the glow of the halogen lamp. The shots were all from the same frame, but each was a little different, depending on the zoom. In the tightest enlargement the resolution was little better than randomly placed dots. She put the fuzzy ones aside and passed a magnifying glass over the largest, clear image. She was trying to zero in on a mysterious imperfection in the photograph she'd taken of the little girl and her dog.

"You've been holed up in here for hours," her mother said.

Cindy looked up from her work. "This is kind of important."

"So is your health," her mother said as she glanced at the dinner plate. "You haven't eaten anything."

"No one ever died from skipping dinner."

She went to Cindy's side, brushed the hair out of her face. "Something tells me that this isn't the only meal you've missed in the last few days."

"I'm all right."

Her mother tugged her chin gently, forcing Cindy to

look straight at her. It was the kind of no-nonsense, disciplinary approach she'd employed since Cindy's childhood. Evelyn Paige had been a single mother since Cindy was nine years old, and she had the worry lines to prove it. Not that she looked particularly old for her age, but she'd acted old long before her hair had turned silver. It was as if her husband's passing had stolen her youth, or at least made her feel older than she was.

"Look at those eyes. When's the last time you had a good night's sleep?"

"I'm just busy with work."

"That's not what Jack tells me."

"He told you about my dreams?"

"Yes."

Cindy felt slightly betrayed, but she realized Jack was no gossip. It was Jack, after all, who'd stuck with her through the darkest times. He wouldn't have gone to her mother if he wasn't truly concerned about her. "What did he tell you?"

"How you aren't sleeping. The nightmares you're having about Esteban."

"They're not really nightmares."

"Just the kind of dreams that make you afraid to close your eyes at night."

"That's true."

"How long has this been going on?"

"October."

"That long?"

"It's not every night. October was when I had the first one. On the anniversary of . . . you know—Esteban."

"What does Jack say about this?"

"He's supportive. He's always been supportive. I'm trying not to make a big deal out of it. It's just not good for us. Especially not now. We're trying to make a baby."

"So, these dreams. Are they strictly about Esteban?"

Cindy was looking in the general direction of her mother, but she was seeing right past her. "It always starts out like it's supposed to be about him. Someone's outside my window. I can hear the blanket of fallen leaves scuffling each time he takes a step. Big, crispy leaves all over the ground, more like the autumns they get up north than we have in Florida. It's dark, but I can hear them moving. One footstep at a time."

"That's creepy."

"Then I walk to the back door, and it's not Esteban."

"Who is it?"

"Just more leaves swirling in the wind. Then one of them slams against the door, and *bam*, he's suddenly there."

"Esteban?"

"No." She paused, as if reluctant to share. "It's . . . Daddy."

"That's . . . interesting," Evelyn said, as if backing away from the word "creepy" again. "You sure it's your father?"

"Yes."

"Does he come to you as an old man, or does he look like the young man he was when he died?"

"He's kind of ghostly. I just know it's him."

"Do you talk to him?"

"Yes."

"What about?"

"He wants Jack."

Her mother coughed, then cleared her throat. "What do you mean, he wants Jack?"

"He wants Jack to come and play poker with him."

"That's . . ." The word "interesting" seemed to be on the tip of her tongue, but it didn't suffice. "I can see why you're not sleeping. But we all have strange dreams. Once I dreamed I was talking with a man who was supposed to be your father, but he looked like John Wayne. He even called me 'pilgrim.' "

"This is different. It's not that Esteban shows up at my back door looking like Daddy. It's more like one thought drifting into another. It's as if Daddy comes in and takes over the dream, forcing me to stop thinking of Esteban."

"That sounds normal. Don't people always tell you to think happy thoughts when you want to stop scaring yourself?"

"Yeah."

"So, you're lying in bed at night thinking of this man who assaulted you. And your mind drifts to happy thoughts of your father to make you stop."

"That was my take on it, too. But it still frightens me. Especially the way he seems to be asking for Jack."

"What does Jack say about that?"

"I haven't told him that part. Why freak him out?"

"Exactly. And why freak yourself out? Esteban is dead. Whatever he did to you, he can never do it again."

"I know that."

"You can't let him creep into your dreams this way."

"It's not that I let him. I just can't stop him."

"You have to force yourself to stop."

"I can't control my dreams."

"You must."

"Can you control yours?"

"Sometimes. Depending on what I read or think about before I fall asleep."

"But not all the time."

Evelyn seemed ready to argue the point but stopped, as if realizing that she wasn't being honest. "No, I can't always keep them under control."

"No one can. Especially when dreams are trying to tell you something."

"Cindy, don't spook yourself like that. Dreams are a reflection of nothing but your own thoughts. They don't tell you anything you don't already know."

"That's not true. This dream I'm having about Daddy and Esteban is definitely trying to tell me something."

"What?"

"I don't know yet. But I've had the same dream in the past, and every time I have it, something bad happens. It's a warning."

"Don't do this to yourself. It's only a dream, nothing more."

"You don't really believe that."

Her mother just lowered her eyes.

"Before Daddy died," said Cindy, "you had that dream. You knew it was going to happen."

"That's overstating it, sweetheart."

"It's not. You saw his mother carrying a dead baby in her arms. A week later, he was dead."

"How do you know about that?"

"Aunt Margie told me."

Margie was Evelyn's younger sister, the family big-mouth. Evelyn blinked nervously and said, "I didn't see it. I dreamed it."

"And why do you think you dreamed it?"

"Because I was worried about your father, and those worries found their way into my dreams. That's all it was."

Silence fell between them, as if neither of them believed what she'd just said. Cindy said, "I get this from you."

"Get what?"

"The ability to see things in dreams. It's something you passed on to me."

"Is that what you think? You have a gift?"

"No. A curse."

Their eyes locked, not with contempt or anger, more along the lines of mutual empathy. Her mother finally blinked, the first to look away.

"Don't stay here too much longer," she said. "Try to get some sleep tonight."

"I will. As soon as Jack gets home."

Her mother cupped her hand along the side of Cindy's face, then kissed her on the forehead. In silence, she stepped outside the glow of the spotlight and left the room.

Cindy was again alone. Her eyes drifted back toward the photographs before her, the shots she'd taken of a little girl and her dog. She was relieved that her mother hadn't asked any more questions. She wasn't sure how she would have explained what she'd been doing. Lying never worked with her mother, and telling her the truth would only have heightened her worries. The dreams alone were strange enough.

Imagine if I'd shown her this.

One last time, Cindy ran the magnifying glass across the enlarged image before her and held it directly over the flaw. An amateur might have been puzzled, but she was looking through a trained eye. In Cindy's mind, there was absolutely no mistaking it. She extended her index finger toward the photograph—slowly and with trepidation, as if putting her hand into the fire. Her fingertip came to rest in the lower right-hand corner.

It was there, in this one photograph out of ninety-six shots she'd taken outside her studio, that a faint shadow had appeared.

A chill ran up her arm and down through her body. She'd examined it from every angle, at varying degrees of magnification. This wasn't a cloud or a tree branch bending in the breeze. The form was definitely human.

"Daddy, please," she whispered. "Just leave me alone."

She tucked the photograph into an envelope and turned out the light.

12

.

Jack and Cindy went out for dinner Friday night, a neighborhood restaurant called Blú, which specialized in pizzas from wood-burning ovens. It was a bustling place with a small bar, crowded tables, and smiling waiters whose English was just bad enough to force patrons to talk with their hands like real Italians. The chefs were from Rome and Naples, and they dreamed up their own recipes, everything from basic cheese pizza like you've never tasted to pies with baby artichokes, arugula, and Gorgonzola cheese. It was Jack's version of comfort food, the kind of place he went whenever he lost a trial.

"How bad was it?" asked Cindy.

"Jury was out all of twenty minutes."

"Could have been worse. Your client could have been innocent."

"Why do you assume he was guilty?"

"If an innocent man were sitting in jail right now, you'd be kicking yourself all over town, not stuffing your face with pizza and prosciutto."

"Good point."

"That's the truly great thing about your job. Even when you lose, it's actually a win."

"And sometimes when I win, it's a total loss."

Cindy sipped her wine. "You mean Jessie?"

Jack nodded.

"Let's not talk about her, okay?"

"Sorry." He'd told her about the latest confrontation with Jessie, though Cindy hadn't seemed interested in the details. The message was pretty clear: It was time to put Jessie behind them.

"Do you think I made a mistake by leaving the U.S. attorney's office?"

"Where did that come from?"

"It ties in with this whole Jessie thing."

"I thought we weren't going to talk about her tonight."

"This is about me, not her." He signaled the waiter for another beer, then turned back to Cindy. "I used to think I was good at reading people, whether they were jurors or clients or whoever. Ever since Jessie, I'm not so sure."

"Jessie didn't just lie. She manipulated you. This latest episode proves what a total wack job she is. You said it yourself, you thought she was on drugs."

"Maybe. But what if these investors really are after her?"

"She should go to the police, exactly like you told her."

"She won't."

"Then she isn't really scared. Stop blaming yourself for this woman's problems. You don't owe her anything."

He piled a few more diced tomatoes atop his bruschetta. "Two years ago, I would have seen right through her."

"Two years ago you were an assistant U.S. attorney."

"Exactly. You remember what my old boss said when we all went over to Tobacco Road after my last day?"

"Yeah, he spilled half of his beer in my lap and said, *Drings are on the Thwytecks.*"

"I'm serious. He warned me about this. Guys go into private practice, get a taste of the money, pretty soon they can't tell who's lying and who's telling the truth. Like ships in dry dock. Rusty before they're old."

"You done?"

"With what?"

"The pity party."

"Hmmm. Almost."

"Good. Now here's some really shitty news. Just because the rust on the SS *Swyteck* is premature doesn't mean this ship is getting any younger, bucko. Even your favorite Don Henley songs are finding their way to the all-oldies radio station."

"You really know how to hurt a guy."

"It's what you get for marrying a younger woman."

"Is that all I get?"

She bit off the tip of a breadstick. "We'll see."

The loud twang and quick beat from Henley's "Boys of Summer" clicked in his brain, triggering a nostalgic smile. *I still love you, Don, but man, it sucks the way time marches on.*

They finished their pizzas and skipped the coffee and dessert. The kick in the ass from Cindy had been a good thing for Jack. Behind the jokes and smiles, however, she seemed troubled.

"Jack?"

"Yes."

"Do you think we're doing the right thing trying to have a baby?"

"Sure. We've talked about this. You're not having second thoughts, are you?"

"No. I just want to make sure you're not."

"I want this more than anything."

"Sometimes I'm afraid you want it for the wrong reason."

"What do you mean?"

"Maybe you think we need another reason to stay together."

"Where would you get an idea like that?"

"I don't know. I'm sorry. I shouldn't have said anything."

"No, I'm glad you said it. Because we need to put that out of your head right now. How long have you been worried about this?"

"I'm not really worried. Well, sometimes I am. It's been five years since . . . you know, Esteban. And people still think of me as fragile. Five years, and I'm still having the same conversations. 'Are you doing okay, sweetie? Getting enough sleep? Have the nightmares stopped? Need the name of a good therapist?' "

He lowered his eyes and said, "You talked with your mother, didn't you."

"Yes. Last night."

"I'm sorry I dragged her into this. I was trying to enlist a little family support. That's all."

"I understand. Look, let's just forget this, okay?"

"You sure?"

"Yes. It'll work out."

"Everything gonna be okay with you?"

"Fine."

"You want another Perrier or something?"

She shook her head. "Let's go home."

He reached across the table and took her hand. Their eyes met as she laced her fingers into his.

"What do you say we stop by Whip 'n' Dip, get a pint of chocolate and vanilla swirl to go, climb under the covers, and don't come out till we kill the whole carton?"

"I'd like that."

"Me, too," he said, then signaled the waiter for their bill.

Jack left a pair of twenties on the table, and in just a few minutes they were in their car on Sunset Drive, moving at the speed of pedestrians. The ice cream parlor was up the street beyond the log jam, though the line was clear out the door, typical on a weekend. Even so, they arrived home before ten-thirty. Cindy went straight upstairs to the bedroom. Jack popped into the kitchen in search of two spoons. It was one of Cindy's pet peeves. If you were going to indulge yourself with dessert, it should be on real silver, not those cheap plastic jobbies with edges so sharp that they could practically double as letter openers.

The master bedroom was on the second floor, directly over the kitchen, and Jack could hear Cindy walking above him. The click of her heels on the oak floor gave way to a softer step, and he realized that she'd kicked off her shoes. A trail of barely audible footsteps led to her dressing mirror. Jack smiled to himself, imagining his wife undressing. But it was a sad, nostalgic smile triggered by what seemed like ancient memories of a time when passions ruled, not problems. She'd reach behind her arching back and unzip her cotton sundress. With a little shrug she'd loosen one strap, then the other, letting the garment fall to her ankles. She'd stand before the full-length mirror and judge herself, unable to see that she didn't really need that push-up contraption. It was a show he'd watched countless times, wishing he could just strip away all the emotional baggage and pull up behind her and kiss the back of her neck, unfasten the clasp, and reach inside, one for the delight of each hand.

But there was never any pulling up behind Cindy, no physical intimacy of any sort, unless she initiated it. That was their life since Esteban. Jack didn't blame her for it. Her only crime had been falling in love with the governor's son. Esteban had been his client, not hers. It was Jack who'd drawn the attacker into their world, not Cindy.

And *that* was something for which he could never forgive himself.

Jack started out of the kitchen, then froze at the sight of some broken glass on the floor. He dropped the frozen yogurt on the kitchen counter and ran to the French doors in the family room. One of the rectangular panes had been shattered. Jack didn't touch anything, but he could see that the lock had been turned. Someone had paid them a visit.

"Cindy!"

His heart raced as he grabbed the cordless telephone and ran to the stairway. He was gobbling up two and three steps at a time and was about to call her name again when he heard her scream. "Jack!"

He sprinted down the hallway. Just as he reached the bedroom door, it flew open in his face. Cindy rushed out. They nearly collided at full speed, but he managed to get his arms around her. He saw only terror in her eyes.

"What is it?" he asked.

She grabbed him but never stopped moving, her momentum dragging him back into the hallway. Her voice was filled with panic. "In there!"

"What's in there?"

She pointed inside the master suite, in the general direction of the bathroom. "On the floor."

"Cindy, what is it?"

She fought to catch her breath, on the verge of hyperventilation. "Blood."

"Blood?"

"Yes! My God, Jack. It's—there's so much of it. Back by the tub."

"Call 911."

"Where are you going?"

"Just call."

"Jack, don't go in there!"

He dialed 911 and handed her the phone. "Just stay on the line while I check this out."

He hurried across the room to the dresser and took the gun from the top drawer. He quickly removed the lock and started toward the bathroom. Jack didn't think of himself as a gun person, but one attack against your wife has a way of making you forever mindful of self-defense. Cindy called his name once more, a final plea to keep him from doing something stupid, but she was soon in conversation with the 911 operator.

"My crazy husband is going in there right now," Jack heard her say. But that didn't stop him. Too many weird things had happened in the last two weeks. He wasn't about to let something—or *somebody*—bleed to death in their bathroom while they waited for the cops.

He stood in the bathroom doorway with arms extended and both hands clasped around the gun. He was aiming at nothing but at the ready. "Who's in here?"

He waited but got no answer.

"The police are on their way. Now, who's in here?"

Still no answer. He stepped inside and checked the floor. He saw no blood, but he'd ventured no farther than the first of two sinks—his sink. It wasn't quite far enough inside their bathroom to see into the back area by the big vanity mirror and Roman tub—the place where Cindy had seen the blood.

He took two more steps and froze. He was standing at Cindy's sink. Her medicine cabinet was half-open, and in the angled reflection he saw it: a glistening, crimson line of blood on a floor of white ceramic tile.

His pulse quickened. Jack had seen plenty of blood before, visited many a crime scene. There was nothing like seeing it in your own house. "Do you need help?"

His voice echoed off the tiled walls, as if to assure him that no answer would come. He took two more steps, then a third. His grip tightened on the gun. His steps became half-steps. Weighted with trepidation, he turned the corner. His eyes tracked the bright red line to its source. He faced the Roman tub and gasped.

A bloody hand hung limply over the side—a woman's hand. For an instant Jack felt paralyzed. He swallowed his fear and inched closer. Then he stopped, utterly horrified yet unable to look away.

She was completely unclothed, only blood to cover her nakedness. An empty bottle of liquor rested at her hip. It was literally a bloodbath, her life seeming to have drained from the slit in her left wrist. Red rivulets streaked the basin, the thickest pool of blood having gathered near her feet.

"Jessie," he said, his voice quaking. "Oh . . . my . . . God."

13

·

The Swyteck house was an active crime scene. An ambulance and the medical examiner's van were parked side by side on the front lawn, a seeming contradiction between life and death. The driveway was filled with police cars, some with blue lights swirling. Uniformed officers, crime scene investigators, and detectives were coming and going at the direction of the officer posted at the door. The first media van had arrived soon after the police. More had followed, and six of them were parked on the street. Neighbors watched from a safe distance on the sidewalk.

Assistant State Attorney Benno Jancowitz tried not to smile.

Jancowitz was a veteran in the major crimes section, with two dozen murder trials under his belt, and he had the seemingly carved-in-wax worry lines on his face to prove it. The Miami-Dade office kept at least one prosecutor on call to attend crime scenes, but it was no coincidence that Jancowitz was on this particular assignment. A buddy had tipped him off that the body was at Jack Swyteck's house, knowing that it would be of special interest to Jancowitz.

After four years of death-penalty work for the Freedom Institute, Jack was persona non grata at the state attorney's office. In fact, he'd handed Jancowitz his first loss ever in a capital case. Jack's stint as a federal prosecutor had only worsened things. He was assigned to the public-corruption section and put two cops in jail for manufacturing evidence in the prosecution of a murder that was only made to appear gang-related. The assistant state attorney in the case was Benno Jancowitz. He was never accused of any wrongdoing himself, but the controversy had definitely bumped him off the fast track within the state attorney's office.

Jancowitz caught up with the assistant medical examiner just as she was hoisting her evidence into the back of the van.

"Hey there," he said.

"Mr. Jancowitz, how are you, sir?" It was her style to be rather stiff and formal even with people she liked.

"You about finished in there?"

"Almost. Pretty messy scene, I'm afraid."

"I know, I saw."

She removed her hair net and latex gloves. "Was the victim a friend of the Swytecks?"

"No. A client, as I understand it."

"Ah," she said.

He wasn't sure what the "ah" meant. Maybe something along the lines of *All lawyers at some point in the relationship are capable of killing their client.* "How soon before she'll be coming out?"

"*She* won't be coming out. It's a body now."

"That's one of the things I was going to ask. How long has she been an it?"

She laid a hand atop her evidence kit and said, "I should be able to give you a better idea once I get these maggots under the microscope."

"You got maggots?"

"I scraped them from her eyes. Some in her nose, too. Looks like they're hatching, or about to hatch."

"Where does that put the time of death?"

"Twelve hours, give or take. Not everyone puts as much stock in forensic entomology as I do, but I'm a firm believer that the insect pattern that develops on a corpse is about as reliable an indicator of time of death as you'll find. Absent a witness, of course."

"But you need flies to have maggots."

"Right. Flies are drawn to the smell of a dead body within ten minutes. They lay thousands of eggs, usually in the eyes, nose, and mouth. That's why the hatching is so crucial in determining time of death."

"But this body was indoors."

"Well, they don't call them *house* flies for nothing."

"I didn't really notice any flies inside."

"Doesn't mean they aren't there."

"House was all sealed up, too. Air conditioner was on."

"There was that broken window pane in the back, on the French door. Flies could have easily come in through that."

"Yeah. Or the flies that laid the maggots could have found the body outside in the open air. Before it was moved inside."

"That would sound a lot more like homicide than suicide."

"Yes," he said, thinking aloud. "It would, wouldn't it."

•

Cindy was waiting in the car. She and Jack had been backing out of the driveway, on their way to her mother's house, when a detective arrived on the scene. Cindy was eager to get away from the chaos, but the detective promised to keep Jack only a few minutes. A few minutes had turned into half an hour.

She peered through the windshield, her stomach churning at the sight of her house being transformed into a crime scene. Long strands of yellow police tape kept the onlookers at bay, which triggered a wholly incongruous thought in Cindy's mind. Strangely, it reminded her of the day Jack had asked her to move in with him before they were married. He'd tied yellow ribbons to the dresser handles as a way of marking the drawers that would be hers. If only it were possible to go back to simpler times.

A knock on the passenger-side window startled her. To her relief, it was a police officer. Cindy lowered the window.

"Would you like some coffee?" It was a female officer who spoke with a hint of a Jamaican accent. The voice was mature and confident, which made Cindy realize that this cop wasn't as young as she looked.

"No, thank you."

"It's Starbucks. Still hot."

"Thanks, but caffeine is the last thing my nerves need right now."

"I can understand that." She rested the paper cups on the car hood, reached through the open window, and offered her hand. "I'm Officer Wellens. Call me Glenda."

"Nice to meet you," Cindy said as they shook hands.

Glenda glanced casually toward the house and asked, "You know the woman?"

"She was one of my husband's clients."

"Wow."

"Why is that a wow?"

Glenda shrugged and said, "That was just the first thought that popped in my head. Isn't that what's going through your head right now? Like, 'Wow, how did this happen?' "

"My thoughts are more along the lines of, 'Why did this woman kill herself in my house?' "

"I could give you my two cents' worth. 'Course, you're talking to a woman who's seen about a million domestic violence calls."

"What makes you think this has anything to do with domestic violence?"

"Didn't say it did. It's just my point of view, that's all. Gorgeous young woman strips herself naked and slits her wrist in her lawyer's bathtub. All I'm saying is that I'm trained to think a certain way, so certain thoughts go through my head."

"Like what?"

She leaned against the car and struck a neighborly pose, as if talking over the kitchen windowsill. "I look at this situation and say, 'This woman was trying to make a statement.' "

"You mean she left a note?"

"No, honey. Maybe ten percent of the folks who commit suicide actually leave a note. Most of them let the act speak for itself."

"What kind of statement does this make?"

"I warned you about my point of view, now. You really want to hear what I'm thinking?"

"Yes."

Glenda narrowed her eyes, as if she suddenly fancied herself an FBI criminal profiler. "I look at this crime scene, I see a woman who's obviously at the end of her rope, flipping back and forth between fits of anger and bouts of depression. She can't take it no more. She's so wigged out she can't even express herself in words. So she does this. This is her message."

"What's the message?"

"You askin' my opinion?"

"Yes, your opinion."

"Something along the lines of: 'You think this was a fling, sucker? You think I was your little plaything? Well, guess again. I'd rather kill myself in your bathtub than let you and your pretty wife go on living happily ever after as if I never even existed.' "

Cindy looked away. "That's not what this is."

"Or, it could be she didn't want to die."

"What do you mean?"

"If she really just wanted to off herself, she could have crawled in her own bathtub and slit her wrists. But no. She does it in a place where she knows her lover will find her. She's maybe played out this fantasy in her mind a hundred times. Her man comes home, finds her on the brink of death, he rushes her to the emergency room. Her hero rescues her. He waits at her bedside all night long at the hospital, clutching her hand, praying for her to come to. He realizes how she doesn't want to live without him. And he realizes he can't live without her either."

"That's too weird."

"That's the real world, sister. Tragic. Lots of people

end up killing themselves when what they really wanted was someone to find them in the nick of time and save them."

"Everything you're saying is . . . it all assumes that my husband was having an affair."

Glenda raised an eyebrow, as if to say, *Well, duh!*

"That's not the way it is with Jack and me."

"I'm glad to hear that. 'Cause to look at this, I surely would have thought otherwise."

"Jack would never cheat on me."

"Good for you. My boyfriend's the same way."

"Really?"

" 'Course. He knows I'd cut his balls off if he did."

"How romantic."

Glenda laughed, then took another hit of coffee. She scrunched her face, as if confused, but Cindy was already onto the fact that Glenda was much smarter than she let on. "One thing I was wondering about. The house alarm."

"What about it?" asked Cindy.

"I notice you have one. But it didn't go off when that glass on the French door got busted."

"It wasn't on."

"You don't use your alarm?"

"We only set it when we're home."

"How's that?"

"I've had some bad—" She stopped, not wanting to reveal too much of herself and her dreams. "I've had some trouble with prowlers in the past. I'm kind of a 'fraidy cat."

"Aren't we all?"

"I'm worse than most. I have the motion sensors turned up so high, all it takes is a strong puff of wind to trigger the sirens. That used to happen all the time when we weren't home, and the city of Coral Gables ended up socking us with seven hundred bucks in fines for false alarms. Finally Jack said enough. We don't activate the alarm when we're not home. If somebody wants our stuff, we have insurance. The only thing we care about is whether someone is trying to break into our house while we're still inside it."

"Makes sense, I guess."

"At a hundred bucks per false alarm, you'd be surprised how many people use their alarms that way."

"You're right, I see it all the time. But one other thing makes me curious: How do you suppose Jessie knew that you guys don't set your alarm while you're away?"

Cindy thought for a moment, then looked at her and said, "Maybe she thought we had a silent alarm. It could be as you said, she wanted someone to come save her before she died."

Glenda screwed up her face and said, "Nah, doesn't work."

"Why not?"

"Like you said, your husband wasn't having an affair."

Cindy didn't answer.

Glenda finished her coffee. "Then again, maybe we should ask Mr. Swyteck about that. What do you think?"

"I'm not going to tell you how to do your job."

"Fair enough. Nice talkin' to you, Mrs. Swyteck."

"Nice talking to you, too."

She handed Cindy a business card. "I'm sure you're right. I'm sure things are just fine and dandy between you and Mr. Swyteck. But just in case there's something you want to talk out, woman to woman, my home number is on the back. Call me. Anytime."

"Thank you."

"You bet."

They shook hands, and Cindy raised the passenger-side window. She watched from behind tinted glass as Officer Wellens cut through the chaos in the front yard and returned to the scene of the crime.

14

It was the most unpleasant evening Jack had ever spent on his patio.

Assistant state attorney Benno Jancowitz was bathed in moonlight, seated on the opposite side of the round, cast-aluminum table. Between his chain-smoking and the burning citronella candle, it was olfactory overload. Yet at times Jack could still almost smell Jessie's blood in the air, his mind playing tricks on the senses.

"Just a few more questions, Mr. Swyteck." Smoke poured from his nostrils as he spoke, his eyes glued to his notes, as if the answers to the world's problems were somewhere in that dog-eared notepad. So far he'd spent almost the entire interview combing over the civil trial Jack had won for Jessie.

Finally he looked up and said, "Know anybody who'd want Jessie Merrill dead?"

"I might."

"Who?"

"The viatical investors who I beat at trial."

"What makes you think they'd want to kill her?"

"She told me in those exact words. She thought they were out to kill her."

"Pretty sore losers."

"They apparently thought she'd cheated them."

"Did she? Cheat them, I mean."

Jack paused, not wanting to dive headlong into the matter of a possible scam. "I can't really answer that."

"Why not?"

"Because we're getting into an area protected by the attorney-client privilege."

"What privilege? She's dead."

"The privilege survives her death. You know that."

"If there was foul play, I'm sure your late client would excuse your divulgence of privileged information."

"She might, but her heirs will probably sue me."

"I don't follow you."

"Right now, Jessie's estate has at least a million and a half dollars in it. Hypothetically, let's say I breach the attorney-client privilege and tell you she scammed the investors out of that money. Her estate just lost a million and a half bucks. Her heirs could have my ass in a sling."

"You want to talk off the record?"

"I've said enough. If something happened to Jessie, I want to help punish the people who did it. But there are some things I can't speak freely about. At least not until I've talked to her heirs."

The prosecutor smiled thinly, as if he enjoyed having to pry information loose. "Did Ms. Merrill call the police about this alleged threat on her life?"

"No."

"Did she tell anyone else about it?"

"I don't think so."

"So she was in mortal fear for her life, and the only person she told was her lawyer?"

"Don't taunt me, Benno. I'm trying to help, and I've told you as much as I can."

"If you're implying there's a possible homicide here, it would help for me to understand the motive."

"The investors reached a viatical settlement thinking Jessie would be dead in two years. It turns out they might have to wait around for Willard Scott and Smucker's to wish her a happy hundredth birthday. In and of itself, that's pretty strong motive."

He wrote something in his pad but showed no expression. "Answer me this, please. When's the last time you saw Ms. Merrill?"

"Last night."

"What time?"

"Around midnight."

"Where'd you two meet up?"

"She was waiting for me."

"Where?"

"The parking lot."

"You go anywhere?"

"No. We talked in my car."

He raised an eyebrow, and Jack immediately regretted that answer.

"Interesting," he said. "What did you two talk about?"

"That's when we had the conversation I just told you about. When she told me she thought the investors might kill her."

"Is that when she told you she'd scammed the investors?"

"I didn't say there was a scam. I told you twice already, I can't talk about that."

"Suit yourself."

"I'm not being coy. I may end up telling you every-thing. Just let me do my job as a lawyer and sort out the privilege issue with her heirs, whoever they might be."

"Take your time. Get your story straight."

"It's not a matter of getting my story straight. It's a thorny legal and ethical issue."

"Right. So, other than this sacred attorney-client relationship that you've chosen to carry into eternity, did you have any other kind of relationship with Ms. Merrill?"

"We dated before I met my wife."

"Interesting."

It was about his fifth "interesting" remark. It was getting annoying.

He glanced at his notes once more and said, "Just a few more questions. Some mop-up stuff. Ever hear her threaten to kill herself?"

"No."

"She ever make any utterances of farewell or final good-byes—like, those bastards won't have me to kick around anymore?"

"No."

"Ever hear her say she can't go on anymore, that life isn't worth living?"

"No."

"Did she have any kind of physical pain that she couldn't deal with?"

"Not that I know of."

"Were you fucking her?"

"Huh?"

He seemed pleased to have set up the question so nicely, having caught Jack off-guard. "You heard me."

"The answer is no."

"Other than those viatical investors you mentioned, can you think of anyone else who'd want her dead?"

"From the looks of things, maybe she wanted herself dead."

He nodded, as if he'd already considered Jack's theory. "Breaks and enters through the French door, grabs a bottle of vodka from the liquor cabinet, goes upstairs, slits her wrist. Which leaves one gaping question: Why would she kill herself in your house?"

"Who knows? Maybe to make some kind of statement."

"Exactly what kind of statement do you think she was trying to make?"

"I can only guess. I was her lawyer. Maybe she didn't like the job I did."

"You'd just won her a million and a half dollars."

"That's a complicated situation. I already told you, I need to sort out some privilege issues before I can talk freely."

"Ah, yes. The scam."

"I never said there was a scam."

The prosecutor's nose was back in his notes. The silence lasted only a minute or two, but it seemed longer. "Lots of nice pictures in your house," he said finally. "I like that black-and-white stuff."

Jack had no idea where he was headed. "Thanks. My wife took them."

"She's good with the camera, is she?"

"She's a professional photographer."

"That what she does for a living?"

"Partly. She's gotten into design work lately. Graphic arts. She's really good on the computer."

"Pretty busy lady, I would imagine."

"It's a full-time commitment."

"And your job? Hell, that's more than a full-time commitment."

"I'm busy, yeah. We're both busy people."

Jancowitz glanced toward the house and then back. "How are things with you and your wife?"

"Couldn't be better." He felt a bit like a liar, but his marriage was no one's business. Jancowitz didn't seem to believe him anyway.

The prosecutor said, "I couldn't help noticing earlier. You seemed pretty eager to get her in the car, off to the sidelines, as soon as the police started showing up here tonight."

"Cindy was attacked by a man five years ago. Turning her house into a crime scene is a pretty upsetting experience for her."

Again, Jancowitz offered that long, slow nod of skepticism.

"What are you trying to say, Benno?"

He gnawed his pencil. "Well, so far we got a gorgeous young woman, who used to be your lover, dead and naked in your bathtub. Blood is dry, body's still not at room temperature, rigor mortis is fading, but the larger muscle groups haven't completely relaxed. Medical examiner will pin it down better, but I'd guess she's been dead no more than twenty-four hours."

"Which means?"

"Which means that the little talk you had in your car last night certainly puts you in contention for the last person to see her alive. And we've already established that you were the first person to see her dead."

"You're ignoring the empty bottle of vodka, the slit wrist. I told you about those viatical investors just to give you the whole picture. It could be just me, but this maybe, kind-of, sort-of, looks a little like suicide, don't you think?"

"One thing I've learned after twenty-two years. Looks can be deceiving."

He gave Jack the kind of penetrating look that prosecutors laid only on suspects. Jack didn't blink. "Sorry. I don't scare easy. Especially when I've done nothing wrong."

Jancowitz closed his notebook, rose slowly, shook Jack's hand, and said, "I just love a challenge. I'll be in touch."

"Anytime."

He crossed the patio and walked back inside the house. Through the bay window Jack saw him stop in the family room to admire a long wall that was lined with Cindy's photographs. He turned, grinned, and gave the thumbs-up, as if he were admiring her work. He seemed pleased to see that Jack had been watching him.

"Twit," Jack said quietly as he returned the phony smile.

Jack waited for him to disappear into the living room, and then he took out his cell phone and dialed.

It was late, but somehow he sensed he was going to need a lawyer. A good one.

15

.

Jack had a noon meeting with Rosa Tomayo at his office. It was literally a matter of walking across the hall. Her office suite was on the same floor, same building as his.

Rosa's firm was three times bigger than Jack's, which meant that besides herself she had two much younger partners to help carry the workload. Not that she needed much help. Rosa was a bona fide multitasker, someone who felt hopelessly underutilized if she wasn't doing at least eight different things at once, all with the finesse of a symphonic conductor. Jack had personally engaged her in spirited debates over lunch only to have her later recount conversations she'd simultaneously overheard at nearby tables. That kind of energy and brain power had landed her among Miami's legal elite, though some would say her reputation was equally attributable to the quick wit and enduring good looks she employed with great flair and frequency on television talk shows. She definitely had style. But she wasn't

the typical showboat criminal defense lawyer who proclaimed her client's innocence from the hilltops when,
in truth, the government had merely failed to prove
guilt beyond a reasonable doubt. If Jack ever decided to
seek out a partner, Rosa would have been first on his
list.

When he needed representation, Rosa was the obvious choice.

Calling her from the crime scene last night had turned
out to be the right thing to do. Even though he'd walked
hundreds of his own clients through similar situations, the
perils of a lawyer representing himself were endless. Rosa
helped him focus objectively. They'd agreed that, first
thing in the morning, she would meet with the prosecutor
assigned to the case.

At 12:15 Jack began to pace. *Rosa, where are you?*

The wait was only made worse by the barrage of
calls from the media. Jack dodged them all. As a lawyer
he didn't normally shy away from reporters, but in this
case Jack was avoiding any public statements at least
until Rosa confirmed one way or the other if he was a
suspect.

At 12:45, finally, she was back.

"I think it's solved," she said.

Jack chuckled nervously from his seat at the head of
the conference table.

"I'm serious." She was picking over the deli sandwich platter he'd ordered for lunch. She removed the
sliced turkey from between two slices of rye bread,
rolled it up, and nibbled as she spoke. "I honestly think
it's resolved."

"Already?"

"What can I say? I'm damn good."

"Tell me what happened."

She tossed the rolled turkey back on the platter and started on the ham. It was the way Rosa always ate—two bites of this, a bite of that, talking all the while.

"The meeting was just me and Jancowitz. He claims you all but admitted that Jessie scammed the investors."

"I didn't go that far. I was just trying to give him some insight into the motive they might have to kill her."

"Well, the motive cuts two ways. He sees it as *your* motive to kill Jessie."

"How?"

"Self-righteous son of a former governor gets scammed by a client who used to be his girlfriend. His ego can't handle it, or maybe he thinks it will ruin his stellar reputation. He snaps and kills her, then makes it look like suicide."

"That's weak."

"That's what I said. Which is why I don't think it's their real theory."

"Then where are they headed?"

"Same place you'd go if you were still a prosecutor. You and Jessie were having an affair. She threatened to tell your wife unless you played along with her scam. You got tired of the extortion and whacked her."

"When?"

"Good question. I pressed Benno on the time of death. They're not committing to anything, but bugs don't lie. The medical examiner says that the maggot eggs in Jessie's eyes were already starting to hatch. If you work backward on the timeline of forensic entomology, that puts her time of death somewhere about midday."

"Good for me," said Jack. "I was in trial all day and then went straight to dinner with Cindy."

"That's what I told Benno."

"Except the maggots give us something else to think about. Aren't they more prevalent on a body found outdoors than indoors?"

"Not necessarily."

"But you see my point. Is anyone considering that Jessie's body was moved from somewhere outside the house to my bathtub?"

"I'm pretty sure they've ruled it out. With all the blood that ran from her body, her heart had to be pumping when she was in your tub, which means she was alive when she got there."

"Though not necessarily conscious."

"True. But there are other indicators, too. Benno was talking pretty fast, but I think he said something about how the livor mortis pattern on her backside suggests that she died right where she was found."

"When can we find out something definite?"

"We have to be patient. You know how this works. It could be weeks before the medical examiner issues a final report. Until then, all we get is what Benno deigns to share with us."

"Does that mean I'm a suspect or not?"

"I don't think you're high on the list. In my opinion, he just wants to tweak you, embarrass you a little."

"Oh, is that all?" he said, scoffing.

"Better than making your life miserable for the foreseeable future as the target of a homicide investigation. All you have to do is give him a little of what he wants."

"What are you telling me? You and Jancowitz sat around a table all morning negotiating how best to embarrass me?"

She bit off the tip of a pickle spear. "Basically."

"This is crazy."

"Just listen. Here's the deal. We put down in writing the whole conversation you and Jessie had the night before she died. She was afraid for her life, she admitted that she had scammed the viatical investors, they were threatening to kill her. Then we put in your side of the story. She acted like she was on drugs, you told her to go to the police, blah, blah, blah. And most important, we put in bold and all capital letters that you knew absolutely nothing about the scam until after the verdict was rendered."

"You're confident that there will be no repercussions about breaching the attorney-client privilege?"

"A lawyer can breach the privilege to defend himself from possible criminal charges."

"I know that. But nobody's talked about charging me yet."

"There was a dead body in your house. Trust me. They're talking about it."

Jack glanced at the untouched sandwich on his plate, then back at Rosa. "What kind of immunity are they offering?"

"They won't prosecute you on the scam. No promises on the homicide investigation."

"You think that's enough?"

"Let's be real, okay? You're never going to get immunity on a homicide charge. You're the son of a former governor. Prosecutors cut deals with the little guys so they can nail people like you."

"Then why are you so sure that this letter is the right thing to do?"

"First of all, it's the truth. Second, even though you weren't part of Jessie's scam, you should sleep better at night knowing that the prosecutor has agreed not to try to prove you were involved."

"That's something, I guess."

"Especially when you consider that we're not giving them anything they haven't already deduced from your conversation last night. Like I said, they're assuming there was a scam. This just puts it on record that you knew nothing about it."

"So, in your view, we're giving them nothing?"

"Exactly. It serves the same purpose as a press release, only not as tacky. And it may help down the road, too. Worst-case scenario, Jancowitz asks the grand jury to indict you for the murder of Jessie Merrill. Your involvement in her little scam is sure to play some part in your alleged motive. Somehow, he'll have to explain that from day one of the investigation he had a letter sitting in his file in which you unequivocally denied any involvement."

"You know as well as I do that a prosecutor doesn't even have to mention that letter to the grand jury."

"No, but we can make some hay in the press if he doesn't."

"So, why do you really think Jancowitz even wants the letter?"

"My opinion? He doesn't like you, never did. He can't wait to use your own words to show the world how stupid you were with your own client."

Jack cringed.

"Sorry," she said. "But that's the way he's going to play it. Slick defense lawyer gets outslicked."

"The media will have a feast."

"Yes, they will. But today's newspaper is tomorrow's paper-hat."

"Gee, thanks. I feel better already."

She came to him, laid a hand on his shoulder. "Look, my friend. These are salacious facts. Innocent or not, you won't come out of this smelling like a rose."

Jack knew she was right. The hardest part about being a criminal defense lawyer was defending the innocent. Even when they won, they lost something—status, reputation, the unconditional trust of friends and peers.

"I suppose it will all come out in the end anyway," he said. "I might as well lay it all out from the get-go, do what I can to make sure the investigation heads in the right direction."

"That's exactly where I came out. Of course, we're making certain assumptions. One, you didn't kill her, which goes without saying. And two, she was not your lover."

"Definitely not."

"I'm not just talking about getting naked. I don't want to find some string of flirtatious e-mails down the road somewhere."

"There's none of that."

"Then I say we go public with the scam. Jancowitz is happy because it embarrasses you professionally. We're happy because the truth focuses the attention where it belongs, on the viatical investors."

"You don't think that sounds too simple?"

"I'm not saying we write Jancowitz a letter and then sit on our hands. If they start thinking homicide and definitely not suicide, he might still hound you as a suspect. In that case, we need to be ready to hand them something on a silver platter, something so compelling that it almost forces them to focus their investigation on another suspect. Hopefully, the right suspect."

"We've got two pretty solid theories."

Rosa started to pace, as if it helped her think. "One, the viatical investors killed Jessie. They put the body in your house to deflect guilt from them to you. Or two, Jessie feared a horrible death. She was convinced they were going to kill her. So she killed herself, but she did it in a way and in a place that, as you say, makes a statement. She wanted to create havoc in your life because you refused to help her."

"It has to be one of those," said Jack.

"Lucky for us, there's a common thread to both of them: The viatical investors threatened to kill Jessie. We need to find out who's behind that company."

"Jessie didn't give me much to go on. She basically just said the company itself was a front. The real money was a bunch of bad operators."

"You know what I always say. Bad money has a stench. Follow your nose. You up for it?"

"What's my alternative?"

"You can sit back and hope your love letter to Jancowitz does the trick."

He shook his head, not so sure that Jancowitz would be satisfied in merely embarrassing him. He looked at Rosa and said, "I'll take care of the letter. Then it's time to go fishing."

"You have any particular investigator you'd like to use?"

"The official answer to that is no."

She gave him a knowing smile. "You know, it's really too bad Theo is a convicted felon. I'd use him too, if he could get a license."

"That's the beauty of the arrangement. It keeps me from having to pay him."

"Something tells me you'll find a way around that."

Jack nodded, knowing that with all the freebies Theo had given him, someday he'd owe him his car.

Rosa checked her watch. "Gotta run. If you need me, you know where to find me."

Jack walked her from the conference room to the

lobby. They stopped at the double doors. "Rosa. Thank you."

"No problem. You'd do the same for me. But let's hope you never have to."

She was out the door, but Jack answered anyway, for no one's benefit but his own. "Let's hope."

16

•

It was two A.M., and Jack sat alone at the kitchen table wearing the pajamas his mother-in-law had given him for Christmas. They were a grotesque paisley print, the kind of garment that might ordinarily sit in a dresser drawer until old age seized his senses. So long as he and Cindy were in Mrs. Paige's house, however, he figured he'd be the good son-in-law and wear them.

Since "the incident," as they'd come to call it, Cindy and Jack had been staying in her old room in her mother's house in Pinecrest. It was a temporary arrangement until they could find an apartment. Moving back into their house would never be an option, and Jack feared that even a fast-talking realtor would have a tough time selling it. *And over here, Mr. and Mrs. Buyer, is a spacious master bathroom, which the owners have quite tastefully painted a very lovely shade of red to disguise the blood splatter on the walls.*

The light from under the range hood cast a faint glow across the room. Beads of condensation glistened on the glass of water before him. A seriously flawed segment of Jack's brain was forcing him to play the half-empty/half-full guessing game, so he raised the water glass and guzzled.

There, damn it. Empty.

Jack's letter had gone off to the state attorney's office that afternoon. It recounted his entire conversation with Jessie the night before her death. He'd labored over the wording for several hours before enlisting Rosa's help to massage the final draft. She was totally sold on the concept. Jack hadn't realized how *un*sold he was until after he'd wasted four hours trying to fall asleep. A written acknowledgment to the state attorney that his own client had scammed him would hardly bolster his standing in the Miami legal community.

"Are you okay?"

He turned and saw Cindy standing behind him. He'd tried not to wake her when he'd crawled out of the little bed they were sharing, but he'd obviously failed.

"Can't sleep," he said.

"Me neither. I thought I'd check the real estate section for rentals once more."

"Good idea."

As she searched through the recycle bin for yesterday's newspaper, she looked up and asked, "Are you still thinking about that letter you wrote to the state attorney?"

"How did you know?"

"Because I know you."

He lowered his eyes. "I feel like the teacher kept me after school to write five hundred times on the blackboard, 'BULLWINKLE IS A DOPE.' "

"You're not stupid. You're the smartest lawyer I know."

"I did a pretty stupid thing."

"You had no choice. Writing that letter is the only way to focus the state attorney's attention where it belongs—on those investors who were threatening your client."

"I didn't mean writing the letter was stupid. I meant letting Jessie fool me in the first place."

She quit searching for the newspaper and lowered herself into the chair beside her husband. The look in her eye told him that he was in for a reality check. "Jessie's doctor was one of the most respected neurologists in Miami. How could you possibly have suspected that a man of his stature would falsify a diagnosis and defraud a group of viatical investors?"

"I deal with clever thieves all the time. I let my sympathy for Jessie get in the way."

"Of course you did. Even *I* felt sorry for that woman. I'm the one who told you, 'Go ahead and take the case, I don't care if she's your old girlfriend.' Remember?"

"It still blows me away."

"Me too. Especially the doctor. The more I think about this, the crazier it seems that Dr. Marsh would jeopardize his whole career that way."

"Money," he said, shaking his head. "I know a few doctors who love it."

"There has to be something more at work. Something that we don't understand."

He could have detailed some of Jessie's other persuasive powers, but that didn't seem like a smart road to travel with his wife. "Let's not worry about him," he said. "How are you doing?"

"Okay."

She'd averted her eyes when answering. He turned her chin gently. "What's wrong?"

"I got my period," she said quietly.

Jack tried not to show disappointment. "It's okay. We'll keep trying."

"We've been trying for eleven months now."

"Has it really been that long?"

"Yes. And I'm still not pregnant."

"Maybe we should try doing it without our wedding rings. That never seems to fail."

She almost smiled, but this was clearly weighing on her. "How worried are you, honey?" he asked.

"Very."

"Maybe it's me," said Jack.

"It's not you."

"How do you know?"

"I just know."

He wasn't sure how she knew, but debating it wasn't going to cheer her up. "There are plenty of things we haven't tried yet."

"I know. And there's always adoption, too. But I'm almost afraid to think about that."

"Why?"

She paused and said, "Because of the relationship you had with your stepmother."

"That's totally different from adoption."

"It's not, at least from a bonding standpoint. You were just a newborn when your mother died. Agnes raised you from infancy."

"The fact that my stepmother and I never bonded has nothing to do with the fact that she was not my biological mother. My father was so desperate to find me a new mother that he married a woman who turned out to be a drunk."

She took his hand, lacing her fingers with his. "How often do you wonder about your real mother?"

"I go in spurts. Times when I'm really curious, other times when I don't think about her at all. Fortunately, I have my *abuela* to tell me all about her."

"Doesn't that concern you, about adoption? The idea of this mysterious person becoming part of our lives?"

"Adoption isn't like that. There's no *abuela* around to tell stories about the biological mother."

"I didn't mean an actual living person. I meant more like the essence of the birth mother."

"That doesn't seem to bother the millions of other couples who adopt."

"I don't think other people are as in touch with that sort of thing as I am."

"What sort of thing?"

"Feeling someone's . . . presence."

Jack knew that she was talking about her father, and he feared that Jessie's death had triggered something. "Is that why you're awake? Were you having that dream about your father again?"

"No."

"Are you sure?"

"Come on, I didn't want to make this conversation about that. I'm sorry."

"Don't be sorry. This was a traumatic event for both of us. If you want to talk to me or someone else or even a counselor, it's okay."

She fell silent, then looked at him and said, "Actually, there's something I've been wanting to show you."

"What?"

"Wait right here."

She rose and followed the dark hall to the spare bedroom that she'd turned into her temporary home office. In a minute she returned to the table and laid a ten-by-twelve photograph before him and said, "I shot a few rolls of film a couple weeks ago. Just a run-of-the-mill outdoor portrait of a little girl and her dog."

Jack studied the photograph, shrugged, and said, "It's a nice picture."

"Look at the lower right-hand corner. See anything?"

He zeroed in. "Like what?"

"Does that not look like a shadow to you? As if someone might have been standing behind me?"

He looked again and said, "I don't see any shadow."

"You don't *see* that?"

"The entire corner is a little darker than the rest of the photograph, but it doesn't look like a person to me. Was someone there with you?"

"No. That's the whole point. It was just me, the girl, and the dog. Yet I had a weird sensation that someone else was there during the shoot."

"Cindy, please," he said with concern.

"No, it's true. Then I went back and took a really good look at the proofs, and I saw this."

"Saw what?"

"This silhouette."

"It's just a dark spot."

"It's a *person*."

"Cindy—"

"Just listen to me. I'm not losing my mind. I thought I was, to be honest. Between my creepy dreams and this shadow in the photograph, I was starting to think— well, I didn't know what to think. But ever since this thing happened with Jessie, it's beginning to make sense to me."

"What's making sense?"

She paused, as if to underscore her words. "Maybe someone's following me."

"What?"

"Jessie told you that some thugs were behind that viatical investment. She said they were going to kill her, didn't she?"

"Yes."

"What if those same thugs think her lawyer helped her pull off the scam? They could be out to get you, too. They could be out to get *us*."

"No one's going to get us."

"Then why is this shadow in my picture?"

"I honestly don't see it."

Her eyes seemed to cloud over. She looked at the photograph, then at Jack. "You really don't see anything?"

He shook his head. "If you want, we can hire another photographer to examine it. See if their professional judgment squares with yours."

"No."

"You sure?"

"Yes. You're right. It's not there."

Jack recoiled, confused by her sudden reversal. "It's not?"

She shook her head. "The first time I examined this proof, I was sure I saw a human shadow. Then I looked at it again tonight and I wasn't so sure. You just confirmed it for me. I'm seeing things that aren't even there." She chuckled mirthlessly and said, "I really must be freaking out."

"What happened to us is enough to push anyone to the edge."

She moved closer, as if telling him to hold her. He took her in his arms and said, "Everything's going to be okay."

"You promise?"

"Everyone has fears. The imagination can run away with you."

"Tell me about it."

"It'll pass. Believe me. We'll be fine."

"I know. Tonight's just been especially tough. The whole day, really."

"What happened?"

"It's just that . . ."

"What?"

"After this horrible thing happened in our own house, I'd managed to convince myself that God had something really good in store for us. That's why it hit me pretty hard today when I found out I wasn't pregnant."

"Good things *are* in store for us. There are so many options we haven't even talked about yet. Fertility drugs, even artificial insemination, if you want."

She smiled weakly.

"What?" he asked.

"An absurd image just flashed into my head. You sitting all by yourself in the back room of some doctor's office, flipping through the pages of a dirty magazine . . ."

"It's not like that at all."

"Oh, really, stud? How do you think they collect their specimen?"

"I dunno. I just always assumed that's why nurses wear rubber gloves."

"Perv," she said as she pushed him away playfully.

He pulled her back into his arms. "Come here, you."

She settled into his embrace, put her head against his shoulder, and said, "A baby. What a thought."

"*Our* baby. Even more amazing."

"You ready for this?"

"Heck, no. You?"

"Of course not."

"Perfect," he said. "Why should we be different from everyone else?"

She flashed a wan smile, her voice seeming to trail off in the distance. "If only we were just a little bit more like everyone else."

Jack wasn't sure how to answer that, so he kept holding her. After a minute or two, she started to rock gently in his arms. It was barely audible, but she was humming the lullaby, "Hush, Little Baby." In his head Jack was following along and enjoying the melody, until she stopped suddenly in midverse. It was a cold and abrupt ending, like hopes and dreams interrupted. He waited for her to continue, but she didn't.

They stayed wrapped in each other's arms, saying not another word, neither of them wanting to be the first to let go.

17
·

In the morning Jack went jogging. He pushed it far-ther than his normal run, following the tree-lined path along Old Cutler Road all the way to Coco Plum, an exclusive waterfront community. The leafy canopy of century-old banyans extended from one side of the road to the other, a tunnel Miami-style. Salty smells of the bay rode in on a gentle east wind. Traffic was sparse, but by the morning rush hour a seemingly end-less stream of BMWs, Jaguars, and Mercedes-Benz con-vertibles would connect this wealthy suburb to the office towers in downtown Miami. Certain American-made SUVs were acceptable in this neighborhood, but only if they were big enough to fill two parking spaces at The Shops of Bal Harbour and were used primarily to drive the future Prada-totin', Gucci-lovin' generation to and from private schools.

Jack was approaching the four-mile mark of his run and feeling the pull of a restless night. He and Cindy had gone back to bed around three A.M. Their talk had put his worries about Jessie and his letter to the state attorney on the back burner, but Jack's thoughts of his mother were percolating to the surface.

The only thing he knew for certain about his mother was that he'd never known her. Everything else had come secondhand from his father and, much later in his life, *Abuela*. Jack's mother was born Ana Maria Fuentes in Havana and grew up in Bejucal, a nearby town. She left Cuba as a teenager in 1961, under a program called *Pedro Pan* (Spanish for "Peter Pan"), a humanitarian effort that was started by an Irish Catholic priest and that enabled thousands of anxious Cuban parents to spirit away their children to America after Castro took over. Ana Maria was eventually linked up with an uncle in Tampa, and *Abuela* had every intention of joining them just as soon as she had the chance. Unfortunately, that chance didn't come for almost forty years, when *Abuela* was finally able to get a visa to visit her dying brother. For Ana Maria, that meant making a new life for herself without her mother. She worked menial jobs to learn English, and moved to Miami, where she met Harry Swyteck, a handsome young college student who happened to be home on summer break. From the old photographs Jack had seen, it was obvious the boy was totally smitten. Jack was born eleven months after they were married. His mother died while he was in the nursery. Doctors weren't as quick to diagnose pre-eclampsia in the 1960s as they are today, or at least they weren't as accountable for their screwups.

It hadn't dawned on Jack until the homestretch of his morning jog, but maybe *that* was the reason he'd jumped into Jessie's case.

He wondered what his mother would think now, her

son duped by a respected doctor and a woman who'd only pretended to be misdiagnosed. He knew too little about her to hazard a guess. His father had remarried before Jack was out of diapers. Agnes, Jack's stepmother, was a good woman with a weakness for gin martinis and an irrational hatred for a woman she feared Jack's father would never stop loving—his first wife, Jack's mother. She went ballistic each time a letter from *Abuela* arrived from Cuba, and many of them Jack never saw, thanks to her. "Dysfunctional" was the politically correct label that experts might have placed on the Swyteck family. Jack tended to think of it as a royal freak show. But he could still laugh about some things. He was a half-Cuban boy raised in a completely Anglo home with virtually no link to Cuban culture. That alone guaranteed him a lifelong parade of comedic moments. People formed certain impressions about the Anglo Jack, only to do a complete one-eighty upon hearing that he was half-Hispanic. Take his Spanish, for example. Jack was proud of his heritage, but it was with some reluctance that he shared his Cuban roots with anyone impressed by the way this presumed gringo named Swyteck could speak Spanish. It was a conversation he'd had at least a thousand times:

"Wow, Jack, your Spanish is really good."

"My mother was Cuban."

"Wow, Jack, your Spanish really sucks."

It was all how you looked at it.

Jack finished the run and showered long before his normal breakfast hour. The commute from his mother-in-law's house was a little farther than his usual drive, but he still arrived before his secretary. Jack stood outside the double-door entrance, fumbling for the master key, as the elevator opened behind him. He glanced over his shoulder, then did a double take.

"Good morning," said Dr. Marsh.

Jack turned but didn't answer. He hadn't seen the doctor since the last elevator ride, when he and Jessie had held hands. Marsh came forward but didn't offer Jack his hand.

"I said good morning, Mr. Swyteck."

"Oh, it's you, Dr. Marsh. I didn't recognize you without your girlfriend."

"I thought we should talk."

Jack gave him a quick once-over and said, "Come in."

He opened the door and flipped on the lights. Dr. Marsh followed him through the small reception area to the main conference room. They sat on opposite sides of the smoked-glass table top.

The doctor was a handsome man who tried way too hard to look younger. Flecks of gray added distinction to his black hair, but it was coated with a thick styling gel that reflected badly in the light. Beneath his seven-hundred-dollar Armani jacket he wore a Miami Heat T-shirt that was given away at last year's NBA playoffs. It was a look that a twenty-nine-year-old tech-stock millionaire on South Beach might get away with, but not a doctor who'd reached the age where he was lucky to still have all of his hair. Purely on a physical level, he didn't strike Jack at all as Jessie's type. For one, Jessie had hated beards, even well-groomed ones. At least that was what she'd told Jack when he'd let his stubble grow for a week while they were still dating. Maybe she'd just hated them on Jack. Or maybe Jack didn't have a clue as to her likes and dislikes.

Jack said, "Before we start, it should be made clear that you're not here as a client or prospective client. Anything we talk about here is not protected by the attorney-client privilege."

"That's fine. I'm confident you won't be repeating this conversation to anyone anyway." He pulled a package of cigarettes from his inside pocket. "Mind if I smoke?"

"Yes."

He smiled a little, as if he liked Jack's combative edge, then put away the cigarettes. "I hear you've been talking to the state attorney's office."

"That's true."

"What are you telling them?"

"The truth."

The doctor paused, as if he needed a moment to recall what was "the truth." It lasted just long enough to let Jack take control of the conversation. "Who told you I was talking to the state attorney?" asked Jack.

"A detective came to see me last night. Him and an assistant state attorney."

"Benno Jancowitz?"

"Name's not important."

"What did you talk about?"

"They told me you'd given them a written statement."

"That's between me and them," said Jack.

"Don't try to get all legal on me. I know what it says. They read it to me."

"Good. Get used to hearing it. It'll be public information by the end of today."

"Don't you want to know why they read it to me?"

"To give you a chance to confirm or deny your role in the scam, I presume."

"You presume wrong."

"Is that so?"

"Yeah. They wanted me to confirm that *you* were part of it."

"I wasn't part of it," Jack said, without so much as blinking.

Dr. Marsh leaned into the table, not quite as smoothly as he might have, as if he'd overrehearsed the cherished line he was about to deliver. "Trust me, Mr. Swyteck. If there was a scam, you were part of it."

"Are you threatening me?"

"I'm appealing to your sense of reason. We're both smart men, but nobody's perfect. Shit, till I saw what that woman could do with a zucchini squash, I was never one to eat my veggies. Jessie Merrill was one tasty dish."

"She was just another client."

"Yeah, and Anna Kournikova is just another tennis player. My point is this. You and I both made mistakes with the same woman. You got a little more crazy than I did, but you're a criminal defense lawyer, so you know people who do that kind of stuff."

"What kind of stuff?"

"Fixing things. You know, getting rid of problems like Jessie Merrill."

"Are you saying—are you *accusing* me of having hired someone to kill her?"

"The detective told me you were in court the day Jessie died. Ironclad alibi. How else could you have done it?"

"That's the whole point. I didn't do anything."

"I heard about you and that friend of yours who went to visit my wife. You know who I'm talking about: Theo Knight, former death-row inmate."

"Theo is not a murderer. And neither am I."

"Come on. I don't give a rat's ass if you had her whacked. Nobody's saying we have to like each other, but we have to be together on this. I can help you on the back end. You just gotta help me on the front end."

"What front end?"

"That's my boy. 'What front end?' I like that. Lost your memory already, have you?"

"What are you talking about?"

"The front end—the scam. There was none, right?"

"No, not right."

"Careful there. With that murder for hire, the back end's the much uglier rap."

Jack felt the sudden urge to kick his teeth in. "Get out of my office."

"You need me."

"Get out."

"If you say there's a scam, I say you're part of it. If you're in on the front end, you're in way deep on the back end."

"You have ten seconds to be outta here."

He stayed put, defiant, but a nervous stroke of his beard told Jack that he was cracking. Finally, he rose, and Jack showed him to the lobby. They stopped at the double glass doors that led to the elevators.

"You sure you won't play ball?" said Marsh.

"Get out before I bat your head across the room."

"Lay a hand on me, counselor, and I'll sue you for assault."

"I'll look forward to it. No better place than a courtroom to beat your ass."

"Yeah," he said with a smirk. "Just like the last time."

"It won't be like the last time."

"Got that right," he said as his expression ran cold. "I won't have to worry about Jessie fucking things up."

He pushed open the door and left. Jack watched

through the beveled-glass window as the doctor entered the open elevator and checked his handsome facade in the chrome finish.

The doors closed, and for the first time since Jessie's death Jack was really beginning to wonder: Just who was the brain behind the scam?

18

.

When Jack first met Cindy, she was a wimp when it came to drinking. "Tying one on" meant an extra splash of Bailey's Irish Cream in her heaping bowl of Häagen Dazs. She'd been raised in a strict Methodist household. Her mother sang in the church choir and her father, Jack was told, had just one vice, a little nickel-and-dime-poker game on Tuesday evenings. She'd loosened up over the years, but Jack rarely saw her sloshed.

So, when he came home early at five o'clock and found a completely empty bottle of chardonnay on the kitchen table, he knew something was amiss.

"You share that with anyone?" asked Jack.

She shook her head. Her mother wasn't home. She'd been drinking alone.

Time had passed slowly since Jessie's death, and the media had not yet tired of speculating as to the "true nature" of the "tragic relationship" between Jack and his attractive client. It was obviously beginning to take a toll.

"You lied to me," she said.

He looked at her but couldn't speak. It hurt more than being called a murderer. "What are you talking about?"

"She was your lover, wasn't she?"

"Do you mean Jessie?"

"Who else?"

"No." He hurried to the table, sat in the chair beside her. "Who told you that?"

"A couple of investigators were just here."

"What kind of investigators?"

"Homicide."

"You let them in this house? Cindy, you have to stay away from those people."

"Why? So I don't hear the truth?"

He looked into her eyes. She'd been drinking, for sure. But he could see way past that, to the part that really hurt. She'd been crying. "What did they tell you?"

She took a sip from her wine glass, but it was dry. "They said you and Jessie were having an affair."

"Not true."

"I trusted you, Jack. I felt sorry for Jessie, I told you to take her case. How could you do this?"

"I didn't do anything. It's so obvious what they're up to. They lay this cockeyed romance theory on you to get you mad enough to turn against me. They're fishing, that's all."

"You really think she killed herself?"

"I don't know. But whatever happened to her, we weren't lovers."

"Damn you! The woman slit her wrist in our bathtub—*naked*."

"Looks bad, I know."

"Yeah, all over the news for over a week it's been looking bad. There isn't a person in Miami who doesn't think you two were doing it."

"Everyone but the person who mattered. You believed me."

"I *wanted* to believe you. But sooner or later, even I have to face facts."

"The fact is, it didn't happen between me and Jessie. And there isn't a bit of proof that it did."

The anger drained from her voice, and she was suddenly stone-cold serious. "That's the problem, Jack. Now there is proof."

He could almost hear his own heart pounding. "What?"

"The investigators. They left it for me."

"Left what?"

She pushed away from the table, crossed the kitchen, and stopped at the cassette player on the counter. "This," she said as she ejected the tape.

"What's that supposed to be?"

"Seems your friend Jessie—your *client*—taped one of your little episodes in her bedroom."

"That's not possible. There were no episodes."

"Stop lying! It's your voice. It's her voice. And the two of you aren't talking sports."

He was speechless. "This is crazy. We were never together. And even if we had been, why would she record it?"

"Get real. She's a swindler, and you're a married man with an awful lot to lose. She wouldn't be the first woman to slip a tape recorder under the bed."

"I want to hear it."

"Well, I don't. I've heard enough."

She grabbed her purse and dug for the car keys.

"Wait," he said. "Give me a minute to listen to it."

"No." She started for the door.

"Cindy, please."

"I said no."

He stepped between her and the door. "You're not driving anywhere. You just drank a whole bottle of wine."

She glared, then started to tremble. A huge tear streamed down her check. Wiping it away only brought replacements, a flood. Jack went to her, but she backed away.

"Just stay away from me!"

"Cindy, I would never cheat on you."

"What about Gina?"

He froze. Gina Terisi, years earlier. "That was before we were even engaged. You went to Italy on that photo assignment and told me we were through before you left."

"You obviously took it very well."

"No. I was a wreck. That's how it happened with Gina in the first place."

"Were you a wreck this time? Is that how it happened with Jessie?"

"No. It didn't happen with Jessie."

"It's on tape!"

"I think I know what this is. Just let me hear it."

"I'm not going to sit here while you play that thing."

As she tried to pass, he backed against the door. "You're not driving drunk."

"Let me out!" She punched him in the chest, not a boxer's punch but more like beating on a door in frustration. She practically fell against him, partly catharsis, partly the alcohol. He tried to take her in his arms, but she kept fighting for the doorknob.

"I'll go," he said. "Just give me the tape and promise you won't drive anywhere."

Their eyes locked—those beautiful, blue, moist eyes filled with doubt and disappointment. Quickly she went to the cassette player on the counter and threw the tape at him. He caught it.

"Knock yourself out, Jack. Now leave me alone."

He didn't budge, couldn't move his feet. "Cindy, I love—"

"Don't even say it. Just go!"

He hated to leave on that note, but he didn't want to make things worse by trying to explain the tape before hearing it. He lowered his head, opened the door, and went without another word. He was halfway down the steps when the porch light switched off. It seemed that Cindy wanted it that way—Jack walking to his car in total darkness, alone.

Jack listened to the audiocassette in the car. Immediately, he knew what it was. The bigger question was, Why was she doing this to him?

Jack had one good friend who'd known the old Jessie. Not in the same way Jack had known her, but they used to hang out together back when Jack was dating Jessie. He'd first met Mike Campbell in Hawaii. Jack spent a summer slumming it in Maui before law school, one last blowout before immersing himself in the study of law. Mike had done him one better, having spent his entire senior year as a transfer student at the University of Hawaii before starting law school in Miami. He'd simply packed up his old Porsche at the landlocked University of Illinois, driven to Los Angeles, hopped on a ship, and finished out his undergraduate degree surrounded by palm trees and beautiful women. They were a couple of young immortals, crazy enough to night-dive in the black ocean beneath the fishing boats, living for the rush of adrenaline that came each time they'd spot holes in the nets that sharks had torn through. Mike was always a bit more fearless, which is why he now lived on the water, with a forty-three-foot Tiara open-fisherman docked in his backyard. He'd second-mortgaged his house and risked everything to wage a ten-year battle against the makers of a polybutylene piping that was supposed to replace copper plumbing in homes across the United States. Turned out that even the minimal levels of chlorine in normal drinking water disintegrated the stuff. Darn. It only ended up costing the big boys 1.25 billion dollars. At the time, it was the largest settlement ever in a case that didn't involve personal injuries. Mike walked away with twenty-two million bucks, thank you very much.

The best part was, it was still impossible to hate the guy.

"You and Jessie on tape?" said Mike.

Jack had stopped by his house and caught him tinkering with the stereo system on his boat. They were sharing a couple of beers on deck, Mike leaning against the rail and Jack reclining in the hot seat, as they called it, a bolted-down fishing chair that made Jack want to strap himself in and reel in a monster sailfish. It was well past sunset, but the landscape lighting from the expensive homes on the other side of the canal shimmered on the waterway.

"Yeah. On tape."

"Like, screaming and everything?"

"Mike, you're not helping."

"Every good lawyer needs all the facts."

"The most important fact, buddy, is that this tape is ancient. It was made before I'd even met Cindy Paige."

"So, was it a high-pitched scream, or more of a guttural—"

"Mike, come on."

"Sorry." He swiveled in his chair and grabbed another Bud from the cooler. "So, it's an old tape. Did you even know she had it?"

"Not really."

"What do you mean, not really?"

Jack tipped back his beer, took a long pull. "Jessie was a lot of fun, but she wasn't nearly as promiscuous as people thought. We didn't jump in bed together, by any means. But once we dated awhile, things progressed. And once we got there, things got kind of . . . interesting."

"Interesting?"

"She wanted to make a videotape."

"What?" he said, smiling.

"I wouldn't go for it. But for about a two-month stretch, she brought it up almost every time we got naked. One night we were out dancing, got pretty drunk. About thirty seconds after we get back to her apartment, we're in bed rolling all over each other. She reaches for the remote control on the nightstand, and I think she's switching on the television to throw a little light on the subject. We're about five seconds away from doing it when I realize that there's a tape recorder on the nightstand. She figures that maybe we'll ease into this with just the audio, then maybe I'll warm up to the idea and do a video. I tell her to turn it off, but at this point I don't care if we're live on National Public Radio. That's how it happened."

"You made an X-rated audiocassette?"

"It was awful. It sounded like a couple of drunks going at it in the dark."

"So, you got rid of it?"

"I told her to, but she kept it. It became a little gag

between us. I'd be working late at the office till maybe ten or eleven o'clock. Instead of getting a nagging call to come home, I'd pick up the phone and on the other end of the line would be this tape of Jessie outdoing Meg Ryan in the *When Harry Met Sally* restaurant scene."

"Beats all heck out of clanging the dinner bell."

"It was good for a couple of laughs, and then she dropped it."

"But she kept the tape?"

"Evidently."

"For how many years?"

"Seven, closer to eight. I don't read much into that. She could have just stuffed it in a shoebox somewhere and forgotten about it."

"And the homicide investigators found it."

"Yeah. Or, more likely, Jessie's estate handed it over to them as evidence."

"As evidence of what? That you and Jessie had sex before you and Cindy even met?"

"I guess it never occurred to anyone that the tape might be from another decade."

"How could they not see it?" said Mike. "You ever gone back to one of your old cassettes? They look *old*."

"But a copy doesn't look old. Cindy's looked brand-new. Unless you have the original, it wouldn't be so obvious that the tape is eight years old."

"So, where's the original?"

"I don't know. The police might have it, but that would be really scummy of them to copy an old cassette onto a new reel and pass it off to my wife as a recent affair."

"So, presumably Jessie's estate kept the original, and for some reason they gave the police a copy that makes it look new."

"Or, I suppose, the original could be gone, and the

only thing Jessie left behind was a copy that looks brand-new."

"Why would she do that?"

Jack paused, as if afraid to come across as paranoid. "Because she wanted someone to think that she and I were having a recent affair."

"Ah, I see," he said, smiling. "And which conspiracy theory do you subscribe to on the Kennedy assassination? Would it be the Mafia, the Cubans, or perhaps the cluster of icebergs that got the *Titanic*?"

"Okay, it's a little out there. But whatever went on here, it sure convinced my wife."

Mike leaned forward in his captain's chair, looked at Jack with concern. "How is Cindy doing?"

"So-so. This doesn't help."

"I thought about you two when I saw this on the news. I called you."

"I know. I got the message. So many people called, I just didn't have a chance to return them all."

"I thought about calling Cindy, but I didn't know what kind of shape she'd be in. Bad enough finding a body in your house. But it has to be especially hard on her, after the nightmare she went through with that psycho former client of yours."

Jack looked down at his empty beer bottle. "First him, now Jessie. Guess I need to work on my choice of clients."

"Water through the pipes, as I always say."

"Polybutylene pipes."

Their bottles clicked in toast. "God love 'em," said Mike.

They shared a weak smile, then turned serious. "Tell me the truth," said Jack. "After all these years, why do you think Jessie had that tape?"

"Could be as you said. She packed it away in her closet and forgot it even existed."

"Or?"

"I don't know. You are the son of a former governor. Maybe she thought you'd run for office some day and she could embarrass you."

Jack peeled the label from his beer. "Possible, I suppose."

"Or it could be that she's been listening to that tape over and over again for the last decade, turning away the likes of George Clooney and Brad Pitt, crying her eyes out night after night for Jack Swyteck, world's greatest lover."

"You think?"

"Oh, absolutely."

"Wow. I never would have figured that out on my own. You're a genius."

"I know."

"Seriously," said Jack. "You're a plaintiffs' lawyer."

Mike glanced around his gorgeous boat. "Last time I checked."

"Go back in time eight months. On the face of it, Jessie Merrill had an attractive case. Sympathetic facts, a young and beautiful client."

"I'll give you that."

"She could have gone to a zillion different lawyers. Most of them would have taken the case. Hell, some would have signed on even if she'd told them flat-out in advance that the whole thing was a scam."

"Not me, but some of them, yeah."

"Yet, she picks me. A guy whose practice is ninety-percent criminal. Why?"

Mike didn't answer right away, seeming to measure his words. "Maybe she wanted a really smart lawyer who she knew she could fool."

"Thanks."

"Or, for some bizarre reason, she wanted you back in her life."

"But why? After all these years, why?"

He shrugged and said, "Can't help you there, my friend. You'll have to answer that one yourself."

Jack leaned back in the deck chair, watched the moonlight glistening on the little ripples in the brackish water alongside Mike's boat. "I wish I knew," was all he could say.

Mike tossed his empty into the open cooler. "You need a place to stay tonight?"

He considered it, then said, "No. I can't let this fester."

"What are you going to do?"

"Tell Cindy the truth."

"That won't be easy."

"Cake," Jack said. "The hard part is getting her to believe it."

He grabbed an end of the cooler, and Mike grabbed the other. They climbed from the boat, the empties rattling against the cold ones as they walked toward the patio.

20

·

The chain lock was on the door when Jack got to his mother-in-law's house. It opened about six inches and then caught.

"Cindy?" he called out through the narrow opening.

"Go away, Jack." It was her mother's voice, coming from the other room.

"I just want to talk."

"She doesn't want to talk to you."

Part of him wanted to plead directly with Cindy to let him in, but he knew there was no getting through to her as long as her mother was acting as gatekeeper.

"Cindy, it's just as I thought. That tape is old. It was made before I'd even met you."

No one answered.

"Call me, please. I'll leave my cell phone on."

"Better get an extra long–life battery," her mother said.

"Thanks a ton, Evelyn." He closed the door and retreated quietly to his car.

He wasn't sure where to go. He drove around the neighborhood for a few minutes, heading generally in the direction of U.S. 1. He considered going back to Mike's, then changed his mind. Cindy was foremost in his thoughts, but his earlier talk with Mike had helped frame another question that, on reflection, just might tie in with his current marital woes: Exactly what information about Jack had Jessie's estate handed over to the state attorney?

This wasn't a job for Theo. He turned down Ludlam Road and decided to pay a visit to Clara Pierce.

In Florida, the executor of the estate is called a personal representative, and with Clara the term "personal" seemed particularly appropriate. It had been years since Jack had been to Clara's house. They'd first met when Jack was dating Jessie. She was a lawyer and one of Jessie's oldest friends, which was how she ended up drafting Jessie's will and being named the PR. Jessie and Jack had actually double-dated with Clara and her then-husband. David and Jack had stayed friendly through the divorce, though Jack had tried not to take sides. David was a real estate attorney who'd given up his own career to be their son's primary caretaker. He did it all—the bottle feedings, the diapers, the back-and-forth from school, homework, soccer, Little League. He fought for custody when they divorced, and lost. At the time, Jack didn't blame Clara for turning on the tears to convince a judge that a boy needed his mother. Having never known his own mother, Jack was perhaps an easy sell. But it bugged him to no end when she'd packed up the boy's things and shipped him off to boarding school two months after the court awarded her custody. It only confirmed that she hadn't really wanted her son, she just didn't want her husband to have him. The only thing that mattered to Clara was winning.

Clara didn't seem shocked to see Jack. She invited him into the kitchen for coffee.

"Your son still a hotshot center fielder?" Jack asked, baiting her.

"Oh, yeah. He's always been, you know, really centered."

Typical of Clara not to know that her own son was a pitcher, not a center fielder. Even Jack's stepmother would have known the difference, and she thought Mickey Mantle was a mouse that sat over your fireplace.

"Cream and sugar?" she asked.

"Black's good."

She sat on the bar stool on the other side of the counter, facing Jack. She was still dressed in office attire, a basic navy blue business suit and white silk blouse. Clara wasn't big on style. She'd worn her hair the same way for eight years, tight and efficient curls as black as her coffee. She took a sip from her cup and eyed him over the rim, as if to say, *What gives?*

"A couple of homicide investigators came to see Cindy today," said Jack. "They gave her an audiotape of me and Jessie. Know anything about it?"

"Of course. I gave it to them."

"Why?"

"I've inventoried every item of her personal property. That's my job as PR. The police asked me for anything that might shed light on the nature of the relationship between you and Jessie. So I gave them the tape."

"You could have called to give me a heads-up. It's the least I would have done for an old friend."

"You and I were never really friends."

She wasn't being acerbic, just brutally honest. Jack said, "I didn't side with David over you. I was subpoenaed for the custody hearing. I told the truth. David was a good father."

"That has nothing to do with this. Jessie was my friend, and the police are trying to find out how she died. I intend to cooperate, and I'm not going to pick up the phone and call you every time something happens. That's not my job."

"Did you know that the audiotape was made back when Jessie and I were dating?"

"No. It looked brand-new."

"You mean the copy you gave to the state attorney looks brand-new."

"No. I'm talking about the only tape I've ever seen."

"You mean the tape you found among Jessie's possessions looked like new?"

"Yes."

Jack tried not to look too puzzled, but his conversation with Mike about being paranoid was echoing in his brain. *Maybe it was icebergs that got Kennedy.* "Jessie must have copied it onto a new tape and destroyed the original."

"Why would she do that?"

He had a theory, but not one that he wanted to share with Clara. "I'm not sure. You got any ideas?"

"I don't even want to guess what kind of games you and Jessie were playing. I just want to help the police find out what happened to her."

"I didn't kill her."

"I hope that's true. I sincerely mean that."

"Come on, Clara. You don't really believe I'm a killer."

"You're right, I don't. But I didn't believe Jessie

would scam a viatical company out of a million and a half dollars, either."

"She did."

"So you say."

"I saw her and Dr. Marsh holding hands just minutes after the verdict."

"So what? He was happy she won. That doesn't mean the two of them were partners in crime."

"She told me it was a scam, and he practically admitted it too. Right in my office."

"He's a respected, board-certified neurologist."

"Evidently, he's also a thief."

"If he's the thief, then why is it your name instead of his on the joint bank account?"

Jack nearly choked. "What bank account?"

"Grand Bahama Trust Company. The offshore bank where Jessie put the money she got from the viatical investors. She had an account there. Jessie *and you* had an account there."

He blinked several times and said, "There must be some mistake."

"Account number zero-one-oh-three-one. A joint account in the name of Jessie Suzanne Merrill and John Lawrence Swyteck. That is your name, isn't it?"

"Yeah, but—a joint account?"

"Don't get any ideas. If you even try to touch that money, I'll be right in your face. Those funds are staying in her estate."

"Don't worry. I want no part of any money she got in a scam. I'll stipulate that it's not mine."

"Good. I'll get you the papers tomorrow."

"Fine. But I need to get to the bottom of this joint bank account. This is the first I ever heard of it."

"You expect me to believe that?"

"It's true."

"Why would Jessie put your name on an account worth a million and a half dollars and not even tell you?"

"Maybe for the same reason she wanted to make that old audiotape look new again."

She narrowed her eyes, as if he were insulting her intelligence. "Let me give you a little advice. Just admit that you and Jessie were doing the deed. This Clinton-like denial is only going to make people think you killed her."

"They won't think that. No more than you do. You wouldn't have invited me into your house if you thought I was a murderer."

She didn't answer.

Jack said, "If anyone killed Jessie, it was the investors whom she scammed."

"That's a theory."

"It's more than that. The night before she died, Jessie came to me, pleading with me to help her. She was sure these investors were going to kill her."

"I know all that. The detectives showed me the letter you wrote to the state attorney. But your investor theory just doesn't add up for me."

"I don't see why not."

"Simple. If the viatical investors were the killers, they wouldn't have made her death look anything like suicide."

"What makes you say that?"

"I'm the PR of her estate. I've seen her life insurance policy. She bought it twenty-two months ago. It's void if she took her own life less than two years after the effective date. It's a standard suicide exclusion."

His response came slowly, as if weighted by the

implications. "So, if her death is ruled a suicide, the investors lose their three-million-dollar death benefit."

"Bingo. I don't care how bad you say those guys are, they can't be idiots. If they were behind it, Jessie would have been found dead in her car at the bottom of some canal. Her death would have looked like an accident, not suicide."

Jack stared into his empty coffee cup. It suddenly seemed like a gaping black hole, one big enough to swallow him and his whole theory about the investors as killers.

"You okay?" asked Clara.

"Sure. That suicide exclusion is news to me, that's all. I guess that's why the cops are looking at me and not the investors."

"You got that right."

Jack sipped his coffee, then caught Clara's eye. "You seem to know more than you say."

"Could be."

"Is there anything else I should know?"

"Yes."

"What?"

"Don't piss me off. Because if I wanted to hurt you, believe me: I could really hurt you."

Her tone wasn't threatening, but he still felt threatened. She rose, no subtle signal that it was time for him to leave. Jack placed his coffee mug on the counter and said, "Thanks for the caffeine."

"You're welcome."

She walked him to the foyer and opened the front door. He started out, then stopped and said, "I didn't kill Jessie."

"You said that already."

"I didn't have her killed, either."

"Now there's something I hadn't heard yet."

"Now you have."

"Yes. Now I have. Finally."

They said good night, and Jack headed down the steps, the door closing behind him.

21

•

By nine o'clock Jack was on a second plate of *ropa vieja*, a shredded-beef dish with a name that translates to "old clothes." According to his grandmother, the name only described the meat's tattered appearance and had nothing to do with the actual ingredients. Then again, she'd fed him *tasajo* without disclosing that it was horse meat, and she would argue until her dying breath that Cubans do so eat green vegetables, as fried plantains were the tropical equivalent thereof.

Jack had a lot to learn about Cuban cuisine.

The stop at *Abuela*'s was yet another diversion. He'd tried to call Cindy but had gotten nowhere, which was perhaps just as well. Perhaps he needed to take a little time to refine an explanation that, as yet, sounded only slightly better than "Good news, honey, it's been at least a decade since my last sex tape."

"*Más, mi niño?*" Predictably, *Abuela* was asking if he wanted more to eat.

"*No, gracias.*"

She stroked his head and ladled on more rice. He didn't protest. Jack could only imagine what it must have been like to enjoy cooking, more than anything else in the world, and yet have practically nothing in the cupboard for thirty-eight years. *Abuela* had a great kitchen now. The townhouse Jack had rented for her was practically new, and she shared it with a lady friend from church. She'd lived with him and Cindy for a short time. They'd sit around the dinner table every night, Jack speaking bad Spanish and *Abuela* answering in broken English, each of them trying to learn the other's language in record time so that they could communicate freely. But having a place of her own made it easier to get out and enjoy herself.

Hard to believe, but almost three years had passed since Jack's father called to tell him that *Abuela* was flying into Miami International Airport. Jack had nearly dropped the phone. Never had he expected her to come to Miami at her age, even on a humanitarian visa to visit her dying brother. He'd tried many times to visit her in Cuba, and while many Americans did visit relatives there, Jack was never approved for travel. His father's staunch anti-Castro speeches as a state legislator and later as governor had surely played a role in the Cuban government's obstinacy. She'd come over on a temporary visa, but she was on her way to U.S. citizenship and would never go back. Their initial face-to-face meeting evoked a whole range of emotions. For the first time in his life, Jack had a profound sense that his mother had actually existed. She was no longer just an image in a photo album or a string of anecdotes as told by his father. Ana Maria had lived. She'd had a mother who'd loved her and who now loved Jack, gave him big hugs, fed him till he could have exploded—and then served dessert.

"I made flan," she said with a grin.

"Ah, your other invention."

"I only perfected flan. I didn't invent it."

They laughed, and he enjoyed her warm gaze. All his life he'd been told that he resembled his father, a well-intended compliment from people who had never met his mother. *Abuela* saw him differently, as if she were catching a precious glimpse of someone else each time she looked into his eyes. Those were the rare moments in his life when he actually felt Cuban.

She served an enormous portion of the custardlike dessert, spooning on extra caramel sauce. Then she took a seat across from him at the table.

"I was on the radio again today," she said.

Jack let the flan melt in his mouth, then said, "I thought we agreed, no more radio. No more stories about inventing *tres leches*."

She switched completely to Spanish, the only way to recount with proper feeling the entire fabricated story. With a totally straight face, she told him yet again how she'd invented *tres leches* a few years before the Cuban revolution and shared the recipe with no one but her ex–best friend, Maritza, who defected to Miami in the mid-sixties and sold out to a Hialeah restaurant for a mere twenty-five dollars and a month's supply of pork chunks.

Abuela was the only bilingual person on the planet who was patient enough to endure his stilted Spanish, so he answered in kind. "Abuela, I love you. But you do realize that people are laughing when you tell that story on the radio, don't you?"

"I didn't tell that story today. I talked about you."

"On Spanish radio?"

"The news people all say terrible things. Someone has to tell the truth."

"You shouldn't do this."

"It's okay. They like having me on their show now. What does it matter if they tease the crazy old lady who says she invented *tres leches*? So long as I get to slip in a few words about my grandson."

"I know you mean well, but I'm serious. You can't do that."

"Why can't I tell the world you are not a murderer?"

"If you start talking publicly about this case, people will want to interview you. Not just reporters. Police and prosecutors, too."

"I can handle them."

"No, you can't." He was serious without being stern. She seemed to get the message.

"Bueno," she said, then switched over to English. "I say nothing to no one."

"It's best that way. Any media contacts need to be approved by my attorney and me. Even Spanish radio."

Her eyes showed concern. Jack pressed her hand into his and said, "It was nice of you to try to help."

She still looked worried. Finally, she asked, "How are you and Cindy?"

"We're . . . okay."

"You tell her you love her?"

"Of course."

"When?"

"All the time."

"When last?"

"Tonight." *Just before she kicked me out of the house*, he thought.

"Is good. Is *muy importante* that you tell your wife how you feel."

"I did."

She cupped her hand, gently patted his cheek. "Maybe you should tell her again."

From the moment Jack had walked into her apartment, he thought he'd managed to keep his problems with Cindy to himself. It amazed him how well *Abuela* had come to know him in the short time she'd been in this country. "Maybe you're right."

He rose to help with the dishes, but she wouldn't allow it. "Go to your wife. Your beautiful wife."

He kissed her on the forehead, thanked her for dinner, and left through the back door.

Jack had a renewed sense of energy as he followed the sidewalk around to the back of the building. He definitely had some smoothing over to do with Cindy. But for the moment it was refreshing to step outside the cynical world and let himself believe, as *Abuela* did, that love conquers all.

His car was parked in a guest space, two buildings away from *Abuela*'s townhouse. He followed the long, S-curved sidewalk through a maze of trees. A rush of wind stirred the waxy ficus leaves overhead. He reached for his car keys, stopped, and glanced over his shoulder. He thought he'd heard footsteps behind him, but no one was in sight. Up ahead, the sidewalk stretched through a stand of larger trees. The old, twisted roots had caused the cement sections to buckle and crack over the years. It was suddenly darker, as the lights along this particular segment of the walkway were blocked by low-hanging limbs.

Again, he heard footsteps. He walked faster, and the clicking of heels behind him seemed to quicken to the same pace. He stepped off the sidewalk and continued through the grass. The sound of footsteps vanished, as if someone were tracing his silent path. He returned to the sidewalk at the top of the S-curve. His heels clicked on concrete, and a few seconds later the clicking resumed behind him.

He was definitely being followed.

Jack stopped and turned. In the darkness beneath the trees, he could see no more than twenty meters. He saw no one, but he sensed someone was there.

"*Abuela*? Is that you?" He knew it wasn't her, but somehow it seemed less paranoid than a nervous "Who's there?"

No one answered.

Jack waited a moment, then reached for his cell phone. Just as he flipped it open, a crushing blow to the center of his back sent him, flailing, face-first to the sidewalk. The phone went flying, and his breath escaped with nearly enough force to take his lungs right along with it. He tried to get up and wobbled onto one knee. A second blow to the same vertebrae knocked him down for at least another eight-count. This time, he was too disoriented to break the fall. His chin smashed against the concrete. The hot, salty taste of blood filled his mouth.

With his cheek to the sidewalk, he counted two pairs of feet. Or was he seeing double?

"What . . . do . . ." He could barely form words, let alone sentences.

His hand exploded in pain as a steel-toed boot smashed his fingers into the sidewalk. He tried to look up, but it was futile. In the darkness, it would have been hard for anyone to make out a face. In Jack's battered state, the attacker was a fuzzy silhouette.

"Consider yourself warned, Swyteck."

The voice startled him. It sounded female. *I'm getting whooped by a woman?*

He laid still, playing possum. The boot extended toward him, gently this time, poking his ribs, as if to see if he was conscious. Somehow, he found the strength to spring to life and grab an ankle, pulling and twisting as hard as he could. His attacker tumbled to the ground, and Jack tumbled with her. His arms flailed as he tried to get hold of another leg, but she was amazingly strong and quick. They rolled several times and slammed into a tree. Jack groaned as his attacker wiggled free. He started toward her, but she threw herself at him, legs whirling like a professional kickboxer. Her boot caught him squarely on the side of the head, and down he went.

He was flat on his belly as someone grabbed him from behind, took a fistful of hair, and yanked his head back.

"One more move, and you bleed like a stuck pig."

Jack went rigid. A cold, steel blade was at his throat. The voice was a man's. He hadn't been seeing double; there were two attackers. "Take it easy," said Jack.

"Silence," he said with a slap to Jack's head. "Like we said, consider yourself warned."

"Warned—of what?"

"Pin Jessie's murder on whoever you want. Just don't pin it on us."

"Who . . . you?"

The man pulled Jack's head back harder. "We don't like to hurt grandmothers, but if you keep putting her on the radio to point fingers where she shouldn't, it's on your head."

He focused long enough to regret he'd ever told *Abuela* about the viatical investors. "She's not part of this."

"Shut up. You don't know who you're fucking with.

Get your grandma off the radio, or there'll be another bloodbath. Understand?"

"You don't—" Jack stopped in midsentence. The blade was pressing harder against his throat.

"Yes or no, Swyteck. Do you understand?"

"Yes."

"Make sure you do," he said, then slammed Jack's head forward into the sidewalk one last time. Jack fought to stay conscious, but he was barely hanging on. He saw nothing, heard nothing, as his world slowly turned darker than night itself, and then all was black.

22

•

Cindy's brain was throbbing. She lifted her head from the pillow, and it weighed a ton. She'd had even more wine after Jack left, putting herself way over her limit. She closed her eyes and let her head sink back into goose down, but it felt like a vise grip pressing at either ear.

She had to move, or, she was certain, she would die.

Her hand slid across the sheet and found the edge of the mattress. She pulled herself up onto her side and checked the digital alarm clock on the nightstand. The numbers were a blur without her contact lenses, and she couldn't reach to pull it closer. There was no telling what time it was.

Just like in her dream. *That awful dream.*

She didn't think she was dreaming. But she didn't feel awake, either. Never in her life had she been hungover like this, not even from those prom-night slush drinks spiked with Southern Comfort. Slowly, her eyes adjusted to the dim lighting. The blinds were shut, but the faint outline of dawn brightened the thin openings between slats. She took a moment, then sat up in bed.

The sound of footsteps thumped in the hallway.

"Mom?"

No one answered, but her voice was weak, stolen by the effects of too much alcohol. Cindy looked around the room. The empty wine bottle was on the bureau, and the mere sight of it was enough to make her sick. She felt a need to run for the bathroom, but, mercifully, the nausea quickly passed. How ironic, she thought, all the school mornings she'd lain in this very room just *pretending* to be sick. She'd hated school as a kid, and, for the longest time, she'd hated this house. She didn't think of it as the house she'd grown up in, at least not entirely. Only after her father was dead had the rest of the surviving family moved there, the widow, two daughters, and three very young boys. Yet it seemed full of memories. Or, at least, at the moment, it was filling her head with memories. Through her mind's eye, she was looking at herself again, the way she could in her dream, except this wasn't a dream— or at least it wasn't *the* dream. The Cindy she saw was nine years old, in their old house, the one before this one, the house in New Hampshire.

•

The leaves rustled outside her bedroom window. As she lay awake staring at the ceiling, the wind plucked the brown and crispy ones from the branches and sent them flying through the night sky. Some were caught in the updraft and swirled high. The others fell to the ground, weaving the endless carpet of dead leaves across their lawn. Tourists came from all over the country to see autumn like this. Cindy loathed it. For a brief two weeks, the green leaves of summer turned themselves into something that no living thing could become without courting disaster, blazing flickers of flame at the end of twisted branches. And then, one by one, the flames were extinguished. It was as if the leaves were being fooled. Tricked into death.

A gust of wind howled outside, and a flock of dead leaves pecked at her window. Cindy pulled the covers over her head. *Stupid fools.*

She heard a noise, a slamming sound. It was as if something had fallen or been knocked over. It had come from downstairs.

"Daddy?"

She was alone with her father in the house for the weekend. Her mother and older sister had traveled to Manchester for a high school soccer tournament. The boys, more than her father could handle, were with their grandmother.

Cindy waited for a response but heard nothing. Only the wind outside her window, the sound of leaves moving. She listened harder, as if with added concentration she could improve her own hearing. Swirling leaves were scary enough, all that pecking on the glass. But it was the crunching sound that really frightened her—the sound of leaves moving outside her bedroom window, one footstep at a time.

"Is that you, Daddy?"

Her body went rigid. There it was. *The crunching sound!*

Someone was walking outside her house, she was sure of it, their feet dragging through the leaves. Just the thought frightened her to the core, brought tears to her eyes. She jumped out of her bed and ran down the hall.

"Daddy, where are you?"

The hallway was black, but Cindy could have found her way blindfolded. She'd run there many nights screaming from nightmares. She pushed open the door to the master bedroom and rushed inside. "Daddy, there's a noise!"

She stood frozen at the foot of the bed. Her eyes had adjusted well enough to the darkness to see that it was empty. In fact, it was still made. No one had slept in it, even though it was long past her bedtime, long past her father's. At least it felt late. The digital clock on the nightstand was stuck on midnight, the green numbers pulsating the way they always did with the power surges on windy nights.

Am I by myself?

Cindy ran from the bedroom. Fear propelled her down the stairs faster than she'd ever covered them. Her father had fallen asleep on the couch many times before, and maybe that was where he was. She hurried into the family room. Immediately, her heart sank with despair. He wasn't there.

"Daddy!"

She ran from the family room to the kitchen, then to the living room. She checked the bathrooms and even the large closet in the foyer, doors flying open like so many astonished mouths. He was nowhere. Tears streamed down her face as she returned to the kitchen, and then something caught her eye.

Through the window and across the yard, she could see a light glowing inside the garage. Her father's car was parked in the driveway, so she knew he was home, perhaps busy in the garage with his woodworking. That could have been the noise she'd heard, his scuffling through their leaf-covered yard, the sound of her father carrying things back and forth from the garage.

After bedtime?

Part of her wanted to stay put, but the thought of being alone in the big house was too much for a nine-year-old. She let out a shrill scream and exploded out the back door, into a cold autumn night that felt more like winter's first blast. She kept screaming, kept right on running until she passed her father's car and reached the garage at the end of the driveway. With both fists, she pounded on the garage door.

"Daddy, are you in there?" Her little voice was even more fragile against the cold, north wind.

She tried the latch, but it was locked, and she was too small to raise the main door anyway. She ran to the side door and turned the knob. It, too, was locked. On her tiptoes she peered through the window. The light inside was on, but she didn't see any sign of her father. The angle gave her a view only of the front half of the garage.

"Daddy, are you—"

Her words halted as her eyes fixed on the dark patch on the floor. It wasn't really a patch. It moved ever so slightly, back and forth. A spot with a gentle sway. Not a spot. A ghostlike image with arms at its side. Feet that hovered above the ground. A rope around its neck.

And a hunter's cap just like her father's.

She fell backward to the ground, pushed herself away from the garage door, and ran back toward the house. Except she didn't want to go back inside, didn't know where to run. She ran in circles around the big elm tree, crying and screaming, the sound of fallen leaves crunching beneath her feet.

•

A pounding noise jostled her from her memories. She blinked hard, trying to focus. It sounded like the footsteps in the hall she thought she'd heard earlier, but it was louder, like galloping horses. Another round of pounding, and she realized it wasn't footsteps at all.

Someone was knocking at the front door.

Her heart raced. She couldn't even begin to guess who would come calling at this hour, and she didn't want to think about it. She had yet to clear her mind of the memories she'd stirred up. That unforgettable image on the garage floor. The one that looked so much like the dark spot in her photograph of that little girl and her dog. The shadow that had never existed.

Or that had disappeared.

With the third round of knocking, Cindy's feet were on the floor. A voice inside her told her not to answer the door, exactly like her dream. And just like the dream, she found herself ignoring the warning, putting one foot in front of the other as she slowly crossed the bedroom.

A light switched on at the end of the hall. Her mother peeked out of her room and said, "Cindy, what the heck is going on?"

"Don't worry," she said. "I'll get it."

23

•

Jack woke to a shrill ringing in his ear. His pillow felt hard as concrete, and then he realized it *was* concrete. His cheek was pressed against the sidewalk, exactly where he'd fallen.

At first, he had no memory of where he was. Dawn was just a sliver of an orange ribbon on the horizon. Jack tried to sit up, but his body ached all over. It was as if he'd been hit by a truck. Finally, he forced himself onto his knees. The ringing in his ear was gone, but he felt nauseous. Probably a concussion. He closed his eyes and tried to stop the spinning. He opened them and strained to focus on something, anything, in the middle distance. Slowly, he began to get his bearings, and the memory of last night came back to him. The footsteps behind him. The blow to his back that sent his cell phone flying across the lawn. His chin banging on the sidewalk.

He touched his jaw. It was definitely sore. His gaze drifted toward the fence, and he spotted a little orange light blinking in the darkness. He squinted, then realized what it was: His cell phone emitted that light whenever he had a message. He tried to stand up, then yielded to the pain. He rolled like a dog and grabbed the phone, then dialed Cindy at her mother's. She answered after just three rings.

"Hi. It's me."

"Jack, where have you been? I've been calling your cell, but you didn't answer."

His head was pounding. "What time is it?"

"Almost five."

"In the morning?"

"Yes, the morning. What's wrong with you? Have you been drinking?"

"No. I got beat up."

"What?"

The simple act of talking made him short of breath. He groaned lightly and said, "Somebody beat the holy crap out of me."

"Are you okay?"

Jack forced a yawn in an effort to loosen his jaw. A sharp pain ran though his head like a railroad spike. "I think I'll be okay." *In about a month*, he thought.

"Who did this to you?" she asked, her voice quaking.

He started to explain, but it hurt too much to talk. "Don't worry. It's going to be okay."

"It's not okay! They just left, and you weren't even here. I had no idea what to do."

He sat bolt upright, concerned. "Who came?"

"The marshals."

"Federal marshals?"

"Yes. They had a search warrant."

"What did they want?"

"Your home computer."

That spike was back in his head. He grimaced and said, "Did you give it to them?"

"Yes, of course. Rosa said I had to."

"You spoke to Rosa?"

"Yes, I couldn't find you. They wanted your office computers, too. Rosa's going ballistic."

"What's the federal government doing in this? Did you ask Rosa?"

"No. But she did say something about the IRS."

Jack was silent. Three little letters no one liked to hear. "You sure that's what she said—IRS?"

"No. She said 'Internal Revenue Service.' "

He took a deep breath, which was a big mistake. All it took was a little extra air in his chest cavity to press against the spine and send him reeling with pain. It was as if he were being kicked in the back all over again.

"Cindy, I'm going to call Rosa now. But as soon as I talk with her, we all need to talk."

"You and I need to talk first. Alone."

Between last night's beating and now the IRS, he'd almost forgotten about the Jessie sex tape. "You're right. We need to talk."

"Sooner rather than later."

"That sounds good to me."

"Okay. Just call me as soon as you finish with Rosa."

"I will."

"Jack?"

"What?"

"What's going on with the IRS?"

"I'm not sure. Listen, I'll get there as soon as I can."

They said good-bye, and Jack switched off the phone. His mouth hurt, partly from having talked too much, mostly from having kissed the sidewalk last night. He spat a little blood into the grass and slowly pushed himself up onto two wobbly feet.

"Wonderful," he said as he tried to straighten his back. "The IRS."

Macon, Georgia, was a good place to die. And that was exactly his plan.

He called himself Fate, the favorite word of Father Aleksandr, the priest in his native Georgian village—the *other* Georgia, the lands beyond the Caucasus Mountains—who'd told him since boyhood that everything happened for a reason. The concept had always overwhelmed him, the very idea that every thought and every deed, every action and every inaction, was part of a bigger plan. The problem was, he didn't know what the plan was, couldn't fathom what it should be. What if he made a decision that somehow managed to screw everything up? He preferred to lay that kind of ultimate responsibility on somebody else, even when doing the very thing he did best.

That made him a peculiar killer indeed.

He was seated behind the wheel of his rented van, parked on the street corner a half-block away from the chosen household. The sun had set several hours earlier behind an overcast sky. The nearest street lamp was at the other end of the street, leaving him and his van in total darkness. Frost from his own breath was beginning to build inside his windshield. No matter how cold it got, he didn't dare start the engine for fear of drawing attention to himself. He didn't need the heater anyway. He had his own source of warmth, a fifth of *slivovitz,* a potent brandy made from plums. "Peps you up, colors the cheeks" was a slogan known to millions of Eastern Europeans. At seventy-percent alcohol, it was also the ultimate insurance against the inhibitions of conscience. The Budapest whores knew it well. So had the snipers in Chechnya, who'd dosed themselves heavily on the devil's drink before potting away at women and children caught in their crosshairs. On occasion, Fate had known it to make him braver too, though he drank it simply because he liked it even more than *chacha,* a grape brandy popular among Georgians. So long as he followed his own rules, he enjoyed his work; he didn't need any vodka to ease his conscience.

He poured another capful of *slivovitz* and then lit it with his cigarette. The genuine stuff burned a pretty blue flame. He watched it flicker for a moment, then tossed the flaming cocktail down the back of his throat.

It was a ritual he'd performed since his teenage years, when Fate had found his first victim—or, more appropriately, when his first victim had found Fate. He and the other hoodlums in his gang never selected a target. Victims identified themselves. The boys set the criteria and waited for someone who fit the bill to come along. The next guy to walk by wearing sunglasses. The next woman with brown eyes. The next kid on a bicycle. Back then, it was just for fun, perhaps an initiation or other gang-related right of passage. That kind of silliness was behind him. His work now had a purpose. He murdered only for hire.

It was the perfect arrangement for a killer who didn't want his work to upset the larger plan. Victims were preselected, not by him but by someone else. He didn't even have to choose the manner of execution. His victims did. It could be a complete surprise, the sleeping victim never regaining consciousness. Or death could be days, even weeks in the offing, a protracted path of suffering punctuated by sharp, futile screams. The decision-making process was deceptively simple. He'd follow his targets home at night and watch them go inside. If they left the porch light on, death would be quick and painless. Porch light off, not so quick—and definitely not painless. The choice was theirs. They sealed their fate without effort and without even knowing it.

Everything happens for a reason. Not even the smallest act is meaningless. It all determines one's fate.

He took another hit of *slivovitz* and turned his eyes toward the front porch. Jody Falder was standing outside her front door. She shifted her weight from one foot to the other, apparently trying to stay warm. A cold wind had kicked up at sunset, transforming a mild afternoon into a dark, cold reminder that the South did indeed have winter. She wore no coat. Obviously, she hadn't anticipated the drastic change in temperature, or maybe she hadn't expected to return home so late.

Peering through night-vision binoculars, he watched her fumble for her house key, unlock the door, and disappear inside. Patiently he waited, his eyes glued to the porch light. Two minutes passed, and it was still burning brightly. He gave her more time, careful not to rush things. He couldn't actually see her moving about inside the house, but it was easy enough to monitor her movement from room to room. Kitchen light on, kitchen light off. Bathroom lit, bathroom dark. Finally, the bedroom light came on and remained lit for several minutes. Then it switched off.

He narrowed his eyes, as if peering into the bedroom window, though he was merely imagining the scene unfolding behind drawn curtains. The unexpected cold front had surely left her bedroom colder than usual. Nipples erect, for sure. She'd shed her clothes quickly, slipped on a nightgown, and jumped beneath the covers. At that point, only a lunatic would jump out of a warm bed, run downstairs, and flip off the porch light. It appeared as though she'd made her decision. Porch light on. Quick and painless.

Lucky bitch.

He lowered his binoculars, then did a double take. The porch light had suddenly switched off. A twist of fate. It was apparently controlled by electronic timer. Arguably, it wasn't her decision, but rules were rules. Porch light off: No more quick and painless. A sign of the times. We are all slaves to our gadgets.

Doesn't that just suck?

A perverse smile crept to his lips as he slipped on his latex gloves, like the hands of a surgeon. It was a real source of personal pride, the way he managed to inflict all that suffering and still make death look like anything but homicide. He grabbed his bag of tools and pulled a black knit cap over his head, the same cap he'd worn on every job since his first mission as a mercenary soldier, a sneak attack on a rebel camp—six women, three old men, and two teenage boys, the first in a long line of noisy amusements for his knives. This job would be much cleaner and quieter, but the hat was still his lucky charm of sorts.

He moved quickly across the yard and toward the darkened house, yearning for that look on her face when she'd look up into his eyes, unable to move, unable to scream, unable to do much of anything but accept the fact that Fate had found her.

25

•

"I'm back," said Rosa as she entered Jack's conference room.

"That was quick," he replied.

There was nothing like the government overplaying its hand to set off a career criminal-defense lawyer, and the morning raid by the IRS had propelled Rosa into orbit. She'd insisted that he go to the emergency room while she marched off to an emergency hearing to block the IRS from accessing his computers. Thankfully, his tests had ruled out serious injury. A mild concussion, at worst. He was discharged with some Tylenol and a sheet of preprinted instructions about things he should avoid over the next few days—loud noises, sudden movements, general stress and aggravation. A trip to Disney World seemed out of the question.

"I still can't believe those sons of bitches took your computer," she said. "You're a criminal defense lawyer, not a hardware store. There's privileged information in there."

"What did the judge say?" asked Jack.

"He wouldn't invalidate the warrant. But I persuaded him to appoint an independent special master to examine your hard drive."

"So the government won't see anything that's on my computers?"

"Not unless the special master determines that there's something the government should see."

"What exactly are they looking for?"

"I'm glad you asked that question. Because we need to talk."

Jack grimaced. No matter what the context, the words "we need to talk" could never be good. "Okay, sure."

"Basically, the government wants anything that shows money flowing back and forth between you and Jessie Merrill. Particularly, they want to know if you ever accessed that Bahamian account that named you and Jessie as joint account holders."

His head was suddenly hurting again. "Oh, that."

"Is there something you forgot to tell your lawyer, Mr. Swyteck?"

"I just found out about that last night from the PR of Jessie's estate, Clara Pierce."

"She obviously told the IRS, too. But let's go back to what you just said: What do you mean, you just found out about it? Your name's on the account."

"I don't know how it got there."

"Well, think hard. Because I don't want to walk into a courtroom ever again without an explanation for it."

Jack went to the window, shaking his head. "I didn't share this theory with Clara, but I'm pretty certain it ties in with Jessie's threats."

"What threats?"

"I told you before. After I figured out she'd scammed

me, she threatened me. She said if I told anyone about it, she'd make them believe I was part of it from the beginning."

"So she put your name on her bank account?"

"Sure. You know how some of these Caribbean banks are. Most of them never meet their customers. Adding a name is a snap."

"But why would she do it?"

"It makes sense," he said, convincing himself as he spoke. "It was the only way she could give teeth to her threat. If I leaked the scam, I'd take myself down with her. The joint account would make it look as if we were splitting the pie, fifty-fifty."

"Pretty risky on her part. As a joint account holder you could have cleaned out the entire account."

"Not if I didn't know about it. It's an offshore account. No tax statements, no IRS notices to tip me off that it even existed."

"What about bank statements?"

"Mailed to her address, I'm sure. Probably a post office box in Katmandu. Assuming a bank like Grand Bahama Trust Company even issues bank statements."

"So you say this was her little secret?"

"Her secret weapon. Something she'd spring on me if I ever threatened to expose her scam. It makes me look like I was part of it."

"Now that she's dead, it also has a way of making it look as if you killed her."

Jack knew that the conversation was headed in that direction, but her words still hit hard. "The million-and-a-half-dollar motive. With no more Jessie, I'm the sole account holder."

"Murder among coconspirators. That's about the size of it."

"You think that theory flies? That I killed her for the money?"

"Not with me it doesn't."

"Thanks, but you're not the jury. Honestly, what do you think?"

"I think we just take this one step at a time. Right now, we have the IRS breathing down your neck. The ugliest beast in the bureaucratic jungle. So let's talk philosophy."

"By 'philosophy,' I assume, you don't mean the great thinkers—Hegel, Kant, Moe, Larry, Curly."

"I mean my own philosophy on how to deal with the IRS. I put criminal tax investigations in a class by themselves. I want to be completely upfront about this, because not everyone agrees with my views."

"Let's hear it."

"Here's a good example. Let's say you're going to have to testify at an evidentiary hearing, and I'm preparing you beforehand for the prosecutor's cross-examination."

"I know the drill. Answer only the question asked. Don't volunteer information. If a question can be answered with a simple yes or no, answer it that way."

"Exactly." She glanced at Jack's wristwatch and asked, "Do you know what time it is?"

"Rosa, I know that game. I'm only supposed to answer the question asked. So, if you ask me if I know what time it is, the answer is not 'It's ten-fifteen.' The answer is 'Yes, I know what time it is.' That routine is so old, I think I've seen it on *L.A. Law, The West Wing, The Practice,* and, if I'm not mistaken, two or three times on *Law & Order.*"

"Leave it to television to give you the wrong answer."

"What?"

"Do you know if your watch is accurate?"

"I set it myself."

"Do you know that it's accurate? To the second?"

"To the exact second, no."

"Let's say you're standing outside Westminster Abbey and staring straight at Big Ben. If somebody asks you if you know what time it is, do you know that Big Ben is accurate?"

"I have no way of knowing that."

"Exactly right. Unless you're Father Time, if someone asks you what time it is, your answer can only be what?"

Jack paused, then said, "I don't know."

"You got it, my friend. And *that* is the way you deal with the IRS."

Jack didn't say anything, though it struck him as a little too cute. There was a knock at the door, and Jack's secretary poked her head into the room. "Jack, you have a call."

"Can you transfer it into here?"

"It's personal."

He assumed that meant Cindy. He excused himself and followed his secretary down the hall to his office.

"It's not Cindy," she said. "It's your old boss."

"Chafetz?"

She nodded. Jerry Chafetz was a section chief at the U.S. attorney's office. He'd been Jack's mentor back when Jack was a federal prosecutor. Maria had been Jack's secretary since his days with the government, so they all knew each other.

"What does he want?" asked Jack.

"Not sure. I told him you were in a meeting, but he was emphatic that I interrupt. And he was even more insistent that I not announce who it was in front of Rosa."

Jack entered his office alone and closed the door. He

stared at the blinking HOLD button for a second, then answered.

"Swyteck, how are you?"

Jack managed a smile. They were old friends, but there was something about working for the government that seemed to put friends on a last-name basis.

"Been better, Chafetz. I have to say, the timing of this call is pretty peculiar, even from an old friend like you."

"Timing's no coincidence. I hope you already know this, but I didn't have anything to do with your computers being seized."

"You're right. You didn't have to say it."

"In fact, no one in Florida was behind it."

Jack's pulse quickened. "This was ordered out of Washington?"

"It's the organized-crime strike force." He'd almost sighed as he said it.

"They think I'm with the mob?"

"I can't tell you what they think."

"Who's the bag boy?"

"Sam Drayton. Pretty big player, but I'm so pissed at him right now I can hardly see straight. This predawn-raid bullshit isn't the way to treat a former prosecutor like you."

"I can fight my own battles," said Jack. "Don't get yourself caught in a bureaucratic crack over this."

"I'm not crossing any lines. All I did was get you a meeting."

"A meeting?"

"Somehow, you fit into Drayton's strategy. I can't tell you how, but I was at least able to convince Drayton that your come-to-Jesus meeting ought to be sooner rather than later. It just isn't right for him to string you along like a common criminal."

"So, does Drayton want to offer me a deal?"

"All I'm saying is that you need to meet with Drayton."

"Fine. Rosa's my lawyer."

"You can't bring a lawyer. You can't even tell her we've talked."

"He wants me to go unrepresented?"

"You're a criminal defense lawyer and a former prosecutor. You'll hardly be outmatched."

"It just isn't reasonable."

"What Drayton has to say can't be said in front of your lawyer or anyone else. It's for your ears only, and this is your one and only chance to hear it. Those are his terms, not mine."

Jack fell silent, concerned. He'd seen the rivalries between the strike force and local prosecutors before. The stench of internal politics was almost bubbling over the phone line. "I appreciate our friendship, but don't be sticking your neck out too far, all right?"

"Don't worry about me. This is all about you." There was an urgency in his voice, an edge that Jack almost didn't recognize. "You don't even have to respond to what Drayton tells you. Just listen. Think of it as free discovery."

Jack glanced out the window at downtown Coral Gables, mulling it over. Experience had taught him that it was best not to overanalyze some opportunities. At some point, you had to trust your friends, go with your gut. "All right. Where?"

"Downtown."

"When?"

"As soon as possible. Drayton's here today only."

"Give me an hour."

"Great. See you then."

"Yeah," said Jack. "Can't wait."

26

·

At eleven-thirty, Jack was at the Federal Building in downtown Miami. It was familiar territory.

Chafetz was the man who'd convinced him to become a federal prosecutor, and he was the reason Jack had stayed with the U.S. attorney's office far longer than originally planned. At the time, Chafetz was in the special investigations section, a trial-intensive team that handled complex cases ranging from child exploitation to gang prosecution. It was hard work, high stakes, and never boring. A perfect fit for Jack. He and Chafetz worked side by side, liked each other's style, liked each other. But nothing lasts forever. Chafetz was promoted to section chief, and Jack moved on to private practice. They tried to stay in touch, but it just wasn't the same after Jack started working the opposite side of the courtroom.

Chafetz led Jack to a conference room near his office. Two men were inside, waiting. From the hallway, Jack could see them through the window on the door.

"I'll take Drayton, you can have the little guy."

Chafetz smiled, then turned serious. "I wish I could prepare you better, but you and I don't need anyone accusing us of exchanging favors on the side. Just remember, whatever happens in there, it isn't my show. It's Drayton's."

"I know what you're saying. It's no secret how Drayton operates."

"You know him?"

"Only by reputation. A conceited tight-ass who thinks anyone who lives outside the 202 area code just fell off the turnip truck."

"Dead on, my friend. Just do me a favor. Don't mention turnips in the meeting, all right?"

"Come on, you know me better than that."

"I'm serious. This wasn't easy to pull off."

Jack wasn't sure how Chafetz had convinced Drayton to lay his cards on the table sooner than he otherwise might have. But things like this didn't happen just because you said "pretty please." He looked him in the eye and said, "Thanks."

"You're welcome."

He opened the door, Jack and he entered, and the introductions followed. First was the portly guy with tortoise-shell glasses, a crew cut, and virtually no personality. The letters "IRS" might just as well have been tattooed across his forehead. At his side was Sam Drayton. Instantly, he struck Jack as a walking fraud. It was well known that his wife was a millionaire, but he still wore the cheap, off-the-rack suits of a government lawyer because that was the image he wanted to cultivate. The wristwatch was a forty-dollar Timex, and the pungent cologne smelled like some homemade concoction of Aqua Velva and a three-dollar jug of berry-scented massage oil that could have masked the odor of a moose in a spinning class. Jack would have bet his liberty that Drayton had never paid more than six dollars on a haircut.

All of that is fine, if that's who you are. But there's nothing more pretentious than a wealthy lawyer who has to work at being a regular Joe.

Jack took a seat at one end of the table, opposite Drayton and his IRS agent. Chafetz excused himself and reached for the door.

"Hey, Chafetz," said Jack as he flipped him a quarter.

He caught it in midair, puzzled.

Jack said, "My turnip truck is parked out front. Feed the meter, would you?"

They exchanged glances, the way they used to communicate silently as cocounsel in a courtroom. "Sure thing," said Chafetz as he left the room, suppressing his smile.

The others looked at one another, clueless as to the inside joke. Drayton turned to the business at hand. "Thanks for coming, Mr. Swyteck."

"I wish I could say it was good to be back."

"We know it's an inconvenience. Especially in light of what happened to you this morning."

"You mean those thieves who took my computers?"

"No. I mean that bruise on your jaw."

"Seems that someone is really ticked off that I might blame the viatical investors for Jessie Merrill's death."

"We know. We've read the police report you filled out in the emergency room."

"Seeing how you're part of the strike force, am I correct in assuming that my little incident may have had something to do with an element of organized crime?"

"To be honest, we want you to help us pinpoint the exact criminal element involved."

"I wish I could, but I can't. Never got a look at who jumped me last night. And I've already told the state attorney everything I know about the threats against Jessie. Unfortunately, she didn't get very specific."

Drayton said, "We hear from a reliable confidential informant that the beating you took last night came on a direct order from a known underworld operative."

"How does your CI know that?"

Drayton didn't answer, didn't even seem to acknowledge the question. He simply rose and went to the whiteboard, rolling a felt-tipped marker through his fingers as he spoke. "For about eight months now, we've had our eye on Viatical Solutions, Inc., or VS, as we call it."

"I didn't know that."

"From the outside, VS appears to be nothing more than a viatical broker. The deals are structured like a legitimate viatical settlement, with one major difference." Drayton marked a red dollar-sign on the whiteboard, then drew an X through it. "The money from the investors is always dirty."

"VS is laundering money?"

"As if you didn't know." The prosecutor leaned into the table and said, "How did your name end up on an offshore bank account with Jessie Merrill?"

"She obviously put it there. How or why, I can only guess."

"How did the investors pay her the one-point-five million?"

"I don't know. That happened before she hired me."

"Was it in cash or a wire transfer from another offshore bank?"

"I said I don't know."

"Perhaps it was a combination," said Drayton, suggesting an answer. "Was it paid in a lump sum, or in installments from various sources?"

"I can't answer that."

"That's unfortunate. Because if you can't help us, we can't help you."

"Help me what?"

"It's no secret that the state attorney suspects foul play in the death of Jessie Merrill. The way the evidence is playing out, you're pretty high on the list of suspects."

"Plenty of innocent people have found themselves on a prosecutor's list of suspects."

"No question. And if just half the glowing things your old boss says about you are true, then you probably will be exonerated. Eventually. But wouldn't it be nice to speed up that process?"

"I'm listening."

"The quickest way to get off the list of suspects is for you to convince the state attorney that someone else did it. We might be able to help you with that."

"Are you sitting on evidence that Jessie Merrill was murdered?"

"This is a money-laundering investigation. All we can tell you is that the people we're investigating—the people who we believe are in control of Viatical Solutions, Inc.—are certainly capable of murder. Your cooperation with us on the money-laundering investigation may well provide the jump-start you need to prove your innocence on the murder charge."

"What do I have to do?"

"Just answer all our questions about the source of the funds, the structure of the transaction. Who did you meet with? How was the money transferred? From what accounts?"

"I told you, I wasn't there."

"And I keep coming back to the same question. Why is your name on that joint account? Just what secrets were you trying to cloak in the shroud of the attorney-client privilege?"

"I can only say it again: I don't know anything about that."

"Obviously, we don't accept that. You have a pretty stainless reputation, but an argument could still be made that you and your client knowingly entered into a transaction that allowed these investors to launder one and a half million dollars in dirty money."

"There's no reason for anyone to believe that."

"Yes, there is. I don't care how clean you are. A married guy makes a mistake, there's no telling what he might do for his girlfriend to keep her from sending an audiotape of their little escapade to his wife."

Jack's heart sank. *Is there anyone Clara Pierce didn't send that tape to?* "That's an old tape. Jessie and I dated before I was married."

"That's a likely story."

"I didn't have anything to do with that joint bank account."

"We'll see what your computers show."

"If that's why you seized them, you're going to be sorely disappointed."

"Computers are just one angle. Fortunately, we have ways of stimulating your personal memory."

"Is that a threat?"

Drayton resumed his position at the whiteboard. "Simply put, you owe the Internal Revenue Service some serious money."

"What?"

Drayton and the IRS agent were suddenly making goo-goo eyes at each other. "Peter, what's the exact number?"

The bean counter flipped open his notebook. "Our latest calculation is in the neighborhood of three hundred thousand dollars."

"That's ridiculous."

"Hardly," said Drayton as he wrote the number on the board. "You and Jessie Merrill were joint account holders on her one and a half million dollars. It's our position that your half of that account is taxable income for legal services rendered. You owe income tax on seven hundred fifty thousand dollars."

"Sorry to disappoint you, but I've already spoken to the PR of Jessie's estate and disavowed any interest in my alleged half of those funds."

Drayton's eyes brightened. "Thank you for sharing that. Peter, make a note. It seems Mr. Swyteck has made a gift of his seven hundred fifty thousand dollars. So, in addition to income tax on that sum, he now also owes gift tax."

The bean counter scribbled in his pad and said, "That brings the total closer to four hundred thousand."

"You arrogant prick," said Jack. "I dedicated a big chunk of my career to this office. And now this is what I get? Trumped up charges from Washington?"

"Calm down, all right? I didn't want to have to threaten you, and I'm not going so far as to say you killed the woman. But there was something funny going on between you and Jessie Merrill. This is an eight-month investigation that needs your help. Fact is, you need our help too."

"I don't need anyone's help. No juror in his right mind is ever going to believe I'm a murderer. I mean, really. If I wanted Jessie Merrill dead, would I kill her in my own bathtub?"

"Good answer, Mr. Swyteck. Did you think of it before or after you murdered Jessie Merrill?"

He knew that Drayton was just role-playing, stepping into the shoes of a state attorney on cross-examination. Still, it chilled him.

"You done?" said Jack.

"That's all for now."

He rose and started for the door.

"Hope to hear from you," said Drayton. "Soon."

"Hope springs eternal," said Jack. He left the room, steadily gaining speed as he headed down the hall to the elevator.

27
·

A blast of chilly air followed Todd Chastan out of the autopsy room. He wadded his green surgical scrubs into a loose ball and tossed them into the laundry bag in the hallway outside the door. A soiled pair of latex gloves sailed into the trash. His pace was brisk as he headed down the gray-tiled hallway.

Dr. Chastan was an associate medical examiner in Atlanta. The office served all of Fulton County and, on request, certain cases from other counties. Chastan had spent nearly the entire morning exploring the internal cavity of a sixteen-year-old boy who'd botched his first attempted robbery of a convenience store. He'd left a loaded .38 caliber pistol, twenty-eight dollars, and about two pints of blood on the sidewalk outside the shattered plate-glass window. Just a few hours later, his young heart, lungs, esophagus, and trachea were resting on a cold steel tray. The liver, spleen, adrenals, and kidneys would be next, followed by the stomach, pancreas, and intestines. His brain had already been sliced into sections, bagged, and tagged. It was all part of a typical medical-legal autopsy required in the seventy or so homicides the office might see in an average year. Over the same period of time, ten times that number of examined deaths might be classified as "natural."

An urgent message from a medical-legal investigator didn't usually spell "natural."

Dr. Chastan made a quick right at the end of the hall, knocked once, and entered the investigator's office. "You paged me?"

Eddy Johnson looked up from the papers on his desk. "It's about the Falder case."

"Falder?" he said, straining to recall.

"The woman you did yesterday. The one with AIDS."

"Yeah, yeah. Her medical history painted a bleak picture. By all accounts, she was on borrowed time. Full autopsy didn't seem necessary. I did an external and sent some tissue and blood samples to the lab."

"Got the report right here," Johnson said as he pulled a file out from under two empty coffee cups and the sports section.

"Something give you concern?" He smiled impishly, but realized that he was in a medical-legal investigator's office, and answered his own question. "Obviously, something gives you concern."

Johnson was deadpan. "Plate's under the microscope. Have a look-see for yourself."

Chastan maneuvered around the swollen folders on the floor and stepped up to the microscope that was resting on the countertop, right beside *Gray's Anatomy*. He closed one eye, brought the other to the eyepiece, and adjusted the lens. He twisted it to the left and then to the right, but something didn't seem quite right. He stood up, scratched his head, then gave another look. Finally, he faced Johnson and asked, "What the hell is that?"

"It's the blood you drew from Ms. Falder."

He blinked, confused. "It's like nothing I've ever seen before."

"That's why I have the file," he said with a wink. Johnson was known around the office as a strange-case specialist.

"What do you think it is?"

"I couldn't even guess. Some kind of virus, maybe."

"We need to send it off to the Center for Disease Control right away."

"I already did, this morning. But there's more to this case that troubles me."

"Such as?"

"She came here with just over two liters of blood in her body."

"I took only three vials."

"That's my point. Where are the other three and a half liters?"

"I don't know. I looked at the photos. No blood at the scene of her death."

"That's right."

"She couldn't have donated it before she died. AIDS aside, nobody walks around with sixty percent of the blood in their body missing."

"Right again," said Johnson.

"Which means what? Somebody took it?"

He gave the doctor a serious look. "I think you and I are now on the same page."

"She had multiple injection marks all over her body. I didn't think anything of it. She had AIDS. She was getting injections almost every other day."

"Looks like one of those holes was used to siphon out her blood."

"That changes everything. If that much blood was drawn while she was alive, it would have sent her into cardiac arrest."

"Which means the cause of death was anything but natural."

"I need that body back," said Chastan. "We need a full medical-legal autopsy. I can get on it this morning."

"Go to it."

He started for the door, then stopped. "Ed, why do you think someone might have wanted this woman's blood?"

"Don't know. But I have a feeling we'll have a better idea when we hear back from disease control."

"You think someone out there is into collecting blood infected with strange organisms?"

"Collecting. Or harvesting."

With all that he'd seen over the years—dismembered bodies, charred babies—it took a lot to get a reaction from Dr. Chastan. But the thought of someone cultivating disease in human hosts was up there. "This could be one sick son of a bitch."

"You got that right." Johnson switched off the light on the microscope and put the blood plate back in the file. "I'll put homicide on notice."

"Sure," he answered. "The sooner the better."

28

.

Jack couldn't get The Beatles' "Tax Man" out of his head. It reminded him of Sam Drayton—an old, annoying song that he didn't like in the least, but it was embedded in his brain.

After the meeting, Jack stopped to collect his thoughts at an open-air café on Miami Avenue. Just down the street from the old federal courthouse, it had been one of his favorite coffee spots during his years as a prosecutor. The smell of *arroz con pollo*, today's lunch special, wafted from the noisy kitchen in back. A guy with no shirt, no shoes, and practically no teeth was selling bags of *limas* from a stolen shopping cart at curbside. A largely Spanish-speaking crowd sipped espresso at the stand-up counter along the sidewalk. Jack found a stool inside and ordered a *café con leche,* a big mug of coffee that was half milk. The woman behind the bar remembered him from his days as a prosecutor. She smiled and worked her old magic, frothing up the milk with the steamer just the way Jack liked it.

"*Muchas gracias,*" he said.

"You're welcome," she replied.

It was the same routine they'd followed for eight years, Jack's wooden Spanish evoking a reply in English. The story of his barely Cuban life.

Jack's meeting had gone even worse than he'd feared, but he tried to shake it off. He needed a contingency plan, but he had other things to deal with, too. Things more important. He needed to talk to Cindy.

He took his cell phone from his pocket, flipped it open, and froze.

What the hell?

He hadn't noticed anything unusual at five A.M. when he'd called Cindy. It had been dark then, and he was too incoherent to have noticed. But now it was broad daylight. His head was no longer swirling. It was obvious to him.

The cell phone wasn't his.

He sipped his *café con leche* and took a closer look. The phone looked exactly like his, a black Motorola issued by Sprint. He and Cindy used to have the exact same model, until they'd tired of getting them mixed up. He'd ended up buying Cindy a Nokia that looked completely different. It was just too easy to grab the wrong phone when you were racing out of the house in morning.

Someone, it seemed, had made the same mistake last night.

Jack flipped open the Motorola. He was familiar with all of the functions; they were the same as his own phone. He checked the message center. Nine voice mails were stored in the memory. He hit the PLAY button. "*Message one,*" the recorded voice said. "*Yesterday, eleven-thirty-two A.M.*"

The message was in a man's voice. The language was foreign. It sounded like a cross between Boris Yeltsin and Robin Williams in *Moscow on the Hudson*. Jack skipped to the next one. *"Message two, yesterday, ten-twenty-one A.M."* A different voice but the same language.

The messages seemed bizarre now, just minutes after hearing that Viatical Solutions was controlled by some "criminal element" that was involved in money laundering. Until now, he'd had little recollection of his attacker's voice, having been pounded so mercilessly. He couldn't say the messages were in the same voice, but he was at least beginning to recall an accent that he'd been too groggy to discern last night. He skipped through the third and fourth messages, the fifth, and on and on. All nine were in the same language.

Russian.

In his mind's eye, he saw himself walking to his car from his grandmother's townhouse last night. A punishing blow from behind sends his cell phone flying out of his hand. In the ensuing fracas, his attacker's cell phone is yanked from her pocket or belt clip. A final blow to his head, and Jack is out cold, leaving the rest to conjecture—perhaps his attacker searching frantically in the darkness until she finds a phone that looks just like hers.

But it wasn't hers. It was Jack's.

Ho-lee shit. He smiled, then chuckled out loud. It was about damn time something had cut his way. *We swapped phones!*

"*Señora,*" he said to the hostess. In his best Spanish, he asked for bread and cream cheese. It was a heart attack in the making, but *Abuela* had sold him on the pleasures of slathering Cuban bread with cream cheese and dunking it into his *café con leche*.

She handed him two long strips on wax paper. "Enjoy."

Jack was dunking at a near-frenzied pace, his mind awhirl. When they'd talked that morning, Cindy had told him that she'd called him on his cell but got no answer. It made sense that his attacker wouldn't have answered before five A.M. But just as soon as someone dialed his number at a decent hour, she *would* answer, and then she'd realize that they'd swapped phones. If she were smart, she'd cancel her cell service and erase the messages.

He dropped his bread and cream cheese, hurried to the pay phone and dialed his office voice mail. He replayed each message onto the recording, then relaxed, suddenly feeling in control. She could cancel away, but Jack would forever have her messages.

Now what? he thought as he returned to his seat.

The fact that she hadn't canceled her service and erased the messages told him that she wasn't onto the swap just yet. He could call the cops, but they couldn't trace the phone until she used it. Unless she tried to use it in the same battered and confused state that Jack had found himself in earlier that morning, she'd realize that the phone wasn't hers, and she'd pitch it in the Dumpster, for sure. This might be his last chance to call and open up a dialogue. He grasped his attacker's phone and dialed his own number. It rang twice before connecting.

"Hello."

His heart was in his throat. The voice on the other end of the line was one of the voices he'd heard last night—the woman's. "Good morning. This is Jack Swyteck. Remember me?"

She didn't answer. Jack was feeling pretty smug,

imagining her shooting a confused look at the phone in her hand.

He said, "I think you have something of mine. And if you check the number on this incoming call on your Caller ID, you'll see that I have something of yours."

She took a moment, and Jack was certain she was checking. Finally, she said, "Well, now. Isn't this interesting."

"Yours is especially interesting. The messages in your voice mail, all in Russian. I don't speak the language, but I'm sure the FBI or vice squad downtown would be happy to translate for me."

There was a brief but tense silence on the line. "What do you want?" she asked in a low, serious tone.

"I want to talk to you."

"We're already talking."

"No. Unlike you, I'm not stupid enough to transact business over nonsecure airwaves. I want to meet."

"That would be a mistake."

"Perfect. I'd say it's about time I made one of my own. I'm tired of paying for everyone else's."

"I'm not kidding. A meeting would be a terrible mistake."

"It would be an even bigger mistake if you stood me up. So, listen good. You know where the Metro-Dade Government Center is?"

"The tall building downtown next to the museum."

"Right. At four o'clock go into the lobby. Right in the middle, there's a planter with a bronze plaque in memory of a man named Armando Alejandre. Wait for me there. Or I'm going straight to the FBI, and your phone comes with me."

"How do I know you're not going to have me arrested if I show up?"

"Because I want to find out who's trying to hide what really happened to Jessie Merrill. And if I have you arrested, you're not going to tell me a thing, now are you?"

More silence. Finally, her answer came: "You sure this is what you want?"

"Yes. Oh, and one other thing."

"What?"

"When I was a prosecutor, this was my favorite place to meet reluctant witnesses, snitches, the like. It works very well because at least a dozen security guards are always wandering around. So leave your steel-toed boots at home. If you try anything, you'll never make it out of the building." He hit the END button, put the phone in his pocket, and finished off his coffee.

"You like something more?" asked the woman behind the counter.

"No, *gracias. Todo está perfecto.*" He handed over a five-dollar bill.

"Thank you. Have nice day."

Have nice day, he thought, smiling to himself. Once again, bad Spanish begat bad English. *Why do I even try?*

"Thank you, ma'am. It already is a nice day."

29

.

Her work didn't require a visit to the studio that morning, but Cindy went anyway. Jessie's death had rendered her own house unlivable, and her mother's house was feeling none-too-cozy after the raid at sunrise by federal marshals. She was running out of places to hide from the rest of the world. Not even her dreams offered any solace. The studio seemed like her only sanctuary.

Her portrait work was strictly by appointment, but she had nothing scheduled today. She'd driven into South Miami looking forward to a solid eight hours alone, a day to herself. There was always work to do, but she wasn't in the mood for anything challenging. She opted for organizing her office, the perfect mindless task for a woman who wasn't sure if she was married to a cheater.

She started with the mound of mail in her in-box, which was no small assignment. She actually had four in-boxes, each created at a different stage of procrastination. There was "Current," then "Aging," followed by "I'll Get to It on a Rainy Day," and finally, "I'll Build the Ark Before I Sort Through This Crap." She was only a third of way through the "Aging" stack when a knock at the door interrupted her.

She double-checked, and sure enough, the sign in the window said CLOSED. She stayed put, hoping that whoever it was would just go away. But the first knock was followed by a second, then another. She finally got up and was about to say *There's no one here,* but then she recognized the face on the other side of the glass. It was Jack's *abuela.* She unlocked the door and let her inside. The little bell on the door startled the old woman as she entered.

"Ooh. Angel got his wings."

Cindy smiled as she recalled that it was two years ago, Christmas, when *Abuela* had come over from Cuba, and her first lesson in English was the movie *It's a Wonderful Life*—over and over again.

"How are you?" said Cindy as they embraced warmly.

"*Bueno. Y tú?*" she answered in Spanish, though Cindy's ear for the language was even worse than Jack's.

"Fine. Come in, please."

Abuela followed her zigzag path through canvas backdrops and lighting equipment, stopping at a small and cramped office area. Cindy cleared the stacks of old photo-proofs from a chair and offered her a seat. She would have offered coffee, but *Abuela* had tasted hers before, and it had just about sent her back to Havana.

"I hope you not too busy," said *Abuela.*

"No, not at all. What brings you here?"

"Well, sorry, but I not here to get picture taken."

"Oh, what a pity."

She smiled, then turned serious. "You know why I here."

Cindy lowered her eyes. "*Abuela,* I love you, but this is between your grandson and me."

"*Claro.* But this just take a minute." She opened her purse and removed a stack of opened envelopes.

"What are those?" asked Cindy.

"Letters. From Jack. He wrote these when I live in Cuba."

"To you?"

"*Sí.* This is before I come to Miami."

"Jack wrote all those?"

"*Sí, sí.* Is how Jack and I got to know each other. Is also how I got to know you."

"Me?"

Abuela paused as if to catch her breath, then continued in a voice that quaked. "These letters. They are all about you."

Cindy again checked the size of the stack. Her heart swelled, then ached. "*Abuela,* I can't—"

"*Por favor.* I want you to see. My Jack—our Jack— maybe is no so good at saying things in words. If his mother lived, things would be different. She was loving person. Give love, receive love. But Jack, as *un niño,* no have her love. In his home, love was inside. *Comprendes?*"

"Yes. I think I understand."

"If you are Swyteck, sometimes only when heart is broken can love get out."

"That I do understand."

Abuela sifted through the stack of letters in her lap, her hands shaking with emotion. "This is *mi favorito.* Is when he asked you to marry. And this one, too, is very good. About your wedding, with pictures."

"*Abuela,* please. These letters were written for you, not me."

She laid the stack aside, clutching one to her bosom. "I wouldn't ask you to read them. I just want you to know they exist."

"Thank you."

"But there is one you must see. *Es especial.*" She fumbled for her reading glasses and dug the letter from the last envelope. "Is the oldest. Very different from others. See the top? Jack wrote the time. Two-thirty A.M. What make a man write a letter at this crazy hour?"

Cindy felt that this should stop, but she couldn't bring herself to say it. She just listened.

Abuela read slowly, trying hard to make her English perfect, though her accent was still thick. " 'Dear *Abuela.* It's late, and I'm tired, so I will keep this short and sweet. Do you remember the letter you wrote me last June? It would have been your fiftieth wedding anniversary, and you told me the story of how you and *Abuelo* met. It was a picnic, and a friend introduced you to her older brother. He ended up walking you home. You said you didn't know how you knew it, but by the time you got home you knew he was the one.

" 'I went back and re-read that letter tonight. I don't know why. I just did. That's not true. I do know why. I had a date tonight. Cindy is her name. Cindy Paige. I don't really know her that well, but I have that same feeling you described in your letter. It's weird, *Abuela.* But I think she's the one.' "

Abuela looked up, and their eyes met.

Cindy blinked back a tear. "He never told me that story."

"I no can explain that. But I know my grandson pretty

good. The young man who sit at his kitchen table and write this letter at two o'clock in the morning . . . he not really writing to his grandmother. He just being honest with his feelings. This letter is like talking to himself. Or to God."

"Or to his mother," said Cindy, her voice fading.

Abuela reached forward and took her hand. "I don't know what he did this time. I don't know if your heart can forgive him. But I do know this. He loves you."

"I know," Cindy whispered.

She handed Cindy a tissue. "Sorry I do this to you."

"It's okay. Maybe it's what I needed."

"Smart girl," she said with a little smile, then rose. "You excuse me now, please. I go home, put on my kicking boots, and give my grandson what *he* needs."

"I might actually pay money to see that."

"Ah, but we both love him, no?"

"Yes," she said, squeezing *Abuela*'s hand. "We do."

Cindy watched as *Abuela* gathered up her letters and put them back in her purse. Then she put her arm around the old woman, thanked her, and walked her to the door.

At four P.M., the main lobby of the Government Center was abuzz with rush hour. Jack headed against the stream of homebound workers. Theo was right along with him. Jack knew better than to face an attacker without a big ugly at his side.

Jack had gone straight to Rosa's office after making the phone call from the café. Immediately, it was decision time. Sam Drayton had confirmed that Viatical Solutions, Inc., was controlled by some element of organized crime. Why not tell the cops that his attacker had dropped a cell phone filled with Russian messages?

Why not? That was a question Jack the Client had been asking himself. Jack the Lawyer knew better. So did Rosa. The feds were going after him through the IRS, and that might only be the beginning. The state attorney had him on the short list of suspects for the murder of Jessie Merrill. In that posture, you didn't simply hand over anything to the police. You negotiated. And to negotiate properly, Jack had to know what he was selling. That was especially important here. From the moment he'd made the phone call, Jack had a strong feeling that his attacker wasn't what she appeared to be.

Not even close.

In less than twenty minutes they'd summoned a Russian linguist to translate the recorded messages. In thirty, they had a good criminal mind translating the literal English translations into something the lawyers could understand. Theo was perhaps the more indispensable of the two. Three of the messages dealt with, literally, "taking the ponies for a boat ride," which, Theo figured, was probably code for shipping stolen cars out of the port of Miami. The other six sounded as if the caller had a plumbing problem. A sink needed to be unclogged. Jack didn't need Theo to tell him that a sink was the repository in a money-laundering operation.

Theo checked his watch and asked, "You think she'll show?"

"A *musor* always shows."

"A what?"

"Didn't you listen to anything that Russian translator said?"

"Only the part that was in English."

As the name implied, Government Center was the nerve center of Miami-Dade County. Offices in the thirty-story tower housed various local departments and officials, including the mayor and county commissioners. The bustling lobby area served not only the office tower but also the largest and most crowded stop along the Metrorail. It was a three-story, atrium-style complex with a glass roof that allowed for natural lighting. Flags of all fifty states hung from the exposed metal rafters overhead. Long escalators carried workers and shoppers to a two-story mall called Metrofare Shops and Cafés. At the base of the north escalators was a large planter in the shape of a half-moon, where bushy green plants flourished. Between two large palms was a simple bouquet of white daisies and carnations in a glass vase. Above the vase was a bronze plaque that read: "Dedicated to the Memory of Armando Alejandre Jr., 1950–1996, Metro-Dade employee, volunteer of Brothers to the Rescue. His airplane was downed by the Cuban Air Force during a routine humanitarian flight over the straits of Florida."

Seated on the ledge of the planter in front of the plaque was a young woman wearing dark sunglasses, even though it wasn't very sunny inside the building. She was alone.

"That must be her," said Jack.

Theo gave him a thin smile. "Let's go."

As they rode down the escalator, Jack's eyes fixed on the woman. He'd never gotten a good look at his attacker, but from the beating he'd taken, he'd built her up to be at least eight feet tall, three hundred and fifty pounds. She was more like five-six, with slender-but-muscular arms, and the nicest set of legs that had ever kicked the daylights out of him. With her long, dark hair and olive skin, she looked more Latina than Russian. It surprised him how attractive she was.

"You got beat up by *that*?" said Theo as they glided into the lobby.

"Just shut up."

"I mean, some guys in my bar would pay money to get her to—"

"I said shut up."

They wended their way through the crowd and

approached from the side. She caught sight of them about ten feet away and rose to meet them, though she skipped right over the hello.

"Who's your friend?" she asked.

"You get my name when we get yours," said Theo.

A group of pedestrians passed by on their way to the train. She asked, "Is this a good place to talk?"

"Perfect," said Jack. "Nobody stands still long enough to hear what we're saying. And like I said on the phone, plenty of security guards around if you decide to get stupid."

She paused, as if to get comfortable with the setting. Then she looked at Jack and said, "That was a gutsy phone call you made."

"Not really."

"Threatening me after I'd already warned you not to mess around with us? I assure you, *that* was risky."

"I just listened to my instincts."

"Exactly what did your instinct tell you?"

"Maybe I'll let my friend tell you." He looked at Theo and said, "Here's a hypothetical for you. One, a woman attacks me in the dark and threatens me."

"Check," said Theo.

"Two, the feds haul me downtown and tell me they have it on good authority from their confidential informant that the order to rough me up came straight from a mysterious organized-crime figure."

"Double check."

"Three, this same woman has nine messages saved on her voice mail, all in Russian. But she speaks English without a hint of a Russian accent."

"Double check and a half."

"I call her and tell her I want to meet. And she just shows up, apparently not the least bit concerned that fifteen police officers might pounce on her the minute she arrives. Now, you tell me: Who do you think this woman is?"

He looked at Jack, then straight at her. "Either she's really stupid."

"Or?"

"Or *she's* the fucking snitch."

"Or as they're known in the Russian mob, *musor*. Rats. The lowest form of life on earth."

"You're a genius, Jacko."

"I know."

"But if we take this one step further, what she's really afraid of is not that we're going to take her cell phone to the police. She's afraid that someone might find out she's a snitch."

"You think?"

"Absolutely. But maybe we should ask *her.*" Theo took a half step closer, gave her his most intimidating look. "What do you say there, gorgeous? Think maybe you wouldn't be so pretty anymore if the wrong person were to find out that you are a *musor*?"

She glared right back at him. It impressed Jack that she didn't seem to back down from Theo the way most people did. *Careful, Theo, or she'll kung-fu your ass, too.*

"Aren't you smug?" she said. "Think you got it all figured out, don't you?"

"Not all of it. Just enough to get you to tell us the rest."

"I can't talk to you."

Theo said, "What a shame. Looks like I'll have to float your name on the street as a snitch."

"And then I'll watch Jack's *abuela* wishing to God she'd never left Cuba."

"Takes real guts to threaten an old woman. Who's next on your list, the Teletubbies?"

"Enough with the threats," said Jack. "Let's just talk."

"I can't tell you anything."

"That won't do," said Jack. "You may think we're just a pain in the ass, but refusing to talk to us won't make us go away. No matter what you do, my only option is to keep on plugging away at this viatical company to figure out who threatened Jessie Merrill and why she ended up dead."

"That's very dangerous."

"My alternative is to stand aside and get tagged with a murder I didn't commit."

"That's a bitch. But there's very little I can tell you."

"See, we're already making progress. We've gone from 'I can't talk to you' to 'there's very little I can tell you.' "

Jack detected a faint smile. She glanced at his swollen jaw and said, "Sorry about the bump."

"No problem."

"Didn't really want to do it."

"I know. Sam Drayton said the order came from high up."

She didn't deny it.

Jack said, "Who gave you the order?"

"You know I can't tell you that."

"Who controls the money behind Viatical Solutions, Inc.?"

"You're going to have to figure that out for yourself."

"Is it the same people who threatened Jessie Merrill?"

"If you're trying to pin a murder on the viatical investors, I couldn't help you if I wanted to."

"Why not?"

"Because you're looking in the wrong place."

"Stop with the threats."

"It's not a threat," she said. "Listen carefully. I'm giving you something here. If you think Jessie Merrill was murdered, you're not going to find her killer by looking where you're looking."

"Where should we be looking?"

She answered in the same matter-of-fact tone. "Somewhere else."

Theo groaned. "Come on. Like you don't know anything?"

"I know plenty. I just don't trust you to deny you heard it from me when someone hangs you upside down and shoves a cattle prod all the way up your ass."

Theo blinked twice, as if the uncomfortable image was taking form in his brain.

Jack gave her an assessing look. "How do you know we're looking in the wrong place?"

"Because I've been working this gig long enough to know the people I'm dealing with. I know what one of their hits looks like."

"Come off it," said Theo. "Not every hit is the same."

"Trust me. If Jessie Merrill had been murdered over her viatical scam, you wouldn't have found her body in the Swytecks' bathtub. You wouldn't have found her body at all. At least not in one piece."

Jack and Theo exchanged glances, as if neither was sure how to argue with that.

She said, "You two have no idea what you're stepping into."

"It's money laundering. I know that much from your phone messages and from talking with Sam Drayton."

"Big-time money laundering. Hundreds of millions of dollars. I tell you this only so you can see that Jessie Merrill and her one and a half million is a speck on the horizon. Now go away, boys. Before you get hurt."

"We can take care of ourselves," said Theo.

She extended her hand and said, "Phone, please."

Jack said, "I kept all the messages on tape."

"And you probably hired someone to dust for fingerprints, too. But I don't care."

"Of course you don't," said Theo. "Why should a snitch care about fingerprints?"

"I still want it back."

Jack removed her phone from his pocket and handed it over. She gave him his, then turned and walked away, no thank-you or good-bye. Jack watched as she moved with the crowd toward the escalators that led to the Metrorail gates.

"What do you think?"

"Two possibilities," said Theo. "Either she's protecting someone. Or someone has her scared shitless."

"Or both."

"You want me to tail her?"

"Nah, thanks. Got someone a little less conspicuous covering that already."

Jack caught one last glimpse of her as she reached the top of the escalator. Then, from afar, he gave his friend Mike Campbell a mock salute as he put aside his newspaper, rose from the bench, and followed her to the train.

Jack skipped dinner. He had a rental house to check out and could only hold his breath. *Abuela* had found it for him.

Jack had planned on staying in a hotel until Cindy took him back, but *Abuela* seemed to think she'd be more inclined to patch things up if he had a place for them to be alone together, away from Cindy's mother. She probably had a point.

The house was in Coconut Grove on Seminole Street, a pleasant surprise. It was small but plenty big for two, built in the forties, with all the charming architectural details that builders in South Florida had seemed to forget after 1960. The lot was huge for such a small house, but there was no grass. The lawn was covered with colorful bromeliads, thousands of green, purple, and striped varieties, all enjoying the shade of twisty old oak trees. An amazing yard with nothing to mow. To heck with the rental. Jack was barely inside and was already thinking of buying.

"You like?" asked *Abuela*.

Jack checked out the pine floors and vaulted ceiling with pecky-cypress beams. "It's fabulous."

"I knew you would like."

A man emerged from the kitchen, *Abuela*'s latest beau. Jack had met him before, the self-proclaimed best dancer in Little Havana. At age eighty-two he still seemed to glide through the living room as he came to greet Jack, smiling widely.

"Jack, how you been?"

He pronounced "been" like "bean," but he insisted on speaking English to Jack, as did most of *Abuela*'s friends, all of whom considered him thoroughly American, at best an honorary Cuban. Jack knew him only as *El Rodeo*, pronounced like "Rodeo Drive" in Beverly Hills, except when Jack was around and everyone referred to him as "The Rodeo," as if Jack were a native Texan and his middle name was Bubba.

"Is beautiful, no?"

"I love it. How much is it?"

El Rodeo pulled out a pen and scribbled a phone number on the inside of a gum wrapper. "You call."

"Whose number is this?"

He continued in broken English, and Jack was able to discern that the house was owned by *El Rodeo*'s nephew, who had just relocated to Los Angeles. Jack tried asking for details in Spanish, but again *El Rodeo* insisted that English would be easier. They were doing fine until he started telling Jack more about his nephew, a guy whose name apparently was Chip, which struck Jack as odd for a Latino.

"Chip?"

"*Sí*, chip."

"He's cheap," said *Abuela*.

"Ah, cheap."

"*Sí, sí*. Chip."

A nice enough guy, this El Rodeo, but if his English is better than my Spanish, I truly am a disgrace to my mother's memory.

Jack tucked the phone number into his wallet. "I'll call him tonight."

"Call now," said *Abuela*.

"I need to think about it. With everything Cindy and I have been through, I wonder if she'll be afraid to move back in with me unless it's a condo with twenty-four-hour security."

"Don't have fears control life. You and Cindy want children. House is better, no?"

He wasn't thinking that far ahead, but her optimism warmed him. "I should at least see the rest of the house."

"Okay." *Abuela* took *El Rodeo*'s arm and led him out the door. "We give you time to look around more on your own. You decide quick."

Jack hadn't intended to kick them out, but they were out the French doors before he could protest. He drifted toward the kitchen.

The window was open, and he could hear his *abuela* and *El Rodeo* outside on the patio talking about the busloads of tourists that cruised through Little Havana, where *El Rodeo* and his friends played dominoes in the park. It bothered *El Rodeo* to be treated as a spectacle, an ethnic oddity that these tourists only thought they understood. Not even Jack had understood until *Abuela* had moved to Miami. The evening newscasts had a way of conveying the impression that the only thing fueling the Cuban-American passion was hatred—hatred for Castro, hatred for any politician who wasn't staunchly opposed to Castro, hatred of yet another Hollywood star who thought it was cool to shake hands and smoke cigars with the despot who'd murdered their parents, siblings, aunts, and uncles. That emotion was real, to be sure. But there were neighborhoods filled with people like *El Rodeo,* a man who'd quietly tended bar in Miami for the past four decades, a photograph of the restaurant he'd once owned hanging on the wall behind him, the keys from his old house in Havana resting in a jar atop the cash register. He just refused to give up on something he loved, refused to admit he'd never get it back.

Tonight, as Jack wandered through a house that might be his, without a wife for the foreseeable future, he could relate more than ever.

"Hello, Jack."

He turned, startled by the sound of her voice. "Cindy? How'd you—"

"Same way you got here. *Abuela* invited me."

"She has a way."

"She definitely does. We had a nice talk in my studio. She got me to thinking." Her voice quaked, not with anger but emotion. "Maybe I overreacted."

"You believe me, then? That the tape of me and Jessie is B.C.? Before Cindy?"

She gave him a little smile, seeming to appreciate the humor. "Now that I've had time to think about it, yes, I believe you."

"We're going to prove it, if we have to."

"I'm sure you will."

"We hired an audio expert. It could still be tough, since we're working from a copy."

"The police won't give you the original?"

"From what Clara Pierce tells me, there is no original. It was destroyed, which tells me that Jessie went the extra mile to make it look as if she and I were having a recent affair. I think she was getting ready to blackmail me into staying quiet about her viatical scam."

"You don't have to convince me. Once I sobered up, I realized that the tape couldn't have been what it appeared to be. If you two were having an affair, I would have known it. I'm not that blind."

He went to her and held her tightly.

"I'm sorry I doubted you," she said.

"I understand. I mean, the way her body was found in our bathtub—"

"Let's not recount the details, okay? Let's just . . . be happy. Happy we have each other. That's all I want, is to be happy."

"Me, too," he said, still holding her tight.

A squeal of delight emerged from the patio. They turned and saw *Abuela* standing at the French door and peering in through the glass, blowing them kisses.

Jack smiled and mouthed the word *"Gracias."*

"Let's go," Cindy said softly. "It's time to start packing."

"I'm right behind you."

In less than five minutes Jack was in his convertible following Cindy back to Pinecrest. It would take at least a couple of days to arrange for a mover to bring their furniture to the new house, so they would have a few more nights with his mother-in-law. The plan was for Cindy to arrive ten minutes ahead of Jack and break the news that Jack was moving back in until the rental was ready. Apparently, her mother was less convinced of Jack's fidelity than Cindy was. Jack waited in his car in the driveway until Cindy came out to give him the all-clear.

His car phone rang, startling him. After the cellular swap, the car phone was his only wireless number. He answered. It was Mike Campbell.

"How'd you make out?" asked Jack.

"Well, there was a time in my life when it would have bothered me to follow a woman around for almost two hours and not even be noticed, but I guess in this context, that's a success."

"Nice work. Where'd she lead you?"

"Some pretty bad neighborhoods. She likes to mingle with the homeless. Especially if they're junkies."

"Damn. Sounds to me like she knew she was being followed. Took you on a wild goose chase."

"Except that she didn't seem to be wandering around aimlessly. She stopped at two places, and both times it looked to me as though it was her intended destination. As if she had some kind of business there."

"You mean drug business?"

"No. Blood business."

"Blood?"

"Yeah. She visited a couple of mobile blood units. You know, those big RV-looking things where people come in, let a nurse stick them in the arm, and walk out with cash."

"What the hell's that all about?"

"I didn't want to give myself away by asking any questions. I was hoping it would mean something to you."

"No," said Jack. "Not yet."

"The first truck was parked just off Martin Luther King Boulevard and Seventy-ninth Street. The other one was about a mile west. Both had GIFT OF LIFE painted on the side with a phone number underneath. You want it?"

"Yeah," he said, then wrote it down as Mike rattled off the numbers.

"I got a name for you, too. I asked one of donors who came out of the bloodmobile after she left. Said he thinks her name's Katrina. Didn't get a last name."

"That's a good start."

"You want me to follow up?"

"No, thanks. You go back to practicing law."

"Aw, this is so much more fun."

"Sorry. I'll take it from here."

"Let me know if there's anything else I can do."

"Thanks."

Jack noticed Cindy standing on the front porch. She was smiling and waving him inside.

"And Jack?" said Mike.

"Yeah?"

"Be careful with this woman, all right? Anyone who beats up my friend by night and deals with blood by day kind of worries me."

Me too, thought Jack. He thanked him once more and said good night.

32

.

Yuri Chesnokov was in his favorite getaway on earth, a city of two hundred thousand thieves, swindlers, whores, hit men, gangsters, kidnappers, drug runners, drug addicts, extortionists, smugglers, counterfeiters, terrorists, and well-armed revolutionaries, some with causes, most without. It was the kind of place where you could get anything you wanted, any time of day, any day of the week. You might also get a few things you didn't want, things you wouldn't wish on anyone. It all depended on what you were looking for.

Or who was looking for you.

Ciudad del Este is a festering urban sore in the jungle on the Paraguay side of the Paraná River. It's difficult to get there, unless you really want to get there. Amazingly, people come in droves. More than a hundred landing strips have been cut into the forests and grasslands in the "Tri-border Region," as the area is known. All are in constant use by small airplanes, not a single flight regulated by authorities. The two-lane bridge from the Brazilian border town of Foz do Iguacu brings in thirty thousand visitors a day, serving as the principal passageway for convoys of buses, trucks, and private cars entering from neighboring Brazil and Argentina. It's a daily ritual, shoppers leaving Rio de Janeiro and other cities late at night and arriving the next morning in the midst of the noisy, fume-filled traffic jam that is the center of Ciudad del Este. Most of the scruffy, bazaarlike shopping centers are on Avenida Monseñor Rodriguez, the main drag from which another five thousand shops fan out in all directions for a twenty-block area. Cheap electronic equipment and cigarettes are big sellers, but only to the truly unimaginative buyers. Behind the scenes is where the real money exchanges hands—cash for weapons, sex, sex slaves, pirated software, counterfeit goods, cocaine by the ton, murder for hire, and just about everything else from phony passports to human body parts for medical transplants. Miami and Hong Kong are the only two cities in the world that see a higher volume of cash transactions. In a country that boasts an official GDP of just $9 billion, Ciudad del Este has risen to a $14 billion annual industry of sleaze, Paraguay's cesspool on the Brazilian border.

Yuri walked from his thirty-dollar-a-night room at the Hotel Munich to a Japanese restaurant on Avenida Adrián Jara, the heart of the Asian sector. An ox cart bumped along the street, maneuvering its way past a pothole large enough to swallow it whole. Mud and ruts were typical for February, when temperatures averaged a humid ninety-five degrees and summer rains were at their peak. It was better than the dry season, when red dust seemed to coat everything, though Yuri saw irony in the pervasive red grit that got in your eyes, your hair, your clothes, as if it were symbolic of the growing influence of the Russian mob, the Red *Mafiya*.

"*Cerveza, por favor,*" he told the waiter. Nothing like a cold beer in the middle of a hot summer afternoon, and the *cerveza* in Paraguay was consistently good.

It was Yuri's sixth trip to the city in the past three months, all successful. He was seated at his usual table in the back of the Café Fugaki, angled in the dark corner with a direct line of sight to the entrance. No one could approach from behind him, and he could see all who entered. At the moment, he was the only customer; a heavy downpour outside keeping away even the most loyal patrons. His beer arrived in short order, and a minute later two men joined him. Fahid was Yuri's middleman, and he'd brought his supplier with him.

Fahid greeted him in Russian, but the pleasantries had exhausted his limited knowledge of the language. They continued in English, their common tongue. The third man, the source, introduced himself as Aman. He had cold, dark eyes—as cold as Yuri's—and a flat scowl beneath his black mustache. Yuri offered drinks, but they declined.

"Fahid tells me you have some problem with the merchandise," Aman said with a heavy Middle Eastern accent.

Yuri sipped his beer, then licked away the foam mustache. "Big problems, yes."

"You asked for a virus that easily injects into the bloodstream and is fatal to people with weak immune systems. That's exactly what we gave you."

"That may be. But West Nile virus is too . . . how do you say—exotic?"

"We sold it to you for the same price as much cheaper products."

"The price isn't the issue."

"If you wanted something specific, you should have said so before we filled the order."

"Five orders you filled, not once did I get West Nile virus. The sixth order, everything changes."

"Not a change. It was within your parameters."

Yuri shot an angry look at Fahid. "I was told it was going to be a strand of pneumonia."

Fahid shrugged and said, "That's what I thought it was going to be."

"The end result is all the same," said Aman. "What's the big deal?"

Yuri's voice tightened. "I'll tell you what the big damn deal is. We stuck a woman in Georgia. Now, instead of a routine death of an AIDS victim from any one of the million or more run-of-the-mill viruses that could have killed her, there's going to be a full-blown investigation into how she picked up this weird virus from someplace in western Africa."

"So what? Investigations blow over."

"I asked you to supply me with something AIDS patients die from every day. Not some bizarre virus that in the last twenty years has killed maybe two dozen people in the entire United States."

"But this is expensive product. I give you the best price anywhere."

"I told you, it's not a question of price, asshole."

"Don't call me an asshole."

"Then don't act like one."

"What you want us to do?"

"I want my money back."

"Oh, for sure. Would you like that with or without interest?"

"You think I'm joking?"

Aman leaned into the table. "Mr. Yuri, you are in Ciudad del Este, not Bloomingdale's. There are no refunds."

Yuri reached across the table and grabbed him by the throat. "You move, and I'll crush your windpipe."

Aman's eyes bulged as he gasped for air, but he didn't dare fight with Yuri. Fahid looked on, too afraid to intervene.

"Stay right there, Fahid. I'm aiming straight at your balls."

Fahid glanced down to see a .22-caliber pistol with a long silencer between his knees. Yuri still had his other hand around Aman's throat. The man's face was turning blue.

Fahid said, "Yuri, come on. Can't we work this out?"

"Just give me my money back."

Fahid glanced once more at Yuri's pistol. "I'm sure that won't be a problem."

"I want to hear it from Aman."

"Take your hand off his throat, and he'll tell you."

He didn't let go. "A simple nod will do. What's it going to be, Aman? Do I get my money?"

Saliva dribbled from the corner of Aman's mouth. He grunted, but the response was unintelligible.

Yuri tightened his grip. "Am I going to get my money back or not?"

Beads of sweat ran from Aman's brow as he struggled to breathe through his compressed windpipe.

"I'm waiting," said Yuri.

His eyes rolled back in their sockets, and his lashes fluttered, as if he were on the verge of losing consciousness.

"Let go of him," said Fahid.

"Shut up. You got five seconds, Aman."

Aman stiffened. His nostrils flared and whistled as he sucked desperately for air. He raised his right hand and curled his fingers into a fist. It shook unsteadily for a few seconds, and then he slowly raised the middle finger.

"You son of a bitch!"

Yuri lunged forward, knocking over the table as he pounced on Aman and flipped him onto his belly. With a knee against Aman's tricep for leverage, he jerked back on the forearm. It was like a gunshot, the sound of bone snapping, and Aman let out a horrible scream as his elbow bent in the wrong direction.

It all happened before Fahid could even blink. Yuri flipped Aman over and jammed a gun into his crotch.

"Stay back, Fahid, or your friend gets an instant vasectomy."

Aman was screaming in pain. There were no other patrons in the restaurant, but the waiters caught a quick look at the commotion and didn't stop running until they were across the street, all in keeping with the silent code of survival in Ciudad del Este: Look the other way.

Yuri grabbed Aman's hand and shoved his middle finger into his mouth. "Give it to me!"

Fahid stepped forward, but Yuri pressed the gun deeper into his friend's groin. "Back off, Fahid, or I'll shoot him."

Fahid froze. Yuri crammed the finger farther down Aman's throat, past the second knuckle and all the way to the base. "Bite it! I want that finger!"

Aman pleaded with a whimper, his eyes watering. Yuri answered with a muffled shot from his silenced pistol. It shattered Aman's left foot. His leg jerked, as if jolted by electricity, and even with his finger halfway down his throat he managed to emit a muted scream.

"Bite it off, right now!"

Aman grimaced, but his jaw tightened at Yuri's command.

"Harder. Bite it all the way through!"

Aman's body shook. Blood ran from his mouth as the teeth tore through the skin and tendons.

"Yuri, stop," said Fahid.

"All the way," he told Aman.

"He's going into shock," said Fahid.

Blood was running down both sides of his face, pooling in the ears. His teeth clenched even tighter as the incisors crushed the bone.

"Let me hear it snap!"

Fahid said, "Stop, okay? I'll get you your money. Consider it my debt. Just let him go."

Yuri looked up at Fahid, then down at Aman. Blood covered his cheeks, his foot was a mangled mess, and his left arm resembled a pretzel. Yuri yanked the middle finger from the clutch of Aman's jaws. It was a broken and twisted stick of raw meat, bitten down to the bone.

"You disgust me," said Yuri. As he rose, he gave two quick punches to Aman's busted elbow, eliciting the loudest scream yet. Aman rolled on the floor in agony, as if not sure which of his painful wounds to tend to.

Yuri said, "I want every penny before I leave town. Not just this order. All six orders."

"I'll deliver it to your hotel tonight," said Fahid. "Then we're square, right?"

"We'll never be square. You assholes cost me my biggest contract ever."

"What?"

"Those bastards I lined up from my Miami office.

They cut me off. And it's your fault. You and your fucking West Nile virus."

He turned and stomped on Aman's bloody foot, drawing one last cry of pain.

Fahid said, "Yuri, I'm sorry about this."

"Not half as sorry as those boys who pulled my contract are going to be."

He tucked his gun into the holster hidden beneath his shirt, dropped twenty dollars' worth of Paraguayan *guaranies* on the chair to cover the beer and the smashed table, and walked out of the restaurant, leaving Fahid to tend to his bloodied partner.

33

.

At 8 A.M. Jack was ready to leave for the courthouse. Cindy had gone into the studio two hours earlier, something about morning light being best for an outdoor shoot. He went to the kitchen for a cup of coffee to go. Cindy's mother was at the table reading the paper.

"Have a good one," said Jack.

"Mmm hmm," she said, her eyes never leaving the crossword puzzle.

Jack started out, then stopped. "Evelyn, I just wanted to thank you."

"For what?"

"For letting Cindy and me stay here with you."

She looked up from her newspaper. "You know there's nothing I wouldn't do for my daughter."

If the words hadn't completely conveyed it, the tone made it clear that she wasn't doing it for his sake. "Can we talk for a minute?"

"What about?"

Jack pulled up a chair and sat across the table from

her. "You've been cool toward me ever since this old audiotape surfaced. Cindy has obviously gotten past it. What do I have to do to make things right with you?"

"There's nothing you need to do."

"Nothing I need to do, or nothing I can do?"

"My, that's the kind of question that certainly brings matters to a head, isn't it?"

Jack looked her in the eye and said, "I wasn't unfaithful to your daughter."

"That's between you two."

"Then why are you making me feel as though I've done something wrong?"

"If you feel that way, then maybe you have."

Jack knew that it was probably best to back away from controversy, the way he always had with Evelyn. But this time he couldn't. "Do you wish I had?"

"Had what?"

"Cheated on Cindy."

"What?

"Do you?"

"What kind of ridiculous question is that?"

"One that you're trying not to answer."

"Why would I ever wish that on my own daughter?"

"You still didn't answer, but here's one possibility: so that she'd leave me."

Her voice tightened. "Do you really want to have this conversation?"

"It's time, don't you think?"

She looked away nervously, then lowered her eyes and said, "It's nothing against you, Jack. Honestly, I don't think you're a horrible person."

"Gee, that's the nicest thing you've ever said to me."

"There was a time when I said nothing but nice things about you."

"And then things changed."

"Esteban changed everything," she said.

Five years after the attack, the mere mention of his name still made his skin crawl. "Cindy told me how you feel. That her nightmares will never end so long as she's with me."

"She was attacked by your client."

"That was when I did death penalty work. I don't anymore. Haven't for years."

"The association is still there. Always will be. Cindy needed to make a break from all of that, and she didn't."

"She's happy with the choices she made."

"She's more fragile than you think."

"She's stronger than you think."

"I'm not just talking about Esteban."

"I know what you're talking about, and I'm nothing like her father."

She paused and settled back into her chair, as if suddenly aware that the intensity of the exchange had her leaning into the table. Her voice dropped to a softer but serious tone. "Do you know why my husband committed suicide?"

"I didn't think anyone really knew why."

"Do you know what his death did to our family?"

"I can only imagine."

"I didn't ask you to imagine. I asked if you knew."

"No. I wasn't there."

"Then you don't know Cindy. And you shouldn't pretend to know what's best for her."

The words angered Jack, not only because they hurt, but because it was so evident that she'd felt that way for a very long time. "You were right from the outset, Evelyn. We shouldn't have had this conversation."

"It was so unnecessary, wasn't it?"

"Some things are better left unsaid."

"Yes. Especially when we both know I'm right."

Jack grabbed his mug of coffee and left the house, down the front steps and across the driveway, thankful for a fast car as his squealing tires carried him away from Cindy's mother and her painful truths.

34

Jack returned from a hard-fought morning in federal court feeling pretty good about himself. A suppression hearing had gone his way, and it was gratifying to know that, despite the personal hassles, he was still able to do impressive work for his clients. Even the guilty ones.

Jack had barely settled into his office when Rosa popped in from across the hall. It was their habit to kibitz after a court hearing, and he was eager to share the details. She beat him to the punch.

"Jessie Merrill named you in her will."

Jack did a double take. "Named me what?"

"A beneficiary."

The words almost didn't register. He hadn't really been focusing on the probate of Jessie's estate as of late. In fact, he'd given it little thought—perhaps too little thought—since he'd spoken with Clara Pierce, the personal representative. "That can't be."

"I just got off the phone with Clara. Apparently she'd rather deal with your lawyer than with you."

"What did she say?"

"There will be a reading of the will today in her office at three-thirty. You're invited, since you're a beneficiary."

"Did she say what I'm getting?"

"No."

"Then it's probably the Charlie Brown special."

"She intimated that it bolsters your motive to murder Jessie. That hardly sounds like a lump of coal."

"You don't think she left me the money, do you?"

Rosa considered it. "It seems incredible. But I'm beginning to think maybe she was at least a little crazy."

"I'll vouch for that."

"I'm saying something a little different. I'm talking about the kind of mental impairment that's medically verifiable."

"Do you know something I don't know?"

She walked to the window and said, "I hear the medical examiner is about to issue a report."

"I hadn't heard."

"Nothing's official yet. But I have it on pretty good authority that higher-than-normal levels of lead were found in tissue taken from her liver and kidneys. You know what that means, Jack?"

He was looking at his lawyer, yet it was as if he could see right through her. "Jessie did have lead poisoning."

"At one time, yes. It was no longer in her bloodstream by the time she died, but traces of it had deposited in her major organs."

Jack was talking fast, his thoughts getting ahead of him. "Okay, she really was sick at the outset. But that doesn't prove that there was no scam. Somebody, somewhere along the line, got the bright idea to take lead poisoning and turn it into a phony case of ALS in order to dupe a group of viatical investors. Maybe it was her idea, maybe it was her doctor's. Maybe it hit them both at the same time while they were lying in bed together."

"I agree with you, but that's not my point."

"What is your point?"

"Lead poisoning has other ramifications, medically speaking. Even personality problems. Paranoia, hallucinations, irritability."

"The kinds of things you'd expect from a suicide candidate."

"Except that this isn't a normal suicide."

"Is there such a thing?"

Rosa took a seat on the edge of the desk, facing Jack. "Let me explain what I mean. So far, we've uncovered what seems to be a string of some pretty peculiar things that Jessie did before she died. She named you as beneficiary in her will. She named you as the co–account holder of her bank account. She used that audiotape to make it look as if you two were recently in the sack together."

"It's pretty clear she was trying to set me up as an accomplice."

"Most likely to keep you from blowing the whistle on her scam."

"Right. As soon as our audio expert finishes her analysis, we can show the state attorney exactly what she was up to."

"With the original missing, it won't be easy to show that the taped love-making session between you and Jessie happened seven or eight years ago."

"Still, any expert worth her salt can verify that the only tapes in existence are copies. The only reason for Jessie to have made a copy and destroyed the original is to create the impression that she and I were having a recent affair."

"That's all true," said Rosa. "But I'm not sure your extortion theory accounts for the full range of emotions behind that audiotape."

"What are you talking about?"

"As you say, we know that she copied the tape from an old original so it would look new. But that begs the question: Why did she keep the original all these years? You can't tell me that she was planning this scam for seven or eight years."

"I explained all this before. That tape became kind of a running gag between us. She probably ended up stuffing it in a shoebox somewhere and forgetting about it. Until recently, when she needed it."

"I'm not convinced that her keeping it all these years was as innocent and meaningless as you think. I've listened to it."

"So have I."

"Maybe you should listen to it again."

"I really don't want to."

"I want you to. Come on." She started out of the office.

"Where we going?"

"The tape. It's in the file."

"I don't need to hear that again," he said, but she was already down the hall. Jack followed. Rosa dug the tape from a locked filing cabinet, then ducked into the conference room. Reluctantly, Jack caught up just as she was putting the audiocassette in the stereo.

"We don't have to listen to all of it. In fact, the only part that piques my interest is at the very end." She hit FAST FORWARD till the tape ended, then rewound briefly.

"Ready?" she asked.

Jack shook his head. "This is embarrassing."

"It's not that bad. This isn't the two of you grunting and groaning. It's the afterglow. Just you and her talking, when she tries to coax you into going from audio to videotape. Listen." She hit PLAY.

The hiss of recorded silence flowed from the sound system, and then Jack heard his own voice.

"Can you put the damn camera away, please?"

"Come on. We did it on audio. Why not try the video?"

"Because it's like a one-eyed monster staring at me."

"I stare at your one-eyed monster all the time."

"Don't point that thing at my—"

"Oh, now you're Mr. Modest."

"Just turn it off."

"Why?"

"Why do you think?"

"Because you don't like to have it on while we're talking."

"No, I just don't like the thing staring at me like that."

"So it's okay to have a tape recorder running while you're fucking me. But it's time to put everything away when we talk about how we feel about each other."

"That's not it."

"Are you afraid to say how you feel about me, Jack?"

"No."

"Then say it. Say it on tape."

"Stop playing games."

"You're afraid."

"Damn it, Jessie. I just don't want to do this."

"You big chicken. Look, I'm not afraid. I can look straight into the camera and tell you exactly how I feel."

Again the speakers hissed throughout the conference room, a pregnant pause before Jessie's final words on tape.

"I don't want to live without you, Jack Swyteck. I don't ever want to live without you."

Rosa hit END, and the tape clicked off. She looked across the room and said, "Well?"

"Well, what? It's lovers' banter. People say that all the time: I don't want to live without you."

"Sure. And probably ninety-nine times out of a hundred it means simply that they'd rather live with you than live without you. But in that rare case, it might have a more literal meaning: If the choice is between death and living without you, then death it is."

"Those words are said in thousands of bedrooms every day. I'd rather die than lose you, blah, blah, blah. It doesn't mean they're going to go off and kill themselves."

"Most of the time, no. But sometimes it does."

"This was almost eight years ago."

"You don't know what happened in Jessie's life after your split. Her life could have been one long string of personal disasters from the day you broke up."

"You're overlooking the fact that she's the one who dumped me."

"Did she? Or did you force her to break it off by refusing to tell her how you felt? You said it yourself, she wanted to get back together with you six months later."

"Stop the pop psychology, okay? This tape, that relationship—it's all old news. And everything you're saying is totally speculative."

"Don't knock it. If you're indicted for murder, this just might be your defense."

"Yeah, right. Old girlfriend carries a torch for over half a decade. Makes me a joint holder of her bank account, leaves me a pot of money in her will, and doctors up an old tape of us making love, all just to give me motive to kill her. It's ridiculous."

"Listen to me. From the very beginning, we talked about how Jessie might have been trying to make a statement by killing herself in your bathtub. Well, maybe the statement she was trying to make is simply this: 'Jack Swyteck killed me.' "

"You're serious about this? You think she killed herself and framed me for doing it?"

"Think about it. The trick only works once, but it could be the perfect frame-up. Kill yourself, but do it in a way that makes it look like someone else did it. If it's done right, it's ironclad. The real killer is beyond suspicion."

Jack took a seat, thinking. Maybe he had overlooked a plausible defense, perhaps even the best defense, all because he feared his wife's reaction to his past with Jessie. "I swear, every time I think I'm getting my arms around this thing, it slips away from me."

"That's good. I'm not saying an indictment's inevitable, but if the worst comes to pass, confusion is the wellspring of reasonable doubt."

"For my own sake, I'd kind of like to know the truth someday."

"Would you?"

"Of course."

"Then maybe you will. Let's just hope it doesn't scare you."

Jack nodded slowly, saying nothing as he watched Rosa remove their copy of the old audiotape.

Katrina Padron had blood on her hands. It was all in a day's work. The vial had leaked in her hand. One of the idiots at the mobile unit had failed to seal it properly, something that occurred far too often in the shipment of product from the source to the distribution warehouse. Mishaps were inevitable when dealing with untrained workers. What else could she expect? A month earlier the crew had been operating a video rental shop, next month they might be hawking gemstones. For now, it was human blood. Diseased blood. Lots of it.

Thank God for latex gloves.

Katrina was in the back of the warehouse, scrubbing her hands with a strong soap and disinfectant, when her assistant emerged from the walk-in refrigerator. He was dressed in a fur-lined winter coat and carrying a box large enough to hold a dozen vials packed in dry ice and wrapped in plastic bubble wrap.

"Where's this one going again?" he asked.

"Sydney, Australia."

He grabbed a pen and an international packing slip. "I saw a travel show about Sydney on the TV a while back. Isn't that where England used to send its worst prisoners?"

"A long time ago."

"So that means everybody down there descended from some guy who was in jail."

"Not everyone."

"Still, prison is prison. You'd think they'd have enough AIDS-infected blood already. What do they need us for?"

Katrina just rolled her eyes. *Morons, I work with. Total morons.*

He sealed up the box with extra tape and attached the shipping label. "All set. One Australian football ready for drop-kick shipment," he said as he went through the pretend motion.

"Don't even think about it."

"What do you think, I'm stupid or something?" He removed his coat, hung it on the hook beside the big refrigerator door, and started for the exit.

"Hey, genius," said Katrina. "Aren't you forgetting something?"

He turned, then groaned at the sight of the unfinished paperwork in her hand. "Aw, come on. I've been in and out of that refrigerator for three hours. Can't you at least do the invoicing for me, babe?"

"Only if you stop calling me babe."

He winked and smiled in a way that was enough to make her nauseous. "You got it, sweets."

She let him and his remarks go. It was easier that way. She wasn't planning on working this job forever, and if she wasted her time trying to get others to do their fair share she'd never get home at night. The paperwork wasn't really all that time-consuming anyway. One genuine invoice for a legitimate purchase and sale of diseased blood, four phony ones to fictitious customers for extremely expensive inventory that never existed. Bio-Research, Inc., had just enough employees, just enough inventory, and just enough sales to look like a real company that supplied real specimens for use in medical research. It was anything but real.

Most amazing of all, the blood business was a huge step up from her first job.

A dozen years earlier she'd come to Miami from Cuba by way of the Czech Republic, having spent four long years in Prague under one of Fidel Castro's most appalling and least known work programs. At age seventeen, she was one of eighty thousand young Cuban men and women sent to Eastern Bloc countries to work for paltry wages. The host countries got cheap labor for jobs that natives didn't want, and Castro got cash. Katrina had been lured across the ocean by the prospect of exploring a country outside her depressed homeland. Once there, she'd ended up seeing little more than the inside of a sweatshop and the two-bedroom apartment she shared with seven roommates. Not even the wages were as promised, which only galvanized her determination never to return home to Cuba. In time, her sole mission devolved into nothing more than getting out of Prague alive.

At times even that had seemed too lofty a goal.

"Katrina?"

She looked up from her paperwork to see her boss standing in the doorway. Vladimir was strictly a front-office guy. He didn't usually spend any time in the warehouse. Especially since they'd gotten into the dirty-blood business.

"Yes, sir?"

He came toward her, stepping carefully around the boxes scattered about the concrete floor. Under his arm was the glossy red folder that held the latest slick marketing brochure for Viatical Solutions, Inc., which told her that he'd come to see her about his other business. The two companies shared office space.

"I just got off the phone with some guy who says you referred him to me."

"Says *I* referred him?"

"Big, deep voice. Sounds like a burly old football player. Says he wants to meet and talk about a huge book of viatical business for us."

"What's his name?"

"Theo. Theo Knight. You know him?"

Katrina instantly recognized the name but forced herself to show no reaction. "I do."

"I told him I'd meet him at the Brown Bear for dinner. He pretty much insisted you come along. Can you join us?"

She put the blood invoices aside, struggling to keep her own blood from boiling. "Sure. I'd love to chat with my ol' pal Theo."

Jack and Rosa reached the Law Offices of Clara Pierce & Associates at precisely 3:29 P.M. The reading of Jessie Merrill's will was scheduled for half-past three, and one extra minute was plenty of time for Jack to sit in enemy territory.

A receptionist led them directly to the main conference room and seated them in chairs of ox-blood leather at the long stone table. From the looks of things, Clara's practice was thriving. Plush carpeting, cherry wainscoting, silk wall coverings. The focal piece of the room was the exquisite conference table. It was cut from creamy-white natural stone, rough and unfinished, one of those expensive excesses that interior decorators talked lawyers into buying and that was completely nonfunctional, unless you were the type of person who liked to try to put pen to paper on the Appian Way.

The receptionist brought coffee and said, "Please be sure to use coasters. The stone is porous and stains quite easily."

"Sure thing," said Jack. *Beautiful, impractical,* and *high maintenance,* he thought. *Jessie would so approve.*

She closed the door on her way out. Jack and Rosa looked at each other, puzzled by the fact that they were alone.

"Are you sure Clara said three-thirty?" asked Jack.

"Positive."

The door opened and Clara Pierce entered the room. A leather dossier was tucked under one arm. "Sorry I'm late," she said as she shook hands without a smile. "But this shouldn't take long. Let's get started."

"Isn't anyone else coming?" asked Jack.

"Nope."

"Are you saying I'm the only heir?"

"I think I'll let Jessie answer that. Her will is as specific as it can be."

Jack didn't fully understand, but Rosa gave him a little squeeze on the elbow, as if to remind him that they had come only to listen.

Clara removed the papers from the dossier and placed them before her. Jack sipped his coffee and absentmindedly set the mug on the table. Clara's eyes widened, as though she were on the verge of cardiac arrest. With a quick snap of the fingers she said, "Jack, please, coaster."

"Oh, sorry."

"This table is straight from Italy. It's the most expensive piece of furniture I've ever purchased, and once it's stained, it's ruined."

"Just lost my head there for a second. Won't happen again."

"Thank you."

"Can you read the will, please?" said Rosa.

"Yes, surely. Let me say at the outset, however, that

it was not my idea to have an official reading of the will. I would have just as soon let you see a copy when I filed it with the probate court. But it was Jessie's specific request that there be a reading."

"No explanation needed, but thank you just the same."

"Very well, then. Here goes. 'I, Jessie Marie Merrill, being of sound mind and body, hereby bequeath . . .' "

Sound body, indeed, thought Jack. Perhaps it should have read, "I, Jessie Marie Merrill, being of sound mind and body that's a whole heck of a lot more sound than I've led everyone to believe, including my dumb-schmuck lawyer, Jack Swyteck, without whose unfathomable gullibility I wouldn't have diddly squat to hereby bequeath, bequest, and devise . . ."

Jack listened to every word as Clara continued through the preamble. After a minute or two she paused for a sip of water, carefully returned her glass to a coaster, and then turned to the meat of Jessie's will.

" 'My estate shall be devised as follows,' " said Clara, reading from page two. " 'One. Within six months of my death, all of my worldly possessions, including all stocks, bonds, and illiquid assets, shall be sold and liquidated for cash.

" 'Two. The proceeds of such liquidation shall be held in a trust account to be administered by Clara Pierce, as trustee, in accordance with the terms of the trust agreement attached hereto as Exhibit A.

" 'Three. The sole beneficiary of said trust shall be the minor male child formerly known as Jack Merrill, born on October 11, 1992 at Tampa General Hospital, Tampa, Florida, and released for adoption by his mother, Jessie Marie Merrill, on November 1, 1992.

" 'Four.' "

It was as if Jack's mind had slipped into a three-second delay. He put down his coffee and said, "Excuse me. Did you just say she had a kid?"

Again, Clara snapped her fingers. "Coaster, please."

Jack moved his coffee mug, but he was almost unaware of his motions. "And his name was Jack?"

"Please," said Clara. "Let me get through the whole document, then you can ask questions."

Rosa said, "Actually, we won't have any questions. We're just here to listen, right, Jack?"

He felt his lawyer's heel grinding into his toe. "But Clara just said—"

"I heard what she said. Please, Ms. Pierce, continue. There won't be any further interruptions."

Clara turned the page. " 'The beneficiary's present whereabouts and current identity are unknown as of this writing. Should he not be located within one year from the date of my death, the trust shall be dissolved and my entire estate shall issue to the beneficiary's father, John Lawrence Swyteck.' "

"What?"

"Damn it, Jack. For the last time, use the stinking coaster."

"Jessie never told me she had a kid."

"Quiet, Jack," said Rosa.

"Coaster, *please*," said Clara.

"And she sure as heck never said I was the father."

Rosa grabbed his arm. "Let's go."

"No, I want to hear this."

"Your coffee mug is still on my table."

"Jack, if you can't shut up and listen, then it's my duty as your lawyer to get you out of here."

"No!" he said as he yanked his arm free of Rosa's grasp. His arm continued across the table in a sweeping motion and collided with the coffee cup. Hot, black liquid was instantly airborne. In what seemed like slow motion, Jack leaped from his seat to catch it, but to no avail. Clara's mouth was agape, her eyes the size of silver dollars. The three of them looked on in horror as a huge black puddle gathered in the dead center of her creamy-stone table and then disappeared, soaking into the porous stone, leaving behind an ugly brown stain. The meeting suddenly took on the aura of a funeral.

Her expensive stone table now resembled fossilized dinosaur shit.

"Clara, I am *so* sorry."

"You bastard! You did that on purpose!"

"I swear, it was an accident."

"It's ruined!"

"I'll pay to have it cleaned."

"It can't be cleaned. You destroyed my beautiful table."

"I just don't know how that happened."

"I think we should go now," said Rosa.

Clara was on the verge of tears. "Yes, please. Both of you, get out of here."

"But we haven't heard the whole will," said Jack.

"You've heard the part that matters."

Jack wanted to hear more, as if he might hear *something* that made sense to him. But Clara seemed impervious to whatever plea he might have pitched. She hadn't moved from her seat. Her elbows were on the table—one of them on a coaster—as she held her head in her hands and stared blankly at the big brown stain.

Jack said, "Sorry about—"

"Just leave," she said, not even looking up.

He and Rosa slipped away in silence, showing themselves to the door.

37

•

Slivers of late-afternoon sunshine cut through the venetian blinds. It was annoying to the eye, but Assistant State Attorney Benno Jancowitz left things just the way they were. Any time he hammered out a deal with a witness who was willing to turn state's evidence, he didn't like his guests to get too comfortable.

Seated across the table from the prosecutor was Hugo Zamora, three hundred pounds' worth of criminal defense lawyer with a voice that boomed. At his side was a nervous Dr. Marsh. The desktop was clear, save for the one-page proffer of testimony that had been prepared by Zamora. Typed on the proffer were the exact words that the doctor would utter to a grand jury, assuming that the prosecutor would agree to grant him immunity from prosecution.

Jancowitz pretended to read over the proffer one last time, drumming his fingers as his eyes moved from left to right, line by line. Finally, he looked up and said, "I'm not impressed."

"We're certainly open to negotiation," said Zamora. "Perhaps put a finer point on some of the testimony."

"It just doesn't help me."

"I beg to differ. Your case against Mr. Swyteck rests on the assumption that Jack Swyteck and Jessie Merrill were having an affair. I presume your theory is something along the lines of Jessie Merrill was threatening to reveal the affair to Swyteck's wife, so Swyteck killed her."

"I'm not going to comment on my theories."

"Fine. Let's talk evidence. The proof you have of an affair is the audiotape that came from the inventory of property in Ms. Merrill's estate, correct?"

"I'm not going to comment on the nature of the evidence we've gathered."

"You don't have to. We both know that police departments are sieves. I won't name names, but it has come to my attention that your own expert has confirmed that this so-called smoking gun of an audiotape is not an original. There is no original. All you have is a copy, which leaves the door wide open for Swyteck to argue that the missing original was made before he was even married. It doesn't prove anything."

Jancowitz said nothing.

Zamora continued, "Now, Dr. Marsh here is ready, willing, and able to plug this gaping hole in your case. He, of course, denies that he was ever part of this alleged scam that Mr. Swyteck talks about. But he will tell the jury that after his serving as Jessie Merrill's doctor, they became close friends. That on the night Jessie won her trial against the viatical investors, she came by his apartment to thank him personally. That one thing led to another, and they ended up making love."

"I know, I've read the proffer."

"Just play the tape."

"I don't need to play it."

"I've already fast-forwarded to the important part. It's less than twenty seconds."

He thought for a moment, sipping his lukewarm coffee. "How is it that this tape came into existence?"

"It was something that this Jessie apparently liked to do. You already know that from the other tape you have."

"So you're telling me you have a tape of Dr. Marsh and Jessie Merrill actually having sex?"

"Yes. It's not a very good tape. She just set the camera up on a tripod and then the two of them . . . you know, did their thing."

Jancowitz glanced at Marsh, a man older than himself, and said, "Is it really necessary for me to watch this?"

"No. We can kill the video portion. The only thing that matters is what was said."

"I can live with that," said Jancowitz.

Zamora handed him the tape. There was a small television set with built-in VCR player on the credenza. Jancowitz inserted the videotape and dimmed the screen to black, for the sake of his own eyes and Dr. Marsh's modesty. Then he hit PLAY. Jancowitz returned to his seat, then leaned closer to the set.

"I don't hear anything."

"Turn it up," said Zamora.

He increased the volume. A rustling noise followed, some kind of motion. A woman laughed, though it sounded more evil than happy. A man groaned.

"It sounds like bad porn," said Jancowitz.

No one argued. Dr. Marsh sank in his chair.

On tape, the voices grew louder. The heavy breathing took on rhythm, and Jessie's voice gained strength.

"That's it. Harder."

All eyes in the room were suddenly fixed on the screen, even though it was black. No one wanted to make eye contact.

"Harder, baby. That's it. Give it to me. Come on. Come on, that's it, yes, yes! Oh, God—yes, Jack, yes!"

Zamora gave the signal, and the prosecutor hit STOP. He gave Jancowitz a moment to take in what had just played and said, "You heard it?"

"Yes."

"She clearly said the name Jack."

The prosecutor grimaced and shook his head. "It just doesn't do it. All you've got is a woman crying out another man's name."

"Not just any name. Jack, as in Jack Swyteck."

"That doesn't establish that she and Swyteck were having an affair. At most, it just establishes that she fantasized about Swyteck while she was making love to Dr. Marsh."

"Right now, you have nothing to prove the existence of an affair. This is a lot better than nothing."

"I think there's plenty more to this triangle than you're telling me. If you want immunity from prosecution, you'd better fork it over."

"We're giving you all we have."

"Then there's no deal."

"Fine," said Zamora. "We're outta here."

"Wait," said Dr. Marsh.

Zamora did a double take. "Let's go, Doctor. I said, we're outta here."

"I'm a respected physician in this community, and the stink from this Jessie Merrill situation is tarnishing my good name. I won't allow this to drag out any longer. Now, Mr. Jancowitz, tell me what you want from me."

"I want the truth."

"We're giving you the truth."

"I want the whole truth. Not bits and pieces."

Zamora said, "Then give us immunity. And you get it all."

The prosecutor locked eyes with Zamora, then looked at Dr. Marsh. "I'll give you immunity, but I want two things."

"Name them."

"I want everything the doctor knows about Swyteck and Jessie Merrill."

"Easy."

"And I want your client to sit for a polygraph. I want to know if the doctor had anything to do with the death of Jessie Merrill. If he passes, we got a deal."

"Wait a minute," said Zamora, groaning.

"Done," said Marsh. "Ask away on the murder. But I won't sit for a polygraph on the viatical scam."

"You got something to hide?" asked Jancowitz.

"Not at all. With the complicated relationship I had with Jessie, I'm concerned that you might get false signs of deception, depending on how you worded the scam question. But if you want to ask me straight up if I killed Jessie Merrill, I got no problem with that."

"Fine," said the prosecutor. "Let's do it."

"Hold on, damn it," said Zamora. "My client obviously wants to cooperate, but I'm not going to sit back and let the two of you rush into something as important as a polygraph examination. Right now, Dr. Marsh and I are going to walk out that door, go back to my office, and talk this over."

"I want to get this done," said Marsh.

"I understand. A few more hours isn't going to kill anyone."

"I'll give you twenty-four hours," said Jancowitz. "If I don't hear from you, I'll subpoena Dr. Marsh to appear before a grand jury."

"You'll hear from us," said Zamora.

"You know the deal. Pass the polygraph on the murder and tell all."

Marsh rose and shook the prosecutor's hand. "Like my lawyer said: You'll hear from us."

The prosecutor escorted them to the exit, then watched through the glass door as they walked to the elevator. He returned to his office, tucked the videotape into an envelope, sealed it, then took out his pen and drew a little star on the doctor's witness file.

38

.

The smoke was thick at Fox's. Just the way Jack wanted it.

Fox's Lounge had been at the same location on U.S. 1 forever, and the decor probably hadn't changed since Gerald Ford was president. It was a time warp with dark-paneled walls, booths trimmed with leather so worn that it felt like plastic, and enough secondhand smoke to gag even a tobacco-industry spokesman. Jack didn't care for cigarettes, except when he really needed a drink. Even then he didn't light up. He just basked in the swirling clouds around him and belted back bourbon until his clothes reeked and his eyes turned red.

It seemed like the perfect way to toast the reading of Jessie's will.

"Make it huge," Jack said into his cell phone. He was speaking with Hirni's Florists, arranging for the immediate delivery of the biggest damn floral centerpiece they'd ever constructed—big enough to cover a stain as big as a manhole cover on Clara's priceless stone conference table. While he was at it, he ordered some roses for Cindy. In a perfect world he would have been home, packing for the scheduled moving day, but somehow he didn't envision himself dashing off to a new house with Cindy happily at his side after telling her about Jack Junior. He needed a little counseling, and for that he turned again to his friend Mike. He was uniquely qualified. He'd known Jack since college, he'd known Jessie when she and Jack were dating, and, most important, he knew they weren't twenty-one anymore and had no business getting drunk on anything but premium brands.

"Old Pappy on the rocks," he told the bartender.

"What the heck's Old Pappy?" asked Jack.

"A little treat I discovered at the Sea Island Lodge. Best bourbon you'll ever drink."

Jack was a little surprised that the bartender had it, but Fox's was a pretty reliable place to find obscure brands, especially old brands, and, if the label was to be believed, no one drank Old Pappy unless it was at least twenty years old.

"What do you make of this mess?" asked Jack.

It had taken him five minutes to bring Mike up to speed. It took less than five seconds for Mike to render his verdict.

"She's a nutcase," he said as he selected a jalapeño popper from the plate of hors d'oeuvres. "She always was."

"What does that mean?"

"Nothing with her ever added up. She did everything for shock value, just to see how people would react."

"This is more than shock value."

"I didn't say she wasn't vindictive."

Jack sipped his bourbon. "This was a stroke of

genius on her part. Her objective was to leave everything to a child she'd given up for adoption. Rather than find him herself, she drops the whole thing in my lap. It's up to me to find him."

"Technically, you don't have to look. If no one finds the kid, you inherit a million and a half dollars."

"That's exactly my dilemma."

"Not sure I follow you."

"The money came from a scam. If I find the child, I'll be handing him a million and a half dollars that I know is dirty. But if I choose not to look for him, I'll forever be accused of cheating my own flesh and blood out of an inheritance from his birth mother."

"Accused by whom?"

"Everyone."

"Everyone? Or yourself?"

"What do you mean by that?"

"I'm just trying to think like Jessie. Maybe her objective wasn't simply to get the money in the hands of the child she gave up for adoption. Maybe she was just as interested in making you feel guilty as hell about the whole situation."

"Years of pent-up anger, is that it?"

"It's a long time, but who knows what was going through her head?"

Jack took another long sip. "I think I know."

"You want to share?"

Jack glanced at the mirror behind the bar, speaking to Mike without looking at him. "Jessie couldn't have kids."

"She apparently had one."

"I mean after that one. I saw her whole medical file during our case. She had PID."

"What?"

"Pelvic inflammatory disease. It's an infection that goes up through the uterus to the fallopian tubes. It was cured, but the damage was done. Doctors told her she'd probably never have kids."

"How did she get it?"

"How do you think?"

Mike nodded, as if suddenly it was all coming together. "You and her break up, she finds out she's pregnant. She comes back to you before she's really started to show and tells you she wants to get back together. But you've already met Cindy Paige, so she keeps the baby a secret. Last thing she wants is you coming back to her just because she's pregnant."

Jack filled in the rest, staring through the smoke-filled room. "She gives up the baby for adoption, meets some guy who gives her PID, and just like that, she finds herself in a situation where she's given away the only child she's ever going to bring into this world."

They glanced at one another and then looked away, their eyes drifting aimlessly in the direction of whatever nonsense was playing on the muted television set.

"Hey, Jack," said Mike.

"Yeah?"

"I think I figured out why Jessie came back to stick it to you as her attorney after all these years."

Jack swirled the ice cubes in his glass and said, "Yeah. Me too."

Katrina walked into the Brown Bear around six-thirty with Vladimir at her side. The restaurant was about half-full, and she spotted Theo instantly. They walked right past the sign that said PLEASE WAIT TO BE SEATED and joined Theo in a rear booth.

Katrina made the introductions, and they slid across the leather seats, Katrina and her boss on one side of the booth, across from Theo.

The Brown Bear was in East Hollywood, just off Hallandale Beach Boulevard. It had a huge local following, mostly people of Eastern European descent. The newspaper dispenser just outside the door wasn't the *Miami Herald* or the South Florida *Sun-Sentinel* but *eXile,* a biweekly paper from Moscow. Behind the cash register hung an autographed photo of Joseph Kobzon, favorite pop singer of former Soviet leader Leonid Brezhnev and a household name to generations of Russian music lovers, known best for his soulful renditions of patriotic ballads. The buzz coming from the many crowded tables was more often Russian or Slovak than English or Spanish. Meals were inexpensive and served family-style, gluttonous portions of skewered lamb, chopped liver, and beef Stroganoff. Caviar and vodka cost extra. On weekends, a three-piece band and schmaltzy nightclub singer entertained guests. Reservations were essential—except for guys like Vladimir.

Katrina wondered if Theo had any idea that the Cyrillic letters tattooed onto each of her boss' fingers identified him as a made man among *vory*, a faction of the Russian *Mafiya* so powerful it was almost mythical.

"Katrina tells me you used to work together," said Vladimir.

She shot Theo a subtle glance. Vladimir had quizzed her on the car ride over, and she'd been forced to concoct a story. Revealing the true circumstances under which she and Theo had met would only have exposed herself as a snitch.

"That's right," said Theo, seeming to catch her drift.

Katrina took it from there. "I've come a long way from slogging drinks at Sparky's, haven't I, Theo?"

"You sure have."

"I like that name," said Vladimir. "Sparky's."

"I came up with it myself. The old electric chair in Florida used to be called 'Old Sparky.' When I beat the odds and got off death row, I thought Sparky's was a good name for a bar."

Vladimir smiled approvingly, as if serving time on death row only confirmed that Theo was all right. "Do you own this Sparky's?"

"Half of it. I'm the operations partner. Buddy of mine put up all the money."

"Other people's money," Vladimir said with a thin smile. "We should drink to that." He signaled the waitress, and almost immediately she brought over three rounds of his usual cocktail, one for each of them.

"What's this?" asked Theo.

"Tarzan's Revenge."

"Ice-cold vodka and Japanese sake poured over a raw quail's egg," said Katrina.

"I didn't know Tarzan drank."

She didn't bother explaining that Tarzan was not Johnny Weissmuller but a flamboyant, muscle-bound Russian mobster famous for wild sex orgies on his yacht and a hare-brained scheme to sell a Russian nuclear submarine to the Colombian cartel for underwater drug smuggling.

"Cheers," said Vladimir, and each of them belted one back.

Just as soon as the first round was gone the waitress brought another. Katrina joined in the second and third rounds but passed on the fourth and fifth. She'd seen Vladimir operate before, knew he could outdrink any American, and knew that Tarzan's Revenge was Vladimir's way of loosening tongues and tripping up rats.

"Tell us more about your proposal," said Vladimir.

"Let me start by being upfront with you. I'm not gonna try to hide the fact that I'm a friend of Jack Swyteck."

"You mean the lawyer?"

"You know who I mean."

Vladimir was stone-faced. "You said you had business."

"That's right. And for me, business is business. Swyteck's not part of it. So, it's your choice. You can tell me to shut up and go away, that you don't want shit to do with any friend of Jack Swyteck. Or you can put my friendships aside and act like a businessman, which means both of us make a lot of money."

Vladimir removed a cigar from his inside pocket, unwrapped the cellophane. "Everyone I do business with has friends I can't stand."

"That's what I thought you'd say. You look like a very smart man."

"What are you offering?"

"Viatical settlements."

"How much?"

"The sky's the limit."

Vladimir laughed like a nonbeliever. "I've heard that one before."

"Maybe so. But not from someone who understands your business the way I do."

"You know so much, do you?"

"You got a lot of cash on your hands."

"What makes you think that?"

"It's written all over your face. And your hands," he said as he glanced at the Cyrillic letters on Vladimir's fingers.

Katrina said nothing, but she was starting to reconsider. *Maybe this Theo isn't as dumb as he looks.*

Vladimir said, "A guy could have worse problems."

"But too much cash is still a problem. So I figure it works this way. You got a pot of dirty money."

"I have no dirty money."

"Just for the sake of argument, let's say you got fifty million dirty dollars. Some from drugs, some from prostitution, extortion, illegal gaming, whatever. We can all talk freely here. We're among friends, right, Katrina?"

"Old friends are the best friends," she said.

"Okay," said Vladimir. "Let's say fifty million."

"Let's say I got a hundred guys dying from AIDS who

are willing to sell their life insurance policies to you for five hundred thousand dollars a pop. You do a hundred separate deals, all impossible to trace, and pay out fifty million in cash. My guys name some offshore companies formed by your lawyer as the beneficiary under their life insurance policy. When they die, the life insurance company pays you the death benefit. Clean money."

"How much?"

"Double. You start with fifty million in dirty money. In two years you got a hundred million in clean money straight from the coffers of triple-A-rated insurance companies."

Vladimir glanced at Katrina. Again she said nothing, though it impressed her the way Theo had put so much together. She suspected that Jack had done at least some of the unraveling.

"Sounds intriguing," said Vladimir. "I might be interested under the right circumstances."

"If you had fifty million dirty dollars?"

"No. If you actually had a hundred fags with life insurance in the pipeline."

"A buddy of mine owns nine AIDS hospices. Three in California, four in New York, two in south Florida. All high-end, all wealthy clientele. No one who checks into these places is long for this earth."

"That could be a very useful connection."

"I thought so."

Vladimir's cell phone rang. He checked the number and grimaced. "I gotta take this. Back in a minute."

Katrina waited until he was safely outside the restaurant, then glared at Theo and said, "What in the hell do you think you're doing?"

"Going to the source."

"What for?"

"It's like Jack and me figured. We find out who's laundering all that viatical money, we find Jessie Merrill's killer."

"Do you have any idea who you're dealing with?"

"Yes. Do you?"

"Eventually Vladimir is going to see right through you. You can't bluff these people."

"Why not? You did."

"That's different. I'm working from the inside."

"Give me a little time. I'll be right there beside you."

"Have you lost your mind? You're going to get yourself killed."

"Only if you blow my cover. But you won't do that. Because if you do, I'm taking you down with me."

She was so angry she could have leaped across the table and strangled him. But Vladimir was back, and she quickly forced herself to regain her composure.

He sank back into the booth and snapped his fingers. The waitress brought another round of Tarzan's Revenge.

"To your health," said Vladimir.

He belted back the drink. Katrina did likewise, keeping one angry eye on Theo.

Vladimir put the unlit cigar back in his pocket, as if signaling that it was time to leave. He looked at Theo and said, "I'm afraid I have to go, but before I do, I want to leave you with this story. You ever heard of the money plane?"

"Money plane? I don't think so."

"Delta Flight 30. It used to leave JFK for Moscow at 5:45 P.M. five days a week. Rarely did it leave with less than a hundred million dollars in its cargo belly. Stacks of new hundred dollar bills, all shipped in white canvas bags. Over the years, about 80 billion dollars came into Russia that way. Just one unarmed courier on the flight, no special security measures. And not once did anyone even try to hijack the plane. Why do you think that is?"

"The food sucked?"

"Because anyone who knew about the money also knew that it was being bought by Russian banks. And if you rip off a Russian bank, nine chances out of ten says you're ripping off the Russian *Mafiya*. Nobody has big enough balls or a small enough brain to do that. So that plane just kept right on flying."

"Very interesting."

"You understand what I'm saying?"

"I'm pretty sure I do."

"Give us two days. If you check out, you meet Yuri."

"Sounds good."

Katrina said, "Tell him what happens if he doesn't check out."

"I think he gets the point," said Vladimir.

"I like to be explicit with my friends. He should hear."

Vladimir leaned forward, a wicked sparkle in his eye. "You don't check out, you meet Fate. And he has not a pretty face."

Theo gave an awkward smile. "Funny how you talk about fate as if it's a person."

"That *is* funny," said Vladimir. "Because we all know that Fate is an animal." He laughed loudly, pounding the table with his fist. Then all traces of a smile ran from his face. "Good-bye, Theo."

Theo rose and said, "You know where to reach me, right, Katrina?"

"Don't worry. We won't have trouble finding you."

She watched as he turned and walked away, then headed out the door, not sure if she should be angry or feel sorry for him.

Theo, my boy, you were safer on death row.

D r. Marsh sat in silence in the plush leather passenger seat of his lawyer's Lexus. They were just a half-block away from Mercy Hospital, an acute-care facility that sat on premier Miami waterfront, the Coconut Grove side of Biscayne Bay. Year after year it was voted "best view from a deathbed" by a local off-beat magazine. Dr. Marsh had missed his morning rounds at the hospital, and they were popping by the parking lot just to pick up his car. But Jessie Merrill was still weighing on his mind.

"Funny thing about that videotape," said Marsh.

Zamora stopped the car at the traffic light. "How so?"

"I don't know if Jessie was sleeping with Swyteck or not. But she definitely wasn't obsessed with him."

Zamora rolled his cigar between his thumb and index finger. "You'd never guess that from the tape. She screamed his name while having sex with you."

"These tapes she did were purely shock value. There's nothing honest about them."

"I'm not following you."

Marsh looked out the window, then back. "This was exactly the kind of thing that bitch liked to do. She'd get me all hot and then say something to spoil the mood and set me off."

"How do you mean?"

"The tapes weren't the least bit erotic for her. It was all about her warped sense of humor. One time, before I'd decided to get a divorce, she had me on the verge of orgasm and then pretended my wife had just walked into the room. That was her favorite tape of all, watching me fly out of the bed butt-naked. Other times she'd just scream out another man's name. She used my seventeen-year-old son's name once, my partner's another time. But her favorite one was Jack. She knew that one really got me."

"Why did that name bother you so much?"

"I don't know."

"Is it possible that you were a little jealous of Jack Swyteck?"

"No."

"Maybe you had reason to be jealous. Maybe when she screamed his name, it wasn't just for effect."

"It was totally for effect. She just wanted to make me crazy."

"Crazy enough to kill her?"

Their eyes locked. "I told you before, I didn't kill her."

"Then the polygraph should be a breeze."

"I think I've changed my mind on that. I don't want to take a polygraph."

"Why not?"

"I swear, I had nothing to do with Jessie's death. I just don't believe in polygraphs. I think liars can beat them, and I think innocent people who get nervous can fail."

Zamora twirled his cigar, thinking. "I have a good examiner. Maybe I can get Jancowitz to agree to use him."

"I really don't want to take one. I don't care who's administering it. Hell, it tests your breathing, your heart rate, your blood pressure. I get so furious whenever anyone asks me about Jessie Merrill, I'm afraid I'll fail even if I tell the truth."

"Then you shouldn't have acted so eager to do it back in Jancowitz's office."

"I was bluffing. I figured the more willing I seemed to take one, the less likely he was to push for it."

"Prosecutors can never get enough. It's going to be hard to get him to back down."

"Maybe if the testimony we offer is so good, he'll do the deal even if we refuse to sit for a polygraph."

Zamora gave his client a look. "How good?"

"We already have a good base. That joint bank account is pretty damning for Swyteck."

"Why *did* she put him on that account?"

"Damned if I know."

"Why weren't you on it?"

"The money was never intended for me. This was something I was doing for her."

"Got to keep the high-maintenance other woman happy, eh?"

"Do you have any idea how hard it is to provide for another woman when your wife of twenty-four years is suing for every penny in divorce?"

"I understand."

"But let's not lose focus here. We got Jessie Merrill naming Swyteck as her co–account holder on the one-point-five million dollars, and we got her on tape screaming out his name. That's a damn good start. The prosecutor says he wants more, so I'll give him more."

"He doesn't just want more."

"I hear you."

"I'm serious," said Zamora. "There is no upside in lying to a grand jury. We need to comb over every word you say. It all has to be true."

"Sure, I love a true story."

"Just so the emphasis is more on 'true,' less on 'story.' "

The doctor flashed a wry smile. "That's what the truth's all about, isn't it?"

"What?"

The traffic light turned green. Zamora steered his car toward the hospital entrance. Dr. Marsh looked out the window at the passing palm trees and said, "It's all just a matter of emphasis."

41

.

It was almost midnight as they lay together in Cindy's
old bedroom, their last night at Cindy's mother's. A
small twenty-five-year-old lamp on the nightstand cast
a faint glow across the bedsheets. It was a girl's lamp
with a pink-and-white shade. Jack wondered what had
gone through Cindy's head as a child, as she'd lain in
this very room night after night. He wondered what
dreams she'd had. Nothing like the nightmares she had
as a grown-up, surely. It pained him to think that perhaps Evelyn was right, that he only added to Cindy's
anxieties.

"Are you really okay with this?" he said.

Cindy was on her side, her back to him. He'd told
her everything about the will and the child Jessie had
given up for adoption. She'd listened without interruption, without much reaction at all.

She sighed and said, "Maybe I'm just getting numb
to the world. Nothing shocks me anymore."

"I know I keep saying this, but it's so important:

Everything that happened between me and Jessie was before you and I ever met."

"I understand."

"Don't go numb on me."

Jack was right beside her but still looking at the back of her head. She wouldn't look at him. "What are you going to do about the boy?" she asked.

"I don't know."

"Are you going to try to find him?"

"I might have to."

"Do you want to?"

"It's all so complicated. I don't think I'll know the answer to that question until some of the dust has settled."

Silence fell between them. Cindy reached for the switch on the lamp, then stopped, as if something had just come to mind. "When did Jessie make her will?"

Jack paused, wondering where this was headed. "About a year ago."

"That was before she came to you and asked you to be her lawyer, right?"

"Yeah, it's when she supposedly was diagnosed with ALS."

"Why do you think she did that?"

"Did what?"

"Wrote her will just then."

"It was part of the scam. She had to make it believable that she was diagnosed with a terminal disease, so she ran out and made a will."

"Do you think it's possible that she really did think she was going to die?"

He thought for a second, almost found himself entertaining the possibility. "No. She told me it was a scam."

"Did she tell you it was her scam or Dr. Marsh's scam?"

"It doesn't matter. They were in it together at the end."

"If they were in it together, then why wasn't his name on the joint bank account?"

"Because they were smart. Only the stupidest of coconspirators would put their names together on a joint bank account."

Silence returned. After a few moments, Cindy reached for the light switch, then stopped herself once again. "In your heart, you truly believe that Jessie ended up dead because she scammed those viatical investors, right?"

"One way or the other, yeah. Either they killed her or she killed herself because they were about to get her good."

"Down the road, if you have to prove to someone— to a jury, God forbid—that Jessie scammed the investors, how are you going to do it?"

"I saw her and Dr. Marsh holding hands in the elevator after the verdict. And then she admitted to me that it was a scam."

"So, really, your only proof of a scam is what you claim you saw in the elevator and what you claim she said to you afterward?"

He felt a pang in his stomach. It was the toughest cross-examination he'd ever faced, and he was staring at the back of his wife's head. "I guess that's what it boils down to."

"That's my concern," she said quietly.

"You shouldn't be concerned."

"But maybe you should be."

"Maybe so."

Finally she rolled over, looked him in the eye, and gently touched his hand. "You and Jessie weren't having an affair. You didn't know about the child. You didn't know about the joint bank account in the Bahamas. You didn't know that she'd left you all that money in her will. She turns up dead, naked, in our bathtub, and the only evidence that someone else might have killed her is your own self-serving testimony. You claim that she admitted the whole thing was a scam, even though you, as her lawyer, knew nothing about it until after the trial was over. I would never tell you and Rosa how to do your jobs, but I've gained enough insights from you over the years to know that it's looking harder and harder for you to avoid an indictment."

"Don't you think I realize that?"

"I'm not saying it to make you mad. My only point is that unless there are twelve Cindy Swytecks sitting on the jury, how do you expect them to believe you? How could *anyone* believe you, unless they wanted to believe you?"

He brushed her cheek with the back of his hand, but even though she'd been the one to initiate physical contact a minute earlier, she felt somewhat stiff and unreceptive. "I'm sorry," he said.

"Me too." She rolled over and switched off the lamp. They lay side by side in the darkness. Jack didn't want to end it on that note, but he couldn't conjure up the words to make things better.

"Jack?" she said in the darkness.

"Yes?"

"What does it feel like to kill someone?"

He assumed she meant Esteban, not Jessie. Even so, it wasn't something he liked to talk about, that battle to the death with his wife's attacker five years earlier. "It feels horrible."

"They say it's easier to kill again after you've killed once. Do you think that's true?"

"No."

"Honestly?"

"If you're a normal human being with a conscience, taking a human life under any circumstances is never easy."

"I didn't ask if it was easy. I asked if you thought it was easi*er*."

"I don't think so. Not unless you're miswired in the first place."

She didn't answer right away. It was as if she were evaluating his response. Or perhaps evaluating him.

She reached for the lamp, and with a turn of the switch the room brightened. "Good night, Jack."

"Good night," he said, trying not to think too much of her decision to sleep with the light on. And then there was silence.

Yuri was chasing flies. They were all over Gulfstream Park. Not the kind that race horses swat-
ted away with their tails. These were flies with money
to wash.

Yuri loved thoroughbred racing, and in Florida's winter
months the name of the game was Gulfstream Park. The
main track was a mile-long oval wrapped around an inviting blue lake that even on blistering-hot days made you feel
cooler just to look at it. Gulfstream was a picturesque
course with over sixty years of racing tradition, host to premier events like the Breeders Cup and Florida Derby. It sat
within fifty miles of at least ten casinos that were more than
happy to take back your winnings, everything from bingo
with the Seminole Indians to blackjack and slot machines
on any number of gaming cruises that left daily from Palm
Beach, Fort Lauderdale, and Miami. This was as good as
gambling got in Florida, and Yuri was in heaven.

But he hated to be ripped off. Especially by his own
flies.

"Pedro, got a minute?"

Pedro was a new guy, early twenties, pretty smart, not nearly as smart as he thought he was. He was standing at the urinal in the men's room beneath the grandstands. Hundreds of losing tickets littered the bare concrete floor at his feet, but at the moment the two men were alone in the restroom.

He looked at Yuri and said, "You talking to me?"

"Yeah. Come here. I got a big winner for you."

Pedro flushed the urinal, zipped up, and smiled. It was his job to buy winning tickets, all with dirty money. It was one of the oldest games in the money-laundering world. Take the dirty proceeds from a drug deal, go buy a ticket from a recent winner at the track, cash it in and, voilà, your money's legit. You had to pay taxes on it, but that was better than having to explain suitcases full of cash to the federal government. Pedro might wash ten thousand dollars a day this way. He was a fly, always hanging around race tracks the way insects of the same name buzzed around a horse's ass.

"I hit the trifecta in the second race," said Yuri. "Twenty-two hundred bucks."

Pedro washed his hands in the basin, speaking to Yuri's reflection in the mirror. "I'll give you two thousand for it."

"You charge commission?"

"Sure. You still come out ahead. You turn that ticket in to the cashier, you end up paying the IRS five, six hundred bucks in income taxes. You sell it to me, you get fast cash for a measly two-hundred-dollar transaction fee."

"I gotta tell you, Pedro. Every time I've done this in the past, it's been at face value. A twenty-two-hundred-dollar purse gets me twenty-two hundred bucks from a fly."

"Must be a long time since you won anything. I been doing it this way for at least two months."

"Is that so?"

"Yeah."

"Business good?"

"Excellent."

"What does your boss say about that?"

"Nothing I can tell you."

"I think he'd be pissed. Because you haven't been telling him about your ten-percent commission, have you?"

"That's between me and him. You want to sell your ticket or not?"

Yuri grabbed him by the back of the neck, smashed Pedro's head into the sink. A crimson rose exploded onto the white basin. Pedro squealed and fell to the ground, his face bloodied, a broken tooth protruding through his upper lip.

"What the . . . hell?" he said, dazed.

Yuri grabbed him by the hair and looked him straight in the eye. "Two months, huh? That's a thousand bucks a day for fifty race days you been skimming. You got two days to cough up a fifty-thousand-dollar present to your boss. Or I'll come find you, and you'll be spitting up more than just your teeth."

The bathroom door opened. Two men walked in, then stopped at the sight of blood on the sink and Pedro on the floor.

Yuri walked past them and, on his way out, said, "It's okay. He slipped."

The door closed behind him, and Yuri walked calmly into the common area beneath the grandstands. A group of dejected losers watched the replay of the third race on the television sets overhead. Winners were lined up at the cashier window. Dreamers were back in line for the next race, wallets open. Yuri bought himself an ice-cream bar and returned to his box seat near the finish line. It was an open-air seat in the shade, with a prime view of the nine-hundred-and-fifty-two-foot straight-away finish from the final turn.

Vladimir was in the seat next to him. "Flies all under control?"

"Totally."

"I think I'll call you the bug zapper."

"You do and I'll squash you like a cockroach."

Horses with shiny brown coats pranced across the track. The big black scoreboard in the infield said it was five minutes until post time.

"I had an interesting meeting last night. A friend of one of my employees from the blood center claims he can hook us up with fifty million dollars in viatical settlements."

"How?"

"He has connections with some AIDS hospices."

"Fucking AIDS. That's how we got into the mess we're in. All those homos were supposed to be dead in two years. Then they get on these drug cocktails, AZT, whatever, and live forever."

"Well, not forever. We both know that a weak immunity system offers a great many opportunities to expedite the process. How'd your meeting in Paraguay go?"

"I set them straight, but it doesn't do us any good."

"What do you mean?"

"Brighton Beach canceled our contract."

The trumpet blared, calling the horses to the gate. "What?"

"No more money. Not fifty million, not fifty cents."

"Why?"

"They didn't give me a reason. I think it's because of all the attention this West Nile virus is getting from the Centers for Disease Control. They're probably getting nervous."

"Why would they be nervous?"

"Because there just aren't that many cases of West Nile virus in the United States. It could start to look pretty fishy when the authorities figure out that half the reported cases in the United States involved AIDS patients who had viatical settlements."

"How many of our targets ended up getting West Nile?"

"One woman in Georgia's dead from it already. Could be a few more to follow."

"You don't know how many?"

"Not off the top of my head. You know how Fate works, his little game. Only the ones who chose a slow, painful death would have gotten stuck with West Nile. The others got something quick and painless. Relatively quick and painless."

"I'm beginning not to trust this Fate. I think I should meet him."

"I can probably arrange that," said Yuri. "Someday."

Vladimir pressed his fingers to the bridge of his nose, as if to stem a migraine. "I don't understand this. This was such a perfect plan."

"It was never perfect. Look at the Jessie Merrill situation. The minute we branch out from AIDS patients who need a little help dying, we get scammed."

"That's a whole 'nother situation."

"Yeah," said Yuri. "Whole 'nother situation."

The bell rang and horses sprang from the gate. Yuri and Vladimir raised their binoculars and watched through the cloud of dust as the sprinting pack of thoroughbreds rounded the first turn.

43

.

Saturday was moving day for Jack and Cindy. Theo was supposed to have dropped by at noon to help with the big stuff, but by one o'clock he was looking like a no-show.

Jack was hauling boxes up the front steps of their new rental house when his cell phone rang. He was pretty sure it was Theo, but the caller's voice was drowned out by loud rap music playing in the background. It was one of the few forms of artistic expression that Jack just didn't get. The lyrics, especially. *Junkies in the gutter all better off dead, Blow-Job Betty sure gives good head*—rhymes for the sake of rhymes, as if the next line might as well be *I like to drive barefoot like my Stone Age friend Fred.*

"Can you turn the music down, please?" Jack shouted into the telephone.

The noise cut off, and Theo's one-word response confirmed that it was indeed him on the other end of the line. "Turkey."

"How can you listen to that stuff?"

"Because I like it."

"I understand that you like it. The implicit part of my question is *why* do you like it?"

"And the implicit part of my answer is what the fuck's it to you? Got it?"

"Got it."

"Good."

"So," said Jack. "What's up?"

"What do you mean, what's up? You called me."

"No. I'm quite certain—oh, what does it matter? When you getting your butt over here?"

"Not today, man. Gotta work. I was just calling to tell you about my meeting with the folks from Viatical Solutions."

"What?"

"After our meeting with Katrina the Snitch, we both agreed that the only way to find out who might have killed Jessie Merrill is to find out who the money people are behind the company. So I met with them."

"What do you think you're doing?"

"Just a little digging, that's all."

"Theo, I mean this. I don't want you messing around with these people."

"Too late. I gotta do it, man. You got me off death row. I can't go around owing you forever."

"You don't owe me anything."

The rap music was back on, even louder than before. Theo shouted, "What did you say?"

"I said, you don't owe—"

Gonna find that motha' an' pump him full a' lead.

"Sorry, Jacko, can't hear you, man."

Jack tried once more, but the music was gone, and so

was Theo. "Damn it, Theo," he said as he hung up the phone. "Sometimes you help too much."

Jack went back inside the house. The rental furniture was stacked in the middle of the living room, and it was up to him and his own aching back to rearrange things the way Cindy wanted them. "And sometimes you help too little," he said, still thinking of Theo.

"What?" asked Cindy.

"Nothing. Just a little sole-practitioner syndrome."

"Huh?"

"Talking to myself."

She gave him a funny look. "Ooo-kay. How long has *that* been going on?"

"Long enough for me to think it's normal."

"We should get out more." Cindy gave him a little smile, then returned to her unpacking in the kitchen.

The move was actually quite manageable. The old Swyteck residence was still a crime scene, and the prosecutor had released only limited portions of it, which basically meant that Jack and Cindy could take to their new house only those things that the forensic team had determined were irrelevant to their investigation of Jessie's death. They'd been able to take a few things with them to Cindy's mother's. Earlier that day, a police officer had met Jack at their old house and told him exactly what more he could take. It amounted to an additional thirty-seven boxes, a television set, some clothes, a few small appliances, and their stereo, all of which Jack had packed into a U-Haul van and hauled out by his lonesome. Cindy just didn't want to go back there, and the prosecutor had refused to allow more than one person inside the house anyway.

Jack was up to box twenty-two on the unloading end, moving at a fairly good clip. But Cindy was falling way behind him on the unpacking, still working on the first wave of boxes they'd brought from her mother's. Jack flopped on the rented sofa and closed his eyes, more tired than he'd realized. He was almost asleep when he heard a shrill cry from Cindy.

"Jack!"

He sat bolt upright, but he was still only half-awake.

"Jack, come here!"

He got his bearings and ran to the kitchen. She was seated at the counter surrounded by open boxes and scattered packing material.

"What is it?"

"Look," she said. "Our wedding album."

Photo albums, home videos, and the like were among the things they'd taken from their house long ago in the first wave of personal possessions that the prosecutor had released from the crime scene. Jack glanced over her shoulder, and the sight sickened him. "What the hell?"

Cindy flipped from the first page to the second, and then the next. The bride and groom at the altar, Jack and Cindy getting into the white limousine, the two of them stuffing cake into each other's mouths. All were in the same condition: sliced diagonally from the top left corner to the lower right by a very sharp knife.

"How did this happen?" he asked.

"I don't know. This is the first I noticed it."

"Did you check it before we took it from the house?"

"No . . . I don't know. I don't remember. I can't believe she did this," said Cindy, her voice quaking.

"I can."

She looked up and asked, "What should we do?"

"Put it down, gently."

She laid it on the table.

"Don't touch another page," said Jack. "Our wedding album has just become Exhibit A."

"As evidence of what?"

His eyes locked on the slashed photograph before him. He was beginning to think that perhaps Rosa was right, that Jessie had killed herself. Or that at the very least she'd been driven to suicide.

Or that somebody had done an awfully convincing job of making it look like suicide.

"I wish I knew," he said.

•

The blood business was booming, and Jack wanted a firsthand look. He found the Gift of Life mobile blood unit just a block away from the same street corner that his friend Mike had told him about after tailing Katrina. Mike, however, had only watched from a distance. Jack was there on business.

It was a cool afternoon, which made his disguise easier. He stopped at Goodwill and bought a crummy sweatshirt, a pair of old tennis shoes that didn't match, black pants with a few paint spots around the cuffs, and a knit cap that was frayed around the edges. Then he went home and burned a pile of garbage in the backyard, standing close enough to the cloud of dirty smoke to overpower the smell of mothballs. With his bare hands he dug a little hole in the earth, doggy-style, getting dirt under his nails, soiling his arms up to his biceps. A swig of cheap bourbon gave his breath the right adjustment. Streaks of engine grease on his hands, face, and clothes provided the finishing touches, compliments of the grimy engine block on his old Mustang.

A half-block away from the blood unit, he stopped along the sidewalk and checked his reflection in a store-front window. He genuinely looked homeless.

Not that his disguise needed to be foolproof. He wasn't hiding from Katrina. In fact, he wanted to talk to her, but a visit to her house or the main office of Viatical Solutions, Inc., could have put them both at risk, depending on who might be watching. A phone call wouldn't work, either, since her line might be tapped. Staking out the blood unit, dressed like a homeless guy, seemed like the best alternative. He was pretty sure that the low-level goons who worked with her in the truck had no idea who Jack Swyteck was, and the disguise was enough to fool them.

"Need twenty bucks, buddy?" said the guy outside the unit.

Jack looked around, not sure he was talking to him.

"Yeah, you," the guy said. "Twenty bucks, and all you gotta do is roll up your sleeve. You interested?"

Jack thought for a second, but this was even better than he'd hoped for. Here was a chance to look around inside. "Sure."

"Come on."

Jack followed him toward the unit, stopping just outside the door to let the latest donor pass. It was a woman, probably in her thirties, who looked about seventy. She appeared to be wearing every stitch of clothing she owned, several dirty layers that smelled of life on the streets and dried vomit.

She smiled at the doorman, half of her teeth missing, and then laid her hand on his belt buckle and said, "How's about I collect some of your specimen, honey?"

"Get away from me," he said, wincing.

"Whatsa matter? Your nice little nurse stuck me with her needle. You don't want to stick me with yours?"

"Get lost."

She snarled and said, "Needle dick."

He pushed her to the pavement.

"Hey, go easy on her," said Jack.

"Needle dick!" she shouted.

"You shut your trap, lady," the doorman said.

"Needle dick, needle dick!"

He stepped toward her, fists clenched, but Jack stopped him. "Come on. I ain't got all day."

The man seemed torn, but finally his business mind prevailed. He hurled a few cuss words at the woman and led Jack up the stairs.

The air inside was stale, trapped by windows that probably hadn't opened in years. The staff was minimal, just a phlebotomist, a cashier, and a thick-necked thug seated near the door. Jack presumed he was packing heat. Donors were paid in cash, so a guard with good aim and plenty of ammunition would have been indispensable, even if he was a blockhead, a matching bookend for Jack's escort.

"Got another one for you," the man said.

The phlebotomist put her cheese sandwich aside and said, "Come on over."

Jack took a seat. A rubber strap, gauze packages, several plastic blood bags, and a needle with a syringe were spread across the table.

"You HIV-positive, partner?" asked the phlebotomist.

Jack looked around. The floors looked as if they hadn't been mopped in months, plenty of dried blood spots on grimy, beige tile. The seats and tabletop weren't much cleaner, and the windows were practically opaque with dirt. How this woman could eat in this place was beyond him. He wasn't about to let her poke him with one of her needles.

"Yeah, HIV," said Jack. "As a matter of fact, I got full-blown AIDS."

"Perfect," she said. "Roll up your sleeve."

He tried not to look confused. "You want bad blood?"

"Of course. Now, come on. Show me a vein."

He didn't move fast enough, so she grabbed his wrist and pushed his sleeve up to his elbow. "Hmm. No tracks."

"I shoot between my toes," he said.

"Make a fist."

Jack obliged, keeping an anxious eye on the syringe. "Is that a new needle?"

She chuckled, still searching his arm for the right vein. "Only been used once by a little old lady who likes needle dicks."

"Don't you start," said Needle Dick.

She tied the rubber strap around his elbow like a tourniquet. If he didn't think fast, he was about to share a junkie's needle. "This is fifty bucks, right?" said Jack.

"I told you twenty," the goon said.

"I ain't doing this for no twenty dollars."

"Shut up and be a good boy. Maybe I'll throw in a half-pint of whiskey."

"No. It's fifty or I'm outta here."

The other goon stood up beside his buddy. With the two of them together, it was like trying to blow by a couple of pro-Bowl linebackers. "Sit down and shut up," he told Jack.

Jack was half-sitting, half-standing. Getting stuck

with a dirty needle wasn't an option, but he wasn't quite sure how he was going to get past these two pork chops.

"I said, sit!" the guy shouted.

"What's going on?"

Jack looked past the goons, relieved to see Katrina.

"Just a little matter of money," said Needle Dick. "Junior here thinks his blood's worth fifty bucks."

She took a good look at Jack, and he could see in her eyes that she'd recognized him instantly, even with the old clothes, knit cap on his head, and grease on his face. He wasn't really worried about a confidential informant giving him up and blowing her own cover, but his heart skipped a beat as he waited for her to say something.

"This jerk's blood isn't worth fifty cents. He scammed us on Miami Beach two weeks ago. His veins are clean. Get him out of here."

The men came toward him, each grabbing an arm. They kicked open the door and threw him out. He landed on the pavement right beside the bag lady.

She looked at him with disgust. "You gonna let a needle dick push you around like that?"

Jack picked himself up, checked the scrape on his elbow where he'd hit the pavement. He glanced toward the van, then answered. "It's okay. I'm a hotshot lawyer. I'll sue his ass."

She flashed a toothless grin, said something about him looking more like a senator, and then just kept talking. Jack listened for about a minute, till he realized that she was chatting with herself.

He felt as though he should walk her to a shelter or something, but he had to stay focused. She went one way, and he went the other, continuing a half block north, where he found a bus bench at the corner and waited. Getting inside the mobile unit had been a bonus, but he still hadn't spoken to Katrina, his main objective. He sensed she wouldn't be far behind him. In ten minutes, his hunch proved correct.

"What the hell were you doing in there?" she said as she took a seat on the bench beside him.

"Funny, I was going to ask you the same thing."

"You and your friend Theo have to stay clear and let me do my job."

"Just exactly what is your job?"

"None of your business."

"You're not even going to let me guess?"

She shot him a look, as if not sure what to make of him. "Okay, Swyteck. Show me how smart you are."

"It's interesting the way you set up these mobile units in high-crime areas, places where the average Joe walking off the street might carry around any number of infectious diseases in his bloodstream."

"Hey, if Mohammed won't come to the mountain . . ."

"So, for twenty bucks and a half-pint of cheap booze they'll gladly drain their veins of infected blood. Then what?"

"What do you think?"

"I don't think Drayton would let you work undercover in this operation if you were using bad blood to contaminate the blood supply or some other terrorist activity. So, I figure you must be selling it to someone who actually wants infected blood for legitimate reasons. Like a medical researcher. Am I right?"

She didn't answer.

Jack nodded, figuring he was right. "Good money in that. I think I saw something on the Internet where some diseased blood can fetch as much as ten thousand dollars a liter on the medical research market."

She focused on the bus across the street. "I'm not talking to you."

"Extremely high margins, I'd say. Especially when the company that collects and sells the blood doesn't even try to comply with the multitude of regulations governing the drawing, handling, storage, shipping, and disposal of blood specimens that, because of their diseased state, technically meet the legal definition of medical waste."

"How do you know we don't comply?"

"I didn't come here without doing my homework."

A low-riding Volvo cruised by, music blasting from the boom box in the truck. Saturday night was starting early.

Jack said, "From the looks of things, I'd say your crew is a lot more interested in appearances than profit. Like every good money-laundering operation."

She looked him in the eye and said, "You have no idea how much money there is in blood."

"My guess is that you sell a whole lot more blood than you ever collect."

"You're a very lucky guesser, Swyteck."

"You produce just enough product to make things look legitimate, but it's a limitless supply of inventory. You create as many sales as you want, no one the wiser. Nice money-laundering operation."

"You're learning a lot more than is healthy for you to know."

"Maybe."

"The irony is, this could really be a good business for someone. All these goons on my crew care about is generating phony invoices to legitimize the cash that washes through our company. With a little effort to collect more specimens, the blood research business could be the most profitable money-laundering operation around."

"Except for viatical settlements," said Jack.

She smiled thinly. "Except for viatical settlements."

Jack crossed his legs, picked at the hole in his old tennis shoe. "Of course, now the million-and-a-half-dollar question is: What's the connection between the two businesses?"

"None. It's just another way of laundering money. Like going into video rentals and opening a Chinese restaurant. No connection, really. Just another sink to wash your dirty money in."

"I think differently."

"Is this another one of your guesses?"

"No. This time it's research."

"A sole practitioner who does research? I'm impressed."

"When I took Jessie's case, I subscribed to an on-line news service about the viatical industry. Kept me right up to date on any development in the industry—trends, lawsuits, whatever."

"And they said something about Jessie?"

"They did, but that's not my point. I've been following it more closely since Jessie's death. What really caught my interest was a recent write-up about a case in Georgia."

"Georgia?"

"A thirty-something-year-old woman had AIDS. They found the West Nile virus in her blood. First documented case in Georgia in decades."

"Not a good thing for someone with a weakened immune system."

"No. But it might be a very good thing for her viatical investors."

"You're being way too suspicious. Viatical settlements are pretty common among AIDS patients."

"Yeah, but this one has a twist. Not only did she have this rare virus, but she was missing three liters of blood."

"She bled to death?"

"No. Somebody took it."

Her look was incredulous. "What?"

"You heard me. Somebody drained three liters of diseased blood from her body and sent her into cardiac arrest."

"And triggered payment under a viatical settlement," she said, finishing his thought for him.

"No one's proved step three yet. That's why I'm here."

"What do you want from me?"

"I want to know about step three."

"You're talking about Georgia, a whole different state."

"We're talking about the Russian *Mafiya*. It's a very small world."

"Look, my plate is full working for Sam Drayton and his task force. I don't have the time or the inclination to be playing Sherlock Holmes for you and your wild-ass theories about some woman in Georgia."

"You need to work with me on this."

"I don't need to do anything with you."

"I can help you."

"How?"

"I know that my friend Theo's been poking around your operation."

"Poking's a good word for it. Like a finger in my eye."

"I don't know exactly what he's up to, or how much danger he's gotten himself into. But I don't want him doing it."

"And neither do I, damn it. Eight months I've been working undercover. I know this blood and viatical stuff inside out, partly from running this hellhole of an operation, but mostly from risking my neck and snooping after hours. All of it's at risk now, thanks to Theo Knight."

"That's what I was afraid of."

"So what are you proposing?"

"Help me out on this Georgia angle. See if my hunch is correct."

"And what's in it for me?"

"I'll get Theo out of your hair, before my big-hearted buddy with the good intentions gets us all in trouble."

She thought for a moment, then said, "I'm not promising I'm going to find anything."

"Do the best you can."

"You're just going to trust me?"

"Yeah. Money laundering is one thing. But I don't think you'd knowingly be involved with a company that's killing off viatical investors."

She paused, as if sizing him up. Then she pulled a pen from her pocket and took Jack's hand. She inked out a phone number as she spoke. "This is another level of snooping, and snooping is dangerous stuff. If you get any inkling that your friend Theo is going to do anything stupid, I want a heads-up in time to get out alive."

Jack checked the number on the back of his hand. "Is this a secure line?"

"No cell is secure. But it's safer than calling me at home or the office, where I can never be sure who's listening. Just keep it to yourself."

"You're just going to trust me?" he said, using her own words.

"Yeah," she said, responding in kind. "Jessie Merrill is one thing. But I don't think you'd knowingly blow your only shot to find out if this company's killing off other viatical investors."

Their eyes met, and Jack felt that an understanding had been reached. She rose and said, "So, exactly how are you going to keep Theo under control?"

"Don't worry. I can take care of Theo Knight."

"That's good," she said. "Because if you don't, I promise you: Someone else will." She started up the sidewalk, then stopped and said, "By the way. Nice outfit."

Jack struck a model's pose, showing off the Goodwill special. "Thanks."

She smiled a little, then continued on toward the blood unit. Jack had a slight bounce in his step as he crossed the street and headed for the Metrorail station, digging his hands deep into his pockets, keeping Katrina's phone number to himself.

It rained on Jack and Cindy's first night in their new house. With no shades or curtains on their windows yet, each bolt of lightning bathed the bedroom with an eerie flash of light. Thunder rattled the windows, seeming to roll right across their roof. A steady drip from the ceiling pattered against the wood floor in the hallway. They had a leak.

Cindy rose in the middle of the night and went to the kitchen. The counter was still cluttered with cardboard boxes, some empty, some yet to be unpacked. She had hoped that her old demons wouldn't follow her to her new house, that she might be able to leave the past behind. But no. The nightmares had come with her.

Lightning flashed across the kitchen. Outside, the falling rain clapped against the patio like unending applause. A river of rainwater gushed from a crease in the roof line, splashing just outside the sliding glass door. The run-off pooled at one end of the patio and rushed in torrents toward a big rectangular planter at the lower end.

Cindy watched from the kitchen window. It was as if the water was being sucked into the deep planter, an opening in the earth from which there was no return. The harder the rain fell, the thirstier the hole seemed to get. There seemed to be no end to the flow into that planter, no limit to what that big, black hole in the ground could hold. It was hypnotic, like nothing she'd ever seen before, except once.

The dark, rainy day on which her father had been buried.

•

Nine-year-old Cindy was at her mother's side, dressed in black, the rain dripping from the edge of the big, black umbrella. Her sister, Celeste, was standing on the other side of her mother. Her grandmother was directly behind them, and Cindy could hear her weeping. Her little brothers were too young and stayed home with relatives. It was a small gathering at graveside, just the four of them and a minister.

"Alan Paige was a righteous man," the minister said, his eulogy ringing hollow in the falling rain. "He was a man who lived by the Scripture."

That was true, Cindy knew. Church every Sunday, a reading from the Bible every night. Her father had only one known vice, a little nickel-and-dime poker game every Tuesday night. Some said it was hypocritical, but Cindy thought it only proved him human. Either way, it hadn't stopped him from leading the charge against the teaching of Darwin's theory of evolution at her school, or from grounding Celeste when she dared to bring home a D. H. Lawrence novel from the public library.

"From dust we come and to dust we return. In Jesus' name we pray, Amen."

The minister gave a nod, and Cindy's mother stepped forward. The cold rain was falling harder, until it seemed that a muddy river was pouring into the open grave. Cindy watched as her tearful mother dropped a single red rose into the dark hole in the earth.

She said a short prayer or perhaps a silent good-bye, and then returned to her daughters. Cindy clung to her, but Celeste stepped toward the grave.

"May I say something?" asked Celeste.

It wasn't part of the program, but the minister rolled with it. "Why, of course you may."

Celeste walked around to the other side of the grave, then looked out over the hole toward her mother, sister, and grandmother.

"Hearing my father eulogized as a man who lived by the Scripture was exactly what I expected. He did know his Scripture, I can say that. I think now is the time for me to share with everyone the part of the Scripture that he often read to his daughters. It's from the Book of Genesis, 19:3, a passage I heard so many times, starting before I could even read, that I've committed it to memory. It's the story of Lot and his two daughters."

Cindy glanced at her mother. The expression on her face had quickly changed from grief-stricken to mortified.

Celeste continued, reciting from memory. " 'Lot and his two daughters left Zoar and lived in a cave. One day the older daughter said to the younger, "Let's get our father to drink wine and then lie with him and preserve our family line through our father." That night they got their father to drink wine, and the older daughter went in and lay with him. The next day the older daughter said to the younger, "Let's get him to drink wine again tonight, and you go in and lie with him so we can preserve our family line through our father." So they got their father to drink wine that night also, and the younger daughter went in and lay with him. So both of Lot's daughters became pregnant by their father.' "

Her voice shook as she finished. The minister stood in stunned silence. Cindy's mother lowered her head in shame. From the hole in the earth, raindrops beat like a drum against her father's casket.

"It's a lie!" shouted Cindy.

No one else said a word.

"You are a *liar*, Celeste! That wasn't the way it was!"

Celeste glared at her younger sister and said, "Tell the truth, Cindy."

Cindy's face flushed with anger, her eyes welling with tears. "It's not true. That's not the way our daddy was."

Celeste didn't budge. She looked at the minister, and then her angry glare moved squarely to their mother. "You know it's true," she said, her eyes like lasers.

All the while, the rain kept falling.

●

Lightning flashed across the kitchen. Cindy was bathed in white light, then stood alone in the darkness.

"Cindy, are you okay?"

She turned to face Jack, but she didn't answer.

He came to her and held her in his arms. "What's wrong?" he asked.

She glanced out the window, one last look at the rainwater rushing across the patio toward the gaping hole in the earth. "Nothing new," she said.

"Come back to bed."

She took his hand and followed him back to the bedroom, ignoring another flash of lightning and one last clap of thunder.

46

.

At nine o'clock Monday morning, twenty-three grand jurors sat in a windowless room one floor below the main courtroom, waiting for the show to begin. Expectations were high. They'd seen the flock of reporters perched outside the grand jury room.

By law, grand jury proceedings were secret, no one allowed in the room but the jurors and the prosecutor. The constitutional theory was that the grand jury would serve as a check on the prosecutor's power. In reality, the prosecutor almost always got the indictment he wanted.

"Good morning," he said, greeting his captive audience.

Jancowitz was smiling, and it was genuine. This was a murder case with stardom written all over it. A sharp criminal defense lawyer in a scandalous love triangle. The victim his former girlfriend. Lots of grisly and salacious details, many of them corroborated by a highly respected physician. This case could be his break-out case, his ticket to the talk-show circuit, and he'd been waiting long enough.

At 9:35 he had his first witness on the stand, sworn and ready to testify.

"Your name, sir?" said Jancowitz.

"Joseph Marsh."

"What is your occupation?"

"I'm a board-certified neurologist."

With just a few well-rehearsed questions he led Dr. Marsh toward pay dirt, establishing him as Jessie Merrill's physician and, of course, laying out the kind of professional credentials that commanded a certain level of respect and instant credibility.

Then he turned to the evidence.

"I have here what has been previously marked as state's Exhibit 11. It is a letter from Jack Swyteck to me. It was written just days after Ms. Merrill's lifeless and naked body was found in a pool of blood in his home."

The prosecutor paused. The location of the body was a theme in his case, one that he gladly allowed the jurors a little extra time to absorb.

He continued, "In Mr. Swyteck's letter, he explains an alleged scam that his client, Jessie Merrill, perpetrated on the investors of a company known as Viatical Solutions, Inc. Dr. Marsh, please take a moment to review this exhibit."

The witness looked it over and said, "I'm familiar with this."

"In the first paragraph, Mr. Swyteck states that, quote, Jessie Merrill admitted to me that she and Dr. Marsh falsified her diagnosis of amyotrophic lateral sclerosis, or ALS. End quote. Dr. Marsh, what was your diagnosis of Ms. Merrill's condition?"

"Based upon the initial tests I performed, my diagnosis was 'clinically possible ALS.' "

"Did you falsify any of the tests that led to that initial diagnosis?"

"Absolutely not."

"Did you later change that diagnosis?"

"After further testing, I concluded that she had lead poisoning. Her symptoms mimicked those of ALS."

"Does that mean your initial diagnosis was incorrect?"

"Not at all. As I said, based upon the tests I conducted, my diagnosis was *possible* ALS."

"Now, Dr. Marsh, I've already explained to the grand jurors what a viatical settlement is. My question to you is this: Were you aware that, based upon your initial diagnosis, Ms. Merrill attempted to sell her life insurance policy to a group of viatical investors?"

"I was."

"Did you at any time mislead those investors as to the nature of her illness?"

"Never. Their reviewing physician did press me for a more firm opinion. I told him that if I had to make a judgment at that particular moment I would probably bet on ALS, but by definition any bet is a risk. It was no sure thing."

"Was there ever any collusion between you and Ms. Merrill in an effort to defraud the viatical investors?"

"Absolutely not."

"Thank you. I refer you again to state's Exhibit 11. In paragraph two, Mr. Swyteck states, quote, on the night before her death, Jessie met me outside my office in Coral Gables. She appeared to be under the influence of drugs. End quote. Dr. Marsh, in the six months that you acted as treating physician for Jessie Merrill, did you ever see any signs of substance abuse?"

"Never."

"Next sentence. Mr. Swyteck states, quote: Ms. Merrill said to me in no uncertain terms that she was in fear for her life. Specifically, she told me that the viatical investors had discovered that she and Dr. Marsh had perpetrated a fraud against them. Ms. Merrill further stated to me that the viatical investors were thugs, not legitimate businesspeople. According to Ms. Merrill, someone acting on behalf of the viatical investors had warned her that she was going to wish she had died of ALS if she did not return the one-and-a-half-million-dollar viatical settlement to the investors. End quote."

Jancowitz gave the jury a moment to digest all that. Then he looked at Dr. Marsh and said, "Are you aware of any threats Ms. Merrill received from anyone acting on behalf of the viatical investors?"

"No, sir. None whatsoever."

"As her alleged coconspirator in this supposed scam, were *you* ever threatened by anyone acting on behalf of the viatical investors?"

"Never."

"Were you ever threatened by *anyone* in connection with this matter?"

"Yes."

"Who?"

"Jack Swyteck."

"Tell me about that."

"After Jessie was found dead in the Swyteck house, I went to his office."

"How did that go?"

"Not well. It took only a few minutes for him to realize that I suspected he had something to do with Jessie's death."

"What happened?"

"He went ballistic. Told me to get my ass out of his office before he batted my head across the room."

"As best you can recall, what exactly were you talking about before he threatened you?"

"As I recall, we were talking about whether he was having an extramarital affair with Jessie Merrill."

"What prompted that discussion?"

"I asked him about it."

"Why?"

Dr. Marsh turned his swivel chair and faced the jury, just the way the prosecutor had coached him earlier in their prep session. "My wife and I are separated and we will soon be divorced. I was . . . vulnerable, I guess you would say. I felt sorry for Jessie and took a special interest in her case. That developed into a friendship, and by the time her lawsuit was over it had blossomed into romance."

"So, when Mr. Swyteck states in his letter that he saw you and Jessie Merrill holding hands in the elevator just minutes after the verdict, that statement is true?"

"That is *not* true. I went over to congratulate her. Mr. Swyteck twisted things around to try to put a sinister spin on the whole episode. That was one of the reasons I went to his office to confront him."

"Do you know why he made that up?"

"In a general sense, yes. Mr. Swyteck was extremely jealous of the relationship between me and Jessie. It was becoming irrational, to the point where he'd accuse her of things like this alleged scam on the viatical investors. Things that never happened."

"Did you ever ask Mr. Swyteck if he and Ms. Merrill were involved in a romantic relationship?"

"Yes, in the conversation in his office, I asked him."

"What was his response?"

"He denied it and became extremely agitated."

"Is that when he threatened to bat your head across the room?"

"No. It's my recollection that he didn't actually threaten me until I asked him point blank whether he had hired someone to kill Jessie Merrill."

Jancowitz checked his notes at the lectern, making sure that he'd set the stage properly for his big finish. "Just a few more questions, Dr. Marsh. You testified that you are *not* aware of any threats that Jessie Merrill may have received from anyone acting on behalf of the viatical investors."

"That's correct."

"Are you aware of any threats that she received from anyone other than the investors?"

"Yes."

"How did you become aware of those threats?"

"We talked on the telephone after it happened. She told me."

"What was the nature of those threats?"

"She was told that if she said or did anything to tarnish the name and reputation of Jack Swyteck, there would be hell to pay."

"Did she tell you who conveyed that threat to her?"

He leaned closer to the microphone and said, "Yes. A man by the name of Theo Knight."

The prosecutor struggled to contain his excitement. It wasn't the whole story, but it was more than enough at this stage of the game. "Thank you, Dr. Marsh. No further questions at this time."

47

.

Vladimir had a business meeting at "the club," a generic term that lent the place much more dignity than it deserved. The actual name on the marquee was "Bare-ly Eighteen," a strip joint where any middle-aged man with ten bucks and an aching hard-on could watch recent high school dropouts dance naked on tables. No jail bait, but not a single dancer over the age of nineteen, guaranteed. Of course, if *60 Minutes* ever called, the girls were all honor students in premed who simply liked to dance naked for extra money.

Vladimir knew the truth, which was why he never showed up at the club with less than a pocketful of ecstasy pills, a wildly popular, synthetic club-drug that acted both as a stimulant and a hallucinogen. The distribution pipeline was largely European, so Russian organized crime had found huge profit in it. Each aspirin-sized tablet was manufactured in places like the Netherlands at a cost of two to five cents and then sold primarily in the over-eighteen clubs for twenty-five to forty bucks a pop. A girl—*any* girl, not just a stripper—could go nonstop for eight hours on one pill, dancing, thrusting, craving the caress of strangers. At his cost and with those kinds of results, Vladimir was happy to give it away to his own dancers, especially when he had guests to impress.

He handed the bag of pills to the bouncer at the entrance. "One for each girl," he said, then pointed with a glance toward the double-D blonde on stage showing off her tan lines. She had a pacifier in her mouth, a telltale sign that she was already on ecstasy. The drug sometimes made users bite their own lips and tongue, and a pacifier was a curious but commonly accepted way of preventing that. In a strip club, it had the added bonus of making it look as though she really loved to suck.

"Give her two," said Vladimir.

"Yes, sir." The guy was a brute, and no one but Vladimir was ever a "sir."

Vladimir had with him two men dressed in expensive silk suits. One was big and barrel-chested, with a neck like a former Olympic wrestler's. The other was shorter and overweight with the round, red face of a Russian peasant who'd somehow found money. Vladimir led them through the lounge area, a circuitous route to his usual booth in the back. It gave them a chance to enjoy the scenery before turning to business. The bar was basically a dark, open warehouse with neon figures on the walls and colored spotlights suspended from the ceiling to highlight each dancer. Young, naked flesh was everywhere, surrounded by men who coughed up the cash to gawk, talk, laugh, and shout at women as if they owned them. A numbing sound system drowned out most of the obscenities, blasting the perennial bad-girl anthem, the old Robert Palmer hit "Addicted to Love."

At the snap of his fingers, Vladimir's two hottest dancers hopped off nearby tables and assumed new posts at the brass firehouse pole closer to his booth. Vladimir sat with his back to the stage, facing a mirrored wall of cheap thrills. His guests sat across from him with an unobstructed view of the show. As if the girls cared or would even remember, he introduced his guests. The wrestler's name was Leonid, a Brighton Beach businessman whose business was best left unexplained, though it was pretty common knowledge around the club that Miami was second only to Brighton Beach in terms of number and organization of Russian *Mafiya*. The short guy was Sasha, a banker from Cyprus.

"Where's Cyprus?" asked the Latina girl. She had the habit of running the tip of her tongue across her front teeth, which could have been the ecstasy. Or perhaps her braces had just been removed and she liked the smooth sensation.

"It's an island in the eastern Mediterranean," Sasha said.

"A suburb of Moscow," said Vladimir.

She licked her teeth and kept dancing, having no way of knowing what Vladimir really meant. Cypriot bankers laundered so much money for the Russian mob that the city of Limasol might as well have been a suburb of Moscow.

A topless barmaid with a gold ring through her left nipple brought them a bottle of ice-cold vodka and poured three shots. The bottle was gone in short order, and halfway through the second Vladimir steered the conversation toward business, speaking in Russian.

"You like my club?" he asked.

His guests couldn't take their eyes off the girl in the long, red wig swinging naked on the pole.

Vladimir said, "I have to run this joint seven days a week for an entire month to clean the amount of cash I can wash in a single viatical settlement."

Leonid from Brighton Beach shot him a steely look. "We didn't come here to talk viatical settlements. That's off the table."

"I just don't understand why."

The banker raised his hands, as if refereeing. "Let's not go down that road. The fact is that Brighton Beach was planning to flush ten million dollars a month through viatical settlements for the foreseeable future. That option is no longer attractive. So all we want to know, Vladimir, is this: What alternative are you offering?"

He sipped his vodka. "The blood bank is coming along."

"Ha!" said the wrestler. "What a joke."

"It's not a joke. It's on the verge of taking off."

"Will never work. You can't possibly do enough volume to wash ten million dollars a month."

"How would you know?"

"The best money-laundering operations have some amount of legitimate business. You have two stinking vans. You can't even draw enough blood off the street to fill the handful of orders you get each week."

"We've filled every single order."

"Yeah. And you had to take blood from cadavers to do it."

The banker grimaced. "You took blood from cadavers?"

Vladimir was smoldering.

"Tell him," said the wrestler.

"It's not important."

"Then I'll tell him. We had a woman in Georgia with a two-million-dollar viatical settlement. AIDS patient. Should have been dead three years ago, so the order went out to expedite her expiration. Vladimir farmed out the job to some joker who injected her with a bizarre virus, which is a whole problem by itself. But to make matters worse, he took three liters of blood from her."

"Is that true, Vladimir?"

He belted back the last of his vodka, then poured himself a refill. "Who would have thought they'd notice?"

"Ever heard of an autopsy, you idiot?" said the wrestler.

"It was an honest mistake. Why leave perfectly good AIDS-infected blood in a dead body when you can sell it for good profit?"

"It's that kind of small-time, foolish greed that makes it impossible for us to do business with you people in Miami."

"So this is why Brighton Beach canceled the viatical contract?" said Vladimir.

"Your man shot her up with a virus so rare that the National Center for Disease Control has her blood under the microscope. And then he took three liters of her blood with him. Why not just paint a big red 'M' on your chest that stands for 'murderer'? You're going to get us all caught."

"So you admit it. One mistake in the whole arrangement, and the hot shots in Brighton Beach think they can just walk away from our deal."

"We don't have to explain ourselves to you people.

The decision was made, and it was blessed at a high level. End of story."

"It's not the end of it," Vladimir said as he pounded the table with his fist. "We put a lot of time into this viatical deal. Things are in place. And you just think you can pull the plug, see ya later?"

"We have good reasons."

"None that I've heard."

"I've said all I'm going to say."

"Then fuck you!" said Vladimir as he threw a glass of vodka in his guest's face.

The wrestler lunged across the table. Dancers screamed and ran for it as the banker ducked to the floor. Three huge bouncers were all over the wrestler before he could get a hand on Vladimir.

The wrestler was red-faced, eyes bulging. But the bouncers had both his arms pinned behind his back.

"This is the way you treat your guests?" he said, huffing. "I was *invited* here."

"And now you're invited to leave." Vladimir jerked his head, a signal to his boys. "Throw his ass out."

The wrestler cursed nonstop in Russian and at the top of his lungs as the bouncers put the strong-arm on him and dragged him away.

The banker peered out from under the table.

"You too, Sasha. Beat it."

The little man scurried away like a frightened rabbit.

The barmaid immediately replaced the spilled bottle of vodka. Vladimir refilled his drink, and with a snap of his fingers the dancers resumed their posts at the brass poles, backs arched, breasts out, hair flying. The music had never stopped, and the scuffle was over.

Or maybe it had just begun.

Either way, the girls kept right on dancing.

48

·

Jack watched the six-o'clock evening news from the couch in his living room. Cindy was right beside him, their fingers interlaced. She was squeezing so hard it almost hurt, and Jack wasn't sure if it was a sign of support or anger.

Rumors of an impending indictment had been flying all afternoon, and in a competitive news market where a story just wasn't a story unless "You heard it here first," the media was all over it.

A silver-haired anchorman looked straight at him as the obligatory graphic of the scales of justice appeared behind him on the screen. "A former girlfriend is dead, and a questionable million-and-a-half-dollar deal is under scrutiny by a Florida grand jury. Jack Swyteck, son of Florida's former governor Harold Swyteck, may be in trouble with the law again."

"Why do they have to do that?" said Cindy.

"They always have." His entire life, any time he'd

gotten into trouble, he was always "Jack Swyteck, son of Harold Swyteck."

Trumpets blared and drums beat, the usual fanfare for the *Action News* opening.

"Good evening," the newsman continued. "We first brought you this exclusive story several weeks ago, when the dead body of thirty-one-year-old Jessie Merrill was found in the home of prominent Miami attorney Jack Swyteck. At first blush her death appeared to be suicide, but now prosecutors aren't so sure. *Action News* reporter Heather Brown is live outside the Metro-Dade Justice Center. Heather, what's the latest?"

The screen flashed to a perfectly put-together young woman standing in a parking lot at dusk. The Justice Center was visible in the distant background, and a half-dozen teenage boys wearing bulky gang clothing, thick gold chains, and backward Nike caps, were gyrating behind her, as if *that* added credibility to her live report. Long strands of black hair slapped at her face like a bullwhip. She'd obviously committed the cardinal rookie mistake of positioning her roving camera crew downwind.

"Steve, sources close to this investigation have told *Action News* that a grand jury has been looking into the death of Jessie Merrill for some time now. Information obtained exclusively by *Action News* indicates that Miami-Dade prosecutor Benno Jancowitz has presented to the grand jury something that one source calls substantial evidence that Ms. Merrill's death was not suicide but homicide. This source went on to tell us that indictments could come down at any time now."

The anchorman jumped in. "Is there any indication who may be charged and what the charges may be?"

"That information has yet to be released. But again,

the operative word here is 'indictments,' plural, not just the indictment of a single suspect. Sources tell us that this could turn into a case of alleged murder-for-hire. Right now, the spotlight is on Jack Swyteck and his former client, Theo Knight. Mr. Knight has a long criminal record and even spent four years on Florida's death row for the murder of a nineteen-year-old convenience store clerk before being released on a legal technicality."

"Technicality?" said Jack, groaning. "The man was innocent."

Cindy gave him a soulful look, as if she fully understood the telling nature of the media's negative spin on Theo's belated vindication. It would probably be the same for Jack. In the court of public opinion, it didn't matter what happened from here on out. The stigma would always be there.

Jack switched stations and caught the tail end of the anchorwoman's report on *Eyewitness News*: "Repeated calls to Mr. Swyteck this afternoon went unanswered, but I understand that *Eyewitness News* reporter Peter Rollings has just managed to catch up with his famous father, former Florida governor Harold Swyteck, on Ajax Mountain in Aspen, Colorado, where he and the former first lady are enjoying a ski vacation."

"What the heck?" said Jack.

The screen flashed to a snow-covered man on the side of a steep mountain. It was a blizzard, nearly white-out conditions. Jack watched his father stumble off the chair lift, practically assaulted by some guy in a ski mask who was chasing him with a microphone.

"Governor! Governor Swyteck!"

Harry Swyteck looked back, obviously confused, one ski in the air in a momentary loss of balance, poles flailing like a broken windmill. He finally caught his balance, and momentum carried him down the slope.

The shivering reporter looked back toward the camera and said, "Well, looks like the former governor won't speak to us, either."

Jack hit the OFF button. "I can't watch this."

The phone rang. For an instant, Jack was sure that his father was calling from deep in some snow bank to ask "What the hell did you do this time, son?" The Caller ID display told him otherwise. Jack hadn't been answering all afternoon, but this time it was Rosa.

"Well, the wolves are out," she said.

"I saw."

"Your old man should take up hot-dog skiing. He must have skidded at least fifty yards on one ski before sailing down that mountain."

"That's not funny."

"None of this is. That's why I called. I want to meet with both you and Theo. Tonight."

"Where?"

"I'm home already, so let's do it here."

"How soon?"

"As soon as you can get your buddy over here. We need to get to Theo before the prosecutor does."

"You don't seriously think that Theo would cut a deal with Jancowitz, do you?"

"You just heard the news as plainly as I did. Theo is targeted as the gunman in a murder-for-hire scheme. It's standard operating procedure for a prosecutor in a case like this: You get the gunman to flip in order to nail the guy who hired him."

"I agree that we should meet, but you need to understand. I didn't hire Theo to do anything. And even if I had, Theo would never testify against me. I'm the guy who got him off death row."

"Let me ask you something, Jack. How many years did Theo spend on death row?"

"Four."

"Now answer me this: You think he wants to go back?"

Jack paused, and he didn't like the direction his thoughts were taking him. "I'll see you in an hour. Theo and I both will be there. Together. I guarantee it."

49

•

Katrina picked at the peas in her microwaved-dinner tray. The evening news had drifted into the weather segment, but she was still pondering the lead story. Two things were clear to her. The indictments were a foregone conclusion. And the timing of the leaks had a funny smell to them. She pushed away from the kitchen table and grabbed her car keys.

It was time to call Sam Drayton.

Rarely did she make a call directly to the lead prosecutor, but this was no time to get caught up in Justice Department bureaucracy. In less than five minutes she reached the 7-Eleven on Bird Road. She jumped out of her car, hurried past the homeless guy sleeping on the curb, and called Drayton from the outside pay phone.

"Moon over Miami," she said into the telephone. It was the code phrase that would immediately convey to him that she was talking of her own free will, not with a mobster's gun to her head.

"What's up, Katrina?"

"Swyteck and his friend Theo are all over the local news tonight. Story has it that they're going to be indicted in a murder-for-hire scheme."

"Is that so?"

"As if you didn't know."

"I'm in Virginia. How would I know?"

The homeless guy had his hand out. Katrina gave him a quarter and waved him away. "Look, if Swyteck and his friend are going to be indicted, that's fine. That's the way the system works. But these leaks aren't fair."

"I can't control what comes out of the state attorney's office."

"Like hell. You asked Jancowitz to leak it, didn't you?"

"Grand-jury investigations are secret by law. That's a pretty serious accusation."

"Two days ago, after Swyteck paid me a visit at the blood unit, I called and told you I needed him and Theo Knight out of my hair. Suddenly it's all over the news that they're about to be indicted in a murder conspiracy. You expect me to believe that a leak like that one is just a coincidence?"

"Totally."

"Stop being cute. Swyteck's bad enough. But do you know what it means to a guy like Theo Knight to have the word on the street that he's a grand-jury target on a murder charge?"

"I told you, I can't control what Jancowitz does."

"Don't you understand? Theo sat across the table from my boss at the Brown Bear and talked viatical business. He made it clear that he's figured out the money-laundering scheme. Vladimir isn't going to let a guy like that just sit around peacefully under the threat of an indictment. He'll put a bullet in his brain before he can cut a deal with the prosecutor and tell everything he knows about the money-laundering operation."

"I can't control what the Russian mob does."

"Is that all you can say, that everything's out of your control?"

"I can't control the things I can't control."

"Then maybe you can't control me, either."

"Watch yourself, Katrina. Don't bite the hand that feeds you."

"You've got nothing on me. I went to the U.S. attorney's office the minute I discovered that my employer might be doing something illegal. I volunteered for this undercover work because I wanted to nail these bastards worse than you did."

"Ah, yes. Katrina the Whistleblower."

"It's true. I was squeaky clean coming in."

"You're not squeaky clean anymore, honey. You turn against me, I'll turn against you. As far as I'm concerned, you've been part of an illegal operation for the past eight months."

"You son of a bitch. You just see this as a cost of doing business, don't you? If someone gets in your way, you just push them aside for good."

"I'm simply trying to preserve the integrity of an eight-month investigation that has cost the U.S. government over a million dollars."

"And a bullet in the back of Theo Knight's head is a small price to pay. Is that it?"

"Listen, lady. We wouldn't be in this mess in the first place if you hadn't fumbled around in the dark and picked up the wrong cell phone."

"Actually, we wouldn't be in this mess if you hadn't told me to beat the holy crap out of Jack Swyteck for treading too close to your blessed investigation."

"I never told you to do that."

"Maybe not in so many words. But I told you that Vladimir was going to make me prove myself somehow, and you said go ahead and do what I had to do. I'll stick to that story until the day I die."

Silence fell over the line, then Drayton finally spoke. "I'm warning you, Katrina. Don't you dare do anything stupid."

"Don't worry. If I do, you'll be the last to know." She hung up the phone and returned to her car.

50

Jack picked up Theo from Sparky's, and the two of them reached Rosa's house in Coco Plum around eight o'clock. Hers was typical for the neighborhood, a thirteen-thousand-square-foot, multilevel, completely renovated, Mediterranean-style quasi hotel with a pool, a boat, and drop-dead views of the water.

"Nice digs," said Theo as they stepped down from Jack's car.

"Yeah. If you like this sort of overindulgence."

"Spoken like a true have-not."

They climbed thirty-eight steps to the front door but didn't have to knock. Rosa spotted them in the security cameras. She greeted them at the door and then led them to her home office, a term that struck Jack as especially meaningful, as this particular office did seem larger than the average home.

Rosa's former law partner was already inside waiting for them. Jack knew Rick Thompson. They shook hands, and he introduced himself to Theo. Then Rosa explained his presence.

"I invited Rick because it seems appropriate for Theo to have his own lawyer. From what we've heard so far, you two may end up being codefendants on a conspiracy charge."

Rick said, "You never want alleged coconspirators to be represented by one lawyer. It tends to reinforce the idea of a conspiracy."

"I agree with that," said Jack.

"Sounds good to me, too," said Theo. "Except I doubt I can afford my own lawyer."

Rosa said, "No problem. Jack will pay for it."

Jack did a double take, but before he could say anything, Theo slapped him on the back and said, "Thanks, buddy."

"You're welcome," was all he could say.

Jack and Theo seated themselves in the armchairs on one side of the square coffee table in the center of the room. Rick sat on the leather couch. Rosa stood off to the side as her housekeeper brought pitchers of iced tea and water on a silverplated tray. Jack glanced discreetly at his lawyer and caught her taking in a long, meditative eyeful of the framed work of art that hung behind her desk. It was a contemporary piece by the late Cuban-born artist Felix Gonzalez-Torres, a renowned boundary-buster who was best known for ephemeral pieces made of candies or printed paper that visitors could touch or even take home with them. Rosa liked to call her little share of Felix "the stress-buster," as it calmed her just to look at it. Jack wasn't sure if the magic flowed from the innate beauty of the work or from the sheer joy of having acquired it long before the artist died and his work started selling at Christie's for seven figures.

When the housekeeper was gone, Rosa turned to

face her guests. Her expression was noticeably more relaxed, as if Felix the Artist had done his job, but her delivery was still quite serious. "I'm told we could see target letters as early as tomorrow, indictments by the end of the week. Two defendants, one basic charge: Murder for hire."

Theo said, "I heard that on the news two hours ago. You sure you're getting your money's worth here, Jacko?"

"Just listen."

Rosa continued, "It's important for us all to agree that anything we say in this room is privileged. This is one setting in which it's worth stating the obvious. This is all joint defense."

"Of course," said Jack.

"Theo?" asked Rosa.

"Whatever Jack says."

"Wrong answer," said Rick. "Jack's not your lawyer. I am."

"Like I said. Whatever Jack says."

Rick grumbled. "I can't represent someone under those circumstances."

Jack looked at his friend and said, "You have to listen to your own lawyer. Not Rosa, and not even me. Those are the rules."

"If you say so."

"Good," said Rosa. "Now that that's settled, let's talk turkey. Rick, tell Jack and Theo what you found out."

Rick scooted to the edge of his chair, as if sharing a national-security secret. "Dr. Marsh is represented by Hugo Zamora. I know Hugo pretty well, pretty good guy. I called him up and just asked him point-blank, hey, what did your client tell the grand jury?"

"I thought grand-jury testimony was secret," said Theo.

"It is, in the sense that grand jurors and the prosecutor can't divulge it. But a witness can disclose his own testimony, which means that his lawyer can, too."

Jack asked, "What did Hugo tell you?"

"The most important thing has to do with Dr. Marsh's testimony about the threats against Jessie Merrill. Marsh did testify that Jessie was in fact threatened before her death."

"That's fantastic," said Jack. "That corroborates exactly what I've been saying all along. The viatical investors threatened her."

"Not exactly."

"What do you mean?"

"Marsh didn't say that it was the viatical investors who threatened Jessie. He said it was Theo."

"Theo? What kind of crock is that?"

Rick continued. "Marsh claims that Theo met with Jessie the night before she died and told her straight out that if she said or did anything to hurt Jack Swyteck, there would be hell to pay."

Jack popped from his chair, paced across the room angrily. "That is so ridiculous. The man is a pathological liar. The very idea that Theo would go to Jessie and threaten her like that is . . . well, you tell him, Theo. That's crazy."

All eyes were on Theo, who was noticeably silent.

"Theo?"

Finally, he looked Jack in the eye and said, "You remember that night we met in Tobacco Road?"

"Yeah. You were playing the sax that night."

"And you said Jessie Merrill admitted to the scam but told you to back off or she'd tell the world that you were part of it, too. You were all upset because she and her doctor boyfriend were so damn smug.

And so I says maybe we should threaten her right back. Remember?"

"What are you telling me, Theo?"

A pained expression came over his face. "I was just trying to scare her, that's all. Just get her and Swampy to back down and realize they can't push my friend Jack Swyteck around."

Jack felt chills. "So what did you do?"

"That's enough," said Rick.

Theo stopped, startled by the interruption. His lawyer continued, "This discussion is taking a completely different track from what I expected. As Theo's lawyer, I say this meeting's over. Theo, don't say another word."

"Theo, come on, now," said Jack.

"I said that's enough," said Rick. "I don't care if you are his friend. I won't stand for anyone pressuring my client into saying something against his own best interest. You told him to listen to his lawyer, not to you or to Rosa. At least play by your own rules."

"Let them go," said Rosa.

Theo rose and said, "We'll get this straightened out, man. Don't worry."

Jack nodded, but it wasn't very convincing. "We'll talk."

Rick handed Jack a business card and said, "Only if I'm present. Theo has counsel now, and you talk to him through me. Those are the *new* rules."

Jack could only watch in silence as Theo and his new lawyer turned and walked out, together.

51

.

Katrina switched on the lights at 8:00 A.M. As usual, she was the first to reach the combined offices of Viatical Solutions and Bio-Research, Inc. That hour to herself before nine o'clock was always the best time to get work done.

And it was the best time to snoop.

She walked by her work station in the back, past the filing cabinets, and down the hall to Vladimir's office. The door was locked, but a little finesse and a duplicate key solved that problem. She was sure she was alone, but it still gave her butterflies to turn the knob and open the door.

Over the past eight months she'd had her share of close calls. Rifling through the files of a money-laundering operation was dangerous work. Sam Drayton was a prick, and she hadn't gone undercover with any illusion that the U.S. government would bail her out of trouble. Truth be told, she'd gotten everything she'd wanted from the feds, which was nothing more than a chance to get inside the Russian mob without risk of going to jail. Katrina had her own agenda, and she was closer than ever to reaching it—at least until Theo Knight had come along. With him sticking his nose where it didn't belong, time was truly of the essence.

She walked carefully around Vladimir's massive desk to the computer on his credenza. It had taken nearly sixteen weeks of casual conversations about his mother's birthday, his dog's name, his old street-number in Moscow, but finally she'd cracked his password.

She typed it once on the blue screen, then again at the prompt: KAMIKAZE.

It stood for "Kamikaze Club," a Moscow bar where Russian mobsters used to gather with their well-dressed mistresses to get smashed on vodka and bet on the fights. Young men were pulled off the streets, thrown into the ring, and ordered to slug it out with their bare hands. Only one would walk out alive. The loser ended up in a landfill, eyes gouged out, jaw torn off. After five impressive victories, Vladimir earned himself a job as a bodyguard for a *vor v zakone,* "thief in law," the highest order of made men in the *Mafiya.*

Katrina logged on to his Internet server and scrolled down the e-mails he'd sent over the last week. She recognized the usual money-laundering contacts, but this morning her focus was on that shipment of blood to Sydney. The buyers had requested a specimen from an AIDS-infected white female, but the only blood in their vault was typical of junkies, filled not just with AIDS but also hepatitis, and any number of parasites and street illnesses that made their blood unsuitable for strict AIDS research. Somehow, Vladimir had come up with three liters of AIDS-infected blood from an otherwise clean source.

Only then did Swyteck's theory about that woman in Georgia seem not so cockeyed.

The fifth e-mail confirmed it. The message was to an investor in Brighton Beach, written in Vladimir's typical bare-bones style, the less said, the better. "Insurer: Northeastern Life and Casualty. Policy Number: 1138–55-A. Benefit: $2,500,000. Decedent: Jody Falder, Macon, Georgia. Maturity date . . ."

The date chilled her. All within a matter of days, Vladimir had fresh, AIDS-infected blood to ship to Sydney, and his viatical investors were in line for a big payday. It hardly seemed coincidental.

Swyteck was right. *This isn't just about money laundering anymore.*

A door slammed, and her heart skipped a beat. It was the main entrance, and she was no longer alone. She switched off the computer, ran to Vladimir's office door, and fumbled for her key.

A man was singing to himself in the kitchen, fixing himself a morning coffee.

Vladimir! Her hand was shaking too much to insert the key and lock the door.

"That you, Katrina?" he said, calling from the kitchen.

His voice startled her, but on her fifth frantic attempt at the lock she felt the tumblers fall into place. She thanked God, hurried down the hallway, and forced herself to smile as she entered the kitchen. "Good morning."

"Coffee?" he asked.

"No, thanks. I had some invoicing work to do." She could have kicked herself. He hadn't even expressed any surprise at seeing her, and she was already offering some knee-jerk justification for being in the office a little early.

"Good." He sipped his coffee. It was so strong, the aroma nearly overwhelmed her from across the room. Then he stepped toward her and said, "Let's you and me take a walk."

The words chilled her. She'd known Vladimir to take many a walk with employees and even a few customers. None of them ever came back smiling.

"Sure."

He grabbed his briefcase, took it with him.

This is it, she thought. Although she'd never been caught snooping, the scenarios had played out in her mind many times. Never did it turn out well for her. Vladimir didn't take chances with a suspected *musor*.

He led her out the back door, the warehouse entrance. It was a hot, sunny morning, and the smell of baked asphalt-sealant stung her nostrils. They crossed the parking lot and walked side by side beneath the black-olive trees that lined the sidewalk, heading toward the discount gasoline station and the perpetual roar of I-95. Rush-hour traffic clogged all eight lanes on Pembroke Pines Boulevard.

"I've been thinking about your friend Theo."

She caught her breath, relieved to hear that someone else was on his mind. "I figured."

"The three of us talked openly at the Brown Bear."

"Of course. Talk among friends."

"He seemed to have the viatical settlements all figured out."

"He's a pretty smart guy."

"Yuri thinks maybe he's not so smart. He thinks maybe you told him something."

"I told him nothing."

Vladimir stopped. The traffic light changed and a stream of cars and huge tractor trucks raced toward the

I-95 on ramp. "I believe you," he said. "But Yuri has his questions. So there is some repair work that needs to be done there."

"Repair work?"

"Rebuilding of trust."

"Vladimir, I've worked here like a dog for eight months. Guys come and go all the time. But I'm right here at your side, day in and day out."

"I know. That's why I don't want you to look at this as a test of your loyalty. Think of it as an opportunity to prove yourself worthy of advancement."

"What are you asking me to do?"

"Your friend Theo got himself in some serious trouble."

"I know. I saw the news last night."

"So we both know this prosecutor is going to lean hard on him."

"Theo's no *musor*."

"I wish I could believe that. But the good ol' days are gone. No more honor among thieves, the old code of silence. These days, people get caught, they talk. We can't risk Theo cutting a deal and telling that prosecutor what we talked about at the Brown Bear. Hell, I think I even mentioned Yuri and Fate by name."

Katrina knew this was coming. She'd even shared those exact fears with Drayton. "Like I said, what are you asking me to do?"

He lit a cigarette, then flipped his lighter shut. But he just looked at her, saying nothing.

"Please. Theo is my friend. Don't ask me to be part of any setup."

He took a long drag, exhaled. "All the time you've worked here, I've never once so much as seen you hold a gun."

"Never had a need to."

"Seems like a waste. Two years in the U.S. Marines, you must be a decent shot."

"Sure, I can shoot."

He handed her his briefcase. "Take it."

She hesitated, knowing full well what was inside.

He narrowed his eyes and said, "Friend or no, Theo has to go. And the job is yours."

"You . . . you want me to take out my friend?"

"We've all taken out friends. We make new ones."

She couldn't speak.

"Is there a problem?" he asked.

She fought to keep her composure, then took the briefcase and said, "No. None at all."

He put his arm around her, and they started back to the office. "This is a good move for you. An important step. I can feel it."

With each footfall, the briefcase seemed to get heavier in her hand. "I feel it, too," she said.

Katrina was crouched low behind the driver's seat of a Volkswagen Jetta, waiting. The floor mats smelled of spilled beers, and the upholstery bore telltale burn marks of many a dropped joint. She was dressed entirely in black, and with a push of a button the green numbers on her wristwatch glowed in the darkness.

One-fifty A.M., just ten minutes till the end of Theo's bartending shift at Sparky's.

Laughter in the parking lot forced her closer to the floor. A typical ending to another "Ladies' Night," a totally drunk chick and three horny guys offering to drive her home. *Their* home. It was almost enough to make Katrina jump from the car and spring for cab fare, but she didn't dare give herself away.

She had a job to do.

From her very first meeting with Vladimir, she'd decided that if it ever came down to a situation of either her or someone else, someone else would get it. But she'd always thought that the "someone else" would be another mob guy. She hadn't figured on someone like Theo.

A rumbling noise rolled across the parking lot. Katrina could feel the vibration in the floor board. A moment later, diesel fumes were seeping in through the small opening in the passenger side window. She lifted her head just enough to see a huge tractor trailer parked two spaces down. The motor was running, and the fumes kept coming. But the driver was nowhere to be seen. The odor was making her nauseous. She had the sickening sensation that the truck wasn't going anywhere soon, that the driver had simply climbed inside and started the engine to sleep off his liquor in the comfort of an air-conditioned rig.

The fumes thickened, and she could almost taste the soot in her mouth. A dizzying sensation buzzed through her brain. The noise, the odor, the steady vibration—it all had her desperate for a breath of fresh air, but she forced herself to stay put. The very act of telling herself to tough it out and stay alert was eerily reminiscent of her life in Prague, not the beautiful old city as a whole but the noisy textile mill where she'd worked more than a decade earlier.

Back when her name was Elena, not Katrina.

There, in an old factory that still bore the scars of Hitler's bombs, the oldest machines ran on diesel fuel, not electricity. The engines were right outside the windows, and even in the dead of winter, enough fumes seeped in through cracks and crevices to give Katrina and her Cuban coworkers chronic coughs, headaches, and dizzy spells. It was just one more hazard in a fourteen-hour workday, six days a week. Katrina had often pushed herself to the verge of blacking out, but the fear of falling perilously onto one of the giant looms around her kept her on her feet. Safety guards and emergency shut-offs were nonexistent, and the machines were unforgiving. Hers was one of the newer ones, about thirty years old. The one beside her was much older, predating the Second World War and constantly breaking down. Each minute, countless meters of thread fed through the giant moving arms. At that rate, you didn't want to be anywhere near one of those dinosaurs when it popped, and you could only hope to find the energy to duck when a loosened bolt or broken hunk of metal came flying out like shrapnel.

Katrina had prayed for the safety of her coworkers, but she also thanked the Lord that she wasn't the poor soul working one of those man-eaters. Years later, she still felt guilty about that. One nightmare, in particular, still haunted her. Never would she forget what happened on that cold night in January when machine number eight turned against its master, when her name was still Elena.

•

A loud pop rattled the factory windows, rising above the steady drone of machinery. Instinctively, Elena dived to the floor. One by one, the machines shut down like falling dominoes. A wave of silence fell over the factory, save for the pathetic screams and groans emerging from somewhere behind machine number eight, a tortured soul with a frighteningly familiar voice.

Elena raced across the factory, pushed her way through the small gathering of workers around the accident, and then gasped at the sight. "Beatriz!"

She and her best friend Beatriz had joined Castro's Eastern Bloc work program together, with plans to defect at the first opportunity. Each had pledged never to leave without the other.

Elena went to her, but Beatriz lay motionless on her side, a thick pool of blood encircling her head. She checked the pulse and found none. She tried to roll Beatriz onto her back, then froze. The left side of her face was gone. A sharp hunk of metal protruded from her shattered eye socket.

"My God, Beatriz!"

The ensuing moments were a blur, her own cries of anguish merging with the memory of Beatriz's painful screams. Tears flowed, and words came in incoherent spurts. Beatriz never moved. Kneeling at her side, Elena lowered her head and sobbed, only to be ripped away by a team of men with a stretcher.

"It's too late for that," she heard someone say. But the men rolled the body onto the stretcher anyway, then hurried for the exit.

Elena followed right behind them, through a maze of machinery, passing one stunned worker after another. The doors flew open, and a blast of cold, winter air pelted her face. They put Beatriz in the back of a van, still on the stretcher. Elena tried to get in with her, but the doors slammed in her face. The tires spun on the icy pavement, then finally found traction. Elena stood ankle-deep in dirty snow as the van pulled away.

In her heart she knew that this was the last she'd see of Beatriz.

She couldn't move. It was well below freezing, but she was oblivious to the elements. Half a block away she spotted a police car parked at the curb. It seemed like a sign, Beatriz whisked away in an ambulance right past the police. It was time for someone in a position of authority to see the deplorable conditions they worked under.

On impulse, she ran down the icy sidewalk and knocked on the passenger-side window. The officer rolled down the window and said something she didn't understand.

"Come see," she said, but her command of the language was still very basic. "The factory. Come see."

He gave her a confused look. His reply was completely unintelligible, a dialect she'd never heard before. She'd learned Russian as a schoolgirl in Cuba, but there was surprisingly little crossover to Czech.

"What are you doing, girl?"

She turned and saw her foreman. He was a stocky, muscular man with extraordinarily bad teeth for someone as young as he was.

"Leave me alone. I want him to see what happened."

He said something to the cop that made him laugh. Then he grabbed Elena by the arm and started back toward the factory.

"Let go of me!"

"Are you stupid? The police can't help you."

"Then I'll talk to someone else."

"Yes, I know you will. We're going to see the boss man right now." His grip tightened on her arm till it hurt. He took her down a dark alley that ran alongside the factory. The pavers were frozen over with spilled sludge and dirty run-off from the roofs, and about every third step her feet slipped out from under her. At the end of the alley were two glowing orange dots, which finally revealed themselves as the taillights of a Renault.

Her foreman opened the door, shoved Elena in the back seat, climbed in beside her, and closed the door. The motor was running, and a driver was behind the wheel in the front seat.

"This is her," said the foreman.

"Hello, Elena," the driver said.

It was dark inside, and from the back seat she could see only the back of his head. "Hello."

"I heard there was an accident with your friend. I came as soon as I could."

"What do you care?"

They made eye contact in the rearview mirror, but she could see only his eyes. "Do you think it makes me happy when someone gets hurt in my factory?"

Elena didn't answer, though she was taken aback to realize that she was talking to the owner of the factory.

"Listen to me," he said. "I know it's dangerous in there."

"Then why don't you fix it?"

"Because that's the way it's always been."

"And you can't do anything about it?"

"I can't. But you can."

"Me?"

"You can make things safer, at least for yourself."

"I don't understand."

"It's very simple. This is a big factory. There are many jobs. Some are dangerous. Some are very dangerous. Some are not dangerous at all."

"Seems to me that the women are always getting the most dangerous jobs."

"Not all women. Some get the dangerous jobs, some get the not-so-dangerous jobs. It all depends."

"On what?"

"On which part of your body you want to sacrifice."

"What is that supposed to mean?"

"Machine number eight should be up and running in a day or two. You'll be taking over Beatriz's spot."

"What?"

He shrugged, as if it were none of his doing. "Or I suppose I could tell your foreman to assign it to somebody else. It's up to you."

"What choice are you giving me?"

He turned partly around, as if to look at her, but his face was blocked by the headrest. He spoke in a low serious voice that chilled her. "Everything happens for a reason. No decision is meaningless. We all determine our own fate."

"Like Beatriz?"

"Like you. And like hundreds of other girls much smarter than your friend."

She could have smashed his face in, but an Eastern Bloc prison was no place for an eighteen-year-old girl from Cuba.

"Sleep on it," he said. "But we need your answer."

The foreman opened the door and pulled her out into the alley. A cold wind swept by her, stinging her cheeks. She stood in the darkness and watched as the car backed out of the alley.

She brushed away a tear that had frozen to her eyelash, but she felt only anger.

You pig, she thought as the car pulled away. *How dare you hide your evil behind such twisted views of fate.*

•

The lock clicked; a key was in the car door. Katrina cleared her mind of memories and sharpened her focus. The door opened, but the dome light didn't come on. She'd taken care of that in advance to reduce the risk of detection.

Theo climbed inside and shut the door.

She was close enough to smell his cologne, even feel

the heat from his body. Her pulse quickened as she rose on one knee. With a gloved hand, she guided the .22-caliber pistol toward the back of the headrest.

Theo inserted the key.

As the ignition fired she shoved the muzzle of her silencer against the base of his skull. "Don't make a move."

The engine hummed. His body stiffened. "Katrina?"

"Shut up. Don't make this any worse than it already has to be."

53

.

Jack went into the office as if it were a normal day. He was following the same advice he'd given countless clients living under the cloud of a grand-jury investigation: If you want to keep your sanity, keep your routine.

He was doing pretty well, until a certain hand-delivery turned his stomach.

It was a letter he'd expected but dreaded. As a prosecutor, he'd sent many of them, and he could have recited the language from memory. *This letter is to inform you that you have been identified as a target of a grand jury investigation. A "target" means that there is substantial evidence to link you to a commission of a crime. Blah, blah, blah. Very truly yours, Benno Jancowitz III.* The only surprise was that Benno Jancowitz was "the Third."

Who in his right mind would keep that name around for three generations?

Line one rang, and then line two. Jack reached for

the phone, then reconsidered. The target letter would surely push the media to another level of attack. He let his secretary answer. Screening calls was just one of the many ways in which Maria was worth her weight in gold.

He answered her on the intercom. "How bad is it?"

"I told Channel 7 you weren't here. But line two is Theo Knight's lawyer."

"Thanks. I'll take it." With a push of the button Rick Thompson was on the line. Jack skipped the hello and said, "I presume you're calling about the target letter."

"Not exactly."

"Theo didn't get one?"

"I don't know if he did or not. I can't find him."

"What?"

"We were supposed to meet in my office three hours ago. He didn't show. I was wondering if you might know anything about that." Rick's words were innocent enough, but his tone was accusatory.

"No, I don't know anything about that," said Jack, a little defensive.

"I called him at home, called him at work, tried his cell, and beeped him five times. Not a word back from him."

"That's weird."

"I thought so, too. Which is why I'm calling you. I was serious about what I said last night at Rosa's house. I appreciate Rosa bringing me into this case. But just because she's my friend doesn't mean I'm going to treat you and Theo any differently than another client and codefendant. If I'm Theo's lawyer, I'm looking out for his best interest."

"I don't quibble with that one bit. All I'm saying is

that if you can't reach your client, it's none of my doing."

"Okay. I'm not making any accusations. It just concerns me that all of a sudden he seems to have dropped off the face of the earth."

"That concerns me, too."

"If you hear from him, tell him to call his lawyer."

"Sure."

As he said good-bye and hung up, his gaze settled on the target letter atop his desk. It had been upsetting enough for him, and he could only imagine how it might have hit a guy who'd spent four years on death row for a crime he didn't commit.

Jack faced the window, looked out across the treetops, and found himself wondering: *How big was the "if" in "if you hear from him"?*

Jack turned back to his desk and speed-dialed Rosa. Her secretary put him straight through. It took only a moment to recount the conversation with Theo's lawyer.

Rosa asked, "You don't think he split, do you?"

"Theo? Heck, no. He doesn't run from anything or anybody."

"You really believe that?"

"Absolutely."

"Why?"

"I represented him for four years."

"That was for a crime he didn't commit."

"Are you saying he killed Jessie Merrill?"

"Not necessarily. Just that people naturally draw inferences when the accused makes a run for it."

"Nobody said he's running."

"Then where is he?"

"I don't know."

"You sure?"

He paused, not sure what she was asking. "Do you think I told him to run?"

"Of course not. But maybe Theo thinks you did."

"You're losing me."

"The conversation you had at Tobacco Road is a perfect example. You told him that Jessie Merrill threatened you, and he took it upon himself to go threaten her right back. Maybe this is the same situation. You could have said something that made him come to the conclusion that you'd be better off if he just hit the highway."

"I haven't spoken to Theo since he and Rick Thompson walked out the front door of your house."

"Then maybe his sudden disappearance has nothing to do with you at all. Maybe it's all about what's best for him."

"Theo didn't kill her. He wouldn't. Especially not in my own house."

"Think about it, Jack. What was the first thing you said to me when we talked about Jessie's body in your house?"

He didn't answer right away, though he recalled it well. "I said, if I was going to kill an old girlfriend, would I really do it in my own house?"

"It's a logical defense. You think Theo was smart enough to give it to you?"

"It's not that smart. I said the same thing to Sam Drayton at the U.S. attorney's office. He tore it to shreds, asked me if I thought it up before or after I killed Jessie Merrill."

"Theo's not a prosecutor."

"Theo's not a lot of things, and he's especially not a murderer."

"I hope you're right. But if you're going to look for him, which I know you are, let me ask you this. You call him a friend, but how well do you really know Theo Knight?"

Jack's first reaction was anger. Serving time for a murder he didn't commit had forever put Theo in a hole. But he was no saint, either, and Jack knew that.

"Jack, you still there?"

"Yeah."

"Honestly. How well do you know him?"

"Do we ever really know *anyone*?"

"That's a cop-out."

"Maybe. I'll let you know what I find out." He said good-bye and hung up.

54

.

It was almost midnight, and Yuri was ready to make
a move.

He and Vladimir had spent the last six hours in their
favorite hotel on the Atlantic City boardwalk. The
Trump Taj Mahal was renowned for its understated ele-
gance—but only if you were a Russian mobster. To anyone else, it was flash and glitz on steroids. Fifty-one
stories, twelve hundred rooms, and restaurant seating
for three thousand diners, all complemented by such
subtle architectural details as seventy Arabian-style
rooftop minarets and no fewer than seven two-ton ele-
phants carved in stone. The chandeliers alone were
worth fourteen million dollars, and each of the big ones
in the casino glittered with almost a quarter million
pieces of crystal. Marble was everywhere—hallways,
lobbies, bathrooms, even the shoe-shine stands. Miles
of tile work had actually exhausted the entire two-year
output of Italy's famous Carrera quarries, Michelangelo's marble of choice for his greatest works of art.

There was even a ten-thousand-dollar-a-night suite that bore Michelangelo's name. Fitting. It was impossible to walk through this place without wondering what Mich would think.

"Let's go," said Yuri.

"What's your hurry?"

"Enough fun and games. It's time we got what we came for."

Vladimir grumbled, but he didn't argue. Blackjack was considered a house game, and for the past two hours he'd conducted himself as the perfect house guest. He was down almost twenty grand at the high-limit table. He gathered up his few remaining chips and stuffed them into the pockets of his silk suit. Then he ordered another drink for the woman seated beside him, a statuesque redhead with globes for breasts and a tear-shaped diamond dripping into her cleavage.

"I'll be back," he said with a wink.

"I'll be waiting."

Yuri grabbed his elbow and started him toward the exit. They were in the Baccarat pit, a special, velvet-roped area in the casino where the stakes were high and drop-dead-gorgeous women sidled up to lonely men with money in their pockets and Viagra in their veins. No one seemed to care that most of the babes were planted by the hotel to encourage foolish wagering.

"You think she's a prostitute?" asked Vladimir.

Yuri rolled his eyes and kept walking, making sure that Vladimir stayed right with him. He made a strategic decision to avoid the temptation of the craps tables by leading him through Scheherazade restaurant. It overlooked the Baccarat pit, making it one of the few five-star restaurants in the world where you could eat lunch and lose your lunch money at the same time.

"These guys aren't the kind of people you keep waiting," said Yuri.

"We're not late."

"Not being late ain't good enough. You get there early and wait. It shows respect."

"Sorry. Didn't know."

They hurried down the long corridor and ducked into one of the tower elevators just past the Kids' Fun Center. An elderly couple tried to get on behind them, but Yuri kept them at bay.

"All full," he said as he pressed the CLOSE DOOR button. He punched forty-four, and the elevator began its ascent, the two of them admiring their reflections in the chrome door. Then Yuri turned and straightened Vladimir's tie.

"Just do what I say from here on out, all right? This meeting is too important to fuck up."

"What should I say?"

"Just answer the questions asked. That's all."

Vladimir rearranged his tie, making it crooked again. "I look okay?"

Yuri gave him a friendly slap on the cheek. "Like a million bucks."

The elevator doors opened and Yuri led the way out. Vladimir seemed almost giddy as they walked briskly down the hallway.

"*Bratsky Krug,*" said Vladimir. "I can't believe it."

"Believe it," said Yuri.

"I laid eyes on one of these guys only once before. I ever tell you that story?"

"Yes." Only a thousand times, the guy who plucked him out of the Kamikaze Club in Moscow, the bare-knuckled fights to the death. *Bratsky Krug* was Russian for "circle of brothers." It was the ruling council of the *vory*, a powerful alliance of Russian mobsters. It didn't have the power or structure of the Italian *Cosa Nostra*, but it had been known to settle inter-gang disputes. Yuri hadn't promised his friend that the council would settle the viatical disagreement between Miami and Brighton Beach. For someone as starstruck as Vladimir, he knew, the prospect of meeting one of these "brothers" was reason enough to make the trip.

The corridor was quiet. Door after door, the whole wing seemed to be asleep. Most of the rooms were under renovation and unoccupied, which was precisely the reason Yuri had chosen the forty-fourth floor for the meeting. He stopped at 4418 and inserted the passkey.

"You don't knock?" said Vladimir.

"You expect them to pay for the room? Like I said, we get here early, they come to us. We're the ones who wait."

He pushed open the door, then stepped aside, allowing Vladimir to enter first. It was dark inside, the entranceway lit only by the sconces in the hallway. Vladimir took a half-dozen steps forward and stopped. Yuri was right behind him. The door closed, and the room went black.

"How about some lights?"

Yuri didn't answer.

"Yuri?"

With a click of a lamp switch on the other side of the room, bright white light assaulted his eyes. Vladimir reached for his gun.

"Don't," said Yuri as he pressed the muzzle of his silencer against the back of Vladimir's head.

Vladimir froze, then chuckled nervously. "What's— what's going on, man?"

Yuri watched the expression on Vladimir's face as a man stepped out from the shadows. It was Leonid, the Brighton Beach mobster whom Vladimir had thrown out of his strip club.

"What the hell are you doing here?" asked Vladimir.

Two more thugs stepped into the light. Instinctively, Vladimir went for his gun again, but Yuri pressed the pistol more firmly into his skull.

"I wouldn't," said Yuri.

Vladimir lowered his arm to his side. All color seemed to drain from his face as the reality of the setup sank in.

"Yuri, what's this all about?"

"Leonid told me about the meeting he and his banker from Cyprus had with you at Bare-ly Eighteen. Seems you were extremely rude."

Vladimir squinted into the spotlight. "They canceled our contract for no good reason. We skimmed a little blood, used a virus they didn't like. What's the big deal? You don't walk out on a deal over little shit like that."

"I hear different. Seems the straw that broke the camel's back was the Jessie Merrill hit."

"We didn't have anything to do with Jessie Merrill's death."

"No," said Yuri. "*I* didn't have anything to do with it. You, I'm not so sure of."

"You were in charge of the hits, Yuri. Not me."

A kick to the left kidney sent Vladimir to his knees. "You keep pushing it on me, don't you? Jessie Merrill was the job of an amateur. You think I'm an amateur?" he said, giving him another kick.

Vladimir doubled over in the spotlight, his face twisted with pain. "No."

"No, what?"

"No, you're not an amateur."

"That's right. You're the only amateur in this bunch, Vladimir. Piece of dirt from the Kamikaze Club."

"I didn't do Jessie Merrill."

Yuri walked beyond the glow of the spotlight, faced Vladimir head-on, and then kicked him once more, this time in the groin. Vladimir cried out and fell face-down.

Yuri said, "You're not thinking the way Brighton Beach thinks. If you didn't hit Jessie Merrill, that means I did."

Vladimir struggled for his breath. "That's not . . . what I'm saying."

"But that's what *they're* saying, asshole. If I don't get the truth out of you, they pin it on me. Isn't that right, Leonid?"

"That's my orders," Leonid said flatly. "If I don't hear a confession out of Vladimir's own mouth, both him and Yuri is in the shithouse."

Vladimir tried to get up, but made it only to one knee. A trickle of blood oozed from the corner of his mouth. "I don't confess to things I don't do."

Yuri grabbed him by the throat and pulled him up, eye-to-eye. "It was a perfect plan. AIDS patients die every day. All we had to do was find the right virus, and we were clear to call home as many viatical settlements as we wanted, no one the wiser. But Jessie Merrill was a healthy broad. You kill her and it's all over the newspapers that she had a viatical settlement."

"I totally agree with you. I would have to be an idiot to kill her."

"A fucking idiot, Vladimir. Because only a fucking idiot would be stupid enough to kill her and then make it look like suicide. The insurance company doesn't pay if she killed herself!"

"I know that. I swear, it wasn't me."

Yuri pressed the gun to the bottom of his chin, aiming straight for the brain.

"It wasn't you or me!" said Vladimir. "If we did it, it would have looked like an accident for sure."

"You're lying!"

"No, I swear. When we found out she scammed us, all I did was scare her. I *didn't* kill her."

"Then who did?"

"I think it's them," Vladimir said, his voice cracking. "Brighton Beach hit her, and now they're blaming us just as an excuse to get out of their deal."

Leonid stepped forward, his eyes bulging as if he were about to explode. "You see what I'm saying, Yuri? It's the same attitude I got at his club. The man's rude."

"I'll handle this." Yuri got right in his face and said, "So, you think Leonid is stupid enough to make Jessie's death look like suicide?"

"I didn't say that."

"I definitely heard you say that. You hear him say that, Leonid?"

"That's the way I heard it. Fucking rude, I tell you."

"If they're so stupid, maybe I should show these boys in Brighton Beach what an accident looks like? What do you think of that, Vladimir?"

Vladimir blinked rapidly, as if on the verge of tears. "Yuri, please. I got kids."

Yuri pushed him to his knees, then stepped away from the spotlight and into the darkness. He grabbed a two-foot pipe from the corner, then returned to Vladimir, tapping the pipe against his palm to the rhythm of each footfall.

Vladimir lowered his head.

Yuri stepped past him. Then he whirled on one foot, swung his arm back toward Vladimir, and slammed the pipe across the bridge of his nose. Vladimir screamed and fell over backward, blood gushing from his smashed nostrils.

"Ouch," said Yuri, mocking him. "Did you see how hard that poor slob's face hit the steering wheel?"

"Must have been going at least thirty miles an hour," said Leonid.

Yuri stepped closer, took a good look at Vladimir's bloodied face. In a blur of a motion he unloaded another hit, this time to Vladimir's jaw. It was a quick one-two, the deep thud of pipe followed by the crisp cracking of bone.

"Looks more like fifty miles an hour to me," said Yuri. Then he looked around the room, the wheels turning in his head. "You know, he wasn't wearing his seat belt, either. Who's got a fucking tire iron?"

"That's enough," said Leonid. "I want him to taste that river water."

"Fine by me," said Yuri.

Leonid gave a quick nod, and on command the two thugs lifted Vladimir from the floor. He was unconscious and bleeding on them, but they didn't seem to mind the occupational hazard. They dragged him across the room to a room-service cart. Vladimir folded in half quite easily, but he was still too big to fit inside the lower food-warming compartment. Yuri walked over with the pipe, wedged it against the cart for leverage, and jerked Vladimir's left shoulder in such a way that his left elbow could touch his right ear.

"Perfect," said Yuri as he closed up the cart with Vladimir inside.

Leonid opened the door, and his men started out with the cart.

"Hey, idiots," said Yuri. "Jackets, please."

They stopped and saw that Vladimir's blood was on their sleeves. They slipped them off and stuffed them into the cart with the body.

"Much better," said Yuri.

They wheeled the cart into the hallway. The door closed, and Vladimir was gone.

Yuri tossed the bloody pipe in the corner. "We square now?"

"I never did hear Vladimir's confession," said Leonid.

"I just bashed my partner's face in, and Brighton Beach still wants to hold Jessie Merrill against me?"

"Don't worry. We're fine on that score. I was just thinking that you worked him over pretty good, and he still didn't admit it. He swears all he did is scare her."

"So?"

"So, maybe he didn't hit Jessie Merrill."

"Which means what? Our viatical business is still on?"

"Sorry, Yuri. Too much heat around that. It's over."

"Damn it. Now whose fault is that?"

"Not mine, not yours. Could be nobody's fault."

"It's always *somebody's* fault. Someone needs to take the blame."

Leonid shrugged. "You want to blame someone, blame whoever it was who killed Jessie Merrill."

Yuri smiled thinly, as if it were a revelation. "You're right. That's exactly who's to blame."

"I'm always right. Come on. I'll buy you a drink."

They started toward the door, then Yuri said, "Hey, if you think Vladimir wasn't behind the Merrill hit after all, you want to call back your men?"

He thought for a second. "Nah. I still say he's rude."

"King of the Kamikaze Club. No fucking class."

They shared a little laugh, then Leonid held the door open as Yuri went back and switched off the spotlight.

55

·

Cindy hadn't intended an ambush, but it was beginning to feel that way. Ever since Jack had told her that he was a beneficiary under Jessie's will, she'd wanted to talk straight to the lawyer who had drafted it. She feared she might chicken out if she made an appointment, so she showed up at Clara's office unannounced.

"Ms. Pierce is with a client," said the receptionist.

"I'll wait," said Cindy.

"It could be a while."

"No hurry." Cindy took a seat in the lobby beside the big spider plant. It had long, beautiful leaves that seemed a little too perfect in shape and color. *Real,* she wondered, *or a convincing fake?* An amusing thought. From what Jack had told her about Clara, the question could have applied to more than just the potted plants.

She flipped through the entire stack of old magazines before the receptionist finally called and led her down the hall, past the main conference room. Cindy caught a glimpse of a monstrous white-stone table that wasn't at all her taste. It had a nice centerpiece of dried flowers, however.

Looks like something Jack would order.

At the corner office, Clara stepped out from behind her desk and shook hands. Cindy had never met her, but the introductions had an uneasy quality that marked any meeting between two people who knew they would never, ever be friends.

"I've heard a lot about you," said Clara.

"Likewise."

She offered Cindy a place at the end of the couch. Cindy seated herself, and Clara sat in the armchair facing her. Clara said, "I wouldn't say I'm shocked to see you, but it is a surprise."

"I'm a little surprised myself."

"Did Jack send you?"

"No. He doesn't even know I'm here."

Clara arched an eyebrow, as if the admission interested her. "Would he be unhappy if he knew?"

"That depends on what you tell me."

"That depends on what you ask."

Cindy scooted forward to the edge of her seat and looked her in the eye. "I want honest answers."

"I won't lie to you. But I do owe a fiduciary obligation to Jessie's estate. If there's something I can't reveal, I'll tell you I can't discuss it. Fair enough?"

"I suppose it's the best I can hope for."

"It is. So, what is it that you'd like to know?"

Cindy took a breath. "I want to know . . ."

Clara waited, but Cindy didn't finish. "Know what?"

"I want to know if my husband has done anything to find the child that Jessie gave up for adoption."

"Has he done anything? You mean you don't know?"

"We don't really talk about it."

"Have you asked him?"

"I told you: We don't discuss it."

"Why not?"

"I'm not here to talk about what goes on between Jack and me. Do you know what Jack has done to find the child?"

"Why would I have that information?"

"You were Jessie's friend. You drafted her will. If I were looking for a child that Jessie had given up for adoption, you're the first person I would talk to. Maybe you'd have some leads. At the very least, you'd know which blind alleys your friend Jessie had followed in her own efforts to find her child."

"I have some insights, yes."

"Have you shared any of that with Jack?"

"No."

"Why not?"

"He hasn't asked for it."

Their eyes locked. "Will you share it with me?"

"Why do you want it?"

"As I understand it, everything Jessie owns goes to Jack if the child isn't located."

"That's correct."

"Then it's important that we find the child. As Jack's wife, the last thing I want is for him to inherit something he doesn't really deserve."

"The last thing you want is for him to inherit something from his old girlfriend."

"Is there some reason I shouldn't feel that way?"

"No. But the very fact that you're here underscores the question: Why *doesn't* Jack feel that way?"

"He does, I'm sure."

"How can you be sure?"

"Because he's my husband."

"Interesting answer."

Cindy narrowed her eyes, confused. "Why is that interesting?"

"Jessie told me about a conversation she and Jack had right before the jury returned its verdict. She asked him why their reunion, if you will, hadn't really blossomed into anything. Jack's answer was like yours. He said, 'Because I'm married.' "

"So?"

Clara shrugged and said, "A nicer explanation might have been something along the lines of because Jack loves you. At the time, I thought Jessie was being a little harsh in her judgment. But now that I've met you, maybe she's right. Maybe Jack is just a poor, lost soul who's playing by the rules."

Cindy struggled not to say what she was thinking. "Are you going to answer my questions about this adopted child or not?"

Clara looked away, as if mulling it over. "I'm not sure I can help you."

"Why not?"

"It's awkward. I don't care to get caught in the middle of whatever's going on between you and your husband."

"The only thing going on is that Jack is too shocked by all of this to do anything about it. Somebody has to step up to the plate and find this child, so we can all put it behind us and move on. That's all I'm here for."

"No. You're here because you don't believe whatever it is your husband is telling you about this child."

"You're reading way too much into this."

"Am I?"

The doubtful expression made Cindy feel small. Finally, Cindy lowered her eyes, rose from the couch, and said, "This was a bad idea. I think I'd better go."

Clara followed her to the door. "Jack always did like kids."

"Excuse me?"

"He and Jessie used to double date with my husband and me. Even way back then, he said he wanted kids. He was so good with my son David."

Cindy blinked, confused.

Clara said, "As I recall, Jack had a pretty rocky relationship with his own father. Guys like that often go the extra mile to keep history from repeating itself. He probably would have made a pretty good dad."

"I'm sure he would."

"Seems ironic, then, doesn't it?"

"What?"

"You never gave Jack a child. Jessie did."

Cindy didn't know how to answer, but it didn't matter. She couldn't speak. She just stood numbly for a moment, ice-cold, waiting for the pain to pass.

"Thanks a lot for your time," she said, then closed the door on her way out.

56

It was late Friday afternoon, and Jack was at his *abuela*'s when Rosa phoned him on his cell. Expecting bad news, he ducked out of the kitchen and took the call in the living room, out of his grandmother's earshot.

"Indictment is down," said Rosa.

He closed his eyes and slowly opened them, absorbing the blow. "How bad?"

"One count, one defendant."

"Me?"

"No. Theo."

The knot in his stomach twisted. A moment of relief for himself, a deep-felt pain for his friend. "No murder for-hire-scheme, like we thought?"

"Not yet."

"You think it's coming?"

"Could be like we talked about earlier. The prosecutor will use the indictment as leverage against Theo, try to get him to turn against you."

"He could have done that even if he'd indicted both of us."

"He's being cautious, as he should be. You're a respected lawyer, the son of a popular former governor. You can bet that the state attorney herself is insisting that the evidence against you be ironclad."

"Marsh's testimony obviously wasn't enough."

"Or the prosecutor has some reservations about it. I heard a rumor that Marsh refused to take a polygraph."

"That's just great. They're not sure if their star witness is telling the truth, so they can't indict me. But it's fine and dandy to indict Theo."

"Theo's a former death-row inmate. I don't care if he was innocent the last time, the bar's a lot higher for you than for him."

"This really pisses me off."

"Calm down, okay? We don't know what additional evidence they have against Theo. It could be worse than we think."

Jack sighed, realizing she was right.

Rosa said, "Right now we have to focus on making sure they don't convince Theo to flip against you. That would be all the evidence they need to go after you on murder for hire."

"The only way they can do that is to get Theo to lie. That'll never happen."

There was a brief pause, then Rosa shifted gears. "Where are you now?"

"My grandmother's house. I didn't want to be home or at the office when the indictment issued. Just can't deal with the media right now."

"Where's Cindy?"

"With her mom."

"Are you two . . ."

"I don't know what's happening with us."

"Have you heard anything at all from Theo?"

"Not a word."

"Well, his arraignment is set for Monday morning at nine. If we don't hear from him by then, he'll officially be a fugitive."

"I've been trying to find him ever since his lawyer told me he couldn't reach him. I called his friends, talked to his partner, the people he works with. No one seems to know anything."

"Then do more."

"I will. But the indictment isn't going to make it any easier. There's no bail for murder in the first degree. The thought of going back behind bars isn't going to sit well with him."

"You need to find him and convince him that he has no choice. A no-show on Monday only digs a deeper hole for all of us."

Jack started to pace. Through the archway at the end of the hall, he could see his grandmother standing at the kitchen island preparing dinner. Strange, but he suddenly smelled jail food. "I need to get on this. Where can I reach you tonight?"

"I'll be here in my office pretty late. You should come by. Jancowitz is delivering the grand-jury materials to Theo's lawyer tonight, and he promised to share with me. Could be interesting stuff."

"Yeah. Like reading my best friend's obituary."

"We're a long way from that, Jack."

He thanked her, said good-bye, and hung up. He took a few steps toward the kitchen, then stopped. Only one thing seemed worse than telling *Abuela* that an indictment might be around the corner, and that was letting her hear it first on television. He drew a deep breath and entered the kitchen.

"Who called?" she asked.

"Rosa."

She was flattening a mound of dough into a paper-thin sheet, back and forth with a rolling pin. It was for her famous meat-filled pastry shells that were tasty enough to tempt even a life-long vegetarian. "What she tell you?"

"Not good news."

"How not good?"

Jack stood on the opposite side of the island, grabbed a sliver of extraneous dough, and rolled it into a ball as he told her about Theo, and how they might still come after him. He could see the emotion in her eyes, but she kept working the dough faster and faster as the news unfolded. He finished in a minute or two, but the silence lingered much longer. Just the sound of the rolling pin and the slice of the knife on the granite countertop—rolling the dough, flattening it into sheets, slicing it into triangles.

"Careful," said Jack. "You're going to cut yourself."

Her pace only quickened. Another wad of dough, another flattened square, a diagonal slice that turned the square into two triangles.

After the third cut, Jack grabbed her wrist and said, "Do that again."

"*Como?*"

"The slicing motion. Do it again."

She flattened another sheet, put the rolling pin aside. Then she took her knife and sliced diagonally across the sheet of dough.

"You slice from top right to bottom left," he said.

"*Sí.*"

"Not from top left to bottom right."

She tried it. "*Aye, no.* That would be very awkward for me."

"Of course it would be," he said, looking off to the middle distance. "You're left-handed."

"*Toda esta bien?*" she asked. Is everything okay?

"*Perfecto,*" he said as he leaned across the island and planted a kiss on her cheek. "*Gracias, mi vida.* I love you."

"I love you, too. But what this about?"

"It's complicated, sort of. But it's really simple."

"What you talk about?"

"You made it all so simple."

"Me?"

"Yes, you. You're beautiful. I'll explain later. I gotta go."

He grabbed his car keys, ran out the front door, and jumped into his Mustang. The traffic lights were all green on his way to Rosa's office, a minor miracle that he interpreted as a sure sign that he was onto something. He was in a hurry, to be sure, but the need for speed was more a matter of adrenaline than timing. Less than fifteen minutes later he was banging on the entrance doors to Rosa's office suite. She let him in and then backed away, as if fearful that he might ricochet off the walls and knock her flat.

"What's with you?" she asked.

Jack caught his breath and said, "Do you have the grand-jury materials yet?"

"Yeah. Just came."

"I need to see the autopsy photos."

"I'm sure they're in there."

He followed her to her office. The materials were in two boxes atop her desk. Jack sifted through one; Rosa, the other.

"Here they are," said Jack. He removed the photographs from the envelope and spread them across the desktop. The gruesome sight cut his enthusiasm in half. Jessie's lifeless body on a slab evoked chilling memories of the bloody scene in his bathroom.

"What are you looking for?" asked Rosa.

"This." He cleared away the other photographs and laid one on the desktop. It was a close-up of the wound to Jessie's wrist. He examined it carefully and said, "Bingo."

"Bingo what?"

"Jessie's left wrist was slashed, which is exactly what you'd expect from a right-handed person."

"Are you saying Jessie was left-handed?"

"No. She was right-handed."

"Then what's the big revelation?"

"The slash mark runs at the wrong angle."

"What?"

He turned his palm face-up, demonstrating. "Look at my wrist. Let's call the thumb-side the left and the pinky-side the right. A right-handed person would probably slash top left to bottom right, or even straight across, left to right. But top right to bottom left is an awkward movement."

Rosa checked the photograph once more. "It's not a severe angle. But now that you mention it, Jessie's appears to be top right to bottom left."

"Exactly."

"So what does this mean? She didn't kill herself? We sort of knew that all along."

"It means more than that." Jack took the letter opener from her desk, then grabbed Rosa's wrist to make his point more clearly. "I'm right-handed. Let's say I'm facing you and cutting your left wrist, trying to make your death look like a suicide. My natural movement is to cut from top left to bottom right. That leaves a wound at the exact same angle you would leave if you had cut your own wrist. Try it."

She took the letter opener, ran it across her veins. "You're right."

Jack took back the opener and switched hands. "But if I'm a left-handed person, and I cut your left wrist, the cut runs at the opposite angle. From your vantage point, it's top right to bottom left."

She simply nodded, following the logic. "So exactly what are you saying?"

"I'm saying that the only way you end up with a slit at this angle is if a left-handed person is facing his victim just as I'm facing you right now and slashes her left wrist."

Rosa looked at the photo, then at Jack, her expression stone-cold serious. "Know anyone who's left-handed?"

"I think I've got a pretty good idea."

"Who?"

He tapped the blade of the letter opener into the palm of his hand and said, "Someone I've suspected since the day he came to my office, talking about Jessie's death as if it were just a business hassle."

"One Dr. Joseph Marsh?"

"You got it," said Jack.

57

Dr. Marsh lived in a Mediterranean-style house near Pennsylvania Avenue, a few blocks west of where the noisy Miami Beach nightlife began. The neighborhood was once a haven for retirees, but with the overall revitalization of South Beach, mountain bikes and Rollerblades had long since replaced the wheelchairs and walkers. It was an eclectic area, lots of artists, musicians, gays, and young people—the perfect relocation spot for a rich, recently divorced doctor in pursuit of hard bodies.

Jack parked on the street and killed the engine. It was a dark night, and the canopy of a sprawling oak tree blocked most of the light from a distant street lamp. Rosa was barely visible in the passenger seat beside him.

"This is the last time I'm going to say this, Jack. I don't think a confrontation with the government's chief witness is a good idea."

"I don't intend to get in his face. I've met him several

times but I've never really focused on whether he's left-handed or right-handed. I just have to see with my own eyes."

"What are you going to do, ask him to grab his glove and have a catch?"

"No, I thought I'd just tell him to slap you upside the head."

"I just want you to be sure about this."

"I am. This thing I figured out with the angle of the slash on Jessie's wrist is only one piece of the puzzle. Even if Marsh is left-handed, that's not the only thing that points to him as the killer. I think she screwed him over."

"How do you mean?"

"Somehow, the entire million and a half dollars that Jessie wormed out of her viatical investors ended up in a bank account that didn't have his name on it. I'm sure that Marsh went along with that arrangement because he wanted to prevent his wife from getting her hands on it in the divorce. But something tells me that when it came time to give the doctor his half of the loot, Jessie gave him the heave-ho—'It's been nice, doc, thanks for helping with the scam, now see ya later.' "

"You realize we're totally shifting gears. The whole defense we've been crafting so far is that Jessie was murdered by the investors she scammed."

"Which is probably why we aren't making any head-way. One thing has always bothered me about that any-way. Why would they kill Jessie and let the doctor live?"

"I don't know."

"And how do you think Dr. Marsh is going to react when I ask him that question?"

"I think he'll say exactly what he said to the grand

jury: *you* killed her. So, please, don't have that kind of talk with him. Just get him to sip coffee or write something down, anything to satisfy yourself that he's left-handed. Don't take it any further than that."

"We'll see how it goes."

"No, I already see where it's going. If all you really wanted to know was whether Marsh is left-handed, you could go ask his wife. You want to get in there, go toe-to-toe, get your friend Theo off the hook, and stem off your own indictment. He got the best of you in that last conversation you had in your office, and now you want to even the score."

"I'm just feeling him out, okay? From what I've seen of Dr. Marsh, he's way too impressed by his own cleverness. If I keep my composure and push the right buttons, I honestly think he's arrogant enough to say something we can use to hang him."

She shook her head, as if she didn't approve. "I see there's no talking you out of this."

"Nope."

"You realize I'm not going with you. The last thing I need to do is be a witness to a conversation that might disqualify me from being your lawyer."

"I agree."

"Good luck."

"Thanks." He stepped down from the car, pushed the door shut, and headed up the walkway. It was a short walk, but it seemed long. The small front lawn was well kept, surrounded by an eight-foot-tall cherry hedge that was trimmed and squared-off neatly to resemble fortress walls. Jack almost checked for a moat. Long rows of colorful impatiens flanked either side of the curved path of stepping stones that led to the front door. The driveway was off to the left, and the doctor's

Mercedes was parked in it. That was promising, almost as good as a sign on the door saying THE DOCTOR IS IN.

Jack climbed one step at a time, three in total, acutely aware of the scratchy sound of his soles on rough concrete. This was technically no sneak attack, but the closer he got to the front door, the less welcome he felt. It wasn't anything he heard or saw. Just vibes.

He drew a breath and knocked on the door.

A full minute passed. Jack heard nothing. He knocked again, a little harder. Then he waited. He checked his watch. Almost ninety seconds. It was a small house. Even from the most remote corner, it couldn't possibly take more than a minute or so to reach the front door. Unless he was showering or sleeping or—

Who the hell cares if I'm bothering him? He knocked a third time, a good solid pounding that could easily have preceded the announcement, *Police, open up!*

He waited a full three minutes. No one home. Or at least no one was willing to come to the door. In the back of his mind he could almost see Rosa smiling and saying something along the lines of *Just as well, God's doing us a favor.*

He turned away and climbed down the stairs. Instead of taking the serpentine footpath, he exited by way of the driveway, a more direct route to the street. The silver Mercedes was a ghostly shade of gray in the moonless night. It seemed odd that the car was in the driveway and yet the doctor hadn't answered the door. Jack took two more steps toward the driveway, then froze. He hadn't noticed in the darkness, but on the other side of the big Mercedes was a smaller, black vehicle, almost invisible in the night. It was a Volkswagen Jetta, and in an instant, Jack recognized it.

Theo?

He sprinted toward the Jetta, pressed his face to the glass and peered through the dark, tinted windows. Theo's windows were so dark they were illegal, making it impossible to see in. Jack walked around to the windshield, but he saw nothing inside. He tried the doors, but they were locked. He stepped back and nearly bumped into Dr. Marsh's Mercedes. As he turned, something inside caught his eye. The driver-side window wasn't as dark as Theo's, so he could make out the image inside.

His heart was suddenly in his throat.

A man was slumped sideways over the console, his torso stretching from the driver's seat to the passenger side. On impulse, Jack opened the door and pulled him straight up in his seat.

"Dr. Marsh!" he said, as if he could revive him.

The doctor was staring back at him, eyes wide open, but the stare was lifeless. The back of his head was covered with blood.

Jack released his grip, his hands shaking. The body fell face-first against the steering wheel. He backed away, grabbed his cell phone, and dialed 911, his mind racing with one scary thought.

Theo, where on God's earth are you?

58

.

Before Dr. Marsh's death hit the late-evening news, Jack was at Theo's townhouse. He'd driven Theo home from his late-night gigs often enough to know that a key was behind the barbecue in the backyard. Technically speaking, he was still trespassing, but a true friend didn't stand on the sidelines at a time like this.

The police arrived at Dr. Marsh's house within minutes of the 911 call. They'd asked plenty of questions about Theo's whereabouts. Jack didn't have any answers, and he quickly realized that it was up to him to go out and get them.

Jack turned the key in the lock, then pushed the door open. He took a step inside, and switched on a light. Almost immediately his heart thumped, as the big cuckoo clock on the kitchen wall began its hourly ritual. In a minute, Jack could breathe again, and he watched the wooden characters continue their little dance around the musical clock. They weren't the typical cuckoo-clock figures. Instead of the little man with the hammer who comes out and strikes the bell, this one had an axe-wielding woodsman who lopped off a chicken's head. Theo had ordered it from some offbeat mail-order catalog and given it to Jack after his successful last-minute request for a stay of execution. Jack gave it back when Theo was finally released from prison. Death row did weird things to your sense of humor.

But I still like having you around, buddy.

Jack continued down the hall and headed for the bedroom. In Jack's mind, it wasn't even within the realm of possibility that Theo might have killed the doctor. Jack hadn't exactly spelled it out this way to the police, but even if you believed that Theo was capable of murder, he was way too savvy to pull the trigger and then leave his car parked on the victim's front lawn.

Still, there were two most likely possibilities. Either Theo was on the run or something awful had happened to him. After mulling it over, Jack settled on a surefire way to rule out one of them.

The bedroom door was open, and Jack went inside. A small lamp on the dresser supplied all the light he needed. This wasn't the kind of search that required him to slice open seat cushions, upend the mattress, or even check under the bed. Jack went straight to the closet and slid open the door.

Instantly, he saw what he was looking for. It was in plain view, exactly where Theo kept it. He popped open the black case to reveal a high-polished, brass instrument glistening in the light.

Jack took the saxophone in his hands and held it the way Theo would have. He could almost hear Theo playing, felt himself connecting with his friend. Jack had no idea where Theo was, but this much he knew:

Theo had lived without his music for too long in prison, and he would never do it again. Not by choice.

His heart sank as he considered Theo's fate—as the least scary of possibilities evaporated in Jack's mind.

No way he ran.

Carefully, almost lovingly, he placed the sax back on the closet shelf, then headed for the door.

59

The Luna Lodge was the kind of seedy motel that could be rented by the week, the day, or the hour. Katrina didn't want to stay a minute longer than necessary, but she wasn't feeling optimistic. She'd sprung for the weekly rate.

She'd chosen a ground-floor room in the back where guests could come and go from their cars with virtually no risk of being spotted. Privacy was what the Luna Lodge was all about, with an extra set of clean sheets coming in at a close second. She could hear the bed squeaking in the room above her. For a solid thirty-five minutes, it sounded like the bedposts pounding on her ceiling. The guy upstairs was Superman, but that wasn't what was keeping her awake. She'd spent hours seated in a lumpy armchair that faced the door, wondering how deep was the mess she'd gotten herself into.

The chain lock was on, the lights were off, the window shades were shut. The room smelled of mold, mildew, and a host of other living organisms that she didn't even try to identify. The sun had set hours earlier, but a laser of moonlight streamed through a small tear at the top of the curtain. Until just then, she hadn't noticed that the big amoeba-shaped stain on the carpet was actually the color of dried blood.

Her eyes were closing, and her mind wandered. Being so close to all this sin evoked a flurry of memories. She suddenly felt cold, though the chill was from within her. It was like a winter night in Prague, the night she'd parted with her pride. She was just nineteen, a mere teenager, locked in a bathroom she shared with seven other roommates in a drafty apartment.

•

A brutal February wind poured through cracks around the small rectangular window. She was sitting on the edge of the sink, a battered metal basin so cold that it burned against the backs of her bare thighs. It was meticulous work, but she did it quickly. Then she pulled up her panties, buttoned her slacks, and put the scissors back in the cabinet.

The fruits of her efforts were in a small plastic bag. She hid it in her pocket so her roommates wouldn't see. Three of them were sharing a couple pieces of bread and a bland broth for dinner as she made her way past them. They didn't ask where she was going, but it wasn't out of indifference. She sensed that they knew, but they'd chosen not to embarrass her. Without a word, she stepped out of the cluttered apartment, then headed down the hall and out the back door of the building.

A black sedan was parked at the curb. The motor was running, as white wisps of exhaust curled upward in the cold air. A sea of footprints in frozen slush covered the sidewalk. The ice crunched beneath her feet as she headed for the car, opened the back door, and climbed inside. She closed the door and handed the bag to the man in the driver's seat. It was the same man she'd met in the alley the night her friend Beatriz had been killed at the factory.

"Here you go," she said.

He held the bag up to the dome light, eyeing it with a disgusting fascination. It was a peculiar fetish among certain Czech men, one that kept many a young Cuban woman in Castro's work program from starving. There was decent money to be had from a bagful of pubic clippings.

"Too short," he said.

"It's only twenty-days' growth. What do you expect?"

"I can't use this."

"Then give me more time between collections. At least six weeks."

"I can't wait that long."

"Then what do you expect me to do?"

He opened the bag, smelled it, and smiled. "I think it's time we expanded our line of merchandise."

"No way."

"Not a good answer."

"I don't care."

"You'd better care."

"I don't. This isn't fair."

"Fair?" he said, chuckling. Then he turned serious. "It's like I always say, honey. Everything happens for a reason. No decision is meaningless. We all determine our own fate."

"If that's what you say, then you're an asshole."

"Yeah. I'll be sure to make a note of that. Meanwhile, you think about the choices you want to make. Think about your fate."

•

A low, throaty groan startled her. It was a man's voice, definitely not the hooker next door. She focused just in time to see Theo's eyes blink open.

"How's your head?" she asked.

He was lying on his back, his body stretched across the mattress like a drying deer skin. Each wrist and ankle was handcuffed to a respective corner of the bed frame. He tried to say something, but with the gag it was unintelligible.

Katrina rose and inspected the big purple knot above his left eyebrow. It was squeezing his eye half shut, and he withdrew at her slightest touch.

"That was a stupid thing to do," she said. "Next time you try to escape, I'll have to shoot you."

His jaw tightened on the gag, but he uttered not a sound.

She returned to her chair and laid her pistol across her lap. "I suppose you're wondering how long I think I can keep you tied up like this."

Short, angry breaths through his nostrils were his only reply.

"The answer is: Long enough for me to figure out what to do. See, if I don't kill you, they're going to kill me. And then they'll come and find you and do the job that I was supposed to do. So it's really in everyone's best interest for you to behave yourself and let me figure this out."

His breathing slowed. He seemed less antagonized.

"Now, I'm sure you'd love to lose that gag in your mouth. And after lying here unconscious for so long, you must be dying to use the bathroom. So nod once if you think you can behave yourself."

He blinked, then nodded.

"Good." She went to him and stopped at the edge of the mattress. Then she aimed the gun directly at his head and said, "You try anything, I'll blow your brains out."

She took the key from her pocket and unlocked the left handcuff. She handed him the ice bucket. "Roll over and pee into this."

Still gagged, he shot her a look that said, *You gotta be kidding.*

"Do it, or hold it."

Begrudgingly, he rolled on one side, unzipped, and did his business. From the sound of things, Katrina was beginning to think she might need a second bucket. Finally it was over. He rolled onto his back, and Katrina locked the handcuff to his wrist.

"Thirsty?" she asked.

He nodded.

"If you scream . . ." She pressed the gun to his forehead, as if to finish the sentence.

She reached behind his neck, loosened the knot, and pulled the gag free. She offered him a cup of water, which he drank eagerly. When he finished, he stretched his mouth open to shake off the effects of the gag, then winced. The mere use of any facial muscles was a painful reminder of the bruise above his eye.

"Damn, girl. Where'd you learn to kick like that?"

"Where'd you get those tattoos?"

He looked confused, then seemed to understand. "You served time?"

"I think of it that way."

"What for?"

"What's it to you?"

"Just curious."

The creaking noise resumed overhead, the steady squeak of the bed in the room above them. Katrina glanced at the ceiling, then shot Theo a look that required no elaboration.

"You were a hooker?" he said.

"No. I refused to be one."

"They put you in jail because you *wouldn't* ho'? I don't get it." The squeaking stopped. Theo lay still for a moment, still staring at the ceiling. "To be honest, I don't get any of this. You're a government informant. If someone is making you do something you don't want to do, just go to the police."

"It's not that simple."

"Just explain to them that things have gotten out of hand. Someone wants you to hit me or they're gonna hit you."

"I can't do that."

"Why not?"

"Because if I go to the police and tell them the fix I'm in, they'll pull me from the assignment."

"Exactly. Problem solved."

"You just don't understand." Her gaze drifted across the room, then settled on the brownish-red spot of dried blood on the carpet. "There's an old Russian proverb," she said vaguely. " 'Revenge is the sweetest form of passion.' "

"What does that have to do with calling the police?"

"If they pull me off the job now, I stifle my own passion."

He looked straight at her, seeming to understand that somewhere behind those troubled brown eyes was an old score to settle.

"I'm good at revenge. Maybe I could help."

"This is something I have to do myself."

He nodded, then gave a little tug that rattled the chains of his handcuffs. "Funny."

"What?"

"When I was fifteen, I used to have this fantasy about being kidnapped by a Latina babe."

"Not exactly living up to the dream, is it?"

"Nope."

"Hate to break this to you, pal. Life never does." She stuffed the gag back in his mouth and cinched up the knot behind his head.

60

.

Jack went from Theo's to Sparky's. It was getting late, but the crowd had found its collective second wind. Loud country music was cranking on the sound system, and a group of Garth Brooks wannabes were twirling their women across the dance floor.

Theo's gone one night, and the place is already swarming with rednecks.

Like most dives, Sparky's was the kind of place where liquor flowed freely but everything else came at a price. All day long, theories about Theo's disappearance had been bouncing off the walls. For twenty bucks the barmaid steered Jack in the most promising direction.

"Buy you a drink?" said Jack as he sidled up to the bar.

A skinny guy with weathered skin looked up from his glass and said, "You queer?"

"No, sorry. But I have a couple friends who are, if you're interested."

He popped up from his barstool. "Watch your mouth, jackass."

"Easy, friend. Just a little joke."

"I don't think you're so funny."

Jack took a moment. Usually he tried to befriend people before bullying them into divulging information, but this guy was too much of a jerk to waste time schmoozing.

"You're a truck driver, aren't you?"

"That's right."

"That's your rig parked out back?"

"What's it to you?"

"I hear you sell drugs out of it."

"That's bullshit."

"Don't worry. I'm not a cop."

"I don't sell nothin' to nobody. Just drive my truck, that's all."

"Well, I hear differently. So let me spell this out for you. Theo Knight left this joint around two o'clock this morning. Nobody's seen him since. His partner tells me the cops have been here asking questions. I hear you're the only one around here who seems to have any idea what might have happened to him."

"I didn't tell the cops nothin'."

"I'm sure you didn't. That's because you were out cutting a deal in your truck when you saw what you saw."

He smiled nervously. "You heard that, huh?"

"From a good source. So, you want to tell me what caught your eye? Or should I call my old boss at the U.S. attorney's office and tell him to get a search warrant for your rig?"

The trucker swirled the ice cubes around in his glass, sipped the last few drops of bourbon. "Tough guy, are you?"

"Just a man with a mission."

He checked the door, as if it were some big secret,

then glanced back and said, "Your friend Theo left with some chick."

"Who?"

"A brunette. Black clothes, nice body. Could have been Latina. She was hanging around his car out back in the parking lot, then she got in. He came out about twenty minutes later, and they drove off together. That's all I saw."

"Did they seem friendly together, were they arguing, or what?"

"I didn't see them together. His Jetta has dark-tinted windows, so I couldn't see inside. Like I say, I saw her get in, then a little later he gets in. I don't know if she was smoking a joint in there or what. She waited for him, then they left. That's it."

"Anything else you remember?"

"Yeah. The bumper sticker. It said, I BRAKE FOR PORN STARS. It just kind of stuck in my brain."

Definitely Theo's car, thought Jack. "That's all I need to know. Thanks."

Jack climbed off the barstool and headed out the door to the parking lot, leaving the loud music and stale odors behind him. The moon was almost full, bright enough to cast his shadow across the parking lot. He leaned against his car, thinking, but he didn't have to think long. Brunette, good-looking, nice body. It was just as he'd suspected, and the trucker's story was all the ammunition he needed.

He pulled his phone from his pocket, then stopped, not sure whom to call first. If he notified the cops, Katrina would probably hire herself a lawyer and never talk. He gave it another moment's thought, then went with his gut and dialed the cell-phone number Katrina had given him outside the mobile blood unit.

"What did you do to Theo Knight?" he said when she answered.

There was silence. Jack said, "Don't hang up, Katrina. I'm onto you. Theo's missing, and you left Sparky's with him last night."

"Says who?"

"I have a witness who saw you waiting in the car."

She didn't answer. Jack said, "I'm giving you one chance to tell me what happened to Theo. If you don't, I'm going to the police."

She paused, a long, tense silence that bespoke her angst.

Jack said, "What's it going to be?"

"Don't go to the police."

"Why shouldn't I?"

"Because if you do, there's a good chance Theo could end up dead."

"Is that a threat?"

"No."

"Is he alive?"

"Yes."

"Do you know that for a fact?"

"Yes."

"Let me be clear about this. Are you saying you kidnapped him?"

"No. I mean, not really. It's not like I'm asking for a ransom or anything. It's more like he's in hiding, for his own safety."

"Say what?"

"All I can tell you is that I'll do everything I can to keep him safe. But if you butt in, there's a good chance he'll end up dead. And it won't be my fault."

"What's going on?"

"I can't explain now. Just give me twenty-four hours to sort some things out."

"Are you out of your mind?"

"You just have to trust me on this. I'm a confidential informant, I'm not a criminal, remember?"

"I'm not trusting you anymore. I'm going to the police."

"Fine. Go. But after keeping your friend alive on death row for all those years, it seems pretty stupid of you to sign his death warrant now. And that's exactly what you'd be doing if you run to the cops."

Jack gripped the phone, thinking. "I don't like this. After that meeting at the blood unit, I thought we had a working relationship. But I haven't heard a thing from you about that Georgia case, or anything else, for that matter."

There was silence, but finally she answered. "You were right about Georgia."

His heart sank a bit. "They're killing viatical settlors?"

"I checked the computers. That woman in Georgia was one of our clients."

"So if they got Jessie, too, that means Viatical Solutions, Inc., murdered two clients in less than a month."

"It's not for sure. And it's not just Viatical Solutions, Inc., either. We created dozens of viatical corporations, most of them just shells that we activate whenever we need one. When I first started this job, I thought all these companies were just a lot of needless paperwork, but now it makes sense. Every client does business with a different company. The one in Georgia was called Financial Health, Inc."

"Smart," said Jack. "It would look pretty suspicious if any single company showed too good a rate of return."

"I am so close to blowing the lid off this."

"You have to come forward."

"I need more time."

"You can't have it. What if they go out and murder another client next week?"

"I'm not talking a week. Twenty-four hours is all I need. Then Theo will be back safe, and this whole operation will be blown wide open. I promise."

He weighed it in his mind, but he and Theo both needed someone on the inside. Busting her chops over a few hours would only push her out of their camp. "All right. I'll give you twenty-four hours. But I want proof that Theo's alive, before noon."

"Like what?"

The image of Theo's saxophone suddenly flashed in his brain, giving Jack the perfect proof-of-life question. "Ask him for the title of his favorite Donald Byrd album."

"Okay. You'll have it by noon."

"One last thing."

"What?"

"Theo Knight is my friend. If you're playing me for a fool and something happens to him, I'm coming after you. You understand me?"

"More than you know," she said.

Jack switched off the phone and buried it in his pocket.

61

At 5:30 A.M. the runners were gathering at Cartagena traffic circle. This was a regular Saturday morning ritual in Coral Gables, the predawn gathering of bodies clad in Nike shorts and spandex, ready to head out on a ten- or fifteen-mile run before the rest of the world rose for breakfast. Himself an occasional runner, Jack admired them in a way, but mostly he regarded them as the South Florida version of those crazy Scandinavians who cut holes in the Arctic ice and jumped in for a refreshing dip in mid-January.

Rosa wasn't answering her cell phone, but Jack found her exactly where he'd expected, her leg propped up on the fence as she stretched out her hamstrings.

"What are you doing here, Swyteck?"

"I have to talk to you."

"I have to run. Literally."

Her friends seemed annoyed by the intrusion, each of them checking their ultraprecise wristwatches/heart-monitors/speedometers.

Jack whispered in her ear, "Theo's been kidnapped."

She shot him a look, as if to say, *Are you shittin' me?*

"I'm totally serious," he said.

Rosa told her friends to go on without her, then followed Jack to an isolated spot beneath a banyan tree where they could talk in private. In minutes he brought her completely up to speed, ending with his conversation with Katrina.

"Why didn't you call me last night?"

"I wasn't sure I should call anyone, since I agreed not to call the police."

"So why are you telling me now?"

"Because I haven't been able to sleep. Things are happening so fast, I need another brain to process it all. I don't want to be wrong."

"You were right about one thing. Theo didn't run."

"I knew Theo was no murderer."

"Well, back up a second. Just because he didn't run doesn't mean he didn't kill Jessie Merrill."

He considered her words, appreciating the distinction. "You still think he might have killed her?"

"I don't know."

"Katrina told me on the phone that her company probably killed a woman in Georgia to cash in on a viatical settlement. Seems to me they did the same thing with Jessie."

"Except that Jessie was healthy."

"What difference does that make?"

"Someone with AIDS is expected to die. So it doesn't raise red flags if the viatical company hastens the process. Especially if you go to the trouble of doing ten different clients under ten different company names, which is apparently the way they did it. But Jessie Merrill was a totally different situation. She wasn't sick, wasn't expected to die. Killing her immediately raised red flags. The thugs that Katrina worked for had to be smart enough to have known that."

"We're talking about the Russian *Mafiya*, not Russian scientists. You get these guys pissed enough, all intelligence goes out the window."

"Maybe."

"It's not just a maybe. It's certainly more likely that they did it than Theo."

"Yes, if you look at it strictly from that perspective. But there's other evidence to consider."

"Like what?"

"For example, what does this new information about the viatical companies do to your theory about the angle of the cut?"

"I don't think it affects it one way or another."

"You said it was probably a left-handed person who slit Jessie's wrist."

"So what? I'm sure the Russian *Mafiya* has plenty of left-handed hit men."

"I'm sure they do. But answer me this: Is Theo right-handed or left-handed?"

"Right-handed. Ha! In your face."

"In your dreams."

"What does that mean?"

"This theory you have about the angle of the cut. Don't you find it odd that the medical examiner's report doesn't even make mention of it?"

"No. The angle is subtle, I'll admit. And a left-handed killer doesn't fit the prosecutor's theory of the case, so, of course, the report doesn't mention it."

"That's a little cynical," she said. "Don't you think?"

"Theo sat on death row for a murder he didn't commit. We have a right to be cynical."

"We? *We* have a right? You're not his lawyer anymore, Jack."

"No. I'm his friend."

"Which is why I'm so worried. Just a take step back, play devil's advocate the way any good lawyer would."

"How do you mean?"

"You say the medical examiner doesn't see the same angle on the cut because a left-handed killer doesn't suit the prosecutor's theory of the case. Well, maybe—just maybe—you do see the angle because a *right*-handed killer doesn't fit *your* theory of the case."

"But you saw it, too. I showed you the autopsy photo, and you said you saw the angle."

"Damn it, Jack. *You're* right-handed. Don't you think I wanted to see something that says the killer was left-handed?"

"Are you still wondering if I killed Jessie?"

"No. Not at all. But believe me, the way the evidence is falling out, I'll grab at anything that makes it easier for me to prove you didn't."

"When I showed you the photo of Jessie's wrist, did you see the angle or not?"

"I saw it, but only after you insisted that it was there. I'd feel a whole lot more sure of this theory if the medical examiner had seen it first."

Jack searched for a rebuttal, but nothing came. "Okay," he said calmly. "Okay."

"All I'm saying is that maybe you shouldn't be so sure about this left-handed, right-handed stuff."

"You're saying more than that. You're saying, don't be so sure that Theo isn't the killer."

"Okay. Maybe I am."

"Don't worry. Right now, the only thing I'm sure of

is that I came here hoping that you'd help me sort things out."

"And?"

He walked toward the fence, watched the line of runners streaming down the footpath along the canal. "And now I'm just more confused."

62

•

After a long night with Theo, Katrina went home for supplies. It was early Saturday morning, and she was working on little sleep. She went to the refrigerator and poured herself a little pick-me-up, a mixture of orange and carrot juice. Then she crossed the kitchen and switched to the early-morning local news broadcast. She caught the tail end of the morning's lead story, the indictment of Theo Knight for Jessie's murder. It was the same lead as last night, with slightly more emphasis on the shooting death of Dr. Marsh and the fact that his body was found in his car by Jack Swyteck, right beside an abandoned Volkswagen that belonged to Theo Knight.

Katrina kept one eye on the television screen as the news anchor closed with a comment that Katrina could have scripted: "Neither Theo Knight nor his attorney were available for comment."

She switched off the set. Just what she'd needed, another kick-in-the-head reminder that she had to do something about Theo. Twenty-four hours was all the time she'd bought from Swyteck. She hoped it was enough.

"Good morning, Katrina."

She whirled, so startled that she dropped her juice glass. It shattered at her feet. A man was on the patio outside her kitchen, just on the other side of the sliding screen door. She was about to scream when he said, "It's me, Yuri."

She took a good look. She'd heard plenty about Yuri, but during her eight-month undercover stint, she'd met him only once, briefly, when he'd come to do business with Vladimir.

"You scared me to death."

"Am I not welcome?"

She opened the screen door and said, "To be honest, a knock would have been nice."

He stepped inside. Then he knocked—three times, each one separated by a needlessly long pause. It might have been his idea of a joke, but he wasn't smiling. He didn't look like the kind of guy who smiled much.

He pulled the screen door shut, and the sliding glass door, too. Then he locked it. "You have no reason to be afraid of me. You know that, don't you?"

He gave her a look that made her nervous, but she tried not to show it. "Of course."

His expression didn't change. It was the same cold, assessing look.

Katrina grabbed a paper towel and cleaned up the broken glass and juice on the floor, then tossed the mess in the trash can. Yuri was still watching her every move.

"Can I get you anything?" she asked. "Coffee, juice?"

No response. He pulled a chair away from the kitchen table, turned it around, and straddled it with his arms resting atop the back of it. "Where you been all night?"

"Out."

"Out where?"

"Just out." She folded her arms and leaned against the refrigerator, as if to say it was none of his business.

Again, he was working her over with that penetrating stare, making her feel as if it were her turn to talk even though he'd said nothing.

"You sure you don't want anything to drink?"

"Tell me something, Katrina. How's the dirty-blood business?"

She shrugged, rolling with his sudden change of subject. "Fine."

"You know, we invented the blood bank."

"We?"

"Russians. Most people don't know it, but blood banks never existed until the Soviets started taking blood out of cadavers in the 1930s. This was something I didn't believe until a doctor showed me an old film about it. Soviet doctors figured out that there was a point, after someone died, before rigor mortis, and before the bacteria spread throughout the body, where you could actually take the blood from the dead body and use it."

She said nothing, not sure exactly what point he was trying to make.

"Can you imagine that, Katrina? Taking blood from cadavers?"

With that, she realized where this was headed. It was as if he somehow knew that she'd snooped through Vladimir's computer and discovered the truth about that woman in Georgia who'd turned up dead—short about three liters of AIDS-infected blood.

"Have you ever heard of such a thing?" he asked more pointedly.

"No."

He smiled, but it wasn't a warm smile. "Vladimir always trusted you, you know that?"

"We worked well together."

"I always thought it was because he wanted to get you into bed."

"So did I, until I saw a picture of his daughter. We look a lot alike."

"Lucky you. I, on the other hand, don't care who you look like. And I am far less trusting."

"He told me."

"Of course he did. Vladimir had a habit of sharing things he didn't need to share. That's why he had to leave."

"He's gone?"

"He had some vacation time coming. But that's neither here nor there. What's important is that you and I have to get past this trust issue."

"I thought the Theo Knight hit was supposed to resolve all that."

"It was."

"So, what's left to resolve? You found his car, didn't you?"

"Right where you said it would be. As a matter of fact, I drove it over to Dr. Marsh's house last night."

"What for?"

"Theo had good reason to kill him. Thought I'd do my part to make sure the cops keep racing right down that rabbit hole."

"I saw the news. Dr. Marsh is dead."

"You bet he is. Deader than Theo Knight."

Katrina felt chills. "What's that supposed to mean?"

"Just that I know for certain that Dr. Marsh is dead."

"So is Theo Knight."

"Is he?"

"You think I'd lie about something like this?" she said with a nervous chuckle.

"Probably not. But humor me. Tell me exactly how Theo Knight went down."

"Not much to tell."

"I'm a detail guy. Let's hear 'em."

"I hid in the back seat, waited for him to come out from the bar when his shift ended. Put a gun to his head and told him to drive out west to the warehouse district. Found us a suitable canal. Told him to get out and walk to the edge of the water. And that was it."

"You're leaving out the best part. I want to know exactly how you did it."

"Shot him in the head."

"Silencer?"

"Yes, of course."

"Which side of the head?"

"Back. One shot."

"How close?"

"Less than an inch."

"The end of the barrel touching his skull or not?"

"Uhm, could have been touching. Real close."

He rose and walked across the room, straight toward her. Katrina didn't move, but she felt her body tense up, bracing for something.

He stopped at her side, formed his hand into the shape of a gun, and pressed his finger to the back of her head. "Like this?"

"More or less."

"At that range, the bullet must have exited through his face."

"It did. Right through the forehead."

He stepped away and nodded, but she could tell he didn't believe her. In fact, she felt baited.

"That's strange," he said. "All the hits I've ever done with a .22-caliber, never once has there been an exit wound."

"Is that so?"

"That's the beauty of a .22. That's why it's the pre-ferred weapon of professionals. Doesn't have enough force to pass through the skull twice. It's not like a .38 or a 9-millimeter, in the left side, out the right. A .22 goes in one side and bounces off the inside of the skull, ricochets around until it turns the brain to scrambled eggs."

She fell silent.

"Are you absolutely sure that your little .22-caliber slug came out his forehead, Katrina?"

"Of course I'm sure. Maybe it never happened that way for you, but there's a first time for everything."

"Except the first one doesn't count if there are no witnesses."

"You expected me to off him in public?"

"No. But if I'm ever going to trust you, I expect you to do it in front of me."

"Too late. Theo's dead."

"Then we find another."

"Another?"

"Yeah." His dark eyes brightened, as if this was what he lived for. "There's always another."

63

.

Jack returned home at dawn. He tiptoed past the bed, squinting as the first rays of morning sunlight cut across the room. Cindy stirred on the other side of the mattress.

"Where you been?" she asked, yawning.

"All over, checking things out."

"I was worried about you. I tried calling you."

He dug his cell phone from his pocket. The battery was dead. "Sorry. I've been unreachable and didn't even know it."

"Did you find out anything about Theo?"

"I think so. Go back to sleep. I didn't mean to wake you."

He watched her head sink back into the pillow, then lowered himself gently onto the edge of the mattress. The doorbell rang, giving them both a start.

"Now what?" he said, groaning.

"Probably a reporter. Ignore it, please."

"I'd better check it out." He took the long route

through the kitchen, where he dropped his cell phone in the battery charger on the counter. The doorbell rang once more as he reached the foyer and peered through the peep hole. The sight of Katrina on his front porch kicked up his pulse a notch.

"Just a minute," he said, then quickly returned to the bedroom. Cindy was out of bed and pulling on her blue jeans. "Who is it?" she asked.

"Katrina. That government informant Theo and I were dealing with."

"What does she want?"

"I'm not sure," he said as he walked to the dresser. He opened the top drawer, removed the trigger lock from his revolver, and slipped the gun into his pant's waist. He pulled on a long, baggy sweatshirt to hide the bulge.

"Jack, what are you doing?"

"Don't worry, she works for the government as a CI. I'm sure it's fine. But with Theo missing and Dr. Marsh dead, we can't be too careful."

"Jack—"

"Just stay here until I say it's okay to come out. And keep one hand on the telephone. If it sounds like anything is going wrong out there, you dial 911."

"You're scaring me."

"Just stay here. I'll be right back."

He returned to the foyer, took a deep breath. *She's a government informant*, he reminded himself, though as a former prosecutor he knew better than to put much trust in that. At the moment, however, he didn't see a better way to find his friend. With caution, he opened the door.

"Can I come in?" she said.

With a jerk of the head he signaled her inside and let

her pass. Then he locked up behind her and led her into the living room.

She took a seat on the edge of the couch and asked, "Are we alone?"

"Yeah," he lied. "Cindy's at her mother's house."

"Good. Because it's time we talked."

"I'm all for that. But first, Theo. Do you have the answer to my question—the album title?"

"I do." She handed him a small slip of paper.

Jack recognized the handwriting as Theo's, and the answer was exactly what he was looking for: *Thank You for . . . F.U.M.L. (Fucking Up My Life)*.

He smiled to himself, then tucked the paper into his pocket. "All right. You just bought yourself a few more hours. But I want to know what's going on."

She took a seat on the leather ottoman, then popped back onto her feet. She seemed wired, and Jack sensed it was nerves, not coffee.

"I'm not sure where to start."

"Why did you take my friend? I want the real reason."

She looked away, then back, as if not sure how to answer even a simple question. "I've been undercover for almost eight months. You know that from our first meeting."

"Our second meeting. At our first, you kickboxed me into the emergency room."

"Good point. Because you understand that it's impossible to play this role without being asked to do things I don't want to do."

"It's every informant's dilemma."

"And I've been fine with it. Until last week. I was given an assignment. Basically, it boiled down to this: Kill Theo or be killed."

Jack went cold. "So you kidnapped him."

"I hid him away. For his own safety."

"You're an informant. Don't you think it would have been smarter just to go to the police?"

"Theo had the same reaction," she said, shaking her head. "But I can't hand this off to the police now. I've invested too much."

"Invested what?"

She was pacing again. "It's no coincidence that I work at Viatical Solutions. I sought this company out, gathered up all the dirt I could, then went to the U.S. attorney and offered to work as an informant."

"And they just went for it?"

"I played it pretty smart. They thought I was a mobster's ex-girlfriend, pissed off and eager to blow the whistle."

"But you weren't."

She shook her head. "I knew I was going to steep myself deep in this company to get the information I needed. The only way to avoid going to jail some day was to turn government informant."

"So what's your real agenda?"

She stopped pacing and looked right at Jack. "There's a guy I've been looking for. He used to own a factory in Prague, which was basically a front for a criminal racket he ran. Drugs, prostitution. It took me a long time, but I finally tracked him to Miami. From everything I've found so far, I'm pretty sure he's working for Viatical Solutions."

"And you want to find him because . . ."

"Because of what he did to me and to a friend of mine named Beatriz. It's personal."

Jack wanted to ask, but she didn't seem inclined to elaborate. "What's his name?"

"I don't know. I'm not even sure what he looks like,

exactly. The closest I ever got to him was looking at the back of his head from the back seat of his car."

"Aren't you worried that he might recognize you first?"

"I looked much different then. Short hair, thirty pounds thinner."

Jack found it hard to imagine her thirty pounds thinner, but it gave some insight into how she must have lived. "How will you know you've got the right guy?"

"I just need a little more time to check things out. Then I'll know."

"Then what?"

"After all this time and effort, I don't intend to shake his hand. But I got a bigger problem right now. As my Russian friends like to say, the house is burning, and the clock is ticking."

"What does that mean?"

She stepped toward the window, peeled back the drapery panel just enough to see across the lawn. Then she faced Jack and said, "I've got a new boss at Viatical Solutions. And something tells me he's looking for the hat trick."

"Hat trick?"

"A little Russian hockey analogy. A hat trick is three goals."

"I know. But I don't understand the context."

"First Jessie. Then Marsh. Now he wants the third son of a bitch who scammed him."

"Are you saying . . ."

"He doesn't believe Theo's dead, so I've got one last chance to prove myself. Which means I have to think fast and figure out what I'm going to do with you."

Jack took a half-step back. "*Do* with me?"

She looked him in the eye and said, "You're my next assignment."

64

Each breath carried Cindy more deeply into sleep, though it felt like something beyond the realm of sleep, a numbing paralysis that tingled all the way to the tips of her fingers. A simple effort to raise her heavy eyelids was enough to send the room spinning. A burning sensation tinged her nostrils. It wasn't that she couldn't remember what had happened. It had all just happened so fast, the moment she'd stepped into the master bathroom—the blur of motion behind her, the muscular arm around her waist, and the pungent rag that covered her mouth and nose. In a matter of moments, she felt limp. But she was battling it, refusing to be overpowered.

She'd managed to hear most of what Jack and Katrina were saying. The living room was down the hall from her, but sound traveled well in their little two-bedroom house, especially in the stillness of morning. She'd heard enough to know that it was time to dial 911. That was when she'd grabbed the cordless telephone on the nightstand and run into the bathroom. It was suddenly coming clearer to her now. The perfectly round hole that had been cut into the glass door that led to the solarium outside their bathroom. The ambush from behind her. And something else was coming back to her, too.

She seemed to recall that there had been no dial tone.

Yes, the phone was dead. That much she definitely recalled, and the fear that flourished in that brief, lucid moment gave her another kick of adrenaline. Part of her knew that she should have been completely unconscious by now, but she wouldn't allow it. Instinct was taking over. It was an almost inexplicable, involuntary, high-gear response to the realization that someone had broken into their house and that Jack was with Katrina, completely unaware. He was in danger and she needed to help. She liked to think it was love that drove her, a kind of love she'd harbored for a long time, as long as she could remember. The feeling was familiar to her, but she was somehow finding it easier to associate that feeling with the distant past than with present events. She tried to resist whatever it was that was pulling her in that direction, fought off the effects of the drug. But she could feel her mind slipping. She found herself retreating to that time and place long ago, where she'd first been tempted to act on her impulse, the God-given instinct to protect a man she loved. Or at least to protect his name.

It had happened when she was nine years old, just two months after her father had committed suicide.

•

A grinding noise emerged from behind the bathroom door, the girls' bathroom on the second floor. Cindy stepped out of her room and listened. It definitely wasn't an electric hair dryer or anything else she'd ever heard coming out of the bathroom. She started down the hall and tried the door knob. The noise stopped.

"Go away!" her sister shouted.

"What are you doing in there?"

"Get out of here!"

The grinding noise was back. Cindy shrugged, then took a bobby pin from her ballerina-style bun and stuck it in the key hole. The lock clicked, and the door popped open.

Celeste grabbed the blender and screamed. "You idiot!"

Cindy was unfazed. She walked in and inspected the mess on the counter. "What are you making?"

"A milkshake. Now will you get out of here, please?"

"Can I have some?"

"No. But if you're going to come in here, at least close the door."

Cindy pushed the door shut, and Celeste locked it. Cindy leaned over the blender and smelled the concoction. "Yuck. It smells like fish."

"Things that are good for you never smell good."

"Is there really fish in there?"

"No, genius. It comes in a bottle."

Cindy checked the label. "Is it really good for you?"

"Yes."

"Then let's pour in some more," she said as she tipped the bottle.

Her sister grabbed it, stopped her. "No. A little is good for you. Too much can kill you."

"Kill you?"

"Yes. Too much is like poison."

"What's in it?"

"Medicine."

"What kind of medicine?"

"None of your business."

"Where'd you get it?"

"One of the high school girls. A senior."

Cindy grabbed the bottle and read the label. "E-R-G-O. What are you taking that for?"

"I said, it's none of your business."

"Tell me or I'll ask Mom."

Celeste shot her an angry look and snatched the bottle back. "I'm taking it because I think I'm pregnant, okay?"

Cindy's mouth fell open. "You were with a boy?"

"No."

"Then how'd you get pregnant?"

Celeste lowered her eyes and said, "I've been having dreams."

"What kind of dreams?"

"About Dad. He comes to me."

Cindy felt her blood begin to boil. "And?"

"At night sometimes, I hear him outside my bedroom window. The leaves crunch every time he makes a step. Then I get up, but I'm not really awake. I can see myself walking down the hall, downstairs. I go to the back door and open it. I see nothing but these swirling leaves in the wind. But then suddenly he's there, and I don't know how, but I'm naked, and he's there, like it used to be, and—"

"Stop it!"

"He pulls me on top of him, and—"

"Celeste, you're a liar!"

"I'm not lying! You were just too young. He would have come for you too, if he hadn't killed himself. He might still come."

"Girls!"

They froze. Their mother was outside the door.

"What's going on in there?"

Celeste went to the door and opened it a crack. "It's okay, Mom."

Cindy listened as her sister and mother talked it out through the slightly opened door. Celeste had turned her back on her sister, and Cindy felt a sudden urge to grab something and hit her over the back of the head, exactly the way she'd felt when Celeste had ruined their father's graveside service with her lies. Cindy could even see it in her mind, Celeste falling to the floor all bloody and unconscious. Celeste and her false accusations. No one had ever spelled it out for her, but Cindy knew it was true: Celeste had driven their own father to suicide, taken him away from her.

Celeste was pleading with their mother, trying to assure her that they weren't up to any mischief and that there was no reason for her to barge in. Cindy grabbed the bottle of ergo and took a good, long look at the label. She wasn't sure what it was, but Celeste had given her all the information she needed. A little was medicine; a lot was poison. She glanced at the "milkshake" on the counter, and a thought came over her.

What might happen if she poured Celeste a little more?

•

"Welcome back," the man said.

Cindy looked up into his cold, dark eyes. Her face was right in front of her, then gone, then back again. It was as if each blink of her eyes lasted several seconds. He put something beneath her nose, and she jerked back violently. Smelling salts, she realized. Slowly, she felt her body coming back to life.

"I need you to stand on your own two feet now," he said as he pulled her up from the bathroom floor.

Her legs wobbled, and she braced her body against his.

"That's it," he said. "You'll be fine in a few minutes. Unless you do something stupid."

Cindy tried to speak, but her mouth couldn't form words. He pried her jaws apart and shoved something long and cold into her mouth until it pressed against the back of her throat. She could taste metal. She could smell the powder from a gun that had been fired many times before. She saw the evil look in his eyes. It felt a lot like a place she'd been before, five years earlier, with a madman named Esteban—a place to which she'd never wanted to return. Her heart pounded, and she was suddenly alert.

"Nothing stupid, you hear me?"

Cindy nodded.

"Okay," he said as he nudged her forward. "Let's go."

65

.

"Nobody move," said Yuri, his voice booming across the living room.

Katrina and Jack froze. Yuri had Cindy in front of him with a gun to her head, using her as a human shield. The fear in her eyes was more than Jack could handle.

"Let go of my wife!"

"Shut up!" said Yuri.

"Who are you?" said Jack.

"His name's Yuri," said Katrina. "What do you want?"

"I want you to do as you're told."

"I can't do that."

"So I heard. Did you really think I was foolish enough to send you here alone and not follow you? I heard everything you said."

"Then you're the man. I guess you're just going to have to do Jack Swyteck yourself."

He shoved the gun into Cindy's cheek. "You'll do as you're told. Or I'll kill his wife."

"You're going to kill her anyway."

"Stop," said Jack. "Let her go, Yuri, or whatever your name is. Then you and I can get in your car, and we'll go to a nice quiet place in the woods. You can do whatever it is you need to do with me. Just let Cindy go."

"Oh, aren't you the hero?" he said, scoffing. Then his smile faded. "Down on the floor, Swyteck. Face-first."

Jack didn't move. Yuri tightened his grip on Cindy's throat. Her eyes bulged, and she gasped audibly. "I said, get down!"

Jack lowered himself to the rug.

"Hands behind your head."

Jack locked his fingers as commanded.

"Very good. Now, Katrina. Let's do what we came here to do."

She glared at Yuri, then glanced at Jack on the floor. The room was silent. Slowly, she reached inside her jacket and removed her .22.

" 'Atta girl," said Yuri. "Now move closer. Remember what I told you about the bullet in the brain. I want to see you use that .22 the way it's supposed to be used."

She crossed the living room, then stopped at the edge of the rug. She was close, but not so close that Jack could reach out and grab her ankle.

"Don't do this, Katrina."

"Put a sock in it, Swyteck," said Yuri. "I'm trying to be a nice guy. I'm giving you the privilege of dying with the faint hope that I might actually let your wife live. One more word, and I'm taking that away from you."

A tense silence fell over the room. Katrina could hear the sound of her own breathing.

Yuri narrowed his eyes and said, "Do it, Katrina."

She could feel her palm sweating as she squeezed the handle of her gun and pointed the barrel in Jack's direction.

"That's it," said Yuri.

She had one eye on Jack, the other on Yuri. Her finger caressed the trigger.

"Do it!"

Her hand was shaking, but her thoughts were coming clear. "This doesn't make sense."

"Stop stalling."

"There are so many easier ways to do this."

"This is the way I want to do it. Now pull the trigger!"

"Why? Why are you making *me* do it?"

"Because I can. Now shoot him!"

"Why? Why is it so important to you that *I* do it?"

"Don't you dare disobey me. I know who you are, you little slut. Did you honestly think you could fool me?"

"What?"

"If I can get you to snip the hairs off your pussy and hand them over to me in a plastic bag, surely I can talk you into pulling the trigger. This is what you are. I know what you're made of, and I own you. It's like I used to say, remember? No decision we make is meaningless. We all determine our own fate. Now do as you're told. Kill him!"

It was him, she realized, and the discovery cut to her core. Bits and pieces of information she'd gathered over the last few months had suggested that he was the man she'd been looking for, and now there was no denying it. Something snapped inside her, a fury sparked by the sickening reality of what drove this pervert. It was all about domination and control, from her friend Beatriz who was killed in his factory for refusing to give her body to him, to her own indignity of selling pubic clippings in a bag—and the truly unspeakable things she was forced to do at gunpoint when the clippings just weren't enough. She couldn't be certain that he'd murdered that woman with AIDS in Georgia, but only this creep was low enough to sell the blood of his victims. *We all determine our own fate.*

She wheeled and fired a shot across the room. Muffled by a silencer, it whistled past Yuri and shattered the vase on the wall unit.

Yuri fired back, another muted volley. But this one found its mark. Katrina fell to the ground. A hot, wet explosion erupted beneath her jacket. Her gun fell to the floor, then she fell beside it.

"Cindy!" said Jack.

A final, deadly quiet shot hissed from Yuri's pistol, and Jack went down behind the couch. Katrina tried to raise her head, and managed to get it an inch above the floor. Just enough to see Yuri ducking into the kitchen with his hostage in tow.

66

Jack kept moving, rolling from his hiding place behind the couch toward Katrina. Yuri's bullet had torn a hole through a sofa cushion. On his hands and knees he snaked his way past the ottoman and found Katrina on a blood-soaked rug. She was lying on her back, grimacing with pain.

"How bad is it?" she asked.

Jack tugged at her neckline to expose the wound. It was just below the collarbone. "Didn't hit a major organ. Just gotta stop the bleeding."

"Pressure," she said.

He grabbed a pillow from the couch and pressed it to the wound. Out of the corner of his eye he spotted the cordless phone on the cocktail table. He grabbed it and hit TALK. "Dead," he said.

"I'm sure he cut the phone lines."

"Do you have a cell phone?"

"Not on me. You?"

"In the freakin' kitchen. It's in the battery charger."

A voice boomed from the other side of the swinging door. "How's everybody doing out there?"

"Fantastic," said Jack. "You really know how to throw a party."

Katrina grabbed his elbow, shushing him. "Don't answer him. I'll talk. Keep this between me and him."

"It's *not* between you and him. He's got my wife."

Yuri said, "Everybody stays put. If I hear a door open, a window slide, anything that remotely sounds like someone running for help, I put a bullet in this pretty head. And don't even think about using a cell phone."

Katrina replied, "Whatever you say, Yuri." Then she looked at Jack and whispered, "So long as I keep him talking, you'll know where he is. Is there another way into that kitchen, other than through the swinging doors?"

"Off the hallway to the bedrooms."

"Good. That's your entrance. If I keep him talking, he'll be distracted. How good are you with a gun?"

He pulled his Smith & Wesson from under his sweatshirt. "Good enough to have shot you before you shot me."

"I wasn't going to shoot you," she said.

"I know. That's why I didn't pull it."

"Pulling it is one thing. Can you use it?"

"I carried a gun as a prosecutor. I've taken tons of target practice."

"Then we're in business."

"What's the alternative?"

"There is none. If I'm right about this guy, he's Georgian, part of the *Kurganskaya*. Elite hitmen. Even the Italian Mafia uses them. He's not going to let anyone walk out of here alive. So, you up for it or not?"

"Yeah. I'm in."

"Good. You'll have the advantage with the .38. Yuri's shooting a .22. Smaller slugs, a little more erratic from a distance. That's why he only winged me. You're actually better off not getting too close."

"How close do you think I should get?"

"You'll get one shot. That's all. Get close enough to make it count."

Jack felt butterflies in his stomach. "All right. Let's go."

"Hey, Yuri," she shouted. "This is pretty funny, isn't it? After eight months of collecting blood for you, here I am, bleeding to death on the floor."

Jack waited for an answer, but none came. At Katrina's signal, he started his crawl across the living room toward the main hallway.

"It was a good plan, Yuri. I thought it was especially clever the way you set up all those dummy viatical corporations. One for Jessie Merrill in Florida. One for Jody Falder in Georgia. Tell me something, though. Is there another victim for every single one of those companies you created?"

Jack kept moving across the oak floor, elbows and knees. He was trying to stay focused on his mission, play out the attack in his mind. But it was hard to ignore the things Katrina was saying.

"Every last one of them was going to die anyway," said Yuri.

"Except for Jessie Merrill."

"You think I killed her?"

"Seems exactly like the kind of person you'd love to kill. A young and beautiful woman who played you for a fool."

Jack stopped. Katrina's voice was growing weaker in the distance. He was within two meters of the hallway entrance to the kitchen. He waited for Yuri's reply to gauge his distance from the target.

"Fuck you, Katrina."

Short and sweet, but it was enough for Jack to guesstimate that Yuri was on the far side of the kitchen, near the two-way swinging door that led to the dining room.

"Touchy subject for you?" she said.

"Cut the crap, Katrina. I know what you're trying to do."

Silence fell over the entire house. Jack was inches away from making the turn into the kitchen. He grasped his revolver with both hands, drew his body into a crouch. He was at the ready.

"Swyteck!" said Yuri. "Where are you?"

The question sent Jack's heart racing.

"Answer me," said Yuri. "Reveal your position right now."

Jack braced himself against the wall. He had to make a move. Charge in? Roll and shoot? He wasn't sure. He said a five-second prayer.

"I'm going to count to three," said Yuri. "If I don't hear your voice, that's how long your wife has left on this planet. One."

Jack took a deep breath.

"Two. Th—"

Jack dived through the opening and took aim with his .38. In the blur that was his entrance, he caught sight of the swinging door flying open at the other end of the kitchen. Katrina rushed Yuri, screaming wildly to unnerve him, and Cindy screamed back. Yuri fired a shot, but it came just as Cindy was breaking free from his grasp. The bullet sailed wildly across the kitchen and took out the window over the sink. Cindy dived to the floor, and for a split second Yuri was standing in the center of the kitchen without his human shield.

Jack kept rolling to make himself a moving target. Yuri fired again but hit the oven door. Jack returned the fire, his .38 clapping like thunder in comparison to Yuri's silenced projectiles. It happened fast, but it seemed like slow motion. The recoil of the revolver. The shot ringing out. The flash of powder from the end of the barrel. The look on Yuri's face that changed in an instant. In what felt like the very same moment in time, Yuri was staring at Jack through the penetrating eyes of an assassin, and then the eyes were gone. His head snapped back in a blinding crimson blur.

Yuri fell to the floor, a lifeless thud, blood oozing from his shattered eye socket.

Jack was momentarily frozen, until he could comprehend what he'd seen. Then he ran to Cindy. She was crying, crouched in the corner beside the refrigerator. Jack held her. She was shaking in his arms.

"Are you okay?"

Tears ran down her face, but she nodded.

Katrina groaned from the other side of the room. Jack rose and saw her lying on the floor. He rushed to her side. "Hang on, Katrina. I'm going to get help."

"I'll be okay. I think."

"Cindy, my cell phone's in the charger. Call 911. Hurry!"

Jack checked Katrina's wound once more. It was still bleeding, but he sensed there was still time. If they were quick about it.

"Cindy, did you hear me?"

She didn't answer.

He rose and started toward the phone, then froze. Cindy was standing in the center of the kitchen, visibly shaken, yet managing to point Yuri's gun straight at her husband.

"Cindy, what are you doing?"

"I'm sorry," she said, her voice quaking. "This craziness. I can't take it anymore. It's all your fault."

"Cindy, just give me the gun, okay?"

"Stay away from me!"

He stopped in his tracks. She wiped tears from her eyes with the back of her sleeve, but she kept the gun pointed at his chest.

"Have you found your son yet?" she asked.

"What?"

"The son she gave you. She told me all about it herself."

"When?"

"After you discovered that she'd scammed you. She called me."

"For what?"

"She played that audiotape for me. The one of you two in bed."

"You told me that it had come from the detectives."

"It did. But by then I'd already heard it from the source."

Jack winced, confused. She was starting to scare him. "Why did she play you the tape?"

"She wanted to tell me that she'd had your baby. And that you two were together again."

"If she said that, she was lying."

"Was she?"

Jack heard a gurgling noise behind him. Katrina was fading. "Cindy, give me the gun. We can work this out. This woman needs a doctor."

Her voice grew louder, filled with emotion. "I don't care what she needs, damn it! Can't you just take ten seconds of your life and let it be about me?"

"She could die, can't you see that?"

"She's dying, you're dying, we're all dying. I'm sick of this, Jack. I swear, the only time I see love in your eyes is when I wake up from a nightmare in the middle of the night or hear a strange noise outside my window and need you to hold me and tell me everything's going to be okay."

"What are you talking about?"

"You know what I'm talking about. Isn't that what you really love about me?"

"No."

"Liar! You love it that I *need* you. That's all you love. So you and your Jessie Merrill can just burn in hell together. I don't need you anymore."

Jack couldn't speak. He tried to make eye contact, but it was as if she were looking right through him. She was crying, but it didn't seem like tears of sorrow. Just an outpouring of some pent-up emotion he'd never seen before.

"Cindy," he said in a soft, even tone. "What did you do to Jessie?"

Her expression went cold, but she said nothing.

"Cindy, talk to me."

A calmness washed over her. Jack no longer saw tears, and her body seemed to have stopped shaking. He watched the barrel of the gun as it turned away from him.

"That's it. Give me the gun."

It kept moving, first to one side, then up. Farther up. She glanced at Yuri's body on the floor, then spoke in an empty voice. "It's like the man said: We all determine our own fate."

Jack watched in horror as she took aim at her own temple.

"No!" he cried as he lunged toward her. He fell with his full weight against her, taking her down, grabbing for the gun, trying to avert one more senseless tragedy. Somewhere in the tumble he felt her hand jerk forward.

The next thing he heard was the sickening, muffled sound of one final bullet blasting from the silencer.

67

Jack had a view of the restrooms from his seat in the hospital waiting room. Cindy's mother was off to his left, several rows of seats separating them. Over the course of two hours, they'd made eye contact once. He'd just happened to look up and caught her shooting death rays in his direction.

A little after eleven o'clock, the doctor came out to see them. "Mr. Swyteck?"

Evelyn jumped from her seat and came between them. "I'm Cindy's mother."

"I'm Dr. Blanco. The good news is your daughter—your wife—is going to be just fine. She dodged a bullet. Literally. It scorched a path right past her ear. Right down to the skull. Still, it's in the superficial category."

Jack asked, "What about Katrina, the woman who came in the same ambulance? How's she?"

"She's in recovery. Lost a lot of blood, but she made it here in time. I'd expect a full recovery. Probably a couple months of rehab on the shoulder."

"Can we talk about my daughter, please?" said Evelyn. "When can she come home?"

"That's a little problematic. With any self-inflicted wound, we don't want to rush these things. Before I make any promises, I want to get a psychiatric evaluation."

"That seems wise," said Jack.

"Psychiatric?" said Evelyn. "She's not a—I mean, she's a bright girl. She's just been under so much stress."

"Stress may be part of it. But let's get a professional to take a look at the whole picture. Then we can make a judgment."

"When can I see her?"

"That's something our psychiatrist should determine. You can wait here, if you like. I'll send someone down from psych just as soon as I can." He offered a polite smile, shook their hands, and was on his way.

Jack returned to his seat. Evelyn started toward hers, then stopped and turned back. She took the seat across from Jack but said nothing. She just stared.

"I'm sorry for all this, Evelyn."

"You should be."

"No need to beat me up. I'll be beating myself up over this for a long time. It's so obvious to me now."

"What's so obvious?"

"Cindy and Jessie. There's no good reason for Jessie's body to have been found in my own house. Unless Cindy killed her."

"Do you honestly believe that Cindy is capable of murder?"

"No. But the little things are starting to add up now. I remember one of the first nights we spent in your house. Cindy was all upset because she found out she wasn't pregnant. We started talking about fertility, and she was so certain that the problem was with her, not me. Neither one of us had been tested. How would she have known it was her, unless Jessie had told her . . ." He stopped himself, suddenly uncomfortable about having this conversation with his mother-in-law.

"Told her that you had already fathered a child?"

"All I'm saying is, I just can't believe it."

"Then don't believe it. Look, Jessie may have died in your house, but Cindy wasn't even home when it happened. She was with me that whole day."

"Nice try, Evelyn. But you're not the first parent to concoct an alibi for her child."

"You listen to me, smart guy. Cindy's not well to begin with. That man Yuri knocked her out with some kind of drug and then put a gun to her head. How coherent would you be after all that? You can't take anything she said this morning at face value."

The elevator doors opened, and a woman stepped out. Jack caught her eye, and she walked toward him. Jack hadn't seen her in a while, but it seemed that the older Cindy and her sister got, the more they looked alike.

"Hello, Celeste," said Jack.

"Thanks for calling me. How's Cindy?"

"She's going to be fine."

Evelyn turned and walked away, saying nothing to her older daughter. If there was ice between her and Jack, she and Celeste were glaciers apart. Jack had never fully understood it, just accepted it as part of a strange family dynamic.

He escorted Celeste to the vending machine, well away from Evelyn, then took a few minutes to explain everything over a cold soda. He glanced toward the intake desk and saw Evelyn talking with another doctor, presumably the psychiatrist.

"Excuse me one second." He quickly crossed the waiting room and introduced himself to the doctor. As Jack had figured, she was from psych.

"As I was telling your mother-in-law, I will probably want to keep Cindy in the hospital at least overnight, mostly for observation."

"That's fine."

"If she does become violent or show some signs that she might injure herself, we may need to sedate or even restrain her. I'm not saying that's going to happen, but to be on the safe side, I'd like your written authorization to do that."

"You really think that's necessary?"

"I'm her mother. I'll sign."

Jack deferred. The doctor handed a pen and clipboard to Evelyn. She looked over the form, then took the pen. Jack watched her sign.

He tried not to show it, but it was as if he'd been hit by lightning.

"There you go," she said.

The doctor thanked her and tucked the executed form under her arm. "I should have an update for you later this evening. I'll phone you."

"Thank you, doctor."

She turned and headed for the elevator. Jack checked his watch and said, "I have to go, too."

"Fine. You're not needed."

"I'd like to stay, but the homicide detectives are already breathing down my neck."

"What's that all about?"

"Something to do with knives. Whoever killed Jessie also slashed up some pictures of me and Cindy from our wedding album. With everything that's happened now, they want to check out our collection of knives, see if the slashes in the wedding photographs came from any we own."

"They think Cindy slashed her own wedding photos?"

"If she killed Jessie out of jealousy, that would fit, wouldn't it?"

Evelyn mulled it over, then shook her head. "Just go, please. Can't you ever bring anyone good news?"

"I'll be sure to work on that." He walked away but took the long route back to the elevators, making a point of passing by Cindy's sister.

"How about a cup of coffee?" he said.

"Sure."

He led her to the elevator and punched the DOWN button. The doors opened, and they got inside. "There's something I have to talk to you about," he said.

"What?"

"Dreams."

She rocked on her heels. "What kind of dreams?"

"For a few months now, Cindy's been having this same nightmare about your father coming to her. And when he leaves, he wants to take me with him. Do you have any idea what that might be all about?"

She didn't answer.

From inside the elevator, he took one last look at his mother-in-law seated on the other side of the waiting room. Then the doors closed, and the car began its descent.

The color had drained from Celeste's face.

"I thought you might," said Jack.

"I guess maybe it's time you learned our dirty little family secret."

"I'm all ears," he said as the elevator doors parted.

68

Jack waited in the dark with the window shades shut. He was in the TV room, though he hadn't so much as switched on a light bulb, let alone the set. For almost two hours, he sat alone, familiarizing himself with every sound of the empty house. The air conditioner kicking on, then off. The hum of the refrigerator. The Westminster chime of the grandfather clock.

Celeste had given him plenty to think about. She told him how her accusations had torn the family apart. Cindy had so fervently believed that her lies had driven their father to suicide that she'd even told Celeste of her fantasies about poisoning her older sister or causing her other bodily harm. Their mother had also turned against Celeste, but there was one major difference. Cindy had eventually made peace with Celeste and came to believe that the accusations were true.

Their mother had never made peace, and she'd known the truth from the beginning.

The clock chimed. It was quarter past two. Jack

started to rise, then stopped. He heard something. He listened, then settled back into his chair. It was the sound he'd been waiting for. At last, a key turned in the lock on Evelyn's front door.

•

Evelyn hooked her umbrella on the hall tree and switched on the light. It had been raining off and on since lunchtime, and, as usual, the gods had really turned on the faucets the moment she'd decided to sprint from her car to the front door. Even a hurricane, however, would not have kept her from coming home.

She walked down the hall and headed straight for the kitchen. There was an urgency to her step. She'd played it cool for over an hour at the hospital, fighting the impulse to rush home, which would have only raised suspicions. She'd used the time wisely, considering the things Jack had told her, weighing her options. This was no time for knee-jerk reactions, but now her mission was clear. She had to get home and secure one last loose end.

She flipped on the kitchen light. Her eyes fixed on an empty space on the countertop, which puzzled her. Her heart began to race. She canvassed the entire counter, one end to the other, then back again.

How can it not be here?

She went to the cabinet, opened it. Bowls, mixer, can opener—everything was in its place, except the one thing she was looking for.

Her hands began to shake. It *had* to be there. She tried the cabinet under the sink, but there was only a dish rack, detergents, and some paper towels. She went down the entire row of cabinets, flinging one door open after another. She found plates, her bread maker, pots and pans. Still, no luck.

A thought came to her, and she raced to the pantry, threw open the door, then gasped.

Jack was standing inside.

"What—" she started to say, then stopped. She saw it. He was holding it, protecting it the way a running back guards a football at the goal line. Only this pigskin was made of butcher block, and it came with an assortment of handles that protruded from the slots on the top. Knife handles. He had her collection of kitchen knives.

"Looking for this, Evelyn?" he asked.

•

Jack stepped out of the pantry. Evelyn slowly backed into the kitchen. He said nothing, waiting for her to speak. She continued stepping backward until she bumped against the sink.

"What are you doing here? I thought you had a meeting with the police."

He stopped at the kitchen table and placed the knives on top of it. "There is no meeting. I lied."

"Wha-a-a-at?" she said, a nervous cackle.

"I made it up."

"Why?"

"It's the strangest thing. I was watching my grand-mother slicing sheets of dough the other day. She's left-handed, so she typically cuts from the top right to the bot-tom left. To make a long story short, it helped me figure out that Jessie Merrill was probably killed by someone who is left-handed. It all has to do with the angle of the slash on her wrist."

"And to think you were ready to convict your wife, and she's right-handed. Shame on you."

"No, shame on you. It didn't occur to me until you and I met with the psychiatrist at the hospital. You so graciously took it upon yourself to sign the forms for Cindy's treatment. And that's when it hit me: *You're* left-handed."

"How dare you!"

He glanced at the cutlery on the table. "Which knife did you use, Evelyn?"

"This is ridiculous. The police have the knife. It was from your own kitchen. It was found floating in the bathtub with Jessie's body, exactly where you'd expect to find it with a suicide."

"I don't mean the knife you used to slash Jessie's wrist. I mean the knife you used to slash up our wedding album."

Her mouth opened, but she didn't speak.

"That's what you were looking for, wasn't it? I bluffed you into thinking that the police were looking for a match between our knives and the slashes in the wedding album. It got you to thinking: Maybe they'll come looking in your house, too."

"You're talking nonsense."

"When Cindy and I moved in with you, we took just a few personal things with us. The wedding album was one of them. Funny, but it wasn't until after we'd spent some time with you that Cindy noticed it had been mutilated. Someone had taken a knife to it."

"Probably that tramp, Jessie."

"Not her. You did it when I decided it was time to move out of your house. Cindy decided to come with me, rather than stay with you."

"You are so wrong."

"Am I? Then I don't suppose you'll mind if I take these knives downtown to have them analyzed. I noticed that one of them has a nice serrated edge. There might even be a few microscopic traces of photo paper on the blade. You'd be amazed by these lab guys and the things they can find."

Her bravado slowly faded. Her eyes filled with contempt. "This is all your fault."

"That's what Cindy said."

"If you'd truly loved her, you would have stepped aside and made it possible for her to move on and start a new life without you, without the nightmares about that deranged client of yours."

"The nightmares aren't about me or Esteban. They're about your husband. I know. I talked to Celeste."

"Celeste," she said, practically spitting out the name. "You two are just alike. But I see through your phony concern. You don't love Cindy. You love rescuing her all over again every two months, six months, a year—however long it takes for her nightmares to start up again. That's your kind of love."

"What do *you* know about love?"

"I've known this much for a very long time: Cindy will never be happy so long as you're in her life."

It was like hearing Cindy's speech all over again, only this time it was coming from the speechwriter. "You fed this to her, didn't you? You convinced her that I'm the source of all her fears."

She flashed an evil smile. "It didn't take much convincing. Especially after Jessie 'fessed up about you and her."

"Jessie was a liar. This was how she got even with me when I refused to help her wiggle out of her scam. Ruin my marriage."

"She did a very convincing job."

"Are you saying you heard her story?"

"I was sitting next to Cindy in the car when she got the call. I heard everything. Cindy didn't want to believe it. But Jessie said she had proof. She wanted to meet at your house to deliver it personally to Cindy."

"The tape?"

"Yes. The tape."

"So you and Cindy went to our house together."

"No. *I* went. Alone."

Jack paused, stunned by the admission. "You were there waiting when Jessie came by?"

"What decent mother wouldn't do that much for her only daughter?"

The reference to her *only* daughter wasn't lost on Jack. "What did you do?"

She walked as she talked, not a nervous pacing, but more like a professor who was enjoying her speech. "I was extremely polite. I just asked her to remove all of her clothes, get in the bathtub, and drink from a quart of vodka until she passed out."

"How did you get her to do that?"

"How do you think?"

"The knife?"

"Hardly." She walked a few more steps, then stopped at the end of the counter. She opened a drawer, then whirled around and pointed a gun at Jack. "With this."

Jack took a step back. "Evelyn, don't."

"What choice have you left me?"

"You won't get away with it."

"Of course I will. I came home, you startled me, I thought you were an intruder. What a tragedy. I shot my own son-in-law."

"This won't solve anything."

"Sure it will. Right now, it's my word against yours."

"Not quite."

She tightened her glare, then blinked nervously, as if sensing that Jack had something to spring.

"I'm afraid your timing is really bad," he said. "You caught me right in the middle of a conference call."

"What?"

He pointed with a nod toward the wall phone beside the refrigerator. The little orange light indicated that the line was open. "You still there, Jerry?"

"I'm here," came a voice over the speaker. It was Jerry Chafetz from the U.S. attorney's office. Jack had dialed him up the moment he'd heard Evelyn put the key in the front door.

"Mike, you there?"

He gave Mike Campbell a moment to reply, then Jack said, "Turn off the MUTE button, buddy."

There was a beep on the line, and Mike said, "Still here."

"You guys didn't hear any of that, did you?"

"Sorry," said Mike. "Couldn't help but listen. Hate to admit it, but I heard everything she said."

"Ditto," said Chafetz.

Jack tried not to smile, but he knew he had to be looking pretty smug. "Tough break, Evelyn. I'm really sorry. Your bad luck."

The gun was still aimed at Jack, but she seemed to have lost her will. Her stare had gone blank, and her hands were unsteady. It was as if she were shrinking right before his eyes.

Jack went to her and snatched away the gun. "You're right, Evelyn. I do love this rescue stuff." He took her by the arm and started for the door. "Even when Cindy isn't around."

69
•

The message on his answering machine was short and matter-of-fact. Cindy wanted to meet for lunch.

It was their first direct communication in six months, since the shoot-out in their house. Cindy had refused to let him visit in the hospital, and after her discharge they'd separated on the advice of her therapist. From that point forward, Jack's only way to contact his wife was through professionals, either her psychiatrist or her lawyer.

The blame game was deadly, but Jack found it easy to count up any number of reasons she might hate him for life. Her mother was a biggie. She'd pleaded guilty to second-degree murder, a plea bargain on a slam-bang case of murder in the first degree that at least allowed her to avoid the death penalty. And of course there was the irresolvable Jessie problem. Cindy was never going to believe that nothing had been going on between them. In truth, it didn't matter anymore.

Jack was through blaming himself.

He waited at a wrought-iron table beneath a broad Cinzano umbrella. It was a humid, sticky afternoon on South Beach, typical of late summer in the tropics. This particular café was one they'd never visited together, and he suspected that was precisely the reason Cindy had chosen it. No memories, no history, no ghosts.

"Hello, Jack," she said as she approached the table.

"Hi." Jack rose and instinctively helped with her chair. She got it herself and sat across from him, no kiss, no handshake.

"Thanks for coming," she said.

"No problem. How have you been?"

"Fine. You?"

"As good as can be expected."

The waiter came. Cindy ordered a sparkling water. Jack ordered another bourbon.

"Pretty early in the day for you, isn't it?" she asked.

"Not necessarily. I haven't slept since I got your message last night, so I'm not really sure what time of day it is."

"Sorry."

"Me, too. About a lot of things."

She looked away, seeming to focus on nothing in particular. A pack of sweaty joggers plodded by on the sidewalk. A loud Latin beat boomed from the back of a passing SUV on Ocean Drive.

"Have you found your son yet?"

Jack coughed into his drink. He'd suspected that might come up, but not right out of the starting blocks. "Uh, no."

"Are you looking?"

"No. No reason to look."

"What about the money? Jessie left the entire million and a half dollars to her son, if you can find him."

"To be honest, I'm not much interested in trying to funnel stolen money to a child who's probably perfectly happy not knowing me or his biological mother."

"But what's the alternative? Give it back to the Russian mob?"

"If I have any say, it'll go to the relatives of people like Jody Falder, and anyone else Yuri and his pack of viatical investors eliminated in order to cash in on their investments."

"That's probably as it should be."

"In due time. But at the moment, Dr. Marsh's widow is trying to prove that half of that loot is hers. She's suing Clara Pierce for fraud and mismanagement of Jessie's estate. I'm content to let those two tear each other to shreds before I take a stand."

"Good for you."

"Yeah. I guess it is."

Cindy squeezed the lemon wedge into her water. A breeze blew in from the Atlantic and sent their napkins sailing. They reached across the table to grab the same one. Their hands touched, their eyes met and held.

"Jack, there's something I want to say."

He released the napkin, broke the contact. "Tell me."

"That day in the house, when I had the gun. I said some things to you."

"You don't have to explain."

"Yes, I do. I said some very harsh things. And I want you to know that part of me will always love you. But those things I said. Some of them . . ."

"Cindy, please."

"It really is the way I feel."

He felt as though he should have been devastated, but he wasn't. "I know that."

"You know?"

"Yes. For years, your mother held such obvious hatred for me. I always wondered, why can't Evelyn put this all behind her, especially since her own daughter has forgiven me for what happened with Esteban? But now I know: You never really did forgive me, either."

"I tried. I wanted to. I've thought about this so much."

"I've been doing a lot of thinking, too. And as much as I loved you at one time . . ."

"You stopped loving me."

"No. It's not that. It's just that it wasn't love that was keeping us together. When you get right down to it, I think you stayed in this marriage because you were too afraid to be alone. Or worse, afraid of spending the rest of your life living with your mother."

"And why did you stay?"

Jack struggled, wondering if some things were better left unsaid.

She answered for him. "You stayed because you felt guilty about what happened with Esteban."

Jack lowered his eyes, but he didn't argue. "Somehow I thought that if we worked long and hard enough, things would get back to where they were. Before Esteban."

"That's fairy tales, Jack. It doesn't usually work that way in real life."

"So where does that leave us?"

"You know, I used to think that people who bailed out on a marriage were just quitters. But that's not true. Sometimes, the so-called quitters are really idealists. They know there's something better out there for them, and they have the courage to go out and look for it."

"You're ready for that?"

"After all these years together, I think the one thing we owe each other is honesty. Since we've been apart, I haven't had a single nightmare."

"What does that tell you?"

"The nightmares will never go away. Not unless . . ."

"Unless I go away," he said.

"I'm not trying to say it's anyone's fault. It's just the way it is. Can you understand that?"

"I more than understand. I agree."

She gave a weak smile, as if relieved to see that he wasn't going to put up a fight. "That's all I wanted to say," she said.

"So, this is it?"

She nodded. "I should go."

She rose, but he didn't.

"Cindy?"

She stopped and looked at him. "Yes?"

"There's one thing I need to know."

"What is it?"

"Did you think something was going on between me and Jessie even before she called and told you there was?"

"What makes you ask that?"

"For months now, I've been trying to put a timeline together in my head. As best I can figure, Jessie came to me and said that the viatical investors found out that she'd scammed them and were out to kill her. Then, after I didn't help her, she called you and said we were having an affair."

"That's right."

"So, I just wonder: How did the viatical investors find out Jessie had scammed them?"

"Someone obviously told them."

"Yeah, but who?"

"Could have been anyone."

"Not really. There aren't that many possibilities. It wasn't me. It wasn't Jessie. It wasn't Dr. Marsh. Just makes me stop and think: Maybe it was someone I confided in."

She showed almost no reaction, just a subtle rise of the left eyebrow. "That's something you may never know," she said, then turned and started away.

He downed his drink and took solace in the knowledge that he had a little something to counterbalance it all. In a way, it was Cindy who'd started the whole Jessie mess.

"Cindy," he called again.

She stopped, this time seeming a little annoyed. "What now?"

"There's something else that's bothering me."

"If you've got something to say, just say it."

"All right, I will. This is going to sound weird, because your mother has confessed and is sitting in jail. But the idea that she killed Jessie doesn't ring completely true to me."

She made a face, incredulous. "What?"

"Maybe it's because I'm a criminal lawyer, but motives are a bit of an obsession for me. Your mother's don't quite add up in my mind. What she wanted more than anything was for you to find the courage to leave me. Killing Jessie wouldn't necessarily have accomplished that. But your finding her passed out naked in our bathtub might."

Cindy didn't answer.

"Is that how you found her, Cindy? After your mother went to our house and forced her to drink so much that she passed out, was Jessie still alive?"

She flinched a little, virtually unnoticeable to anyone

who didn't know her as well as Jack did. But he definitely caught it.

She said, "What about the angle of the cut on her wrist? That was your whole theory, that someone who was left-handed cut her wrist to make it look like suicide."

"That sounded like a neat idea at the time. But the angle wasn't that pronounced. I was having second thoughts about it even before I accused your mother, when Rosa and I talked that morning before Katrina showed up at our house. The medical examiner didn't put any stock in it at all. Your mother wouldn't have spent a day in jail without a confession."

"But there was still an angle, and my mother is left-handed."

"It isn't foolproof. The killer could have been in a hurry. Maybe she was even enraged, filled with jealousy. There's no telling what angle the slash might take in those circumstances."

"Exactly what is it you're trying to say, Jack?"

"It's an idea that's been floating around in my head the last six months. I'm just trying to go back in time, trying to understand the mind-set. For your own good, your mother is desperate for you to find the courage to leave me and start a new life with no nightmares, no reminders of Esteban. She's so desperate that she finally does something that she hopes will utterly shock you. Instead of shocking you into leaving me, she pushes you into a crime of passion. At the end of the day, she takes the rap for Jessie's murder. After all, it was her plan that went awry."

"So who do you think slashed up our wedding photos? Me?"

"No. That was definitely your mother's work. But she was hoping you'd think it was Jessie who'd done it.

Mom's way of making you feel a little less guilty about having killed my old girlfriend."

"Do you really believe my mother would do this for me?"

"You *were* the 'good' daughter, weren't you? The one who protected her husband's fine reputation long after your sister revealed the truth about him."

Her glare was ice-cold.

He looked into her eyes, searching. There was a time when he could have looked straight into her soul, but this time he saw nothing.

Finally, she answered. "Like I said before, Jack. Sometimes in life you just never know."

He stared at her, waiting for some sign of remorse.

"I deserve to know," he said.

"And I at least deserved a husband who played by the rules."

"Funny. Those were the exact words Jessie used to describe our marriage. Playing by the rules."

"How 'bout that."

"Yeah. How 'bout that."

"Good-bye, Jack."

He watched her turn and walk away. He kept a bead on the back of her head as she flowed with the crowd along the sidewalk. She was a half-block away when she disappeared amid the sea of bobbing and weaving pedestrians. He spotted her once more, then lost sight of her. For good.

●

It was Saturday night, and Jack escaped to Tobacco Road. When it came to broken spirits, there was no better salve than a dark club with live music and a bartender who'd never been stumped by a customer's request for a cocktail. The really beautiful thing about the Road was the lack of beauty—no glitz, no palm trees at the door, no neon lights of South Beach. It was just a great bar by the river that catered to everyone from Brickell Avenue bankers to the likes of Theo Knight.

"Hey, Jacko, you came." Theo threw his arms around him, practically wrestled him off his bar stool.

"Of course I came. Why wouldn't I?"

"Oh, I don't know. Possibly because the only thing worse than having no date on a Saturday night is watching your old pal Theo blow on his saxophone and fight off hordes of groupies."

Jack looked around, spotted a woman at a table who looked as though she'd been there since last weekend. "I can live with it."

Theo laughed, then turned serious. "How you been, man?"

"Okay."

"Hey, I hear Benno Jancowitz is leaving the state attorney's office."

"I heard the same thing," said Jack. "Guess he got tired of prosecuting parking tickets."

"That blowhard deserved a demotion. I mean, it's one thing to go after the son of a beloved former governor. But if you're gonna indict an upstanding character like Theo Knight, you better be damn sure you're right."

Jack chuckled, though evidently not hard enough to suit Theo.

"You sure you okay, Jacko?"

"Fine."

He laid a huge hand on Jack's shoulder, as if to console. "Sorry about you and Cindy, man."

"Don't be. It was over for a long time. Now it's just official."

Theo gave a nod, as if promising never to bring it up again, then ordered himself a club soda. "Hey, there's someone I want you to see."

"Please, don't start setting me up already. I just want to have a couple drinks and listen to music. When's your set starting?"

"Five minutes. But I'm serious. I got someone who's dying to talk to you."

He was about to protest, but Theo had already signaled to the other side of the bar. Two women started through the crowd, and at least from a distance it appeared that his friend Theo was doing him quite the favor. One was wearing black leather pants and a fitted red blouse, and Jack wasn't the only man watching her cross the room. The other was equally striking. He was beginning to think that this single life wasn't going to be such a bad thing, until he got a good look at the tall brunette. Not that she wasn't attractive. He was simply taken aback.

"Katrina?"

"Hello, Jack."

Last Jack had heard, Katrina had helped the feds piece together computer records from Viatical Solutions, Inc., and identify more than a dozen *Mafiya*-controlled viatical companies, thereby preventing any further suspicious deaths and expedited payoffs. With both Yuri and Vladimir dead, however, the focus of the overall money-laundering investigation had shifted elsewhere, taking Katrina off the hook. It was evident to Jack that she'd resolved to return to a normal life.

Katrina said, "This is my friend Alicia."

Jack looked at Theo and said, "What's going on here?"

"I just thought you and Katrina should get to know each other better. Especially since, you know, she and I have become such good friends." He put his arm around her, pulled her close. They were suddenly making eyes at one other.

"You mean you two are . . ."

"Does this surprise you?"

"No, no. Not at all. What better way to start a relationship than by putting a gun to a man's head and kidnapping him?"

"She saved my life."

"Technically, yes. But wasn't it a little bit like setting your house on fire and then calling the fire department?"

Katrina's friend said something to her in Spanish. Jack knew it wasn't intended for his WASPy ears, but he understood every word. For effect, he answered her in Spanish. "You're right, Alicia. I'm no Brad Pitt. But once you get to know me, I usually turn out to be slightly smaller than the biggest asshole you've ever met."

Her shock was evident. "Wow. Your Spanish is really good."

"His mother was Cuban," said Theo.

"Wow. Your Spanish really—"

"I know, I know. It sucks."

The way he'd said it, it was clear that he'd been through that routine a thousand times. The reaction was delayed, but finally the four of them shared a little laugh. The ice had broken.

Katrina said, "Can I buy you a drink, Swyteck?"

Jack thought for a minute, then smiled. "What the heck."

Theo's band was tuning up on stage. "My gig's up. Time for me to blow."

"Just a sec," said Jack. "How about playing that Donald Byrd song for me. You know. The one from the album, *Thank you for . . .*"

"Fucking up my life?"

"That's the one."

The threesome laughed, to the exclusion of Katrina's friend. They alone knew that it was the album Jack had requested when Katrina was holding Theo hostage.

"I'll play it," said Theo. "But only if you promise not to make it your theme song."

"Just this one last time, and that'll be it."

"Then what?"

"Who knows?"

"That's such a great thing, isn't it? If you ask me, it's the only way you know you're alive."

"What?"

"The fact that you just never know."

Jack wasn't quite sure what he meant.

"I'm right, ain't I?" Theo said with a wink. Then he grabbed his saxophone and ran to the stage.

Jack still didn't get it, until Theo took center stage and drilled them with the sax, an overly sharp note worthy of Kenny G. He glanced at Katrina, this gorgeous woman with her eyes locked on Theo. At that moment, on some level, it all made incredible sense to him.

He smiled and thought, *You're exactly right, buddy. You just never know.*

Photo by Jeffrey Camp

JAMES GRIPPANDO is the bestselling author of *Got the Look, Hear No Evil, Last to Die, Beyond Suspicion, A King's Ransom, Under Cover of Darkness, Found Money, The Abduction, The Informant,* and *The Pardon,* which are enjoyed worldwide in twenty-one languages. He lives in Florida, where he was a trial lawyer for twelve years. Visit his website at *www.jamesgrippando.com.*